ONE SMALL
CANDLE

The Story of
William Bradford
And the
Pilgrim Fathers

EVELYN TIDMAN

One Small Candle

The Story of William Bradford and the Pilgrim Fathers

Fiction
First edition

ISBN-13: 978-1482792416
ISBN-10: 1482792419

ONE SMALL CANDLE

CONTENTS

ACKNOWLEDGEMENTS

Cover by Laura Wright LaRoche,
LLPix Photography:
www.llpix.com

Thus out of small beginnings greater things have been produced by his hand that made all things of nothing, and gives being to all things that are; and as one small candle may light a thousand, so the light here kindled hath shone to many, yea in some sort to our whole nation; let the glorious name of Jehovah have all the praise. —William Bradford.

ONE SMALL CANDLE

ONE
Hard Beginnings

Near Boston, England, 1607

Pulling the thick travelling cloak tighter around him in a forlorn attempt to keep out the penetrating cold of a November night, William Bradford shifted on the bare board seat. Thick damp darkness obscured the faces of the others, but he could hear them; the rustle of clothing as someone moved, quiet breathing, a stifled cough. Yet no-one spoke. Men, women and children sat in tense silence, fearing the slightest sound drifting across the Lincolnshire salt marsh. Every squeak of the oars in the rowlocks, every creak of boat timbers, every ripple in the black river water jangled taught nerves. A suffocating fog of fear hung over them.

A child wailed suddenly, a clanging alarm in the stillness of the night, hushed quickly by a mother's breast. It was enough to rouse a man dozing on the watch and it set Will's heart banging against his ribs in sudden terror. Everyone in the boat shuffled uncomfortably. They all knew what it would mean if they were discovered. Their plans for escape foiled, and themselves, at best, incarcerated. It was better not to think about the worst.

With his hands on the gunwale, Will raised himself carefully off the bench, peering over the shadow of the bank. In the grey distance, the tower of St Botolph's church, the Boston Stump, glowed eerily, guiding sailors, and travellers alike. But that was the only light. No torches, no shouts. Relieved, he sat down again, and wished his heart would not thud so loudly in his ears.

'Anything, young Will?' William Brewster beside him spoke in an anxious whisper.

'No sir.' *Young Will.* It was the way they all addressed him, and he supposed he was young at seventeen to have made a decision such as this, to leave family and inheritance for the freedom to worship as God's Word said. Imagining the reaction of his guardian uncles when they found him gone, he knew they would say William Bradford had thrown in his lot with outlaws.

He cast his eye over the outline shapes of these 'outlaws' barely visible in the dark of the night. They were ordinary men, women and children huddling together in the boats. They were outlaws because they dared to disagree with the Established Church, because they wanted freedom to worship their way.

Silently the boats slid down the river hidden by the darkness. Will shifted his position again. His back ached where it rested against the side of the boat, the ridged gunwale pressing against his bruises. But the physical discomfort was nothing compared to the churning in his insides, part fear, part excitement.

As always, Will found the presence of William Brewster reassuring, calming and positive. Of all of them, he felt closest to this man, who stood in place of the father he had never known.

'Nervous Will?' William Brewster's disembodied voice came out of the darkness.

'A little.' He peered at the shape beside Brewster, Mistress Mary Brewster, barely visible in the darkness. She had a child on her lap, probably Fear, their youngest. ''Tis hard on the children,' Will observed.

'Aye.' There was an edge to Brewster's voice. The responsibility of fatherhood weighed heavily upon him at this time. 'Be grateful that you have no children of your own, Young Will.' But it was jest. Brewster adored his family.

As the river widened and the banks drifted away into the night the sailors hoisted the sail. At last they had reached the sea—the Wash, which the crew said was not true sea. Out there beyond the Wash, the German Sea was true sea. True sea or not, the water grew in power, a sudden wind rocking the boat, spraying the passengers and waking the children. They began to wail, their voices rising shrilly as desperate mothers tried to hush them.

Will strained his eyes forward, peering into the night but the sea ahead was disappointingly empty, a frightening black void.

'Where are they?' William Brewster hissed anxiously.

The question flew round the open boat. Cold dread pulled at his belly as Will, too, searched the sea. He felt sick. The ship was not there. Had the captain dealt treacherously with them, taking their money and not kept his part of the bargain? What would they do now, at sea in an open boat? Panic-stricken rage boiled up from deep inside him.

The hired men at the prow of the boat struck a tinder box and lit a small single candle lantern, and when it flickered, held it aloft. Will wanted to cry out in alarm. It made them visible to anyone within a five mile radius, and not just to the ship they hoped would be there. Didn't they understand the danger? Then, out on the black water, two lights appeared twinkling like stars in the blackness of the night, allowing them to pick out the castellated stern of the waiting ship.

Will uttered a little prayer of relief in his heart. A collective sigh seemed to escape the rest, and the mood lightened perceptibly.

Looming large out of the night, the ship towered over them as tall as a house, and Will's heart soared. In a few days, just a very few days, they would be in Amsterdam, free.

The sailors brought the boat's sail into the wind, and the boat crossed the black water to slip beneath the ship's towering bow, and then alongside on the starboard side in the full glare of the lights, but away from the shore. They scrambled up the ladder, the women with children tied to their backs, hampered by full and heavy skirts which got in the way of wooden ladder rungs. A slip, a misplaced foot or a child wriggling free would mean certain death in the icy black water.

Then it was Will's turn with sea lashing up the side of the ship, snapping at his heels. Moments later strong hands heaved him roughly over the side and he landed on the deck in an ungainly heap.

Grinning, William Brewster helped him to his feet. 'You'll never make a sailor,' he said, his eyes twinkling.

Will grinned in response. 'I could have done it if they had let me do it by myself.'

Brewster laughed out loud. It was a reassuring sound and Will took it in good part.

Although the ship rocked in the swell, it was good to feel something more solid beneath his feet. Above deck in the cold wind, the ship reeked of wet wood, of mouldy cordage and canvas, of tar, and the sickening stench of sweaty unwashed humanity. This last was almost certainly the sailors, filthy, dour, rebellious, watching the boarders with ill-concealed hostility.

Huddling together in an attempt to keep warm, the passengers began to relax a little now that they were actually on board, allowing themselves to talk, although they feared to raise voices still. The mood had changed from dread to hope, and even excitement. They dared to believe they might make it this time.

'Soon be in Holland,' Brewster said encouragingly and gave Will a fatherly slap on the shoulder. A sharp pain made Will winced and stifle a cry. Brewster's eyes narrowed suspiciously. 'What ails thee, Will?'

Will shook his head and gave his shoulder a rub. 'Just a bit sore, that's all.'

'A bit sore, eh?' Brewster frowned and Will wished he would not speak so loudly. 'Your uncles?'

Will's lips formed a tight line. It still hurt, not only physically but mentally as well. 'They said they would disinherit me.'

Brewster sucked in his lips, concerned. 'They cannot do so, not legally at any rate. You are your father's heir. The farm and all that was his belongs to you. Not even your sister had any claim on it.'

Will nodded. He didn't want to think of Alice, dear sweet Alice, his only ally. Her death had been a terrible blow. 'They think I will fritter my inheritance away. There was talk of ancestors and tradition.'

'They are uneducated men, Will. Ancestors and tradition are all they have to hold on to. We have something of far greater worth.'

'Perhaps if I had tried again to explain—'

'You have already explained. How many times? They refuse to understand.' Brewster dismissed the guardian uncles with an impatient wave of his hand.

Will grinned, a mischievous twinkle that betrayed his youth. 'They rue the day they let me learn to read and write!'

'Aye, that they do.' And he raised his hand to give Will another clap on his shoulder, and then remembered and turned it away instead to scratch his beard, before wandering over to the gunwale, leaning on it and looking out over the black sea to the faint glow of the Boston Stump. 'Do you look back Young Will?'

Will joined him. 'No.'

Brewster chuckled. 'Everything they hold dear you have shown to be of no value. Of course they are angry. You were once a sickly lad, unable to stand up for yourself. Now look at you! Tall, and a man grown, and not so pliable as they would have you. You can understand their frustration. After all, they still think of you as a mere boy.'

'And so do you, it seems!' Will countered. 'How long will I continue to be "*Young Will*"?'

Brewster laughed. 'Perhaps you are young, Will Bradford. But this I tell you, there are men not with us right now because they were afraid to take the step you have taken. It seems to me that it takes manly courage to leave everything behind.'

Will held his chin up. 'This is what I have been called for.'

Brewster nodded and grinned appreciatively. 'Not such a boy after all!'

John Robinson joined them and caught Brewster's eye. 'What are they doing?' he hissed. 'By my life, they tarry long enough!'

Will looked about him. The passengers were all loaded, and their belongings too. A great heap of boxes and bundles were piled on the deck. But instead of stowing it, or ushering the passengers below, or going about the tasks associated with putting to sea—raising the anchor, setting the sails—the sailors stood idly together, staring at the passengers, pretending to fiddle with unattached bits of rope, whittling bits of wood.

'Do they have to wait for the tide or something?' Will asked, puzzled, and in his own ears he sounded naive.

'Not in deep water and with such a favourable wind they don't,' Brewster replied, his voice loud enough for the whole ship's company to hear.

A sickening slide in his insides warned Will of imminent danger. Catching his eye, one of the crew curled an unshaven lip, hawked and spat disparagingly onto the deck. Another, a mere boy, looked away, and yet another growled low in his throat.

An air of growing malevolence hung over the ship. Will focused on Brewster waiting for some reassurance. The other passengers grew silent.

John Robinson glanced at the women huddled together in the lee of the raised quarter-deck. While old Brother Clifton was the leader of the congregation, John Robinson, a much younger man, was also an elder, and the one the brethren looked to for practical guidance, as well as spiritual enlightenment. He was responsible for their wellbeing. He marched over to the captain. 'Why haven't you taken the women and children below?' he demanded.

The captain regarded him steadily, but said nothing.

'Do you not answer me?'

When the man still did not reply, but instead turned contemptuously away to walk aft, John Robinson followed him and grabbed his arm. 'Answer me! What goes on here?'

The captain shook his arm free, and completely ignoring Robinson, he continued walking.

Angry, Robinson came to join Brewster and Will at the gunwale. 'That rogue will not speak to me.'

'We're betrayed,' Brewster said, his eyes fixed on the distance, and the note in his voice was of defeat. Robinson followed his gaze.

At first all Will could see was the light from the Boston Stump in the distance for the ship's lights bounced off the black waves, and beyond the lantern beam the darkness was impenetrable. His stomach jolted. A boat— or rather a sail, the pale canvas glowing ghostly in the available light— came into view on the heaving black sea. This was what the captain had been waiting for. He felt the sick slide of fear in his stomach. He knew what the boat carried without even needing to see them: officers of the law. The captain had betrayed them.

A low murmur spread through the waiting passengers like a man in pain. Not after all this work, this effort, and the money spent! It was a bitter pill to swallow.

Brewster uttered an unchristian oath, an expression of impotent fury. It was futile to attempt an escape. The officers would be upon them long before they could get off the ship, even if the sailors did not interfere, which they probably would. Brewster thumped the gunwale with his fist. 'Damn them!' he hissed under his breath. 'Damn them all!' He meant it literally.

Mary, Brewster's wife appeared at his side. 'What is happening?' she asked her husband, and Will heard the alarm in her voice.

'I don't think we will be going to Amsterdam today, Mistress,' John Robinson said grimly.

Will's heart had started that dreadful thudding again.

A man in the boat hailed them. 'Ahoy there!'

Someone from the ship answered, 'Halloo!'

'Stand fast there in the name of the King!'

Will found his hands were shaking. He hid them beneath his arms, as though they were cold, which they were. He kept his eyes on the oncoming boat. Another appeared behind it.

The passengers watched in silence, tired, shivering, and defeated.

'Betrayed, by God!' Brewster exploded. Then to the captain, 'What is the meaning of this? Have you taken our money and betrayed us?'

The captain eyed him malevolently, sneered and turned his back. As Brewster made to follow, three sailors stood together blocking his way.

John Robinson took Brewster's arm and pulled him away. There was nothing to be gained by pursuing the captain. 'Betrayed certainly, but not by God, brother,' he agreed quietly, but there was an edge to his voice.

'What will they do with us?' Will asked.

'No doubt put us in prison.' Old Richard Clifton's voice was flat, and when Will turned to look at him, he saw his body sag as though someone had taken the breath from it. He was too old for this, too old for prison, and weary of the fight. He drew a thin knobbly hand over his wrinkled face, and tugged at his magnificent snowy white beard in a gesture of defeated despair. 'Let the Lord's will be done,' he said resignedly.

Brewster grunted. 'More like Satan's will.' He gripped the gunwale and ground his teeth with anger. Mary put a restraining hand on his.

Will, standing beside them was angry also, but he knew the futility of anger.

'Damn the captain who has betrayed us!' Brewster exploded suddenly. 'May God do to him as he deserves!'

'No doubt he will,' John Robinson replied and there was an edge to his voice.

The intruders had come alongside, and now clambered up the ladder and onto the deck, six unwashed and unshaved ruffians, armed with pistols, pikes, halberds and bills with evil-looking curved blades, glinting menacingly in the lamplight. Their captain, distinguished by the metal helmet he wore on his head, approached the ship's master.

'Is this them?' he demanded jutting his chin in the direction of John Robinson.

'Aye.'

The captain of the guard cast a look of pure dislike on the men women and children huddled in the lee of the stowed longboat. He held out his hand imperiously. 'Permits!'

Richard Clifton took a step, but John Robinson stopped him and went forward himself. 'What permits?'

The captain of the guard was a slight man, and he had to look up at Robinson. He looked around at the huddle of men and women and said with a sneer, '*Travel* permits.'

There was a tense silence before John Robinson said innocently, 'Do we need travel permits?'

The man swore, betraying his irritation. He was cold and wet and no doubt unhappy about leaving his bed. 'Permits from the King,' he snapped. When John Robinson did not move, he added deliberately slowly as though he addressed an idiot, 'The papers that say you can leave the country.'

John Robinson met his eyes fearlessly. He had the quiet bearing and innate authority of a much older man, a man certain of the rightness of his convictions. 'We are Separatists, sir. You must know that permits for us to leave England will not be forthcoming from the King.'

'No permits? Arrest them!'

Another man grabbed John Robinson's arm and spun him around so that he fell against the gunwale and proceeded to search in his pockets. As if it were a signal, the deck erupted into chaos. Will found himself thrown against a deck housing, his face pressed into wet wood which smelt of stale urine, and huge hands deftly worked over his person taking everything in his pockets, his Bible, his money, and a lace handkerchief his sister Alice had given him. He could see little, but could hear women and children crying, men protesting. They left him and he stood.

'How dare you touch me!' John Robinson's young and pretty wife Bridget protested vehemently, her voice ringing across the deck. A man held her arms, while the other slid his hands lasciviously over her body, and rifled through her petticoats, showing her shapely white legs to all who would see. She struggled, kicking furiously, and when he bellowed in pain as her boot hit the mark, she added crossly, 'I'll thank you to mind your manners!' They pushed her over the side into the waiting boat.

Mary Brewster, outraged at the improper body search, dealt her assailant a resounding slap. 'Let me go!'

'By God, I'll kill him—' William Brewster began, stepping forward. The pike pointing at his belly stopped him.

'One more step and I'll run you through!'

John Robinson took advantage of the man's distraction to step forward, his customary calmness deserting him in the face of his wife's distress. 'This is an outrage. How dare you lay hands on gentlewomen!'

Another man held up one of the evil-looking bills, the threat implicit. A tool for cutting hedges, a single blow from the curved blade would take a man's head clean off. 'Turn the other cheek, brother,' he mocked.

TWO
Awaiting the Assizes

Boston, England, 1607

It was growing light by the time they entered the mouth of the Haven, which meant it was about seven of the clock. Another hour saw them right into Boston.

A crowd had gathered by the time the officers ordered the prisoners out of the boats. Will shivered violently in the cold air, but the fear and disappointment coiling inside him were much harder to bear than the cold or the curses of the officers. He had been robbed of his Bible, which was an expensive and precious item, spare clothes, and what little money he had managed to muster.

Around him the others stood with calm dignity awaiting their fate. Bridget Robinson struggled to suppress tears, as she looked imploringly at her husband. As if he could do anything. Brewster put his arm around his wife, only to have it knocked away again. They were ordinary families not criminals, gentlewomen with young children crying in terror and hiding in their mothers' skirts, anxious husbands and fathers. He wanted to protest. Why couldn't they just let them go to get on with their lives?

The mob jostled each other and murmured. 'Who are they?' The reply was full of hatred, 'Brownists.' This because they were thought to follow the teaching of the man Brown. The murmurs turned to jeers and insults became a menacing rhythmic chant. They would have to run the gauntlet of this terrifying angry mob. Will's mouth went dry. Beside him Mary Brewster pushed her little ones behind her protectively. Bridget Robinson clung to her husband John, but she had to let go of him to hold on to her children. Her sister Katherine Leggat took one of the little ones and clutched her to her breast tightly, protectively.

The men tried to surround their womenfolk, to keep them from the baying mob, but the guards pushed them roughly into the crowd. The mob surged, raining blows down on them, cursing, screaming, swearing. Just ahead of Will John Robinson fell but big John Carver hauled him quickly to his feet before he could be trampled. Will hunched over, trying to protect his head.

The officers tried to push them through the mob. 'Clear the way there, in the name of the King!'

A woman spectator cried out from a blow to her shoulder, and the mob parted reluctantly. Now people lined the narrow, cobbled street beneath the overhanging houses, and the prisoners were forced to run the gauntlet of abuse.

'Move!' Something struck Will in the small of his back and he staggered into Katherine Leggat in front of him. Half turning, she just saved him from falling.

The crowd closed in around them again. The noise roared in Will's head, a noise of menace and hatred. Ugly twisted faces. Spit and violence.

'Antichrist!'

'Traitors!'

'Filthy Separatists!'

'Puritan Dung!'

'Heathen Whores!'

Bridget Robinson clutched a child to her and presented her back to the mob. Women cried out in fright. Children screamed. The blows came thick and fast. Kicks, sticks, stones. The crowd pressed against them in the confined space, screaming abuse, a heaving terrifying mass.

Will lost his hat as something struck him on the side of the head. He stumbled at the shock of it, stunned, the tumult echoing in his ears. Brewster grabbed his arm. 'Steady Will.' And his voice was calm, imperative. Will touched the place on his temple and his fingers came away sticky with blood. He took another blow, this time to the stomach, and he doubled over. If he'd had food in his stomach he would have disgraced himself. As it was he staggered half blinded and winded. Brewster held him upright, despite the punishment to his own body. Still the blows rained down. Would it never end?

They reached the Guildhall, and were hustled inside and the noise died away as the doors closed behind them.

The relief was short-lived. Will, sore and bruised, had a pain in his head. He trembled with shock, his legs so weak he thought, ashamedly, that they might buckle beneath him. Disgusted, he hid his hands in his pockets, lest anyone should see the palsy there.

They stood quietly trying to tend to each others' wounds, dignified despite the ordeal, comforting the sobbing children. The soldiers separated them into two cells, one for women and children, the other for the men.

The room was hardly big enough. Looking around it with disgust, Will wondered how they thought so many would fare in such a small space. There were more women and children than men, but he supposed the women's cell was hardly bigger than this. There was no straw on the flagstone floor to insulate them from the cold, no blankets, no wooden pallets lining the walls to use as seats or beds. A bucket in the corner served as a privy, another contained fresh water. The gaoler slammed the door on them, and turned the key in the lock.

Brewster banged on the door. 'We'll freeze to death in here!'

''Tain't no more'n dung like you deserve,' the gaoler growled, and walked away.

Brewster ground his teeth. He stood a moment longer and then turned away.

He spotted Will and came over to him. 'Are you all right, young Will? You look like death!'

The pain in Will's head had grown rapidly and now it crashed in his temples, blocking out everything else. 'I—I do not feel so good,' he confessed.

'Sit down!' Brewster commanded. 'Master Carver, make room for the boy.'

Gratefully sinking to the cold damp flagstone floor beside John Carver, Will leaned against the dirty wall. Brewster knelt beside him. John Carver slapped him on the knee. 'You'll be alright, Young Will,' he said in his bluff jolly way.

Brewster dabbed at a spot on Will's temple with a white lace-edged handkerchief, one of his finest which had escaped the hands of the officers, and it came away crimson. 'You took a blow to the head,' he said.

John Robinson joined him, his concerned face coming into Will's line of vision. 'I don't like the look of him.'

Will managed a smile. 'You've never liked the look of me!'

Robinson chuckled. 'No. You were always a sickly-looking lad, though of late much improved, I have to say.' His eyes grew serious again. 'You are as pale as death, boy. Do you feel sick?'

'Very.'

John Robinson stood up. 'Do we have a bucket?'

It came only just in time, but with nothing in his stomach Will retched on empty air. As he lay back against the wall again, Brewster dabbed his face with a handkerchief soaked in water.

'They have sent messengers to inform their lordships of the Council,' big bluff John Carver said. 'What do you think they'll do with us?'

'That depends.' William Brewster brought the ladle from the water bucket and offered some to Will who sipped at it. 'It depends on whether their lordships care to bother themselves about us.'

'They are stirred up by the priests,' John Robinson said. Since the King was head of the church, to disagree with the church and the bishops and the clergy was to disagree with the king, which was treason.

'Well you'd think the King would be pleased to let us go,' Brewster said, 'seeing as we're so much trouble!'

'If he lets us go to Holland then we have won and he has lost face. He would rather we stayed here and be forced to acknowledge that he is right.'

'Will we ever get there?' Will asked and even in his own ears his voice was feeble. John Robinson crouched down to have another look at the wound on the side of Will's head. 'Of course, with God's help.'

Old Richard Clifton said, 'I think we should ask for the Lord's protection and help.'

Immediately, out of respect for the proposed prayer, those who had been sitting down or crouching, stood up. Will too made an effort but Brewster held him down with a hand firmly on his shoulder. As old Richard Clifton, their respected shepherd and pastor, began what looked like a lengthy prayer, Will tried to concentrate, but the pounding in his brain grew, and before long he drifted.

The prisoners, men, women and children filed into the court, bringing with them the peculiar stench of the prison. A month in the Guildhall had taken its toll on them. To a person they were thin and the men had raggedy beards and that strange white prison pallor mixed with dirt that characterised anyone who had not seen even winter sunlight in many days. Yet despite being manacled, they assembled in the courtroom with quiet dignity. They were not felons, but people of faith.

The courtroom was too small for all seventy or so of them. The benches on either side, partially filled with interested observers, took up the available space. So they had to squeeze together tightly, with some of them spilling into the hallway behind.

The magistrate, a local gentleman, walked in and took his seat, studied the papers before him, and then peered at the prisoners over his spectacles.

'Ah—yes. Well, now that we have heard back from the Council in London, we know what to do with you,' he said. 'The Council has been magnanimous. Generous to a fault. You can all go except for the leaders.' He picked up a paper and read out the names of seven men including John Robinson, William Brewster, Richard Clifton and John Carver. 'These men will be remanded in custody for the Assizes.'

From where Will stood, he saw Brewster square his shoulders, and lift his chin, and John Robinson waited quietly, his voice grave. Old Richard Clifton, with his white shaggy beard, bowed his head, shaking it sadly, while big John Carver gritted his teeth, suppressing anger at the injustice. They had got it wrong, of course. They were not all leaders. Will wanted to protest. He wanted to tell the magistrate what he thought of him. But Brewster looked at him and gently shook his head. It would serve no purpose and might, in fact, make things worse. They led them away in their chains.

The magistrate glared at Will and at everyone else. 'The rest of you may go home, and do not try such dangerous dealings again.' The magistrate banged the gavel. 'That is all.'

So that was it. They were free. Well, most of them.

Will found himself ushered outside the courtroom and marched with the other freed men and women to the blacksmith to have their irons removed.

When it was his turn to come to the anvil, the blacksmith put the cutter on the rivet, struck a mighty blow with the hammer, and the irons parted, freeing Will's hand. A second blow to the other wrist, and Will walked away a free man, examining the raw skin where the irons had rubbed.

Mary Brewster waited for him. 'We'll have to go home, Will,' she said wearily.

'We're not done,' Will told her with solid determination. 'They'll not beat us.' He looked at Mary, uncomfortably aware of his own lack of compassion. 'None of us,' he added meaningfully. 'Brother Brewster will be home soon.'

She smiled wanly, wanting to believe him. Her two oldest children, Edward, the same age as Will, and fifteen year old Jonathan, joined them, having been freed from their manacles.

It seemed strange not to have Brewster or John Robinson, or Richard Clifton at the meeting, Will thought, as he struggled to find a seat in the crowded room. Of course the meetings continued as they always had for no man was indispensable, and Thomas Helwys and Gervaise Neville had taken over the role of elders to the remaining congregation. However, to Will's mind neither man had the fire or the knowledge of John Robinson.

They no longer had the Scrooby Manor House, Brewster's former home, for meetings of course. Instead the remainder of the congregation met in Thomas Helwys' home, and modest it was at that. They squeezed in with hardly enough elbow room to turn the pages of their Bibles, and the usual segregation of men and women which they viewed as a moral propriety, had to be limited. It only added to the aggravation of having to wait for their pastor's return.

From where he sat, Will had a good view of Bridget Robinson cuddling her youngest also called Bridget on her lap. The child was hot and fidgety, and Mistress Robinson would struggle to concentrate on the meeting. And if the child cried, everyone else would struggle too. Bridget showed the strain she was under. Her small pointed face looked drawn and pinched but her eyes were bright and her shoulders square and straight. A puffiness around her eyes betrayed that she wept lonely tears, struggling to have confidence that her husband would come back to her, bravely trying to face life if he didn't.

Then there was Mary Brewster, once plump and motherly, and at thirty-nine much older than Bridget, also with a little one on her lap, her face now pale and thin, for as she had lost a great deal of weight, her clothes fitted her ill.

By contrast Mary Clifton was serene and outwardly calm. Their husbands and the other men were due at the Assizes, and everyone knew that the Assizes judge had the authority to hang a man, or to have him flogged. It was a gnawing fear.

Thomas Helwys, a tall thin man with a little beard and pert moustache, said an extemporaneous prayer which included asking for the men to be returned to the congregation safe and well. The congregation had just said *Amen* when a rap on the door brought instant tense silence. Helwys glanced anxiously at Gervaise Neville, alarm in his eyes. In these days you never knew. It could be the militia come to arrest them all again. No-one was safe.

As the householder, Thomas Helwys had to go to the door while the congregation waited in silent suspense. The door opened and William Brewster burst in, filling the room with his presence, closely followed by the others. 'We're free!' he cried unnecessarily.

Mary Brewster fell into her husband's arms. Bridget also stood but she was not very tall, and could not see her beloved John for so many bodies, for everyone had stood up and in the confined space it was difficult to see anyone, but with hardly room to move John still managed to come to her, take her in his arms, and hold her to him.

Will grinned at the heart-warming spectacle as the congregation cried out welcome and demanded information. 'This is an occasion for laughter and joy!' someone bellowed.

Robinson spoke to his wife, and then turned to the congregation. 'Do we not have a meeting this evening?'

Gervaise Neville grinned. 'A prayer of thanksgiving would be appropriate, do you not think?'

THREE
Another Attempt

Yorkshire, 1608

William Brewster turned his back to the fire, lifted his coat and warmed his nether regions. In all his life he did not think he had ever been as cold as he was now, having spent the entire day on the dockside in the freezing fog of a Hull winter. Except when he was in jail, of course. Well, the calendar might say spring, but to Brewster's mind it was still winter. His fingers inside his leather gloves had turned blue, and his face beneath his golden beard seemed to have set solid. And all for nothing, he thought disgustedly.

'I'll get the ale,' John Carver volunteered, and Brewster nodded gratefully.

A good man, John Carver. Big, bluff, noisy and dependable. The sort of man you would want on your side in a fight. So dependable, in fact, that he had recently become a deacon in the congregation, a helper to the elders.

'I ordered boiled mutton,' John Carver said when he came back and handed a steaming mug of mulled ale to Brewster. They sat down at one end of the long table, opposite each other.

Brewster sipped the foaming ale, savouring the warmth as it stung his tongue, the sweet spiciness of it, and wiped his moustache with the back of his hand. Only two other men were in the taproom, seamen by the look of them, at the other end of the table, and they were deep in conversation. 'I confess I could eat an ox,' he said.

One of the other men looked up. 'Where ye from, stranger?' he asked.

William Brewster nodded acknowledgement. 'Nigh Gainsborough.'

'Gainsborough? Ye don't sound like a Yorkshireman to me.'

It was true, for Brewster's clipped accent betrayed him as a man who had spent time at Cambridge University and he had he been at Court, too. 'Spent time in the service of the old Queen, God rest her soul.'

'Here on business?'

'We seek a ship to take us to Holland.'

'Holland is it?' The man surveyed Brewster with red-rimmed eyes, noting his clothes, the rich blue embroidered doublet, an extravagant ruff around his neck. Brewster had wanted to impress a ship's master that they had the ability to pay, and while the Puritans generally felt that it was more Godly to wear drab clothes of black or grey or brown, with no decoration, the Separatists did not agree with them. 'You ain't had much luck, then?'

William Brewster didn't believe in luck, but he said simply: 'No.'

The man was silent for a while and Brewster and John Carver exchanged glances.

'There be a Dutchman in the harbour,' the seaman said at length.

William Brewster frowned at him. 'We saw no Dutchman,' he said carefully.

'Came in late this evening. Her master be signing up hands tomorrow.'

John Carver said, 'Must have missed her.'

'Well, I don't know how.'

Brewster and Carver moved, sliding along the benches to join the two men. The landlord brought two plates of boiled mutton and dumplings. They thanked God for their food—William Brewster saying a brief prayer—which was common enough practice not to occasion comment. 'Does the captain own the ship?' he asked. It was important that the master was his own governor.

The seaman shrugged. 'Dunno. Happen he'll be willing to take you and your brood to Holland.'

'You know about us, friend?' John Carver asked uneasily.

The man shrugged. 'Plain as the nose on yer face. I heard about you people at Boston. I know who you be and what you be about.'

'And so?' Brewster asked quietly, outwardly calm, but his heart began to thud hard in his chest and his food became unappetising. He had a sword on his hip, perhaps not a Christian thing to have but a safeguard just the same. And he knew how to use it.

'And so it ain't no bother to me what a man believe, as long as he don't tell me what I ought to be doing! And if he want to leave England, I say, let 'im!'

Brewster relaxed. 'If only others thought as you do, friend.'

'Aye, well ye'd best be quick, like. I don't know how long the Dutchman be here.'

John Carver grinned. 'Looks like the Lord is with us, brother,' he boomed.

William Brewster wasn't so sure. Satan had led them into a trap before and he might well do so again. Look what happened at Boston.

It made Brewster decidedly uneasy when others knew his business. One thing civil service had taught him was to be very careful of other people.

However, there were the others to think of, for the congregation, now in desperate straits back in Scrooby, relied on them to act quickly. With no homes, and no jobs, they were a drain on the congregation. They could afford no more delay.

He glanced at John Carver. Not a man of great perception, John

Carver, but steady and reliable. He said, 'Perhaps.'

The master of the Dutch ship, a stocky man with a full red-gold beard, cared not what faith these strange English were as long as they were not Papists. He had been brought up to believe that what a man believed was his own affair and the government of his country agreed with him. Still, he understood the dangers for the Englishmen. They had got away with it last time, they might not be so fortunate next time. He suggested, therefore, that they board his ship at a deserted part of the beach between Grimsby and Hull near Stalingsborough, where a tributary of the river met the sea. The women and children should travel by boat along with their belongings and the men should walk to meet them.

'Do you think we can trust him?' John Carver asked as they rode back to Scrooby.

Brewster shifted in his saddle and frowned. 'I trust the man. But it seems to me that we would all of us be much better off making our own private arrangements instead of trying to go together. How can you hide a whole congregation of a hundred people? How can you keep it secret? Might as well print tracts advertising our intent and post them on the trees for all to read!'

'We must trust to the Lord, I suppose,' Carver said gruffly.

Brewster grunted. They had trusted to the Lord before but the opposition always seemed to have the upper hand.

Will looked up when Brewster and John Carver came in to Charles White's library, and set aside the Latin he had been studying. For some years William Brewster had encouraged him to sharpen up his Latin, the language of study and knowledge, the language of the Universities, teaching him how to speak it, and learn from it and Charles White, a scholar himself, invited Will to make use of his well-stocked library.

Charles followed the visitors into the room, and John Robinson got up from the chair by the fire to greet them.

Brewster slid his travelling cloak from his shoulders and shook off the rain onto the flagstone floor. 'We have found a ship to take us,' he said to John Robinson.

Robinson glanced meaningfully at his brother-in-law. Charles backed out. 'I will leave you to it,' he said. 'I don't want to be accused of being a spy if something goes wrong.'

'Nonsense,' Robinson began, but Charles closed the door firmly and they could hear his footsteps as he retreated down the tiled hall.

Shaking hands warmly with the newcomers, John Robinson beamed from one to the other of them. 'The Lord has indeed been with you!'

Brewster frowned. He didn't like so much assumption as to the work of the Lord. 'Perhaps.'

'What is the ship?' John Robinson wanted to know.

'A Dutchman. We sail in a week. From a place the master pointed out on the chart. It will take some arranging, but we all need to be at the rendezvous promptly. The women and children and belongings to go by boat, the rest of us to walk.' He moved to the table and leaned on it, glancing at Will's study. He slapped Will on the shoulder. 'We shall soon be in Amsterdam, young Will.'

Young Will nodded. 'Aye.'

Brewster searched his face, his eyes narrowing in concern. 'Not seen your uncles then?'

Will put his chin up, his eyes meeting Brewster's. 'No.' He tried to sound careless but he heard his own voice wobble with hurt.

John Robinson heard it too and created a diversion. 'Run and tell Mistress Brewster that her husband is home, Will.'

Taking this to mean that the men wanted to be alone to discuss matters and that he was not included, Will put a small piece of thread in the book he had been reading, closed it, and put it back on the shelf where he had found it. Then he left them.

'I think we have arrived.' Bridget Robinson craned her neck to peer at the sea ahead.

'Already?' Mary Brewster also peered forward but could see nothing. Beneath the cover of her shawl she had been suckling Fear, now a boisterous two-year-old, crooning to her to soothe her. 'It didn't take as long as I thought it would,' she said cheerfully.

Bridget scowled. 'No. And not as long as John thought, either. We are a whole day early! Just what are we supposed to do with ourselves for a whole day?'

Mary said bracingly, 'Well, I dare say exactly the same as if the journey had taken longer.'

Bridget made a noise in her throat of impatience, and Mary smiled. Poor Bridget! So impatient, her temper always frayed. Motherhood did not sit well on her. Although she loved her children, she viewed them as a hindrance, getting in the way of other things she would rather do. Bridget, if she had been a man, would easily have rivalled her husband for teaching ability. Her knowledge of the scriptures was frightening, her tongue incisive. For all her youth, many stood in awe of her, some of the men as well. It was no surprise to Mary to see that the journey irked her and the children irritated her, for she was not one to endure without protest.

'Brother Helwys did his best in arranging the boat for us, and he was anxious for us not to miss the rendezvous with the ship,' Mary said without much hope of being heeded.

Katherine Leggat added, 'He had to make sure we would be in good time in case the sailors had to row all the way.'

'Well, they didn't have to row,' Bridget snapped. There had been a brisk breeze to keep the barque moving at a fair speed.

The biting north easterly wind whistled about them, and tugged at her cloak where she sheltered her youngest, also called Bridget. 'I *hate* the cold!' she added with feeling.

Katherine was sympathetic. 'So do I.' She reached over and took the young John Robinson from her sister's side and pulled him onto her lap to give Bridget some peace. 'Now what are you grizzling about, young man?'

Three year old John knuckled his eyes. He was cold and tired, like all the children. 'I know you are wet and cold, and so are we all. We have to be patient and bear it.'

'I wish the men were here,' Bridget said.

Katherine cuddled little John closer. She had a daughter, Marie who had to be a comfort to her since her husband's death. But Katherine still yearned for more children.

Seeing her sister's reaction to the child on her lap, Bridget patted her hand. 'One day, sister.'

Mary knew to what she referred, and she hoped that one day Katherine would find a loving husband who would give her another child.

Katherine pursed her lips and looked down at little John in an attempt to hide her discomfiture from her sister.

Suspecting Katherine was near to tears, Mary rushed into speech. 'The men will be here shortly. They cannot be far away.' she stretched up to peer at the land around them. It was flat enough, the grasses not yet grown in the cold spring, and she could see some distance. What she saw dismayed her. The sea reflected the sky—cold and grey—save for the white foam which was a sure sign of a rough sea.

'There is no ship,' she confirmed to the others, sitting down again.

'Ship won't be here yet, Mistress,' one of the hired sailors answered her, revealing that he had been listening in to their conversation. 'We be a day early on account of the wind, see.'

'What shall we do then?' Mary Brewster asked.

He shrugged. Already they were at the mouth of the river. A moment later the full force of the sea wind hit the barque amidships, rocking it alarmingly.

'We'll have to heave to and put down the anchor,' he said. As he said it, the barque turned until the wind roared at them from over the prow, and two other burly men stepped across their passengers to reach the sail and pull it down.

Icy water splashed up against the side of the barque, and Bridget took little Anna from Marie and gathered her into the confines of her cloak, wrapping the two children up against her body to try to warm them.

Mary curled down lower into the boat with her little one, Fear, in a futile attempt at avoiding the wind. 'We cannot stay here all night,' she told the sailors. 'We'll freeze to death!'

They paid her little heed. They had other concerns. The wind was rising and hefty gusts blew rain into their faces, and howled through the lines on the single mast. The waves on this part of the shore open to the German Sea grew into fearsome rollers, breaking over the beach in a flurry of foam and spray. The boat rocked dangerously as each wave lifted it and dropped it again, the sea splashing over the occupants' who huddled together in their cloaks which proved woefully inadequate.

Mary's head, reacting to the motion, beginning to buzz, and everything seemed very far away. She felt suddenly icy cold, and the nausea in the pit of her stomach which had been present since they had embarked, intensified.

Jane White, Bridget and Katherine's younger unmarried sister who had also been fighting nausea before they reached the Wash was the first to lean over the side, retching uncontrollably until her stomach was empty, and Mary groaned. There was nothing more contagious than vomiting in company, and sure enough the sight of her set everyone else off. The other White sister, Frances Jessop was next, and Mary straight after her.

The sailors looked at each other despairingly and consulted together.

'We'll put into the shore,' one of them told Mary who peered at him almost unseeing, her suffering acute.

She nodded acquiescence, feeling too ill to do much else. Indeed, in that moment she would have given up everything she possessed just to be on dry, still land.

They hoisted the sail again, pulled up the anchor, and heaved the barque along the coast until they came to a small sheltered creek where they were out of the worst of the wind. However, by this time Mary felt so ill she thought she would die. Her head ached, her whole body shivered as though she had the ague, and her stomach heaved continually. As night fell she began to wish she had never left Scrooby, and she longed for the comforting arms of her beloved husband. 'If we could just go ashore,' she whispered to the sailor.

'Sorry, Mistress, but 'tis all mud and marsh. You'll sink right in and be swallowed up.'

It was a miserable night of cold and discomfort and little sleep. The chill morning brought some relief. Mary awoke from a light, exhausted doze to find her headache had become a pounding migraine and her bones and muscles ached. Then slowly, as she massaged life back into her arm, she realised something else was wrong. The barque listed to one side, and there was no movement at all. Where she had prayed for it to stop moving last night, it looked as if the Lord had taken her request rather too literally. With a growing sense of unease, she sat up and looked over the side, and to her horror saw beneath the keel not water, but mud.

'We're stuck on the mud!'

Her voice woke the others. Bridget stretched her back and frowned at Mary from across the barque. 'What did you say?'

'We're stuck on the mud,' Mary repeated and looked at the sailors accusingly.

'What happened?' Bridget demanded of the sailors.

'The tide, Mistress. The tide went out and left us high and dry as the saying is.'

She glared at him. She was cold, tired, and sick, her children cried in distress, and fear shook her to her very bones. 'You knew this would happen!' she accused.

The man's eyes grew round with denial. 'I swear Mistress I did not.'

Out on the sea the ship had arrived and now rode quietly at anchor. A great lot of help that was! 'How are we to get to the ship now?' she demanded angrily.

The sailor shrugged philosophically. 'We'll wait till the tide rises— should be about noon—then we'll float off the mud.'

Bridget ground her teeth. 'You are the most incompetent—'

'Sister!' Mary brought her up sharply, and she stopped.

It was hardly part of the Christian personality to tell the man what she thought of him, and it would not win him, or his acquaintances to their cause. Bridget struggled for self control, and then sat down again, taking little Bridget into her arms to suckle beneath the confines of her cloak. This was another of the indignities they had to suffer, that and the bodily necessities which had to be screened from the eyes of the interested sailors at the boat's prow. It made them all vulnerable before strangers.

Mary said, as much to hide her own fears as to calm the others, ''Tis a terrible thing, having to spend the night in an open barque. And we're all cold and tired. But we'll be all right when the tide rises and we can board.'

Bridget didn't look at her.

'Well, there is the ship, as promised,' William Brewster announced. Then glaring at young Edward Southworth, who had voiced his doubts, added with great relish, 'As I told you!'

John Robinson screwed up his eyes to have a better look. In the cold grey light of morning, the ship looked sound enough, riding at anchor, her sails furled, flying the Dutch flag. He searched as far as he could see in either direction before giving voice to the question they all asked. 'Where are the women?'

Brewster frowned, as the other men gathered to them. 'I can't see them. They should be here.'

'Perhaps they are already aboard,' John Carver suggested hopefully.

Will climbed up a small mound, giving him the extra height to see over the bumps in the shoreline. 'I can see them,' he cried. 'They are in a creek about a mile to the left.'

John Robinson also climbed the mound. 'They do not appear to be moving. Something's wrong. Why do they not go out to the ship?'

Will felt the uneasiness squirming again in the pit of his belly. *Not this time. Please, not this time. Don't let something go wrong now that we have come this far.*

'The ship has launched a boat,' John Carver said.

Will watched with the others as the boat came closer, oars dipping into the heaving grey water. John Robinson took a deep breath, his calm outer manner belying the anxiety he felt inside, the terror he felt for his wife, his children. Only the clenched fist at his side betrayed him to Will.

It took half an hour for the boat to reach them. As it ran onto the shore, William Brewster was there to meet the sailors. 'Why are not the women being taken to the ship?' he demanded of them before even greeting them.

'They be stuck in the mud,' one of the sailors, an Englishman, perhaps from the West Country, replied and smiled reassuringly. 'They'll float off alright when the tide rises.'

'And when will that be?'

'About midday. Meantime, Cap'n says to get you men aboard. He don't want to be here longer'n he must.'

John Robinson and William Brewster looked at each other. 'Very well.'

It would take two boat loads to get them all aboard, and they decided to send the younger men first, those less experienced, allowing the older men to control matters on shore. Will was in the first boatload, and although he protested Brewster told him sharply not to waste everyone's time by arguing.

He sat in the prow, his back to the ship, his face to the shore, watching the men left behind as the boat pulled away, a feeling of uneasiness creeping through his belly. It had all gone wrong before, now this.

The sea was very rough away from shore, and he felt the beginnings of the churning in his stomach. By sheer effort of will he struggled to overcome it. He could see now where the women were stranded, and frowned in frustration. *Dear God, protect them.*

The ship loomed large above them, a towering giant, seemingly enormous compared to the boat, and he felt the leap of excitement in his belly. Cold and wet from the sea spray, he clambered aboard, thankful to have the relatively solid timbers of the deck beneath his feet. Soon he was joined by his companions.

The ship was adequate for their needs—a three-masted square-rigged vessel with a high castellated stern and raised foredeck and forecastle. Will joined the others at the gunwale looking over at the wide flat shore. Over there, the men walked about on the beach. Further across, the women huddled in the boat.

'They wait for the high tide, the ship's master explained from behind them in his thick accent. 'They are stuck on the mud.'

Will turned towards him. 'What are they doing on the mud?' The captain looked like a capable man, and he smiled at Will. Not likely to betray them, Will thought.

'I think they take refuge from wind and waves—and what is this?' As he spoke he raised the telescope to his eye and peered across at the beach.

Will followed the direction of his gaze and felt his heart crash against his ribs. A crowd of people on horse and on foot crossed the marsh at a great rate, carrying bills and guns and swords and they were bearing down on the women in the boat. Catchpole officers.

The captain swore. '*Sacramente!*' The oath was Spanish in origin, and no doubt gleaned from the long war the Dutch had fought with the Spanish.

He left the passengers on the deck, marching towards the helm, firing out orders in Dutch and English.

Men ran up the ratlines and out onto the swaying yards, releasing the sails. Others took the spars from the store and slotted them into the holes in the windlass to haul up the anchor. They were making ready to sail.

'What are they doing?' Francis Jessop asked, his face paling in the white light of the early spring morning.

'They are making ready to sail,' Will said. 'They are going to desert them!'

Francis Jessop stared at him, wild-eyed with panic. His wife, also called Frances, was in the boat. 'No! We cannot leave them!'

Will ran aft, skipping over ropes and obstacles to reach the captain. 'Captain—we cannot leave without the others!'

The captain looked up at this young man and turned his back on him continuing to give his orders in Dutch.

Will grabbed hold of his arm. 'You cannot sail without them, Captain.'

The captain looked down at his arm meaningfully, and Will let it go. This man may have been shorter than Will, but he was at least twenty years older with the full weight of authority and confidence on his side. The other passengers added their own arguments. 'We cannot go,' Francis Jessop cried. 'My wife is on that boat.'

The captain turned to them angrily. 'And what would you have me do, Gentlemen? Go to help them? And how may I do that, pray? I cannot bring my ship close to shore. I fire my cannon. Act of war. Your sisters and wives will be hurt. If we wait for your men, we get caught.'

Francis Jessop, usually a gentle man, began to panic. 'But my wife!'

Will said, 'We have nothing but the clothes on our backs, no money, nothing! Everything else is in the boat. You must send us back to the shore!'

'There is no time and I will not risk my ship!' the captain declared, his eyes flashing. He was angry and he was afraid, and Will knew that a frightened man could not be persuaded.

'My wife! My dear wife!' Francis Jessop wailed.

'This is my ship, and we do what I say,' the captain barked at them.

'Then send us ashore again!' Will demanded. 'We cannot desert our friends and families.'

'No time for that!' The Captain brushed past them impatiently.

Thomas Tinker also burst into tears. 'My dear wife! What will become of her?'

The captain cast them a contemptuous look. 'She is in the hands of God. And what can you do if you go back, eh?'

Will was furious. 'You cannot leave. We cannot leave our families and friends! You would have us cowards, and destitute at that!'

'*I* am captain of this ship, not you. You are a boy to have much to say!' The ship began to move, jerking as the wind took up her sails and the captain marched smartly away from them. 'You go below!' They refused and stood still at the taffrail, watching the drama on the shore unfold as the armed mob surrounded their helpless women and children, taking them ashore. The men waiting farther along the shore scattered and disappeared.

Francis Jessop hit the gunwale with his clenched fist, railing at his helplessness, tears pouring down his cheeks. Will put his hand on his arm in a gesture of understanding. Yet he didn't understand, not really. He couldn't understand a husband's desperate need to protect wife and family.

'What will happen to them?' Digorie Priest asked.

No one answered him, for no-one knew, and Digorie Priest cursed the ship's captain and the authorities that treated them so harshly.

They were powerless. As the wind filled the Hollander's sails, she picked up speed and carried them away from England and out into the stormy German Sea.

The lower deck, the gun deck and mess deck where the crew of twenty-four slept and ate together, was dark and airless, and the ceiling, or rather the deck head was so low that they could not stand upright. A stench of bilge water and wet cordage, rotting wood and mildew, tar and unwashed humanity overpowered the passengers. Will felt his stomach heave anew but he controlled it with determination. They sat down where they could, some on a bench, others on barrels, others on the deck squeezed between black cannon and barrels. All the sailors were topside getting the ship under weigh. But without the others, they had plenty of space, and no luggage either to fill it.

Will looked around him sadly. They should have had the whole congregation with them, a hundred and twenty people, but instead they were just twenty. And a sorry lot they were, Will thought. Men continued to weep openly at having left their wives and children behind in the hands of the mob. And they all knew what that meant. It would be the magistrates, and perhaps the Assizes. Again.

Will tried to encourage them. 'Brother Brewster, and Brother Robinson will be there to look after them.'

'And what can they do against the might of the judges?' Digory Priest demanded. 'Men have been hanged—'

'We don't need reminding,' Edward Southworth stopped him. He lay in a corner, white as a sheet, seasickness already affecting him.

The trouble with Digory Priest, Will thought, was that he had a negative way of looking at things. A good enough man, but so miserable at the best of times.

Francis Jessop, a man of maturity took a steadying breath. 'Our sisters are not men, and as of the gentle sex, will be treated more leniently, like before. We can confidently leave them in God's hands. They will be safe.' He hoped.

'You think so?'

'Perhaps a prayer?' Thomas Tinker suggested, and without waiting for others to agree or not, removed his hat and began an extemporaneous prayer. Belatedly Will also removed his hat and bowed his head with the others, but from topside the sounds of shouted commands in a language they did not understand interrupted his concentration. *How shall we go on in a country where we do not speak the language?* They must learn, of course, if they were to earn a living.

Will shot a look at Edward Southworth who was near his own age. Edward's brother had been left behind. The colour had completely drained from his face.

'You feel ill?' Will asked solicitously, trying to find a space in the corner to sit beside him, and reached for an empty bucket for him.

'Don't you?' Edward replied tetchily.

Yes he did, but he wasn't going to admit it.

As they headed away from England out into open sea, the ship's gentle rocking became a severe pitching. Nausea caused by the stench and pitching of the ship now took all of them, and Will's head started to feel like a fog had descended on it. A nagging pain began behind his eyes. But Edward Southworth was the first to throw up. That set everyone else off, and they were all retching into available buckets.

Finally, exhausted and wishing he had never left England, Will lay down, wrapped himself in his cloak, and fell into merciful sleep.

He awoke reluctantly a few hours later to unfamiliar noise. The intensity of the wind had increased to a roar and it buffeted the ship. The pitching had intensified too. It became necessary to hang on to anything that was stable, for Will could feel himself rolling about on the deck with the movement of the ship. He sat up, and even then he found himself sliding first one way then another. The lantern which had long gone out swung precariously almost at right angles to the deck head.

Digory Priest cried out, 'What is happening?'

'A storm,' Will stated the obvious, and smothered his impatience. He felt too ill for more. He simply lay down again but hope of sleep vanished.

The storm raged for the better part of two weeks. The sailors fought to keep the ship on course, and cursed the weather. The passengers endured endless misery. They could not eat, for their stomachs would hold nothing and they could not sleep, for the continual crash of waves against the ship, the riding up one wave and crashing down into the next jarred the very teeth in their heads. Water cascaded through the deck head beams, and hatches, soaking their clothes so that they chafed their skin, and the cold seeped into their bones so that they developed coughs and colds and fevers. Fearing for their lives, they begged God to save them. Those with wives and children who had been left behind now thanked their God that they had not been able to join them on the ship.

Without sight of sun or stars for days on end, the captain could not determine their position, and they drifted hopelessly off course. A journey of two days took fourteen. When they eventually spotted land, the captain announced they were in sight of the towering fjords of Norway, not the flat landscape of Amsterdam.

But at last they hove into Delftshaven. Never had Will been so thankful to put his feet on dry land. Holland, with its strange flat landscape of windmills and canals, seemed like paradise compared to the heaving ship. He fervently hoped he would never have to set foot on board any ship ever again.

As they stood on the dockside wondering what to do next, Francis Jessop voiced all their thoughts. 'Well we've arrived! I wonder when the others will come over.'

'They will come,' Will said and he knew they would.

FOUR
Apostasy

Amsterdam, 1609

As the sailors, standing on the small footrope slung beneath the yards reefed the sails and the hawser slipped over the bollard to secure the ship to the quay, Mary Brewster let out a sigh of relief.

So this was Holland. *At last!*

She had heard that Holland was flat, of course—hadn't everyone? But Mary hadn't expected it to be so—well—foreign! The people dressed differently, they spoke differently, they even appeared to act differently. The buildings, what she could see of them, were strange too. Similar in some ways—the usual array of sheds and huts and warehouses adorning the edge of the quayside—but beyond them the houses were all closed in together. In fact the whole place seemed closed in to one who had spent many years in the English countryside.

She moved to join Bridget Robinson at the taffrail to look out on this new land, this Holland, which was to be their new home.

It seemed an unpromising sort of place, not only flat with no hills or landmarks, but all she could see were roofs and chimneys, and the sky above them was leaden with the threat of rain, making the whole scene appear depressingly grey. So much for Holland in August! Mary had a sudden pang of homesickness, a longing for the pretty greenness of England, for the hills and cliffs, for the emptiness.

Not that England had been anything but a trial she remembered, shaking herself from her daydream. It had been persecution, prison, and living with kind brethren, not in their own home. She had felt distressed, and displaced. Not that she would ever have complained, for the brethren had been so kind. Not that she ever doubted that the decision to move to Holland was the right one. But that last time, it had been hard on them all, especially on the children. She tried to push the thought away for it had taken great resolution to keep herself together. Children weakened a woman. Just the thought of her little ones clinging in terror to her skirts brought the tears to her eyes.

'Look! There's Jonathan!' Bridget cried referring to Mary's son. 'And Will Bradford! And Edward Southworth, and all of them!'

Mary saw them too, waiting beside the quay with some of the others, looking for them, and she waved, her heart skipping to see her boy.

However, while these men had got away safely, others, her William among them, had to hide themselves, for fear of arrest. She knew her William was always nearby, though, looking out for her, for all of them.

Even if she hadn't seen him, she had felt his presence. And the Lord never left them.

The magistrates hadn't known what to do with a group of homeless women and straggly children. They pushed them from one place to another, until they decided that their only crime had been to obey husbands and fathers, just as Christian women ought—even though the same husbands and fathers eluded them.

'Go home,' they told them.

'We cannot go home,' Bridget had spoken for them all in her clear young voice, her chin up proudly, her eyes defiant. 'We have no homes to go to. They have all been sold. Why cannot you let us leave? You do not want us here.'

The magistrates frowned at her, for they did not have the answer. Still, they let them go, glad to be rid of them. And now here they were at last, in Holland. Free. No, hilly and pretty England might be, but it was a dangerous place for Separatists.

A short while later Mary followed Katherine down the gangplank to the quay and found herself in a huddle of brothers and sisters as they noisily greeted each other.

'How goes it young Will?' Brewster asked as he hugged Will to him as a son, and slapped him hard on the back.

'Well enough,' Will assured him with a fleeting grin. 'We have found lodgings and I have apprenticed myself to a silk maker.'

Mary felt her husband brace himself, and his eyes narrowed. She felt it too, the reserve in those cool blue eyes. 'There is something you are not telling me. Is it the congregation?'

Will took a breath, and evidently searched for something to say. Now was not the time. 'We wrote to you about it. Did you get the letter?'

Brewster frowned. 'Yes.'

'Everything in the letter was true. But you will see for yourself, sir. But come. Jonathan and I have secured lodgings for ourselves and for you.'

Now that Mary had let her son go, she gave Will a sisterly kiss on the cheek. He had grown up since she last saw him, now almost a man. He had procured lodgings for them. She knew it had not been Jonathan's doing. He would not have thought of it. No, this was Will's thoughtfulness. Practical as ever. No matter how rudimentary they might be, she was so grateful. She needed to get her little ones out of the weather, for already it began to spot with rain.

Brewster did see at the first meeting they attended the following Sunday.

The shabby rented hall in the centre of Amsterdam was a dark cavernous wooden building, and it was the only one John Smith could find to cope with the number of Separatists who had arrived from England. To Young Will it was a place to meet, functional, if not the height of comfort. To some in the congregation, it was the object of much murmuring.

The Scrooby newcomers occasioned no small comment when they joined the congregation, but they were received warmly. Brewster felt the comfortable familiarity about meeting with people they had known in Gainsborough, about the order of the meeting, the kind of things discussed. Yet Brewster felt the tension in the air, and no wonder, for Will had told him in his letters that the pastor, John Smith, had been coming out with all sorts of odd things, and making the congregation uneasy. He wondered if John Robinson noticed it too.

The meeting began in the usual way with a long prayer and then the congregation sat down on the wooden benches, Bibles on their knees, to hear Master Smith's lesson.

He began by reading a long portion in Exodus, and then spoke of faith, the faith of Abraham and of Moses. They had heard it all before. It occurred to Brewster that it would be good if Master Smith could find other subjects for his sermons. He found his wits wandering, as he studied the congregation. They had a large congregation here, he thought with approval. Men and women who reverenced God, who sought truth in the scriptures, who had left England for the same reasons that they all had. The hall was packed tight with bodies. Perhaps the Lord would bless them with more increase.

Suddenly he forgot about increase and the congregation. Admittedly his wits had gone begging, but had he heard right? *What* had Smith said? He turned shocked eyes to John Smith who stood on the platform, a man of average height, with wild hair, and to Brewster's mind, a superior attitude.

'I repeat,' Smith said helpfully, 'the scriptures you hold in your hands, brothers, the Bible you refer to, are *not* the word of God.'

Brewster couldn't believe his ears. He wasn't the only one. The startled congregation shifted uneasily and looked at one another. Had the man taken leave of his senses?

Brewster tried to jump to his feet, but John Robinson pulled him down again, and made a warning signal with his hand.

Reluctantly, Brewster did as he was bid, even though rage fizzed in his veins. His fingers gripped his Bible and he had a burning desire to speak, but John kept his hand on his arm as a warning. He knew why. *Give a man enough rope and he will hang himself.*

And Smith obligingly proceeded to do so. 'The scriptures in the original languages are the Word of God,' he explained further. Well no-one could disagree with that! 'In Greek, or Hebrew, or in Aramaic, that is God's word. But in English, no,' and he paused dramatically, raising his voice to a crescendo to add, 'for the *translation* is the work of men!'

'This is outrageous!' Brewster fumed.

'Quiet brother!' Robinson hissed.

But Brewster could not keep quiet. He jumped to his feet, shaking Robinson's restraining hand from his arm. 'So perhaps you could explain, Brother, just how are we to read the scriptures, since few of us here have the ability to read Hebrew, or Greek, or Aramaic?'

Smith glared at him. It was unheard of for someone to challenge him directly in a meeting. He managed a sort of half-smile. 'Of course, Brother, we must read the scriptures in the original language, and then a brother will translate.'

This was too much for John Robinson also. He came to his feet beside Brewster. 'How do you suppose that every individual in the congregation will know that what the translator says is an accurate translation?' he demanded.

'Because he will have the Lord's spirit.' Hoping that was the end of the argument Smith waited for John Robinson and William Brewster to resume their seats.

'So does the translator who writes it down, surely?' Brewster countered, and his voice was rising.

'We cannot be sure of that.'

'So neither can we be sure of your translator, sir!' Brewster bellowed. Again John Robinson's hand was on his arm.

John Robinson took up the fight. 'And surely such a translation as you speak of must also be the work of men! How can it be any different to the printed translation?'

It was John Carver's turn. 'Why do we need such translator when we already have a translation here?' He waved his own Geneva Bible in the air for all to see.

The congregation's murmur of agreement grew in volume. Smith could see his hold on his flock disintegrating before his very eyes. The half-smile vanished from his face and he cast Robinson a look of pure dislike. 'Because that is not the word of God,' he repeated.

'Rubbish!' John Robinson thundered. 'Did not Wycliffe, and Tyndale, and Coverdale and others translate the holy writings into English so that we could see for ourselves and not have to rely on someone else—a priest—to tell us? Did some of them not die for that privilege? Or is it that you would take us back again to Romanism where the priests keep the sole right of scripture reading and translation for themselves so that they may control what people believe? Do you, sir, put yourself in the role of a Romish priest?'

'No, no,' Smith cried tremulously.

Big John Carver put his two pence worth in. 'I ain't no scholar,' he said. 'And I ain't learning no Hebrew. Not when I have the English here in my hand!' And he again waved his Bible in the air emphatically.

There was noisy agreement among the congregation.

Seeing that the meeting had degenerated into chaos, Smith said placatingly, 'Come now, brethren. There is no need for—'

Brewster raised his voice to be heard over the general hubbub. 'You want to control the brethren,' he accused Smith. 'You want them to believe everything you tell them instead of them searching out the scriptures for themselves.'

Smith panicked. 'No, no, I assure you, brethren, that is not the case!' he cried desperately.

No-one was listening to him. They were all talking at once. 'Ridiculous!' 'Apostasy!' 'Papist doctrine!'

John Robinson pressed his advantage, 'A translation puts the ancient writings into a form we can understand. Or should God's Word be kept only for those able to study Hebrew and Greek? Is not God's Word to be available to all?'

'Aye! Aye!' cried the congregation.

Furious now, Smith's voice trembled. 'You mistake, sir. A careful examination of scripture reveals differences between the original text and the English.'

'How can that be otherwise, sir?' John Robinson countered angrily. 'In English we say the same thing in several differing ways. Does that mean we have said something different each time? No. What we have in our hands is essentially the same as the disciples and prophets wrote down all those years ago, all inspired by God. It is scripture!'

Brewster could keep quiet no longer and again joined John Robinson in the fray. 'So you think the Lord expects all of us, little ones as well, to learn Hebrew, do you? And Greek? May God condemn you for a nave, sir!'

'I ain't learning no Greek,' John Carver said again mulishly.

'I would ask you to leave my church, sir!' Smith announced. 'And may God forgive your ignorance!'

'And may God forgive your lies,' John Robinson retorted and walked out.

Brewster followed, and the whole congregation of Scrooby and not a few of Smith's congregation went with them.

'The man's a madman!' John Robinson thundered in the sanctuary of William Brewster's rented home, pacing back and forth in the kitchen.

Old Richard Clifton sat down with difficulty on one of the wooden chairs, and rested on his stick. He frowned in perplexity, fingering his frothy white beard. Never could he agree to calling one of the Lord's elect a madman, no matter how odd his ways. 'Well,' he said mildly, 'he does seem a little muddled.'

'Muddled? *Muddled?*' Robinson stopped to glare at the old man. 'Satan has overreached him! 'Tis outright apostasy.' He glanced at Will, half hidden in the corner. 'Seems you were right about Smith, young Will.'

'What is apostasy?' Jonathan, Brewster's son asked Will quietly, ashamed to show his ignorance.

John Robinson overheard him. 'It means to turn away from the truth and promote untruth.'

Mary paused in the act of pouring ale into some mugs and turned her eyes on her husband. 'I hope that doesn't mean we are all expected to learn Hebrew and Greek.' she said.

Brewster was for once a little calmer than John. 'No, my dear, that is not the case. You may be easy.'

'We must, of course, change congregations,' Richard Clifton said, shaking his head dolefully. 'We can't stay here after this.'

Will said, 'Quite a lot of people left when we did. But I do not understand. Why did not all of them leave? Surely it must be obvious that Brother Smith is promoting Romish doctrine?'

'They follow a man rather than the Lord,' Brewster said dismissively, and Will, belatedly remembering that he was not part of this conversation wished he had not spoken.

Thinking he had a valid point, John Robinson took pity on him. 'When people follow a man, rather than what God's word says,' he explained, 'they will make excuses for him.'

'But we have all suffered so that we might find the truth of God's word. We have fought so hard—'

'The fight goes out of them, Will. They want an easy life. Remember they have been with Smith for many years.'

'I was with him once, in Gainsborough,' Will said and he was sad.

Brewster growled low in his throat. 'Smith's got the very Devil in him! I never did hear the like in all my life!'

Old Richard Clifton made a noise of protest in his throat. No-one should say that of one of the Lord's elect!

John Robinson met his gaze and said his voice heavy with irony, 'His instability and wantonness of wit is his sin and our cross to bear.'

Unhappy at their anger, Richard Clifton banged his stick on the flagstone floor. 'Brothers, please! Remember he is one of the Lord's elect.'

'Perhaps,' Brewster said pointedly. 'Perhaps not for much longer!'

John Carver who had sat silent and morose in the corner,

contemplating his beer mug now said, 'So what can we do about it?'

John Robinson drew a breath to clear his head. For a moment no-one spoke as he paced the floor, brows drawn together, his finger thoughtfully on his lips. 'The brethren are in danger from this apostasy,' he said at last. 'We cannot allow them to continue subject to it.'

'So you also think we should leave this congregation?' Brewster asked pointedly.

The room fell silent as they all waited for John Robinson's answer. By tacit consent he had supplanted Richard Clifton as their leader, the man they looked to for decisions. Even so, he deferred to the older man. 'What do you think, Brother Clifton?'

Clifton sighed with weariness. 'He began with such promise. Such a bright man who gave up holy orders for the Lord. I am surprised at him!'

In the face of no clear answer, John Robinson made a decision. 'We cannot stay under the leadership of a man who decries the holy scriptures.'

Will was moved to speak. 'It seems to me that we've already left.'

Brewster laughed suddenly. 'Well said, Young Will. I agree! I think we have no alternative but to leave Master Smith's congregation.'

'We could meet on our own,' Richard Clifton suggested. 'We did so before.'

John Robinson shook his head. 'And where will we meet? With two congregations here in Amsterdam already, how can we form a third?'

John Robinson said, 'There is a congregation of Ancient Brethren here under a man called Francis Johnson. They meet in Brownists' Alley.'

''Tis said they were the people associated with brothers Barrow and Greenwood who suffered for the Lord's sake at Tyburn,' Will supplied.

John Robinson knew that. 'Aye.'

Brewster said, 'Were they not exiled to Newfoundland or some such place before coming here? And wasn't there some scandal over their pastor's wife?'

Clifton, ever on the defence of his fellows, said, 'Only for the woman's love of finery. 'Tis a small thing.'

'What do we know of this Master Johnson?' Brewster demanded, putting his beer pot down on the table.

John Robinson said, 'He seems a God-fearing man, from what I've heard, and he has suffered much for the Lord, what with the exiling to Newfoundland, and prison and such. I know the Ancient Brethren have similar views to our own. I think we should pay Master Johnson a visit.'

FIVE
Brownists' Alley

Amsterdam, 1609

Neglecting the book on her lap, Alice Carpenter absently watched a bumblebee settle on a flower on a foxglove stem, buzzing his way inside. Here in the courtyard garden the city seemed so far away, the noise of the carts and the horses and the people outside, and the smell that went with them, distant on the late summer air. She looked up at the clear blue sky and took a deep breath enjoying the scent of lavender and stocks. It was a perfect day, a day of sunshine and ease.

From inside the house, her father's voice filtered through the hum of insects, and so did Master Ainsworth's. She knew what they discussed for the whole of Amsterdam seemed to buzz with the gossip.

She shook her head. *Don't spoil the peace. Don't let ugly things spoil the beauty of this garden.* But even though she fought it, the whole scandal came flooding back to her, things so terrible that to know about them brought a shameful blush to her freckled cheeks.

Her father's voice, gruff on the hot morning air, drifted to her through the open window. 'Do you think it to be true?'

Henry Ainsworth must have followed him to the window. 'I know not. But this I do know, and Brother Johnson agrees with me, that the Lord has not blessed us.'

Alexander Carpenter grunted and Alice winced. It was what they were all thinking. How they had worked and saved and struggled to get the meeting place in *Bruingang* (Brownists' Alley, so-called because opposers insisted on calling them Brownists). No sooner had they put it up than a storm blew it all down again. So just where was the Lord's blessing? Certainly not in a strong construction! They had to start again.

Alexander Carpenter said, 'We cannot act on mere hearsay. But we must look into the matter. If it is found to be true—'

'Well, yes. But you have to remember that some will hear no ill of Studley.'

'Well, he has fooled them with his piety. False piety. I have no truck with the man.'

'Be careful, you know he is an elder!'

Alice closed her eyes. She felt sick at the thought. This was talk unfit for delicate female ears, and she realised all at once why it was that men were elders, and not women, be they ever so capable.

Abruptly she got up and walked away from the house, away from the conversation, following the little brick path as it wound its way first of all through the herb garden, past the huge apple tree, and on to the roses.

The garden was her mother's project, a labour of love, not only providing a refuge in good weather, but food for the house. Alice liked to come here, to seek solitude, hidden from prying eyes by the jungle of plants where she might pray or just think.

Now she prayed, *Dear Lord, please don't let it be true.* Yet even then she knew it was true. She just could not bear to think of the gossip that buzzed through Amsterdam bringing reproach on the congregation of which she was a part, and on the Lord himself.

She was eighteen years old, the fourth of six children, and not one of them married—not one of them even with a suitor in sight, as her mother was fond of lamenting. It was not that the Carpenter girls were ill-favoured, although neither could it be said that they were outstanding beauties. Still, she would like to be married, and settle down with her own home, her own husband and perhaps children.

The door opened and the two men came out of the house and into the garden. Her father stood still talking with Henry Ainsworth, and she thought how different they were. Alexander Carpenter with his large over-fed belly, and full magnificent golden beard, and the younger Henry Ainsworth, tall, slender, clean shaven with his little darting eyes and fair hair. Alice liked Henry Ainsworth in a friendly sort of way. He was a common visitor to their house, a man known for his faith and good humour, yet he was modest to the point of shyness. He and her father always got on well. They trusted each other.

Henry Ainsworth caught sight of her. 'So Mistress Alice, enjoying the sunshine?' he asked and a ready smile came to his lips.

'Good day to you Master Ainsworth.' Alice dropped a curtsey. 'Yes indeed. How is Mistress Ainsworth?'

'Very well, I thank you.' He smiled broadly, his eyes lighting up. 'Recovered from her cold. She will be at the meeting tonight.'

'Is it true, sir, that we have people from Nottinghamshire joining our congregation?

'And how did you hear that, Mistress?'

'Oh, 'tis general knowledge. 'Tis said they left Master Smith's congregation.'

Her father shot her a look which said, *Keep your peace, young lady.*

Ainsworth frowned as though he did not wish to discuss this subject with her. 'You will see tonight.' He turned to Alexander. 'I'll be on my way.'

'I'll see you out.'

Watching them walk to the gate in the wall, Alice wondered what had caused the Scrooby people to leave the other congregation. But she thought how exciting it would be to have newcomers. She knew her mother would be hoping that there would be eligible young men among them. After all, when you had five daughters to marry off, it was a matter of constant concern as to who was in the congregation. Alice smiled to herself. Well, one never knew.

Will always found it nerve-wracking going into a new congregation. No matter how he tried to think of them as fellow-believers, which they were, the kindest people in the world, nevertheless he knew that he and the others would be objects of curiosity, that they would be assessed as to what kind of people they were, whether they were zealous, or just going through the motions. He knew that because he had done the same to others.

Francis Johnson's congregation in Brownists' Alley was large and they filled their new hall, without the newcomers making it a tighter squeeze. Yet still they shuffled up and made room on the benches—the men on one side, the women on the other, and the children looked after by an older strict matron, a deaconess, who used a birch twig to keep them in check.

Feeling everyone's eyes upon him, Will sat down between an older man with large white whiskers who smelled of strong drink, and fortuitously thin Edward Southworth. Even so he felt squashed, and his elbows dug into his sides. Turning the pages of his Bible was going to be some feat. Moreover, it was hot, searingly hot, and airless in the dark hall, and he felt the heat building inside his coat, and sweat break out on his forehead. He fingered the large white collar at his throat and ached to remove his coat. Not that he could do so, for that would not be seemly.

The speaker on a raised platform at one end of the hall—who Will learned later was Henry Ainsworth—waited patiently for them all to settle. Will took a moment to study him. A serious man, he thought, but with a twinkle in his small eyes. Then, as the hall fell silent again, he addressed the congregation.

'Brethren, we must welcome our friends from Nottinghamshire.' He beamed in the general direction of the newcomers. 'First we will sing Psalm 55 *Give ear to my prayer, O God,* after which we will pray.'

This was new—singing during a meeting. Will wasn't sure what to make of it. But as it was a psalm, well that must be all right. After all did not Jesus sing psalms? But the rest of the meeting was very much like the Separatist meetings in England, a portion of scripture read, talks on it, explanations, applications. He was right, also about the twinkle in Brother Ainsworth's eye. Ainsworth had an animated way about him, and he caused a chuckle during his address. That was also new, and Will found that he paid closer attention because of it.

Then Master Francis Johnson took the platform. He was altogether a different man. Flamboyantly dressed, with a large starched ruff around his neck, and bright red doublet, he was obviously a man of means and he liked others to know it. Will had also noticed a woman in the congregation—his wife?—dressed very stylishly. They looked like they might fit together.

Master Johnson was a good orator. He had a way with the audience and used the Bible freely to prove his point. He was a man of medium height, with long dark hair Will knew a little about him, how he had suffered in prison, been exiled, and so on, so obviously he was a man of great faith, and that commanded respect.

Will shifted uncomfortably in his seat and leaned forward to try to catch some cooler air, and the man with the whiskers grumbled in his throat. The man directly in front of him sat slumped, dozing perhaps, his rounded back intruding on what little space Will had. He shifted again and unintentionally glanced across to the women's section. A young woman sat on the end of the bench nearest to him, her head bent as she searched her Bible, a concentration frown on her face. She was not pretty, but pleasant enough, Will thought, with tawny hair scraped back severely under her cap, and freckles on her nose. As though feeling his eyes upon her, she looked up suddenly and caught his eye.

Will looked away quickly. He should not be distracted by young women. His business was to study the scriptures as expounded by the Lord's elect.

As the meeting wore on, his discomfort grew. But at last, the meeting closed with a final sung psalm and a prayer.

Thankfully, Will stood up.

The congregation came to life again, the noise of excited chatter, of introductions and comments, of greeting and welcomes becoming a surprisingly large sound in such a confined space.

A man greeted Will. 'Alexander Carpenter is the name, sir,' he said. 'Welcome to Amsterdam.'

Will shook his hand. 'William Bradford. We have been here some weeks, sir.'

'I know it. Allow me, sir, to introduce my daughters to you.' Three young women, one of them the girl who had caught his eye earlier, appeared from behind him. 'My eldest, Julianna.' The tallest of the three, and perhaps the prettiest, bobbed a curtsey. 'Agnes.' A thin small slip of a girl with lighter hair just visible beneath her cap also curtseyed. 'And my middle daughter Alice.' The girl who had caught his eye earlier also bobbed a curtsey, keeping her head bowed. Then as she rose she smiled at him. He liked the look of her, of her wide smiling mouth, and of her eyes a luminous green colour, like clear sea. There was sensibleness in Alice's eyes, and an air of quiet calmness about her person. She moved with easy grace, with dignity. 'My dears, this is Master William Bradford.'

At that moment as Edward Southworth and George Morton joined Will, he had to introduce them.

But his attention was claimed by another man waiting with growing impatience beside him. 'Henry May, sir, and pleased to meet you.'

'William Bradford,' Will said, 'Edward Southworth and George Morton.'

All the gentlemen bowed and then Edward and George made their excuses and left Will to the mercies of Master May. The Carpenters also moved away, and he was dismayed that they may think him rude for allowing Henry May to cut in.

'Allow me to introduce my wife, sir.' Will greeted Mistress May suitably, a pretty but plump woman with large grey eyes. 'And these are my daughters, my elder daughter Jacqueline, recently married to Master de l'Ecluse, and my younger, Dorothy.'

Both girls curtseyed and said what was proper. However, it was the younger girl, Dorothy who caught his attention.

Dorothy May had to be the prettiest little thing he had ever seen. She gazed up at him with eyes as blue as summer sky, so round and innocent that she reminded him of a painting of a child he had once seen. She had ethereally white skin, smooth as wax, and small, plump dark red lips. Hair of glossy pale gold silk cascaded from a crisp white cap to her waist. Her body was still young, with the promise of womanhood. Nevertheless, Will felt the breath catch in his throat, and was shocked at himself.

He said, 'Mistress de l'Ecluse, Mistress Dorothy,' and bowed.

The two girls left them, and their father watched them for a moment, fondly. 'Dorothy is twelve,' Henry May told him.

Twelve! Will felt the floor rock beneath his feet. 'I thought she was older than that,' he said lamely. He had thought her to be about fourteen.

'Yes, she looks older than her years.' He went on to ask Will where he had come from. 'You are a man of property, I understand,' he said.

Will was not used to the wiles of match-making parents and, although he was surprised at the question, answered, 'There is a farm and a house in Austerfield in Nottinghamshire which will become mine when I am twenty-one.'

'Ah, you must manage your assets wisely, Master Bradford.'

William Brewster came to his rescue and Will was obliged to perform introductions. 'Mistress Brewster is getting supper for us, Will. We must not tarry.'

Will excused himself to Master May and left with Brewster.

'So, you made the acquaintance of Master May,' Brewster said pointedly as they walked over the canal bridge.

'As you saw.'

Brewster chuckled low in his throat. 'And Alexander Carpenter.'

Will frowned. 'And so?'

Brewster's chuckle grew and he put his hand on Will's shoulder. 'Oh Will, you have a lot to learn.'

'I fail to understand.'

'Can you really be so slow, I wonder? Master Carpenter has no less than five unmarried daughters. Can you imagine the difficulty in finding suitable husbands for them all?'

Will saw it suddenly. 'Oh.'

'And Henry May has one daughter suitably married, and wants to find a good husband for the other.'

'She is only twelve.'

'No matter. Once you are betrothed, she will keep. I am surprised you were not asked about your inheritance.'

Will chuckled ruefully. 'As a matter of fact, I was.'

'Then I should watch your step if I were you! Be sure, he means to have you!'

Will shook his head, but thinking of Dorothy May, it occurred to him that there could be worse things.

'I don't like it,' John Robinson said quietly to Brewster some days later when they left the meeting in Brownists' Alley.

Brewster said, 'You've heard the gossip about Studley then?'

'Aye. How did you hear about it?'

''Tis common talk.'

'I've just spoken to Master Ainsworth, and Master Johnson about it.'

Brewster looked at him sharply in the bright moonlight. 'And?'

'It hasn't been handled right. Johnson is particularly close to Studley. He is protecting him out of misplaced loyalty, I think.'

'But surely, if the man has been committing fornication—'

'Not just fornication,' John Robinson said very quietly, so as not to be overheard by the late leavers from the meeting, 'but with small girls.'

'Dear God!' Brewster was so shocked the blasphemy burst from him, whereupon he looked skywards and uttered a quick apology. Then after a moment, 'Is it true?'

'Don't know. Evidently some time ago a tract was circulating with the allegations, and Studley sued for libel in the Dutch court. The court, however, found against Studley and for the publishers of the tract.'

Brewster let his breath go in a low whistle. 'Was there no sentence imposed upon him? No fine, no punishment?'

'It would seem not. I don't know how the law goes on in this country.'

'Law or not, it should have gone to the congregation.'

Robinson took a breath. 'No, it didn't. No-one went to court to view the proceedings, and since there were no witnesses that I know of, no actual accusers, but rather Studley's word against the publishers', Johnson decided there was no case to answer.'

'But the man is no longer in good standing! Even if it cannot be proved, he should not be an elder! Does not the scripture say such a man should be *"unreprovable"*, and *"well reported of, even of them that are without"*?'

'I does. And I would certainly allow no man found guilty of such a crime to be an elder. I think Henry Ainsworth has allowed himself to be taken along by Johnson who will admit no accusation against Studley.'

Brewster raised a sceptical bushy eyebrow. 'Oh. In each others' pockets, are they?'

They walked together over the bridge, and John Robinson paused again to lean on the parapet and look down at the black water. 'What can we do? We don't even belong to the congregation yet! We have no option but to leave it to God to deal with.'

Brewster could see he was unhappy. He changed the subject. 'Have you heard about Smith?'

John Robinson looked at him sharply. 'No.'

Brewster took a breath, knowing he had startling news. 'He has rebaptised his flock.'

Robinson stared at him for a long minute, bereft of speech.

Satisfied with his reaction, Brewster went on, 'He has decided that our baptisms in the Church of England are not baptisms.'

'The man's an idiot!' Robinson snapped impatiently. He walked on quickly, then stopped and turned back to Brewster who, taken by surprise, belatedly followed him. 'We were all baptised in the name of the Father and of the Son and of the Holy Spirit. So how can he say that?'

'Well, he says that since the Church of England is Babylon itself, and we do not recognise the ordination of their priests, we didn't ought to recognise the baptism either. Further, he says that the scripture says that baptism is an act of faith by believing disciples, so how could an infant make such a declaration of faith?'

'Ah, so now he says we should not baptise infants?' He turned to walk away again, clearly agitated and again came back. 'How can he do that? How can he refuse believing parents the comfort of knowing their little ones are safe with God?'

He glared at Brewster as if it were his fault. Brewster shook his head. Scripturally speaking, he had an uneasy feeling that Smith might just be right. But at the same time, what Smith proposed was too controversial. True, infant baptism had been brought in by the Catholic Church sometime in the dark ages as insurance against the appalling infant mortality rate, and absorbed into the Protestant faiths as the Reformation took hold. Children were routinely baptised within a day or two of birth. It had never before occurred to anyone to question it. Every family could expect to lose one or two or more infants to the grave, and their comfort was in thinking that the child had gone to be with God in heaven. It was unthinkable to deprive them of that one comfort.

'No,' Robinson said again after a long moment's thought, 'we cannot deny parents the need to bring their offspring into the true church. Surely believing parents have that right?' He paused again. 'The man's a madman! He has a vacillating mind.'

'Well, he has rebaptised all his flock.' Brewster repeated.

'By whose authority?'

'His own, I think.'

Robinson took a deep decisive breath. 'I think we should distance ourselves from Master Smith,' he said to Brewster.

Brewster had seen it coming. Smith with his strange ideas was like gunpowder, likely to explode in the faces of the congregation.

Old Richard Clifton saw them talking on the bridge and walked towards them, bent over his cane, treading with difficulty on the cobbles.

'All this argumentation is not good for the church,' Robinson said as Clifton came near. 'The brethren are being torn one way and then another. And I don't think Ainsworth and Johnson have handled the Studley affair properly.'

'We have an obligation to protect the flock,' Brewster pointed out.

'I don't want the brethren to be caught in the middle of scandal and controversy. They have enough to do with making a life for themselves in this country which is not England.'

'So—you have heard about Studley, then?' Clifton said.

John Robinson looked at him accusingly, 'You knew of these things?'

'Aye. I dismissed them. When you get to my age you'll realise it don't do to listen to gossip.'

'What if the gossip is true?' He took a frustrated breath. 'But we were discussing John Smith.'

'Ah yes. The baptism affair.'

'You know of that too?' John Robinson demanded.

'Of course.'

John Robinson controlled himself with an effort. 'You might have told me.'

Clifton shrugged. Having begun the congregation in Scrooby, he did not want to share the leadership with Robinson. It was natural, but it wasn't right.

Robinson swallowed his pride. 'There is trouble on every hand,' he said. 'Trouble with Johnson's church, trouble with Smith's. I don't want the brethren caught up in scandal. I think we should move again. Perhaps to Leyden.'

Richard Clifton's eyes mirrored his disapproval. 'I don't like that idea. We are united in the basic doctrines of separation from the church.' He stamped his stick on the cobbles. 'We all recognise the Church of England as popish, Babylonish. We know much of her practice is idolatry and her clergy lord it over the common people. These things we are agreed. And a man stands condemned for supporting the whore, Babylon.'

'Did we not repent of the Church?' Brewster dared to suggest.

Clifton delivered the death blow, 'Aye. And our baptism? Do we repent of that as well?'

Robinson stifled an oath. How difficult it was to find the truth of the scriptures at this time. If only the Lord would reveal things more clearly!

'Well I am not for moving,' Clifton stated. 'I have moved enough. Besides, we have distanced ourselves from Smith's congregation so as not to be affected by whatever he does.'

'It's not just Smith,' Brewster said.

Robinson sighed. 'All this business with Studley. There is something dangerous afoot there, something which I fear may well split the congregation and cause untold trouble for the brethren. I don't want them mixed up in it.'

'You worry too much.'

Brewster intervened again. 'I think Master Robinson is right. There is trouble brewing. I feel it in the air. The brethren have been through enough.'

John Robinson nodded. 'Yes indeed. Furthermore it is difficult enough keeping to the way of the truth as it is without adding to our burdens. As elders it is our duty to protect the flock.'

Again Richard Clifton stamped his stick on the cobbles. 'I am an old man,' he said. 'Like you, John Robinson, I have been to Cambridge and I have learned to question. Like you, I have searched the scriptures and done my best to serve God. I too renounced my orders. But this you know. This I do say, my brothers, that the scriptures say we should all speak "*one thing*", and that there should be no dissensions among us. The truth does not allow for dissensions. I am saddened at this state of affairs, for we are disunited.' He pulled his cloak tighter about his body. 'But I am cold and tired and I am going home to my wife and children.' He started off carefully in the direction of his home and then turned back to them. 'My family and I are not moving anywhere else. We are staying here. So whatever you decide, you decide it without me.'

John Robinson didn't answer him, but allowed him to make his way slowly along the canal path.

Robinson and Brewster watched him until he disappeared from view.

'We have differences of thought, John,' Brewster said. 'Things that cannot be resolved easily. How can we say we believe something when we do not? How can we fall into line with Smith when he speaks as he does? No. The man is apostate, and those who adhere to his church apostate.'

'It's not so much Smith,' John Robinson answered him, 'for Master Clifton is right, we are distant from that. My worry is the growing problem with the Ancient Brethren for Ainsworth and Johnson will be at each others' throats before long.'

'You think so?'

John Robinson started to walk slowly towards his own home. 'I think we should move. I think we should put it to the others, and apply to move to, say, Leyden, to be on our own.'

Brewster fell into step beside him. 'And Master Clifton?'

John Robinson's lips set in a tight line. 'He must decide for himself what he will do, as must all of them.'

However, the decision to move to Leyden did not go down well with the Scrooby people. They had just managed to settle in Amsterdam and it meant uprooting yet again. It had already been a great upheaval to leave their farms and other work in England to come to Holland. With great difficulty the men had found jobs and homes for their families and had begun the difficult task of integrating into Dutch society. Now, suddenly, they were expected to leave.

'May I ask why?' Mary Brewster demanded with uncharacteristic abruptness as she ladled bacon stew into a dish and slammed it down in front of her husband.

Brewster looked at her, surprised at her evident dislike of the idea. 'No,' he said bluntly. 'You may not.'

Will got his stew next, and it nearly landed in his lap from the force with which Mary set it down. A glance at her stormy face did not encourage him to say anything about it. Instead he said to Brewster, 'Excuse me, sir, but I am apprenticed to a silk maker, and now we must leave. Can we not know why?'

Brewster eyed his wife warily. 'It isn't for no reason, Will. There is very good reason, but your elders do not think it right to discuss it with you, for it would be wrong to gossip, would it not?'

'Is it because of Daniel Studley?' Anne Peck asked with simple directness.

They all looked at her. Anne Peck was a distant relation of Brewster and at twelve years old had come to Holland with him as his ward. To Will, she was like a sister—an annoying sister who heard too much gossip.

Mary, who stood in place of her mother snapped, 'That is something you should know nothing about, young lady!'

Anne would not be silenced. 'I don't see why! Everyone in the congregation knows about it. Everyone is talking.'

'Anne!' Brewster snapped the reprimand. She immediately clamped her mouth shut in a sulk.

Will had heard the gossip, too, and had tried not to think about it. Now he felt himself blushing at the sheer shamefulness of it.

'By that she means all the young ones,' Jonathan Brewster said scathingly. He was three years older than Anne, and had all the superiority of an older brother.

'Well, the young ones shouldn't be talking about things they know nothing about,' Mary snapped. She sat down at the table.

'Let us thank God for our food,' Brewster interrupted, and they all bowed their heads.

Later, Will raised the subject with Sam Fuller.

Sam was older than Will by five years, a member of the original Ancient Brethren, and a married man. His sister Susanna was his ward. Will liked Sam for his gentleness, his obvious intellect, his love of books, and scripture. Sam loved people. All people. But most of all Sam loved his companions in the congregation. More to the point, Sam Fuller was a deacon in the congregation, and therefore, Sam Fuller would know what was afoot.

'You know, Will, if Master Robinson and Master Brewster think it wise to move to Leyden, they must have an excellent reason.' He took the plane to a length of wood he had fitted in the vice on the bench and began to stroke it rhythmically, taking off fine slivers of wood. The loft was an excellent place to use as a work shed.

Will perched on the other side of the bench. He trusted both men. 'I know that. But it is a lot to ask of the brethren when they have to uproot, sell houses they have just bought, and get new jobs all over again, without explanation. Some say that Master Studley is the reason.'

He waited for Sam's reaction, watching him carefully, and although Sam continued stroking the wood, Will could see the inward struggle he had with his conscience. After all, he really should not gossip. 'I am not surprised,' Sam managed at last, trying to sound non-committal.

With all the directness of youth and a burning desire to understand, Will would not let him off so lightly. 'So that's it.'

Sam hesitated, then continued working on the wood. 'I am unsure what to think.'

'You think him guilty, then?' Will pressed.

'I have no idea. It is not my problem. Leave such things to the elders to deal with.'

'Mmm.' Will was thoughtful, but if Sam hoped that was the end of the conversation, he should have known better. 'And there is something else, isn't there?'

'Perhaps.'

'John Smith?'

'Perhaps.'

Will studied him with that direct gaze, trying to read his thoughts, to understand what it was that Sam was not telling him. 'I knew Master Smith when he preached in Gainsborough. I belonged to his congregation until Brother Clifton set up the congregation in Scrooby. I always thought he was a good man, knowledgeable and Godly. Now I am not so sure. He has twice come out with some odd things.'

Sam abandoned the wood, stood up straight and allowed himself to be drawn in. 'Master Smith is like everyone else, struggling to find the truth of God's Word. Unfortunately, he does tend to veer towards any new kind of teaching.'

'You know he dared to question whether the Bible was God's Word,' Will said. 'We walked out of the meeting, all of us!'

Sam smiled. 'I wish I had been there!'

Will tried to make sense of it. 'You are right. Our elders would not act unless they thought it absolutely necessary. So we go to Leyden.'

'You sound like you do not wish to go.'

'I have reasons for wanting to stay in Amsterdam.'

It was Sam's turn to probe. 'Something to do with a pretty little blonde sister?'

Will blushed fire red. 'What makes you think that?'

'Something my wife said.' Sam frowned at him. 'She is too young, Will.'

'So, I have a long wait. And while I don't want to do the waiting in Leyden, I think it will be more sensible to be apart until she is old enough.'

'You want to marry her?'

Will looked down at the floor. He was eighteen, and he knew it was irresponsible to be thinking of marriage at such a young age. But he had lost his heart to her. To his mind, Dorothy was the epitome of beauty, of grace, of modesty. When she looked up at him from under her lashes with those large cornflower blue eyes his heart melted. He wanted to protect her, to care for her, to give her everything she could ever want. Oh yes, he wanted to marry Dorothy.

He stood up. 'I must be going. It grows dark.'

Sam turned back to his work. 'Yes—and I have a table to make. So get on your way.' His grin took the sting out of his words.

Will went to the trap door with the ladder jutting out from it. Then Sam checked him. 'Will—you'll change your mind before she is old enough, you know.'

Will looked at him straightly. 'I think not, sir.' And he disappeared.

Contrary to what he had told Will, Sam left the woodwork and also went downstairs, closing the trapdoor behind him. It was bitterly cold in the eaves of the house, and he sought the comfort of the huge fire in the kitchen. Will was too young to be thinking of marriage, he thought with disquiet. And Dorothy May was too young to be the object of courtship. Yet he knew Henry May encouraged it. Well, Will was a good catch in anyone's language. A strapping lad, with good looks, well connected in the congregation, and an inheritance in England. Still, very likely he would grow out of his infatuation, especially if he were in Leyden, some twenty-five miles distant.

SIX
Leyden

Leyden, 1610

Will paused to wipe the sweat from his face with the back of his hand. Despite the lateness of the hour, the heat of early summer reflected off the uneven cobbles beneath his feet, and he knew it would be an uncomfortably sticky night. Still, the warmth brought out the flowers, little daisies in the grassy banks alongside the canals, strange plants growing out of the mortar in the walls of the typical stepped and curved gabled buildings, and in between the bricks in the bridges. The air was alive with the hum of insects, and he knew that by tomorrow it would be a miracle if he did not find an itchy lump or two on his bare skin.

Unfortunately, the heat brought with it too, the stench from the canal as he made his way over the *Hoogewoerds* bridge towards the little house the Brewsters rented in the *Stinksteeg* which certainly lived up to its name. Covering his nose and mouth with his forearm in a vain attempt to stop his stomach contracting, he willed himself not to vomit. He had been used to strong aromas on the farm back in Austerfield, but nothing resembling the noisomeness of this canal.

Austerfield. How far away it seemed now. Even further now that Uncle Robert Bradford had died, his last close relative, for he did not count Uncle Robert's children—his cousins—close relatives, especially as the children were still minors. When he came of age in two years' time and received his inheritance, he would sell the farm and free himself once and for all of England.

Taking off his hat, he again wiped his brow on his shirtsleeve. It came away stained black from the black fabric he had been weaving. The dust stuck to a sweating oily brow, and clogged the lungs as well. And that was another thing. He hated weaving. In England weaving was considered women's work. Men worked the land, women—poorer women—spun and wove cloth. Like most of the brothers, he had been of yeoman stock, from a family of some consequence in the neighbourhood. When he came of age he had known he would inherit the comfortably sized farmhouse, and the acres that had been in his family for over a hundred years. But Leyden was renowned throughout Europe for its textile industry, not its farming. The immigrant had no choice but to join the army of weavers and accept the pitifully low wages that were on offer.

Low the wages may have been, but without Will's income the Brewsters would have starved. For although William Brewster tried to find work, he had been unsuccessful. He was considered too old, and too gentlemanly for work in textiles. Indeed, William Brewster was a scholar, not a weaver.

'You could earn a living by teaching English,' Will had suggested on more than one occasion. Brewster sighed wearily; these days he looked tired and aged. The move from Amsterdam had exhausted the last of his fortune, and the tiny house in the *Stinksteeg* was all he could afford. It tortured him that he could not care for his family, and that he had to rely on the wages of a mere boy for all of them to survive. It wouldn't have been so bad if his son Jonathan had not decided to marry his childhood sweetheart and find a house of his own.

'I'll look into it,' he had promised.

Will found Mary Brewster where she usually was, in the kitchen, sitting on a bench at the table, her Bible open in front of her, her sewing on her lap, but she looked up as Will's shadow fell across the floor, and struggled to her feet. For Mary was at the end of her pregnancy, and her enormous bulk made her awkward and lethargic. 'I didn't expect you yet, Will.'

Will put his hat on a peg behind the door and said, 'Don't get up on my account, mistress.' Her size alarmed him; it always worried him that she might suddenly go into labour when he was the only other person in the house and he would have to act as midwife. She sat down again, her legs apart beneath the grey skirt, to accommodate her massive belly. She looked tired and pale, her face greased with sweat, the tendrils of brown hair which escaped her cap, sticking to her cheeks. He felt a rush of protective love towards her, the way a man might feel for his mother, for indeed Mary Brewster was the nearest thing to a mother Will would ever know.

'There's ale in the jug,' she said.

Will went to the larder and pulled out the large earthen jug and removed the stopper, pouring ale into a mug. 'Is Jonathan here yet?'

'Not yet,' Mary snapped.

Will wished he hadn't asked. Jonathan's parents were not happy that their son should have taken on the responsibility for a wife while still only a child himself. And his wife was newly pregnant.

'And the children?' Will asked.

'At the Robinsons'. Anne is upstairs. She's got a fever.'

Will swigged the ale. It was lukewarm, and thick, like honey, but he looked at her an eyebrow raised. 'There is fever in the city.'

'There is fever in this street,' Mary corrected him. 'In this house. And 'tis no surprise, either, with the vapours rising from that pestilential canal.'

''Tis an open sewer,' Will agreed. He looked around him. The house was small, similar to the one in Amsterdam. Two rooms up and one room down. Where they were going to put a new baby heaven only knew. But then the house in *Stinksteeg* was only meant to be a temporary affair. Even now William Brewster searched for something better.

'I ought to look in on Anne,' Mary said.

'I'll do it.' Will couldn't let Mary waddle and puff her way upstairs when he could do the errand for her.

Anne Peck was growing into a young woman, and his relationship towards her had become more distant now that she was obviously not his sister. He now had to be more careful in his dealings with her.

He found her sitting up in the bed she usually shared with the Brewster girls, her blonde plaits falling over her shoulders, the covers pulled up to her chin when she saw who had come in.

'Oh, 'tis you, Will.'

'Mistress Brewster is feeling the heat,' Will explained. 'Did you want anything?'

''Tis only a slight fever. I am surprised I should have to go to bed.'

'Well, you are better off here than mixing with company and giving your sickness to Mistress Brewster now that she is so near her time.' He poured a drink from the brew Mary had left beside the bed and gave it to her. 'If there is nothing else?'

There wasn't, so he went downstairs again.

Brewster was home now, his booming voice rising up the closed stairwell.

'And how goes she?' Brewster greeted him by asking after his ward.

'Not too bad. I've seen a deal worse.'

''Tis hot today.'

'Aye. And the canal stinks more than usual.'

'Aye. Well, they don't call this street *Stinksteeg* for nought.' He poured some ale for himself. Suddenly he said, 'It seems we were right about Studley.'

Will's thoughts flew to Amsterdam, to the girl he had left there. Dear sweet Dorothy. His heart turned over with dread. 'How is that, sir?'

Brewster sat down with his ale. 'Henry Ainsworth has accused Studley of misbehaviour with his young daughter. And he is not the only one.'

Mary Brewster brought the cold bacon from the larder. 'No! It cannot be true!'

Brewster shook his head. 'I'm afraid it is! I knew there would be trouble over that. It wasn't dealt with properly at the time.'

Will felt sick. Ainsworth's daughter was about seven years old.

Mary said with more venom than Will had ever heard her use before,

'The man should be hanged!'

'He will be expelled?' Will asked.

'Perhaps. Certainly Brother Ainsworth is furious and if he has anything to say to it, Studley will be out.'

Mary regained her customary calmness. 'God will sort it out,' she said as though it were a *fait accompli*.

'He hasn't done thus far,' Will said, his anger getting the better of him.

'You know how He works,' William Brewster reminded them both. 'He waits until the situation comes to ripeness, then He acts.'

'Meantime innocent children—' Will began.

'If you are thinking of the May girl, be easy. Henry May is aware of the danger. Which reminds me.' He reached in his doublet and pulled out a letter and handed it to Will.

He knew before he opened it that the letter was from Dorothy. It was typical of her, a chatty letter, full of news, but no malicious gossip, which he approved of. Nothing about Daniel Studley, which was just as well. She was a good and dutiful girl, was Dorothy. She helped her mother bake bread, oversaw the servants, helped her sister. She called him her dear Will, and begged him to write soon and tell her all about the things that happened in Leyden.

Dear Dorothy. He smiled when he remembered her beautiful childlike face, the huge blue eyes, the long corn-coloured hair which shone like burnished gold. He longed to see her again, but it was doubtful that he could get away from work for the foreseeable future. He just hoped Brewster was right and Henry May kept his daughter from the clutches of Daniel Studley.

Mary arched her back, massaging the muscles above her waist. 'Well, I must get supper. Will—would you mind getting the children for me from the Robinsons'?' Bridget Robinson had been helping out at this late stage of Mary's pregnancy by taking the children off her hands.

'Of course.' Will reached for his hat.

Outside, the alley where they lived was dark and empty, the sun rarely seeing the track between houses with overhanging upper storeys. There was no open sewer, but with the stench from the canal and the natural damp of a dark hole, the smell was unhealthy.

He had taken no more than three paces when he heard Mary cry out, a shrill sharp cry, more of surprise than pain, and his heart froze. Her time had come. He wanted to go on, to the Robinsons and to stay there until it was all over, but they might need him, so he turned back to the house.

'I hate this time, Will,' Brewster said a short while later as a shrill scream followed by obscene grunts, groans and moans poured through the planks of the ceiling above, Will thought that he could not but agree. He said as much to comfort himself as Brewster, 'It will soon be over.'

'Aye. But this is the part no man likes. I have prayed often enough about it, but you never know. Each time, I think I will never put her through this again.'

Will walked over to the tiny window which opened out onto the dark street. It was perhaps two o'clock in the morning, and the night seemed to have dragged. He knew that childbirth was a hazard women had to go through. And Mary, he knew, had put by a fresh winding sheet for her burial if necessary. If a woman survived the ordeal then it was something indeed to be thankful for.

Upstairs the English midwife and the women who were there to witness the birth, (the gossips as they were called) and who included Bridget Robinson and her sister Frances Jessop, encouraged Mary in her labours. It always puzzled Will why so many women needed to be present at the birth of a child when only one man was needed to see to a lambing, but Brewster explained, 'It is something women do, and it is good to have others at the birth in case the child dies. Then there are witnesses to show the mother did not smother the child.'

Mary gave one enormous scream and suddenly there was the plaintive wailing of the new-born.

The women upstairs all gave a cry of triumph, as though they had borne the child themselves. Downstairs William Brewster's legs buckled and he had to sit down. Come to that, so did Will for his legs wobbled.

Presently the midwife came down the stairs with a bundle of linen in her arms in which, Will realised, there must be a baby. 'It is a girl,' she announced dourly to Brewster.

'And my wife?'

'Mistress Brewster is very well. Do you not wish to see the child?'

Brewster opened the wrapping and peered at a healthy baby girl. 'She is beautiful!'

Will came to have a look. The baby was pink, and seemed to have some kind of grease on its scrub of black hair, and the umbilical cord, cut and tied with a piece of string dangled grotesquely from where its navel would be. Its face was screwed up and fat, and its little fists punched the air. It was the ugliest baby Will had ever seen, yet it evoked in him a strange paternal feeling, a hint perhaps of things to come.

'Can I see my wife?' Brewster asked.

'Soon,' the midwife said, and took the baby back upstairs.

Brewster beamed at Will with relief.

But the fever raged and it took its toll.

When Will entered the house in the *Stinksteeg* a few days later, he sensed the atmosphere immediately. Something was wrong. The place, usually bustling with excitement was so quiet. The girls, Anne Peck, Patience, nine and Fear, three, sat together on the settle against the wall, silent and sombre. Brewster sat at the table, his head in his hands. And although Will could hear footsteps upstairs, he heard no voices. Which was strange. For Mary was still lying-in, and the 'gossips' were an ever-present feature.

'What is it?' he asked, his stomach contracting in dread.

Brewster looked up at him, his face a mask of agony. 'The baby's dead.'

Will stared at him. The baby had been all right that morning—at least he hadn't seen it, but he had heard it crying lustily for its feed. Had it not been for the lines of grief etched on Brewster's face, the shock in his eyes, he would not have believed it. 'Dead? How dead?' he asked.

'Fever.'

'Where is the body?' Will needed to see for himself.

Brewster indicated the cradle in the corner. Will had not noticed the tiny body at first, for it was covered over. He pulled back the sheet with a shaking hand. The baby was firmly swaddled, as all babies were, and its eyes were closed, but not quite. There was that glaze of death in them, the stillness of death, the paleness of death, the smell of death. And his stomach turned over.

Gently he put the sheet back in place and went to Brewster. 'I am so sorry.' How inadequate! What could he say in such a circumstance?

Brewster swallowed painfully. 'It was all so quick. The fever came on this morning. By this afternoon she was dead. We haven't even named her.'

Will said tentatively, 'We know there is a resurrection.'

'I know.' Brewster thumped the table, unable to contain his grief. With a supreme effort he struggled to control himself. 'I know. But that doesn't help right now.' He paused, and the tears flowed. 'She had all her life ahead of her,' he managed in a small voice. 'Why? Why does this happen?' He thumped the table again in pent-up anger. ''Tis this house, with this terrible stench.'

His grief frightened the two little girls, and they clung to each other wailing. Will put his hand on Brewster's shoulder wishing he could think of something constructive to say. 'The fever strikes where it will,' he said. 'Half of Leyden has it.'

'Dear God, that we have come to this—this poverty!' Brewster exploded. Will quailed in the face of such raw pain. 'God forgive me, I have not taken enough care of my family.'

Will said, 'But you are not at fault, sir. It is not your fault. There is fever in the house.'

'I have failed them, Will.'

A shadow crossed the open doorway and to Will's immense relief, John Robinson stood there.

'Come in, Brother,' Will said.

Robinson sat down with Brewster. 'I came when I heard,' he said gently, and Brewster broke down and sobbed.

They buried the child in the churchyard of *Pieterskerk* the next day.

A week later they moved to a better situated and slightly larger house in *St. Ursulasteeg.*

However, the Brewsters were not the only ones to suffer loss. Three weeks later Mary Carver gave birth only to lose her baby also. A few days later, she followed her child to the grave.

SEVEN
Trouble in Amsterdam

Winter 1610

It was cold and dark, filthy December weather, and William Brewster muttered under his breath as icy water trickled down his neck. It was not a night on which to be out, and when he saw the welcoming light in John Robinson's house as he turned the corner, he uttered a prayer of thanks.

Bridget Robinson met him at the door. 'Come on in,' she said, taking his cloak from him. She was pregnant, and a white apron perched pertly on her growing belly over her dark blue dress. Momentarily Brewster thought of his harrowing loss, but he put it firmly out of his mind. He hoped the same would not happen to Bridget and John.

John Robinson's house was small, considering the number of people expected to live there, but there was a decent fire which drew Brewster to it, where he could warm his hands, face and nether regions.

Brewster greeted the deacons—Sam Fuller and John Carver who, like himself, had arrived early for this meeting. They waited while John Robinson dismissed the women to an upstairs room—'to read and sew, and I have allowed them a fire'—for elders' meetings were not for the ears of delicate females, nor, come to that, for the ears of the rest of the congregation—and then he too sat down.

They asked God's guidance on their meeting, and then John Robinson opened the discussion by reading a scripture. *'That there be no dissensions among you but be ye knit together in one mind and in one judgement.'*

Then he looked at them one by one, his face grave. 'It has come to my attention, brothers, that the brothers in Amsterdam are not joined in unity. Indeed, there is strong disunity.'

'Well, I am not surprised,' Brewster said bluntly. 'I always thought there was trouble brewing.'

John Robinson ignored this comment and went on. 'Firstly, the news is of John Smith and his congregation, and it is not good news brothers. Master Smith has now decided that his new baptism was all wrong after all.'

They all groaned, and John Robinson nodded his understanding. He added, 'Helwys and Murton have expelled Smith and the others—including Hugo Bromhead and Thomas Piggot—for teaching false doctrine—apostasy.' This was grave, for expelling put the group firmly outside any fellowship they might have had with the Leyden congregation. It put them outside the Lord's church altogether.

The men murmured again and William Brewster said, 'It had to happen. I saw it coming.'

'As did we all, Brother. Smith has applied to the Mennonites to be admitted but Helwys and Murton contacted the Mennonites and informed them of Smith's dealings.'

'What will happen now?'

'I suppose Smith's group will have to found a congregation on their own, if that is what they want.'

'I don't understand,' John Carver boomed. 'Why don't they see what kind of idiot Smith is, and leave him?'

'Because they follow a man, not the Lord. Depend on it, Jehovah will deal with him. Anyway, that is not the reason for this meeting.

'I have had a letter from Henry Ainsworth, an admirable God-fearing man if ever there was one. The matter of Daniel Studley which was not resolved, has brought a problem to the surface. As you know, Studley was accused of behaviour unbecoming a Christian towards Ainsworth's young daughter. Yet despite his own confession that he just wanted to discover the child's sex—would you believe?—he was not removed either from the position of elder nor from the congregation.'

'He said *what*?' John Carver demanded. 'Are they stupid? The man as good as admitted it. And besides, how can he have been in doubt about her sex. Faith! The girl wore petticoats, didn't she?'

'And they allowed him to continue as an elder?' William Brewster put in, unable to hide the righteous anger which surged to the surface. When John met his eyes, he added on a more subdued note, 'Still, that was to be expected, I suppose. Studley and Johnson are close.'

John Robinson looked at them straightly, and said with exaggerated impassivity, 'Brother Johnson believes Studley to be innocent.' Then he raised his eyebrows expressively.

Sam Fuller was outraged. 'He is fooled by him. Well, he has such winning ways, and he makes a show of piety.'

'Furthermore, Johnson has taken the power of expulsion away from the congregation and put it in the hands of the elders only.'

'So he can manipulate them no doubt,' Brewster put in acidly.

John Robinson went on, 'There is a split in the congregation, with Ainsworth and a large number of brethren on one side, Johnson and Studley and others on the other. Thirty members of the congregation have written to ask us for help.'

'Is it official?' Brewster asked.

'No, for Henry Ainsworth is not among the signatories of the letter.'

John Carver dismissed it. 'Then let them sort it out themselves. We moved here to get away from all this.'

John Robinson said in his mild way, 'I agree, brother. But if the brethren need us . . .'

'Perhaps you should wait until Master Johnson specifically asks you to come,' Sam Fuller put in quietly. 'Or Master Ainsworth.'

'Yes, I agree,' John Carver said. 'What say you, Master Brewster?'

William Brewster nodded. 'I think it is a good point. We need to keep out of the controversy if we can. But I feel for our brothers there. Master Ainsworth must be suffering.'

'He is a Godly man, is Henry Ainsworth,' John Robinson repeated. 'I hate to leave him to deal with Master Johnson alone.' He looked at the other three men. 'But you are all right. We need to be invited to go to Amsterdam and talk to them. I think we will write back accordingly.'

'Do you think you will have to go to Amsterdam?' Mary Brewster asked her husband, as they ate dinner around the huge table.

Brewster shrugged. 'I hope not. We are of the opinion that we should not get involved unless we must. The brethren need to sort out their own squabbles.'

Will said, 'It seems to me that the brethren should sort it all out in a spirit of love. Why should this argumentation take place like this?'

'Sometimes, Will, there are false brothers.'

'But all the brothers have been tried and tested and come off faithful in the past. I don't understand it.'

Brewster said patiently, 'People change. Besides, I was talking of Studley.'

'Aye,' Will thought about it. 'Yet he too has taken his share of persecution and stayed faithful.'

'Well there are other things to tempt a man away from the Lord besides persecution, Will.'

He knew it, but he did not yet understand it. How could a man who loved God to the point of risking his life for his faith then fall to temptation? It was incomprehensible to him. Yet he knew that there were those who gave in to immorality, or worse, adultery, or who became apostate, or who were drunkards—the list was a long one. Why did their love for God not stop them from committing such crimes?

Mary changed the subject, 'Jonathan asked me if I would be a 'gossip' at his wife's lying-in.'

Brewster looked at her. 'No,' he said sharply.

'But William . . .'

'I said no! I will not have you exposed to what may cause you pain. No.'

'But . . .'

58

'I have spoken!'

Mary lowered her eyes in submission, and Will was fascinated. He had never known Mary to flout what her husband said. Ten year old Patience looked up. 'Why cannot Mama go, Papa? I do not understand.'

'When you are older, you will understand. Fear! Do not eat the bone!'

Fear had put a small lamb bone in her mouth and now Mary reached across the table and held her hand beneath the child's mouth. Fear obediently spit the bone out into her mother's hand.

The crisis averted, Brewster said, 'I have taken up your suggestion, Will. I have a few pupils to whom I will teach English.'

'Oh?'

'German and French students in the University. Because they all speak Latin, I thought I would use Latin as the common language.'

'That is a good idea, sir. Will you earn enough?'

'I do not come cheap!' Brewster said and laughed. Then he added, 'I've been thinking about it, and I have begun an English grammar primer, on the lines of a Latin primer.'

Will was impressed. 'You will need some kind of logical way to teach English. I hope it will work, sir.'

'It will work.' He finished his stew. 'God is good, Will. He provides for us what we need.'

Alexander Carpenter leaned back in his chair and sipped from the beer mug Henry Ainsworth had just given him. 'So what will happen to Studley?' he asked.

Henry Ainsworth's thin lips set in a bitter twisted line. 'Nothing if Johnson has his way.' He sat down opposite his visitor, and stared moodily at the glowing embers of the fire.

Alexander Carpenter said sympathetically, 'It isn't right.'

'No. I know it isn't right!' Henry Ainsworth audibly ground his teeth. 'Brother Johnson has been fooled by Studley. Completely taken in. So pious, so good, such a fine fellow, so entertaining!' He put his head in his hands suddenly defeated. 'I trusted them. I trusted Johnson, I trusted Studley.' And his voice was thick with hurt anger.

Alexander Carpenter put a comforting hand on his arm. 'We all did, brother.'

'I feel so—so betrayed.'

'I know.'

'And now Johnson says we cannot expel him.' Ainsworth smashed his fist on the table. 'If I didn't know better . . .' He paused, struggling with himself. 'All this time Johnson has been moving us further towards the

Presbyterian leaning at variance with our origins and our Articles of Faith. To protect that—that—pervert! Studley's behind it of course. He pulls Johnson's strings.'

Alexander Carpenter was anxious. 'Be careful what you say, Brother,' he cautioned. 'You are overwrought.'

Ainsworth took a steadying breath. 'I have decided to ask the Leyden brothers for their help.'

Alexander Carpenter nodded his agreement. 'I think that you are wise. *"In the multitude of counsellors there is steadfastness,"* as the scriptures say.'

'Yes. John Robinson knows what he is about, as does William Brewster.'

'And we will accept their counsel?'

He nodded. 'I will.' He looked at Carpenter. 'What has happened to us? This is not how it should be among the Lord's people.'

Alexander Carpenter shook his head. 'You know as well as I do that having the truth is no guarantee of protection from troubles.'

'But these are men who have previously been faithful, and suffered much.'

'But if a man does not continue faithful, then what? The Devil will try to lead any of us astray in a different way if he can.'

Henry Ainsworth nodded. He knew it, of course. But it was still a shock.

Later, as he walked home, Alexander thought over the situation, and with a heavy heart he came to a decision. It was not an easy decision, and in fact he had been considering it for sometime, reluctant to act, hoping it would not be necessary. However, the split in the congregation had become so serious that he felt he had no alternative if he did not want his beloved daughters and son stumbled from the way of the truth. For he knew it could come to that.

The meetings had deteriorated into arguments. He hated the way God-fearing men could degenerate into spitefulness and name-calling. As if seeing the split in Smith's church wasn't bad enough, the Ancient Church was now going through the same. All right, it was a refining work, a sifting out of dead works, but it hurt greatly.

Carpenter was not a fool. He knew there would be serious repercussions, and he did not want to be involved. Why could they not just get on quietly with their worship? he asked inwardly. Why all this arguing and upset? Why didn't Johnson see Studley for what he was?

Because Johnson could not believe his friend guilty of such a heinous crime, that's why.

When Alexander Carpenter reached his home, his wife had dinner waiting for him, and his daughters bustled around to help, chattering away like a flock of birds, crowding the kitchen. His wife greeted him with a kiss, his daughters with a cheery greeting, and his heart wrenched. He did not want any of them in the thick of this. He must get them out of Amsterdam.

He took his place at the head of the table, and his daughter Alice put before him his plate of stew and a spoon, and also before her brother John, who sat on Alexander's right, and then sat down with her sisters who had their own bowls. When all was quiet, they bowed their heads and Alexander thanked God for the meal.

Then he looked up at his family, all seated around the table, one son, five daughters, and his wife. He loved them. God knew he loved them more than his life.

'You are troubled husband?' his wife Mary asked him.

He said, 'I am. I have just spoken with brother Ainsworth. About the problems in the congregation. I don't want anyone in this family involved. I don't want any of you taking sides or voicing an opinion or getting involved in arguments.'

'Why not, Papa?' Mary asked. She was only nine. 'I thought you said that Brother Ainsworth has the right of it.'

'I do not recall speaking of the matter to you, Mary. Could it be that you have been eaves-dropping again?'

Mary coloured. She was not a pretty girl. A bout of smallpox when she was little had left her heavily pockmarked, and she had not been well-favoured to start with. Now her discomfiture brought Julianna to her rescue.

'It is easy to overhear conversations, Papa. None of us mean to, but we all know what is going on.'

Alice said, 'Forgive me, Father, but should we not stand by Brother Ainsworth if he is right?'

'If we stay, we are in danger of being swallowed up by this thing. Already it has split the congregation and it threatens to destroy all of us.'

'If we stay?' John repeated. 'You are thinking of moving, Father?'

Alexander said, 'I think it would be in our best interests to move to Leyden with John Robinson.'

His wife made a sound of dismay. 'Not moving again!'

But excitement flooded through Alice. Will Bradford was in Leyden.

Alexander met his wife's eyes straightly. 'Henry Ainsworth and Francis Johnson will part, and one of them will be destroyed before this thing is over.'

'Surely, if Brother Ainsworth has the right of it, the Lord—'

'Yes, so it would seem. But sometimes the wicked prosper.

Sometimes the Lord allows Satan to win.'

John said, 'So you consider Brother Johnson to be wicked.'

Alexander uttered an explosive sound. 'I did not mean that. At least I don't know. I think he is mistaken that is all. You see this is why I do not want us to be here in the midst of all this. I do not want to be involved, and I do not want you involved. I am writing to the Leyden authorities for permission to bring my family to live there.'

'And what of our living?' his wife asked tartly.

'Do you not think the Lord will provide?' Alexander demanded. 'I am a merchant. I can do that just as easily in Leyden as I can here.'

Julianna exchanged glances with Alice, and Alice's cheeks darkened, her stomach turned. The short time the Separatists from Scrooby had been with the Ancient Brethren in Amsterdam had been enough for Alice to find herself attracted to Will. Remembering how his eyes had been upon her during that first meeting, Alice felt a pleasurable anticipation at seeing him again. In Will she had seen a confident young man, good looking, tall and well-built. The blue eyes that had looked into her own had mesmerised her, convincing her that this young man was special, and the thought of seeing him again made her heart skip within her.

Alexander saw the flush on her cheeks. 'Well, soon we will be in Leyden,' he promised her.

EIGHT
Making Plans

Leyden 1611

As Alice Carpenter looked at her reflection in the small silver-backed hand mirror, she knew that she was no match for the exquisite ethereal beauty of Dorothy May. Dorothy May with her corn-flower blue eyes, her long golden silky hair, her girlish coquettishness, may only have been fourteen years old, but she was a serious threat to Alice's peace of mind. However, Dorothy May was in Amsterdam, whereas Alice had the advantage of being close at hand in Leyden, and she would use the situation to the best of her advantage.

'Alice! Are you ready?' Her mother's insistent voice floated up the stairs.

It was their first congregation meeting since arriving in Leyden two days ago, and Alice felt her heart turn over. *He* would be there. She held up the mirror so that she could check that her white collar was not wrinkled, or had a speck on it, and then she put down the mirror and wrapped the thick winter cloak around her. Picking up her Geneva Bible which was small enough to be held in one hand, she skipped down the twisting wooden staircase.

The others awaited her in the small hallway.

Alexander Carpenter had managed to rent a comfortable house in Leyden, boasting a hall (however small) and a sitting room as well as a kitchen. He was proud of his achievement.

He looked up as he heard her on the stairs. 'At last! What have you been doing? We don't want to be late on our first day. Creates a bad impression.'

'I am sorry, Father,' she said meekly, and followed the others from the house into the cold crisp air of a Dutch winter morning.

Julianna waited for her, and fell into step beside her. 'I feel nervous, don't you?' she whispered.

Alice said, 'A little.'

A little! She wished her stomach wouldn't churn the way it did. She wished she didn't feel the panic which seemed to be washing over her in waves. This was her opportunity to bring herself to Will's attention.

'George Morton will be there,' Julianna said looking down at the stone slabs beneath her feet.

Alice nodded approvingly. 'You could do worse, Ju. He comes from a well-to-do family.'

'He gave all that up when he left the Catholic Church to become a

Separatist.'

'Disinherited was he?'

'So I heard. All he has is what he can earn.'

This was a disadvantage, but they were all of them in the same situation. Alice liked George. 'Still, he is a fine man, and one who loves God.'

The Leyden Separatist congregation used the building of one of the Reformed churches for their meetings, not a satisfactory situation since the church had a cross, and stained glass windows which the Separatists considered idolatrous. Furthermore, the Reformed church held their meetings on Sundays as well, so that it was difficult to fit in their own meetings which ought to last all day on a Sabbath. Nevertheless it served for now.

As soon as Alice walked into the dim church, she saw Will, and her heart crashed in her ribs. He was such a good man, she thought, so kind, so full of faith.

She waited hopefully for him to approach her, or her family, to welcome them, but he did not glance in their direction and he made no move towards her.

John Robinson, however, did spot them. 'You are settled in, Master Carpenter?' he greeted them

'Indeed we are, I thank you, sir.' Alexander looked around him. 'You have a goodly number in the congregation, Master Robinson. Your group has grown!'

'Indeed, sir.' John Robinson inclined his head to the women and moved away.

They sat down, for the meeting was about to begin, and Alice had a view of the back of Will's neck, which took her attention for most of the meeting.

Later, as they walked home again, Julianna said, 'I think you are in love with Will Bradford.'

Alice hedged. 'What makes you think so?'

'It's written all over you! You did not take your eyes off him for the whole meeting. I am surprised Mother didn't notice.'

Alice smiled a tight little smile. 'Well, it is of no consequence, is it? He doesn't even notice me. After all, I do not have vivid blue eyes and long golden hair!'

Julianna took her arm. 'Oh Alice!'

Alice turned her head to look at her. 'At least George Morton noticed you! You seem to have had quite a conversation!'

Julianna smiled. ''Tis early days.'

'There is a house for sale in the *Kloksteeg*,' John Robinson announced tossing his hat aside and sitting down on the settle in front of the fire beside his wife.

Bridget Robinson fiddled frantically with the buttons on her dress while baby Isaac on her lap squalled lustily for his feed. 'Oh?'

John could not talk over the noise of his latest son, so waited patiently until she freed a plump white breast and the baby grabbed the nipple with a searching mouth. John stroked the child's downy head and smiled at Bridget. 'He is a blessing from Jehovah,' he said, unable to better describe the warm feeling washing over him at the sight of his baby son and beautiful wife.

Bridget nodded, smiling, well pleased. Now that she was a little older, she was more content to spend the time cuddling and feeding the new baby. It hadn't always been like that. With the others, the panic of new motherhood and the restless need to be a perfect wife had kept her short-tempered and distant. The change delighted him.

'So what is this about a house?' she prompted.

John took a breath. He wasn't sure how she would take to this idea. 'There is a house for sale in Leyden near the St. Peter's church. 'Tis a big house, not so large at the front—perhaps twenty-five feet wide—but it goes back a long way, and has many rooms. But more importantly there is a large plot of land at the rear, amounting to half an acre.'

'What would we want with all that land? 'Tis too small to farm, too big for anything else.'

John leaned towards her earnestly. 'No, not farming. I have something else in mind. Bridget—we could build a meeting house in the grounds. We need a hall, and there is enough land on which to build one—and some. You know how much we need one.'

'We do,' she agreed, her vivid blue eyes watching him.

'And there would also be room to build tenements. Around the outside wall. For the brethren. It is so difficult for them to find decent accommodation here at prices they can afford. And the wages are so low. I thought that a few decent tenements at a low rent—and Master Jepson is a building carpenter by trade and has volunteered to see to the building of them. That persuaded me that it would be feasible.'

'You've already discussed it with him?'

'He saw it first, and already mentioned to me that if we could just find some land we could build on . . .'

Suspicion crept into her eyes. 'Are you talking of us living there as well?'

'Yes. In the house.'

'And how do you propose to pay for such a property?' She sat the baby up, stretched his neck a little so that he gave a surprised burp, and then put him on the other breast.

John was momentarily diverted by the baby's somewhat puzzled face which smoothed out into bliss as he began to suckle again. With an effort he brought his mind back to the subject in hand. 'Well, there are others in the congregation who have expressed interest in investing in such a scheme.'

'Who?'

John hesitated. He stood up, restless and uncomfortable. He paced the flagstone floor, avoiding her eyes. 'Well, William Jepson of course. Henry Wood.' He glanced at her and away again. 'And your sister Jane and us. We can afford it between us.'

Bridget frowned. John had inherited only a very little from his parents, but she and her brothers and sisters, eight of them altogether, had received sizeable portions from their mother's estate when she died twelve years previously. Jane's was held in trust until either she came of age or she married, whichever came first, and she was just recently twenty-one. 'So you have enticed my sister to spend her inheritance before she is even married! And what, pray, is she to live on in the future?'

She sounded angry, and he watched her anxiously. She could veto the plan and he would not go against her wishes. 'There would be income from the rent.'

'A *low* rent,' she reminded him.

'So you unhappy with the idea.'

'I am—surprised. You intend to use my inheritance as well, I assume.'

In law, when they married, a woman's possessions became her husband's to dispose of as he wished. But he said, 'I hope you know I will not act without your agreement.' He paused, trying to gauge her mood.

'I am pleased to hear it,' she retorted.

'Well, if you do not like it . . .' he trailed off, dismayed. Thought for a moment, and then returned to the plan. 'The house would be for us to live in. And Jane too, if she wills. By the time we have finished it will be worth far more than when we started, so we will not lose by it. Of course, it would all have to be drawn up legally . . . I just thought we could use some of our material wealth to help the brethren with affordable dwellings. But, of course, if you dislike it . . .'

'So I can say nay, can I?' She pursed her lips thoughtfully, but her eyes danced.

He saw it and relief swept through him. 'It would solve all our problems in one swoop. 'Tis a decent house, with several rooms. You will like it, I know you will. Do you wish to see it?'

'Certainly I do!'

'So you agree then?'

She laughed. 'Dear John. You know very well that I trust you absolutely. Of course I agree. How much is it?'

He hesitated again then reluctantly admitted, 'Eight thousand guilders.'

Her eyes grew round. Yes, it was a huge amount of money. '*Eight thousand?*'

He went on quickly. 'Of which two thousand is to be paid down, and the balance on mortgage at five hundred guilders annually. There is also a small yearly ground rent of eleven stivers and twelve pence to be paid to the *Seigneur* of Polheest.'

'John! Are you mad? We cannot afford such a sum!'

'Master Brewster thinks it an excellent idea.'

'And does he intend taking one of the proposed tenements?' she countered tartly.

John put his hand on her shoulder. He said gently, 'I do not know. Perhaps. He would be welcome to do so, although I suspect for his brood that he would find a tenement a little cramped.' He put his head on one side as he studied her. 'You do not mind? You really do not mind?'

Baby Isaac had fallen asleep, letting go of the breast, and she rebuttoned her dress with her free hand. 'John Robinson, when have I ever opposed you in anything you wished to do?'

Oh, how he loved this woman. He bent down and kissed her on the forehead. 'I knew you would understand.'

She stood up and put the baby in the crib. 'You knew I would not deny you,' she corrected, her eyes twinkling.

Now she was free of the baby, he could draw her into his arms, and he kissed her again, this time lingeringly on the lips. She could never resist him, and she responded immediately, melting into his arms, pulling him even closer.

And at that moment the servant, Mary Hardy bustled in, and he drew away.

Accordingly on January 27th 1611 John Robinson in partnership with the three others in the congregation bought the house in the *Kloksteeg,* also called *Pieterskerkhof,* opposite the cathedral church of St. Peter, a few steps from the University, and in the shadow of its library. But they did not take possession of it until May the following year.

Alice frowned at the words on the open page in front of her. She was used to the print used in the Geneva Bible, but what did annoy her was the way the text was at an angle to the page so that the first line sometimes went off the top of the page, or the last line vanished at the bottom. Of course, this Bible could be had relatively cheaply, which was why Alexander Carpenter had bought one for each of his children, but she did wish the printer had taken more care over his work.

She heard the front door, and then Will's voice asking politely to speak to her father. Her heart began to pound and she sat up, straining to hear. He had come, and he was asking to speak with her father. Perhaps she had been wrong about Dorothy May. Perhaps he had seen something in herself that he liked. Her stomach seemed to tie itself in knots, and at the same time be up in her throat. *Will is here to see Father!*

From the room beneath her she could hear just the voices of the two men, but could discern nothing of what they said. An age seemed to pass. Perhaps her father was inquiring about Will's ability to provide for his daughter. Alice's hands clasped so tightly in her lap that her knuckles were white. *Dear God, please may he be making an offer for me!*

At last she heard the front door close again, and the voices ceased. She waited. Surely her father would call her down and tell her?

He didn't

Perhaps he didn't know she was at home. After another five minutes she could bear it no longer, and she came down the stairs.

Her father sat in his small oak-panelled 'drawing room', and he looked up as she entered. 'My dear Alice! I thought you were out!'

Just as she thought. 'I was reading Papa. Was that Master Bradford I heard a minute ago?'

'Yes. He brought me some papers from Master Brewster to look at.'

Her heart dropped like a stone. 'Was that all?'

He looked at her in surprise. 'Yes.'

Alice nodded. 'I see.'

He studied her, a question in his eyes, but she could not endure his scrutiny. Instead she turned and fled upstairs. Her disappointment was acute, but she was not entirely without hope. She decided that the best thing she could do would be to get to know Will better. Even if it did look a little forward, she must contrive to get into conversation with him. Then he would be bound to see that she had much more to recommend her than Dorothy May's pretty, but empty, head.

Mary Brewster was pregnant again and feeling the effects quite severely. Will felt for her. She was constantly being sick, and found it difficult to carry out her housewifely duties. They could not afford a servant, and Anne Peck, now a strapping girl of fifteen, stepped into the breach, as did

Patience, the eldest Brewster girl at nearly eleven.

'So, the Robinsons are buying the house in Peters Church Street,' Mary said, tossing Will one of the new apples she had bought at market. She had not applied her mind to learning Dutch, and had no inclination to use the Dutch place names. 'A fine house by all accounts.'

Snatching the apple out of the air, Will took a bite. 'It is the congregation house. They will build a hall in the gardens for worship and tenements also for those who cannot afford to rent a house.'

'Very noble I'm sure. And you, will you live there when you get married?'

Taken aback, Will said, 'I am not getting married.'

Mary, taking up a rolling pin and dumping a handful of flour paste on the table glanced at him. 'No? When you have been writing to little Dorothy May these last two years? She must be rising fourteen now.'

Will flushed scarlet. 'If and when I do get married—eventually—I will not live in the new tenements. Leave them to those who need them. I have something else in mind.'

Brewster, seated on the settle in front of the fire reading a religious tract he had come by, looked up. 'Oh? And what is that, pray?'

'I come into my inheritance in a week, and I plan to use it. When I have sold the farm in Austerfield, I intend to buy a house, and a loom, and become a citizen of Leyden like Roger Wilson has done. Then I can set up in business for myself.'

He spoke easily, but the farm in England had been in his family since about 1500 when his great-great grandfather Peter Bradford had bought it, and its sale was going to cost him a pang. It would sever his ties with England and his family once and for all.

William Brewster leaned on the rough-sawn beam which served as a mantle. Below, on the hearth, the fire burned big and bright, with a large cooking pot hanging above it. 'You wish to set yourself up in business, then? All for little Dorothy May.'

Mary moved him out of the way, so that she could get to the fire. 'William—do not tease the boy.'

'I must wait until she is old enough,' Will said. 'There is time yet.'

Mary took the lid off the pot and taking the huge ladle began to stir. 'She is only a child, Will. Whatever made your fancy light on her?'

Will struggled for an answer. He knew perfectly well that from the moment he had seen her face he was smitten. He knew also, though, that they would not be impressed by his professions of love for a pretty face. He said, 'In faith, I do not know. She is beautiful, of course. And she has innocence about her which appeals.'

'I should hope so. She is young. Too young.'

Will felt himself blush again. There was an odd guilty feeling inside him.

'And spiritually, Will? What is she like spiritually?' William Brewster pressed.

Will hadn't the faintest idea. Her letters were full of news, not scripture. But he said, 'Well enough, as I see it. Her family has been affected by this split in the congregation, of course.'

Mary and Brewster exchanged speaking glances, which made Will uneasy. They had been discussing him behind his back, he was sure of it, and had decided to tackle the subject together. He drew their fire. 'You think I am making a mistake, then?'

Brewster said carefully, 'Marriage is an honourable estate set up by God for man. There is no revoking it once it is done. It is a lifetime agreement. If you choose unwisely, Will, you will be desperately unhappy, and unable to do anything about it. You must think carefully before you enter such a covenant.'

'I have thought about it,' Will replied defensively. 'I love Dorothy.'

It was Mary's turn. 'But does she love you, Will? She is only fourteen. Too young to have formed an attachment.'

'I can make her love me.'

'No, Will, it doesn't work like that.'

Brewster said, 'I could have had my pick of any of the ladies at Court, well-to-do young women with handsome dowries and pretty faces, all of them sophisticated, casting out lures to a fellow like me. Many a man succumbed, I can tell you, and many came to a downfall at that. But it was Mary Wentworth back home in Nottinghamshire who took my eye and my fancy. By then I was quite a bit older than you are now, and I fell in love with her, and I am still in love with her. None of the others, for all their finery, and their lewd promises, could capture my heart. It was Mary's goodness, her kindness, her love for the Lord which affected me deeply. And, of course, she is a fine-looking woman to boot.'

Will glanced at Mary who had flushed crimson. She said shyly, 'Oh, William!'

Brewster said seriously, 'Dorothy May is too young yet, Will. Give her plenty of time. Time to grow up. Time to decide what kind of woman she will be. Don't be impatient for her.'

Inwardly Will seethed at this seeming intrusion and struggled to remind himself that this couple loved him as a son and therefore had his best interests at heart. If only they would allow him to live his own life! When he spoke his voice was tight. 'Thank you for your advice, sir.'

'And please mind my own business. I know.'

Will stood up. 'I think I will go out for a walk.'

'Supper won't be long,' Mary said.

'Neither will I.'

Will headed for the door before anyone could say more, and let himself out into the street.

'I think he's making a terrible mistake, William,' Mary said after the door closed behind him..

Brewster frowned. 'He is young and in love.'

'Young and foolish more like! The girl's got nothing more between the ears than hay!' She stirred the pot again. 'Oh, I don't doubt she is pretty enough. Perhaps she even has faith, although I doubt it. But what conversation does she have? I tell you, William, I have had occasion when we were in Amsterdam to speak with the girl, and she really is a simple soul. She will bore Will rigid in a fortnight. Nay, less. A day! And tell me this, what will that girl know about keeping house? Her mother has taught her nothing about house management. She thinks her daughter is too dainty for such things as cooking and cleaning, just as she is herself. She leaves everything to the servants!'

'You cannot know that,' William reprimanded her. 'Indeed, you judge the girl and Mistress May harshly, although I don't know why. If Will's got to marry someone it might as well be the May girl.'

'And what, pray, is wrong with one of the Carpenter girls? Oh, I give you, they are none of them pretty, but capable certainly. And clever, all of them. And I tell you this, Alice Carpenter has feelings for Will.'

'How do you know?'

'I'm a woman and I've got eyes in my head. Not like you men!'

'The May girl is young yet. She may well improve. Besides, if Will is bent on it, there is little we can do.'

'There is plenty we can do. We can advise him against such a match! We stand in place of his parents.'

'Will is of age, he will do as he pleases, and in this matter even natural parents have no say. Besides, it may well work out all right.'

'William! Have your wits gone a-begging too? Will is a clever lad— man—bright as a button, quick, restless, and his love for the Lord blazes like a thousand candles. He will be an elder one day. He needs a capable woman, not a ninnyhammer!'

'Do you know something I do not?' Brewster asked quizzically, raising his brows.

'I don't know what you men get up to. But this I do know. That boy has ability, and he will go far in the Lord's work. Of course he'll be an elder. And she—will she make an elder's wife? Will she support him, and care for his needs so that he can concentrate on the matters of the Lord?'

'She might do.' But Brewster spoke without conviction.

Exasperated, Mary slammed down the ladle with which she had been stirring the stew in the pot. 'William—you must speak to him.'

Brewster sighed. Clearly he did not want to meddle in this, but he said, 'Yes, yes, alright.'

Satisfied, Mary sat down beside the fire, for the feeling of nausea had come over her again. 'Well, see that you do,' she scolded.

Will stalked along the canal path angrier than he knew he had a right to be. How dared they interfere! How dared they imply criticism of his beloved Dorothy!

With the coming of dusk the scant warmth had gone out of the day, and the air was clear and crisp. The canal reflected hardly any light, and neither did the buildings.

He paused on the bridge over the *Rapenburg* and leaned on the parapet to peer down into the black water. He could just see himself, for the light faded quickly. He looked like any other man. A mere weaver of fustian, when he would have been a yeoman farmer. He had tried to keep his thoughts positive. He had come here because the congregation had come here, and to escape the persecution in England. He had found himself a job, and he had his eye on a house in the *Achtergracht* which he hoped he could afford. And he wanted a wife. A man needed a wife to settle him down, to make him a man, head of his household, a father. And he loved Dorothy. He wanted Dorothy. And nothing Brewster and Mary could say would change that. *Nothing*, he thought fiercely, clenching his fist.

Yet at the back of his mind a small niggle suggested they might be right. He did not know much of Dorothy, not really. He had been to Amsterdam once since they left, and he had visited the Mays, but Dorothy had been closely chaperoned, as was proper, which meant he never had a chance to have a private conversation with her, to find out the real Dorothy. She always put on her prettiest behaviour, no doubt counselled by her mother. He knew it and it nagged him. Even so, he had a fierce love for her that took his every thought, a kind of distant worship. He looked forward to the time when he could make her his wife. Once they were married he could mould her into the helpmeet he needed. She was young enough to be moulded.

'Why so glum, Master Bradford?'

Will jumped for he had been so deep in thought that he had not noticed Alice Carpenter join him on the bridge, and he looked up and smiled. Alice always made him smile, with her bright cheery face, the dark rosy cheeks, the childish freckles across her nose. 'Good day to you Mistress,' he said and inclined his head. 'How is it that you are abroad at this time of day?'

'I have been to visit with Sister Robinson.' She looked at him, her eyes holding his, and something in their luminous depths puzzled him. She looked down before he could work out what it was.

His protective instinct roused itself. 'You should not be out so late. It is getting dark and not at all safe for a woman on her own. You must allow me to escort you home.'

She smiled, but demurred. 'It will take you out of your way.'

'It will,' he agreed affably. 'But I shall not leave you to the footpads.'

'Well, then, I thank you, sir.' She turned to walk on over the bridge, and he fell into step beside her. She peeked up at him from under her bonnet. 'So what happened to put you at outs, Master Bradford?'

'Am I at outs?'

'You were scowling at the water.'

'Was I?' he asked surprised. 'Well, it wasn't anything really. A family argument, that is all.'

'Oh?'

'Master Brewster dislikes my choice of bride.'

He thought she hesitated, and he glanced at her. She said, not looking at him, 'And who is your choice?'

'Why, Mistress Dorothy May.' The question surprised him. Surely everyone in the congregation knew he had intentions towards Dorothy.

He became aware of a long awkward silence, and again glanced at her, puzzled, but the light was insufficient for him to read the expression on her face.

'She is—very pretty,' Alice said at last in a small voice.

'Indeed she is,' Will breathed with deplorable lack of tact. 'The most beautiful creature I ever set eyes on.'

Again she hesitated, then forced a laugh. 'That is hardly the most gallant thing to be saying to another woman, you know!' Her voice sounded strange, tight.

Will had the feeling he was missing something. He tried to see her face hidden by her bonnet and the growing darkness, but it told him nothing. Trying to make amends he said, 'I am sorry, Mistress. I didn't mean anything by it. I mean, you are not unhandsome yourself.' And he realised that she was indeed quite striking with those clear washed sea-green eyes. Not ethereally pretty like Dorothy, of course, but strong, intelligent, with a curvy womanly figure and a warm smile.

She laughed shakily. 'I know I am no beauty, sir. You do not have to say otherwise out of politeness.'

'No—really!' but awkwardness had settled between them.

'So what did Master Brewster say that upset you?' she asked, forcing a lighter note.

'He thinks Mistress May is a little young.'

'Well, and so she is. Only fourteen by my reckoning. Whereas you are—?'

'Twenty-one.'

'Then you and I are the same age.'

It meant nothing to him and they lapsed into silence. After a while, Will said, 'I have a lot to do before I can ask her to—' He broke off, the suspicion finally occurring to him that there was more to Alice than he had realised. Surely she could not have developed feelings for him! It made him uncomfortable, and he was unsure how to handle the situation. 'Well, there is a lot to do,' he finished lamely.

She did not answer but he thought he saw the merest quiver of her lip, although he could not see properly. His suspicions grew.

'Well, here we are,' he said when they came to the Carpenters' house, grateful that this strange conversation would soon end.

She turned to him, staring at a point somewhere on his chest. 'Well, thank you for seeing me safely home, Brother Bradford. Goodnight.' And before he could say anything else, she fled into the house.

'Goodnight, Mistress,' he called after her, but she had already slammed the door.

He stood looking at it for several seconds, perplexed. Perhaps he had imagined it. Surely she did not like *him*. He thought everyone in the congregation knew he had set his sights on Dorothy. Besides, Edward Southworth was in love with Alice and everyone knew that too. In fact, thinking about it, there wasn't much that escaped the eyes of the rest of the congregation.

He frowned thoughtfully, and turned to walk slowly home.

Inside the house Alice hitched up her skirts and ran up the stairs and into the room she shared with Julianna and Agnes, slamming the door to lean against it, her eyes shut tight against the pain within her. A leaden ball seemed to have settled somewhere in the region of her abdomen, solid, agonising. *Dorothy May!* She should have known it. It had been obvious. Had she not heard the rumours, the hints? *Oh Will, Will!*

Oh yes, she had known it, and denied it. *Fool! Stupid fool!* She clenched her fist and bit into it in an attempt not to cry out. *Oh dear Lord, how shall I bear it?*

Hearing the noise on the stairs and the crash of the door, Julianna followed her upstairs and tried to enter the room. 'Alice?'

Alice moved away from the door and sat down on the bed.

Julianna came in, and came to sit beside her sister, putting an arm around her. 'What is it, dearest?'

Alice couldn't speak. The words stuck in her throat, anchored down by the lead ball in her chest.

'Is it Will?' Julianna pressed in her gentle way.

'He is in love with Dorothy May,' Alice managed and her voice broke.

Julianna was horrified. 'No! You must be mistaken. Who told you?'

'He did. Will. He wants to marry her.' She turned a stricken face to her sister. 'Oh Ju, he loves her. That silly little creature with nothing in her head but yellow hair!'

'Alice, surely you must be wrong?'

'How can I be wrong?' Alice demanded angrily, impatient with Julianna's effort to console her. 'He told me himself. He will have her, even though the Brewsters disagree with him.'

'Oh Alice!'

Alice burst into tears and Julianna took her in her arms. Julianna could think of nothing to say.

After a while of hysterical sobbing, Alice pulled away from her and stopped crying, drying her eyes on the kerchief Julianna handed her. 'Well, I am not going to be an old maid because of *him*!' she said between sobs.

Alarmed, Julianna asked in an anxious voice, 'What do you mean?'

Alice's sobs died away. 'Edward Southworth is particular in his attentions towards me.'

Julianna was appalled. 'Alice, you *can't*.'

Alice's green eyes blazed and her lips set in a determined line. 'I c-can! What is more, I will! Why should I pass up the chance of marriage because of *him*? Edward is a k-kind s-sweet man who loves the L-Lord every bit as much as William Bradford does. I expect he will make a very good husband.'

'Alice!'

Alice said, 'I don't know why you are so shocked, Ju. After all, many people make marriages of convenience.'

'Well, there has to be some liking, Alice.'

'I do like Edward. And next time I see him, I shall make a point of speaking to him.'

'But you don't love him.'

'Love! Huh! Look where love gets me! The man loves a foolish child! A silly little girl with a doll-like face. Well, he'll be bored with her in a day, and good luck to him!'

All gentle Julianna could think of to say was, 'We don't believe in luck, dearest.'

Alice again dissolved into tears.

Pursuing his intention to become a suitable husband for Dorothy, Will bought a small house on the *Achtergracht* just across the *Rapenburg* Canal from where John Robinson had bought *Groeneport.* Feeling pleased with himself, he went home to tell the Brewsters the news.

William Brewster, however, was bursting with his own news. 'I have a son! I have a son!' he cried as soon as Will popped his head in the door.

'That was quick!' Will said. Last time Mary had laboured all night.

Brewster beamed. 'It happened so quickly this morning. Listen, he cries lustily, does he not?'

Will listened dutifully and then grinned. 'Aye, he does. A proper Brewster if I am not mistaken. And what are you going to call him?'

'Love.'

Will raised one eyebrow. 'Love?' Already Brewster had named his daughters Patience and Fear, which seemed an odd choice of names to Will who preferred something more traditional. Love, he felt, was going a little too far. 'Why Love?'

'Why not?'

Thinking he had pressed his point too far already and not wishing to give offence, Will held up his hands and backed off with a laugh. 'No reason at all.' He turned away, keen to share his own news, wondering if this were the best time. He decided that he ought to speak up, so he turned back to face Brewster. 'I've bought a house.'

Brewster was surprised out of his elation. 'You have? Where?'

'On the *Achtergracht.'* Will smiled, pleased with himself.

Brewster pursed his lips. 'Is this for Dorothy May?' he asked.

'First, it is for me,' Will told him seriously.

For an awkward moment Will thought he would counsel him again, and he steeled himself, ready to turn on his heel and leave. But Brewster evidently had decided not to interfere, for he said at length: 'Congratulations.' He managed a tight smile. 'You'll share a jug of wine with me over the safe delivery of my son?'

Relieved, Will nodded. 'That I will.'

NINE
Settling Down

Leyden, 1612-13

The winter had come around again, cold and stark, short grey days punctuated by the whiteness of snow which sank into the cracks between the cobbles. Alice didn't mind the cold, and she didn't mind the snow, but she did so hate the dark days.

As she stood outside the small rented house, Susanna Fuller, Sam Fuller's little sister, finished saying goodbye and joined her. 'So, sister Leggat is to marry Brother Carver.'

Susanna was a pretty little thing of just sixteen, flaming red hair and tawny eyes. She had a quick way about her, a staccato way of speaking at breakneck speed which never failed to take Alice's breath away. It was as though her brain ran on so fast that her tongue had to keep up with it.

Alice said, 'I am happy for them both. They have been alone for too long.' Her heart ached. She would so like to be married. She would so like to have Will look at her the way John Carver looked at Katherine.

'Well I'm happy for them. Oh, look! Is that not Master Bradford on the bridge?'

Alice saw Will marching over the bridge, obviously going to his new little house in the *Achtergracht*, and her heart seemed to stop within her. For all her protestations she was still in love with him. 'Why yes,' she said non-commitally.

Will had not seen them, and did not acknowledge them. Susanna continued, 'He is going to marry Dorothy May, you know.'

'Is he?'

'Have you not heard? Everyone is saying how he is always going to Amsterdam to visit the Mays. My brother says that Master Ainsworth writes that he expects an announcement as soon as Dorothy is old enough. Imagine, Dorothy is so pretty, and they have an understanding already when she is not even of age yet.'

'And you and I old maids,' Alice said, sarcasm in her voice.

Susanna missed it. 'I'm not going to be an old maid. I really shouldn't say anything yet, but I know you can keep a secret. William White has spoken to my brother. He has asked to marry me.'

Alice stopped walking and turned to look at her. 'William White?'

'Yes. Is it not so exciting?'

'And has your brother agreed to this marriage?'

'Yes.'

'And do you wish to marry him?'

'Oh yes. I know he is only a wool-carder, but that is all anyone can get at the moment. But he is cousin to Bridget, Katherine and Frances—'

'Yes, Susanna, I know all about the White family.'

She raced on, 'And he is a faithful servant of the Lord. And surely that is all that counts, although of course, there are other things that matter, but the really important thing is that he loves the Lord, don't you think? I know he does so, because he reads the Bible every day, but there are times when he is so serious with me because he thinks I have too much levity which he says is unbecoming because you know his mother always said that too much levity is wanton in a female—'

'Susanna! Please stop!'

Susanna did stop and looked at Alice with big round eyes. 'What's the matter?'

'I can't keep up with you! Let me tell you that I am pleased for you. You love Master White?'

'I think so, though one can never be sure, can one? But he has the most pleasing manners, and I know he cares for me, and that he will always look after me because he is a hard-working man, and my brother likes him and so does everyone in the congregation so you see he must be a good match for me—'

Alice had to interrupt her again. 'You know you are very young. You may meet someone more to your taste.'

'Everyone could think that, but really, Master White is very much to my taste, seeing as he comes from a good family and seeing that he is industrious and honest. I know we'll never be rich, but then, riches are not everything—oh, is that not Master Southworth yonder?'

Edward Southworth saw them too and raised his hand and walked towards them.

'He comes this way,' Susanna said unnecessarily.

'So he does,' Alice said with just a hint of irony in her voice. 'Master Southworth, well met!'

Edward Southworth smiled and inclined his head. 'Mistress Carpenter, Mistress Fuller.'

Alice found herself studying him. She supposed he was good-looking in a lean, hungry sort of way, with a long face and long nose and prominent cheekbones, as though he hadn't eaten for a month. His eyes were grey, the pupils dilated, and he unnerved her by staring unblinkingly at her face. Even when Susanna spoke he did not take his eyes from Alice.

'We have been visiting Mistress Leggat,' Susanna said.

He said nothing, as though he hadn't heard her. Alice felt obliged to step into the breach. 'We have enjoyed a cosy chat by the fire.'

'Your human kindness does you proud, Mistress Carpenter,' he said gravely.

Feeling left out Susanna took the hint, 'Well, I am near my brother's house. Forgive me, sir. Sister Carpenter, I will see you tomorrow.'

Alice wanted to say, *Don't go and leave me here*, but she had already left them.

Edward said, 'I am glad she is gone.'

'Are you?'

'There is something I wished very particularly to say to you.'

Alice's stomach turned over. *Oh no!* 'Oh?' she invited politely.

'I—I wondered if I might have the privilege of paying my addresses to you.' He coloured as he spoke, and her heart wrenched. Poor man. He was shy and awkward.

Her hands shook, and she knew that she must make some sort of answer. Could she really stick to her resolve to marry Edward when her heart belonged to Will? Trying to give herself time she said, 'I would rather you did not, sir. I do not have any wish to be married to anyone.' She spoke the truth; she wasn't ready yet to pledge herself to anyone yet.

Undeterred, he said, 'I am sure you know that I have a high regard for you, Alice.' He coughed in the cold harsh air, and she thought how his leanness made him look weedy and pale in the wintry sun.

'I have not given you permission to use my forename, sir,' she told him stiffly. If only he would stop staring at her!

'Mistress.' He corrected himself hastily. 'I will come straight to the point. I have come to understand in recent months that of all people, I have the highest regard for you.'

'I see.'

'Alice—Mistress—I am in love with you. I want to marry you.'

She looked at him and thought about it. 'I am not in love with you, sir,' she said bluntly.

'That doesn't matter. I have enough love for both of us! You will grow to love me, Mistress, I know you will. You cannot fail to when I show you how much I love you. I do not ask you to say yes to marriage now, only let me pay my addresses to you.'

She took a breath. Who else was there to marry now that Will had set his heart on the May girl? It might as well be Edward as anyone. She said, 'You must speak to my father, sir. If he does not dislike it, then you may pay your addresses to me. But that is not a betrothal, you understand.'

He took her hand. 'Oh Alice, if only you knew how happy you have made me.'

'I haven't made you happy yet,' she pointed out.

He nodded eagerly. 'I understand, but you will love me, Alice, I promise.'

'And I still haven't given you permission to use my forename,' she added.

In a civil ceremony before the Leyden magistrates, a short time later, Katherine, widow of George Leggat, and John Carver were married, and after an official betrothal according to the Dutch custom, Susanna Fuller became Mrs. William White in February.

The Separatists did not believe in a religious ceremony, viewing such as part of the Romish doctrine they were trying to avoid, but they recognised that to gain God's favour and from the point of view of inheritance and other legalities, it was necessary to be lawfully married. To not be would be unthinkable.

On the twenty-third of July in the same year, Alice's sister Julianna became Mrs. George Morton to the special delight and no surprise of her sisters, and her sister Agnes became the second Mrs. Samuel Fuller, the first having died in childbirth along with the child.

As she stood behind her sister Agnes, watching her repeat her vows to Sam Fuller in front of the magistrate, Alice could not help feeling a pang of envy. It had been the same when her sister Julianna had taken her vows, for Alice was aware that both her sisters adored their new husbands, whereas the man she really loved had set his heart on another.

Edward Southworth was her only hope of a husband now. Who would want plain Alice Carpenter anyway? She was already three-and-twenty, almost an old maid. She had kept Edward dangling long enough. If she did not take him there would be no-one else. She knew that. He was her last chance of marriage.

He was attentive towards Alice and patient. He had a sombre way about him, as though he carried the weight of the world on his shoulders, but when he did smile, his face lit up. He was dependable, hard-working and eager to please. She did not dislike him, but no matter how she tried, she could not feel for him that deep emotion that washed over her unbidden when Will was near.

Not that Will noticed. He only had eyes for Dorothy May.

Edward, on the other hand, did notice her.

'You have eyes the colour of the sea on a cloudless day,' he told her in one expansive moment as they watched the building work going on in the grounds of *Groeneport*.

Alice smiled at it. So she had sea-green eyes, then. Edward was too poetic for her taste. 'Thank you, Edward.'

'Your beauty is the beauty of roses when kissed by the morning dew,' he eulogised.

She stared at him. 'Edward, I am not beautiful.'

'In my eyes you are.'

'Then I can only think your eyes are clouded.'

'Clouded with love.'

'Edward, please!'

He looked suitably crest-fallen, but then said, 'You know, Alice, I am in love with you.'

She was serious immediately. 'Edward I wish you would not.'

'I have asked your father if I might ask for your hand in marriage. He said I could ask you. So, will you be my wife?'

She hesitated. This was it. She had already made up her mind that if he asked her—and she had had no doubt that he would—she would agree. And she had told him that if her father agreed she would have no objection. After all, what other prospect was there? She took a deep breath and said, 'Yes, Edward, I will marry you. And I will do my best to be a dutiful wife.'

His delight was pathetic. And even as he kissed her hand, and told her he would love her forever, she felt a pang of guilt. She was using him, and she knew it. But she would love him to the best of her ability and try to forget Will who would soon belong to another.

Julianna and Agnes were less enthusiastic. They both lived in tenements in the *Groeneport* and it happened that when Alice visited Julianna, Agnes was also present.

Both sisters welcomed her with a hug, and a kiss, and then Julianna turned back to the pot on the stove, stirring it with a huge ladle.

'Alice! You are the first to hear the news!' Agnes began enthusiastically.

Alice sat down on the settle. 'And what news is that, dearest?'

'Julianna is with child.'

Alice looked across at Julianna. 'Is that right, Ju?'

Julianna nodded and smiled. 'I am sure that it is so.' She cast a look of reproach at her sister. 'I have missed three months already but I would have liked to tell you the news myself!'

Agnes wrinkled her nose. 'Well tell her then!'

Alice ignored her. 'Why did you not say before, Ju? My dear 'tis wonderful news. I expect George is pleased.'

'Oh yes.' She stopped stirring and turned her back to the fire, coming towards Alice. 'What is it Alice?'

'What do you mean?'

'Something has happened. I can see it in your eyes.'

Alice forced a smile. 'I am to be married,' she said and hoped she sounded pleased.

There was a long silence. Then Agnes burst out, 'Oh, Alice!'

Alice looked down at her hands, and her lips wobbled. 'You might be happy for me!'

'Is it Edward Southworth?' Julianna asked her straightly.

'You know it must be.'

Agnes leaned towards her. 'Don't do it, Alice,' she said quietly.

Alice bit her lip. 'Edward is a good man, a fine brother, a dependable and hard worker. And he loves me.'

'And you do not love him,' Agnes stated with finality.

'I am sure I will grow to love him as we go on,' Alice said. 'He has many excellent qualities.'

'And what about Will Bradford?' Julianna shot at her.

'What about William Bradford?' Alice countered. 'He cares nothing for me. He is marrying Dorothy May. But Edward loves me. And I will love him well enough, I am sure.'

'But you are not in love with him.'

Alice sat very still and gripped her hands tightly together, fighting the impulse to burst into tears. She forced a quick smile. 'We shall deal well enough together. Many couples marry without being in love.'

'You can't know that.'

'Look, why are you arguing with me? William Bradford does not even know I exist. He does not love me. He loves Dorothy May.'

'That chit of a girl!' Agnes said dismissively. 'His wits have gone a-begging. She has no more sense than a pretty flower! How is she to make a decent wife for a man like William Bradford? He'll frighten her half to death!'

Julianna added her two pence worth. 'Alice—you must tell him how you feel. Before it is too late.'

'It is already too late, Ju. I've agreed to marry Edward. The betrothal is in two weeks. And I have to keep my word. As for Will, he must never know. Promise me, both of you. Agnes, you must say nothing to Sam, or you to George, Ju, because if either of them tells Will, I will not be able to bear it!'

Julianna came towards her and put her arms around her neck. 'Oh Alice, my poor dear Alice!'

Alice disengaged herself from Julianna's embrace, and managed a smile. 'You are supposed to rejoice with me,' she reprimanded gently.

But inside her heart quailed. She would have to live the rest of her life in a lie, pretending that she loved a man she did not love, worthy though he might be. Her life stretched before her, bleak and empty and loveless. For she loved Will with every fibre of her body. She loved his strength, his energy, his faith, his courage. She loved his deep blue eyes, his sense of humour, his quick brain, his cleverness. And she wanted him with a deep earnest need that she felt for no other man.

She changed the subject. 'How is Sam?'

Agnes almost skipped. 'Oh Alice, he is such a good husband, and he does worry about me so. He is learning physic.'

'Like a doctor?'

'I think he hopes to be a physician.'

'I am sure he'll make a good one.'

Julianna said, 'Did you know Mary Brewster is with child again? And Mary Allerton. And Moses Fletcher is marrying Sarah Digby?'

They gossiped for another hour, and it was growing dark when Alice left to go home.

Agnes and Julianna had done much to brighten her spirits, but as she went outside into the cold spring wind, Alice felt them plummet again. Neither Will nor Edward must guess. And she herself must put her own feelings away and out of sight. But she ached and mourned, and found it difficult to look forward to her own formal betrothal in May 1613, and the wedding which must follow three weeks or so later.

Whatever Alice's misgivings, she did marry Edward Southworth.

In August of 1612, John Smith in Amsterdam died of 'quick consumption', broken-hearted and having renounced his faith entirely. He was neither bewailed, nor missed, and his passing went largely unnoticed by the Leyden congregation.

On November the ninth 1613 Will and Dorothy and her father gave notice of their betrothal to the Amsterdam magistrates. A week later Will was back in Leyden to publish the banns. On December 10th that year they were married in Amsterdam.

Dorothy wore a new blue dress with lace on the collar for her wedding, the blue matching the colour of her eyes and Will thought he had never seen a lovelier vision. She also wore her golden hair tied up beneath a lace cap, for now she was to be a matron—at sixteen!

The ceremony was conducted by the Amsterdam magistrates in the chilly courtroom. There was no pomp and ceremony, none of the usual trappings that accompanied a wedding in the Church of England. The magistrate, a grave fatherly man, smiled on the couple, and spoke his lines in heavily accented English.

'Do you, William Bradford, give your faith and fealty to Dorothy May, pledging never to desert her but to live peaceably, lovingly and in concord with her as true children of God, and in awe of Him, following his ordinance until death should you part?'

'I do so swear,' Will said in a loud voice.

'And do you Dorothy May . . .?' and he repeated the same phrases.

'I do so swear,' she said in a small little-girl's voice.

'Then repeat after me, "I call upon Almighty God . . ."'

'I call upon Almighty God,' Will and Dorothy said in unison.'

'". . . to bless our marriage . . ."'

'To bless our marriage.'

'". . . grant us his Holy Spirit . . ."'

'Grant us his Holy Spirit.'

'". . . And crown our union with His grace and favour."'

'And crown our union with His grace and favour.'

The magistrate beamed upon them, and dipping the quill in the ink standish he gave it first to Will and then to Dorothy who accordingly signed the register.

There was nothing else. No singing, no throwing of wheat or rice— for that was a pagan fertility custom and very much frowned upon by Separatists—and no feast. Nor any prayers. Despite the reference to God, which was so commonplace that no-one thought it odd, this was not a religious ceremony.

With Dorothy on his arm, Will swelled with happiness. He had waited four long years for this, and now he had the prettiest little thing in the congregation as his wife.

Henry May shook Will's hand warmly. 'Welcome to the family,' he said, extremely pleased to have caught this young man for his daughter.

Will thanked him.

He looked down at Dorothy. 'Will you bid farewell to your parents, wife?' He liked the word 'wife'.

She looked up at him, tears in her wide blue eyes. 'Do we leave immediately?' she asked in a small voice.

Will frowned. 'Why yes, of course. Our home is in Leyden. You know that.'

'But I had thought we would stay here for a while.' She bit her lip uncertainly.

Will would have done anything for her, but he had a commitment. He said apologetically, 'I have an order to fulfil. I cannot be away from Leyden any longer. We will be there by nightfall.'

She bent her head and her father patted her hand. 'Your trunk is already on the coach,' he told her. 'If you do not go immediately they will leave without you.'

Dorothy nodded.

Henry May took Will aside while Dorothy allowed her mother to put a thick travelling cloak around her. 'Treat her gently, Will. She is young, and so innocent. Do not rush her.'

'I will always take the best care of her, sir,' Will promised solemnly.

Dorothy trembled as she took Will's arm again, but although her mother was in tears, Dorothy was dry eyed. Was she cold, or was it nerves? Well that was to be expected. She was a young maiden, with a new husband. In fact, heavily chaperoned throughout their courtship, they had never even been alone together.

Henry May shook Will's hand again, kissed his daughter, and the newly married couple left to catch the coach back to Leyden.

Treat her gently, Henry May had said. He would certainly do that.

Leyden lay beneath two inches of snow, a dusting of dry powder that seemed to blow off the cobbles without sticking, drifting into strange shapes and columns, decorating the bare twigs with glitter.

The little house in the *Achtergracht*, however, was warm and welcoming. A fire burned brightly in the grate, and even though it was not quite dark, candles burned in the sconces. Even a chicken roasted on the spit before the fire. To Dorothy, who had been dreading coming home in this weather to a bleak cold house, it was a welcome surprise.

William dumped Dorothy's travelling chest on the flagstone floor just as Agnes Fuller and her sister Alice Southworth came in carrying bundles of wood.

'Oh!' They stopped when they saw Dorothy and William. 'We did not expect you just yet.' Agnes spoke for them both.

'You appear to have been working hard,' William said, looking around with approval. They had cleaned and scrubbed and dusted and made everything tidy and welcoming.

Alice put the wood in her arms in the log-bin, and dusted the shavings off her hands and apron. 'We thought how terrible it would be for you to come back to a bleak cold house,' she said, and smiled at Dorothy, while not even looking at William. Then she came forward and kissed Dorothy on the cheek. 'Welcome my dear.'

Dorothy smiled at her. She liked Alice. 'Thank you.'

Agnes, putting down her own bundle, kissed Dorothy too.

'The chicken will be nearly done,' Alice said with practicality, picking up her cloak, and fastening it around herself. 'And there is fresh bread and cheese in the larder, and turnips, carrots and onions.'

Dorothy nodded. 'Thank you,' she said again, and looked up at William. The sisters were all older than she was by several years and she felt young and inexperienced. It had been very kind of them, of course, and but she was, at the same time, a little resentful that complete strangers had taken over what ought to be her duties.

The sisters did not stay, but putting up their hoods over their white caps and hugging their cloaks around them, they departed.

Closing the door behind them, Will thought how small the house looked compared to the May house in Amsterdam. He said apologetically, 'It isn't large, but it is all ours.'

Dorothy hid her disappointment. She had expected something more elegant, more civilised. This was typical of the one-room dwellings in England.

'Where is the loom?' she asked.

'In the attic. Come, I will show you around.' In preparation for his marriage, Will had installed a loom and applied to the Leyden authorities for citizenship so that he could work for himself.

Dorothy went to the cheery fire and turned the chicken on the spit.

Before the fire were two chairs, and behind them a table which was much too large for the house, and benches tucked beneath the table edges. It was spartan to say the least, lacking the womanly touch. Of course, Will lived here alone. And he was a man, and everyone knew men were useless at the fripperies which brought warmth to a house.

He watched her anxiously, and she forced a smile. 'There is a privy out the back and the well is on the corner of the street.'

She nodded accepting this information as inevitable. The privy would be shared, perhaps, and the well probably filthy.

'And upstairs?'

'Come and see.'

The stairs were dark, steep and with small treads and opened onto a yard-square landing with a room each side. In one was a large plain bed, big enough for two people, and it had been made with fresh sheets and a heavy crocheted counterpane. There was no fireplace up here and it was as cold as a frozen lake. A cupboard took up one chimney recess and a huge box-like chest stood in the corner. There was little room for anything else.

Across the minute landing, the other bedroom had no furniture in it at all, but Will evidently used it as a storehouse for bales of black-dyed cotton for weaving into fustian. Lengths of finished cloth had been folded and stacked in a corner.

Trying to think of something complimentary to say, she managed, 'Well, it is a good strong house, William .'

'I know it is small,' William apologised.

She touched his arm. 'It is fine,' she said gently.

It was the closest she had ever been for it was the first time they had been on their own.

He reached out for her, slipping his arms around the tiny waist, pulling her to him, a sudden surge of love overtaking him with such speed that it took his breath away. Her lips, pink and full, were inviting, her breasts pressed against his chest were soft, intoxicating. He bent his head and touched her lips with his.

She did not move, but stood quite rigid, her back arched away from him, and the lips beneath his were hard, clamped shut, unyielding. Still, his arms tightened about her.

She broke away suddenly, moving quickly across the room. 'William! What are you *doing*?'

He stood still, his hands by his side, bewildered, struggling to regain some self-control, aware of a growing sense of disappointment. Slowly, as his breathing calmed, he realised that Dorothy was so young and virginal that she misunderstood his advances. And he who had waited so long did not completely understand the instincts she aroused in him.

He said, 'I am sorry, I did not wish to frighten you.'

Her eyes were round with outraged shock. 'How dare you treat me like that? I am your wife!'

'I love you,' he said, confused. He tried to understand. How could she possibly have sat in the congregation and listened to some of the scriptures relating to married life, and not know what was expected of her? He said, 'Did no-one explain to you about marriage?' and to his chagrin, he felt himself blushing.

'I know what is expected of me, if that is what you mean. I know about cooking and cleaning and—'

'I don't mean that,' he snapped.

'Well, I don't know what you do mean. Tell me.'

He took a breath. 'Between a husband and wife.'

'A wife must be in submission to her husband,' she announced with certainty.

Will groaned. 'At home, in Wisbech, on the farm—'

'Oh, I remember so little about it. I never had much to do with the farm. And, pray, what has the farm to say to anything?'

Will persisted doggedly, 'But you know that the farmer would put the bull in with the cows.'

'Yes. Although I have always wondered why it was necessary to do that.'

He had come this far, he was not going to give up now. He said, 'Well, it was so that the cow could be got with calf.'

She frowned. 'How on earth—' And then as understanding dawned, 'Oh no!' She blushed a deep red and Will did too, but he uttered a silent prayer of thanks.

He went on, 'In the scriptures, when it says Adam *knew* his wife Eve, that is what it meant.'

'You don't mean—s—surely you can't mean . . !'

He swallowed. 'That is why God made them male and female, and said the two would be one flesh.'

'I don't think I can—that is—oh no! I *couldn't*!'

Seeing that she was quite alarmed, Will said gently, 'It is alright. I'll wait.' And he went downstairs to turn the chicken on the spit.

88

TEN
A Time to be Born and a Time to Die

Leyden 1615

John Robinson caught up with Will just as he and Dorothy were leaving the meeting. 'Will—an elders' meeting tomorrow evening, if you please.'

Just a few weeks previously Will had been voted into the position of elder in the congregation, a position he was keen to fill conscientiously. The meetings with the other elders were important to him.

Will nodded, ignoring Dorothy's insistent tugging on his arm. She did not wish to stay and talk at the finish of meetings, which made it more difficult for Will to discuss matters with the other elders.

He said, 'Of course.'

'You do not have time, William,' Dorothy cut in. 'You have an order to finish for Master Gertruycht.'

John Robinson frowned and raised his brows at Will. The inference was plain. A woman ought not to tell her husband what to do. It was not her place, and certainly she had no right to forbid him to attend any spiritual discussion that he chose.

Embarrassed, Will glared at Dorothy, but she met his eyes with determination in her own.

John Robinson too glared at Dorothy, but she did not look up at him. Instead she turned and walked away from them and out of the hall. She would walk home on her own in the dark if Will did not go with her. She knew he could not allow that.

'What is wrong, Will?' John asked gently.

Will shrugged. 'Women.' He smiled but the smile did not reach his eyes. 'Who is there to understand them?'

How could he tell John the truth? That Dorothy had changed from the shy quiet child to a stormy self-centred little cat, intent on bending him to her will? He was ashamed and hurt and confused.

She had no idea of spiritual things, Will thought fiercely, the sick slide of disappointment renewing itself within him. All he wanted, all he needed, was a wife who loved God with the fierce all-consuming love that he felt himself.

'I will come,' he said again to John Robinson.

John glanced at the door Dorothy had just left by and nodded. 'Of course,' he said gently.

Alarmed for his wife's safety, Will ran after her, and caught her up by the bridge.

'I wish you would not go off by yourself at night,' he told her sharply.

'You always do whatever he wants of you,' Dorothy snapped.

'Should I not go?' Will asked, but he was not asking for permission. He did not need her permission. 'Am I not allowed to attend to my duties as an elder, to do the Lord's work?' He was keenly aware of the privilege of being an elder at so young an age, and determined to work extra hard to be worthy of the privilege.

'The Lord's work!' she retorted scathingly. Then she burst into tears. She often wept these days. 'You don't love me. You think only about the Bible, about God, about meetings, about debates!' She walked so quickly in her passion that he almost had to run to keep up.

'You have always known that I am a man of God,' he said.

'If you loved me you would stay at home with me!'

They had come to the house in the *Achtergracht,* and she went in.

Will was so shocked by this outburst that he stood outside for some moments, staring at the door as it slammed behind her. When he went in, he could think of nothing to say. For she was right in a way. His faith, his love of God, his love of truth, were paramount in his life. It was so much part of him, so obvious, that she must have known it long ago. Now he could not understand this jealousy. It was alien to him.

Had he given her cause to be so jealous? He tried to analyse himself. He was a man of fierce energy. His love for God and truth were like a fire burning inside him, a zeal he could not conceal. It was his whole being, his whole life. Dorothy was, or was supposed to be, a pleasurable companion, one who he had thought would share his faith. At least he expected her to understand, for she had grown up in the Separatist congregation—or at least he thought she had. Perhaps she had not. Perhaps her father had not shown the zeal he should have. Perhaps Dorothy did not understand him at all.

True, he was often out in the evenings. As an elder he had a good deal to do in caring for the flock under his care. While the congregation had a deaconess whose job it was to visit the sick, there was much else to do. For there was trouble among the youngsters in the congregation, the youths who had gone into the world, getting caught up in its loose immoral materialistic ways, turning away from God, breaking the hearts of their parents. Some had even gone into the army which was alien to the beliefs of Separatists.

And the congregation was large. The one hundred or so persons who had arrived from Amsterdam in 1609 were now over four hundred strong. Leyden was becoming cramped and it was difficult for these ones to make a living. The number of families on the charity list grew each month.

Caring for the spiritual needs of all these people took time. There were three elders. John Robinson, the pastor, William Brewster the teaching elder, and Will. But three elders were not enough among so many. Sam Fuller as a deacon was an aide to the elders, as was John Carver. Their help was greatly appreciated, but the congregation in Amsterdam had many more elders than Leyden did. Leyden could do with more.

Wives of elders had to be self-sacrificing, everyone knew that. It was part of their own ministry to look after things at home so that their husbands could keep doing what they should. It was a privilege that all Christian wives should cherish. Evidently, Dorothy did not see it that way.

When he entered the house, he found Dorothy sitting at the table, drumming her finger-tips on the table top. He said, 'I am sorry you feel like that, Dorothy.'

She looked at him with ill-concealed contempt. 'Look at you! You're nothing but a weaver of fustian! We have no money William, and you spend time at religious debates when you could be working.' It wasn't strictly true. They had enough money to live on, but there were few luxuries.

'You speak like an atheist,' he told her bluntly. 'Do you not think Jehovah will provide for us? We are here because we need the freedom to worship Him!'

'Oh, that is all you ever think about! Your head is full of cloudy ideas! You are a useless creature, unable to care for your wife and child properly.'

Hurt anger fired up in him. Useless! How could she call him useless, when he worked back-breaking hours day after day to provide for her and—did she say *child*?

'What did you say?'

For a moment she looked guilty, then once more defiant. 'Yes, child. Soon. In the summer.'

'Dorothy!'

He took a step towards her, reaching out for her, but she brushed past him and fled from him, running upstairs sobbing loudly.

Finding himself alone, Will felt cheated. He wanted to discuss this new turn of events, to wallow in the novelty of it, but he had no-one to share it with.

Quietly he went upstairs and into the bedroom. She was lying face down on the bed, weeping loudly into her pillow.

'Dorothy? What does this mean?'

'Go away! You've got what you wanted. Now leave me alone!'

He sat down on the bed, and put a hand gently on her shuddering shoulder. She shrugged him off, and suddenly turned to face him, her face a contorted mask of rage. 'Go away!' she screamed. 'Get out of here!

Haven't you done enough? Leave me alone. I don't want you to touch me ever again!'

Will recoiled in shock, his heart pounding in his chest, his stomach contracting. His eyes filled with tears, his throat swelled with terrible sadness so that it ached. What had happened? How could it be that this girl that he had loved so much, hated him so much? What had he done to deserve this? And in that moment he thought his heart would break.

He did as she bid him, and left her to weep on the bed, going downstairs to put on his cloak. Quietly he let himself out.

He had a desperate need to get away, to be on his own. If he had been in Austerfield, he would have climbed the hill and sat and talked with his God as he had so many times in the past, pouring out his heart while the stars twinkled overhead.

Now, as he made his way towards the *Rapenburg* bridge, three drunks, holding each other up, brushed past him noisily. Others were abroad too, gentlemen in carriages, others who had been to the tavern or to the theatre. It was a city of a hundred thousand people. There was no solitude here.

The streets were damp with winter rain, and it was dark, save for the lights from unshuttered windows. He walked. He needed to be alone, to weep, to pray, to think.

He turned through the passageway of the *Groeneport*, to the garden behind the house. The tenements were not yet finished, and the new meeting place took up quite a bit of space, but there was still a garden, a place to be alone.

He thought of John Robinson in his own house, of his 'father' William Brewster a few houses away, of his friends Edward Southworth, and Sam Fuller and George Morton, in the tenements, any of whom would have taken him in and listened to his tale of woe. But he was ashamed to seek them out. Instead, he went into the remains of the orchard, into the garden, where it was dark and lonely and, unmindful of the damp, sat down with his back to a tree.

He tried to pray, but the words would not come. So he sat in the soft moonlight just asking for help.

He heard the gate as someone came into the garden, the rustle of cloth which told him the newcomer was a woman, and he stood up quickly lest she should fall over him. Had Dorothy relented and followed him?

Hearing his movement the woman stopped. 'Who is it?' she demanded, a note of fear in her voice. 'Who is there?'

'Mistress Southworth?'

'Brother Bradford? Is that you?' The fear left her voice and she came towards him. He could see her silhouetted against the moonlit sky, and he put his hand out and touched her gently to stop her walking into him.

She gasped with the suddenness of it. 'What are you doing here at this time of night?'

'Forgive me, I did not intend to startle you. I—I came here to be alone.'

'Oh, I see.' She assumed he meant to pray, and he did not enlighten her. The Pilgrims often used the garden, as if it were common property. 'Then I will take my leave. I am sorry to have interrupted you.'

Oh, it would be such a relief to confide in her, to unburden himself! He wanted her to stay, but he could not, should not, *must* not ask her. So he said nothing.

She must have sensed something of his agony, for she said sharply, 'Brother Bradford? What is it?'

He struggled with himself. 'My wife is expecting a child,' he said at last, and his voice was flat, strange in his own ears.

After a moment's hesitation, Alice said, 'Oh! That is wonderful news!'

If it were so wonderful, why did he feel so wretched? 'My wife does not seem to think it is wonderful news.'

'Oh?' He could hear the puzzlement in her voice.

'She is upset, angry.' His voice caught, and he knew he had betrayed his hurt to her.

She took a breath. 'Perhaps it is not anger, sir. Perhaps she is afraid.'

'Afraid?' It hadn't occurred to him.

'I am myself,' she went on. 'For I too am with child.'

'I am pleased for you. And you are afraid?'

'Oh yes. Would not you be if it were you?' Too many had died in childbirth recently.

He gave a shaky laugh. 'I find it difficult to picture myself in that position!' There was hope now in his voice.

She laughed too. 'Of course you cannot! But she is young, sir. Still only seventeen. She is probably terrified. She doesn't know what to expect. I shall call to see her tomorrow.'

'Would you? Because I don't know what to say to her. It's like—like she's a stranger to me.' The troubled note returned to his voice. 'I try to make her happy, but nothing I do is right.'

She put a hand on his arm, a mere gesture of sympathy, but he was acutely conscious of it. Her touch seemed to burn through his clothes and into his skin. It occurred to him, belatedly, that they were alone together in the intimate darkness, hidden from others, as good as being in a closed room. If anyone happened upon them there, he realised he would be compromising her good name.

She must have thought the same, for she pulled her hand away. 'I must go. Edward will be wondering where I am.'

'Yes, of course.' And he surprised himself, for his voice was low, gentle.

'I'll call and see Sister Bradford tomorrow,' she said with forced lightness.

'Thank you, Mistress.' He tried for a lighter note in his own voice.

She had already left him and walked through what was left of the orchard back to her own home. He stood still in the darkness, seeing the sudden shaft of light as the door to her tenement opened, and for a moment she was silhouetted there, and then gone.

Something had happened to him. He wasn't exactly sure what, but he realised there was a closeness between him and Alice Southworth that had not been there before. It didn't disturb him, and it didn't worry him, but he did think about it. And strangely, he was not as troubled by Dorothy's behaviour as he had been. Perhaps Alice was right.

When he got home Dorothy was asleep in the bed they shared, and he slid in carefully beside her so as not to wake her, but he lay there a long time awake thinking over what Alice had said, and feeling again her touch on his arm.

Dorothy shifted in her seat and stretched to ease her aching back, and scowled across the aisle at Will who was engrossed, as usual, in whatever was being said. Dorothy had not the faintest idea what John Robinson was talking about, and didn't care much, either. All she wanted was to go home, and she was cross with William because he failed to notice her discomfort.

Sunday, the Sabbath, was a day of meetings. William was always absorbed in the programme of scripture and discussion, and he spent the entire day engrossed, utterly oblivious of anything else that might be going on around him. Or so it seemed to Dorothy.

Since the day she knew she was pregnant she had suffered. Nausea had put her to bed, unable to see to any of William's needs, and other women in the congregation had come to their aid with meals and cleaning. Not that those who helped were not pregnant themselves. Alice, and Sam Fuller's sister Susanna White and his wife Agnes, and Julianna Morton were all expectant mothers.

But 1615 had not begun well. In January Randall Thickens and his wife Jane, sister of Bridget Robinson, lost their baby of a few weeks. In June Edmond Jessop buried his wife Ellen. Three days later Susanna and William White buried their two year old child, a victim of the same fever.

It terrified Dorothy. It was bad enough going through pregnancy, an experience she had no intention of ever repeating, but then to lose the child would be beyond endurance.

As her pregnancy continued the nausea eased, and the backache and headaches and indigestion took over. The baby kicked just when she tried to go to sleep, and pressed up under her ribs and against her stomach when she was awake so that she could hardly eat her food, and when she did it repeated on her in acid heartburn. To sit for two or three hours in the morning and the same in the afternoon on solid wooden benches in a room that was freezing cold in the winter and stiflingly hot in the summer, did not improve her temper.

Alice Southworth, with the calm acceptance of a woman pleased with her condition, assured her that all was perfectly normal. She sat beside Dorothy now, and patted her hand, and when Dorothy looked at her, Alice smiled.

It was alright for Alice, Dorothy thought crossly. Alice's very calmness annoyed her almost as much as William's seeming indifference.

She took a breath and the baby started moving again. A solid lump— perhaps a foot—appeared in her upper right abdomen for a moment and disappeared again. The whole bulk moved to the left. It made her feel quite odd to see it!

Glancing along the row, Dorothy stifled a giggle. All the pregnant women seemed to be sitting together, a row of large bellies beneath grey or brown skirts, the largest being Agnes on the other end of the row. She was near her time.

Agnes stroked her bump as though it hurt, whispered to Julianna and the two of them got up to leave. Clearly Agnes's time had come, and Dorothy suffered an envious pang. Yet at the same time, the fear would not go away. She tried to concentrate on what John Robinson said, but could not. And she could only be thankful when the meeting was over and she could go home.

The room was deathly silent. Julianna stood with Priscilla, their younger sister, beside Agnes's bed, Priscilla stroking Agnes's pale waxen forehead. Alice wrapped up the baby in a sheet, and took it out of the room.

Downstairs Sam Fuller waited for news with his sister Susanna, and his friend Will. Alice paused at the bottom of the stairs, unable to break the news, unable to speak for the tears which choked her.

Will's heart turned over when he saw her, for the child did not wriggle, or move, or cry. This had happened to Sam before. Could anything be so cruel, as to repeat the grief of a few years ago? He glanced at Sam whose face had blanched. Susanna put her hand to her mouth to stifle a cry as tears sprang to her eyes, and she turned away.

None of these women needed to be here at this time, with their own babes on the way.

'The child is dead,' Sam said in a flat voice.

Alice nodded. 'She did not breathe. We tried everything. Do you want to see her?'

Sam came forward and with shaking hands took the bundle from her, opening the covering to look at the child. It was small, and it was blue, so obviously dead.

He just stood there looking at it, and Alice turned agonised eyes on Will. He could read the anguish there, the horror. She swayed, and her legs gave way, and he crossed the room in two strides, catching her before she fell.

'Alice!' Susanna cried.

Will picked her up effortlessly in his arms and set her down gently on a blanket Susanna had the presence of mind to put on the flagstone floor. He stood back to let Susanna take over. 'She should not be here,' Will said severely. 'None of you women should be here in your condition.'

Alice began to come round. Susanna chafed her hands, and tapped her face, and she opened her eyes. She struggled to sit up. 'I'm so sorry. So silly of me!' She struggled to sit up, and Will helped her to her feet, and to sit down on the settle. 'I don't know what came over me,' she said.

'Shock,' Will told her succinctly. 'Ah—Mistress Carpenter!' Mary, the youngest Carpenter aged eighteen now, arrived fortuitously at that moment. 'Go and fetch Brother Southworth to take your sister home.'

'No!' Alice protested. 'I must be here. Mary—go fetch our mother, if you please.'

As Mary departed Will looked from Susanna to Alice and repeated, 'None of you women should be here.'

'We could hardly leave Agnes on her own now, could we?' Susanna pointed out reasonably.

'There are other women in the congregation who can be the gossips,' Will said curtly.

Still holding the dead baby, Sam seemed not to see them.

Will took the baby from him, wrapped it up so that it could not be seen, and put it in the crib standing ready by the fire. 'Agnes will need you,' Will said gently.

Sam nodded, and went upstairs.

Alice, and Susanna, who had joined her on the settle, both wept. 'The baby. The poor little mite did not even cry. It went very hard for her,' Alice said, searching in her petticoat pocket for a handkerchief and blew her nose.

Will drew a stool up and sat down in front of them both.

'It was so terrible Will,' Alice went on after a moment, not realising she had used his forename and beginning to cry all over again. 'It took two days, and then the baby died. All that pain and all that effort and the baby died. And she wanted it so much.'

She broke off, sobbing all the harder, and he put his hand on hers. She looked at him. 'Will, I am so afraid.'

Will said nothing because he could not find the words. He was afraid too. For Sam and Agnes, for Julianna and Susanna, and for Alice, and most of all, for Dorothy. Childbirth was always risky, such a risky business in fact, that women made preparations for their funeral during pregnancy in case it all went wrong. A cold hand of dread squeezed at his heart.

Susanna said, 'Just because the worst has happened to Agnes, it does not mean the same thing will happen to us.'

Will and Alice both looked at her. Will had forgotten her presence, and now he quickly let go of Alice's hand.

Alice nodded, gaining comfort from Susanna's own courage. It was hard on Susanna also, for she had just lost her child aged two.

At that moment Sam came back downstairs. Will stood up. 'How is she?' he asked Sam.

Sam looked at him, stunned, and Will felt that sick dread turn over in his stomach. *Dear God, no!*

Sam shook his head and he looked at Will. 'There is so much blood, Will, so much blood. She is white, like parchment.'

Susanna went to her brother, and put her arms around him. Alice also stood up, and she let out a wail.

Afraid she might swoon again, Will put his hand on her shoulder. She turned in his arm, burying her face in his shoulder, and broke her heart.

Will heard Dorothy's footsteps on the stairs, the pause at the landing, and the climb up the second flight of stairs. He heard her puffing with exertion, and he stopped the loom, arching his aching back as he did so.

Dorothy had been to the Fullers' home behind the *Groeneport* in *Pieterskerkhof*, despite his advising her not to go. She had wanted to comfort Agnes, she said. Now as she came into the attic where he worked, her face had that look of shock that told him the worst had happened. 'Agnes Fuller?'

Dorothy nodded, the tears springing into her big blue eyes, her lip trembling. Will had been expecting it. Agnes had lost so much blood, and there was nothing Sam or any other physician could do. He pushed his stool away from the loom, and got up to take Dorothy in a comforting embrace.

'She bled to death, William,' Dorothy said simply.

'I told you it had not gone well. I wish you had not gone.'

'Well yes, but I thought—that is, I did not think she would die.'

Will was silent, agonised for Sam, worried for Alice, terrified for Dorothy. He struggled to control his fear. 'Poor Sam,' he said after a moment.

Dorothy looked up at him. 'William—what if—'

He cut her off. 'No! You must not think like that!'

'Oh William, I am so afraid.'

He said, 'Come. I will take you to see Mary Brewster. I must go to see Sam.'

It was not the first time he had comforted Sam in an hour of bereavement. Sam Fuller's house had the stillness that followed the shock of death. However, contrary to Will's expectation, Sam, sitting on the settle, was quite calm. But his eyes held the haunted disbelieving look of the newly-bereaved.

'Sam, I'm so sorry.'

Sam looked at him, and the tears spilled from his eyes and trickled unheeded down his ashen unshaven cheeks. 'She just slipped away,' he said. 'We have only been married two years. Such a short while. And I loved her so much, Will. How could this have happened? Twice. Twice this has happened to me. Why, Will? What have I done that God should afflict me like this?'

Will struggled to find the words of comfort. He sat down on a stool opposite Sam and leaned forward. 'You are a good man, Sam. Our heavenly Father would never do this to you. Time and chance happen to us all. We are not perfect. And then there is the Enemy.'

Sam jumped suddenly to his feet. 'Satan! But God could have stopped it.'

Will stood up too, and put his hands on Sam's shoulders. He was bigger than Sam, with a longer reach. ''Tis no use blaming God,' he said.

Sam turned on him. 'What do you know about it? Your wife isn't dead. God hasn't afflicted you! He hasn't taken your child, your wife! Twice over, Will! Damn it all to hell! What is it all for? All this effort and persecution and near poverty for what? To lose one's wife and child—' he struck the table with his fist so hard that it split along the grain.

'Sam, Sam!' Will spoke calmly, hoping his own calmness would take the heat out of his anger.

Sam swept the table of books and papers and a jug which smashed on the floor, pouring ale onto the flagstones.

'Sam!'

He picked up a three-legged stool and threw it across the room, and it smashed against the chimney. A wooden bowl and another earthenware jug followed, accompanied by howls of anguish.

Alarmed by such impotent fury, Will grabbed his friend again by the shoulders and used his own strength to hold him forcibly. Sam took a swing at Will's jaw, but Will ducked backwards and he missed.

Then the fight left him.

'What am I going to do?' he whispered. 'How am I going to go on without her?'

Will said, 'Do you want me to pray with you?'

Sam nodded gratefully. So, just as he was, Will bent his head and prayed. And poor Sam sobbed.

When Will finished and looked up he saw Alice standing behind the settle. She too had been weeping, and her eyes were puffy, the lids swollen and distorted, her nose red. She looked terrible, yet Will knew a sudden and inexplicable urge to go to her, and hold her in his arms. He pushed the thought away, feeling guilty, and turned his attention back to Sam in his distress. He said, 'She is gone for just a while, Sam. She will wait for you.'

'I can't bear it,' Sam cried. 'I can't live without her.'

Will looked up at Alice for help. She stared at the ceiling for a moment, fighting the tears, and then, taking a breath as though summoning every ounce of willpower, she came to sit beside Sam.

'Will is right, Sam,' she said. 'She has gone to be with the Lord and we should be happy about that.'

Sam struggled with himself and nodded.

Alice and Will sat with Sam for a long while, until it was almost dark, when William Brewster and John Robinson arrived.

Will got up to go, and Alice, now much calmer herself, went outside with him. Her home was just across the yard.

'Will you be alright?' he asked her.

She nodded. She looked so tired, so desperate, that he ached to comfort her, but not daring to reach out for her. She was so heavily pregnant herself, the baby due just after Dorothy's. And he felt fear deep in his being, not just for Dorothy, but for Alice, too. It was the shock, he told himself. And the horror.

Dorothy still had a month to go. Alice six weeks. Will was torn between self-preservation and the need to help his friend in his hour of need. However he could not, would not, abandon a friend in need for his own sake, and as a result he found it difficult to think of Dorothy's confinement with anything but dread.

However, Alice's sister Julianna Morton gave birth to a healthy baby girl they named Patience not many days after the Fuller tragedy, and made a full recovery herself so that Will was able to feel a little more positive when Dorothy's time came.

Even so, when Dorothy woke him in the middle of the night to announce that she was having pains, he felt a surge of panic for this woman and child for whom he was responsible.

She sat up in bed beside him and he could see her outline silhouetted against the small window in the greying dawn behind. Her head was bent, and her thick golden plait fell forward across the gross lump that was the child within her.

'Dorothy, what ails you?'

'It damned well hurts!' she swore at him. 'For God's sake go and get Mary!' He swallowed the shock at her language, realising that under other circumstances she would not have given way to profanity, and dived out of bed, hopping on one leg as he pulled on his breeches, searching for his boots, his shirt, his coat in the darkness.

Dorothy let out a cry of pain. 'Hurry up, Will, for God's sake.'

Trying to hurry up made him clumsy, and he knocked over the washstand as he crashed into it, and he heard the jug smash on the floor.

As he went to see to it, she said, 'Never mind that! Just get Mary!'

He raced down the stairs, grabbed cloak and hat on the way out, and ran down the road.

It wasn't that far to William Brewster's house, but it was almost as if it had been moved further away while he was not looking. In his anxiety, he ran all the way, and cursed that he had no other means of getting there. A horse right now would have been a good idea. But at last he reached *St. Ursulasteeg*, and banged with his fist on the door.

Of course the Brewsters were all asleep, and it took several sustained bangs to raise nine year old Fear from her bed, and she answered the door in her night smock.

'Will?'

'Your mother,' he gasped, still panting from his run.

Fear disappeared and Will let himself in, standing awkwardly in the single ground floor room.

Mary came down the stairs a few moments later in her own night shift.

'The baby is coming,' Will said.

'You go on,' Mary told him. 'Go back to her, and I'll get everything ready.' Then, as Will turned, 'And don't worry. It will be ages yet!'

While Will trusted Mary's judgement, he did think that she might be mistaken. He had seen too much tragedy lately to risk anything with his Dorothy.

'Please don't be long,' he begged, and raced off again down the road towards his own little house, praying as he ran.

The horror of Sam's loss was fresh in his mind still, the devastation of losing his wife and child had been hard on Sam. Will couldn't bear to think of the same thing happening to Dorothy.

Back at his house he swept up the broken crockery and got the things ready that Dorothy had prepared, the crib for the baby, the swaddling bands, the wraps, the towels, water, everything he could think of. He brought Dorothy some wine to drink, but she did not want more than a sip, and sat on the bed holding her hand and wishing that someone would come to help him, knowing that he was being unreasonable, for certainly Mary and the others, the gossips, were hurrying as best they knew how.

Meantime the pains grew stronger and closer together, and Will began to wonder if he would be the one to deliver this baby. However, whenever he spoke to Dorothy it was to reassure her that Mary was on her way, and that everything would be fine.

To his immense relief Mary arrived shortly afterwards, and the women, the gossips that Dorothy had chosen. Katherine Carver was one of them. Anne Peck, Brewster's ward was another, but the Carpenter sisters, Julianna a new mother, and Alice so near her time, and after the terrible loss of Agnes and her babe, had not come.

Mary bustled about with the air of a midwife who had attended many birthings, which she had, and her plump jolly presence was a comfort. She went to Dorothy and sat beside her with her hand on her abdomen, as Dorothy had another pain. Mary nodded with satisfaction. 'A good strong pain,' she told Dorothy. 'Not long, I think.' Then she looked at Will. 'This is no place for a husband. Off you go!'

Will stood his ground mulishly. 'I've been at many a birthing, Mistress,' he said. 'And this is my house.' He didn't want to leave Dorothy to deal with this alone.

Mary was shocked. 'Not human ones, you haven't. Lord, whatever next! Out!'

Will moved reluctantly to the door, and said to his wife, 'Not long now, and it will all be over.'

'And not before time!' Dorothy snapped. 'This is all your fault.'

'Now, we'll have none of that talk here!' Mary said briskly. 'Downstairs, Will. Now!'

Will gave in with a show of reluctance, but with inward relief, and went downstairs leaving his wife and soon-to-be-born child in the hands of these experienced women.

He was left with nothing to do but pace the floor anxiously as his wife cried out at intervals in the room above. And far from being quick, it went on all morning.

Edward Southworth came to keep him company, and to help in supplying the midwife with ale and food to keep them going, while

Dorothy laboured.

Alice Southworth looked in, but being near her own time, and with the recent tragedy so fresh in everyone's mind, her husband ushered her out again. He could not risk exposing her to another tragedy.

The baby was born just after midday, the sudden lusty squalling of the infant telling Will it had been born strong and hearty. Relief overwhelmed him, and he sat down and wept.

A short time later Mary appeared at the bottom of the stairs with the child in her arms wrapped in a blanket, and showed it to Will. It was a boy, larger than Sam Fuller's little dead girl had been, all pink and wriggly and with a lopsided head, moulded by the birth—on one side with the eye open and the ear sticking out, and on the other with the eye shut and the ear plastered flat against his head. And he screamed, his little pink tongue curling up with the effort.

'It's a beautiful boy,' Mary beamed as though she had produced him herself.

Will took the bundle from Mary, cradling his son in his arms, and a rush of love overwhelmed him. He counted all the fingers, thumbs and all the toes, on a body that seemed to him to be so small and helpless in his own massive hands.

'Yes, he's all there,' Mary assured him, but Will hardly heard her. His heart was so full of love for this tiny scrap of life in his arms that he could not even speak for several moments. He felt his throat contract, and the tears come to his eyes.

Then he closed the blanket in case his son got cold, and raised him to kiss his forehead. Immediately the child stopped howling and started looking for what he thought might be a nipple.

Seeing it, Mary took him back from Will. 'Time for Mama,' she said.

'And Dorothy?' Will asked belatedly.

'She is fine. Tired, but very well. She'll do.'

'Can I see her?'

'Give us time to make everything tidy. I'll call you in a little while.'

Dorothy was sitting up in bed, propped up on the pillows when Will came in, the baby at her breast beneath a raised chemise. She looked tired and a little pale, her hair wet from the efforts of her labour, but she smiled at Will, and his heart melted.

'A son,' she said.

He kissed her damp forehead. 'Our gift from Jehovah. We will call him Jonathan which means Jehovah's gift.'

She raised her free hand to him, pulling him down against her, kissing his cheek. 'Thank you for giving him to me,' she whispered.

In that moment he loved her, loved them both more than anything else in the world.

Three weeks later Alice Southworth also successfully gave birth to a son, Constant, much to Edward's delight and Will's relief, although why Will should have been so relieved over Alice's safe confinement, he didn't know. It was also a relief for Sam that his sister Susanna White had a son shortly afterwards, called Resolved, and Susanna found some comfort in this child after the harrowing loss of her own child earlier in the year, and her brother Sam's loss.

ELEVEN
Debates

1617, Leyden

It had been advertised as the definitive debate on predestination, with Episcopius on the side of Arminianism, and John Robinson for Calvinism. As Will entered the vaulted University auditorium with Brewster, he could feel the expectation hanging like a thick cloud in the air, and men talked in muted tones, filling the circular auditorium with a murmur.

The subject of predestination had gripped the University for years, and not just the University, but the whole city. It was hotly discussed in taverns and in homes, and wherever people came together. The question was, Had God foreordained that Adam and Eve should sin in the garden of Eden? And if so, was this consistent with a God of love? Everyone wanted to know the answer, and this debate between Episcopius and John Robinson was viewed as providing the defining answer.

Now, as John Robinson, dressed in the traditional gown, made his way to the raised dais, the waiting observers fell silent.

Will, who had accompanied him, took his seat in the centre of the row, jammed in between William Brewster and a man he did not know. The stench from unwashed bodies was overpowering. It was hot in the auditorium too, the air thick with heat and smells.

John Robinson sat quite still and waited. Perhaps he prayed. Certainly he was very calm. Of course, this was nothing new to him. Cambridge had been a hotbed of this kind of controversy when Robinson was there, and he had learned to argue and draw conclusions then about this very subject. Since his enrolment as a student of theology at Leyden not many months past, he had shown himself more than capable. That was why professor John Polyander had asked for his help with this issue, and a great honour it was, too, to be asked. Not that John Robinson viewed it as an honour. He was a humble man, and he saw it as just doing the Lord's work.

'So where is the man Episcopius?' Will asked Brewster, for the opponent had not yet put in an appearance.

He was answered by the man sitting on his other side. 'He is here. He will not be long. I have seen him.'

Will turned to the stranger, a man in his mid-thirties, with a pleasant bewhiskered face, and expensive taste in clothes. 'Forgive me, sir, whom do I have the honour of addressing?' Will enquired.

The man inclined his head. 'Thomas Brewer, sir, of Kent. And you, sir, I collect, are Master Robinson's friends.'

'William Bradford,' Will said. 'And this is Master William Brewster.'

'Well met, gentlemen, well met.'

'Are you for Master Robinson, sir, or Master Biscop?' Will asked. Simon Biscop was the man whose name was Latinised into Episcopius.

'I have not yet made my mind up, sir. I look forward with interest to the debate.'

Will did not answer him, for at that moment Simon Biscop, or Episcopius, professor of theology, ascended the dais wearing his gown, and the auditorium broke into applause.

Will could see little of him from where he sat. The man was tallish, not fat, had a small beard (like everyone else) and was perhaps in his early thirties. John Robinson was a little older.

John Polyander came onto the dais and addressed the audience in Latin. The whole debate was to be conducted in Latin, for that was the common language of the University which people from all different nationalities could understand, and William Brewster whispered to Will, 'Now you will see how useful Latin can be!' Certainly Will was pleased that he had studied Latin himself.

John Polyander introduced John Robinson on the one hand, and Simon Biscop on the other, and the debate began.

From Will's point of view, nothing John Robinson said could be wrong. Certainly Robinson made the best use of his arguments, and in Will's opinion knew better what he was talking about than the Arminian professor.

Will listened in rapt attention as the debate raged. Whatever Episcopius could say, John Robinson countered, using the Bible cleverly. Will in his bias felt that Robinson had the best of it.

Will was jubilant. 'The truth will always win out!' he cried, as he walked home with Robinson and Brewster afterwards.

'You think so?' Robinson looked straight at him. 'I may have convinced others, but if only I could be sure myself. These debates, they prove nothing, only who can argue to the best account. There is more in scripture than we know at present.'

Will frowned. 'I do not think I follow you, sir.'

'Do you not, young Will?' They walked along the canal, and John Robinson was thoughtful.

'At the moment we cannot know definitively,' he said, 'Instead of debating with these men, which means I take one stand, and they another, I would rather sit down with them and discuss it and thrash out all the different aspects of the subject, and probably find there is a compromise somewhere that we had not thought of. We are near the truth but not quite there yet.'

Will was disappointed. 'Yet I have seen your writings on the subject.'

John Robinson sighed. 'Yes. And they are as true as they can be within my own limited knowledge.'

'So it is as if it is just out of reach.'

Robinson nodded agreement. 'Yet we are grateful to have the truth as far as we can. Perhaps it is not yet the Lord's time to reveal all these things.'

They had come to the *Groeneport,* the house in *Pieterskerkhof* where John Robinson lived and which housed the meeting hall and the tenements.

They had stood outside talking for some time, but now John Robinson shivered. 'Do you come in, Will?' he asked.

Will shook his head. At home Dorothy waited for him, and he knew she would already be angry at the lateness of the hour. 'Not this evening, sir.'

John Robinson's eyes reflected pity, and Will flinched. He did not want anyone's pity. So he bowed his head in brief salutation, and went his way.

'You know how it is, of course,' Brewster said watching Will disappearing into the darkness.

Robinson sighed. 'Aye.'

But no-one could know the misery of Will's life. Who could have foreseen that sweet little Dorothy May who he had married when she was sixteen and he twenty-three, should turn into a whining, clinging, bad-tempered little witch? No, he chided himself. That was going too far. He tried to think positively. But all he could think of was his misery.

Dorothy had turned into a complaining, nagging contentious woman. There was no softness in Dorothy now, no love. She was appalled by the intimacy of marriage, and refused the marriage due, giving in only until she conceived the child, the only thing she really cared about. He was hurt and disappointed, and did not understand it. John Robinson might tell the congregation that such intimacy was a joyful gift from God, but Dorothy plainly did not agree. It was a trial for her, and she made it plain that his attentions were unwelcome. Her attitude did little for Will's self-esteem, leaving him angry and tense, and somehow different from everyone else. As the time went on his misery increased. He and Dorothy were growing apart, and he did not know how to prevent it.

He shook his head. He had known almost at the outset that he had made a terrible mistake in marrying Dorothy. He had hoped to find in her the compliant helpmeet he needed. Instead she was too young to help him in anything. She found it difficult to keep the house clean and tidy, particularly after little Jonathan was born. Sometimes there was no supper, because she had not found the time to go to market. She hated him going out and leaving her, and now that he was an elder, with all that entailed, it had come to be a point of contention between them. He went out anyway, for he had to be a man in his own household, and not under any woman's thumb, but he did not like the rows, the tears, the *'You don't love me, you don't. All you think about is the church!'*

He crossed the *Rapenburg* canal towards the *Achtergracht* where he had his own little house, pausing on the bridge to look down into the dark water. He was suddenly reluctant to go back to Dorothy and her constant complaining, and wished he had taken up John Robinson's offer after all. An evening by the fire in the comfort and welcome of the Robinson's house, of easy friendly conversation would have been so good.

He came to his own house and bracing himself, he went in.

The house was surprisingly quiet, still. There was no fire in the grate, no meat roasting on the spit, (their income would just stretch to the occasional meat), no stew in the pot. No wife. No son.

Will's heart lurched. Had she left him? He thought of the atmosphere in the house in the last few days and felt the sickening dread that perhaps she had gone back to her parents in Amsterdam.

On sudden impulse he ran up the narrow stairs, and went into their room. Although Dorothy was not here, her things were—lace collars, caps, hairbrush. So she had not left him. He felt a rush of relief.

He went downstairs again, and found the tinder box to light a candle, for it was growing quite dark. It took several strikes to ignite the tinder, but at last he had a candle glowing and then two or three. Then he saw the scrap of paper on the table, weighted with his own tankard.

I have gone to visit Julianna Morton, was all it said.

That explained it. Probably the Mortons had encouraged her to stay to sup with them. He could not allow his wife to walk home in the dark on her own, and he could not expect George Morton to do it for him, so he would have to collect her. He brightened. In fact, he would be expected to stay as well, no doubt, and if they had not eaten, to sup with them. It was a prospect he found he looked forward to, for he enjoyed these evenings spent with dear friends, people who loved God. It was often a time of laughter and joy, or discussion and conversation.

The Mortons' tenement behind the *Groeneport* was a compact but adequate dwelling, with whitewashed walls and small leaded windows. Julianna had added the personal touches only a woman could add, the crocheted table cover, a sprig of lavender suspended from the ceiling rafter.

They welcomed him with beaming faces, George jumping up from the settle where he sat with Sam Fuller and Edward Southworth, each with a mug of ale in their hands. 'Will! Well come. We have been waiting on you,' George said and immediately poured ale from the jug into another mug and handed it to Will. Will joined him and Sam and Edward by the fire, sitting on a stool to the left of George, and took a large swig of ale to wet a dry throat. Julianna, clad in a large white apron over her brown dress, busied herself tending to the food, and smiled at Will serenely. 'Supper will be ready directly now that you have come.'

'I didn't know I was expected,' Will said.

'But of course. If Dorothy is invited, of course you are too!'

Will glanced at Dorothy who sat on the flagstone floor playing with their son, Jonathan, now a golden haired child of two and, and also with two of Julianna's—Patience also two, and Nathaniel who was six. The youngest, John, just a few months old, was fast asleep in a crib in the corner. Also in the group were Alice and Edward's two year old Constant and their younger son Thomas, a few months old, being cradled in Alice's lap as she sat on a rag rug on the floor with the children. They seemed to be quietly amusing each other, although Will did not suppose for one moment that that would last, and their respective mothers watched over them adoringly.

Dorothy looked up at him, but there was no welcome in her eyes, no smile. He felt excluded and hurt and he hoped the others did not notice it.

Alice also looked up, and she did smile. 'We thought you would have been here hours ago, Will,' she said.

'I've been to the University,' he replied.

Julianna, who had not been paying attention interrupted. 'Will! Sam has some news for us. Sam, tell Will your news!'

'I am to be married,' Sam said quietly to Will, and Julianna nodded with satisfaction, which surprised Will for it was just two years since Sam's wife, Julianna's sister Agnes had died. But then Sam had been sad long enough and it was time to get on with his life.

'You are? To whom?'

'Bridget Lee.'

'She is a fine woman, Sam.'

'And Robert Cushman is to marry Mary Singleton,' Julianna added as she put the wooden dishes and spoons on the table, together with a loaf of bread.

Robert Cushman had buried his wife and then, a few days later, his child last year, the victims of another birthing that went wrong. And he wasn't the only one. Susanna and William White had also buried their new-born in December. It had been a terrible time. Yet few expected anything else. No-one had children and kept them all. It just didn't happen. And childbirth was a risky business at the best of times. They lived with death all around them. It was part of life. Everyone could expect to lose someone dear to them.

Will's eyes rested on Alice who sat on the floor with the children, cradling her baby who was still young enough to be wrapped in swaddling bands, talking gently to him, showing him the wooden toy, a horse, in which he seemed singularly uninterested.

Alice said from the floor, 'You have come from the debate, Brother?'

They all looked at him then, for the debated question of predestination was of great interest to everyone. Except Dorothy, of course. He said, 'I have.'

'Well, and how did it go?' Edward Southworth prompted.

'As you would expect. Brother Robinson had the right of it, and left the great Episcopius with nothing to say.'

'What was the question again?' Alice asked.

'Were Adam and Eve predestined to sin?'

There was a short silence.

'No,' Alice said suddenly filling the gap. 'Of course they were not.' And she looked down at the child.

Edward reprimanded her. 'Woman, you speak out of turn!'

Will, too had been surprised and even displeased by her answer, which was opposed to the argument John Robinson had put forward. It was not a woman's place to question her menfolk, but he was intrigued. He said kindly, 'What brings you to such a conclusion, Mistress?'

'Oh don't mind my wife,' Edward interrupted becoming quite annoyed. 'She has windmills in her head. I keep telling her that it is not a woman's place to question such things.'

Sam Fuller said in his gentle way, 'Do not the scriptures themselves tell us that women were used as prophetesses?'

'That is so,' Will agreed. Unlike many of their contemporaries, the Separatists had a respect for their womenfolk that went beyond the world's view. In a time when women were usually considered little more than chattels, to do the bidding of men, the Separatists viewed their women as worthy of love and consideration, intelligent creatures in their own right. True they were to be in subjection to their menfolk, yet that did not mean they had no say in anything. They had a worthwhile place in their society, and were valued as homemakers and mothers and wives—helpmeets. They were to be treated with respect, older women as mothers, younger women as sisters. True, it was considered unseemly for women and men to sit together at meetings, or for a man to be alone with a woman to whom he was not married, except they be chaperoned, but everyone recognised that as a protection against sin. Still, Will recognised, as Edward had, that Alice had gone further than she ought, but he wanted to know why she said what she did.

'So what is your view, Mistress?' he invited.

Her eyes met his across the heads of the children, and she said, 'It seems to me, sir, that it is unreasonable to believe that God foreordained us to be sick and die. We have lost many in the congregation—little ones and older ones—did God *intend* for them to die? Why a child?'

He frowned at her, for as far as Will was concerned what John Robinson said must be absolutely right, and it bothered him that she had unwittingly taken a stand against him. He could have dismissed it as a subject beyond feminine capabilities, and if it had been another woman he would have done so. However, he recognised in Alice a sharp brain, a superior grasp of matters that put some men into the shadows. Furthermore, her directness was like a challenge. He had to answer the challenge, to explain John Robinson's reasoning.

'Brother Robinson showed that God must have foreordained Adam's sin, for God knows and is capable of foreordaining everything.'

They listened intently, taking in what he said, but Alice came back at him, 'Being capable of it does not mean that He did it,' Alice pointed out. 'What about the scripture which says of God: *Perfect is the work of the mighty God, for all his ways are judgement. God is true and without wickedness. Just and righteous is he.*? Would not deliberately causing Adam and Eve to sin make him an unjust God, since he also made them— and us—to suffer and die?'

'Alice!' Edward remonstrated, horrified. Whatever would people think? That he had an unruly wife who did not keep a civil tongue in her head?

Will put up his hand to silence him. 'Let her be,' he said, then to Alice, 'That is what Simon Biscop—Episcopius—argued.'

She met his eyes straightly, not looking away or downwards in mock humility, but challenging him, and he was struck by the beauty in those green eyes, the intelligence of her face, the parted dark orange lips. He again felt drawn to her as he had the night in the garden, and he wanted to keep her attention. Still, male pride could not allow her to have the insight that a man had, and the others were looking to him to settle the issue.

Edward fidgeted uncomfortably on the settle, glaring first at Alice and then at Will as though he saw something he did not quite like. 'As the foolish women talk, so do you, wife.'

She did not look at Edward, although she obviously heard him. This was not Edward's conversation. But she continued to look at Will, waiting for an answer.

He echoed Robinson's words earlier, 'We cannot know all God's ways. There are many things yet to be learned and understood.'

She came back at Will 'True enough,' she acknowledged. 'But because of Adam we all sin, get sick and die. Did God make us to die? Would a God of love do that?'

Will continued to look into her sea-green eyes. 'But then he fits us for heaven.'

'Why not, then, create us all in heaven, like he did the angels? And besides, do all of us go to heaven?'

'Alice!' Edward snapped again, aware that something was happening here, beyond the debate, that he did not understand.

Recklessly, they both ignored him. Will answered her, 'No, only those whom he chooses. The elect.'

'So those who are not of the elect, he made to be tormented everlastingly in hellfire?' She countered. 'Is that just? Is that the work of a loving God? It seems to me that we condemn the Catholic Inquisition because it tortures people and burns them to death. And that torture is for a relatively short time—certainly not forever. We say it is the Devil's work, yet we ascribe worse to God—tormenting forever.'

Julianna interrupted them. 'I think that is enough theological debate now, you two. If you will all sit around the table, I will serve supper.'

Obediently Alice got up from the floor, picking up her baby and lying him on his back on a blanket a little away from the fire. Will had a chance to whisper in her ear: 'You have an interesting theory, Mistress, but I would be careful to whom you told it, if I were you.'

She stood up and looked at him with those wonderful eyes. 'You mean I could be guilty of apostasy?' She raised her brows, laughing at him. 'It is a good job I trust you, sir.'

He said: 'You are safe with me. But don't repeat it to Brother Robinson.'

'I hope I am not so prideful as to think I know better than Brother Robinson,' she said a little wistfully. 'But there is so much I want to know. I read my Bible every day, and I ask Edward, but he does not have time— or the knowledge—to tell me. He is a man of simple faith. Me I want to *know* so much. Oh, I would that I were a man, able to join in the discussions you brothers have!'

Will laughed and they sat down at opposite ends of the table, as Julianna ladled out the stew she had prepared for them all. Then, as the stew began to cool, George Morton asked for God's blessing on the meal.

Will sat next to his wife and concentrated on what Sam Fuller had to say about what he learned from his medicine books. But all the while he went over the discussion with Alice in his head, and he was acutely conscious of the woman at the other end of the table, of her washed green eyes, her freckled nose, her rounded womanly figure. She had woken something inside him, something sinful, and it disturbed him.

Edward was furious with Alice. 'You have made me a laughingstock!' he told her as he closed the door on their own little tenement.

She felt dismayed. 'I don't know what you mean.' She put the sleeping baby in the crib and began to usher Constant up the stairs to his own room.

Edward detained her. 'Everyone will think I am not master in my own home, that I have a wife who puts herself above her station,' he thundered.

'Because I asked a question?' she countered and followed Constant upstairs.

Yet she had a nagging, guilty feeling inside her. It had been too much temptation. She was still in love with Will, and she knew she always would be. But she had to keep it subdued, locked away deep inside her, and learn to live with it, to keep him at arms' length without him even being aware of it. She had given herself to Edward, and he was her husband.

However, Edward did not live up to her needs for a husband. He was caring enough—indeed he loved her very much. But he was not as strong spiritually as she would have liked. He did not read the Bible with his wife, for example, which other husbands did, or were encouraged to do. He would miss meetings for the least reason; either he was too tired, or he had a headache, or some other reason. He frequently did not work, so that they had little money. And he complained about everything, from the weather to the hardness of the work.

She found it a struggle to cope with their reduced circumstances, his depressive moods, his lack of spirituality. When Will had spoken about the debate she saw the opportunity of engaging in conversation with someone who could meet her intellect and it was too tempting to pass up.

But, giving in to that temptation changed things between herself and Will, and she was afraid. Worse, Edward had recognised it too, and he was jealous.

When she came down, she found Edward pacing the floor agitatedly. 'You think I don't know, don't you?' he said.

Alice took her white starched cap off, and unpinned her hair. It fell to her waist. 'I don't know what you mean,' she lied, but her stomach lurched.

Edward was not impressed, reached forward, and took her arm, turning her to face him. 'I know what you think of Will Bradford,' he hissed viciously.

'There is nothing between me and Brother Bradford,' Alice told him truthfully, putting her chin up defiantly. 'And to suggest anything else is a scurrilous lie. Will is a man of principles, a man who would never betray his vows to his wife, or his vows to God. And I value my faith too much to risk anything that would endanger it. Furthermore, you are my husband, and I have made certain promises to you which I take very seriously. I love you, and I would do nothing to hurt you.'

He searched her eyes. And it was true. She did love him. It may not have been the same as the love she had for Will, which would always be with her, but she had grown to love him simply because he loved her. Furthermore, she would not endanger her marriage, or her position in the congregation, no matter what she felt for Will.

Edward was reassured, but he said, 'I have been thinking. I am not happy here in Leyden. I have decided we shall go back to England.'

Alice felt her heart crash to the floor. 'England?' she faltered. 'But my parents, my sisters, my brother, my friends, they are all here.' And so was Will.

He said, 'I cannot provide for you here, Alice. In London I could get different work. There is a congregation in London led by Henry Jacob, a fine brother, and I feel it would be a good move for us.'

She didn't want to go, but she saw that his mind was made up. She nodded. 'Very well.'

He pulled her to him, and buried his face in her hair, wrapping his arms around her. 'I'm only trying to do the best for you and the boys,' he mumbled. She let herself be persuaded, and went with him up the stairs.

A few days later, Edward and Alice Southworth and their two boys left Leyden and returned to England.

TWELVE
First Suggestions

Leyden 1617

It had been a hot day, made hotter in the close confines of the attic in the house in the *Achtergracht*. The black dust from the cloth Will wove stuck to the sweat on his face, got trapped in the hairs on his arms, and even found its way down his neck. He was glad when Dorothy called up the stairs and announced that supper was ready. She had the meal ready early at his request, for John Robinson had called an elders meeting for that evening, and he could not be late. Quickly he descended the twisting narrow stairs to the bedroom, and washed himself in the water in the bowl, and shaved, and then went on down into the kitchen where Dorothy had prepared an impressive pudding full of vegetables, and a little bacon. He prayed for them and then ate quickly, and as soon as he was able he left the house. For once Dorothy did not complain.

After the heat of the day, Will found the spacious kitchen in the Robinson house, cool and welcoming for there was no fire in the grate. He must have been late, for everyone else had arrived before him. The elders and deacons sat around the huge scrubbed table, and greeted Will as he took a place between big bluff John Carver and Robert Cushman.

Robert Cushman, had recently been appointed deacon, but Will didn't know him well, save that he had a firm faith. To look at, Cushman was middle aged at forty, balding on top with dark greying hair flowing to his white starched collar. He had keen dark eyes which seemed to pierce through to one's soul, and which made others wary of him, and an easy smile. This last year he had suffered much over the death of his wife and child.

Besides Cushman and Carver were Sam Fuller, also a deacon, now married to Bridget Lee, and others not normally present at elders' meetings, brothers who were highly regarded, for their wisdom and faith—William White, Isaac Allerton, and Digorie Priest who was married to Allerton's sister Sarah, George Morton, as well as Brewster, and Robinson of course.

Will was surprised. Their presence told him that this was no ordinary meeting and he peered at two of the books on the table trying to gain some clue as to the reason John Robinson had called them. However, they had been deliberately placed to obscure their titles, and they were at the far end of the table with other books where John Robinson and William Brewster sat.

'So,' Brewster said conversationally across the space that divided him from Cushman, 'I hear you are to be congratulated, Brother.'

Everyone peered at Cushman. Carver said, 'Oh?'

'It appears that our brother is to be married,' Brewster informed them in booming tones.

Will already knew.

Cushman grinned with pleasure. 'That is so.'

'So who is the lady?' Carver asked.

'Mary Singleton.' Everyone knew her as a widow.

'An excellent woman,' Will said. 'She will make you a fine wife.'

John Robinson coughed. 'If we could get down to business, gentlemen? I think we will ask the Lord's blessing and guidance on our meeting,' and he cast a warning eye at William Brewster.

Accordingly they bowed their heads, and John Robinson prayed,

The *Amen* said, they waited while John Robinson took a few moments to collect his thoughts. Will watched him, his hands still clasped together in front of his mouth in an attitude reminiscent of the recent prayer, frowning, looking not at the men but at the books in front of him. He was a fine man, Will thought.. He was forty-one, but with his hair still dark and full, and his beard unmarked by grey, one could easily think him ten years younger. Only the eyes, clear, light grey, intelligent eyes, were careworn, betraying the heartbreak they had all suffered, and which seemed even more part of life here in Holland than in England.

Brewster glanced at Robinson. There was something in that glance that heightened Will's curiosity. Something of moment.

At last John looked at them all, his grey eyes resting momentarily even apologetically on each of them and Will understood that he took his responsibility as their pastor seriously.

'Brothers, we have been in Holland some eight or nine years,' he began, 'and life is not easy for any of us. We have lost men and women, as well as many children, to death, and we are growing older.'

Brewster shifted uncomfortably in his seat, too aware of his own advancing years. At fifty he had a receding hairline, and greying beard, and beginning to look his age.

Robinson went on, 'The hardness of this country is such that although there are brothers in England who would dearly like to join with us, few are prepared for the difficulties, and they do not come, while others who do come, do not bide it out and continue. Why even this week Edward Southworth has removed his family to London.'

Will suffered a shock. Alice had gone and he did not even know it until this moment. It shouldn't matter to him of course.

John Robinson continued, 'We live in poverty here brothers. We struggle to earn a living, while the Dutch abide in well-lit and well-appointed houses, and our brothers have to work looms to earn a crust. It is the hard labour and scant fare that we must endure.'

It was true. Hardly a man of them felt able to provide adequately for his family. The Netherlands was overpopulated. There was not enough work to go around. The only occupations open to untrained English immigrants were in the textile industry where the work was hard labour, and in which the standard of living was low. '*Poverty*' was not too strong a word for it. For people who had been yeoman farmers, and some of them had been gentlemen, if not quite nobility, educated at University, it was a hard lesson in humility and want. Brewster whose age and class were against him found it particularly difficult, although his taking up teaching English brought just enough in to keep his family.

Robinson went on, 'So, although prospective members love us, and approve of our cause, yet they leave us as Orpah left her mother-in-law Naomi. Some even prefer the prisons in England to the enduring of these hardships for the sake of liberty.'

He paused. By now every man around the table was nodding in agreement. Robinson continued, 'I put it to you, brothers, that if we could be in a place where we could have freedom of worship and live comfortably, then we would find others drawn to us.

'Secondly, although we put up with all these difficulties cheerfully for the sake of freedom, that is fine while we are in the best of health and in our youth. But old age is coming in on us, and the hardships we face here make us old before our time. In a few years more we must leave or sink beneath the burdens. You well know the proverb, brothers, that '*a prudent man seeth the plague and hideth himself*'. We do not want to find ourselves surrounded by enemies at a time when we are not able to flee or able to fight. Again it would be the prudent thing to find a better abiding place.'

'What enemies?' George Morton asked.

Brewster explained, 'The peace treaty between the Spanish and the Dutch ends in the year sixteen hundred and twenty-one. If the Spanish go to war and win, just think what it would be like here. And with Spanish occupation comes the Inquisition.'

'Oh!'

They all knew what it meant, and no man was prepared to risk it for themselves or their families. England, by comparison, looked tame.

John Robinson took back the reins. 'Third, because necessity is such a taskmaster over us, so we have to be taskmasters over our servants and our children, which is not the way it should be, and causes great grief to parents and children alike. Those children of the best dispositions who are willing to help their parents in their burdens, are often so weighed down with the heavy labour that their bodies are being destroyed, becoming decrepit in their early youth. And many of our children, unable to bear the burdens, are enticed away by the easy living and licentiousness of the Dutch youth into extravagant and dangerous living, getting the rein off their necks and leaving their parents, some even joining the army, others going to sea, others descending into a life of vice to the grief of their parents and dishonour of God. All this you know. How many have we expelled in the last few years? And as we go on, how many more?'

William Brewster no doubt had his own family in mind when he put in, 'Our children are growing into little Dutchmen. They speak Dutch, like the local people, and they forget they are English. If we stay, they and their children will become Dutch, not English.'

That was something Will, and he assumed most of the men present, could not stomach.

John Robinson continued, 'We all have young children, little ones who will grow up in this place. Soon the truce with Spain will be ended. Will we be drawn into a war we have no wish to be involved in, our young men drafted into the army to fight. And if Spain should overrun this country which is not beyond possibility, then where will our freedom of worship be? We will be eliminated from the face of the earth.'

There was a profound silence, then Robert Cushman stirred in his seat. 'What do you propose Brother Robinson? That we should move again?'

John Robinson paused and looked at them, and Will felt a leap in his chest. Something in Robinson's eyes made Will expectant. 'I need your views, gentlemen.'

George Morton put into words what they were all thinking. 'Are you thinking of America?'

Will's heart jolted. *America*! That vast fruitful, unpopulated wilderness on the other side of the Atlantic, ripe for colonisation. And the English were desperate for people to do the colonising. Anyone would do. Even the cursed Separatists! The English government were keen to encourage everyone who felt they could go and tame the wilderness in the name of the English King, and accordingly they had set up a corporation in London to grant land and to assist those who wished to go, called the Virginia Company.

Sam Fuller tapped the table with his forefinger. 'It is a big step. And not all will want to go, or be able to go.'

'Naturally, we would force no-one. Each man must weigh carefully whether he wishes to go.'

Will could not hide the excitement in his voice. 'What are we talking of? Virginia? Guiana? Raleigh is there now, exploring the Orinoco.'

'Sir Walter Raleigh looks for gold. We look for a place to live. Still he has some interesting things to say about Guiana.' Raleigh had written a book about a previous voyage to this land which he viewed as el Dorado. John Robinson picked up one of the books on the table, opened it to a previously marked page, and read, '"*To conclude, Guiana is a country that hath yet her maydenhead never sacked, turned, nor wrought, the face of the earth hath not been torn, nor the virtue and salt of the soil spent by manurance, the graves have not been opened for gold, the mines not broken with sledges, nor their images pulled down out of their temples. It hath never been entered by any army of strength, and never conquered or possessed by any Christian prince.*"'

'So far,' John Carver added morosely. 'With respect, neither we, nor Sir Walter Raleigh, know what the Spanish have in mind. And as I recollect it, the Spanish are also in South America, and certainly in the West Indies.'

'True. And the proximity of the Spanish must always be a consideration. The other option is Virginia, where there is already an English colony.' He indicated the other books on the table. 'Brother Brewster has found some books about the New World.' William Brewster slid them one by one across the table so that they could each be seen. 'John Smith's *A Map of Virginia; Voyages* by Hakluyt and, of course, Sir Walter Raleigh's *Discovery of Guiana.*'

'Have you read them?' Will asked.

Brewster nodded. 'Not cover to cover,' he admitted, 'but enough. Guiana is on the northern coast of the southern continent of America. Its location is on the equator. Raleigh speaks of it in terms of gold and el Dorado, but it is also a very hot place. I think we, who come from a colder climate, would find it difficult to adjust—particularly the women. But he says the land is lush.'

'Overgrown jungle more like,' John Carver added. 'And I tell you, brothers, heat equals pestilence.'

'Jungle could be cleared and cultivated,' Will said. 'Are there natives there?'

'Indians,' Robinson said. 'Friendly enough. Not cannibals according to Raleigh.'

'And wild animals?'

Brewster said, 'Nothing we could not handle. Well, not if they don't eat us first.'

That brought a small laugh. John Robinson, though, said, 'There are things that are against Guiana—not least the fact that it is near the Spanish territories.'

'The Inquisition,' Sam Fuller murmured.

It was a very real threat. Wherever the Spanish went they took with them the dreaded Catholic Inquisition. Everyone knew the tortures inflicted on those who did not hold to Catholic dogma.

Oh yes, it would be foolish indeed to put the brethren in a situation that could put them in such danger, and would defeat the reason for their emigration, namely freedom of worship. For surely, of all Protestants, the Separatists had to be the most hated by the Catholics. The feeling was mutual.

They moved on. 'Captain John Smith, the explorer, speaks well of Virginia,' Brewster said.

That would be the same John Smith who had found the Indian princess Pocahontas. She had journeyed from Virginia to England the previous year with her husband John Rolfe. According to reports, the princess created a stir in London. She was now of great interest to Will, if he were to meet her kindred in Virginia. Following that thought, Roger voiced another concern. 'Forgive me for saying so, brothers, but I thought the settlement in Virginia was for Catholics also!'

'We could have a separate colony,' William White suggested.

The discussion went on late into the night. Later, as Will walked home with William Brewster, Brewster said, 'So what do you think about going to America, Will?'

Will was excited about it, seeing the possibilities opening up for them. He said, 'I like the idea of a community built on faith in God, on the truth, people who love one another, the way we do in the congregation. I like the thought of farming again, and being able to provide for our families out of the good land that God provides and the work of our own hands.'

'So—has Holland been a disappointment, think you?'

Will hesitated, but Brewster peered at him intently in the moonlight. 'Yes. I had hoped for more from Holland. I do not like living in a city very much. I do not like weaving. I do not like the poverty that we have been brought to, and most of all I do not like the pestilences that have claimed so many lives.'

He paused as he thought about it. So many of them had lost children, and others had lost wives as well. And he thought of his own little family—of Dorothy who now seemed so fragile, and little Jonathan. Fear stalked them all constantly, for no-one was immune.

William Brewster said, 'It has been difficult here. But enough of that, Will. I want to ask your opinion.'

'Opinion?' Will repeated, intrigued.

Brewster linked arms with him and they took the route by the canal. 'I am going into partnership with Tom Brewer.'

Thomas Brewer, the stranger Will had conversed with at the University debate, had put in an appearance at one of the meetings, but his beliefs tended towards Calvinism rather than Separatism. Still they were close enough not to be enemies.

'I heard Master Brewer fled from Kent because of his beliefs?'

'Indeed. More to the point, he is rich—a nobleman actually.'

'So what do you mean by partnership?'

'Brewer has put up the money for a printing press.'

Will turned this over in his mind. 'Why a printing press?'

'There is a need for a printer unafraid of producing certain religious works. In fact we have already started, and we are working on something called, "*A Plain and Familiar Exposition of the Ten Commandments, with a Methodical Short Catechism.*" It is written in Dutch.'

'It sounds impressive. You will need a man who knows about printing.'

'Master Brewer knows of two such men in London—a John Reynolds, who is sympathetic, but not of our persuasion, and a younger man Edward Winslow, who is a Separatist and who has spoken of joining us in Leyden.'

'Mmm. It will be costly.'

Brewster nodded. 'Jehovah will provide. Tom Brewer has already put up a large sum.'

'But you are short?'

'A little.'

They discussed ways of financing the venture. 'Of course finance is difficult to come by here,' Brewster said. 'It is hard enough making a living. No wonder the Southworths moved to England. Their going seemed to be a surprise to you, Will.'

Will looked at him sharply. 'I think Edward is not going to improve his lot, if that is what you mean.'

'No, that is not what I mean.'

'Then I do not understand you, sir.'

Brewster stopped walking, took a breath and stared at the cobblestones beneath his feet. '"*Whosoever looketh on a woman to lust after her hath committed adultery with her already in his heart.*"' He spoke softly, and Will felt his heart lurch and then thud on.

'What are you saying sir?' he demanded dangerously quiet.

Brewster took another deep breath before looking straight at Will. 'I think you know what I am saying.'

Will swallowed convulsively. 'There is nothing between Mistress Southworth and myself.'

'No? I have watched you, Will. You used to sit and watch her during the meetings, you know. You found the merest excuse to talk to her.'

'You are mistaken, sir,' Will said stiffly, by no means pleased to have pointed out to him what he had been denying to himself.

'You think so? I know all is not well between you and Dorothy. I observe you see.' He tapped his face beside his eye. 'I notice things that others do not notice. And do not forget that I know you well.' He put up a hand to stop Will protesting, and said instead, 'I cannot judge what is in your heart. Only God can do that. But I warn you, Will, that many men have trodden that road, and it has led to their destruction.'

'I will bear it in mind,' Will said coldly. He bowed, formally polite to this man who had stood in place of his father for so long, and left him, striding away into the night.

Will was furious. How dared William Brewster speak to him in such a manner! He, William Bradford, an elder, universally acknowledged to be a spiritual man! To imply that he and Alice—he stopped there, for honesty forced him to admit that he did have an affection for Alice that went beyond her being his friend's wife, beyond just that of a sister in the congregation. He enjoyed Alice's company more than that of any other person, enjoyed her conversation, her wit, her softness. But to imply that there was more to it than that—well it was preposterous. Wasn't it?

Hell's teeth! he swore uncharacteristically to himself. Why could not a man be friendly with a woman without everyone assuming they were lovers? But he knew the answer to that. They lived in a time of lax morals on the one hand, and extreme strictness on the other. It simply wasn't done to pay too much attention to a woman to whom one was neither husband nor brother, nor father. Why the women even sat separately at the meetings because of the strict moral code. And he had come close to breaking that code.

He sighed. Brewster was right. He had to acknowledge that he, William Bradford, was not immune to the lures of the flesh. He was as imperfect as the next man. Worse, probably, because he should know better. By the time he got home he had had a long conversation with his God, and decided that it was a good thing that the Southworths were in London. If only it were a matter of 'out of sight, out of mind.'

THIRTEEN
More Plans

1617

The congregation murmured restlessly. Expectation hung in the air. Everyone knew something was in the wind but only the elders, deacons and privileged men knew exactly what. Even their wives had not been told.

When William Brewster took the platform, everyone fell silent, waiting. However, nothing in Brewster's face, or demeanour, gave anything away. They had to wait.

As usual, they began with a sung psalm. Will looked across the aisle at Dorothy where she stood with the child beside her, and he was struck by how much Jonathan resembled her, with enormous blue eyes, and curls so fair that they were almost white. He thought, too, how much he loved this child, the only one they were ever likely to have.

Little Jonathan saw Will watching him, and his face split into a huge grin until Dorothy tapped him on the leg, and he obediently turned around again. Dorothy glanced at Will, but there was no smile. Will was growing accustomed to the way she treated him, so cold, so bad-tempered, so distant, she was a pretty, but empty, woman, and it hurt.

Brewster offered the prayer, which, as custom dictated, went on for twenty minutes, and was punctuated by the occasional squawks of little ones who found standing still for such a long time more than they could cope with. Obliquely, he asked for God's guidance in their decisions, his working in their behalf. Will wondered what the congregation made of it, for the remarks could be general, or they could be specific, depending on what you knew.

The congregation sat down on the long wooden benches, Brewster returned to his place and John Robinson came to the platform. He took a minute to look at the brethren, this flock of God for which he was responsible. The congregation had grown in the years they had been in Leyden. How would they take the proposal? How would they view it?

Robinson began by speaking of the Israelites in 'affliction in the land of Egypt'. He spoke of the faith of Moses, but set more emphasis on the fact that their God saw their affliction and brought them up out of the land of Egypt, and into the promised land. This was all familiar stuff. Then John Robinson went on to make an application as to the congregation in Leyden. 'As you know, brethren, we, the Lord's modern day people, the elect, have been sorely afflicted here in Leyden. True, we have freedom of religion, but we have suffered at the Devil's hands as well. We suffer want and privation, many of the brethren do not have the means to feed and clothe and house their families comfortably, while those around us who do not serve God fare better than we do.' He went on to repeat much of what he had said at the elders' meeting. Will looked around him as whispers floated around the congregation, a look of concentration on some faces, and surprise and shock on others. Robinson finished with, 'In short, brothers, we are like the children of Israel, enslaved to unrighteous Egypt.'

There was a murmur, and Will couldn't tell whether it was approving or disapproving. John Robinson glanced at William Brewster for support. Brewster nodded his encouragement.

'So, we have looked to God to see what his will is on the matter, and there is good reason for us to move on. Already, we have been through much. We have been harried and persecuted in England, and we have come here. We have removed from Amsterdam, and settled in Leyden. But the Lord's elect suffer still at the hands of the great Adversary, Satan the Devil. It would be good for us to settle in a land where there is religious freedom, where we can make our own way in the world, plant our fields, tend our herds and flocks, harvest our own wheat. A place where we can rule ourselves in a manner that is fitting with the Lord. In short, brethren, we propose to remove to the New World. America.'

He paused, to see their reaction. A buzz of murmuring grew louder as the members of the congregation looked at each other and absorbed this new information.

Will looked across at Dorothy to see how she took it. Deliberately not looking at him, she stared hard at John Robinson, her face set. Will felt his heart sink. She did not like the idea, he could tell. Yet he had his heart set on it, and he vowed silently himself, and to his God, that if she should refuse to go, he would go alone, and send for her and Jonathan later.

John Jenney came to his feet. 'America is on the other side of the world, brother. It would take an immense journey.'

'Not quite,' Robinson answered briskly. 'Only across the Atlantic. We are thinking of various possibilities. Guiana was suggested. Also Virginia. But you are right, it is a long journey.'

He outlined the pros and cons of each place. Will glanced again at Dorothy, but she steadfastly ignored him.

John Robinson went on, 'We have discussed the difficulties we suffer here in Holland, and they are many and great. In America, we would have our own rule. We would be answerable to no-one but ourselves and God. We know it is an uninhabited place as far as civilisation is concerned, and we can therefore have complete freedom of worship. Imagine, a new land, fit for the taking, peopled only by those who worship God and keep his laws, people who truly love one another. In short, one congregation, everyone in unity. And the land, fertile land, waiting for our ploughs, our harrows, our seeds. To farm once more, to provide for our children, this is our God-given right. In time, as our children grow, and as the land gives its yield, we will see peace and prosperity for our families. Brethren, we are on the verge of the promised land, and all we have to do is cross the wider Jordan, the Atlantic. As Jehovah said to Joshua before he crossed into the promised land, *"Be strong and of a good courage; fear not nor be discouraged, for I the Lord thy God will be with thee whithersoever thou goest."* Imagine a land, brethren, ripe for the taking, fertile land, good land, a land blessed by God. This land can be ours, belong to us. Where we can farm and care for our families in peace. This can be ours.' He spoke with passion, and they were swayed, Will could see.

John Carver stood up, this bluff no-nonsense man, and he too addressed the congregation, adding his weight, if not substance to what Robinson had already said, adding after a lengthy speech, 'So, then, let us grab what is rightfully ours, grab it with both hands,' he clenched his fists in front of him expressively, 'and build ourselves a congregation in the wilderness.'

The protests came fast and furious. It was a great idea, but subject to too many dangers. The length of the journey—the women and others who were old and the very young would never be able to endure such a journey; the perils at sea; the expense; the wildness of the land; difficulties that might finish off those that survived the journey—famine and nakedness and want in all things; the change of air, diet and the drinking of water which everyone knew was injurious to health, so that there would be sicknesses and grievous diseases; the solitude when they landed—there would be no welcoming inns for them; a country full of savages and wild beasts, the savages known for their cruelty and treachery, the torture of their captives. Cannibals even.

On this last point, Henry Jepson added some detail. 'They are known to be furious in rage and merciless with their captives. Not only do they kill, but they do so in the most bloody manner—flaying men alive with the sharpened edges of sea-shells, cutting off the members and joints of others bit by bit and broiling them on the coals, eating the flesh in the sight of their victims while they are still live—'

John Robinson protested. 'How do you know these things?' he demanded.

'Everybody knows them! Is it not enough to make the bowels of men squirm within them to make the weak tremble?'

'Great designs produce great difficulties,' John Robinson said, but Will could see he was ruffled, dismayed by their lack of faith. 'And the Lord will provide the means and the courage to overcome them.'

John Jenny stood up again. 'And how are we to afford it?' he demanded. 'We expended all our estates in getting to Holland in the first place, and this venture will require greater sums of money to accomplish than all our existing estates will amount to.'

William Brewster stood up. 'There are ways of funding something of this nature. Financial backers.'

'Who will want return for their money,' Jenney added.

Will was beginning to get annoyed. The meeting was degenerating into a bear-pit. Where was their faith, where their courage?

The protests continued. There had been other attempts to colonise America which had met with calamities and miseries. It had been difficult enough to move to Holland, a civilised country, rich and welcoming. America was nothing like as accommodating.

John Robinson calmed them all down again, for he had that serenity which took the heat out of rising disagreements. 'All of what you say is true, brothers. No-one said the project would be without its difficulties. But if we have faith in the Lord, he will help us to overcome them. The hazards are great. We will be going into the unknown. When men go into the unknown there are bound to be risks, and fears that are often unfounded. Probably many of our fears might never happen. And others, by being careful, we might prevent. And everything with the help of God by courage and patience will be borne or overcome.

'True, we must not make such an attempt rashly or without good reason, not out of curiosity as others have done, or for hope of gain. But we are not ordinary men. Our ends are for an entirely different reason, our calling lawful and urgent, and therefore, might we not expect God's blessing on the attempt? God is on the side of the elect.'

'And Satan their enemy!' someone shouted out.

Will stood up and turned to address them all. 'We live here as men in exile and in poverty. Do you fear Indians who are really only men, and probably are not cannibals, more than you fear the Spaniards with their Inquisition? The truce between Spain and Holland ends in two years. And what do you think will happen here then? Do you think you will live in peace? If the Spaniards invade, we will all be at their mercy, and we can expect none from them for such as we are. And of sicknesses, do you think we will have fewer sicknesses here than there? When we have lost untold numbers to sickness in the last few years. Which family has not lost someone, child, or husband, or wife? How can it be worse in America than it is here?'

John Robinson took the reins again. 'We are the Lord's saints, the elect. We have ever been persecuted, but are we prepared to give in to Satan? I say *No*, brothers. We have stood firm in the face of death and come off victorious. Do you think God will abandon us now? Just think what a triumph for God if we succeed in the wilderness, providing a stepping-stone for others to follow! We can do it, brothers. We will do it.' He paused and glared at them all. 'Yet not all of us can go. Not all of us will want to go. Those that do put their faith in the Lord will have the Lord's blessing. I leave it with you, brothers.'

So that was it, then, Will thought. Some will go. Not all of them. Perhaps some never would. But some would. And he was determined to be one of them.

Afterwards, John Robinson said to him, 'I know you wish to go, Will.'

'I do,' Will admitted. 'I want the freedom that America can bring. I want to be able to farm land again, to provide for my family properly, not working at women's work the way I do now.'

'It is a huge risk.'

'I know. But I have faith that Jehovah will look after his people. He will bring this to fruition, whatever the Devil tries to do.'

'It is a dream, Will,' John Robinson admitted. 'The dream of freedom to worship God, of a land free from the tyrannies of the world we have to live in. True, it is a challenge, but it is also a great opportunity.'

'You intend to go, sir?'

'Aye. There is nothing I want more, than to see the Lord's church prosper.'

'It is a big wide and wonderful land,' Will said, his eyes shining at the vision his words created. 'Enough for all who want to go.'

Will walked home alone long after Dorothy had taken Jonathan home to put him to bed. He stood leaning on the bridge over the *Rapenburg* canal, as he often did, and stood looking down into the dark waters. *America!* His stomach lurched with excitement at the thought. America, the land of promise, the wilderness waiting for them to tame it, the way Adam and Eve were to tame the land outside Eden. How he longed to go. It was what he had wanted, what he longed for. To give his son an inheritance after him. *Heavenly Father,* he prayed, *please let it come to be.*

Still, it wouldn't do to spend the night gazing at the water. He turned towards the house, the little house that he had bought for Dorothy, the house she viewed with disdain. He stopped his thoughts there. It wouldn't do to dwell on negative things. Already at the thought of Dorothy his spirits sank. And he wanted nothing to spoil the excitement of the occasion. Even so, he braced himself to go into the house.

Dorothy was waiting for him, sitting on the settle in front of the fire which she had stirred up into a blaze. The room was hot, for the weather was not cold, and Will felt his forehead break out into a sweat. Why did she waste fuel in this way? She knew how tight money was.

She stood up as he came in and turned to face him, a woman in black, with her prim white cap and starched plain collar and cuffs. Her face was dour, her hands clasped forbiddingly at her waist.

'Where have you been?'

He did not want to tell her how he had lingered on the bridge over the canal, so he said with perfect truth, 'You know where I have been Dorothy. You yourself knew I was speaking with John Robinson.'

'All this time?'

'There is much to discuss.'

'You would rather be anywhere than home here with me!'

It was the truth, he thought with a shock, but he replied, 'Don't be ridiculous.'

She walked to the other end of the table, without apparent reason, then she said: 'You intend to go to America, don't you?'

He took a step towards her. 'Oh, Dorothy, it would be such an opportunity for us! Just think—'

'I heard all your arguments at the meeting,' she said shortly.

He stopped, wounded. 'I think it would be a good thing for us.'

'For you, you mean. You have no family.'

He didn't understand her. 'I have you and Jonathan.'

'But you do not have parents. I have my parents who are here in Holland.'

'I dare say they may come as well, if they wish.'

'You know very well they will not wish. My parents are getting older you know. And there is my sister Jacqueline to think of.'

'It is understandable that you do not wish to leave them.'

'And so?'

'If you do not wish to go, I will not force you. Perhaps it would be better if I went alone, and built a house for you and Jonathan. Then you can follow later.'

'And if I do not wish to follow later?'

He stared at her, and said very quietly, 'You are my wife.' The implication was clear. As his wife she must go. Even so, he knew, and she knew, he would not force her.

She put her head up. 'I see. I have no choice in the matter.' She took a deep breath. 'It seems to me, William Bradford, that you would be pleased to be rid of me. Perhaps you do not wish to be married to me. Certainly you find no pleasure in my company, nor I in yours.'

It was like a slap in the face. He reeled from the shock of it. Was this the Dorothy he had courted so ardently, had waited so long for, had prepared a house for? Was this the sweet angelic child he had fallen in love with?

'What do you say, wife?' he demanded. 'Do you wish to separate from me?'

Her eyes glittered with unshed tears, and he was at once contrite. 'Dorothy—.' He took a step towards her.

'Do not touch me!' she spat at him like a cornered cat. 'I know what you want, and I tell you, you won't get it from me!'

He ignored the jibe. 'Dorothy, you are my wife,' he said gently, 'I love you.' But even as he said it, he realised that it was no longer really true. She had killed the love he had once had, that youthful love, that perfect love, with her waspish nastiness, her biting sarcasm, her tongue which slashed like a sword. She denied him the love he had so looked forward to, the needs of a man. She had shown no pleasure in it when, for the sake of a child, she had given in to him. And after that, terrified that she might again have a child, she had refused him. She had shown no consideration for his needs. Gradually, bit by bit, it had eaten away at his love for her, had killed it, as it withered from the root upwards until it became a dry desiccated thing, ready to be blown away on the wind. What he felt now was a deep longing for what it had once been, the need to be loved, the need to love. He wanted warmth and companionship, the relationship he saw between John Robinson and his Bridget, between William Brewster and his beloved Mary. But he knew that with Dorothy it was finished. His life stretched ahead of him barren, empty, a desert. Yes, he would be happier without her in some ways. Yet he grieved over it.

'If you wish to stay behind, Dorothy, I will understand,' he said simply.

'But you will go.'

He looked at her. 'Yes, I will go. I have to look after them.'

'You do not have to look after them. Brothers Robinson, Brewster and Carver will do that! If you go, it will be because you want to go.'

'Yes, I want to go. I want to be able to provide for you and Jonathan. I want to be free of this toil, this women's work of weaving. I want Jonathan to grow up English, not Dutch, and to stay in the truth. I want to give him land to work, good land, productive land, for him and for his sons after him. I want us all to be there, all together.'

'My son is not going on a sea journey across the Atlantic!' she stated.

'What do you mean?'

'I will not allow it.'

'*You* will not allow it? You speak out of turn, madam. *I* am his father.'

'And I his mother. *I* gave birth to him. *I* bore the agony of it. *I* produced him, not you! And I will not put him in such danger. He stays here.'

'We shall see.'

'We shall not see. He stays here!'

'So I go alone?' It was a rhetorical question, for he had every intention of taking Jonathan, regardless of whether Dorothy went.

There was a long silence, broken by the crackle of the fire, and the sound of someone walking past the door in the street. *It is hopeless,* Will thought. *She intends to take my son away from me now. What will she do— go back to her parents? Stay with her sister? Is this it? Am I to lose them both?*

'Yes,' she said quietly, 'you go alone.' And she turned away from him and opened the door to the stairs, pausing to say, 'But that is your choice.' And she began to climb the stairs, closing the door behind her.

Will stood just as he was in the middle of the room, still wearing his coat and hat, too stunned to move. He felt so helpless. His wife and his child were going to leave him. It wasn't in him to force her to stay. In any case, he could not force her. Her father was only twenty-five miles away in Amsterdam. Forcing himself to move, he removed his hat, took off his coat, and put them on the pegs by the door. She did not love him. She had said so. But then it had been obvious for some time. What had happened to that dear sweet little Dorothy, the pretty little girl, with the pretty little lisp, and the dainty manners? A great sadness welled up from what seemed like a solid ball in the pit of his stomach, washing over him in a great wave of despair. The trouble was, she was right. They did not love each other. Where there had been love, there was now emptiness. Nothing.

Yet he still felt something. He still loved her, in a way. He still wanted her. But not like this. He wanted the old Dorothy. But she wasn't the old Dorothy. He couldn't make sense of it.

He stood by the pegs where he had hung his cloak and found he still held the coat, leaning on it, oblivious to it. A terrible noise surprised him, and he realised that it came from himself, and he broke down and wept.

The meetings were dominated by the proposed move, both in discussion and in prayer. Those who wanted to go came forward and put their names down on a list. Since that was more than half the congregation, it was clear they would not all be able to go on one ship. But the more pressing question was where to go.

They discussed Guiana at length, the land Sir Walter Raleigh had spoken about so glowingly. However, in the end it was decided to reject it. Guiana was too hot. Hot climates bred diseases. They were not used to such weather. Some would find it intolerable. Besides, the Spaniards were too close to Guiana, having already founded colonies in the Caribbean and also it was rumoured that they had interest in the salt pans of Venezuela at present in the possession of the Dutch.

Virginia was a better option. But the colony in Virginia had been settled by Catholics also, fleeing from religious persecution in England. There was strong antipathy between Catholics and anyone who was remotely connected to Protestantism, even if the Separatists had nothing to do with the Church of England. If anything, the Catholics hated the Separatists more than they did the Anglicans, and the feeling was mutual.

However, the majority of those who wished to go were in favour of Virginia. There were already people there, and they could, they said, live as a distinct and separate colony although under the general government of Virginia, and ask the King to grant them freedom of religion.

'We might do that,' William Brewster suggested, 'And with some success. In the Virginia company is one Sir Edwin Sandys, son of Edwin Sandys, the lord of the manor at Scrooby where I had the honour of residing for some years, the lease of which is now owned by his son Samuel, Sir Edwin's brother. Sir Edwin is known to me personally, and is known for his Puritan leanings, and therefore favourable to our cause. Sir Edwin himself is a leading promoter of the Virginia Company, interested in seeing the country settled.'

'I don't like the word 'Puritan', John Robinson growled.

William Brewster grinned, and ran his fingers over his moustache. 'Well he ain't a Separatist,' he said, his eyes flashing mischievously, 'and he ain't a Puritan. Merely sympathetic.'

John Robinson nodded. He understood. Sir Edwin was not a man to draw unwanted attention to himself religiously, but he was one who might help them.

Will asked, 'What do the Virginia Company do?'

'They grant tracts of land known as *Hundreds* or *Particular Plantations* in Virginia,' William Brewster answered. 'Up to eighty thousand acres to groups who agree to cultivate them and populate them, and they have the rights of self-government, jurisdiction, fishing, and permission to trade with the natives.'

'So that is settled, then,' Robinson said. 'We will send someone to speak to Sir Edwin Sandys.'

'Who?'

'I'll go,' Will said.

Brewster met his eyes and shook his head slightly, then put forward, 'What about Brother Carver? Or Brother Cushman?'

So it was decided. Will was disappointed. 'You did not wish me to go,' he said later to Brewster as they walked home.

Brewster met his eyes. 'Dorothy needs you.' It was true. Both Carver and Cushman had enough money behind them to provide for their wives in their absence. Dorothy, who had not, after all, deserted him, had no-one to provide for her if he did not continue doggedly at his loom. If she were left, she might return to her father, and Will had no intention of allowing that. If he could help it.

He did say, however, 'With Sister Carver's child due soon, I would have thought she needs her husband as much as Dorothy needs me.'

'She has her sisters to help her,' Brewster pointed out. He could have added that the Carvers were happily matched, unlike Will and Dorothy.

Swallowing his disappointment, Will turned the conversation. 'How goes it with the printing press?'

'Oh, well enough,' Brewster replied guardedly. 'And the less you or anyone else knows about it, the better.'

Will smiled. 'Very well. But we have three new members of the congregation very much in evidence.'

John Reynolds the printer had arrived from London, and he married Prudence Grindon in August. In a congregation of over four hundred members, Will had made only the briefest acquaintance with him, but he was suitably impressed, for Reynolds had arrived as a non-believer, and had come into the congregation.

The other printer, Edward Winslow, however, was very much in evidence, a man that Will had taken to. Tall, good looking and blond with blue eyes, he was only twenty-two, and had taken a stand for the Separatist faith. Like Will he picked up the Dutch language with no difficulty, and in no time was speaking it like a native.

The printers, Brewster and Thomas Brewer, risked a great deal to print the tracts, books and news sheets which their press produced. In England there were those who would dearly love to eradicate them if they could have laid hands on them.

'Anyway,' William Brewster finished off their conversation, 'Carver and Cushman will no doubt stay with the Southworths in London, and I am sure that is a situation you would do well to avoid.'

Will flushed, but he met Brewster's eyes straightly. 'You are mistaken, sir. There is no reason why I should not stay with the Southworths if I should have been sent on the Lord's work,' and he turned and marched towards his home.

Brewster shook his head disbelievingly, and then turned towards his own home.

A short time later, the Carvers buried their child.

FOURTEEN
The Virginia Company

London, 1618

Alice Southworth had never liked London. It was a cold, wet, grey, smelly, filthy hole of a place, unlike the neatness of Leyden. Edward found them a tenement in Heneage House. Originally the town palace of the Abbot of Bury St. Edmunds in the Middle Ages, Heneage House was part of the sprawling priory of the Holy Trinity, the monastic buildings of which surrounded a large court. The dissolution of the monasteries by Henry VIII saw the eastern half of the property in the hands of the Duke of Norfolk which became known as the Duke's Place. The western end had been given to Sir Thomas Heneage, the two properties separated by Heneage Lane. However London teemed with people, the overcrowding not conducive to the grandeur the Duke of Norfolk and the Heneage family felt they deserved, so they gave up the contest and turned their splendid properties into tenements.

It was a particularly attractive area for immigrants, especially those of faiths differing from the Church of England, for there was no parish church in the area and so the law could not be enforced which required everyone to attend their parish church on Sundays. A Dutch church had been established in the Aldgate Ward, encouraging hundreds of Dutch craftsmen into the area of the same religious persuasion as the Dutch in Leyden. There were many French Huguenots too, and the English Separatists, also, found Heneage House a convenient home. With no parish church, they were free to attend their own meetings.

Even so the tenements had been neglected. The lime plaster peeled off the laths, exposing the horsehair beneath where all manner of insects resided. The rooms were tall and roomy, reflecting the grandeur of a former age, and there were vestiges of ornate plaster work on the ceilings in some rooms. The high ceilings made them more difficult to heat, and to Alice the place never seemed warm. However, there was more room here than there had been in the tenement built in John Robinson's garden in Leyden.

Still, Alice hated the place. She missed her sisters and the brethren back in Leyden, and although there were other Separatists in London, new friends, she felt she did not completely fit in. Worse, the cough that Edward had developed back in Leyden grew more severe in the filthy air, and he worked only sometimes. In fact he began to look ill, his skin pale and clammy, his eyes sunken.

Alice also missed Will. Not that she had seen much of him in

Leyden, but an old familiar longing gnawed at her, robbing her of peace and happiness. There was a void in her life where he had once been. She tried to ignore it, to concentrate on her family, on her faith, on her husband, with limited success.

Oh, how she hated London!

Edward interrupted her thoughts. 'We have Master Cushman and Master Carver coming to stay with us,' he announced, reading from a letter.

Alice looked at him aghast. 'Where will we put them?'

'In with the boys of course. There is room. We will make room.'

'Perhaps they would rather find rooms.'

'Perhaps they will in time. But for now they are coming to stay.'

Alice looked around at her crumbling home. What would they think of them, living in a hovel like this?

'Why are they coming?' she asked.

'On the Lord's business. Some errand of John Robinson's.'

'That will be to do with the proposed move to America,' Alice suggested. Julianna and her mother, and her unmarried sisters Priscilla, and Mary the youngest had all written to her separately, telling her about the meetings that spoke of America. Their letters were full of excitement at the proposed move.

Alice liked the idea of moving to America. It certainly could not be worse than the poverty she endured here in London. Nor could it be worse than the deprivations in Holland. She liked the idea of a free country, of wide open spaces, of fields and crops and a house of her own. But she looked at Edward and she knew that they would not be among those going.

Would Will be going? She knew he would. It would be just like him to want to go to a place like that. However, she also knew that Dorothy would not. Furthermore, she herself did not like the idea of him being in America. It was another world, so far away. It had been a wrench to move away from Leyden to London, but she had grown used to thinking of herself here, and him being there. Now she would have to get used to him being on the other side of the world. It was such a long way, and she missed him so much already. If he were in America, their paths would never ever cross again.

'No doubt if John Carver and Robert Cushman stay here,' Edward cut in on her thoughts again, 'they will contribute for their keep.'

'No doubt.'

'That will help the finances.'

She did not answer, for making money out of the brethren was immoral. 'We need to find somewhere for them to sleep.' She looked around her. 'I must clean and perhaps, Edward, you could whitewash the walls for us.' She did not add that they would need to be repaired first, for she thought this too obvious to mention.

Edward liked the idea, and he came home with a bucket of whitewash that evening, and set to spreading it liberally over the walls and ceilings. However, he did not repair the plaster, but merely spread the whitewash over the hairs sticking out of the laths.

Alice watched him and shook her head in dismay.

Two days later John Carver and Robert Cushman arrived in London.

Sir Edwin Sandys peered over his desk at the two men sitting anxiously on the plush upholstered chairs, before resuming his perusal of the letter they had brought. He leaned back in his chair as he read, one leg hooked negligently over the arm, his eyes scanning the paper.

John Carver exchanged glances with Robert Cushman, keenly aware of the responsibility they had to bring this thing off, impatient to hear what Sir Edwin had to say. He thought of the brothers in Leyden, waiting to hear if they had been successful, hoping they would be bearers of good news by the end of the week.

John looked around him at the opulent luxury of the Virginia Company. Offices, of course, but well appointed offices, with an ornate plaster ceiling that must have cost a fortune. The table behind which Sir Edwin took his time over John Robinson's letter, was made of oak, highly polished, with beautifully carved legs. A huge fireplace housed a few burning logs which hardly dispelled the raw chill of early winter; the oak panels were highly decorated. John was not a rich man, not like Robert Cushman who was a wool merchant and who owned two or three houses in Leyden. No, he came from humbler origins, but he appreciated quality craftsmanship when he saw it.

Sir Edwin set the papers aside and pursed his lips thoughtfully as he studied his visitors. 'And how is Master Brewster?' he inquired.

'He is well,' John said, brushing his moustache a little nervously. 'And asks to be remembered to your lordship.' What else could he say? That Brewster had set up a clandestine printing press and was publishing books and tracts that others might consider to be seditious? In fact if Sandys got wind of Brewster's clandestine operations, it would be the end of their quest.

Sir Edwin took a deep decisive breath and unhooked his leg from the chair's arm, and leaned forward, clasping his hands in front of him on the table. He had small delicate hands, John thought, giving his own huge capable paws a quick comparative glance. White and soft with carefully manicured nails. Hands that had never done a day's manual work in their entire lives. Like the man. A nobleman, of sizeable inheritance, he had fine delicate features, almost like a woman's save for the tuft of ginger hair on the end of his pointed chin. His short auburn hair was shiny like it had been washed with soft-soap that morning. He wore fine clothes too, not the homespun drab garments of the poorer man. But a dyed doublet, the colour of the sky on a cloudless day, and a snowy white lace ruff collar. His bearing, his carefully clipped speech, his easy manners proclaimed him what he was—a member of the ruling class.

'So you want to go to Virginia, do you?'

Robert Cushman bowed. 'We do, sir.'

'Well, the Virginia Company is eager for colonists. The Company will be pleased to grant you land in Virginia, up to eighty thousand acres.'

John Carver blinked. Was that it? Just like that? No arguments, no persuasion?

'And government, sir?' Robert Cushman asked.

Sir Edwin waved a delicate hand in the air. 'Of course you would govern yourselves. You cannot expect London to be concerned in your affairs three thousand miles away. However, you will remain subject to the King.'

'Naturally.' Cushman frowned. He had a quicker brain than Carver who felt sluggish and stupid in his presence. Cushman may not have been Sir Edwin's equal, but he felt he was not far off. 'Did not master Brewster and Master Robinson in their letter explain that to you?'

Frowning, Sir Edwin picked up the letter again. Then his face cleared. 'Ah yes! *The King's Majesty we acknowledge for Supreme Governor in his Dominion in all causes and over all persons, and that none may decline or appeal from his authority or judgement in any cause whatsoever, but that in all things obedience is due unto him—*" etcetera. Yes indeed. However—'

He paused and Cushman and Carver waited with growing unease as Sir Edwin frowned at the paper. He raised a sceptical eyebrow which they met with bland stares. 'Gentlemen, is this a true representation of your beliefs? I think not! Article one here: "*To the confession of faith published in the name of the Church of England and to every Article thereof we do, with the Reformed Churches where we live, and also elsewhere, assent wholly.*" Really?'

For once, Robert Cushman was lost for words. John felt his spirits plummet. Clearly they did not agree with the confession of faith of the Anglican Church. That was why they were Separatists in the first place. Still, he felt he could wriggle around this one. 'Do you think, my lord, that we do not hold to the Articles of Religion? We believe in one God, in the Son of God, the Word, and in the Holy Spirit. We believe in the sufficiency of the Holy Scriptures for Salvation. Do I need to go on?'

'And the Trinity?'

John Carver and Robert Cushman were effectively silenced. Denial of the doctrine of the Trinity—the belief that God and Jesus and the holy spirit were all God, and yet there were not three gods but one, the so called three-in-one doctrine—was a capital offence. Of course, once they were in America they could do as they pleased. But they knew that the Articles John Robinson had supplied in the letter were ambiguous to say the least. Sir Edwin knew it too.

Sir Edwin looked at them and smiled. 'You are not under Inquisition here gentlemen. But it may be that there ought to be a larger clarification than Master Robinson has set down here. You see, although as far as the Virginia Company is concerned you may have the patents and welcome, you still need the permission of the King. However,' he added thoughtfully, prodding the papers on the table, 'it may be that the King will not question these Articles. Leave it with me, and I will see what I can do for you.'

John and Robert Cushman left Sir Edwin not unhopefully, and made their way through the tangled streets of London to Heneage House and the Southworths' home.

'Did you see Sir Edwin?' Edward asked before they had even removed their cloaks.

Cushman sat down on the stool before the blazing fire, and spread his hands out to warm them. 'We did.'

Alice said, 'I think Brother Cushman is pleased.'

Edward flashed her a look which she interpreted immediately. This was not women's business, and he did not like her to speak out of turn. He thought she did not know her place, and was always telling her so. It was a dispute which irritated them both constantly. It made Alice rebellious and resentful, and inclined to do it all the more. It took real effort to curb her unruly tongue, and only the presence of Cushman and Carver prevented her from making a suitable retort which would be neither loving, nor Christian, and which would certainly be reported back to Leyden. Sister Southworth, they would say, is not in subjection to her husband. And what a crime that would be!

Still she would not bow out entirely. 'Is it so, Brother Cushman?' Alice asked innocently. 'Have you found favour with the Company?'

'They told us we may have a grant of land,' John Carver said, sitting down and pulling his boots off, exposing his smelly stockings to the heat of the fire. 'Eighty thousand acres.'

'Why that is wonderful!'

Edward said, 'But?'

John Carver admitted, 'But we need permission from the King.'

Everyone knew the King was not favourably disposed towards the Separatists. Alice asked, 'Is that likely to be forthcoming?'

Again that look from Edward.

Robert Cushman shrugged.

'What do you think?' Cushman retorted, his quick anger rising to the surface.

Carver said more calmly, 'Sir Edwin wants a more detailed description of the Articles of our faith. So we must go back to Brother Robinson. Still, all things are in the hands of God.'

'If it is God's will, it will happen,' Alice said with pure simple faith.

Edward said pointedly, 'Is dinner ready yet?'

Alice collected the children from another room where they were playing and sat the little one on the floor. The men sat around the table on the benches.

She had cooked everything in one pot on the fire—pieces of bacon, carrots and onions and a pudding tied up in a cloth. Now she ladled the stew into wooden bowls and the men and her boys sat down at the table to eat.

Edward asked a blessing on the food. It was a plain but wholesome meal, hot and welcome on a cold day.

Alice began to ask after the brothers in Leyden. Edward did not like them talking at mealtimes, but Alice was desperate to hear news. Of her sister Julianna, and her parents, and Sam Fuller, who had once been married for such a brief while to her poor dead sister Agnes.

'Sam is fine,' John Carver said beaming. 'He has married Bridget Lee you know. Sam Lee's sister.'

'Yes, I did know. She is a little young for him, I thought.'

'About the same age as his wife Agnes was. Oh—begging your pardon, Mistress.'

Alice swallowed. It was painful to remember how Agnes had bled to death and no-one able to help her, no-one able to save her.

She said casually, 'And Brother Bradford? How is he?'

Edward cast her another sharp, disapproving look.

John Carver chewed noisily on a piece of bacon and swallowed, then boomed, 'Goes on as usual.'

'He's making a fine elder,' Brother Cushman said. 'Has a way of managing folk, and of making things orderly.'

'And his wife?'

Cushman and Carver exchanged glances. So all was not well with little Dorothy Bradford then.

'She is well.' Carver said at length.

Alice allowed her thoughts to linger on him. She thought she new what the exchanged speaking glances meant, that all was not well with the Bradfords, and she was sorry for it. For she wanted with all her heart that Will should be happy. For a moment he came before her, just on the edge of her vision. In her mind she heard his laugh, and at the same time saw the sadness in his eyes. But it was fleeting, and she put the thought from her. It wouldn't do to dwell on what was not, and never would be.

Edward changed the subject. 'So what happens now then? Do you go back to Leyden?'

John Carver slurped his ale from the mug. 'Well, we must wait and see what comes of Sir Edwin's meeting with Sir Robert Naunton. He is the King's secretary, you know,' he added for Alice's benefit. She did know, but she let it pass. 'And, if all goes well there, then we will be taking good news back to Leyden.'

'You think it will be good news?' Edward asked.

John Carver wiped his mouth with the back of his hand. 'Delicious food, this, Mistress.' Then to Edward. 'Well, Sir Edwyn was hopeful. But it does depend on the King.'

'We will have to wait and see,' Brother Cushman said depressingly.

FIFTEEN
Sabine Staresmore

London 1618

Sir Edwin Sandys was no stranger to the palace of Whitehall, and in particular the offices of the King's Secretary Sir Robert Naunton. The opulence that surrounded him impressed him not a bit, and nor was he intimidated by Sir Robert, who removed his spectacles and looked up as the servant announced Sir Edwin, and beckoned him in.

Sir Edwin bowed as Sir Robert stood and inclined his head.

'You are well come, Sir Edwin.'

'I trust you are well, Sir Robert?' Sir Edwin replied raising his voice, for he was aware of Sir Robert's growing deafness. He and Sir Robert were old acquaintances.

'Fairish, sir, fairish. To what do we owe the pleasure of this visit?'

Sir Robert was a fine intelligent man, a Puritan sympathiser and a staunch Protestant. His eyes searched Sir Edwin's for clues.

'I come on Company business,' Sir Edwin said. 'A group of people have asked the Company for a patent for land in Virginia.'

Sir Robert was well aware of the need to settle land in the Americas, before the Dutch, the French or the Spanish got their hands on it. 'Come now my dear sir. Sit down. You will take a little wine? Miles—some sack for Sir Edwin.'

The servant who had opened the door to Sir Edwin bowed and went away. Sir Robert moved towards the blazing fire and sat down on one of the fine upholstered damask chairs, where Sir Edwin joined him. When he was seated and he had his host's attention again, Sir Edwin repeated his reason for coming.

'So, you wish me to petition the King?'

'How goes it with His Majesty?'

'Considers you his greatest enemy!'

'Does he, indeed?' Sir Edwin laughed, much impressed. 'Well, and I hope he is not right on that! I must be one of His Majesty's most loyal—'

Sir Robert laughed. 'Yes, I know. So who is this group that want to go to Virginia?'

'They call themselves Pilgrims.'

'I've heard of them. Separatists from Leyden. John Robinson's group.'

'You know of them?'

'Who does not?'

'They are prepared to face the wilderness and strengthen the King's dominion in America. They are stalwart and hardworking, men of faith. I have a letter here from Master Robinson and William Brewster, their elders, setting out seven articles which they hope will persuade the King. And I think it may well serve.'

He produced the paper from inside his doublet and gave it to Sir Robert, who perused it carefully while Sir Edwin received the wine from the servant and took a sip from a silver goblet.

'It may well do the trick,' Sir Robert said at length. 'Leave it with me.'

King James was amenable, and Sir Robert was not unhopeful of success. His Majesty looked at the letter but he did not bother himself with the fine details. There was always so much to read, and his eyes got tired. 'So these Puritans want to go to Virginia, do they?'

'Your Majesty did indeed suggest that we need colonists willing to brave the rigours and the hardships of living in a wilderness in order to bring the Americas under the dominion of your great Majesty.'

'For England, eh?'

Sir Robert bowed assent.

'And they want our protection, and no doubt freedom of worship, do they?'

'I believe that is the case, your Majesty.'

The King pursed his lips thoughtfully. 'By what means will they exist there?'

'I believe fishing, sire'

The King laughed. 'God save my soul! 'Tis an honest trade. It was the apostles' own calling!'

Sir Robert, feeling optimistic, bowed his head again. 'Indeed, your Majesty.'

'Well, we see no reason why not.' He paused. 'Freedom of worship eh? Just who are these people?'

'They are known as Separatists, sire.'

'Did they not quit this glorious realm to live in Holland?'

'Indeed, your Majesty remembers well.'

'Well, we think we should see what the Archbishop of Canterbury and the Bishop of London have to say about it. Let them apply to them.'

Sir Robert could do no more than bow, and retreat backwards from the King's presence. But he was not pleased. He knew there was no hope of their lordships the bishops granting anything to the Separatists. They were avowed enemies.

However, he had to obey, and so he applied to the bishops. George Abbot the Archbishop of Canterbury refused point blank. He hated

Puritans, and hated particularly the Separatists whom he disparagingly called Brownists. As a group they challenged his authority. Indeed, they did not recognise his authority in spiritual matters at all, so that he wondered why Sir Robert should think it necessary to ask his permission for these people. If it were left to themhe would be out of office, and reduced to the straightened circumstances of a country parson. As far as he was concerned they were the offspring of the Devil, the Antichrist, and he had no intention of giving them anything at all.

When Sir Edwin heard the news he was not in the least surprised. He had known, just as Sir Robert had known that the bishops were no friends of the Separatists. However, he was not easily put off. It was a setback, true, but the Virginia Company were desperate for willing, foolhardy, settlers no matter who they might be, and he thought the King was being inordinately intractable in handing the matter over to the bishops. He decided to apply again, but when Cushman and Carver learned of the application, they both said *No*.

'We cannot apply to the bishops. You must know, Sir Edwin, that they are our enemies.'

Sir Edwin put his head in his hand, and wrote to John Robinson and William Brewster, sending the letter with Cushman and Carver.

Robinson had known it would not be easy. When had anything ever been easy? Life was full of setbacks. He had been foolish to hope for anything more than they had accomplished. 'So what does Sir Edwin say?' he asked. Robert Cushman produced the letter.

With a sigh, Robinson took it, and broke the seal with the crest impressed in the red wax, and read. He looked up at them. 'Well, you made an impression,' he said, not displeased. 'He speaks well of you, wishes me well, etcetera, etcetera. He seems favourable towards our suit.'

'He is favourable,' Robert Cushman insisted. 'He thinks, though, that the seven articles in your letter are a little—ah—vague.'

'I was afraid of that.' Robinson read quickly then passed the letter to Brewster with a look which said *I told you so*. 'He wants us to send him something more definite, something to set his Majesty's mind at rest.'

Brewster read, 'The Privy Council headed by a Sir John Wolstenholme,' he pronounced it *Worsenam*, 'are deeply interested in our case. They want to know our views with regard to the nature of the ministry, the sacraments, and the oath acknowledging the King as supreme over the church.'

John Robinson sighed deeply. 'They know our views,' he said shortly. 'That is why we are in Leyden.'

'Yes, and as long as we stick to them, they will not budge,' Cushman said. 'They see us as enemies.'

'Faith! Can a man not even go abroad to worship as he pleases!' John Robinson fumed. He knew he was cornered, that if he did not compromise they would never be allowed to go to America.

Yet compromise was not a word in his vocabulary. They had fought hard to come this far, had to stand firm against the beliefs of the Church of England. Craftily, the Privy Council used this against them. They knew well their beliefs, knew well what the Separatists thought of Church structure. They wanted to bring them back into line, to break their integrity.

It was a nightmare. Without compromise they could not go. It was as simple as that. John Robinson agonised over it. He prayed about it. He became uncharacteristically short-tempered, and still he could reach no suitable conclusion. As a writer, he had written countless leaflets and booklets and many letters on Biblical doctrine and church order. William Brewster also did his own writing, as well as running his printing press with the help of Thomas Brewer. Between them it ought to be easy to write something about these matters couched in ambiguous language. Didn't it?

The end result was more compromise than either man wanted to agree to.

They stated seven Articles of Faith:

They assented to the confession of faith published in the name of the Church of England, and with the Reformed churches. (This was stretching it a bit. There were subjects, such as the Trinity, which were a matter of debate. However, it would be downright suicidal to say so.)

They acknowledged the doctrine of faith, of the salvation of conformists and reformists, and desired to keep spiritual communion with them in peace, and would practise all lawful things. (They could have added, not unlawful things, for there were things that were against God's law as they understood them.)

They acknowledged the King's Majesty as Supreme Governor in all causes, and submitted to his authority in all things, either active if the thing the King commanded was not against God's word, or passive if it was, unless pardon could be obtained.

They acknowledged the lawful right of his Majesty to appoint bishops, civil overseers or officers to oversee the parishes, and churches, congregations, dioceses etc. so that they may be governed civilly according to the laws of the land. (However, they did not agree with the hierarchy within the church and it was the main disagreement. Still, John Robinson observed, the King certainly did have the lawful right to appoint Bishops if he so chose. It was nothing to do with the Pilgrims. The same as it was with the appointment of civil officers.)

Similarly they acknowledged the authority of the bishops in the land for the King had appointed them, and '*as they proceed in his name whom we will also therein honour in all things and him in them.*' (That was stretching it a bit, too. However, since the King had the right to appoint bishops, the Pilgrims had to admit their authority.)

They believed that the Synod, Classes, Convocation, or Assembly of Ecclesiastical Officers had no power or authority at all, except that a magistrate should give to them.

Lastly, they desired to give due honour to all superiors, to preserve the unity of the spirit with all that feared God, and to have peace with all men as far as they were able, and to be counselled if they erred in that way.

It was signed by John Robinson and William Brewster.

After more thought, they wrote another letter on the fifteenth day of December 1617 adding further persuasion:

They trusted the Lord was with them, for they had served Him even in the face of many trials and their hearts were whole towards Him; they had already left England and were inured to the trials of a strange and hard land, which they had overcome; the people were industrious and frugal as any in the world; they were close-knit in a strict sacred bond and agreement of the Lord, and violaters were punished; and they looked after each other.

Lastly, they were not to be easily discouraged. For if they should fail and return to England or Holland, they would have nothing left, everything having been spent in their efforts to go to America. Nor would they again be moving on, for life was short and some of them were getting on in years.

'*These motives we have been bold to tender unto you, which you in your wisdom may also impart to any other our worshipful friends of the Council with you.*'

They added further notes:

Concerning the 'ecclesiastical ministry, etc.,' they agreed with the French Reformed Churches, according to their public confession of faith with some small differences:

1. As first, their ministers do pray with their heads covered; ours uncovered.

2. We choose none for Governing Elders but such as are able to teach; which ability they do not require.

3. Their elders and deacons are annual, or at most for two or three years; ours perpetual.

4. Our elders do administer their office in admonitions and excommunications for public scandals, publicly and before the congregation; theirs more privately and in their consistories.

5. We do administer baptism only to such infants as whereof the one parent at the least is of some church, which some of their churches do not observe; though in it our practice accords with their public confession and the judgement of the most learned amongst them.

Other differences worthy mentioning we known none in these points. Then about the oath, as in the former.

Subscribed,

John Robinson
William Brewster

Armed with these letters and statements, Robert Cushman and John Carver once more set out for London, with instructions from John Robinson to give them to a man he knew of in the Separatist congregation there, Sabine Staresmore. Sabine was acquainted with Sir John Wolstenholme of the Privy Council, and therefore in an ideal position to help the cause.

Sabine agreed to do the deed, but he was far from happy. He knew very well how much rested on this meeting. He knew also that the Privy Council had the authority of life or death over those who were unfortunate enough to make enemies of any of its members. But how could he refuse the request from John Robinson that he help them, especially as he was acquainted with Sir John Wolstenholme? Worse, he had a pregnant wife to think of, and it didn't do to put one's life in jeopardy except for a very good reason. Furthermore, he did not entirely approve of the way John Robinson handled the situation. Not that it was Sabine's place to question his elders, of course, but he had been associated with the congregation in Leyden for a year or two before moving to England, and he was well aware of their doctrines. He disapproved of the move John Robinson was making in this letter, a way of compromise in an attempt to get the permission for emigration.

As he waited anxiously for Sir John Wolstenholme of the Privy Council to read the papers sent by John Robinson, he prayed silently that he would not be called on to defend anything John Robinson said. Outwardly Sabine appeared calm, but his black eyes darted nervously around the spacious room.

It was a long letter, and it took time for Sir John to study it, but at last he looked up. 'Who shall make them?' he boomed so suddenly that Sabine's heart flew into his mouth. Faith the man was a monster! And a monster that spoke in riddles at that.

Sabine raised his heavy black brows, and enquired politely, 'I beg your pardon, Sir John, who shall make what?'

Sir John raised one bushy white eyebrow suspiciously and stroked his equally white beard. 'You do not know the contents of this letter?'

Sabine bowed. 'I am a mere messenger. I have not read the letter as you yourself well know, for it was sealed when I brought it to you.' He wished he did know the contents. Perhaps he could have answered.

Sir John's lip curled sardonically. 'Indeed.' He flicked the paper in his hand. 'The Ministers. It says here "*Touching the Ecclesiastical Ministry, namely of the Pastors for Teaching, Elders for Ruling and Deacons for distributing the Church's contribution . . .*" So who shall make them?'

Aha! Suddenly he knew what Sir John meant and he was able to clarify things. 'The power of making ministers is in the Church to be ordained by the imposition of hands by the fittest instrument they have. After all, it must either be in the church or from the Pope and the Pope is Antichrist.'

'Ho! And what the Pope holds good, as in the Trinity, that we do well to assent to!'

Sabine felt his enthusiasm for refuting false doctrine rise up suddenly, but he squashed it down again. It would not help John Robinson's cause for him to enter into a theological argument now, nor would it help his own case. To deny the Trinity was punishable by death.

Sir John saw the shock on Sabine's face and spared him. 'But we will not enter into dispute now.'

'No indeed,' Sabine agreed with relief and another bow.

Sir John paused frowning at the letter. He was a businessman, and keenly interested in promoting the interests of the Virginia Company. He could not see how a man's religious beliefs had any bearing on whether he could make profit for the Company or not. Still, he mused half to himself, 'I am surprised these men are not of the Archbishop's mind for the calling of Ministers.'

Sabine stood still, unwilling to answer.

Sir John leaned back in his chair, resting his hands with the letter on his enormous belly and read it again thoughtfully. It took some minutes. Then he sat upright, and put the paper down on the polished table.

Seeing that Sir John had evidently reached some kind of decision, Sabine asked, 'What news do you have for me to write to Master Robinson tomorrow, sir?'

Sir John leaned back again and folded his hands on his belly. 'Very good news, I think, for both the King's Majesty and the Bishops have consented. I will go to the Master Chancellor, Sir Fulke Greville today and next week you shall know more.' He added thoughtfully, 'I'll keep these letters by me. I think the fewer persons that set eyes on them, the better.'

Sabine's spirits soared, while his knees wobbled with sudden relief. He had no intention of going to America himself, but he did hope for the outcome for those he considered his fellow believers. He wanted to remove with his wife back to Leyden to join the remainder of the congregation there. He thanked Sir John, bowed, and removed himself from his august presence.

It was enough. Sir John was on their side, and he was hopeful of a favourable outcome.

Sabine said as much to Sir Edwin Sandys when he bumped into him the following Wednesday evening in a tavern. 'Well, and I hope you are right,' Sir Edwin said taking a swig of ale. If anyone can help, Sir John Wolstenholme can. Be at Virginia Court next Wednesday.'

Sabine put his own mug down on the table, his black brows drawing together. 'You will be discussing our case?'

'Be there!' Sir Edwin said and tapped Sabine's cloaked shoulder to emphasise the point.

Full of hope, Sabine wrote to John Robinson.

Alice Southworth looked around her as the members of the London congregation filed into the rented hall. Henry Jacob, the pastor, was there. And Sabine Staresmore. John Carver and Robert Cushman, of course, once more in London from Leyden, and Francis Blackwell.

Blackwell. Alice knew him from Amsterdam, but her memory was hazy. She tried to remember what she had heard of him.

Blackwell had been in Francis Johnson's congregation in Amsterdam. The same congregation she and her family had attended. The same congregation whose split into two halves caused such a rift that the Fullers and the Carpenters had gone to Leyden with John Robinson's congregation. Henry Ainsworth had control of one group, Francis Johnson of the other, but John Robinson had made it plain that he considered the Johnson group apostate, and indeed, Francis Johnson showed his unrepentant spirit when he wrote a book in which he turned against the Separatist religion he had once suffered so much for, been imprisoned and deported for, and lived in exile for. He died in his apostasy a few days after the book was published, and Francis Blackwell took over the group.

Francis Blackwell was a true disciple of Francis Johnson, an arrogant overbearing man who liked finery and the praise of men. There was little hope that he would treat the apostate congregation with any more consideration than Francis Johnson had done.

Alice summed him up smartly. 'That man likes first place in the congregation.'

'That is Francis Blackwell,' Edward agreed.

'What is he doing here?' she asked her husband when he came near her.

'His congregation have decided to emigrate to Virginia,' he whispered as he passed and took his seat in the men's section.

Virginia. So Blackwell's group—Francis Johnson's apostate group—were going to Virginia. And here he was sitting with his minions, his Bible open on his knees looking as pious as you please. Well—she tried to be charitable—perhaps he *was* pious, a different man from Francis Johnson. Yet somehow she doubted it.

There was something about the expensively embroidered clothes, the air of self-importance as he spoke to Sabine Staresmore, the way he held his head, the way he seemed to be looking down on a man he considered his inferior. Dear Sabine, with his black short cropped hair, and beard and darting black eyes was a faithful, courageous yet delicate little man. Sabine was a man of faith, well respected in the congregation. Furthermore, Sabine was descended from gentry, and mixed with the nobility, whereas Francis Blackwell's background was something of a mystery. Certainly, Francis Blackwell had no reason to think himself superior to any of them. Did not Christ say, 'All you are brothers'? No, Francis Blackwell was certainly not as God-fearing as he ought to be.

Sabine Staresmore excused himself from Blackwell, moving to take a place beside Edward Southworth, and Henry Jacob began the meeting with prayer, and took up his Bible to read a huge chunk from Nehemiah.

Sabine shifted uncomfortably in his seat. Henry Jacob might have been a man of faith, but he was no riveting orator and Sabine's wits wandered. He wondered how Francis Blackwell was faring in the matter of getting patents for Virginia. Better than those in Leyden?

Fighting his wandering thoughts, Sabine struggled to concentrate. But in a few moments his wits had wandered again as Henry Jacob droned on. He thought of his dear sweet little wife expecting their first child. He had not wanted to risk her safety, and had left her in the care of his servant in the country. But he missed her desperately, and he hoped he could, in a few days, escape the city and go to her.

This would never do. Once more he made an effort to concentrate.

There was a shout at the back of the hall and the door burst open with a crash that made him jump. Faith! Some people made enough noise when they came into a meeting! It was all very distracting, and not at all in keeping with a place of worship. No doubt it was the Tilleys again. They were usually late. He tried to ignore the distraction.

All at once the meeting place erupted into pandemonium. The hall was full of officers, soldiers, with billhooks and swords at the ready. Women screamed, children wailed, and people ran in all directions. The officers shouted above the din.

Sabine's heart flew into his mouth, but he knew he had to get out. To be caught here at a Separatist meeting would be certain to bring him before the court. He sat near the small side door. Instinctively he dived for it and with just a sharp push on the door he found himself in the street with Edward Southworth and Richard Masterson, and the two men from Leyden, Robert Cushman and John Carver. Others poured out into the narrow street with them, and immediately scattered. It would be folly to hang around and be picked up by the officers. However, with Edward and Richard Masterson, Sabine waited on the corner, feigning interest in the pies for sale at the shop, while, with his heart pounding, he watched to see what happened next.

'My wife is in there!' Edward said in Sabine's ear. 'And the boys.'

Sabine looked at him with a good deal of sympathy. He said consolingly, 'They are not interested in women. It is the men they want.' But he silently thanked God that his little wife was not in town.

'They want us,' Richard Masterson agreed.

Sabine said, 'If they could get their hands on us, I fear it would not go well. Ah—see!'

The women began to come out of the hall, running with their little ones away from the terror of soldiers and weapons. Alice Southworth was with them, little Thomas in her arms, Constant held by the hand as she hurried away.

Edward let his breath go in a hiss.

A moment later the guards came out of the meeting house and with them the few prisoners they had managed to capture—and among them was Francis Blackwell, the leader of the Amsterdam group.

Sabine frowned. 'Now what?'

Edward looked at him puzzled. 'What are you thinking?'

Sabine met his eyes with a blithe smile. 'Merely thinking aloud. But to me something does not smell right. I think I will go to my wife in the country.'

He had to be back by Wednesday, though for he had agreed to meet Sir John Wolstenholme at Virginia Court. Still, he knew he was safe. After all, did they not have to catch a man in the act of attending a meeting before they could bring him before the Ecclesiastical Court? Unless, of course, he was denounced.

So Sabine met Sir John Wolstenholme, as arranged, and met disappointing news. Sir John was very apologetic. Problems, he said, had arisen within the Virginia Company's hierarchy itself, which left no room for debating the problems of a small and insignificant group like the Separatists. Sabine was desperately disappointed. Despite Sir Edwin and Sir John's efforts, the hoped-for tolerance from the King did not materialise.

The Ecclesiastical Causes Commission Court had assembled hastily to deal with these hated Separatists, the Brownists as they liked to call them disparagingly, or Barrowists after a man called Henry Barrow, also a Separatist. The two bishops were present, dressed in gorgeous robes to accentuate their standing in the church, and as they entered the entire court bowed. Then the Archbishop of Canterbury, the grossly fat George Abbot, walked grandly up the aisle, acknowledging the bows and praise of all the people, and took his seat in what appeared to be a throne in the middle.

Everyone else then sat down, and the Recorder stood up and addressed the assembled company. 'Office of Court against Francis Blackwell of Amsterdam. The said Francis Blackwell, elder of the sect of Barrowists or Brownists in Amsterdam, holding and maintaining erroneous opinions and doctrine repugnant to the Holy Scriptures and Word of God was apprehended at a meeting of the sect of Brownists or Barrowists conducted by Henry Jacob.'

The prosecutor, a thin angular man stood up, and asked Francis Blackwell his name and age, and asked if he had indeed been apprehended at the meeting.

Francis Blackwell stood tall and proud in the dock. He had an imposing demeanour, a presence that impressed those in the court. 'Indeed, sir, I was apprehended there.'

'And are you, sir, of that persuasion?'

Francis Blackwell lifted his head, looked directly at the pompous, fat and gorgeously robed Archbishop of Canterbury and said, 'I used to favour that direction, your grace, but I have since seen the error of that way and have directed those in my care accordingly.'

A sudden babble broke out as the observers expressed their surprise to each other. The Archbishop leaned forward, his heavy clean-shaven jowls quivering, like a hound on the scent. 'Explain yourself, sir.'

Francis Blackwell bowed. 'Your Grace well knows the error of the Brownists and Barrowists. I admit I was taken in by their lies and disseminations. For a while.'

A woman from the gallery bellowed, 'Traitor!' and the archbishop sighed and put his hand over his eyes. 'Have that person removed,' he ordered in a weary voice.

There was a commotion and then quiet. The Archbishop now nodded graciously to Blackwell. 'So do you admit the Church of England to be the true Church and the ecclesiastical authority of the bishops and archbishops to be true authority, Master Blackwell?'

'In every way, sir.' And for the next ten minutes Francis Blackwell assured the bishops and archbishop that he was no longer one of the so-called Separatists and that he totally repudiated that sect.

At length the archbishop said, 'I understand, Master Blackwell, that you are currently seeking to go to Virginia.'

'That is correct, your Grace.'

The archbishop's tight-lipped smile grew. 'Of course, we could not give our blessing to such an enterprise if we thought that the purpose would be to promote apostate teachings in the New World.'

'I assure your grace that nothing could be further from our minds. We are no longer of the sect of Barrowists or Brownists.'

'Well, we are pleased to hear of your recanting, Master Blackwell. And of course, you will be as anxious as we are to put a stop to furtherance of that sect. Of course, if you could give us the names of the chief members—'

There was a long silence. Francis Blackwell's eyes closed for a moment, and then he said, 'Richard Masterson. Sabine Staresmore. Both men are of that church.'

Sabine Staresmore! The archbishop's little eyes narrowed to mere slits. Sabine Staresmore who had helped in the negotiations between the Leyden Separatists and the Virginia Company in London. Sabine Staresmore who had evidently fooled Sir John Wolstenholme and that pain in the nether regions Sir Edwin Sandys. He hid a grin. That ought to put a halt to the plans of the Leyden church. He had long been wondering how best to fox them. Now he knew.

The archbishop smiled delightedly on Francis Blackwell. 'You, sir, are a true servant of God, a man to be commended for your insight and return to the true fold of God. We applaud you sir. You are herewith dismissed and we give you our blessing to proceed with your voyage to Virginia.'

The bishops rose to their feet, and the whole court stood, and then they filed out.

The Archbishop of Canterbury George Abbott immediately ordered the arrests of Richard Masterson and Sabine Staresmore.

'They have Brother Staresmore under arrest in the Woodstreet Compter,' Edward announced to Alice as he closed the door behind him.

Alice looked at him appalled. 'But his wife is great with child.' Then as she thought about it some more, 'How did they catch him? I mean he escaped. They have no reason to apprehend him.'

'Oh yes they did. When Francis Blackwell came to trial, he renounced the truth, and the Lord, turned his back on his brethren, and denounced Sabine Staresmore and Brother Masterson.'

'He denounced his brothers?' Alice could not believe it.

'I am afraid he is a false brother.'

'A traitor!'

'He did it to secure passage to Virginia for himself and his group.'

Alice sat down, and thought of Sabine. Dark-eyed and dark-haired Sabine, who always dressed in black, a man known for his quick wits and his faith. He had shown courage in approaching Sir John Wolstenholme on the Leyden group's behalf. Now he had been denounced by a man from within.

'Francis Blackwell. That congregation has already brought dishonour to God, scandal to the truth and ruin to themselves under Johnson. Now Blackwell is worse. He denounces faithful men for his own ends. I hope this voyage may prove his ruin.'

'Alice!'

'I am sorry, Edward, but I cannot be forgiving and Christian in this instance. He has disowned the Lord, and betrayed his brothers. I hope he gets what he is owed! May Jehovah see to it.'

'Perhaps it would be better to ask that he repents of his sins.'

'Like Judas whom our Lord Jesus called the son of destruction? I don't think so.' She paused. 'Where is Brother Richard Masterson?'

'He made it to Leyden safely.'

'May Jehovah be praised!'

Edward sat down at the table. 'Is supper ready yet?'

'Yes indeed.'

He put his head in his hands. 'My head aches,' he said.

Sabine Staresmore looked up from the letter he was writing as the key turned in the lock.

'Visitor for ye.'

He shook sand over the wet ink, and shook it, and when he saw who it was that entered, turned the page over so that it should not be read. 'What do you want?' he asked.

Francis Blackwell sat down on the small chair by the meagre fire, and Sabine eyed him with disgust.

'I have come to explain what happened,' Blackwell said.

'You have no need to explain,' Sabine told him. 'I know perfectly well what you are and why you did what you did.'

'Oh?'

'You are a traitor. You have turned your back on the Lord. You have acted as Judas for your own ends.'

'Come now, brother. It was for the best that you were nominated to be apprehended.'

'Forgive me, sir, but I do not see it quite that way. You sold me to save yourself and to get the patents you wanted to go to Virginia.'

'It was for the best,' Blackwell said again.

'Are you telling me that the Lord will make what is evil good for the sake of some point? I see no good in this! My wife is great with child, and my servant who is to look after her is lame, my estates are in turmoil and I am in debt because of this accursed place. Furthermore, I know not how long I will be here, nor whether I shall escape with my life.'

Francis Blackwell gave an unkind chuckle. 'My dear boy, it is not because the Lord sanctifies the evil to good. Of course not. But the action is good. For the best. It will mean the increase in the Virginia plantation, for now people will be more generally inclined to go. Brother, if I had not nominated you, I would not have been free, for it was known that I was at the meeting.'

Sabine stood very still in his anger. His black eyes met those of the bigger man squarely. 'I am sorry for your weakness, sir. But you are no brother of mine. I would ask you to leave.' And he turned away from him.

Armed with the archbishop's blessing, Francis Blackwell victualled a ship with all speed and brought his congregation to Gravesend in Kent. He had one ship and packed one hundred and eighty persons into it, together with their belongings, so that there was hardly room to move. The discomfort and the squalor promised to be appalling, worse than anything they could imagine on dry land. There were many complaints. They had put off their estates, they said, and put the money into the venture, so that there was no turning back now. They were forced to go ahead, men, women and little ones.

Worse, his people did not understand Blackwell's reasons for his recanting. They felt that he had sold them to the enemy, that he had not kept integrity and they no longer trusted him. On the quayside there were arguments and extreme quarrels and even physical fights. 'You have brought me to this!' one man said, and his words were echoed by others.

But there was no going back now. In the summer of 1618 Francis Blackwell and his company sailed from Gravesend for Virginia.

SIXTEEN
Guilt and Conscience

Leyden 1619

As William Brewster followed Robert Cushman and John Carver into the oak-panelled parlour of the *Groeneport* it occurred to him that John Robinson, coming forward to greet them, had aged suddenly. There were deep shadows beneath his eyes, and his dark head had begun to show white strands.

It had been a particularly difficult year for him. The congregation had suffered much. Death had stalked Leyden as it usually did in the form of various pestilences and illnesses. One of the victims had been John's twelve year old daughter Anna, his second child who had slipped away in May. Edmund Jessop lost a child also, and Thomas Brewer who aided and abetted William Brewster in his printing works, lost both his children and his wife.

However, much as the tragedies weighed heavily upon John Robinson, he worried more about the business of trying to get permission for the congregation to emigrate to America. It had been more difficult than any of them had guessed it would be, and as 1618 wore on in frustrating delays and prevarications, they seemed no closer to getting the coveted patent for Virginia.

No-one knew better than William Brewster what John Robinson had been through in the last months, agonising over the compromise he had made in the letters he had written to Sir John Wolstenholme concerning beliefs, the half-truths, the ambiguity. There seemed little evidence of the Lord's blessing on their endeavours.

'We are little better than Francis Blackwell,' he lamented to Brewster on more than one occasion. 'We should have had faith in the Lord, and gone about it some other way. We failed this test miserably!'

'But there was no other way,' Brewster had pointed out reasonably.

'The Lord will always provide a way if it is His will.'

'Well, perhaps He will make the way,' Brewster said.

Now John Robinson looked at the messengers, Robert Cushman standing by the fire in the grand carved stone fireplace, and John Carver sitting down wearily on the settle. Brewster did not need to read the letters to know the news was not good. He saw it in the agony that crossed John's face, and knew what he was thinking.

Between the internal disputes of the Virginia Company regarding their own officers which precluded any other business, and the intervention of the Archbishop of Canterbury, not to mention the betrayal by Francis

Blackwell of Sabine Staresmore, they stood no chance of getting the coveted charter. If anything, things were in a worse state than when they started, for Richard Masterson had arrived back in Leyden a hunted man, and without a penny to his name, and Sabine Staresmore languished in the Woodstreet Compter awaiting sentence. The Pilgrims as they had begun to call themselves were now brought to the attention of the enemy, when it would have been better to keep their heads down.

John Robinson put his head in his hands. He knew Brothers Cushman and Carver had done their best. At the moment he could see nothing more that could be done. He said wearily, 'I thank you for your efforts, brothers.'

'Unless the Lord steps in, we are lost in this,' John Carver said morosely, and William Brewster wished he would keep quiet. It was no good rubbing salt into the wound.

The dismay of the congregation was obvious when John Robinson tried to explain at the next meeting. 'Despite the best efforts of Sir Edwin Sandys and Sir John Wolstenholme, we have to say that George Abbot, the so-called Archbishop of Canterbury is not going to give us his blessing,' he told them. 'But the suggestion of the Virginia Company is that although the King will not give us his public authority in the face of the Archbishop's refusal, he will allow us to go without molestation.'

'But if we sell up our homes and businesses and go on such a sandy foundation we could face collapse,' Sam Fuller pointed out.

George Morton added, 'Indeed, anything we do now will come to the King's notice. It would have been better to have worked without making any application at all than be rejected like this.'

Robert Cushman shook his head. 'I don't think so. I think we might as well go ahead. For the King will not hinder us, even if he feels he cannot give his public sanction.'

John Carver came to his feet. 'The Privy Councillor, Sir John Wolstenholme, as good as promised the thing was done,' he boomed, 'and I say we go with his judgement. Really, if there is no security in the promise, there will be no certainty in a confirmation now. For if later there shall be a purpose or desire to do us wrong, though we had the King's seal as broad as the house floor,' he raised his voice so that it filled the hall, and spread his hands expressively, 'it would not save us. For they will reverse it if they wish. We must leave it in the hands of God.'

John Robinson had the uncomfortable feeling he might have lost God's favour.

He took it to Him in prayer, and begged His forgiveness, and he emerged from a distraught night certain that he had been heard, his faith in God renewed, his certainty that He would be with them unshakeable.

Accordingly he sent his messengers back to London to the Virginia Company to procure a patent with as good and ample conditions as they might obtain.

The year 1618 dragged tediously to a close.

Edward Winslow who had come from England to help William Brewster and Thomas Brewer with their printing press married Elizabeth Barker.

'It seems Brother Cushman has come up with another idea,' John Robinson told Will as he stood on the doorstep and unfolding the letter he had stowed away in his pocket.

Will was pleased to see him looking better than he had for sometime. He had colour in his cheeks again, and his serious eyes lit with a smile more often.

'Do come in and sit down, Brother,' Will said, standing aside to let him pass. The weather was cold, with a good strong gale blowing snow up the road piling it into small drifts on the ice on the canal. John Robinson gratefully took up a seat by the hearth and Dorothy put a rolled up cloth at the bottom of the door to stop the scything draught that hacked at feet and legs.

'Some mulled ale, brother?' she asked.

John Robinson nodded. 'Thank you. I'll give them credit,' he added to Will, talking again of brothers Cushman and Carver, once more in London. 'They are doing their best.'

'I know they are,' Will agreed.

'They have found a clergyman by the name of John Wincob who also wants to go to Virginia.' He studied the script. 'Ah yes, he was tutor chaplain to the now dead Earl of Lincoln. They want to apply for a patent in his name.'

'Well, the Archbishop of Canterbury can have no opposition to his gaining a patent for Virginia,' Will said.

'They ask for my permission to proceed.'

'And do you go ahead?'

'Why not? I see nothing wrong or compromising in that.'

'Neither do I,' Will agreed.

John Robinson sighed wearily as they watched Dorothy plunge the red-hot poker into the mug of ale, making it hiss and bubble. 'This has been going on eighteen months, Will. I must admit, I despair.'

'I know. But we must keep faith, sir. I know it is the Lord's will that we go.'

'You reckon?'

'Absolutely. In fact I—I have accepted an offer for this house from

Jan des Obrys.'

'You are selling up?'

Will avoided Dorothy's eyes. 'Yes.'

'And do you all go?'

'I will go alone. But Dorothy and Jonathan can hardly stay here on their own. They will go to Dorothy's father in Amsterdam. But you need the money for the venture.'

'Don't rush into it, Will,' John warned, alarmed.

'It is a good offer, and if I leave it, I might not get another.'

John Robinson sat staring moodily into the fire. 'And if we do not go?'

'Then I will buy another house,' Will told him imperturbably.

Later, when he had gone, Dorothy who could hardly wait until the door closed behind John rounded on Will. 'So, you sell my home without even consulting me.'

'It is my house,' Will said.

'I see. So, you go, regardless.'

'I told you,' he said and meant it to mean there was to be no more argument. 'When we are settled in America, and I have built a house for you, then you and Jonathan can come to me.' He looked down at Jonathan playing with a wooden horse that he had roughly carved for him from some old wood.

Dorothy said suddenly, 'I will go with you, Will.'

It was so unexpected that he could think of nothing to say.

She went on. 'We will leave the child with my parents in Amsterdam, and then when we are set up, we will send for him.'

He did not know whether to be pleased or sorry. He was wary of her mood swings, of her depressions, and her tantrums. She was not a woman to put up with a hard life. Living in Leyden was hard enough. Witness the lack of attention to their home now. But on the other hand, he knew that a separation would harm them more than anything else and he doubted her resolve to join him in America later.

'Very well,' he said, showing neither pleasure nor displeasure.

'I thought you would be pleased.'

'I am,' he said. 'If you think you are up to the journey, and there is no reason why not, then I am pleased that you wish to come with me.'

'I could not risk it for Jonathan, of course.'

He looked at Jonathan with his blonde curls. 'No, of course not.'

Thomas Brewer sat down on the settle in his kitchen, and leaned against the back combing his fingers through his dark hair in a weary gesture. It had been a long hard night as they stowed the last batch of printed tracts of

David Calderwood's *Perth Assembly,* into vats disguised as fine French wine. They then loaded them onto the cart, which would take them to the boat which would transport them to Scotland. The work had been heavy and completed with the threat of discovery hanging over them, for *Perth Assembly* was a stinging indictment against King James, and it was a treasonable offence to have anything to do with it. They had all known the risks, and had considered the risk worth it. However, the threat of discovery still set nerves on edge.

'So that is the last,' William Brewster said sitting down beside Thomas Brewer on the settle. He took a long gulp of well-earned ale provided by Thomas Brewer's new and enthusiastic wife Margaret, a comely and capable woman in her thirties who had helped with the packing of the kegs.

'It was a damning attack on the King,' Thomas Brewer observed.

'Treasonable,' Brewster agreed cheerfully.

Edward Winslow sat by the hearth with the other printer, John Reynolds. 'You mislike that, Master Brewer?' He tucked his golden hair behind his ear.

'No. I think it to be a vital work,' Thomas Brewer answered leaning forward and putting a hand on his hip to ease his aching back. 'It is nothing but the truth after all. But it seems to me that His Majesty will not take such an attack lightly.'

David Calderwood, the tract's author, was a Scot, and a staunch Presbyterian, another offshoot of the Reformed churches. The main argument the Reformed churches had with the Anglican church was to do with church government. It had caused a rift that could not be healed. The Anglican Church, like the Catholic Church, favoured rule by episcopacy, that is by a system of priests and bishops. The Reformed churches on the other hand, favoured rule by elders (Greek: *presbyteros*, elder, from which the name Presbyterian) and deacons (Greek: *diakonos,* literally minister or servant). King James, as head of the Anglican Church, favoured episcopacy. His youth, spent in Scotland, had been one of continual argument with the Presbyterians, and now that he had power as King of England and Scotland, he intended to force episcopacy on the Scottish Presbyterians and at the same time become head of the Scottish church. He had pressed his plans with vigour at the General Assembly of the Kirk at Perth in August 1618.

This interference infuriated David Calderwood who wrote *Perth Assembly* knowing full well that it would draw the ire of the King.

King James saw the rejection of the bishops whom he controlled and appointed as a rejection of his own tenuous authority on a political as well as a spiritual level. He might be head of the Anglican Church, but clearly he was not head of the Scottish church, nor of the Separatists, nor the Calvinists nor any of the Reformists come to that. It was a situation he could not tolerate, and was intent on rectifying. On a personal level, too, their reasoned scriptural arguments struck at the very heart of his beliefs. He alone had the authority to tell his subjects what to believe, like Queen Elizabeth before him, and they should obey their King. After all, he was king by Divine right, wasn't he? And to disagree with the king was treason.

David Calderwood's attack on the King was direct and unequivocal. When William Brewster had first seen the manuscript, it had provoked a whistle through his teeth. He knew it would bring the King's wrath down not only on the head of Calderwood, but also on the head of the publishers—that meant himself and Thomas Brewer—should they become known. Yet Brewster had not hesitated, for what Calderwood had written was nothing more than truth. The King did not have the authority to interfere in matters pertaining to God. Freedom of religion was involved, a cause dear to Brewster's heart. It was something that must be brought to the notice of as many people as possible.

'I should think the King will be furious,' John Reynolds said now. 'But there is nothing to suggest who the writer is, nor who the publishers are.'

'It won't take a genius to work it out,' William Brewster said sardonically. He looked at the printers. 'We shall keep you out of it, of course.'

'Aye and the King well knows who his adversaries are in this matter,' Winslow put in. He took another gulp of ale. 'He may well guess the identity of the author.'

'You think Calderwood will betray us?' Thomas Brewer asked.

Brewster took a breath. 'I do not know Calderwood personally. I have met his messenger only. But it seems to me that a man who feels so strongly about his church and his God to risk the ire of his King will not lightly betray his friends.'

'Well, and I hope you are right, sir,' Edward Winslow said. He stood up and stretched his back. With his fair looks he appeared ghostly pale in the candlelight, with dark shadows beneath his eyes. 'Well, the tracts are on their way to Burntisland, so there is nothing we can do about it now. Soon they will be safely in Scotland.' He stretched and yawned wearily. 'I am for my bed.'

Brewster also stood up. 'I thank you, brothers, for your help. We could not have done it without you.'

John Reynolds grinned showing a mouthful of overbig but glowingly white teeth. ''Tis a surprise, brother, that you do not know how to set type yourselves by now!'

The Virginia Company was in turmoil. The Company Treasurer Sir Thomas Smith had complained bitterly about the amount of work heaped upon him, whereupon the Company summarily dismissed him and appointed Sir Edwin Sandys as his successor. That had come as a nasty shock to Sir Thomas who had expected to be given help, perhaps the appointing of an underling, or a secretary, certainly not a replacement. He realised that he had lost his position, and his power, and whipped up support among his colleagues. His only way of attack was to harass Sir Edwin, and find some means of disgracing him. If he could provoke Sir Edwin into outright retaliation, he might be removed. Sir Edwin deftly parried the attack, but the Virginia Company was in such a state that they could carry on no business whatsoever, let alone worry about a bunch of religious zealots who had upset the Archbishop of Canterbury.

Robert Cushman wrote to Leyden from England with the news and announced that he was going to Kent for two or three weeks. After all, there was nothing much he could do in London, and he had family in Kent.

But he also had news of another sort, and when John Robinson read it his heart quailed within him.

John Robinson read this section of the letter out at the next elders' meeting.

' *"Captain Argyll is come home* [from Virginia] *this week. He upon notice of the intent of the Council came away before Sir George Yeardly came there, and so there is no small dissension. But his tidings are ill, though his person be welcome.*

' *"He saith, Master Blackwell's ship came not there till March. But going towards winter they had still north-west winds, which carried them to the southward, beyond their course. And the master of the ship and some six of the mariners dying, it seemed they could not find the Bay till after long seeking and beating about. Master Blackwell is dead",'* John Robinson paused as the assembled brothers gasped at this news, and he repeated, ' *"Master Blackwell is dead, and Master Maggner the Captain, yea, there are dead, he saith, 130 persons one and another in that ship. It is said there were in all 180 persons in the ship so as they were packed together like herrings. They had amongst them the flux and also want of fresh water; so that it is here rather wondered at that so many are alive, than that so many are dead.*

' *"The merchants here say 'It was Master Blackwell's fault to pack so many in the ship.'"'* John Robinson looked at his fellow elders, and they all sat silent. 'One hundred and thirty persons dead,' he said solemnly. 'It has wiped out the congregation. 'Tis a terrible tragedy.'

Will took a deep breath. It was more than a tragedy. It was a warning of what might happen if one lost the Lord's protection. Probably it was no more than Blackwell deserved. After all he had sold Sabine Staresmore to gain the Archbishop's favour.

'Heavy news indeed.'

Brewster turned to Robinson. 'You yourself once said, Brother, that we should hear no good of Blackwell.'

'The Lord was not with them,' Sam Fuller said bluntly.

'But they had the *Archbishop's* blessing,' Will put in scathingly. 'If such events follow the bishop's blessing, I'm glad we haven't got it!'

'Blackwell was not a man of faith,' Sam Fuller observed dryly.

Will was blunt. 'Jehovah has judged. He was a traitor, an unfaithful man, disloyal to his God and his brothers. An arrogant man, like his predecessor, Francis Johnson.'

John Robinson sighed. He was weary of it all, and there was still an uncomfortable nagging in his heart. He had compromised. Would that also cause his God to leave them? He said impatiently, 'Yes, yes. Well, it is up to the Lord now. Now what about us? Do you think the brothers will be discouraged?'

'We have the Lord with us,' Will replied confidently, and John Robinson winced inwardly.

'But we still do not have any sort of patent for Virginia,' Brewster pointed out, 'and with the Company in turmoil I do not know how we are going to get it.'

Will said, 'Master Cushman and Master Carver know what they are about, I've no doubt. And we are not as Master Blackwell. We do not compromise to lose the Lord's approval. We keep faith and we do our best, and if God is with us, who will be against us?'

John Robinson buried his head in his hands in a weary gesture. Concerned that his conscience still troubled him, William Brewster said, 'I will go to London to see what I can do.'

'You think you can help?' Robinson asked.

'I can be very persuasive when I like,' Brewster said with a chuckle and twinkle of his hazel eyes.

'That we know!' Robinson retorted. He sighed again. 'I think, brothers, that if I had known what we were taking on when we suggested moving to America, I think I would have voted against it!'

They all laughed, but he meant it.

Sam Fuller said, 'Satan opposes at every turn, but if God is with us, it will come right in the end.'

If, John Robinson thought despairingly. *Oh my God, what have I done?'*

SEVENTEEN
'Who Will Go?'

Leyden, 1619

It all came together with William Brewster's help. On 19th June 1619 the Virginia Company finally sorted themselves out enough to be able to grant 'John Wincob and his associates' a patent for Virginia, although as it turned out, by this time Wincob had changed his mind about going to Virginia.

Victorious, William Brewster and Robert Cushman arrived in Leyden with the precious patent, without which they could do nothing, and the suggestion that they should prepare themselves to go with all possible speed, before the authorities changed their minds.

Accordingly John Robinson called for a solemn meeting of the congregation.

After the usual prayer, John Robinson took for his text First Samuel chapter twenty-three, verses 3 and 4, ' *"And David's men said unto him, So we be afraid here in Judah, how much more if we come to Keilah against the host of the Philistines? Then David asked counsel of the Lord again."*

'And that is what we must do, brothers, take counsel of the Lord— again. Are we afraid, brothers, of what might befall us? Are we afraid that what happened to Blackwell's congregation may happen to us? Then we seek the Lord's direction. Be not afraid. As Jehovah told David to rise up and go down to Keilah, and David was successful, so he tells us to go to Virginia. It is the Lord's will.'

Will felt his heart stir. He wanted to go. So very badly did he want to go. Already he had sold his house, as had others. Now, when the call went out *Who shall go?* he was ready. Those who still had affairs to see to would not be ready in time. Besides, there were too many of them to go all at once.

But there was still the little problem of transport and the means to pay for it. So they discussed that at length. Then another problem arose. Alexander Carpenter summed it up. 'If all our elders go, who will teach us?' he asked the congregation. Then he looked directly at John Robinson. 'You would not abandon those who are left behind, would you Brother Robinson? We need you here.'

John Robinson knew in that moment that he could not go. For Alexander Carpenter was right. He could not abandon them. In fact he had been worrying about just that. They were his flock, and he was their shepherd under Christ. He had a responsibility toward them. Yet his heart had been so set on going. His had been the suggestion to go, his the responsibility to bring it all together. Now they would go without him. It was a terrible blow. However, he had consecrated himself to do the Lord's will, and that meant taking care of the congregation.

'No,' he said quietly. 'I will not abandon you. I will not be going.'

Thomas Blossom rose from his seat. 'If that is the case, brother, that you will stay behind, can we ask that Brother Brewster go with us? For those of us that go also need oversight, a teaching elder.'

John Robinson looked at William Brewster. 'Well, brother?'

'I will go,' Brewster said.

More discussion followed. They agreed that those who went were to be an absolute church in themselves, as would those remaining, for it might be that they never meet again in this world, but that if others did join them, they should be admitted as members without any disputing.

'And we promise you, brothers,' John Robinson concluded, his voice wavering, 'that if the Lord spares you and gives you means and opportunity to make a life in the wilderness, we will come to you as soon as we can.'

To which the others responded, 'Amen!'

All they needed now was the transport and the finances to pay for it. So they sought God's guidance and spent a day in humiliation, or fasting.

John Robinson's disappointment cut him like a sword thrust. He voiced his concern to his friend William Brewster the following day, but added, 'It is God's will. I compromised in the matter of the letters we sent to London, and now, like Moses, I shall not see the promised land.'

'You didn't compromise,' Brewster told him, trying to ease the disappointment.

John Robinson looked at him straightly. 'Oh, but I did.'

Brewster didn't know quite what to say to that, and he hesitated. Words of comfort did not come, for he had to share the guilt. His name was also on the letters. Instead he said, 'Well, perhaps you can go later.'

'Perhaps,' John Robinson said without conviction.

They did not have long to wait before John Robinson received an offer of transport from the New Netherlands Company, which was intent on settling New Amsterdam and Manhattan Island, to take them there, providing ships and even a fleet of warships for protection.

He took the letter to Will and William Brewster.

'What do you think, brothers?' he asked.

Will hesitated to speak before the older men, and waited, unsure of this new proposal.

William Brewster also said nothing, so that John Robinson himself broke the profound silence.

'You do not like the idea?'

'I don't know,' Brewster said. 'Part of our reason for leaving Holland was that our children were growing up to be Dutch. Now we intend to submit ourselves to the Dutch crown.'

Will said, 'We do not involve ourselves in the affairs of the nations, particularly their warfare. What if other people were to be killed on our account?'

John Robinson agreed. 'Perhaps then, we should wait. In any event, our intention is well-known, brothers. We may receive another offer.' With that he folded up the paper, and put it in his doublet.

Unaware that the Pilgrims had decided to wait and see, the New Netherlands Company applied to the Prince of Orange to sanction a settlement of the Leyden congregation in America, but he turned them down flat.

So apparently this was not the Lord's direction.

EIGHTEEN
Hunted

Leyden 1619

While John Robinson worried about funding the emigration to America, William Brewster had worries of his own.

The publication of the *Perth Assembly*, had stirred up the King to demand the blood of the perpetrators. It was short work for the English ambassador to The Hague, Sir Dudley Carleton, to discover just who had been the printer. And even shorter work to track him down to Leyden.

The first inkling of trouble came when a stranger knocked on Will's door and asked for William Brewster.

'He is not here,' Will said perfectly truthfully, for Brewster was not in the house Will now rented, 'and nor is he like to be. He went to England.'

'Where in England?'

'I am not his keeper.'

The messenger was not convinced. 'You people all stick together,' he said.

The warning gave Brewster, who had come back from London and was actually living again in Leyden, time to hide. He fled to Amsterdam for a while.

However, Sir Dudley Carleton was not to be thwarted. He might search for William Brewster, but he knew that Thomas Brewer also had a hand in matters. Accordingly he prevailed upon the Leyden authorities who summoned Thomas Brewer to their presence on 9th September 1619 to answer the King's complaint.

William Brewster, now back in Leyden and lying hidden in an attic room, sick with a fever, was appalled. 'You will not go, surely,' he demanded of Thomas Brewer.

Thomas Brewer sat down on the edge of Brewster's sickbed and nodded. 'Is there reason why I should not go?' he asked mildly.

Brewster wiped his forearm across his forehead in a despairing gesture. He felt ill, cold and shivery, his head ached, his body ached, and he had a great desire to sleep, to drift into those strange delirium type dreams that dogged him. It was an effort to concentrate on anything. Yet he knew why Thomas Brewer would go to the magistrates. He was doing it to shield his friend, sacrificing himself for Brewster. They didn't really want Brewer. He was a Calvinist, not a Separatist, and it was the Separatists the bishops, and therefore the King, saw as such a threat. No, it was William Brewster they sought.

Brewster pulled the bedclothes back and sat up on the edge of the bed. The room spun alarmingly, and he felt as though he could hardly get his breath. He paused there, trying to summon reserves of strength.

'What do you think you are doing?' Thomas Brewer demanded, alarmed.

'It isn't you they want,' William Brewster pointed out. 'It's me.'

'You can't even stand up, man!'

No, and he felt sick as well.

Thomas Brewer shook his head and put his hand on Brewster's shoulder and pushed him back down on the bed. It did not take much effort, for Brewster was weak, his face white as the plaster on the walls, his eyes sunken. All his body wanted to do was rest.

'They asked me to go,' Thomas Brewer said. 'And I go willingly of my own accord. If they ask for you, then you can come forward.'

'What if they put you in prison?' This was no idle threat. King James had at first thought that a man called Cathkin might have had a hand in printing the tract, and had had him brought before him for cross examination. Thomas Brewer could expect no less a fate.

'I doubt very much that the Leyden authorities will dance to King James's tune. Be easy my friend. They will do little to me.'

Brewster did not trust it. But he was too weak to do anything about it just now. Thomas Brewer wrapped the comforting blankets around him again.

Brewster took his hand. 'Be careful, Thomas.'

Thomas Brewer nodded. 'Now you are not to fret yourself, my friend. I go voluntarily.'

But William Brewster did fret.

Thomas Brewer appeared before the Leyden magistrates on Thursday the ninth of September 1619, and it was clear that they were unhappy about being ordered by the British ambassador to arrest him. Still, they went through the motions. The proceedings were conducted in Dutch.

They asked his name, his address, told him of the charge, namely that of printing seditious literature, and asked him what he had to say for himself.

Thomas Brewer was not a man to be easily intimidated. As a Calvinist, he knew they were already on his side. He spoke quietly, with that air of dignity that had won William Brewster as a friend, and he spoke the truth. 'My business until now, was printing, or having printing done,' he told them. 'However, I have ceased printing because of the *Placaat*.' The *Placaat* or Proclamation had been issued to control the printing of books. 'At the time of the *Placaat*, the business was mostly my own.' That was because William Brewster had gone to England to try to forward the plans for emigration.

One of the magistrates, a man with thinning white hair to his shoulders and a tuft of white hair on the end of his chin leaned forward. 'And what of your partner, William Brewster? Is he here in Leyden?'

Thomas Brewer was under oath, sworn before God on the Bible to tell the truth. He said, 'Yes, sir, he is in town, but he is sick.'

The magistrates conferred together, seeking, like Pilate, to wash their hands of what they viewed as a petty charge, yet at the same time not annoying King James and his ambassador, and they found the perfect excuse in William Brewster being a matriculated member of the University. They could hand him over to the University authorities! They let Thomas Brewer go.

The University Council was not much interested in King James's complaint either. They believed in freedom of speech and even encouraged religious dissension. However, they requested Brewster to go to them.

William Brewster got up from his sick bed, shaved, and washed and did his best to make himself tidy, although even to his own eyes he looked like living death. He went voluntarily to the Debtor's Chamber to be examined by the University Council.

He repeated what Thomas Brewer had said. His business was printing, but not since the *Placaat*, and in any case, he had been in England for some time.

It was good enough. They let him go.

The brothers were waiting for him in the dark as he left the University, together with Mary his wife. 'I had thought you in gaol,' she whispered, tears in her eyes.

'Not yet, my sweet.'

Will came to him. 'We have arranged for you to get out of Leyden,' he said. 'Your chest is packed, and passage is booked for England.'

Brewster looked at him with sorrowful eyes.

Will pressed the point. 'Carleton will hunt you down if you do not go now.'

Brewster looked at them all, at their concerned faces, and tears came into his pale eyes. He held out his hand to Thomas Brewer. 'You will not come, my friend?'

Thomas Brewer shook his head. 'I will see to things here.'

Brewster closed his eyes and a single tear escaped. Thomas Brewer was a true and loyal friend. He risked his life if the King could get his hands on him.

'You must go, sir,' Will said urgently.

Brewster clasped his hand. 'Look after Mary for me,' he begged.

'Have no fear. We will look to Mistress Brewster and the children. It will not be for long. When we have everything arranged for America, we will let you know so that you can join us.' Brewster pulled him suddenly and clasped him tightly to his chest like a father would a son.

Then it was John Robinson's turn. 'We will let you know what happens,' Robinson said. 'Be of good courage.' Brewster hugged him too.

Then Brewster held his wife to him, and his son Jonathan who had just buried his own wife and the ridiculously young age of twenty-two. And he wept openly.

'It won't be long, sweeting,' Mary said through her own sobs, 'you'll see.'

He nodded, unable to speak. He turned to get on the barge that was waiting for him. Who could know when they would see him again?

Sir Dudley Carleton, the English Ambassador, was furious that the Leyden authorities had let William Brewster slip through their fingers. He wrote to King James on Sunday the twelfth of September 1619 apologising profusely and saying that the bailiff sent to arrest Brewster had got the wrong man. It was a good enough excuse.

However, he did not sit idle. He sent the representative for the City of Leyden in the Council of the Provincial State of Holland, a man called Jacob von Brouckhoven, from the Hague to Leyden to seize books and type from Thomas Brewer and to further examine Thomas Brewer about all the books printed by him and Brewster in the last eighteen months to two years whether in Latin or in English. So they visited Thomas Brewer's house, and seized the type, nailed the attic door shut and sealed it.

Carleton prevailed upon the University of Leyden to appoint an assessor and a magistrate to investigate the said books but they really were reluctant to get involved. They looked at only a few non-controversial titles. They also appointed John Polyander as the assessor—and he had written a preface for one of the first books printed by Brewster!

Yet Thomas Brewer was not, as such, under arrest. He was free to roam the city—and the Pilgrims kept him hidden while Ambassador Carleton fought for his extradition to London.

However, the Leyden authorities were loathe to dance to King James's tune, so they prevaricated, and then they prevaricated some more.

Thomas Brewer discussed the situation with Will. 'If they send me to England, James will have me hanged and sun-dried. Perhaps even broiled, like Bartholomew Legate.' Legate had been burned at the stake. 'Or perhaps send me to gaol like John Murton and others.'

'There is no doubting the King's anger,' Will said carefully. He felt helpless. He could not help this man, other than to hide him. He could not advise him.

'I cannot stay here, Will. Sooner or later Carleton will have all the brethren arrested just to find me.'

'I doubt Carleton can do that—' Will began, but Thomas Brewer held up his hand.

'I cannot risk it. Besides, it makes it more difficult for you to arrange the passage to America.' He paused, deep in thought. 'Already I've answered the interrogations of Carleton through the University, but that wasn't good enough.'

Will smiled. 'Yes, indeed, you prevaricated very well. Not as much as a single direct answer.'

Thomas Brewer grinned. 'I think the Lord helped me.'

'No wonder Carleton is furious, and baying for your blood!'

Thomas Brewer was serious once more. 'I have it in mind to return voluntarily to England.'

Will knew the risks. 'I don't like it, brother. Once they have you in their clutches they will do what they like.'

'But if the King gives his word?'

Will was not acquainted personally with the King. He did not know if he were a trustworthy man or not. He said, 'We have many enemies among the bishops who may persuade the King otherwise.'

'You think it unwise to go.'

Will took a breath. 'Unwise, certainly. You have no guarantee of safety.'

'You are afraid for me.'

'I am.'

'Yet if it were you, I know you would go.'

'It needs to be dealt with,' Will agreed cautiously. 'However, I think I would require some assurances from His Majesty, particularly for my safety.'

Thomas Brewer nodded thoughtfully. 'I will speak with John Polyander.'

Standing up, Will put his hand on Thomas Brewer's shoulder. 'Let the University make the arrangements for you. They have shown themselves to be our allies.'

Accordingly on the first day of November 1619 a deputation consisting of one of the Curators and the Rector of the University, John Polyander and a Daniel Heinsius, came from Leyden to the Hague to put Thomas Brewer's terms to Sir Dudley Carleton and so to the King. As a dutiful subject of His Majesty, they said, Thomas Brewer was prepared to go to England as a free man, not under arrest. But he required certain conditions: that it was his Majesty's own pleasure to have him sent; that he may not be punished during his abode in England either in body or in goods; that he may be suffered to return to Leyden in a competent time; and lastly, that his journey be without his own charge.

All of which Sir Dudley Carleton assented to in the King's name—and wrote to the King accordingly who, through the Secretary of State, Sir Robert Naunton, assented.

By then Thomas Brewer, in the care of one Sir William Zouche, was on his way to England.

The terms and the conditions infuriated the King and put him at a disadvantage. Worse, when Sir John Bennet and Sir Henry Martin examined Thomas Brewer, they could pin nothing on him, and accordingly King James had to release him, so that Thomas Brewer returned to Leyden a free man. Sir Robert Naunton sent a message from the King to Sir Dudley Carleton suggesting he find William Brewster and bring him to London.

But William Brewster had gone to ground somewhere in England.

NINETEEN
Thomas Weston

Leyden, 1620

The spacious parlour in John Robinson's house *Groeneport* reverberated to the sounds of laughter and clapping, and Thomas Blossom's fiddle. A necessarily small circle of children and primly-clad men and women skipped first one way and then another in time to the music, and then when the music stopped stood panting for breath and clapping, and calling for more, while the less energetic sat close to the walls where the furniture had been moved out of the way, looking on indulgently.

Will smiled at the scene as he came in from the bitter cold of a Leyden winter evening, and picked his way through young bodies to find a place to sit by the fire next to John Robinson. He looked for Dorothy and Jonathan, but Dorothy's fair head was turned away from him, as she tried to hear what Susanna White said to her above the din and chatter of excited voices, and she did not see him. Still she was smiling, and flushed with the effort of dancing, and he entertained hope that the depression which had settled on her since the birth of Jonathan might be lifting.

John Robinson leaned back, his elbow on the arm of the settle so that his hand could prop up his head, his feet crossed at the ankles on the three-legged stool in front of the fire, watching the little ones indulgently. His son John, at fifteen, viewed himself as a man, and disdained the antics of the children, but twelve year old Bridget, Isaac who was nine and Fear who was nearly six enjoyed themselves hugely. Yet John's daughter Anna was missing, dead at just twelve years old, and there was a reflective look in his eyes which made Will think he must be remembering her. It was a hard discipline, one that was all too common.

Mary Hardy the servant pressed a mug of ale into his hand, and Will greeted John, raising his voice to be heard above the din.

'The children are enjoying themselves, Will,' John Robinson said as Will sipped from the tankard.

'Aye. It does the heart good to see it.' Again his eyes fell on Dorothy, pretty today with her corn-coloured hair flowing hoyden-like down her back. Pretty as it was, he wished she would coil it away properly like the other women. Something in him told him that her long hair should be for him to enjoy alone.

She had grown up and put on a little more weight, which not only suited her face which had been a little angular before, but also filled out her figure. Motherhood became her. She had grown less contentious of late, now that Jonathan was out of the baby stage. More content with her lot.

She had been unusually compliant too. A new Dorothy, and he liked it. Not that she was as loving towards him as he wished, but he hoped that perhaps as time went on she might become more loving.

'Do you leave little Jonathan behind, Will?' John Robinson asked.

Will looked at him. ''Tis one thing for adults to take such a risk, quite another to risk a little child. I know others will do it, but I think Jonathan will be safer here until we are settled. He will stay with his grandparents.'

'Perhaps you are wise.'

Will stretched his feet out to the fire. 'Have you decided whether to accept the Dutch offer?'

John Robinson sighed and leaned forward, resting his elbows on his knees. 'It is a good offer. Offers of land and cattle, and so on. But I do not think it wise to settle Dutch land or to live under Dutch rule.'

'And if we do not accept their offer, how can we go?'

'I don't know,' John admitted, shaking his head and Will saw that it worried him. Brewster had hinted to Will that John Robinson's conscience bothered him, that he felt he had made a compromise over the articles of faith and he realised that he did not intend to make the same mistake again. 'I cannot see any other way, though. But I tell you, Will, I do not feel right about it.'

Will frowned. 'Time is marching on. Already we begin the new year. It is three years since we first thought of going, and still we are little further forward.'

John Robinson pursed his lips. 'Unless the Lord comes up with something else very soon, I think we must accept the Dutch offer.'

At that moment the music and the dancing stopped and the participants clapped. 'I see no other option,' he concluded. He stood up and walked towards the centre of the room where he made a little speech, thanking them for coming, thanking Thomas Blossom for playing his fiddle. Will watched him reflectively.

Will had known John Robinson for many years, yet the man was still an enigma. Perhaps because he had 'put on the new man', that is, changed his character to fit in with the Christian ideal, and exercised strict self-control, it was difficult to see just who he was. John Robinson did not reveal his emotions, his thoughts, his anxieties. He was a private man. How he must have suffered over the loss of his daughter, yet unlike William Brewster whose emotions had been agonisingly raw, he had never shown outward sign of pain.

Will respected him, and had love for him because of his zeal for the Lord, yet he had the strange feeling that he did not really know him. He did not know, for example, how John felt about not going to America.

Probably he was disappointed. Yet he still worked hard for the project for those that would go. He bore all his misfortunes with cheerful fortitude.

Not so Bridget, Will suspected. He didn't know Bridget well, for because she was a sister, of necessity he had little to do with her, except that she would be present in her own home when Will came to speak with John. Still, he knew enough to see that Bridget was a woman whose emotions were on the surface, completely opposite to her husband. She was a beauty, even at nearly forty. That John loved her dearly was plain to see; that she exasperated him, as Will suspected she did at times, was less evident. He smiled to himself as he imagined their domestic arrangements. It was possible for people to be so very different and yet get on, then.

Dorothy came over to him, all pink in the face, and still breathless from the dancing, her blue eyes shining like stars, and he remembered how he had fallen in love with her. ''Tis a pity you were not here, Will,' she told him. 'It has been such a grand party!'

'I like dancing and playing,' Jonathan joined in, grinning at Will. 'Father—Bridget gave me this!' he pulled out an old wooden doll, crudely carved and grubby with use. 'May I keep it?'

Will glanced across at John Robinson's daughter, and smiled. 'I hope you thanked her kindly.'

'Yes indeed father.'

'Then you may keep it.'

Dorothy had retrieved her cloak from the pegs by the door, and Will stood up to help her put it about her shoulders. He had to carry Jonathan home, for after all the exertion, he fell asleep before they could leave, little legs unable to walk so far.

Bridget Robinson looked around at her untidy room and shook her head in dismay. She had sent Mary Hardy to bed, telling her she would help her tidy up in the morning, for the hour was late, and Mary had helped daughter Bridget to put the younger ones to bed.

Now the house was silent, save for the whistling of the wind as it found the cracks in the windows, the spaces under the doors, the chimney. She picked up the last of the cups and began washing them in the bucket.

'Well, I think that was a success,' she said. She had planned the entertainment for some days, eager for the children to enjoy fellowship together while they all had the chance. She felt it keenly that they would not be able to go with the others to America, and she would miss those to whom she was particularly close. Further, her own sister, Katherine Carver, was going with her husband John, a circumstance which pained her greatly.

John picked up the cloth and wiped the mugs dry, hanging them on the hooks in the cupboard.

'Everyone enjoyed themselves,' he agreed with Bridget. 'And not least because you worked so hard.' He came behind her and put his arms around her waist. She leaned back against his chest, her face against the wiry springiness of his beard, and he kissed her cheek. He loved her just as much now as on the day he married her, and although she had aged a little, and white strands were sprinkled in her raven-black hair, she was just as beautiful. Perhaps she did not always have supper on the table at the right time, and perhaps she was sometimes a little disorganised, and sometimes she could show the sharp edge of her temper, but she was the finest woman a man could have, and he would never complain.

She turned in his grasp and put her hands around his neck, her beautiful violet eyes twinkling at him. 'Why, John Robinson!'

He grinned and kissed her full on those dark red lips. 'Shocked, wife?' he asked.

'And you a man of God!'

'A grateful man of God,' he said. 'For giving you to me.'

She chuckled in that delightful way she had. He kissed her again, with more urgency, his arms tightening around her slender body. 'Leave the cups,' he whispered in her ear.

'And you'll do them in the morning, I suppose? Fie on you, John Robinson!'

'No—Mary will.

'John!' she protested as he pulled her towards the stairs.

'Bed, wife!'

She giggled girlishly, grabbed hold of the night candle, and began to climb the stairs, when a smart rap on the door startled them both, and they sprang apart, guiltily aware that someone outside would probably be able to see them through the uncurtained windows.

She looked up at John enquiringly, but he frowned and shook his head.

Smoothing her apron, and making sure her cap was straight, she went to the door.

A man she did not recognise stood outside in the street. It had started raining, and he had his hat pulled down over his eyes as some protection from it.

'Good evening, mistress,' he said in English. 'Is this the house of Master John Robinson? I would speak with him if you please.'

Puzzled, Bridget glanced over her shoulder at John. Christian hospitality would not allow John to keep the man outside in such weather, and he resigned himself to the fact that his wife would have to wait for his attention. 'Come in, sir.'

The man came in and stood dripping water on Bridget's clean flagstone floor. He was a man of medium size, with a prominent hooked nose, and small black eyes that put John forcibly in mind of a cunning shrew, all framed by a full but neatly trimmed black beard. He looked to be in his mid thirties. He removed his hat, tipping more water onto the flagstones, then bowed. 'Master Robinson, good evening to you. I am Thomas Weston, and I would speak with you on a matter which I think might be mutually beneficial.'

'It is a little late to come a-calling,' John Robinson reprimanded him. 'Ten of the clock by my reckoning.'

'You were a difficult man to find,' Weston said, but Robinson did not think so. Everyone in Leyden knew they lived at the *Groeneport.*

John Robinson took the man's sodden cloak, and Bridget draped it over a stool to the side of the fire to dry.

Thomas Weston looked around him with blatant curiosity in his small black rodent's eyes, at the ornate plaster ceiling, and at the contrasting plain furniture, and John could see him trying to make some mental calculation as to how much the Robinsons might be worth. Then he moved over to the fire and held out his hands to warm them.

John frowned. Clearly material wealth was important to him. This was a man who liked his finery—witness the expensive clothes, the Flanders lace, the silver buttons.

'Well, Master Weston,' he prompted. 'To what do we owe this honour?'

Thomas Weston turned to face him. 'I understand, sir, that you are planning to move to America and wish for financial help.'

John Robinson stared at him, silently thanked God, and quickly revised his opinion of him. He said, 'Sit down, Master Weston.'

Weston sat down on the settle in front of the fire, and Bridget poured some ale into a mug, mixed with it sugar and spices, and set it on the hearth while she heated the poker in the fire.

'How have you heard about us, sir?' Robinson asked.

'I sell cloth in Holland, sir, through an agent with whom you may be acquainted, one Edward Pickering. I believe his wife is a member of your congregation.'

'Ah!' Mary Pickering was indeed in the congregation, although her husband did not share her faith.

'I believe, sir, you are looking for transport to the New World. And I think I can help you.'

'Perhaps, Master Weston, I should explain that we have had an offer from the New Netherlands Company that we have just about decided to accept.'

'Forget the Dutch! And don't expect much from the Virginia Company either!' Thomas Weston declared with a wave of his hand, and a ruffle of fine lace.

Bridget plunged the red hot poker into the ale and it hissed and boiled, sending off a cloud of scented steam. Then she gave the mulled ale to the visitor. Thomas Weston thanked her heartily and cupped the mug in delicate hands blue with cold. He took a grateful sip and said to John, 'I have friends who can help you.'

'How is this, sir?'

Weston sipped his ale again, savouring the spicy warmth. 'My dear sir, I am a business man, and my friends are like-minded. We invest in projects at the promise of a profit, and I have worked out a proposal which I think might serve each of us. I suggest that we form a joint stock company, with shareholders of two kinds—my friends who we shall call the Merchant Adventurers, who will invest their money, and your friends, who shall be called the Planters, who will invest their hard work—that is the settlers. Shares could be at, say ten pounds and each Planter of sixteen or over, would be given one share, although they could invest too, if they had a mind to. Then all profits will remain in the joint stock for seven years. At the end of seven years, the Planters can keep the houses they have built and the land they have tilled for themselves. All the rest, with the profits from trading and fishing and whatever else they discover will be divided proportionately among all the shareholders, thus giving them return for their investment. Each Planter will work for himself for two days a week.'

John Robinson thought about it. It looked good. The settlers would get a pay-off the same as the investors would at the end of the seven year period, the debt would be paid and the colony would then be self-sufficient.

For another hour the two men talked out the details.

Finally John said, 'Well, Master Weston, you have given me plenty to think about. I will call a meeting of the chief ones in the congregation, and I would be grateful if you would come and present again your proposal for their perusal.'

Thomas Weston smiled. 'Certainly Master Robinson. I shall call on you again tomorrow evening—say at seven of the clock?'

The following evening John Robinson assembled the men, the heads of families who had expressed an interest in going, cramming them all into his own home. Will, arriving with John Carver was surprised to see a stranger in their midst, and eyed Thomas Weston suspiciously. At first sight he didn't like the man, didn't like his calculating shrewish eyes, his expensive garb.

As usual John Robinson began the meeting with a prayer. Then he introduced Thomas Weston to their attention, and gave a brief explanation of his reason for being there.

Thomas Weston stood up and explained his proposal to them, talking at length, adding that his friends had already expressed interest in investing in the enterprise, adding weight to his persuasiveness.

Will could see the possibilities. Indeed, it looked a very good offer. There was money to be made in America, and clearly Weston, who pretended no philanthropic tendencies whatsoever, thought that he could make a tidy sum, inducing investors, and yet making the offer attractive enough to the Pilgrims in that they would gain from it as well.

The discussion went on well into the night, and they agreed to put it to the congregation.

Gratefully, the men went home to their beds. Will however, hung back, the last to leave.

'What do you think about it, Will?' John asked him.

Will pursed his lips thoughtfully. 'I don't know about Master Weston. The man is an adventurer, and he has one aim in life—to make money.'

'Absolutely. He sees our enterprise as a way of exploiting the New World, and believe me, he will exploit us too if he gets the chance. We'll just have to make sure he does not get the chance.'

'It is a good offer,' Will said thoughtfully.

'It is the best offer we have had. I think we must go along with it.'

Will nodded. 'We will need articles of agreement about the terms between us and Master Weston. And those who are to go must sell their estates and put their money into a common fund.'

'That is so.' John Robinson paused, looking up at the black night strewn with twinkling white stars. Then he looked at Will again, his eyes intent. 'With Brother Brewster in England, I will need you to oversee the arrangements, Will.'

He had been expecting it. 'I've been giving it thought,' he said.

John clapped him on the shoulder. 'Good. I knew I could rely on you.'

Will had the level-headed organisational ability that was required for such a project. He needed to bring all the different people and situations together, Weston and his friends, and the Planters and at the same time arrange shipping.

On Thursday evening they put it to the congregation, and they also agreed. Accordingly they drew up articles of agreement for Weston and his associates, and John and Will dispatched John Carver and Robert Cushman to England to make provisions and shipping, and charged them not to exceed their commission but to proceed according to what was stated in the articles.

Then it was a matter of making preparations for those who were to go. Those that had estates sold them and put their money into the common fund which would go to the making of provisions which Brothers Cushman and Carver would see to in England.

Then Thomas Weston came back to Leyden with a different proposal. The King had made a grant of land in the more northerly parts of America derived from the Virginia patent, but wholly separate as to government. This new grant of land was called New England, and Master Weston and his people thought it a better place to go. There was profit to be made from fishing there—better than Virginia.

The congregation agreed.

'Thomas Weston seems to know what he's about,' Sam Fuller observed in his gentle way.

Will put his feet up on the fender around the fire in the house he now rented, and sighed. It had been a long day, with much to sort out, as well as the usual task of earning a living at the loom. He said, 'So you think New England is a good idea.'

'Don't you?'

'Certainly I do. It just worries me that others might not. This is a difficult business, Sam, when we are dealing with men who might not be so keen to keep their word.'

'You do not trust Weston, do you?'

'No. I neither trust nor like him. Still, it is not my place to form an opinion.' He stood up as a rap at the door claimed his attention, and, still in his shirtsleeves and breeches, he opened it.

'Master Bradford?'

'Yes.'

'I am Miles Standish. At your service, sir,'

Will stood looking at him for a long moment. Miles Standish was a short man, thick and stocky, with flaming red hair, uncovered now that he clutched his hat in his hand, and a red beard and moustache to match. '*Captain* Miles Standish,' the man added.

Will invited him in. 'To what do we owe this honour, Captain Standish?' he asked politely.

Standish stood uncertainly in the middle of the room. 'News has it that you are going to America,' he said.

'That is so.'

'My wife and I would like to go to America too.'

Will was completely taken aback by the directness of the statement. 'You wish to go with us to New England?'

'Yes, sir.'

'Are you of our persuasion, then? You know we are Separatists by faith.'

Standish pulled himself up to his not very considerable height, his red moustache bristling with indignation. 'It don't rightly matter to me, sir, what your faith is. I am a Christian. I don't disagree with you, sir, but neither do I agree. I don't see what a man's faith has to do with it anyhow.'

Will smothered a smile. 'I see. Well, I think it fair to inform you that our plan is to form a colony based on our own understanding of God's word. In short, we wish to establish a congregation, in New England, governed by God's laws.'

'I see.'

He looked so crestfallen that Will said, 'Perhaps you can tell me why you think you should go?'

Miles Standish fixed him with pale hazel eyes. 'I am an army captain, sir,' he said. 'I know how to command men, to use weapons. Where you go, sir, there are savages. Indians. People who may be hostile. I know, Master Bradford, that you Separatists don't believe in war. I dare say you don't know how to fire a musket, how to use a sword even, how to fire a cannon. Am I right?'

'Yes you are,' Will admitted. His own abilities with a sword were negligible, and he had never even held a musket.

Standish's eyes widened expressively. 'How then are you to defend your families against Indian attack?' he demanded. 'How will you save your children from being eaten, your wives from being raped?'

Sam, still sitting on the settle beside the fire choked on his ale, and gave vent to a fit of coughing.

Will asked, 'You could help us in this Captain Standish?'

Standish nodded. 'Aye, I could. I could teach you how to use weapons, how to defend yourselves. I am well versed in the army, have fought with the Dutch in the Spanish wars, have commanded men. I know how to defend a position, how to attack.'

'Captain Standish, we wish to convert the natives, not kill them,' Will said.

'Certainly, sir,' Standish replied, not at all put out. 'But you have to be alive to be able to convert them, do you not?'

Will laughed despite himself. 'Very well, Captain Standish, I will discuss this matter with Master Robinson, and I will let you know. If, meanwhile, you wish to join us in worship, we have a meeting on Thursday evening at seven of the clock at the *Groeneport*, in *Pieterskerkhof*, opposite the cathedral.'

Miles Standish's eyes narrowed. 'Rose—my wife—and I will be

there.'

He turned and left them, and Sam gave way to a chuckle. 'Will you take him?'

'I think he could be an asset,' Will said.

'A bit raw, you getting him to a meeting.'

'I see no reason why he should not come,' Will replied with an arch to his brows. 'If Captain Standish should wish to become a member of our church, then that will be all to the better.'

Sam chuckled again, shaking his head.

However, Miles Standish was not the only outsider going to America.

There were some in London, Separatists, some of Henry Jacob's group, who had already made it known to John Robinson that they would like to go to America if there were room for them. But Weston had others who were not Separatists who wanted to go. Furthermore, the law stated that settlers in America must also take certain children with them, those orphans who were a drain on the state.

This was not to the congregation's liking. After all, the whole point of going to America was to found a colony on the precepts of their religion. However, John Robinson saw immediately that if they did not agree Weston and his group would withdraw their support, and having now finally rejected the offer from the Dutch, he was caught in a trap. What he did not want, but saw no way of avoiding, was for the Pilgrims to be diluted by 'strangers', and perhaps not very nice ones at that.

Now the headaches began in earnest, for those in London could not agree on anything it seemed. Some of the London contingent changed their minds about going. That was fair enough. There were others who could go. Then some of the Merchant Adventurers who had put up money suddenly withdrew. They did not like the prospect of settling New England; it had to be Virginia or Guiana, but not New England where there was no white man at all for hundreds and hundreds of miles. Still others decided that they did not want to go to Virginia, and that New England was the best place. The arguments ranged back and forward.

'This is what happens when you get involved with worldly people,' John Robinson said to Will.

Meanwhile the Pilgrims who had sold their estates in Leyden found themselves in a desperate situation. As the seasons moved on they grew impatient with the disagreements and anxieties. John Robinson and Will tried to keep them from giving up entirely, or allowing the situation to degenerate into war between the different factions. John Robinson wrote letters to London—not only to Carver and Cushman, but also to Weston in a desperate attempt to get things settled. But at that distance they could not control things in London.

It was a worrying time. They spent long hours in discussion. John Robinson worried that they would lose the summer, the fine weather required for an Atlantic crossing. To go in the autumn and winter was too dangerous to contemplate.

Finally, at the end of his patience, John Robinson said, 'Will you go to England, Will, and see if you can settle them down there?'

Will frowned. 'You mean meet with Weston and his cronies?'

'And deliver to Master Carver the monies collected for provisions. If he doesn't get on with it, you'll have nothing to go to America with.'

In fact it was necessary for John Carver and Robert Cushman to literally 'make' provisions, salting down pork and beef, making hardtack and so on. It was a lengthy business, and the sooner they got started on it, the better.

Will nodded, but his mind raced. London. He had never been to London. And hard on the heels of that thought another flipped into his mind. Alice Southworth was in London.

As if reading his thoughts, John Robinson said, 'You can stay with the Southworths at Heneage House. I am sure they'll find room for you with Brothers Cushman and Carver. No sense in spending money wantonly on an inn.'

Will had to agree, even though he found he had mixed feelings about the suggestion. 'Very well,' he said.

'And may Jehovah be with you.'

TWENTY
Heneage House

London, Spring 1620

From the Thames, Will could see nothing for London was draped in a thick mist, brought about by a sudden bout of weak sunshine and the promise of spring. As the *Skylark* slithered up the river, he had a strange disjointed sense of isolation as though the city did not exist, yet sounds carried across the water, voices and shouts in English, not Dutch, and the clatter of cart wheels and horses' hooves on cobbles. Where the mist thinned, he could make out the shoreline at Shadwell on his right, Rotherhithe on his left, and then Wapping, once more on his right. A mile or so further on, he was reliably informed, was the grey stone fortress of the Tower, disappointingly invisible in the mist.

The ship moored at Wapping where taverns and bawdy houses and ships' chandlers and victuallers lined the waterfront. Will, with his few clothes tied up in a large bundle, bounced down the gangplank and found himself in the smelly filthy higgledy-piggledy world of dockland London.

Behind the waterfront, cottages and tenements fought for space in impossibly narrow streets and dark alleys with no thought to structure, daylight or sanitation. The unpaved backstreets were little more than thick oozing ditches, filled with sewage, dead cats and dogs, and animal entrails, fish heads and guts, and Will even saw a grotesque horse's head with bulging eyes, all slithering slowly down towards the river. In the midst of this filth, grubby children played with a ball which turned out to be the detached head of a cat, squealing to each other with that peculiar accent of London, the strange flattened vowels and the non-existent aspirates, while the rats danced in and out of the shadows.

To Will, fresh from what now appeared to be the clean and beautiful city of Leyden, London was a shock.

Gagging on the stench, Will covered his mouth and nose with a kerchief. He had instructions and he consulted them now. They did not seem to make a lot of sense, so he asked a man he thought looked relatively friendly—and who turned out to be the local undertaker on a mission—and was directed west along the Radcliffe Highway almost to the Tower itself where Sir Walter Raleigh had recently been beheaded, until he picked up a snaking road known as Minories that took him northwards, past Goodman's Fields to Aldgate. He passed carpenters' yards, kitchen gardens, bowling alleys and tenements, but as he approached the city gate, the state of the dwellings deteriorated. A mess of refuse heaps and tumble-down cottages surrounded the Aldgate and made crude shelters for poverty-stricken families who had nowhere else to go. He sincerely hoped his friends Edward and Alice Southworth lived in something better.

From Aldgate it was a small step to the section known as Cornhill, and just within the city wall the street known as Berys (or Bevis) Marks.

Here the city took on a different picture. In Duke's Place just off Berys Marks he found the once-pretty gardens and squares of the priory that had been bestowed on the Duke of Norfolk during the dissolution of the monasteries and the Abbot's palace that had belonged to the Heneage family. From the outside it was an old-fashioned place with an air of faded grandeur about it. Inside it was a rabbit-warren of tenements.

Will looked at his note, and asked a woman if she knew where the Southworths lived.

He found the Southworths' home at the top of rickety wooden stairs, the rail polished black with the oil and grime of the handprints of centuries and so too the once-whitewashed brickwork. A huge yellow fungus grew out of the corner, along with a fern frond, bearing witness to the damp dark conditions. It smelled of damp, of mushrooms, of wet earth, of cats, and of stale urine.

Standing on the landing, Will rapped smartly at the door he had been directed to. Somewhere in the bowels of the building a woman swore profanely at someone unseen, a dog barked somewhere else, and a child screamed shrilly, but from behind this door there was no sound, no discernible movement. Perhaps no-one was home. Or worse, he might have the wrong door. He peered along the landing trying to decide whether or not the thick arched door at the end might be more productive, when suddenly the door latch clicked, the heavy oak door creaked open, and Alice stood in front of him.

The breath caught in Will's throat. She was as he remembered, chestnut hair, almost hidden beneath a white cap, the pretty freckles across her cheeks and nose, soft red lips, and light green eyes right now large with shock. He was obviously the last person she expected to see. There had been no time to write and inform his hosts of his intention. A letter would have taken as long, or longer, than he did himself to get here.

'Will!'

She smiled, her eyes glowing with pleasure, and the colour rushed to her cheeks.

'Hello Alice—Mistress Southworth.'

From inside Edward called out. 'Alice—who is it?'

She stepped aside and opening the door wide she said to Will, 'Come in, Brother Bradford, come in,' adding to Edward, ''Tis William Bradford.'

A wonderful smell of bacon stew filled the air and made his stomach rumble as Will obediently brushed past her and into a spacious but dark room which had evidently seen much grander times. The remnants of ornate plasterwork on the ceiling, the decorative, and highly impractical marble fire surround did not bespeak a common tenement. The floor of bare boards were black with age and grime, although swept clean, and the walls had lost their plaster covering in places, exposing hairy laths. Whitewash had been applied to the whole, bare laths and all, which at least made it clean, but Will realised with dismay that the Southworths were poor people. Poorer than they had been in Leyden.

Edward came from behind a screen in front of the fire to meet him and took Will's hand in his own. 'Will! My dear fellow! Well come! Well come indeed. Alice! Some ale for Will.' But there was no smile in Edward's eyes.

Will watched her as she went to the cupboard, and he thought how thin she was. She had lost the round womanliness to her figure. He deliberately changed his thoughts. He shouldn't be noticing her figure, he realised with a guilty start.

Alice brought out a large jug and poured ale into two tankards.

Edward said, 'Well, sit down, Will, sit down.'

Coming out of his trance, Will put his bundle down on the floor by the table leg, and sank gratefully onto the stool by the fire, pleased to warm himself after the nip in the early spring air, and accepted the ale from Alice's hand with a smile and a word of thanks. There was a brief answering light in her eyes.

'So what brings you here, Will?' Edward asked, taking his own ale.

Will sipped from his mug. 'John Robinson sent me. There are problems here with Weston's people, and I have the task of making sense of it all. I need to ask if I might stay here while I am in London.'

Edward hesitated fractionally, then said, 'Of course! Where shall we put him Mistress?'

Alice said, not looking at Will, but looking directly at her husband, 'Master Carver and Master Cushman are in with the boys. I trust that will be acceptable.' She smiled at Will and he found himself smiling back at her.

'That will do very well, I thank you.'

She sat down at the table, and picked up the linen she had evidently been mending, and began to sew.

'We heard about the decision to go to America,' Edward said.

Will's eyes stayed on Alice for a moment longer as she bent her head over the work, her fingers small and delicate, nimble but red with the daily chores they had to perform. He turned his attention back to Edward. 'Weston's people are for going to Virginia, or Guiana, whereas our people would like to go to New England. There is much disputing.'

'So Master Carver told us.'

'Where is Master Carver?'

'He does not tell me where he goes,' Edward said almost petulantly.

Will studied him, surprised by the note in Edward's voice, and the thought crossed his mind that all was not well here. Edward looked thin, and Will noticed how pale he seemed. He had never been a robust man, but Will thought he looked worse than he had ever seen him. Edward was unwell. Furthermore, it was the afternoon, and Edward was not at work.

He said, 'Everything goes well with you, I hope?'

'We are well,' Edward agreed, nodding, and sipping at his ale.

Will glanced uncertainly at Alice, suddenly aware that she had not spoken much, and did not seem to be interested in their conversation. Almost as if she were shy, which he knew she was not. However, good manners prompted Will to ask, 'And your good wife?'

Alice glanced up at him, and opened her mouth, but before she could speak Edward said, 'Mistress Southworth is in good health, I thank you.'

Will dragged his eyes from Alice who bent her head again over her work, but not before he had seen her cheeks turn crimson. He did not wish to embarrass her so he asked Edward, 'And you are working?'

'Aye—but I have been unwell lately. I go when I can.'

That would explain it, Will thought. The obvious lack of money. What did these people live on then? From what John Carver gave them, perhaps? He did not ask, however. And neither did he ask what Edward did for a living. Whatever it was, it was not well paid.

The door clicked open and two small boys tumbled in. This then was Constant, at five the same age as Will's Jonathan, and his younger brother, Thomas. Alice set her stitchery aside and stood up to greet the young girl who had brought them home, and the boys saw this as an opportunity to throw themselves at her with obvious delight, hugging her around her legs chattering excitedly.

'Do stop that noise!' their father snapped, and Will looked at him, again surprised. However, both boys cowed immediately, and came to the fire, standing sullenly in front of their father. 'We have a visitor,' he said sternly, and both pairs of large grey eyes, turned on Will who they had evidently not noticed until that moment. 'This is Master Bradford.'

'Well come Master Bradford,' they chorused.

They were too young to have remembered Will from Leyden, and so he took their proffered hands in his by turns, and shook them solemnly. 'Constant, I believe? And Thomas?'

'Yes, sir,' Constant said seriously.

As the young girl left and Alice closed the door on her, Will caught Alice's eye, and there was a strange look on her face. Alice suffered.

'To your room, boys, and wash for dinner,' Edward commanded.

'Yes, sir.' They chorused, and ran towards a door beside the huge fireplace.

'Walk!'

The last boy, Thomas, stopped running immediately, and walked sedately, until he got to the door, then he ran through it, and it closed with a bang.

Edward winced and again turned his attention to Will. 'One has to be strict with boys or they turn into vagrants,' he explained his harsh attitude. Again Will glanced at Alice to see what she thought, but she had gone back to her work and did not look up.

'So how are things in Leyden?' Edward asked conversationally.

Will told him the gossip, spoke of Alice's sisters, of recent deaths, of William Brewster's arrest, and Thomas Brewer's self-sacrificing gamble. All the while Edward encouraged him, asking questions, but Alice spoke not at all, not even when he spoke of her own family, although she did look up at him. He tried to give as full a picture of her family as he could, but it was difficult when no-one asked encouraging questions.

Big bluff John Carver and the richly-dressed Robert Cushman arrived in the middle of Will's news, somewhat to his relief.

'By God, 'tis Will!' Carver exclaimed in his booming voice, then with a glance at Alice, 'Begging your pardon, Mistress.'

Will came to his feet and found his hand shaken in a powerful grip, and grinned with pleasure at John Carver whom he liked a good deal, and greeted Robert Cushman as well.

'How did it go?' Edward asked.

Robert Cushman frowned. 'Difficult,' he said. He sat down on the stool by the fire, and Alice set aside her stitchery again to pour ale for them both. It seemed as if her role in life were to wait on the men around her. 'Weston is as intractable as ever. What are you doing here, Will?'

Will resumed his seat, and resumed his ale. 'John Robinson thinks I may be able to help.'

John Carver looked at him intently. 'Faith! I hope you may at that! The Lord knows we can't get anywhere.'

'Is it time for supper?' Edward asked Alice, rudely cutting across the conversation.

'It isn't quite ready yet,' she replied quietly.

Edward's face turned cold and he said deliberately, 'It *is* time for supper, woman.'

The exchange was low, and it made Will uncomfortable. Alice obediently folded her work and put it in the basket, then got up and went to the fireplace, stirring the stew with the huge ladle. Then without speaking she retrieved pottery bowls from the cupboard, and began to ladle the stew into them.

'Well, sit up at table,' Edward said to his guests, and called the boys from their room. All of them sat around the table in prim silence as Alice finished dishing up the bacon stew, passing it to her guests. Edward said a lengthy prayer and the stew cooled.

Throughout supper Cushman and Carver recounted to Will the details of the situation that existed within the London branch of the prospective emigrants. The arguments and wrangles of the Merchant Adventurers, the complaints of the Settlers, the discord between them all.

Will listened, asked questions, put his own thoughts, yet he was aware that during the whole time Edward spoke not at all, and Alice spoke only to reprimand the boys. The atmosphere between them was thick, tangible. His heart went out to Alice. He had been there just a few hours, yet he could see that she had lost some of her confidence. And Edward was to blame.

Cushman said, 'So John Robinson has sent you to check up on us!'

Well aware how volatile Cushman could be, Will said carefully, 'He is most concerned about the disagreements within the company in London.'

'And well he might be,' John Carver boomed, waving his spoon in the air expressively. 'There is much talk of some of the Merchant Adventurers pulling out.'

'I see.'

'Will, you have no idea what has been going on here. We have tried to tell Brother Robinson—'

'But it is nothing we cannot handle!' Cushman interrupted, bristling.

Will said, 'Brother Robinson is concerned because time is going on. Already it is March, and we have the summer before us, and we need to sail in June if we can to catch the good weather. We do not want to sail in winter or arrive in winter, do we?'

'Are you saying that we are not able to deal with the matter, Brother?' Cushman demanded awfully.

'No.' Will paused. 'But I do have the money for you to make provisions which will keep you busy enough without having to deal with Thomas Weston and his cronies.'

'You should hear it, Will,' Carver confided. 'I tell you, there is so much dissension. They cannot agree on anything.'

'I will speak with them.'

'I cannot see how what you say will make any difference,' Cushman said, peeved.

Clearly he didn't like Will taking over.

'Can't do any harm,' Carver put in, and Will looked at him gratefully.

Later, when Will got his bed ready in the room he shared with Carver, Cushman and the boys, he asked Carver quietly, 'What goes on between the Southworths?'

Carver shrugged. 'You reckon something is wrong?'

'Don't you?'

'Can't say as I've noticed,' John Carver said evasively.

'I expect it's nothing then,' Will replied, and settled down to sleep.

Alice got up early, dressed in the dark, pinned her hair up by guess, pinned on her starched white cap and then went into the main room. She peered in the pot over the fire, and gave the porridge in it a stir, and although the porridge, which had been cooking all night on the highest hook above the fire, had settled at the bottom, it had not burnt because the fire was nearly out. It would have been a disaster to burn the porridge on Will's first day here! She went out and down the stairs to retrieve wood from the log store. She needed to bring the fire to life again, for the mist had settled into a frost, and it had turned cold.

Why does he come here? she asked herself. *Why have you sent him here, Lord?* She demanded of her God. Wasn't life hard enough without this complication? Just the sight of Will sent the blood rushing in her veins, her heart thudding, her stomach churning.

He had changed, subtly. He had become more confident, capable, a man who knew instinctively how to command others. No wonder John Robinson had put such trust in him. He towered above other men not just in height, but with his quiet authority. He might defer to those older than he was, but he would lead them all eventually.

With her arms full of logs she staggered up the rickety stairs, and let herself quietly into the main room of the apartment. She didn't like this place, didn't like London. She was a country girl, from Somerset originally, and it had been a sacrifice to go to Holland. Now she was in London and she hated it, hated the separation from her family and the dear friends in the Leyden congregation.

She poked carefully at the cinders in the ridiculously ornate and woefully impractical fireplace, and coaxed them into life with more tinder and some small sticks. Some logs were damp, and she set them to one side to dry. Others were already dry and she placed them on top of the now ignited sticks.

It wasn't that she did not love Edward, she told herself, and it was true after a fashion. However, Edward was difficult. Edward was always complaining of being ill. Edward was Edward. But he had some good ways. He was kind and loving towards her. A good father. And he did his best by them. But he could also be morose, and he was jealous of her faith and her abilities as he saw them. He manifested that jealousy by stopping her expressing her faith, by keeping her in what he saw as her place. She resented it, but it was easier to keep quiet. For deep down in her heart she knew that he did not arouse an ounce of feeling in her, whether good or bad, and he never had. She had married him because Will was going to marry Dorothy. It was as simple as that. She did not want the ignominy of being left on the shelf. It had been a mistake, she knew, but not one she could not live with. Especially once they left Leyden.

She scooped flour from the sack onto the table, and made a well in the centre, then took the bottle of yeast from the pantry, and poured some into the well, sprinkling a little flour onto it, and then left it to 'sponge'.

The fire was well alight now, and she poured herself some ale and sat down in front of it to warm herself. It was too dark to see enough to sew by, so she sat and stared into the flames, remembering when she had first seen Will, how he looked, different things he had said. *I love him so!*

The door opened to her bedroom and Edward came out, yawning, his hair untidy, his stubble a dark shadow in the dim light on his jaw. 'What time is it?'

'Dawn is not far off I think.'

'You kept me awake with your tossing and turning.'

Since he had steadfastly snored through the whole night, she doubted she had disturbed him more than once or twice. 'I am sorry. I had a restless night.'

'What ails you?'

She shrugged and lied. 'I don't know.'

Edward sat down on the stool and she poured some ale for him. 'Well, I hope you sleep better tonight, or it will be the settle for you!'

She said nothing, but got on with the task of mixing the flour into the yeast and water, and kneading it. She had a large amount to knead, but you could knead a small amount in ten minutes and so you could a large amount. But it was work, and she was pleased to be able to do something.

Edward meanwhile sat by the fire supping his ale, and warming his bare feet.

She sighed within herself. Edward could sit by the fire warming himself; she had to knead the dough and bake the bread; Edward could claim to be ill and not work; she did other people's laundry to make a little money to feed them. Edward was well regarded in the congregation as a man of faith; she was a mere woman and as such hardly noticed. Edward liked London; Alice hated it, and missed her sisters.

She put the shaped loaves to one side to rise. Later she would take it to the communal oven to bake.

The boys, who never slept late, came out of their bedroom, and the quiet of the room turned into the lively chatter of family life. Alice put some of the steaming porridge into the bowls for them, and their father, and herself, and they all sat around the table. She did not expect her guests to be stirring yet, for it was only just light. Edward said the prayer and they ate, the adults in silence, the children chattering excitedly.

The porridge finished, Alice filled the wash bowl in the bedroom for her husband to wash and shave, and then left him to it.

She washed and dressed the boys.

Will emerged from the room he shared with the boys wearing breeches and shirt. 'Is there anything I can do?' he asked.

'I need the water fetched from the well in the yard,' she told him and pointed to the buckets.

Will came back with the water as Edward left for his work, taking the boys with him to their lessons.

'There is porridge for breakfast,' Alice told Will as he emptied the water into the large earthen jar kept for the purpose in the corner. It would take several more trips to the well to fill it, and he would do that for her, he decided, before he went about his business. Apparently it had not occurred to Edward to do any of the heavy work that was necessary to run a household.

'Sit down, and I will fetch your breakfast,' she told him.

He watched her ladle the porridge from the pot. She had a slender waist, but her breasts filled out the dress she wore. He had to look away.

The porridge was steaming hot. Enough to set a man up for the day, washed down by ale.

Alice, with a moment to herself, sat down opposite him, pulling a chestnut curl off her face with a weary gesture. He thought of the proverb. *'Who shall find a virtuous woman? For her price is far above the pearls.'* And Alice was certainly virtuous in every sense of the word. Will, on the other hand felt anything but virtuous.

'Did you sleep well?' she asked him.

'Well enough, thank you. Master Carver and Master Cushman sleep still.'

She nodded knowingly. 'They usually do not rise much before noon unless business calls them out. And Master Cushman takes an inordinately long time to dress himself, let me tell you!' Her eyes flashed expressively as she said it, and Will laughed.

'I can well believe it.'

Then she turned to the task of preparing dinner, peeling carrots and onions and cutting up salt beef for the stew.

He pulled out a leather purse of money, and dropped it with a clatter on the table, and she looked up. 'For my keep,' he explained.

She flushed scarlet. 'There is no need, I assure you. You are a guest here.'

'I think there is every need,' he said quietly, seriously, looking into her eyes. 'And I would consider it only right and proper to pay for myself.'

He held her gaze, making sure she understood. With a nod, she picked up the purse, feeling the weight of it. ''Tis more than it should be,' she said primly and put it down again, pushing it towards him.

'It may not be enough when you see how much I eat!' Will exclaimed. Then more seriously, 'You take it, mistress. Please.' And he picked it up and, taking her small hand in one of his, he pressed it into her palm, closing her fingers over it.

For a long moment neither of them spoke, but sat still at the table, her little hand resting in his much larger ones. The feel of her sent a shiver through him. This was improper. Abruptly, he released her.

Slipping the purse into the opening in her skirt, she smiled shyly at him. 'Thank you.'

His heart twisted painfully. This poor little lass had a hard life, and had been turned into a drudge by a lazy husband. The least he could do would be to make sure she was not left short on his account.

'There is some bread from yesterday and a little cheese if you would like?'

He thanked her and she brought it out of the pantry. The bread was hard, so he decided against that, but swallowed a mouthful of cheese and followed it down with a swig of ale. Then he dared to ask what had been plaguing him. 'Is all well between you and Edward?'

She flashed a startled look at him, then took a deep breath. 'He is— unwell.'

So, *No*, then. Will studied her, and she turned away to hide her embarrassment. 'That makes it hard on you,' he said and his voice softer than he intended.

Her eyes filled. 'Oh Will—if you only knew!' She pulled herself up short. She had spoken out of turn and she knew it. Not only had she betrayed herself by using his forename, but a woman must, of all things, be loyal to her husband, no matter what kind of man he was. She abruptly changed the subject. 'How is Dorothy?'

Will allowed the change. 'She is well.'

'And Jonathan?'

'He grows. He is five now.'

'He must be, for Constant is also five. The boys are at lessons with the Tilleys.'

'It is good to get them to lessons young.'

'Do they go with you to America?' she asked him, 'Dorothy and Jonathan?'

'Dorothy will go, but we have decided to leave Jonathan at home with his grandparents.'

'Oh?'

'Dorothy is concerned that it might not be quite safe for him to go. When we are settled, we will send for him. Sam Fuller is not taking his wife. And the Brewsters are leaving their daughters behind.'

She looked at him wistfully. 'I would that we could go.'

'Why do you not?'

She wrinkled her nose in that delightful way that she had, and he noticed again the sprinkling of freckles across her cheeks. They made her look much younger than her thirty years, childlike. 'Edward does not feel he could survive the journey.'

'We have a saying in Yorkshire—squeaky hinges hang long.'

'What does that mean?'

'It means that those who make the most fuss tend to be around the longest.'

She chuckled. 'Yes, I suppose you are right. But I do worry about him.' She took some more carrots from the basket, and sat down at the table opposite him to scrape them with a small-bladed knife.

He changed the subject. 'You heard that Jonathan Brewster buried his wife last May?'

'I did. Poor Jonathan. A terrible tragedy for one so young.'

'None of us is immune.'

'Master Brewster is in England.'

'Yes indeed. He escaped the authorities at Leyden.' And he went on to tell her the events surrounding the printing of the *Perth Assembly*. As he talked she scooped up the chopped vegetables and put them in the pot. Then it was the turn of the turnips. He watched her efficiency, impressed by her, mesmerised by her.

She made a dough with suet, soaked a cloth and floured it and tied it all up, and put it in the huge kettle she had set on the fire, together with the onions and the carrots and the salted beef. Some herbs went in there too, and some ale, all seemingly without thought. If only Dorothy could learn to cook like this, he thought. If only Dorothy were a capable wife like Alice. Edward was indeed a lucky man. It was a pity he did not know it.

'We have the meeting tonight,' she told him. 'You will come of course?'

'Of course.'

She stopped what she was doing, and looked at him straightly. 'I am pleased that you have come,' she said simply. Her words warmed him, but she had flustered herself, and her cheeks flushed again. How beautiful she was. True, most people did not consider her a great beauty, not like Dorothy, generally holding her to be plain. However, Will saw nothing plain in the intelligent green eyes, not in the fullness of her mouth, nor in the small nose, nor in the strong cheekbones, nor in her now-slender figure.

At that moment the door to the boys' room opened and John Carver in shirtsleeves, untidy hair, and unshaven, came in. 'Good morning,' he boomed. 'And a beautiful morning it is too!'

Alice smiled at him. 'Sit down, sir, and I will fetch you ale.'

The Christian meeting held that night was certainly different to the ones in Leyden. The congregation was large enough, but there was no singing of psalms as they had become used to in Leyden, and Henry Jacob's lengthy and dull sermons were no match for John Robinson's oratory. Still, it was in line with truth, and the scriptures said one should not forsake fellowship. If the Lord chose to use Henry Jacob as his mouthpiece so be it.

Later Will walked home with Alice and Edward, Cushman and Carver, and the two boys through the smelly dirty streets of London, discussing the scripture text used at the meeting.

The men had the discussion between them. Will noticed that Alice stayed silent save to keep the boys under control, and he wondered at it. For in his experience, Alice had not been tardy when it came to such matters. She had a good brain, she studied her Bible often, and she wanted to know the answers to questions every bit as much as the men. Alice was not a Separatist because her father was, or because her husband was, but because she wanted to be.

So why did she not speak now? And Will knew the answer to that, for he caught the warning look that Edward shot at her. Will suspected that Edward feared Alice's intellect. She cast him in the shade and he didn't like it. It occurred to Will that if Dorothy had shown as much interest in the faith, he would have been delighted, and would have enjoyed discussing it with her, so he was dismayed by Edward's reaction.

Inside the apartment in Heneage House, Will watched Alice getting the boys ready for bed, her voice low and kindly, and thought that Edward did not really appreciate what a fine woman he had.

He lay down later on the straw pallet in the room the men shared with the boys, and listened as the others began snoring loudly. It had been a day spent in deep conversation with Carver and Cushman, preparation for the meeting with Thomas Weston's people tomorrow. He was tired, but he found sleep eluded him. If his brain did not go over what he had to say to the London contingent of the America expedition, he thought of Alice. But he also knew that even to think of her put him in spiritual danger, for just thinking of her made him want her with a deep longing. What she said, how she spoke, how she looked at him, all flashed through his mind in continual repetition. He tried to think of it logically, to will it away, but she seemed to plague his every waking moment. Faith! He was becoming obsessed!

Reminding himself that she belonged to another man, and he too was not free, he repeated the scripture to himself that Brewster had quoted to him in Leyden: *Whosoever looketh on a woman to lust after her hath committed adultery with her already in his heart.*

But it was not lust that he had in his heart, he thought, not entirely truthfully. And he certainly had no intention of committing adultery! The very idea was enough to send shivers down his spine! To betray his God, his wife, his friend (Edward), and to be excluded from the church, was so painful to contemplate that it was enough to keep him from doing anything rash. And he certainly would not put Alice through that either. No, he reasoned, for him it was more a meeting of minds. Alice was someone he could confide in, and discuss things with on a level that he could not with anyone else.

Who was he trying to fool? Himself? Or God? No, this was dangerous territory. He must stop it now. But he couldn't stop it. He couldn't stop thinking about her. So he spent most of the night praying about it.

TWENTY-ONE
Difficulties

London, 1620

The meeting place at the Ironmongers' Hall where Thomas Weston had assembled the London contingent, was fairly full. Will looked around him at faces he did not know, and some that were vaguely familiar to him. There was a young man with the same fair looks of young Edward Winslow who helped Brewster with his printing—and he later found out that he was Edward's younger brother, Gilbert.

The meeting had been going on for best part of two hours, the arguments ranged back and forward. The set-up was not to their liking; they wanted more to go who were not Pilgrims. They wanted a better share. They wanted to go to Guiana. Or Virginia. They became heated, and Will and Cushman and Carver came away disheartened and doubting if ever they could all reach an agreement.

Will arranged to meet with Thomas Weston, the following day, and when he did he got no further. For Thomas Weston had his own difficulties. He had to keep his investors happy, and it was becoming apparent that some investors were ready to pull out of the whole shambles.

Frustrated he returned to Heneage House.

The days went by. March became April, not that one would have thought so from the weather, and the situation at the Ironmongers' hall became increasingly fraught. Will struggled to keep his temper.

'All this delay!' he complained to Cushman and Carver when they returned from another fruitless attempt at reconciliation at the hall.

'Well you knew it wasn't going to be easy,' Cushman said reasonably.

John Carver removed his shoes and wriggled his toes about in ecstasy of relief. 'Faith! If these men don't come to some agreement soon we shall all be lost. We can't get on with making victuals when things are at such a shoddy pass.'

Will shook his head. 'We will lose the summer,' he prophesied darkly. Somehow he had to get things moving in a positive direction.

Alice, busying about in the background, spoke up. 'Why don't you address them yourself, Brother Bradford?'

'Me?'

'Yes. If anyone could persuade them, you could.'

He met her eyes, and as he did so, felt a great thud in his chest. It was so unexpected it bereft him of speech, so that he could only continue looking into her eyes, struck dumb like some kind of idiot.

She looked away, breaking the spell, and he tried to recover himself. 'I have refrained from addressing the assembled company for fear I may complicate matters,' he said.

'Mistress Southworth is right, though,' John Carver boomed clapping him on the back. 'You address the company. That is the way forward. When you have commented at the meeting, look how they have listened to you.'

Alice poured water into a bowl. 'You can hardly make things worse, brother.'

This was true. Will had added his word to the debates, but it had been too little, too fragmented. A natural reticence to put himself forward, a desire to act with modesty had meant he had not acted as John Robinson had wanted him to.

'Very well,' he said.

Alice looked at him and smiled, and his heart flipped over.

Robert Cushman was speaking to him, but he had to ask him to repeat himself. Cushman regarded him with justified impatience. 'Where have your wits been, Will Bradford? I said, we must ask Weston to allow you to speak at the next meeting. You could tell them outright that we in Leyden have decided to go to New England.'

'I know what to say,' Will replied acidly.

Cushman scowled at him. 'Well I am glad you do.'

At the next meeting of the Merchant Adventurers and company, Will was ready. His speech prepared, his points written on paper which he could refer to. He had addressed the congregation in Leyden many times, and had not suffered from nervousness. Now, however, his stomach turned over and he felt slightly unwell at the thought. So much was at stake.

Christopher Martin took the floor. He was a small man, but obviously very full of his own importance. Will had seen him at the London Separatist meeting, and recognised him as an ally. Even so, Christopher Martin liked to hear the sound of his own voice—and why use two or three words when a hundred would do nicely? Will's mind began to drift. And it drifted annoyingly toward Alice who was at home looking after her sons.

Whatever was he thinking of? He was married to Dorothy, she to his friend Edward. *Thou shalt not covet thy neighbour's wife.* How could he, William Bradford, one of the Lord's elect, break this most basic of the Lord's commandments? *It isn't as though I am a callow youth with a crush,* Will told himself. *Or that she is outstandingly beautiful. Or that I am unhappy with Dorothy.* But he was unhappy with Dorothy.

Robert Cushman stood up. 'Gentlemen, we need to agree on where we are going and who will go. If we cannot agree, we cannot go. Time is getting on. We have to make our minds up.'

'I'm for Guiana! It's Guiana or nothing!' someone shouted.

'Nay—Virginia is where we should go.'

'I think New England.'

Will put his head in his hands and groaned. This was madness.

Carver pursed his lips. 'I told you so,' he said loudly from his seat beside Will. 'There ain't one of them can agree on a single thing.'

It was time Will made his speech. He stood up and waved his hands at the assembled crowd, walking to the front to take the dais, and they gradually fell silent.

'Men, friends, why do we quarrel? We are all bound for the New World, are we not? Why then do we argue about the details? I understand what the arguments are. But those of us in Leyden have agreed with Master Weston and we voted for New England. By my reckoning, with those here who have put their lot in with New England, we are in the majority. However, if sheer weight of numbers is not enough to convince you, then look at the reasons why we in Leyden liked the thought of New England.

'The reasons, gentlemen, are varied. While Sir Walter Raleigh spoke highly of Guiana, it is worth remembering that Guiana is very hot and liable to sickness. There are fearsome wild beasts there, but most importantly, the Spanish are close by at Venezuela. We would be too few and they too well-armed for us to defend ourselves. If we were to be overtaken by the Spanish, the Inquisition would be our lot. And you do not need me to explain how that would be!

'As for Virginia, already the Catholic church has a hold in the colony there. There has been sickness also, and massacre by the Indians. The Indians there have already formed a dislike for Englishmen. Perhaps in New England they have little experience of the English, and we may have a chance to win their friendship. In Virginia we would be living under Catholic, and therefore Popish domination—and watch out again for the Inquisition. We are not liked by the Catholics.

'Furthermore, we who are English will fare better in a more equable climate. We would be able to govern ourselves with no threat from the Spanish or the Catholics. True there will be no welcome there for us in New England, no inns, no shelter. But we are Englishmen, and bred for sea-faring and are we deterred by such considerations?'

'No!' John Carver bellowed wishing to give Will all the help he could, and Will looked at him gratefully.

'Then I put it to you, gentlemen, that we set our sights on New England.' Will went back to his seat, and Stephen Hopkins came to his feet.

'I have been to Virginia,' he said. 'And all that Master Bradford has said is true. It is hot, it is humid, it is disease-ridden. The colony struggles to survive, and there are constant Indian attacks. My vote is for New England.'

Thomas Weston took his place. 'New England is known for its hunting and fishing. We who are the merchant Adventurers want return for our investment, and it seems to me that we will get it in New England where it is unlikely in Virginia.

'Master Trevor, you have been to New England, what say you?'

William Trevor was only a young man, but he stood up, even though he blushed furiously to the roots of his red-gold hair. 'Aye, I've been to New England. It be a fair country, not unlike England, perhaps, with weather like ours, and good rich land. There are whales and fishing, and animals to hunt.'

'What about natives, Master Trevor?'

'The natives, the Indians, are strange, but friendly. We had no trouble with them.'

He sat down, evidently hoping this was all he had to say.

Will nodded. Yes, Master Trevor had won the day.

The three delegates from Leyden were delighted, and they went to the tavern to celebrate. A little later they went back to Heneage House.

'New England it is,' John Carver boomed as they went into the apartment, to inform Alice and Edward.

'We have an agreement,' Robert Cushman added. 'All thanks to Will here.'

Will sat down on Alice's bench, and watched her as she bathed Constant's knee. Some scrap with other lads had caused him to fall over as children often did. Even so, Alice soothed his tears with comforting words, and as he watched her a great surge of love filled him and with it a sharp need.

'So it worked then?' she said, looking up at Will and smiling, and then, catching her husband's eye, flushed and lowered her eyes. Edward did not like his wife speaking unless she was spoken to directly, it seemed. Or perhaps it was just that he didn't want her speaking to Will.

John Carver didn't notice. 'And I hope that is the end of the disagreements,' he said.

Will shook his head. 'I doubt that very much. There are people here who would far rather have not involved themselves in this in the first place.'

Alice picked Constant up in her arms and walked past Will to the boys' room, and although he felt her presence, smelt the intoxicating scent of her, he did not dare look at her. He made himself focus on the other men, on their conversation.

'I don't know why that should be,' Cushman said. 'I think the deal is good enough.' He went to warm himself by the fire. He looked weary. It had been a harrowing time, and there was still much to do. Furthermore, Cushman had a short temper, which, even if he did not give vent to it, irked him. People irked him. He had a desire to have everything his own way. For Robert Cushman had put quite a bit of his own money into the venture, rather like the merchant adventurers. And he intended to make a profit. Unlike most of the Pilgrims whose sole aim was to get to the New World, his considerations were financial. It made him selfish in his attitude which he did not recognise in himself.

Not so John Carver. As ever he was solid, dependable, a rock in the face of adversity.

'You meet with Weston tomorrow, Will?' John Carver asked.

'I have to present the conditions which were agreed in Leyden to him.'

Cushman leaned on the tall mantle. 'While we have the task of finding the ships and victualling them.'

'It should not be difficult to find ships,' Will said.

Cushman shot him a meaningful look which suggested that it would not be as easy as Will thought.

The following day while Cushman and Carver went in search of suitable ships, Will went to see the shrew-like Thomas Weston.

The meeting was brief. Thomas Weston was a busy man, he said. But he took the conditions which the Leyden folk had decided on, and read them. 'Seems all right to me,' he told Will.

Will's job was done. As he walked back to Heneage House, he knew that he would be leaving London shortly. Leaving London and leaving Alice. The thought stopped him in his tracks. *How am I going to live my life without her!*

He took a deep breath and instead of going straight to Heneage House where he knew Alice would be alone, he veered off towards the River, and walked across the boarded walkway over the oozing smelly sludge which formed the marshy river bank. It was not a pleasant place to be, not like walking in Leyden. He changed direction and walked down to the river by the straight road that led to London Bridge, and began to enquire in the taverns for a ship which would take him back to Leyden. It took a while but he learned of one that was due to leave Wapping on Friday, and after searching out the master and making arrangements, he finally returned to Heneage House, a little light-headed from the quantity of ale that he had consumed. It was growing dark now, and he supposed everyone else would be at home.

Despite his calculations, he found Alice on her own. Probably the others would not be long.

She sat in the chair with a candle near her, sewing, but she looked up as he came in. 'Will!' She recovered quickly, though, asking, 'It went well with Master Weston?'

'I think so. Where is Edward?'

'He sent a message to say he would be late home. And the boys are at the Hicks', playing with young Samuel.'

'I see.' He sat down on the stool by the fire to warm himself, and she got up and brushed past him to stir the pot. The scent of her, which was warm and musky, stirred him, making his heart ache, but at the same time elating him. The sooner he was gone from here the better.

'Stew tonight,' she said cheerfully.

He did not look at her as she stirred, and tapped the huge ladle on the side of the pot and hung it on the hook again. But he was deeply aware of her, of the tendril of chestnut hair escaping from her cap. How he wanted to see that hair cascade down her back!

She moved away from the fire to the chair where she picked up her sewing again.

'You will be going back to Leyden now that your business here is finished,' she said carefully, quietly.

'I will.'

'And then on to America.'

'That is right.'

'How I envy you! All of you.' Her tone was falsely light. He sensed the tension. She added, 'I shall miss you, Will.'

He looked at her sharply, his heart banging in his chest, and saw that she blushed.

He couldn't stop himself saying, 'And I you, Alice.'

A short silence fell between them. He saw her confusion, even though she continued sewing, and she tried to cover her tracks with a lighter note. 'You must know that I—that I have always had a high regard for you. You have been a dear friend, and a—a dear brother.'

He looked down at the floorboards beneath his feet. 'As you are a dear sister,' he said carefully. He looked at her then, and found himself looking deeply into her washed green eyes, and time seemed to stand still. He must speak to her about it. 'Alice—'

Abruptly setting aside her stitchery, she stood up, brushing past him again to go to the pot suspended over the fire. No. He must not say what he wanted to say. He must not go any further. He had made a vow to his God that he would not tell her how he felt. Yet the temptation to get up and go to her, to hold her in his arms, to kiss her was almost more than he could bear.

'I wish we were able to go to America with you, Will.' She stirred the stew with the ladle so vigorously he almost expected her to wear a hole in the bottom of the pot.

He wished she were going too and at the same time was grateful that she was not. 'Perhaps it is just as well,' he said quietly.

She turned to look at him, her eyes full of regret, and in that moment there was no need for words. She knew. 'Yes.'

The door opened and Edward Southworth came in. Alice turned back to the stew, and Will greeted Edward who looked from one to the other of them suspiciously.

'You have been successful?' Edward asked Will. The man had a haggard look, his cheeks sunken, his skin almost yellow.

'Well enough. My business here is done, and I have much to do in Leyden. I will be leaving tomorrow.'

'Do you come to the meeting tonight?'

'Of course.'

Alice said brightly, 'Dinner will be ready just as soon as the boys come home. They are with the Hicks children. Phoebe has promised to bring them back for me.'

Phoebe was the Hicks' daughter, aged ten, considered responsible enough to do the errand.

Edward nodded and sat down also at the table just along from Will. 'So, it is decided to go to New England, then?'

'Everyone seems to be in agreement.' Will's eyes met Alice's for a brief second. 'Do you not wish to go Edward?'

'Later, perhaps. If my health withstands the journey.'

Looking at him, Will didn't think it would. Despite his earlier judgements, he had now concluded that the man was definitely sick. Consumptive maybe.

It was a strain to be pleasant, to act as if nothing had happened. But then nothing *had* happened. He had said nothing at all to Alice, and she had said nothing to him. Yet there was an understanding between them. He felt sure that Edward felt it. That would explain his behaviour towards Alice. Will felt like some kind of Judas. The sooner he was back in Leyden, the better.

Cushman and Carver and the two Southworth boys came in together, creating a hubbub that drowned out everything else. But when Will went to bed that night, he found sleep eluded him, and he spent the entire night—which seemed longer than any night he had ever spent—tossing and turning, alternately praying to his God, and wishing himself elsewhere. He didn't want this. He didn't need things to be complicated like this. He didn't want to love another woman.

———

The following morning, Edward came into the attic room Will shared with the boys and brothers Carver and Cushman. He stood watching Will tie up his belongings in a cloth to make a bundle, and the bundle contained letters for the brothers in Leyden, and a clean shirt which Alice had meticulously washed and flat-ironed, but not much else.

'You go, then, Will.'

Will paused and looked at Edward. Poor Edward. The man had shrunk in the days Will had been in London, and not just vertically, but altogether, as though his collapse was from within. Will had heard him coughing again in the night, harsh tearing paroxysms that left him exhausted, and this exhaustion was reflected in the fever-bright eyes which stared at Will now, hauntingly black in a face so white as to be almost transparent, the veins and few freckles standing out in contrast. His lips were as white as his face.

This, Will thought, was a dying man. No wonder he did not wish to work. And poor Alice, she would have to manage on nothing. Taking in stitchery or laundry or whatever. He could not bear to think of the straits this would put her to.

He took Edward's proffered hand, clasping it warmly. He had once loved this man like a brother, more than a spiritual brother. He had known him in Scrooby where Edward and his brother had been part of the congregation. He knew that he would never see him again. He said gently, 'May Jehovah be with you, Edward.'

Edward nodded but did not smile. 'And with you Will.'

'Later, when we are settled, perhaps you will join us.' Will said. But it was a forlorn hope.

Edward looked at him intently. 'Build a colony, Will. A colony for Jehovah. A land of hope and freedom.'

'Aye, we will that.'

There was a moment's awkward silence. 'I would that I could see you off.'

'I understand. I am nearly done. You must go. I thank you for your hospitality, my friend.'

Edward nodded acknowledgement and then he was gone.

Will stood still, listening as Edward kissed his wife, and then the opening and closing of the outer door.

The two boys played together. He could hear them running around the tenement, and Alice's stern reprimand. And then silence.

Will took up his bundle and came out into the main room. 'Mama says you leave today, uncle Will!' Constant said.

Will put down his bundle and picked him up in his arms. 'Well, you know, I am going a long way across the sea.'

'Is that where you live?'

'Yes.' It did not seem reasonable to explain further to a five year old. Alice smiled. 'Porridge, Will?'

Will sat down, and little Thomas, a year younger than Constant, stood shyly beside him. 'Have you eaten your breakfast?' Will asked him.

'Didn't want none.'

'Any! Didn't want *any*!' Alice corrected.

A scratch at the door and the Hicks' girl, Phoebe, a small delicate little thing with mousy brown hair ventured in. 'Mistress Southworth! Are the boys ready?'

'Ah, Phoebe, I thank you!'

Will watched her kiss the boys goodbye, and then when the door was closed she turned to Will. 'One of the sisters teaches the boys reading and writing and numbers. She is very good.'

She bustled over to the cooking pot, took a wooden bowl, and ladled porridge out for Will. She made perfect porridge. Steaming and wholesome and never burnt.

She sat down to eat also, at the other end of the table, as though she were afraid of him.

Will said a prayer of thanks for the food and then they ate in silence.

He was so acutely aware of them being completely alone and of her sitting five feet away from him at the other end of the table. He felt a pull in his belly and a deep ache. He was afraid of the power of the emotion she created in him. How hard it was to leave this woman who was dearer to him than any other person, to leave her alone in this country with a dying man and two small children. How he wanted to take her with him, to protect her. He pushed the thought away.

Alice gathered up the bowls.

'You are ready to go then?'

His heart began to thud in his chest. 'Yes. You—and Edward—have been very kind to me. I thank you for your hospitality.' He picked up his bundle and threw it over his shoulder.

She came towards him. She stood just in front of him now, and he could see that her eyelids were puffy, with dark shadows, as though she had been weeping. For Edward? Or for him?

'You have a rare privilege before God, Will.'

'Aye.'

'You will write and tell us how you go on?'

'Of course.'

They stood there, helplessly looking at each other, neither of them wanting to make the move that would separate them for ever. And Will knew that if he stayed any longer all his good resolve would be undone. He moved toward the door. She followed him.

'May God go with you, Will.' She reached up, putting her hands lightly on his chest, and kissed him on the cheek. It was a friendly kiss, the way women kissed each other at the meeting, yet they never ever kissed men they were not related to. Her lips were soft and the wispy tendril of her hair floated across his face, and his heart seemed to stop within him. Of its own accord, one hand slipped around her pulling her gently against him, while his belongings in the bundle dropped to the floor. Her face was against his cheek, her breath in his ear. Turning slightly she kissed his cheek again, more gently, lingeringly. He could not think. He knew only that he loved her, wanted her. His lips sought and found hers, gently at first, and then more urgently. His senses reeled, conscious thought disappeared. He registered only that he was kissing her with a passion that seemed to consume him.

Abruptly she pulled back looking at him with panic in her eyes. 'Oh, Will!'

She brought him back to his senses.

Shocked, he could think of nothing to say, no word of apology, no excuse. He could only look at her, horrified at how powerful his desire was for her, and how close he had come to doing something they would both regret. He must leave now. Right now.

But he held her in his arms still, reluctant to release her. In a moment he would go, and he would never see her again, for he would be on the other side of the Atlantic Ocean. This woman whom he loved with every fibre of his soul would be lost to him forever the moment he walked out the door.

She knew it too. Tears filled her eyes, and her lip wobbled. He pulled her against him once more, but this time the passion was subdued and in its place the feeling of his heart being ripped from his chest. He held her tightly, his face against hers. Then abruptly he let her go, picked up his things, and strode purposefully to the door.

He looked back at her for the last time. She stood still where he had left her in the middle of the room, tears pouring down her face. 'God be with you, Alice.' He said quietly.

'And with you, Will.'

He wanted to go back to her, but he made himself open the door.

Appalled at his own lack of self control, he ran down the stairs, and then out into the gardens. He knew as he walked quickly away that she watched him from the window and that her heart was breaking as his was. He knew too that he could turn around and go back to her. But powerful as his love for her might be, his love for his God was even stronger. He had dedicated his life to doing God's will, had taken up the cross of discipleship, denied himself. And no matter how much he loved her, no woman must come between himself and his God. Yet his heart was a leaden ball in his chest, choking him with grief.

But at the same time guilt writhed in his belly. He should never have touched her, never have kissed her. Why had he done it? he demanded of himself. She was another man's wife. He had gone beyond the bounds of propriety, had broken one of the ten commandments, and now stood guilty before his God.

He walked quickly to the Aldgate, retracing his steps of a few weeks ago, down towards Minories, Radcliffe Highway, and then to the river by the Tower. He felt desolate, empty, as though he had left a huge piece of himself behind at Heneage House. Yet he did not look back. With other passengers he boarded the ship, and at midday they sailed for Holland.

TWENTY-TWO
Farewell

1620

Leyden, with its clean streets, and neat little houses, seemed alien to Will after the dismal disarray of London. To save money, Dorothy and Jonathan had given up the rented house and moved in with Mary Brewster and her children but the lack of his own home made Will feel displaced. It made it difficult to return to normality after the events in London, and Will had to fight to keep positive in the face of Dorothy's nagging and the preparations for the voyage to America.

Dorothy, in her muted way, seemed genuinely pleased to see him. There was no display of affection from her, no throwing her arms around his neck and kissing him, which was probably just as well, for he needed no reminders of how Alice had kissed him. But Dorothy smiled quietly as Jonathan ran up to his father like an exuberant puppy, demanding to be picked up.

Will held him in his arms, kissed Mary Brewster on the cheek, which he allowed himself to do, seeing that she was the nearest thing he had to a mother, kissed Dorothy on the cheek, and ruffled Jonathan's white-blond curls. He greeted the Brewster children by turns—the girls, Patience and Fear, and the boys, Love and Wrestling, and of course, Anne Peck.

'What news of my husband?' Mary asked anxiously as Will put his son down again.

'I have had no communication with him,' Will told her. 'But others have reported that he is well, and in hiding.'

'I wish he would write to me.'

'I am sure he will when he feels it is safe to do so.'

Mary nodded, accepting the fact.

Will went to see John Robinson at the *Groeneport* as soon as he had eaten, much to Dorothy's disgust.

John Robinson greeted Will, pleasure in his eyes at seeing him again. 'How goes it in London, Will?' he asked.

'We have the ships,' Will told him. 'The *Mayflower* and the *Speedwell*. The *Speedwell* will come to Holland and will be our ship, the one to stay with us in New England. Then we will meet with the *Mayflower* at Southampton.'

'So things move on.'

'It hasn't been easy,' Will told him. 'It was like a bear pit in London, the merchants and the planters at each others' throats. I tell you I wondered what we were doing trying to form them into a company!'

'You managed to get them to agree?'

'It wasn't easy. And I tell you this, I don't trust Weston.'

John Robinson was thoughtful. 'I am not sure of Weston myself. What has put you at outs with him?'

'I showed him the terms we had agreed on here in Leyden, and he did no more than give them a cursory glance. He agreed too readily to them, without thought, without really reading them, and he did not sign them. I had no choice but to leave them there.'

'I mislike it.'

'I mislike it also. And there is something else. Brother Cushman has gone to Kent to make provisions.'

'Why has he gone to Kent? Would it not make more sense to make provisions in Southampton?'

'Well I thought so. And so did Master Carver. But he did not inform us of his intention before he went, so we could not remonstrate with him.'

'That is ridiculous! He will have to go to the expense and trouble of having everything transported to Southampton.' It was an expense and delay they could well do without. The making of provisions required just that, starting right from the beginning. Brother Cushman had to begin by buying his cattle in the market, and his grain, un-threshed and certainly un-milled, and finding the people who knew how to salt down beef, bake hardtack, provide barrels for beer and water, and other things such as oatmeal and butter which would last a long time.

'Master Carver wrote to Master Cushman in the strongest possible terms.'

'Did Cushman reply?'

'Aye. He said, "I wonder why so negligent a man was used in the business!" It was all Weston's fault for complaining, he said. But he was making good headway with the provisions and all would be ready on time. Why they should fall so readily into dispute he could not understand.'

John Robinson groaned. 'I shall write to him.'

'And so shall I,' Will said, 'since you have given me oversight of the matter.'

'Include Allerton and Fuller in this,' John Robinson advised. 'And I received this from a man Christopher Martin.'

'Oh him!'

'You sound like you do not like him.'

'An arrogant man who wants to have first place among us. He is not of our persuasion, I might add. But he was with me on the matter of going to New England.'

Will took Christopher Martin's letter from John Robinson and read that he was the agent appointed for the Merchant Adventurers. Will could see plainly that he interfered in the matter of provisions, stating how much he thought they should take and would not listen to anything Cushman said. Then he lamented that Master Cushman paid him not the slightest attention. Since Christopher Martin was to be one of the passengers, it did not augur well for good relations later.

'Both of them are hard-necked,' John Robinson observed to Will, as Will folded the paper and handed it back to him.

'I tell you, I did not know what we were taking on when we first decided on this matter,' Will said. 'It seemed like a good idea at the time!'

John Robinson laughed. 'Aye. And it still is. If only Satan would not keep interfering!' He changed the subject abruptly. 'Tell me, how are Brother Southworth and his wife?'

Will felt his colour start to rise at the mention of Alice Southworth, but he controlled himself with an effort, and settled down to give John Robinson the not so urgent news. He stayed late, even taking a little supper with the Robinsons, enjoying the company of a dear and trusted friend. And when he arrived home, Dorothy was furious.

Mary's tempering presence, however, kept her from giving full vent to her fury, but when they were alone in bed in their own room, she took him to task. 'You have been out all afternoon, Will. And you only just back from England.'

'I had things to bring to the attention of Brother Robinson,' he said reasonably.

'All afternoon? Will, did you not think your wife needed you?'

She was right, of course. He knew it. Yet he had not wanted to be with her. His heart ached so much for Alice, that it was impossible to give anything to Dorothy. He had nothing to give. *Oh, God forgive me*, he prayed. *I must forget Alice.*

He looked at Dorothy, easy to see in the candle light. She was young, and beautiful, with her golden hair spread about her, for she never plaited it. Her boyish figure had filled out a little, and he suddenly needed a woman's love. He put his arm across her, gently cuddling up to her.

She turned rigid in his arms, and pulled away. 'No!'

He felt as though she had struck him, and he turned away from her, hurt, rejected, and furious. Why had he bothered, only to be rejected yet again? Why was she so difficult? Why did she not love him? She cared nothing about his needs, nothing about her duty as a wife. He turned on his other side, struggling with his anger, and thought longingly of Alice. Warm Alice. The memory of a few days ago was sharp, causing an ache of loss within him, bringing tears to his eyes. Alice loved him. Dorothy did not. He wanted to go to Alice, to feel her arms around him, taste her warm kisses. He needed her comfort, her strength, her love. And he thought, as he lay beside his wife, that he must be the loneliest man in the world.

Will's 'headaches' intensified. He made the startling discovery that the Leyden people were short of money. That caused arguments in London, and the arguments together with the delays irritated the investors, who threatened to withdraw their money. Some indeed did pull out, so that all they could raise was twelve hundred pounds when they needed fifteen hundred. Will could see the collapse of all their plans, even at this late stage.

So could Thomas Weston in London, and he panicked.

'I tell you, Master Cushman, that we will lose every one of the investors if we do not alter the agreement further in their favour,' he said when they met.

Robert Cushman was not happy. 'Without the agreement of the people in Leyden, I cannot agree to any altered terms. I will write to them and tell them of your new terms.'

'Well it's that or nothing. And already 'tis June, and the summer is passing. And how long does it take to get a letter to Leyden and a reply back again to London?'

'At least two weeks.'

'And very likely a good deal longer.'

'What are your new terms?'

Weston pursed his lips. 'I'll get them drawn up.'

Weston did not have a high opinion of the Pilgrims. Religious fanatics, he thought them, and he had even less opinion of Robert Cushman's intellect. An idea occurred to him. If he worded his terms in such a lengthy way that he lost Cushman, who was an impatient man at the best of times, he could easily fool him into thinking they were almost to his advantage. And if he used a sloping difficult-to-read script, it would make it even more to Weston's advantage. Accordingly he prepared the terms in just such a way and a few days later he presented Cushman with a written agreement.

Cushman groaned within himself. The document was lengthy, it was difficult to read, and it did not appear to him to make sense at all. In fact, although he read the words, they made little impression on his tired and stressed brain. While he tried to take it in, Weston sat at his desk tapping his fingernails in a particularly irritating rhythm suggesting his impatience with the time Cushman was taking, so that he kept interrupting Cushman's thoughts.

Cushman gave it up. 'Yes,' he said at last to Weston. 'It seems to me to be all right. I will send it to my people in Leyden, and they will have to give their consent.'

Weston arched his brows. 'You do not have the authority to consent now?' he asked. 'How is that, since you are their agent in these matters?'

Cushman bristled. 'I have all authority vested in me on their behalf.'

'Then can you not consent?'

Cushman had had a bad day. That fellow Christopher Martin, who he was growing to detest, had done nothing but pick at everything he did. Rattled he said, 'Of course I can consent. I told you. I am sure they will agree in Leyden.'

Thomas Weston grinned, and watched as Cushman signed the new terms. He had what he wanted.

Robert Cushman and John Carver, who had by now made up their differences, sent letters to Leyden in the care of Thomas Nash, a Separatist, who came to Leyden with Robert Coppin, the man who would pilot the *Speedwell* the vessel they hired to take them from Holland to England and on to America.

'You know there has been a change in terms?' Thomas Nash said to the committee who had assembled in the *Groeneport* as he handed over the letters entrusted in his care into John Robinson's hands.

'What change in terms?' Will demanded, a nasty feeling growing in his gut.

'Perhaps Master Cushman has sent you a copy of the agreement. Certainly he has signed it on your behalf.'

'*He's done what?*' Will and John Robinson cried together.

Thomas Nash looked a little sheepish, wishing he had not spoken out of turn. John Robinson broke the seal on two letters he knew were from Cushman, but neither of them mentioned the new terms. John Carver's letter however, besides showing the writer's outrage, was more informative, enclosing a copy of those terms for John Robinson.

John Robinson read them in silence, and Will had to wait his turn with growing impatience, until Robinson handed them to him, his anger evident in the gesture and his tight-lipped silence.

In growing fury, Will read. 'Cushman has given us into Weston's hands! Weston has sold us as bond slaves!' He read on. 'For seven years! All to the benefit of the Merchant Adventurers, leaving *us*, we who take the heat of the day and the toil of the land, and risk life and limb, mind you, leaving us after seven years of work in America with nothing, for ourselves!'

'Surely not!' Sam Fuller was aghast.

Will passed the copy to him. 'The basic agreed conditions were that at the end of seven years everything in the common stock should be divided between everyone participating, Planters and Adventurers. It did not include land and gardens and houses, which must belong to us, the Planters who are to take the greater risk; further the former agreement allowed two days a week for the planters to use for time with their families and to provide for their families. Now he wants all the time to be for the making of profit for the common stock, and houses and gardens and land, everything, to be included in the common stock, and shared among everyone participating. In short, gentlemen, it leaves us with nothing. We who have invested our very lives end up with less than the investors who give just a little money! Everything we will have worked for for seven years will be gone, all the land we have tamed, and worked, and brought yield from, the houses we have built with our own hands, gone, as though it were not ours.' He put his head in his hands. 'What is the point of going then, if we are not to improve our lot by going?'

There was an awkward silence, and Will took a strengthening breath.

John Robinson said quietly, 'Because it is the Lord's will.'

Will looked up again, and nodded. 'Yes, but this is not.' He pointed to the sheet of paper now in Isaac Allerton's hands. 'It might be wonderful for the Merchant Adventurers, increasing their potential profits, and certainly it prevents certain ones from pulling out, and encouraging others to invest, but for us it is a disaster. It will wipe out the colony. We cannot agree to these terms. We *will not* agree to these terms.'

'Whatever was Cushman thinking of?' Samuel Fuller asked aghast. 'Fancy agreeing to it!'

Will shook his head.

It was Isaac Allerton who said, 'Brother Cushman does not understand such things as legal agreements.'

'Weston has fooled him,' Edward Winslow agreed. 'I mean look at this thing. It takes a genius to work out what he is saying!' He flipped the edge of the paper now in his own hands, with his finger.

Will raised a sardonic eyebrow at him, and couldn't help a laugh. 'Well, thank you!'

'I am going to write to him,' John Robinson announced. 'And I suggest you do so too.'

So, with Samuel Fuller, Edward Winslow and Isaac Allerton, Will wrote a strong letter to Cushman and Carver, reprimanding Cushman for being so presumptuous. *'We desire him* [Cushman] *to exercise his brains therein,'* they said and reminded him of John Robinson's former reasons for not agreeing to the new rules. John Robinson also wrote to Cushman which left Cushman in no doubt as to his feelings on the subject.

In London, Cushman showed the letters to Thomas Weston. 'Well in that case I shall pull out altogether!' Weston announced flatly, putting on his hat and making ready to leave the Southworths' tenement.

'You cannot,' Cushman pointed out. 'You have too much invested already.'

Weston paused. 'You are right, my friend. But if it were not for that, I would have pulled out. It is all too big a burden to bear. I tell you, I wish I had not involved myself in this business in the first place. Nothing but trouble.'

Cushman said a quick prayer for help. 'Master Weston, you have shown yourself to be a man capable of managing financial affairs. You know and I know that there is profit to be made in New England. It is a land that is, as yet, untouched. It has resources the like of which we, who are merchants by trade, can only dream of. Furs at a price so low that we can make a fortune out of them. Fish, salted and ready to transport to England. Wood, timber for the use in furniture or wainscoting or whatever. The possibilities are limitless.'

Weston's shrewish little eyes seemed to disappear as he smiled at this image of the reason for investing in the New England venture. He knew that what Cushman said was right. 'Yes, I know,' he said.

Cushman followed up his advantage. 'And these new terms, which they will have to agree to in the end, will bring us rich rewards.' As an investor, as well as a prospective settler, Cushman saw the benefits growing in his own favour. 'If you let this go now, at this late hour, you will lose everything you have put in so far, with no return. And believe me, they *will* agree to these terms. They will have to.'

Thomas Weston nodded. 'Very well, sir. But I want no more of this bickering. Tell them in Leyden.'

'I will sir, I will.'

He conducted Thomas Weston from the apartment, and turned to see Alice Southworth watching him.

'Brother Bradford is not stupid so as to agree to terms that will be detrimental to the brethren,' she told him.

'He has no choice,' Cushman told her flatly. 'And you do not understand the situation, woman, so keep your own counsel.'

Furious, she turned back to stew in the pot on the fire.

In Leyden, John Robinson threw his hands up in despair. 'We have to let it go,' he told the others. 'We have no time now to negotiate. The ships are almost ready, it is late June already, the summer is high, and we need to get going or we will be sailing at the worst time of the year in the worst weather, autumn and winter. We are running out of time.'

But worse was to follow. Some of those in Leyden, misliking the new terms pulled out. Now Will found that instead of having too many to go, there were not enough. He applied to Henry Ainsworth's congregation in Amsterdam inviting any to go who wished, and a few responded.

At last they were ready. John Robinson called for a day of solemn humiliation, which meant a day of fasting and prayer, and they all went to the *Groeneport* for a final meeting together.

John Robinson took for his text Ezra chapter eight, verse twenty-one: *And there at the river, by Ahava, I proclaimed a fast, that we might humble ourselves before our God and seek of him a right way for us, and for our children, and for all our substance.*

He did his best to upbuild them, to encourage them, to send them away with positive thoughts, even though all the women and not a few of the men were in tears.

Will's own stomach was churning. It had finally arrived. At last after all the work, and the effort and the years of struggle, they were going to America. It was a strange unreal feeling, one of excitement and anticipation, of grief at leaving loved ones behind—and they would be leaving little Jonathan—and not a little anxiety at the voyage that lay before them. A vast ocean stretched between England and America, an ocean known for storms and lost ships. And witness Francis Blackwell's terrible voyage. And after the voyage, what then?

Yet Will had confidence in his God. He would be with them.

It was time to depart. The whole congregation, including some who had come from Amsterdam, like the Ainsworths and Dorothy's parents and sister and brother-in-law, went with them the short distance to Delftshaven where the *Speedwell* lay ready, waiting at anchor.

Will had a strange feeling of unreality as he helped load the baggage on the boats, almost as though he were detached from it, or it were not really happening. For it was more difficult to leave Leyden than he had imagined it would be. He had not realised how much he had grown to love the city with its precise order in all things. For eleven years it had been his home. Here he had brought his wife, here his child had been born. And here he had come to know Alice.

With the goods and children and wives piled into boats, they made their way down the Vliet Canal, past The Hague, through Delft with its huge church towers and stepped gables, and towards Delftshaven on the Maas.

It was not Will's first sight of the *Speedwell*, lying quietly at anchor alongside the quay, ready to take them. But Will was struck again at how small it seemed for such a huge undertaking. How would everyone and everything fit in it? This little ship had been re-masted, and re-fitted, and was to stay with them in New England for a time for their use.

The sailors, mostly rough Englishmen with more than their fair share of muscle, set to with the help of some of the men, piling their belongings in cargo nets and heaving them into the hold. Will found himself hauling with two huge men that made him, large as he was, seem puny. His work had not been as physical as theirs, his muscles not so well developed. He caught Captain Reynolds smiling at the sight, and mentally decided that he would help out with some of the heavy work on board if he were not to be as weak as a woman when they arrived in America.

'What in the name of all that is holy is that?' Captain Reynolds demanded suddenly.

Will looked round, and saw Edward Winslow directing the hoisting of a large object in the cargo net.'

'It is a screw captain,' Edward Winslow told him cheerily.

Captain Reynolds was not amused. 'We do not have room for it. Get it off my ship!'

Edward Winslow came running up the gangplank, all blonde curls and boyish looks. 'But Captain, it must go. We need it in the Americas.'

'What on earth is it for?'

'It is part of a printing press.'

'And what do you want with a printing press?' Captain Reynolds demanded.

'To print books and pamphlets.'

'For who to read? The Indians?' He laughed, and his men laughed with him as if he had made a fine joke.

'The books will come back to England, of course,' Edward Winslow told him, by no means cowed. 'As I am sure you know must be the case.'

'You are all mad!'

'Nevertheless, the screw stays!'

Captain Reynolds gave it up. 'Oh if you must!'

'Thank you, Captain.'

Reynolds looked around him, at no-one in particular. 'We sail on the tide in the morning,' he announced. 'Do you come aboard now?'

Will said, 'This may be the last time we see our friends and our families. We will spend the night with them on the dockside.'

Clearly Captain Reynolds thought them queer folk to want to camp out, but that was exactly what they did. Men and women and children settled down in the balmy summer night to talk, and sing a few folk songs just to be together. Dorothy sat with her mother and father and with little Jonathan, beside the fire. Will looked at his son, his blonde curls lit by the firelight, his face serene, unaware of the trauma that the morrow would bring for him. It was not too late to decide to take him, and he knew he wanted to. But he knew also the dangers. *Stupid to expose a child so young to such dangers.*

'You will write to us, won't you Will,' Alexander May, Dorothy's father said for the umpteenth time.

'Have I not promised you?' Will responded, but his tone was kindly, his eyes smiling.

'And take good care of my little girl.' He smiled fondly on Dorothy.

'You know I will.' He looked across at Dorothy. She clung to little Jonathan sleeping peacefully in her arms. She met his eyes. There was something there that he could not fathom. What was it? Regret? Blame? Or merely sadness at parting? But it made him uneasy. She did not want to go. He knew it. He had always known it. So why was she? Why did she not stay behind with Sam Fuller's wife Bridget, and come out when he had prepared a home for her? He did not know the reason.

John Robinson came over and sat down on the blanket beside Will, linking his hands over his drawn up knees. 'I would that I could come with you Will,' he said.

'We will miss you,' Will told him. He paused for his heart was full of love for this fearless proclaimer of God's Word, yet not knowing quite how to express it. '*I* will miss you.' It was no more than the truth. 'I want you to know, Brother, that you, and Brother Brewster, have been like fathers to me. I have learned so much from you both.'

John Robinson smiled that quiet smile of his, and said gently, 'We've watched you grow up, Will, seen you at a tender age take a stand for the Truth. Don't ever compromise the Truth. Stand upright for the Lord. Be strong, Will. The company rely on your good sense and your capableness. You are an elder and you know what you are about. Work together with Master Brewster, and Master Carver and Master Fuller. You have strength in you. Use it.'

Will was silent, feeling that he was unworthy of this great man's accolade, yet deeply grateful for it at the same time.

John Robinson put his hand inside his jerkin and brought out some sheets of paper folded up together and sealed. 'I have written a letter for all the brothers and sisters, and all those going along with you, which I hope will encourage you all.'

Will took the letter and John put his hand on his to stop him opening it. 'No, it is for when you sail from Southampton. Give it into the hand of Brother Brewster when you meet him there.'

Obediently Will tucked it into his doublet. 'Yes, I will.'

'And write to me, Will. Tell me the details Brother Brewster will not think to tell me, for he is lazy when it comes to writing letters, I think. Look how few he has sent since he has been in England!'

'I will write,' Will promised.

John sighed, and the silence between them was awkward. 'I would I were going with you,' he repeated. 'You have no idea how much this means to me, how much I long to go. You are doing the Lord's work in this. Build a settlement, a colony, help others to come after you, to a place where a man may think and worship as he wishes. And one day, perhaps I can come to you, if the Lord wills it.'

'I would you were coming now,' Will told him.

John's eyes took on a glow as he saw America in his imagination. 'This will be our Promised Land, Will. We will build Jerusalem, a cause for rejoicing, in the wilderness. A land built on the free worship of God. You are young, Will. You will bear the burdens well. And God will go with you.'

As the dawn approached on Saturday 22 July 1620 they began to board the *Speedwell*. The warm night had turned to rain, soaking passengers and crew and well-wishers.

To Captain Reynolds' intense annoyance, everyone went aboard, including those saying farewell. The ship's decks were a tangle of people, men and women and children, getting caught up in the ropes, in the way of the sailors.

The moment had come. They wept in each others' arms, and sobbed, and prayed together. Children wept at being parted from parents. Fear and Patience Brewster sobbed in their mother's arms, for she was going and taking her two young sons with her and they were not. Bridget Fuller clung to her husband Sam as he tried to comfort her. Digorie Priest said goodbye to his wife Sarah and his sons who were staying, and Sarah Priest in her turn hugged her own brother Isaac Allerton and his wife Mary and their three young children for they were all going. Nothing, Mary Allerton had declared to her husband when he suggested she and the little ones should stay at home, would prevent her from taking her place at her husband's side, and where she went, her children went, as a matter of course. William White, who was going with his very pregnant wife, Susanna, Sam Fuller's sister, and their sole surviving son Resolved, aged just five, bid farewell to his cousins Roger White and Bridget Robinson. Mary Cushman was a passenger, ready to meet her husband in Southampton. Katherine Carver kissed her sisters Bridget Robinson and Jane Thickens and Frances Jessop, and her brothers Thomas and Roger White. She was also to meet her husband John Carver in Southampton. Edward Winslow and his wife Elizabeth who had become beloved by all the congregation, had no-one to say goodbye to, but the Blossoms, Thomas and Thomas junior who were going wept with Anne, wife and mother to be left behind.

John Robinson fell to his knees on the deck, and, as if it were a signal, the noise suddenly stopped, and with almost one motion everyone of the congregation fell to their knees with him. In prayer, with tears, John

Robinson begged God for his love and help towards the travellers—the Pilgrims.

Now the time had come for Will and Dorothy to part from her parents and her sister, and their five-year old son Jonathan.

The parting was worse than Will had anticipated. An agony that would stay with him a lifetime. For all his youth Jonathan understood that his parents were leaving him, perhaps forever. He clung to Dorothy, sobbing and begging her not to go.

Dorothy sobbed as she held him tightly. 'There, there, don't cry my little man. We'll soon see you again. I promise.' But her efforts at soothing him were hampered by her own sobs.

'Mother! Please don't go! Don't leave me here! Please. I want to go too.'

Will bent down and tried a sterner tactic. 'Now John, no more of this crying. You must be a man and look after grandmother.'

But Jonathan clung all the harder and wailed pitifully.

Will took him from Dorothy, and held him in his own arms. This was his son, his own flesh and blood. Will loved him as a father must, and his resolve weakened. But he was not ignorant of the dangers that lay ahead. No, Jonathan was far too precious to risk on a venture that he knew was fraught with danger.

Deprived of Jonathan, Dorothy threw her arms around her mother and the two women wept, and then her father, as Will gave Jonathan into his grandmother's arms. With promises to write and to the sound of Jonathan's hysterics, Will gently pulled her away, allowing them to leave the ship.

Captain Reynolds's voice could be heard above the tumult. They must make sail or lose the tide.

With all those ashore who were going ashore, Captain Reynolds gave his orders to the mate, 'Make all sail!'

'Lay aloft there, you laggards!' cried the mate, and barefooted sailors ran up the rigging, loosing the sails. Others cast off and the ship began to move.

The passengers lined the gunwales as the wind filled the sails and the *Speedwell* moved away from the quay, slowly at first, then with growing speed, out into deeper water. The passengers waved to their friends and families, calling out last-minute messages.

And there in the front of the bystanders, his blonde curls shining like ripe corn was Jonathan, Will's last sight of him, standing between his grandparents, crying out for his mother, little hand outstretched to the ship.

Will watched him until they were out of sight, as tears streamed down his own face.

TWENTY-THREE
Disagreement

Southampton, England, July 1620

After two days crossing the English Channel, it was with relief that Will saw the hills of England, lush from recent summer rain, the trees gowned with leaves. It was a different landscape to Holland. Towering white cliffs at Dover, topped with a wig of green grass, verdant hills of Kent, the hills of Sussex, and the cliffs again along the Wessex coast and on into Southampton, where idle ships waited for their loads amid a forest of tall naked masts.

As they approached they could see people on the banks and quays. Men heaving on block and tackle; wagons with goods; carriages of the wealthy, with their impressive pure-blood horses; men, sailors in their distinctive garb, ordinary folk, and a few women and children. Some of the women were of the 'loose' variety, with gaudy dresses, obvious even at a distance, but others were modestly dressed, waving at the *Speedwell* as she came to anchor. These were the London contingent, Will guessed hopefully. They would recognise the ship, for no doubt Brother Cushman and Brother Carver were among them.

Captain Reynolds brought the *Speedwell* to rest close to the *Mayflower*. Will recognised her immediately, all ninety feet of her, a beautiful two-masted ship, already loaded with her cargo, it seemed.

Together with Edward Winslow, Isaac Allerton, and the wives of the men who had gone to England, and others, Will clambered into the first boat to go ashore. The brothers on the shore greeted them with enthusiasm. It was Will's first sight of William Brewster in some months, and he hugged him unashamedly.

Almost immediately Mary Brewster elbowed him unceremoniously out of the way and slipped her arms around her husband's waist, and he hugged her in sheer delight, whispering to her, which brought a blush of pleasure to her round cheeks. The boys, Love and Wrestling, danced around their father, and he picked each of them up in his arms in turn and gave them a kiss, before they went off to play. Will felt a sudden surge of acute envy, as he thought of the dry welcome he had received from Dorothy after his sojourn in London, and the loss of the woman he loved in London.

His eyes scanned the crowds in the hope that she and Edward had decided to come to see them off, but there was no sign of them. He felt the lurch of disappointment in his belly, but then he had not really expected to see her. She and Edward could not afford the journey.

'So, Will, you managed to get it all together at last!' Brewster said, turning to face him, his arm encircling his lady's waist.

Will grinned and said lightly, ''Twasn't easy. But now is not the time. I will leave you to it. You and your dear lady have much to make up.'

Mary smiled happily, but said diplomatically, 'Aye—and there'll be time enough for that, young Will.' She knew the men had much to discuss. Her own private conversations with her husband could wait until they were alone.

They were two of Will's favourite people in the whole world, and he was happy for them, and happy to be with them.

Mary excused herself to keep an eye on the boys, for congregation politics were of no interest to her.

Brewster searched Will's face. 'How are things back in Leyden?'

'Fraught. The delays have cost some brothers their nerve and we had to make up the numbers from those in Amsterdam. Indeed, Brother Robinson is angry at the new terms Master Weston has proposed and Brother Cushman has agreed to. Have you seen them?'

'I have,' Brewster said grimly.

'Brother Robinson says we are not to agree to it, not under any circumstances. And I have to say I agree with him. Weston would sell us as bond slaves!'

'That was my thought. It will destroy the colony.'

'Where is Cushman? I think we must discuss this with him.'

Brewster looked around him. 'The general feeling here is that everyone wants to discuss it with him!'

Will nodded. 'I see.' He cast a glance at the people on the quay. 'What think you of the Strangers?' The 'Strangers' were the people they did not know, who had not been of their congregation in Leyden, but who Weston had brought into the company to make up the numbers.

Brewster frowned. 'Some of them are God-fearing families. Others not of our persuasion, but still Godly. And others are . . . well.'

'I met some of them when I went to London.'

'Some have pulled out since then.'

'So I understand.' He shook his head. 'I knew Weston was not to be trusted.'

'Well, I might tell you, some of them here think he is little short of the King in authority!'

'Well, there were ever those short on brain!'

Brewster grinned. 'John Robinson is well?'

'Aye, and he sends his warmest Christian love, and—' he rummaged in his jerkin and pulled out the letter, now a little crumpled around the corners, '—he sent you this.'

William Brewster took it from Will, broke the seal and spread the sheet, and read it. 'For the whole congregation,' he said to Will.

'So I understand.'

Brewster folded it and put it in his own jerkin. 'Fine.' He looked at Will. 'Did Dorothy come after all?'

'Yes.'

Brewster looked at him sharply. 'But?'

Will said as carelessly as he could, 'We left Jonathan behind. Dorothy—that is we—agreed that the journey was too dangerous for him. I know you have brought your little ones with you, but Dorothy was sure he would be safer with her mother until we find out what we are going to. We will send for him later.'

Brewster frowned. 'Of course, you must do what you think is right.'

Will sighed, full of regrets, and he suddenly felt weary with it all. But it was too late now. 'Dorothy now wishes she had him with her. As I do. Perhaps it was not a good decision.'

'She blames you?'

Will winced. She did blame him. She had gone into deep melancholy, sitting in a corner of the deck, weeping to herself, ignoring everyone who tried to speak to her. She hadn't eaten anything since they embarked, and he was afraid that her strength would fail her. Still he managed a wry smile. 'I am the family head!'

Brewster clapped him on the shoulder. 'She will be alright.'

'You reckon?'

'Oh, women come round in time. And you can send for Jonathan to join you when we are settled.'

'It is difficult to part with them when they are so young,' Will said. 'Dorothy feels it more than I do.'

Brewster drew him away towards one of the taverns that lined the quay, and changed the subject. 'Tell me, how is Master Thomas Brewer?'

Christopher Jones, the captain of the *Mayflower* put the great cabin at their disposal for the meeting of the chief ones of the company. The passengers' spartan quarters were on the next deck, their bedding was straw, their only light came from covered lamps, there was no decoration, nor any furniture save for a few small stools and oak chests. The captain, however, had sumptuous carved, polished oak panels lining the great cabin, and a large black oak refectory table almost filled the available space, together with the ten or twelve carved oak chairs surrounding it. A bare wooden cross on one bulkhead, made the Pilgrims look at each other with ill-disguised disapproval, for they viewed such a display as idolatry. Still, they had more important things to worry about.

The men crowded into the room, those that were chief protagonists sat down on chairs, the rest stood leaning against the bulkheads as the ship rocked gently. It was hot in the cabin, even though the windows were open, and Will felt the sweat break out on his forehead. A smell of tar and damp, rotting wood, of hemp, of candlewax, of sulphur, of the sweat of bodies, and unwashed feet mingled in one nauseous odour, and the stays and timbers creaked and whined with the motion of the ship.

The meeting began with a prayer, offered by William Brewster, and straight afterward Will waded in. 'We cannot agree to these new terms, Master Cushman,' he stated bluntly. 'What did you think you were doing?'

Cushman shot him a defiant, and at the same time, hurt look. 'What did you want me to do? What was I supposed to do? If I had not agreed to the terms, Master Weston and his cronies would have pulled out. And then where would you all have been? I tell you, brother, I had no choice. If this expedition were to go ahead, I had to agree to Weston's demands.'

Will put his head in his hands to try and suppress the unchristian anger that surged through him. 'Do you know what you have done?'

'And what exactly have I done—*Brother*?' Cushman demanded awfully.

Will glared at him. 'You have sold us into bondage for seven years. We, who put our all into the project get less out of it than the men who risk only money—and money they can afford at that! We risk our lives, and at the end of seven years we do not even own our own land and houses that we have built with our own hands!'

'I had no choice,' Cushman said sulkily.

'Had no choice? Do you not realise that on these terms, we cannot pay back what we have been given?'

'What would you have me do? I could not ask you—you were in Leyden. So what was I supposed to do? Let Weston pull out? It was a close thing, I can tell you. It took all my persuasion to keep him in the scheme. When he saw your letter—.'

Will was outraged. 'You showed him our letter? You think it was something fit for him to see? A letter from us to you?'

Cushman's eyes flashed defiant again. 'Yes I did! And furthermore, I thought then we had lost it all! But *I* kept it all together.'

'Well I think you have done us ill!'

'And that is all the thanks I get for all my efforts? I tell you, William Bradford, this has been the most thankless task of any I have undertaken for the Lord's sake. I have done my best to make provisions in Kent, where it is cheaper, while that man Christopher Martin has used up money on what I do not know!' Christopher Martin uttered a sound of protest at this, but Cushman paid him no heed. 'I have gone to all the trouble of shipping them here. I have fought—yes sir, I have done battle—with that man Weston. I knew you were depending on me to keep things going here. You men had sold everything you owned in Leyden to finance this. Where would we all have been if Weston had pulled out? Well, I tell you, if this is all the thanks I get, I am sick of it!'

William Brewster flashed a warning at Will, and Will understood, and backed off. Cushman was at the end of his tether. He was tired, and he did not look well, and he had worked hard for the congregation. Brewster said placatingly, 'Well what is done is done. We do appreciate what you have done for us, Master Cushman, but as Master Bradford said, it has put us in a very difficult situation, and we have instructions from Brother Robinson not to agree to such a proposal. Master Weston is the man who has acted roguishly in this, putting everything in his favour.'

Christopher Martin, shook his thin bony head. 'I think that is unfair to Master Weston who has himself put a lot of work into this project to get patents and so on. As well as some of his own assets.'

'But he risks not life and limb like you do, Master Martin,' Will retorted, his anger still near the surface.

'I think you like not Master Weston because he is not of your persuasion, as some others of us are not.'

Will sighed with exasperation. 'You wrong us! We love all of God's creatures.'

'Then why did you speak so of Master Weston?'

Brewster stepped in. 'Because he is a rogue,' he said bluntly. 'An opportunist intent on making a fortune before he dies. And, unless I am much mistaken, at our expense!'

'My thoughts too,' Thomas Blossom added unexpectedly. 'Never trusted the man!'

Christopher Martin's eyes narrowed as he looked at them. 'He has made this project possible by his efforts.'

'We could have taken the Dutch offer,' Cushman pointed out sulkily.

'That would not have been a bad idea,' Brewster muttered.

John Carver leaned forward, putting his elbows on the table. 'It seems to me that all this remonstrating is of no value right now. The deed is done, for better or for worse. Brother Cushman did what he thought was right at the time. The fact that he showed lamentable want of brain is immaterial!'

Cushman made a choking sound but was immediately silenced by John Carver, who was in his stride. 'The situation is as it is. What we need to do now is decide what our next action will be. Brother Cushman, are we to expect Master Weston to meet us here?'

Robert Cushman nodded. 'We owe him some money, and he wants

the agreement signed.'

'Very well. I suggest gentlemen, that instead of arguing among ourselves and beating Brother Cushman about the ears, we should speak to the real perpetrator.'

'Agreed,' Brewster said flatly.

So, when Weston came aboard the *Mayflower* at noon, to his consternation he found everyone awaiting him in the Great Cabin. His shrewish little eyes opened wide, and he expressed surprise, but the Pilgrims were not letting him get away lightly.

William Brewster indicated a chair. 'Sit down, please, Master Weston.'

'What is this?' Weston demanded, alarm showing in his face. 'I seek only formal confirmation of the new conditions.'

Will said flatly, 'That's as maybe, sir, but we are all here to tell you that we disagree with the new conditions.'

Appalled and nervous, Weston looked around at the faces. 'Even you, Master Martin?'

'Even me,' Christopher Martin told him solemnly.

'And you, Master Tilley? Master Chilton?'

'We are all here together,' Brewster said. 'The new conditions are not according to the first agreement.'

'Well, no. But I hope Master Cushman has informed you of the reason for the change. My backers were pulling out. They did not wish to commit themselves to such a flimsy escapade as this—'

'It seemed not so flimsy when they first agreed,' Will said bluntly.

'True. But as time went on—I had to make it worth their while to invest.'

'You mean you hoped to make a tidy profit.'

'Master Bradford—I know you are suspicious of my motives.'

'That's right!'

'But you must consider my position.'

'I am not interested in your position,' Will told him intractably. 'Our responsibility is to the men and women who are risking their lives in this venture when all you are risking is excess money. We are not going to sign this new agreement, sir. None of us.'

Weston's shrew-like face and beady eyes widened in panic. 'But you must!'

Will met his eyes steadily and saw the man wilt. 'No. We refuse to confirm these new conditions. You knew right well that these are not according to the first agreement, and neither could we yield to them without the consent of the rest that we have left behind in Leyden. And indeed, we were especially charged when we came away from the chief ones we left behind that we must not agree to it.'

Thomas Weston's rodent features darkened, and he stood up. 'How dare you suggest, sir, that I am doing something improper.'

'You must think us incredibly stupid, Master Weston,' Will said.

'Well, in that case, sir, you must stand on your own legs.'

'You still owe us a hundred pounds to clear things so we can go.'

'I will not give you another penny,' Weston retorted. 'You must shift as best you can!'

And with that he stalked from the cabin and Will heard him demanding to be taken ashore.

Will put his head in his hands, only too well aware that they were now short of a hundred pounds. And a hundred pounds was a mountainous sum.

'Now what shall we do?' Christopher Martin demanded. 'I rather think that is the end of our voyage. A hundred pounds! And where will we find that?'

John Carver said joyously, 'We can sell some of the provisions.'

'Won't that leave us short?' Isaac Allerton asked.

Strangely, it was Christopher Martin who answered. 'Well actually, owing to someone's over-zealousness,' he glanced at the hapless Cushman, 'we have more butter than we need, or indeed have space for. Captain Jones has lamented long and loud at the amount we have. And we can live without butter.'

'Let's do it!'

They sold some four-score firkins of butter, that is 3,360 to 4,720 pounds of butter, as well as oil, and leather which had been intended to mend shoes with, and some gave up their swords too which caused consternation to the man Will had added to the passenger list, Captain Miles Standish. Standish, lamented long and loud. They would not have enough arms to defend themselves, he prophesied dourly.

But they managed to raise sixty pounds which cleared the debts and allowed them to leave the haven.

On August the fourth 1620, William Brewster gathered all the passengers together on the *Mayflower*'s deck and read to them the parting letter from John Robinson.

Robinson first told them how he wished he were going with them, bearing with them the difficulty of being the first to go. Then he urged them to repent of their sins, in case God should call them to account and swallow them up by some danger or another. At length he warned them about giving offence to each other, and of being quick to take offence. Obviously, not only in the close association they would have during the voyage but also afterwards when they settled, there would be many causes for friction. By being careful not to give offence and not taking offence when none was intended, things would run along more smoothly. Besides, he added, it was the Godly way, as set out in scripture, and he quoted several scriptures to the point. He reminded them also that there were strangers among them, people who were not of their faith, whose imperfections they did not know, and with whom they must learn to live in harmony.

And lastly he advised them as to civil government. They did not have in their midst special men of rank and ability; they were all equal. But they should appoint an honourable man to be governor or magistrate, and they must give him all due honour. He then commended them to God. 'Fare you well in Him in whom you trust, and in whom I rest,' he said.

Thus strengthened, the passengers made ready for the voyage. Those for the *Speedwell* returning to it, and choosing a governor over the passengers, and two or three assistants for each ship at the request of the captains, to see to the management of the passengers and their belongings. Christopher Martin became governor of the *Mayflower,* with Robert Cushman as his assistant. Most of the Leyden people were on the *Speedwell* still, John Carver and William Brewster joining their wives there.

On the morning of fifth day of August 1620, the *Mayflower* and the *Speedwell* set sail from the West Quay at Southampton, later than was prudent, but still within the limits of safety. Ahead of them lay a voyage of perhaps four weeks if they had favourable winds.

Will joined other passengers on deck to watch.

To the rhythm of a chant, the sailors slotted the spars into the windlass which resembled a huge cotton reel lying on its side, and cranked it up, as the great tarred hawser bearing the anchor wound around the reel, bringing the anchor slowly up to the cathead where they fixed it.

A different chant with a different rhythm accompanied the hoisting of the main yard. They sheeted the mainsail home.

Reynolds then gave out the order, 'Make fast the halyards!'

'Make fast the halyards!' echoed the officer.

'Set tops'ls. Haul tops'l sheets!'

Men scrambled up the shrouds and out onto the yards.

Will watched with ill-concealed admiration for the courage of such men. He was no coward, but to actually walk out onto a yardarm, with nothing more to support him than a footrope, and whatever a man might cling to, with the deck or the sea some sixty to a hundred feet below, while the gentle rocking of the ship translated at the top of the mast into terrible dizzying swaying of the yards through a hundred degrees or more, was more than he thought a human being ought to have to do. But these men made light work of it.

Fingers fiddled with reefs, and then at the command the whole ship was gowned in pale grey sail, which glowed white in the dazzling sunlight.

'Master Coppin—keep her full and by . . .'

The men in the yards came down, and the arduous task of tacking into the wind began.

Robert Coppin, the *Speedwell's* pilot guided them down Southampton Water and through the difficult waters of the English Channel.

The *Mayflower* rode with them in stately splendour, a larger ship, a queen with her tiny consort.

Ahead lay perhaps four weeks if the winds were favourable, and then America.

TWENTY-FOUR
False Starts

August, 1620

Will leaned on the gunwale and peered down into the dark blue depths. He fancied he could see the bottom, if he looked hard enough, despite the gentle swell of waves on the surface which caught the light at every movement. The weather was good, and he knew they made good headway.

He was surprised, then, to see Captain Reynolds approaching him, a forbidding expression on his face.

'I don't like it,' he told Will, as he came near enough to be heard above the sound of the wind in the sails, the slap of water against the hull, the cries of the men who 'sweated up', that is tightened the ropes that held the sails which worked loose of their own accord. 'The cargo is overweight. See how she sits in the water! And I don't like the cut of her jib.'

Will raised his brows questioningly.

'Her sails. She needs trimming,' Reynolds explained.

'But she was re-rigged and trimmed with new masts and spars in Holland,' Will pointed out. ''Tis a little late now to decide you don't like what you oversaw then, and later still to criticise the cargo which you agreed to.'

Captain Reynolds looked up into the rigging, frowning and tutting, and so did Will. It seemed alright to him. But then what did he know? A triangle of white sails against a clear blue sky, what could be more perfect?

'So what do you suggest?' Will asked.

Reynolds pulled a face, and shook his head. 'Damned if I know. But it don't look good.'

Will walked away from him. He had not formed a good opinion of the man. Reynolds did not like the Pilgrims—Bible thumpers he called them—and grew impatient with their prayers and their sermons. Since Captain Reynolds had been commissioned with the ship to stay in America with them for a whole year, Will wondered how they were going to get on with such an unfavourable beginning.

He went down to the lower deck, where the passengers had set up some temporary berths for themselves and their families, screened off by curtains. It was dark here, the only light coming from glass-covered lanterns which swung joyfully from the deck head beams. It stank as well. Some had been seasick, and some had used the buckets, which they must. The deck head above was only five feet from the deck they stood on, so that a man could not stand up straight, nor walk upright. There were no proper beds, not even hammocks. They slept on straw on the deck, and Will fervently hoped it was not going to be a long voyage. He foresaw all kinds of difficulties ahead if it were.

He found Dorothy sitting by herself in their own curtained-off berth, her face turned towards the bulwark. His heart sank. He knew the signs of Dorothy in melancholy, and things had only got worse since they left England. 'Do you feel unwell?' he asked.

She shrugged. 'A little.'

He came into the berth and sat down on the chest, which was the only comfortable position for him. 'What ails you then?'

She turned huge saucer-like eyes upon him, and in the small light, her face was ashen. 'I want to go home,' she whispered pitifully.

His heart wrenched and he was wracked by guilt. He tried to reason. 'We have nothing to go home to.'

'Our son. We have our son.'

Will bowed his head in dismay. He had not realised this would be such a problem. He said, 'I miss him too.' Perhaps as a father he missed his son less than the boy's mother would. Certainly he did not understand her distress.

She turned on him then. 'No you do not! You are not his mother, I am. What do you care about him? All you care about is your duties as an elder and—and for the congregation, and this voyage. You haven't had time for us. Our son means nothing to you.'

He was shocked by her outburst, and acutely aware that only a curtain of material separated them from interested ears. 'Dorothy!'

Mary Brewster came over to them. 'Are you ill, Dorothy?' she demanded quite stridently.

Will looked at her gratefully.

Mary jerked her head, a signal for him to go. He obeyed. There was no dealing with Dorothy when she was in this mood.

He joined William Brewster in his corner, and sat down beside him.

'What's the problem?' Brewster asked.

'She misses Jonathan,' Will explained, and he felt his heart turn to lead within him. Ahead of them was a long journey, and a great deal of hardship. He needed a supportive wife, or one that would meet him half way, not this depressive selfish little hellcat who turned on him and belittled him, and worse, embarrassed him before everyone else.

'Well, you knew it would be difficult to leave Jonathan behind.'

'I did. But I thought it was best. Now I don't know.'

'Hear that?' Brewster asked after a moment.

Will knew it alright. Who could forget the rhythmic thud and whoosh, the backbreaking sound of the bilge pump? It had been in operation on that dreadful voyage when he first left England for Holland. He would never forget the terrible sound.

'We are taking in water,' Will said, deliberately keeping his voice low. 'Captain Reynolds told me he was not happy about the ship. He did not like the "cut of her jib".'

'She was careened in Delftshaven, was she not?'

'Careened?'

'Hauled out of the water, her hulls scraped and painted with a mixture of sulphur, tallow and tar to keep out the worm that eats into ships' timbers. If it is not done regularly, a ship will soak up water like a sponge.'

'I don't know. I did not see.'

'Aye—you had enough to do.'

'Well,' Will was not easy on himself, 'I should have taken notice.' He sighed. 'So what now?'

'We'll have to see what the master says.'

'And what'll that be, I wonder.'

He did not have to wonder long. Four days out of Southampton, the weather turned nasty. A gale sprung up and the sky turned a uniform grey. The wind brought up the waves, and tugged at the sails and lines, and the ship began to buck and heave in that peculiar way of rising on one wave and crashing down into the hole between it and the next with a jarring that made those below think they had struck rocks.

And the *Speedwell* began to leak badly.

Captain Reynolds sent for Will.

'We have to turn back and get the *Speedwell* repaired,' he said.

'Turn back?' Will was aghast. 'But we are four days out of Southampton and presumably four days back.'

'We can put in at Dartmouth. But I tell you, Master Bradford, that the ship is leaking badly, and if we do not get her repaired, she will sink before we cross the Atlantic.'

Will had to agree. After all, people's lives were at stake.

Accordingly Captain Reynolds hailed Captain Jones of the *Mayflower* and told him that they must return and get the *Speedwell* repaired.

So they turned back, and put into the lee of the point below the Mewstone at Dartmouth in Devon, and into the sanctuary of the beautiful estuary of the River Dart.

If one had to stop, it was as nice a place as any. The passengers and cargo were put out onto the grassy banks and the *Speedwell* was hauled over onto her side, for all the world like a fat-bottomed woman displaying her nether regions to all, while both crews got to work on solving the problem.

It cost time. Too much time.

'We are eating our supplies and going nowhere,' Will fumed.

For once Brewster was silent, for he was as angry as Will. This was bad management on the part of Captain Reynolds, he felt. It was his responsibility to make sure that he had a sea-worthy vessel.

Robert Cushman joined them from the other ship. 'I am grateful for the chance to be on dry land again,' he remarked, sitting down on the grass beside Will, the upset on the *Mayflower* earlier evidently forgiven or forgotten. 'Been sick as a dog, you know.'

'Aye. So has my wife. And others,' Brewster said. In fact the *Speedwell* passengers were just as pleased to get off the ship, for it reeked of vomit. 'But this delay will cost us dearly.'

'This voyage is full of mishaps,' Cushman said gloomily. 'We have as fair a wind as ever can blow and we wait here for this ship to be mended!'

Will exchanged glances with Brewster. He began to have an uneasy feeling. Did they not have the Lord's blessing after all?

'The *Speedwell* is as leaky as a sieve,' Brewster told them. 'I saw a board a man might pull off with his fingers, two foot long, and the water poured in through it. I saw it myself.'

'Deliberate?' Will asked quietly.

Brewster frowned. 'What think you?'

'I think it sits ill with Master Reynolds to have to spend a year with us in New England. I think he does not like this voyage at all.'

Cushman frowned, and let his breath go in a whistle through his teeth.

Brewster said, 'I sincerely hope you are wrong, Will.'

'He is rarely wrong when it comes to people,' Cushman said disarmingly. 'Are you, brother?'

Will could not make out whether he meant it, or whether Cushman was being sarcastic. 'How goes it on the *Mayflower*?' he asked.

Cushman sighed. 'The passengers fall to arguing. I ain't seen so much arguing since I was in the world. Which I suppose most of them are. As for Master Martin—well I tell you if that man makes landfall in New England without being hanged first . . .'

'Bad as that?'

'I discovered that nearly seven hundred pounds was spent at Hampton on what, I know not.'

'That's a lot of money,' Brewster said.

'What does Martin say?' Will asked.

'He says he knows nothing about it. When I said I wanted to see the accounts, he cried out that we are suspicious of him, and cut up rough.'

'I don't like the sound of that,' Brewster said.

'You mean he stopped you investigating,' Will said.

'Well, I don't want to seem like I am suspicious of him,' Cushman hedged.

'But you are.'

'Yes indeed.' Cushman frowned, perplexed. 'I ought to tackle him, but I tell you, Will, I don't quite know how to go about it.'

It was a dilemma. Whilst the Pilgrims knew that not everyone could be trusted, nevertheless they did not like to accuse anyone of anything improper. For that was what it amounted to.

'And there is another thing,' Cushman added, warming to his theme, 'he insults us and treats us with scorn and contempt, as if we were not good enough to wipe his shoes. The brethren complain to me, but what can I do? If I speak to him, he flies in my face, tells me I'm mutinous, that I can complain to no-one but himself because he is the leader, and says the brothers are discontented people, and bad tempered, and I should not listen to them. Some are actually saying they want to leave everything and go home, even though they would lose everything. But Christopher Martin will not allow them ashore in case they run away! What kind of a situation is this? I thought we were free men!'

Brewster frowned and tugged at a tuft of grass. 'We would have a man like that inflicted on us!'

'How did you manage to come ashore then, brother?' Will asked.

'I slipped off when no-one was looking. Bribed one of the sailors to let me in the boat.'

'Well, I did not think the Devil would let us off lightly,' Brewster observed.

'Well, as to that, perhaps we will get off lightly on that score,' Cushman continued darkly. 'For I tell you, the sailors are ready to do him mischief if he continues to meddle in their affairs.' He shook his head gloomily. 'I reckon that if ever we make a plantation, God works a miracle. Not only that, there is fighting and anger among the company. And I thought these were God's people.'

Will took a deep breath. 'You cannot blame them. We have been many days already cooped up on ships going nowhere, and not all your passengers are the Lord's people. And they are sick and anxious.'

They fell silent and they all looked across the stretch of impossibly blue water to where the *Speedwell* was being mended and the *Mayflower* rode quietly at anchor.

'Well, and you have added to my burdens,' Cushman added sullenly.

Will looked at him. 'Oh?'

'Aye. You came here determined not to confirm the agreement and conditions. You have put me in a difficult position. Weston is not pleased. He will hate us now, and I am sure we will rue the day we crossed him.'

'And ought we to have sold our brothers into slavery?' Will demanded.

Cushman stood up and Will shielding his eyes to look up at him, suddenly saw that he was worn out with the anxiety of it all. He was sick, from grief and anger and worry as well as seasickness, and he was hurt. Will was sorry for it, for he loved all his brothers, and cared about their welfare. He stood up too, and put his large hand on Cushman's arm.

Cushman looked at him with dark sorrowful eyes, and then put his own hand on Will's. 'I can't be putting up with much more.'

'The Lord will sustain us,' Will told him. 'He will sustain us all.'

A few days later the *Speedwell* was righted and they set sail once more.

Will went topside to find some space, some fresh air and some privacy so that he could pray to his God. On open deck the weather had turned cooler, although the days were still bright, the wind ruffling his shoulder-length brown curls, and whipped his cloak about him. Below, the sea rose in sickening peaks and corresponding holes, and the *Speedwell* had taken up that jarring rhythm of riding up and down the waves.

'I hate this ship!' Dorothy announced suddenly in a vicious hiss in Will's ear, and he spun round, by no means pleased to have his solitude interrupted. His heart sank as he registered her words, the crossness on her face. It was that look that he had come to dread, only varying in intensity from the harsh depression which had plagued their married life.

'It will not be long ere we are in New England,' he said consolingly.

As the ship plunged again, she grabbed the gunwale and he put his arm around her to stop her falling. 'New England. America. That is all you care about! What about me?'

Will looked at her straightly. 'What about you?' he countered.

Her anger grew, as he knew it would. He did not have the knack of pacifying her. 'I hate it here! I hate this ship! Everything is damp. It smells. There is no privacy. And I feel sick all the time!'

'We are all suffering discomfort. Your position is no worse than anyone else's.'

'I wish we had not come!'

'I told you how it would be,' Will reminded her. 'I told you it would be uncomfortable crossing the Atlantic. I told you to stay with Jonathan.'

'And leave you alone so that you can dream of that—that witch!'

He reeled as his stomach turned over. He felt as if she had slapped him. 'What did you say?'

She knew she had gone too far, and lowered her eyes. 'Nothing. I said nothing. Forgive me, I feel not myself this morning.' She went to go past him, but he grabbed her arm. 'What did you mean?' he demanded roughly.

She looked up at him then, her lovely face pale with sickness, and contorted with anger. 'You think I don't know. I saw the way you looked at her. When she went away I thought that was an end to it. How wrong I was! You go and you stay with her, and when you come back you think I don't know anything!'

'You speak rubbish, woman.'

'I know you, William Bradford. I am your wife!'

'Well, 'tis a pity you don't show it then!'

'How dare you talk to me like that!'

'Before God I have been true to you, even though you be not a true wife to me! You malign me, and you malign an innocent woman, do call her an adulteress and me an adulterer! You have an evil suspicious mind, and a wicked tongue!'

Her rage was at boiling point now. William Brewster's voice interrupted them. 'Now then, you two, we can hear you all over the ship.'

'I must go below,' Dorothy said, and took herself off.

Brewster joined Will at the gunwale.

For some time neither man spoke, but Will stared broodingly at the rocking sea, at the huge mountains of water, at the clear depths. He felt sick inside, shocked that all this time she had nursed this grievance. At the same time the grief and guilt he felt over Alice washed over him afresh. In any case what did she mean that she had seen the way he looked at Alice? For she must have meant Alice. He had not fallen in love with Alice until London—had he?

'What ails Dorothy?' Brewster asked.

Will shrugged and struggled to control the unmanly tears which had started to his eyes. 'I notice she is crotchety before her menses.'

Brewster frowned. 'Is that so?' And Will had the feeling he did not think for one moment that was the problem.

He wondered how much Brewster had heard. Did he know what Dorothy accused him of? Effectively she had threatened him with denouncing him to the elders. One step to expelling. Even if they could not prove anything, just to make the accusation would cost him his good name, and would mean that he was no longer above reproach, no longer suitable to be an elder. And she threatened Alice's good name also, she too having to face a judicial court in her own congregation and the trouble that would cause her. In the name of all that was sacred, did he not have enough to deal with?

Evidently not.

'You know the ship's leaking again,' Brewster said.

Will looked at him sharply. 'You know this?'

Brewster said, 'You mark the men working on the pump?'

At the moment the pump was quiet, but the men were already taking their positions to work at it, and its rhythmic clanking had kept them awake for most of the night.

Will dropped his head to his forearms resting on the gunwale rail. *No more!* 'What does Captain Reynolds say?'

'Nothing yet. But he will.'

He did.

Three hundred miles off Land's End and he informed them they would have to turn back again. He again consulted Captain Jones on the *Mayflower*.

'This ship is so leaky that I must bear up, or sink at sea.'

Captain Jones swore profanely. Under the circumstances Will and Brewster and Carver excused it. They felt like swearing too. They were heading well into autumn, and they now had to go back to England—again!

So they turned back again, and put into Plymouth, Devon, and once more they hauled her on her side. They could find nothing wrong.

''Tis a general weakness of the ship,' Captain Jones of the *Mayflower* told the passengers, standing beside Captain Reynolds. 'To my mind she is overmasted.'

'And what does that mean?' Will asked.

Captain Jones eyed Captain Reynolds. 'When she was refitted, she was given too much mast, and too much sail. Such a small ship cannot bear it. It causes her to labour in heavy weather, opening up her seams and losing the oakum which plugs the gaps.'

'So what do you suggest, Captain Jones?' Will asked.

'I suggest you dismiss the *Speedwell*, and those of your company who wish to depart—' he cast a weather eye at Christopher Martin whose policies had irritated him beyond measure '—load the remaining provisions and belongings into the *Mayflower*, and proceed alone.'

There was a murmur among the assembled throng, and Captain Jones and Captain Reynolds went off alone together while the company discussed it among themselves.

The situation had assumed nightmare proportions. It was late now. Ridiculously late to be thinking of crossing the Atlantic. But what choice did they have? To give up now would lose them all the money and possessions and the backing they had worked so hard for.

'The Devil has manoeuvred us into an impossible situation,' Will complained to Brewster and Carver. 'We are now to leave at the most difficult time of the year.'

'We have no choice,' Brewster pointed out unnecessarily.

There were many who chose not to go after all, viewing the risks as too great. Robert Cushman and his wife, and Thomas Blossom and his son were among them.

Cushman had had enough. He was fed up with bearing the blame for everything that went wrong, fed up with the recriminations that Will laid at his door. And he was sick. He felt betrayed, and he was physically ill.

The work of off-loading the passengers and their belongings and the provisions from the *Speedwell* and getting them aboard the *Mayflower* began. Captain Jones protested as Captain Reynolds had before him, about the immense screw that Edward Winslow brought aboard, but Winslow disarmed him as he had Captain Reynolds.

At last all was ready.

On the sixth day of September 1620, a month and a day since they first set sail, they put to sea again, one hundred and two passengers, all crowded onto one ship, the *Mayflower*.

TWENTY-FIVE
The *Mayflower*

September 1620

The *Mayflower* was blessed with a prosperous wind. Prosperous, perhaps, but a fair wind meant a rough sea. The *Mayflower* heaved and plunged constantly. It made Will's head ache, and his knees and legs turned to jelly, but he found that as long as he stayed on deck, he could cope without actually giving up the contents of his stomach.

Not so the majority of the passengers particularly the women and children who did not venture on deck because of the weather, or because they were so ill. Each false start had meant that they had to find their sea legs all over again, and some found the rough weather unbearable. They were confined below in a black noisome space some twenty-two feet across the beam narrowing dramatically at each end, and perhaps fifty feet long. They shared the space with their personal belongings, which did not amount to much, and the huge trunk of the mainmast which went through all the decks and into the ballast in the bottom of the ship. Bulkheads divided up the space, and so did black blankets, acting as curtains affording each family a little privacy. A tiny space with a curtain acting as a door, served as privacy so that the women could use the buckets. The men, sailors and passengers, used the head which was on open deck at the bow of the ship and overhanging the sea. A precarious perch in the best of times, in bad weather it was under water half the time as the ship carved a passage through mountainous green waves. A man had to choose his moment carefully if he were not to find himself overboard. As it was he might well get a good soaking. Certainly it was not an option for the women who would have been in full view of the crew, and far too dangerous for the children.

Dorothy found the confinement below decks more irksome than anything she had hitherto experienced, and she suffered from terrible seasickness. She languished in the berth she and Will shared, lying prone on the pallet of straw, and complained that she would surely die.

'Nonsense,' Mary Brewster said briskly when Dorothy confided her fears to her. 'No-one ever died of seasickness. In a few days you will get your sea legs, and then you will feel well again.'

'We have been on one ship or another for nigh on two months,' Dorothy complained. 'Will doesn't understand. He has no sympathy for me. He does not care about me.'

Mary had heard it all before. 'Oh really! I happen to know that Will is not feeling as well as he might, as none of us are. And of course he cares for you. He is your husband.'

'You don't know,' Dorothy said darkly.

Mary Brewster took a breath. 'What don't I know?' she demanded impatiently.

Dorothy turned her face to the bulkhead. 'No-one cares about me. No-one cares how I feel.'

'Fiddle!' Mary snapped. 'You wallow in your own self-pity young lady. You are not the only one to have left your child behind. I've left four behind, and buried a fifth. At least your son is hale and hearty, and in good spirits. And you have a good man in Will. He will never hurt you or do anything wrong. He is strong for the Lord.'

'Yes, he's that alright!'

'Do you know, Dorothy, I have often wondered why he puts up with your continual whingeing, and weeping and self-pity. A man needs a woman who will take care of him, and look after his needs and above all love him.'

Dorothy turned back and raised herself up on one elbow. 'What has he been saying?'

'He has said nothing. He wouldn't say anything disloyal. But I have eyes in my head and you have lived with me for some time. I can see what is going on. In my opinion, Dorothy, you would do well to look to yourself, and to try to mend whatever it is that is causing you and Will to be apart.'

'You always take his part.'

'I take both your parts. But our men have a lot ahead of them. A great deal of responsibility, and a lot of work. It is not going to be easy on anyone. A man does not need a contentious and nagging wife who does nothing but dig at him and holds him back in anything he does. Every time he goes to some meeting, or away for some other reason, he does not need a wife who says that he is neglecting her!'

'I don't.'

'Oh, but you do. Now pull yourself together and stop feeling sorry for yourself. You are not alone in this, you know.'

And with that she got up from the small stool on which she sat and marched across the deck to her own berth, full of righteous indignation.

Mary was right. In three or four days Dorothy's insides settled down. Feeling better physically, she rose from her bed. But she was still unhappy. Whatever Mary might say, she missed her young son so much that it was a physical pain. She was convinced she would never see again that perfect round little face with the shy smile, and the blonde curls. She ached to hold him in her arms, to be there to comfort him. And the more she thought of him, the further down she sank into deep depression.

The days wore on, and the golden September days turned gradually colder. Still, it was fine enough for the passengers to go topside, where they strolled about as if they were walking in an English garden. The children found open deck a wonderful place for playing hide and seek, or for running races up and down, uncoiling ropes and tying each other up in them, and the bolder even dared to swing out onto the ratlines the way they had seen the sailors do and climb up the rigging. They hampered the sailors whose cursing and swearing were not fit for a Christian's ears, let alone the delicate ears of one's offspring.

'I tell you, I shall die of fright!' Mary Brewster complained to her husband about her son Love who had led his younger brother Wrestling in such an escapade which had caused his mother to scream out in terror as she beheld them clinging like frightened monkeys to what appeared to her to be flimsy ropes.

Brewster eyed his sons standing before him, both of them with their heads bowed, their hands behind them. 'Now what have I told you?' he demanded in accents which did not invite an answer.

Both boys mumbled an apology.

'You, Love,' William Brewster said at his most awful, 'are older than Wrestling. You are responsible for him. What if he had slipped and fallen into the sea?'

'I'm sorry, Father,' Love mumbled.

'Sorry? Is that all you can say?'

Love said nothing. He couldn't think of anything else to say. He raised his serious grey eyes to his father's and they were full of tears. He had always been a sensitive boy, the kind of child who rarely did anything wrong. It always came as a surprise to his parents when he did occasionally slip up, for they never expected it. Like now.

'What possessed you?' William Brewster demanded.

'I—I didn't think of the danger. I didn't realise . . . It was only when I looked down and saw the sea below me . . .'

'I saw it all,' Will said approaching them, 'if you will forgive me, Brother Brewster. I saw young Wrestling teasing his brother, and saying he would go to the top of the mast, and when Love tried to stop him, Wrestling got away from him and was up the ratlines before anyone could move. Love went after him to stop him, I think. Without a thought for his own safety. The rest you know.'

Brewster raised his brows at Will, and then turned to his son, a light shining in his own eyes. 'Well, then, Love, it seems you are to be commended. Brother Bradford has saved you from a beating.'

Love turned grateful eyes upon Will. 'Thank you, sir.'

Will nodded.

Brewster turned to Wrestling. 'As for you young man—'

Wrestling was always in trouble, the daredevil, the one who had no fear, who cared not what beatings he incurred. A harsh word could reduce Love to tears. Not even a severe beating could do that to Wrestling, young as he was!

Will left them.

Christopher Martin caught his attention. 'Captain Jones has asked to see us.'

'Us?'

'You and me.'

'Why me? You are the governor of this ship.'

'How should I know?'

They found Captain Jones in the sumptuous great cabin, sitting at the table and writing in a book. He put the pen in the standish as they entered, and stood up. 'Ah, Master Martin. Master Bradford. Thank you for coming.'

'There is a problem, Captain?' Will asked.

Christopher Jones was an experienced sailor of at least forty years of age, with a beautiful full gold and white beard, and a mass of dark curly hair. It was difficult to see what colour his eyes were, for they were swallowed up by the creases around them, the result of years squinting against the sun, but they missed nothing. He went back to his table, sanded the wet ink on the page, blew it off, and then shut the book. 'Gentlemen, as you are aware, this ship was not built for passengers. It is a working vessel and my men must work.'

'So—what is that to me?' Martin demanded.

Christopher Jones stared at the man as though he were an idiot and then turned his attention to Will who he evidently thought more amenable. 'To put it shortly, your people are getting in the way, and you cannot have missed the arguments that have taken place.'

'So what?' Martin said again, deliberately drawing the captain's eyes back to him. 'People argue all the time. Even Bible-thumpers.'

Christopher Jones shot a look at Will who did not betray that the jibe had hit its mark. Will said calmly, 'What would you have us do, Captain?'

'I would like you to confine your people below as much as possible,' Jones said.

'Preposterous,' Martin exploded. 'You cannot keep us cooped up like criminals!'

Will said calmly, 'Perhaps, captain, we could allow the passengers on deck, say, twice a day to stretch their legs and get some fresh air, and see to necessary things?'

'I think that might serve, Master Bradford. The children though are still a worry. The ship is a dangerous place for unsupervised children. It would be wonderful if we made landfall and had not had a fatal accident on board.'

'We will see to it.'

Christopher Martin opened, and then shut his mouth. There was little he could say.

'Thank you gentlemen,' Captain Jones said and inclined his head.

As they left the great cabin Master Martin turned to Will. 'Well, you can tell 'em,' he announced to Will. 'I won't.'

Will knew the passengers would not like it, but he remained unruffled. 'As you wish, Master Martin.'

Christopher Martin stormed off, leaving Will alone on the deck watching his skinny retreating figure.

The thought occurred to him that he did not like Christopher Martin, and he remembered what Robert Cushman had said of him. Usually Will liked most people, or perhaps more accurately did not form an opinion of them but took them as they were. It was unusual for him to take a dislike to someone, particularly a strong dislike. But he had done so for Christopher Martin. The man was insufferable, the irritating kind of tyrant who refused to listen to anyone, who always knew best, who imposed his will without kindness or restraint. And Martin hated the Pilgrims. Why he wanted to join them in the venture in the first place was anyone's guess!

Captain Jones had a point. While the ship pitched and the sailors heaved on ropes to tighten them or 'sweat up' the lines and stays, the passengers were everywhere, in the way.

'Just look at it!'

Will turned. The voice was familiar. Since leaving Plymouth it had been the same taunt. A stocky young man the Pilgrims nicknamed Rabshakeh, because of his constant taunting of their God and their faith. Rab for short, one of the crew, as hale and hearty as anyone could be, stood on the ratlines, at home as if he had been born there. His attention and his vitriolic comments were directed at poor Rose Standish, the army captain's wife, who retched ignominiously over the side while Katherine Carver held her comfortingly. 'Ain't got no stomach, none of you! Milksops the lot o' ye. Where's yer God now? Eh?'

Will went towards him, and stood in front of him. 'Don't you know when to stop?' he demanded, and some of his anger showed in his voice. 'Can't you see that gentlewoman suffer the most?'

'Why don't yer God put a stop to yer agues? If he sees ye that is. Or perhaps he can't. Perhaps he can't hear ye! Damned Bible pushers! Think God is with ye, do ye? Well I tell you I look forward to seeing just half yer number, the rest pitched over the side! You ain't got no business on a ship! Damn me, ye'll all die before we get to Americky, and good riddance!'

Will's anger seethed in his brain, and he felt his hands ball into fists. 'You would do better to hold your tongue, friend,' he said, dangerously quiet.

"Rabshakeh" met his eyes defiantly. 'And what'll you do about it, Puritan?' And he let go a string of blasphemies that drew an exclamation from another sailor nearby.

Will was bigger than this man, yet probably no match for him. For Will had no experience of brawling. Even so, his anger overcame his good sense, and he took a step towards him.

William White put a restraining hand on his arm. 'Leave him be, Will. He ain't worth it.'

No, it wasn't worth it. A fight would prove nothing, and would make him answerable to the congregation. With an effort, he forced himself to turn and go below, the man's laughing taunts stinging his ears.

William Brewster caught him as he passed, and Will turned aside and sat down on the wooden chest in Brewster's berth. 'What ails you, Will?' he demanded abruptly. 'Is it 'Rab'?'

Will gave him the gist of what had happened. 'That young man needs teaching a lesson,' he said.

'And you're the one to do it? I think not.'

Will gave a reluctant laugh. 'No, I think not too.'

'Leave him be.' Brewster advised. 'After all, remember what happened to the original Rabshakeh.'

'The Lord killed him along with a hundred and eighty-five thousand other Assyrians.'

'And our friend will meet his comeuppance once day.' That was the end of that subject and Brewster moved on. 'What did Captain Jones want?'

Will sighed. 'He is concerned about the number of people on deck, particularly the little ones who he says rightly are in danger if they are not supervised. Others get in the way of the work the sailors must do. We will have to limit everyone to just two periods on open deck.'

Brewster grimaced. 'So is Martin going to tell them?'

'No. I am.'

Will put it to them in the most tactful way that he could, but there were groans of dismay. For between decks there was little light, it was cold, it was smelly, the headroom was just five feet, and the conditions cramped.

'Well I ain't staying below every day,' someone said and in the gloom Will saw big John Billington sitting defiantly, his meaty arms folded across his chest, his full-bearded chin raised mutinously. 'I'll be damned if anyone will tell me what to do.'

Will mustered as much patience as he could. 'We are all suffering the same conditions, Master Billington. Of course, we would all like to be on open deck as much as possible. But Captain Jones is master of this ship, and what he says is law. We must not hamper the work of the sailors, and we must be particularly cautious with our little ones.'

'I'll do what I damned well please, and ain't no Bible basher going to tell me what to do!'

'Then you must bear the consequences,' Will snapped at the end of his tether. He'd had enough for one day.

Brewster put a restraining hand on his arm, and Will took a breath and focused on the rest of them sitting in front of him. 'I think if we keep the children occupied, with lessons, with singing songs, stories and the like, and when they are on deck, keep a good eye on them, then I think we will serve. We have a long voyage ahead of us, and we must all co-operate as best we may.'

'I suppose you are going to pray now,' Billington growled sarcastically.

John Carver, who was as big as Billington, boomed, 'And that's what God-fearing folk do, *Master* Billington. If you don't like it, you shouldn't have come!'

After that, the passengers went on deck only at certain times. And the children only under supervision. It meant long tedious hours below in the darkness, and there were times when people defied the orders, but Captain Jones was impressed by the general compliance of the passengers, and impressed with Will whom he saw had the ability to take charge.

TWENTY-SIX
Guilt

The Mayflower, October 1620

Sunday was the Sabbath, the day of Bible study and prayer. William Brewster was a teaching elder, and he led in worship the small congregation which included the Mullins family, the Hopkins, the Tilleys and the Chiltons. It afforded 'Rabshakeh' the opportunity for more verbal abuse, making jokes among his friends at their expense. The Pilgrims ignored him.

Later, Will found Brewster eating his noon-day meal alone at one end of the gun deck and he saw it as an opportunity to speak to him, sitting down on a small stool beside him. 'Why do you think things went so ill with the *Speedwell?*' Will asked.

Brewster carved himself a piece of rock-hard salt beef with his knife and conveyed it to his mouth, where he gave it several chews before sliding it behind his teeth to speak. He cast Will a sideways thoughtful glance.

'What do you think, Will?'

Will frowned as Brewster banged the hardtack or biscuit on the barrel in front of him, leaving little white maggots wriggling on the barrel top. 'I think God is displeased with us,' Will said.

'For what reason?'

'Two things occurred to me. I ask myself, did we do wrong in going to the likes of Weston? Did we compromise there? Was the Lord angry with us?'

'Hmm. And the other possibility?'

The moment had come, but he hesitated. How could he confess? How could he tell this man who stood in place of a father to him about how he felt about another man's wife?

Brewster's brows furrowed as he considered. 'You think it might be you?' he suggested.

Will shrugged helplessly. He thought of Alice, of the hand he had slipped around her waist, of kissing her, of the desire and the frightening lack of self-control only just recovered in time. He thought of the longing he had for her even now, guilty, secret longing.

Brewster swallowed and followed it with a swig of water. 'Is it to do with Mistress Southworth?' he asked gently.

As his belly twisted, Will turned and shot him a look. 'What made you say that?'

'I heard what Dorothy said that day on the *Speedwell*. Is it?'

'It is—'tis not like that.'

'I would have been surprised it were.' Brewster paused, and after a moment he said, 'You know, though, what the Lord himself said. *Whosoever looketh on a woman to lust after her hath committed adultery with her already in his heart.*'

'I know all that,' Will said quietly, and his voice broke.

Brewster probed gently, 'There is trouble between you and Dorothy.'

Will struggled with himself. 'We have one son, and not like to have any more.'

'You can't blame a wife for that! 'Tis in God's hands. Unless—'

Will did not look at him. 'Aye, unless...'

Brewster pushed the rest of his food away from him, his full attention on Will. 'Oh.'

'It don't excuse anything,' Will said miserably.

'No.'

There was a silence, then Will finally spoke in a voice hardly above a whisper. 'I have sinned before Jehovah, sir.'

Brewster closed his eyes, no doubt saying a prayer. He took a deep breath. 'Tell me.'

Will shot him an agonised look. 'It—it is not adultery.' Brewster let his breath go in relief. 'That's only in Dorothy's mind. But it might as well have been.'

Brewster brightened. 'Then you have not sinned.'

'Oh but I have!' Will insisted determined now to make Brewster understand the depths of his iniquity. 'I have sinned in my heart. And I keep sinning in my heart. I can't help it!'

Brewster asked, 'You have spoken with Mistress Southworth?'

'No.' Will hesitated and couldn't look Brewster in the eye. 'Worse! I—' he hesitated, unwilling to say.

'What did you do, Will?' Brewster prompted gently.

Will swallowed convulsively. 'I kissed her.' He rubbed his face with his hands. 'I—I know I should not have done it, and I wish I hadn't.'

Brewster groaned. 'What were you thinking of?' he demanded, and even though his voice was low so as not to be overheard, Will heard his indignation. It was no more than he deserved.

'I wasn't thinking,' Will admitted briefly glancing at Brewster, but unable to meet his eyes in case he saw condemnation there. 'I should never have gone to stay with them. But with Cushman and Carver there, I thought it would be no problem.' He added very softly, 'I had not intended to kiss her. It—it just happened. On the day I left. And when we—I— realised what was happening, I left and came home. Immediately. Nothing further happened between us.'

Brewster drew a breath. 'This is serious, Will. But not as bad as it could have been. You walked away from the temptation. That was the right thing to do.'

Will struggled with himself, and Brewster waited patiently for the rest. 'I was tempted.' Will admitted. 'I didn't realise I was so weak.' He pulled his hands over his face again in a weary gesture. 'I thought I was strong enough to cope.'

'Knowing how you felt about her, you would have done better to stay somewhere else while you were in London.'

'I wasn't aware of any feelings for her before I got there. I liked her, but that was all. And what, pray, could I have said to Brother Robinson who insisted I should stay there?' He paused, struggling with the weight of it. 'I don't know how it happened. When I saw how unhappy she was, I had sympathy for her. She is a good woman. She would not betray God or her husband. No more would I.' He brushed his dark hair from his eyes despairingly.

'Did you not know that she admired you?'

'No. That is, yes, well once I did suspect, but she married Edward. I thought that was an end to it. I don't understand how it happened, how I could feel like this for her.'

Brewster said, 'If Dorothy had lived up to your expectations as a wife—but a man deprived is a man easily tempted.' He took a deep breath. 'If you had not walked away, what would have been the result?'

Will shuddered. 'I can't bear to think of it!'

'I'll tell you what would have happened. You would have hurt Dorothy, and your son, and you would have hurt Edward and his sons. And you would have ruined Alice's good name. And yours. You would have lost your standing with God, and so would she, and you would have been expelled from the congregation, both of you. Would it have been worth it to act so selfishly?'

'No. I wouldn't do that. I hope you know that sir. I must live without Alice, but I cannot live without my God.'

Brewster wasn't going to let him off lightly. 'What you did was serious, Will. Desiring another man's wife, you are breaking the tenth commandment of God.'

'You think I don't know that? You think I haven't prayed about it every day, morning, noon and night? You think I don't feel my guilt every single moment of every day? But however guilty I feel, I still love her. God help me, I cannot stop it. Isn't this why Jehovah is not blessing us?'

'You think He would punish all of us for your sin?' Brewster asked.

'Why not? He has done it before—with Achan in the time of Joshua; with Israel when David took the count. We have lost Jehovah's spirit because of me! Did not Brother Robinson warn us to repent?'

'That would be a heavy burden to bear, Will, and you are not able to bear it. If you have not lain with this woman, then that is an end of the matter.'

'I kissed her,' he reminded Brewster.

'Thankfully, that's all you did! And now that you have confessed, you will be forgiven.'

'I have begged for forgiveness, and begged for my heart to be right. But it doesn't seem to make much difference.'

'Your prayer will be heard.' Brewster seemed eager to comfort him. He went on, 'King David went much further than you did. He committed adultery with Bathsheba, and then had her husband killed! Thankfully you did not do that! But remember, David was still known as a righteous man, and he was still blessed by God. You have repented, and you have confessed your sin to me now. Let that be an end to it.' He paused. 'You will recover from this, you know. Men lose loved ones in death, and they recover from the grief. You will too. And when we get to New England there will be so much to do you will find that it fades. With God's help. Perhaps we should pray together?'

Will was doubtful, but grateful. Perhaps Brewster was right. He would get over Alice. Eventually. So Brewster prayed with him, and Will was comforted.

Brewster returned to his meal. 'I am of the opinion that there are other things which may have displeased Jehovah,' he said presently.

'You reckon?' Will raised his head, hope rekindling.

'Like our taking strangers with us who are not of our persuasion. Unbelievers in many senses, people of the world who do not value freedom like we do. We have entered a contract with them, bound ourselves to them. Ought we to have bound ourselves to worldly people?'

'I see.' Will was struck by the thought.

Brewster went on, 'Worse, it has often struck my conscience, as I know it bothered Brother Robinson, that when we struggled to get a patent for Virginia, we did not set down our articles of faith as they really were. It was not quite—well, the truth. In the end, the Lord provided another way. The patent we got for Virginia we do not need, after three years of struggle! Satan manoeuvres us sometimes into a position where we cannot find the way out unless we do something wrong. So we compromise ourselves.'

'And Weston? Was he from Satan or from the Lord?'

'Time will tell. But he has already tried to sell us into slavery. We are at the mercy of the world in these matters.'

'So Master Robinson erred in his judgement?' It had not occurred to

Will before that John Robinson could be fallible.

'Brother Robinson cannot take all the blame. We all agreed. But I have often wondered about Weston. Look at the way he changed the terms! Then he insists that we take worldlings with us when the whole purpose of our venture was to build a colony of like-minded people who worship God in truth. Like the new world the scriptures speak of.'

'But that is future, surely.'

Brewster shrugged non-committally, not wishing to divert the course of their conversation. 'Perhaps that is why we have hit difficulties. But it is true that whenever the Lord's elect get involved with the world, there is a clash of goals, ideals. We wanted to be free of the world, that is why this venture. Yet we take them with us! And of necessity, we will have to live in close association with them. And they are bad association. Look at Christopher Martin. And that man Billington.'

Involuntarily Will's eyes strayed to the big John Billington. A Londoner, with the flat London accent that grated on northern ears, he had already made a name for himself as a troublemaker, his children undisciplined and as uncouth as himself.

Could Brewster be right? Was it so that he was not to blame after all? 'You think that to be the cause?' he asked.

'I think that is more likely to bring the Lord's displeasure than anything you have done. After all, you did not stay long in London, and you are now going to be an ocean away. I think the Lord will be pleased because you did not give in to temptation.'

I nearly did, though, Will thought. It had been a close thing.

'It is over now,' Brewster finished up. 'Now stop troubling yourself, and forget it.'

Will nodded, and swallowed the lump that had come into his throat. How could he forget? He could not tear out of him the heart that pumped in his chest, where the ache seemed to have lodged. He could not stop loving her. It was as much a part of him as breathing, and he would have to live with it probably till the day he died. But he couldn't tell Brewster that.

Will thought over what Brewster had said as he crawled into the space beside Dorothy that night. She was still, turned away from him, her breathing faint, yet he had a feeling she was awake. She did not acknowledge his presence.

It was hard on Dorothy, he thought. She had given up her son to go with him. And now he needed to spend some time alone with her to rekindle their marriage, perhaps to read to her from the scriptures, to hold her in his arms—if she would let him. He needed it. And he knew she did too. But where could they get privacy here? Their tiny corner of the deck was hardly private.

TWENTY-SEVEN
Storms

The Mayflower, October, 1620

During the night the weather changed. It was the time of the equinox, when the worst storms batter the Atlantic. Will woke from a troubled sleep in which Alice and Dorothy featured strongly, to the howl of the wind through the rigging and the cracks in the planking. The lanterns swung so wildly that the tipped wax had put two of them out, and another smoked and guttered warningly. A child started to cry, and as if that were a signal, others began to cry too.

Will clambered out of his bunk and went up the aft gangway. The hatch was closed but he forced his way through it, to find the most frightful sight. Almost before he had come on deck, in the half light, a wash of icy water hit him full in the face, making him gasp in shock and cold, and he staggered backwards, ready to fall down the steps again.

Gripping the handrail, which was only a length of rope, he peered around him. In this grey half-lit world, a madness had taken hold. Waves the size of three-storey houses lifted the suddenly tiny ship and threw it down again. Grey water crashed over the bow, so that Will thought she would go to the bottom there and then. They had not so much as a knot of sail on her—the wind was so strong that a sail would drive her under. They were at the mercy of wind and current, drifting with the storm.

Will went below again and closed the hatch, a good deal shocked, and not a little afraid. Everyone was awake now. Water found its way through the deck planking above and poured in countless steady rivulets on the hapless passengers. The ship rolled not just backwards and forwards, but side to side as well and it threw Will across the deck so that he crashed into John Billington.

'Damn you!'

'Never mind me,' Will retorted. 'And watch your language in front of Christians.'

The lanterns gave up the ghost, and plunged them into thick choking darkness. Women were crying and screaming now. Some prayed. The children shrieked, and the noise of the ship, battling the tempest rose in a terrible roar and creaking and splintering of wood.

'Will!' Dorothy's terrified voice reached him, and he stumbled towards her in the darkness but could not find her.

Someone was sick, the dreadful acid stench filling the confined space and promoting a sudden epidemic of vomiting.

'Will!' Dorothy's voice rose in fright.

Will shouted to be heard above the noise. ''Tis a storm. No more than that.'

'We will pray!' William Brewster suggested helpfully, but he could hardly be heard above the din. Those who were not Pilgrims took that as a cue to begin to recite the Lord's prayer, although the Pilgrims disagreed with reciting prayers, and believed in praying extemporaneously. Still, since no-one could be heard above the din, it hardly mattered.

Someone managed to get a tinder-box to strike and lit a lantern again, but it guttered and went out almost immediately.

Will staggered across the deck, falling over someone's legs, bending to avoid hitting his head on the deckhead beams, and the vicious protruding iron hooks and ring-bolts which he knew lurked in unexpected places, and finally by following Dorothy's sobs, arrived at her side.

He couldn't see her, but he spoke to her, and she clung to him in the darkness.

Water poured in through the deck beams onto them, soaking clothes and bedding alike. It was agony, for the next few hours. No-one dared move for fear of falling. A broken arm or leg could mean death for the victim. It wasn't worth the risk.

The wind in the rigging, became a low moan. The sailors said that when it sounded low, almost musical, it was the worst wind to be feared. Will wondered if it were like that. And suddenly a noise like the sound of tearing and splintering wood brought prayers and cries to a frightened stop, and daylight appeared above them amidships.

Even in the confines of the lower deck, Will knew it was serious. The timber had split, one of the main structural timbers. Water poured in through the gap in torrents, making a bad situation ten times worse.

'We're going to die!' a woman screamed shrilly.

Will found he shook with fear. Still, they had to wait until the storm blew itself out to find out exactly what had happened.

It looked bad. A beam straddling the ship had buckled. To Will who was no mariner, it looked as though they must turn back—again. The sailors themselves thought the ship unlikely to complete the voyage.

The male passengers met with Captain Jones and his crew to decide what to do.

Some were for turning back to England. The sailors had no desire to risk their lives when there was no need. On the other hand, they were nearly half way across the Atlantic and it was as far to go back as it was to go forward. And the sailors would not get paid if they did not complete the voyage.

Will was loathe to turn back too. Had they not had two false starts already? To abandon it this time would be to abandon it for good. And they would have lost everything for no gain. On the other hand, they could not risk everyone's lives for the sake of the money they had put into the venture.

Captain Christopher Jones had more than once impressed Will with his good sense, knowledge and ability. In his turn Christopher Jones liked Will for his leadership qualities, his own common-sense and good humour. Jones now looked at Will for backing.

'The *Mayflower* is a strong ship,' Jones said. 'She is strong and firm under the water. She will make the voyage to New England.'

'But the buckled beam?' Isaac Allerton asked.

Captain Jones looked at him blankly, his thoughts evidently elsewhere. Then he turned to Will. 'Did you not bring a screw aboard?'

Edward Winslow answered before Will could open his mouth, 'For the printing press we did.'

This was the very screw Winslow had insisted on bringing with them, much to the annoyance of Captain Reynolds on the *Speedwell,* and subsequently to the annoyance of Captain Jones as well. Reluctantly he had allowed the printing press, screw and all, to go into the hold.

'Perhaps we could use it to raise the beam, what think you, Master Alden? Could we then put in a post and secure it, set firm in the lower deck?'

John Alden, the carpenter, agreed. 'Aye. I reckon it could be done, Cap'n.'

'Good! As for the decks and upper works, we will caulk her with oakum. It'll work free again with the ship's movements, but it will serve for a while. I think we might go on very well as long as we do not overpress her with sail.'

So they committed themselves to the will of God, prayed for his assistance, and set to work.

Mariners and passengers bent their backs to the arduous task of winding up the huge black screw to bring the cracked beam into place, and helped the carpenter get a hefty beam to brace it from beneath.

And God was with them, for it worked, and the *Mayflower* was once again under sail, though her speed was much reduced.

Brewster sought Will out on the deck, as he leaned on the gunwale and watched the whales jumping out of the water, their huge flukes flicking in the air. Such marvellous beasts, with their unimaginable power, and immense size, the passengers had never seen anything like them and viewed them as a marvel of God's creation.

'I never get tired of watching them,' Will said to Brewster.

It was a fair day, with the sky a perfect blue, the wind just right for a good speed, and the *Mayflower* went along at a better pace. The breeze blew their hair, ruffled their white starched collars, brought the colour to wan cheeks.

Brewster agreed. ''Tis a fair sight. They could swallow a man whole had they a mind to.'

'Like Jonah.'

'Like Jonah,' he agreed. 'Mind I'd not have relished it much. Just what the inside of a whale's stomach must look like and smell like is anyone's guess! All full of half-digested and rotting fish, I reckon!'

'And Jonah was vomited up onto dry land!'

'Don't speak of vomit young Will if you don't mind!' Brewster said with feeling.

They fell to silence for a while, and Will peered into the depths beneath the ship. It was difficult to see in the sunlight reflecting off the water, but he thought he saw something down there. Another whale? A shoal of fish perhaps?

'You know that young sailor 'Rabshakeh'?' Brewster said suddenly.

Will thought of the young strapping man who had so mocked them in their seasickness, even mocked their God, announcing his hopes of throwing them overboard. 'Aye.'

'He's grievously sick.'

'Oh?'

'Aye, he has a high fever and is vomiting, and he has a pain in the right side of his belly, that makes him scream in agony.'

Will frowned. I've heard of that. A grievous disease if ever there was one. And no cure.'

'The surgeon says he will be dead in a few days.'

A chill ran up Will's spine which had nothing to do with the breeze. 'Dear God!'

'So it is of those who speak ill of the Lord and His elect. Do they think he does not hear?'

Brewster said to Will, 'So you think Jehovah is no longer with us?'

Will met his gaze as a shiver ran up his spine. Just who was this God that they worshipped?

As the man's sickness grew, and his suffering intensified they could hear his groans, and moans through the bulkheads. The surgeon could do nothing. Two days later the young man who had so profanely blasphemed the God of the Pilgrims died. His death shocked the passengers and sailors alike. 'It is the hand of God upon him!' they said to each other, and the sailors treated the Pilgrims with greater respect after that.

———

The lull in the weather did not last long. A few days later another fierce storm hit them and the ship again took up that pitching and rolling to which they had become accustomed.

Once more confined below decks, the passengers groaned and complained and vomited. The thirty-six children among them chafed at being unable to play topside. Wrestling Brewster thought it a good idea to tease the girls, pulling pigtails and generally earning himself a cuff round the ear from his father.

'They are impatient of this place,' Brewster said to Will. He rubbed his hand over his face in a weary gesture, and Will realised he was not a young man any more. Brewster was fifty-four, considered almost elderly in an age when few made it to their seventieth birthday. His coppery hair had faded in colour, so had his beard, and his face was pale and haggard. But then this voyage was enough to turn anyone's hair white.

John Carver was the same age as Brewster, but he did not enjoy Brewster's good health. He suffered more from seasickness, and he found the constant damp and the cramped conditions—particularly the low deck head—made his joints stiff and swollen and painful. The voyage laid this large bluff man low.

Carver said, 'If the Lord be merciful, we will not be much longer.'

Will sighed. He did not wish to remind him that they were just over half way across the Atlantic, and they had been a month out of Plymouth already. He too felt weary of this journey.

Brewster frowned in the half-light of the lantern. 'And when we get to New England, what then?'

Will's first thought was that they must find a place to settle, to build shelters, and so on, but he knew that Brewster was not thinking along those lines—they had already discussed that at length. 'What do you mean, brother?'

Brewster struggled to put his thoughts into words. 'We are a hundred and two people.'

'Soon to be a hundred and three when Mistress Hopkins comes to childbed,' Carver put in.

'And Mistress White,' Will added, thinking of Sam Fuller's sister Susanna, who was also near her time. Isaac Allerton's wife Mary was also due. Why these people had to come on such a perilous journey in such a condition, he could not understand. It seemed idiotic to him to put one's wife in such peril. But then, if things had gone to plan they would have been in America a month since.

But William Brewster was not concerned about the pregnant women in their midst. 'We are a hundred and two people,' he said again, calling them to order. 'Some sixty of us are not Separatists. We who are the Lord's elect are in the minority.'

Will had known it, of course. And had not liked it. A good many of the Separatists had gone home when they parted from the *Speedwell*, reducing their numbers. Thomas Weston must have been hoping for this outcome all along. That was why he insisted that they take with them some of his own people.

Will scanned the people on this deck. Good people, most of them. Yet it was true, the vast majority were 'strangers'.

Brewster went on, 'This was our idea. We wanted to create a colony for our own people. An oasis for the Lord, if you like. A colony based on the congregation and run like the congregation. The body politic must lie with us, the Pilgrims.'

Carver and Will looked at each other. 'How will we manage that when the balance is not in our favour?' he asked.

Brewster drew a breath and watched as John Howland, John Carver's unservant-like servant gathered the children around him and began to tell them stories to keep them occupied. 'We are not without friends among the "strangers",' he said.

Will knew what he meant. For example, William Mullins was a Separatist from Henry Jacob's congregation in London, and therefore not strictly a 'stranger'. Richard Warren, not exactly a Separatist, but with strong sympathies for the Separatists, might convert later and was a potential ally. Stephen Hopkins was another man who had Separatist leanings without actually committing himself.

Stephen Hopkins, a strong dark stocky man, had already been to America once, having sailed on the *Sea Adventure* for Virginia in 1609. He had been wrecked off the Bermuda coast before going on to Virginia, and he was the only person on board with any experience of landing on these shores.

Miles Standish, too had been picked for his experience, this time in the matter of defence. His usefulness to the company was without question, and without doubt he was on the side of the Pilgrims. After all, it was Will himself who had enlisted his help, for one thing the Pilgrims were short of was knowledge in matters of defence. Miles Standish had spent his life in the army, had gone to Holland in his youth to help in the war against the Spanish. He was thirty-six now, but a seasoned army captain, leader of men and capable of organising a defence against, say, a native attack. Killing people was not part of the Pilgrim ethos. However, they recognised that to fail to defend one's friends and family would render a person culpable in their murder. So Miles Standish spent what time he could instructing them in the matter of necessary defence—with limited success.

'And so?' Will asked.

Brewster pursed his lips. 'And so we must think how we are going to keep the balance of power with us. The body politic. If we let those who are not belonging to the Lord rule us we will not have the clean laws that belong to godly people. Look how others have fared, say, in Virginia in the past.'

There had been all sorts of rumours about the colony in Virginia. At one stage the whole colony was wiped out, and no-one knew why. The Pilgrims saw it as an obvious illustration of this point. To succeed, they must have the Lord's blessing. And that meant keeping the Lord's laws.

A woman cried out. The word seemed to echo around the deck—Mistress Elizabeth Hopkins was about to have her child. Now. In the middle of the storm.

Will's thoughts flashed back to Dorothy's confinement with Jonathan. How terrible it had been in a warm house in a decent bed, with light and help. And poor Agnes Fuller, Sam's second wife, sister of Alice who had lost her child, and who had bled to death. And now here on this ship, amid the filth of full slops buckets, and sodden stinking straw, and vomit and darkness, in the terrible pitching and damp of a ship, this woman was about to give birth.

Mary Brewster and Katherine Carver, the matrons of the group, took charge, taking Elizabeth behind a curtain. An uncomfortable silence settled on the passengers as they heard Mistress Hopkins panting, moaning, and finally screaming in her struggle to give birth. It went on for hours.

Kindly Sam Fuller, trained in physic, offered his help and was summarily sent about his business. 'This is no place for a man, Sam Fuller,' Mary Brewster told him briskly.

John Howland led the children in singing songs in an attempt to drown out the woman's cries, but it was difficult to encourage them in the face of Mistress Hopkins' evident distress.

Will shifted uncomfortably. This was terrible. They had endured much, and there was much yet to be endured. How could a child survive, born in such circumstances?

'What's happening?' a little girl asked.

'Sister Hopkins' baby is coming out, silly,' John Billington junior, with all the seniority of eight years to his name, told her.

Will looked at him with dislike. Detestable family, the Billingtons, coarse, common, vulgar Londoners. And they were dirty, too.

'Does it hurt then?' the little girl, who turned out to be Humility Cooper asked again.

John Howland met Will's eyes with a despairing expression.

Suddenly Dorothy let out a cry, and covered her ears and head with her hands. This scene brought back the trauma from which she had never fully recovered.

Will excused himself from Carver and Brewster and went to her, putting his arm around her and cradling her to his broad chest as she sobbed. Part of him understood. Part of him did not. She was a woman, after all. It was her lot in life, wasn't it, to bear children, as was the lot of all women? But he knew she did not ever want to repeat the experience.

John Howland staggered by him, and Will caught him with an outstretched foot. 'Where are you going?'

'I need to go to the head.'

'You can't go on deck in weather like this!'

'You want me to use the bucket, then? Here? In this? With this going on?' He indicated the curtained section, and Will sighed.

'Mind you don't get washed overboard,' he warned. Well, the man was six and twenty and able to decide for himself where he went.

John Howland left the choking atmosphere below and came on deck, gasping in great lungsfull of salty crisp air. Carefully, he began to make his way forward. Strange how short a distance to the head it seemed usually, and how long a distance it seemed now. Not only that, but now he came to think of it, the head was continually beneath the water. He stood there undecided. The ship lurched and swayed frighteningly. He gripped the rope by him and made his way forward. Now he could see it. Well, sometimes he could. As the ship lurched the whole of the bow section dipped beneath the grey sea. The ship seemed to stand on its nose, before rising until it almost stood on its stern, paused for a moment and then crashed down into the next hollow, jarring the whole ship. The sight of it made him feel ill.

'What the devil do you think you are doing?' John Parker, one of the mates had to yell to be heard. 'God, man, you'll be washed overboard.'

Hardly had the words left his mouth when a wave hit them amidships, putting the yardarm under on the lee side, so that the sea cascaded over the whole deck.

John Howland lost his footing and felt himself slithering to disaster. Desperately he thrashed out his hands, trying to stop himself, but the deck beneath him was slippery, like ice, and his fingers found nothing to stop him. Below him now was the sea with a gap in the guard-rail big enough for him to slide through. As he slithered towards it, his hand grabbed a rope.

Icy water rushed over his head. He went right down, the noise of the tempest stopped suddenly, only the strange glugging of water in his ears. Above him the surface of the water washed back and forth. He passed the ship's keel on his way down.

Instinctively he cried for help, but only a bubble and a noise which he supposed must be his own voice, came out.

Frantically he fought against the cold dark water, but suddenly he jerked to a halt. He still had hold of the rope he had grabbed.

On deck, John Parker raised the alarm, giving the bell several clangs, and yelling, 'Man overboard!' It brought the passengers to their feet in sudden anxiety.

John Howland!' Will whispered feeling sick in his stomach. He should have tried harder to stop him.

He ran up the companionway steps, and out on to the deck. Already men were heaving on a rope and Will joined them in their efforts. Then John Howland's head miraculously appeared above the grey surging water.

'Is he dead?' someone asked as they pulled him nearer the ship.

'If he be dead, he's got a grip on that thar rope like a pirate on a rum bottle!'

'Get the boathook!' Christopher Jones had appeared at the scene. 'Get him aboard!'

'Damned landlubbers!' someone else swore, but they worked together and slowly—too slowly Will thought, for he was in an agony of guilt—they heaved John Howland to the side of the ship and manhandled him onto the deck, where he lay in a forlorn heap.

In a moment he was taken below, and laid out on a table. 'He's all yours,' John Parker announced to the passengers in general.

John Carver prodded the man's lifeless sodden body. 'Is he dead?'

Giles Heale, the ship's surgeon arrived, and felt for a pulse, and everyone held their breath while they waited for the verdict. He shook his head, and Will felt a huge lump rise in his throat. This was his fault.

Then Giles Heale suddenly went to the man's head, and took hold of the his arms, raising them right over his head, and then down again, in a pumping action. The Pilgrims needed no further demonstration. Two men took an arm each and did the work, and with each downward thrust, water seeped out of the man's mouth.

'Sometimes it works,' Heale said.

As they worked, Heale forced open John Howland's eyes one at a time and peered into them. What he expected to see, Will had no idea, but the surgeon said, 'Keep trying, you never know.'

'It's useless, he isn't breathing,' Christopher Martin said.

Will took over one arm from Isaac Allerton, and Sam Fuller took over the other. It was hard work, but they kept pumping. And all the while Will was praying.

Behind the curtain, screened from them, another drama neared completion. Elizabeth Hopkins gave a terrible noise, as though she were straining, which she was, and a moment later Katherine Carver's voice reached them clearly, 'The head is out!'

The baby began to mewl in that strange way of the new-born. 'Come on now,' Mary Brewster encouraged the mother, 'let's have the rest of him!'

Elizabeth Hopkins made that straining noise again. There was no dignity in childbirth, especially as upward of a hundred people were listening, and the birthing of a baby waited on no other drama. Suddenly Mistress Hopkins gasped, 'Oh!' and Mary Brewster gave a whoop. ''Tis a boy!' she announced. A lusty boy! Listen to his yell!' And yell he did.

'For God's sake, woman, put a teat in its mouth!' John Billington growled. Evidently she did, for the baby quietened.

Will felt tears stinging his eyes. As one person is born, another dies, he thought. His arms ached with working John Howland's arm.

'Give it up, men!' Christopher Martin urged. 'The man is dead.'

William Button took over from Will, and John Goodman from Sam Fuller. Will stood back, and bit his lip, looking at the man on the table.

William Button was twenty-two, but a tall man, and he peered at Christopher Martin. 'Why don't you shut up?' he said.

And at that moment John Howland coughed, and retched, and they turned him on his side.

The surgeon Giles Heale beamed on them. 'I told you to keep going!' he said as though it was all his own doing.

Will's legs felt as though they would collapse, and he staggered to a chest and sat down shakily on it where he thanked his God.

Alice Mullins and her daughter Priscilla took over the nursing of John Howland, while Katherine Carver and Mary Brewster finished their care of the new mother.

Will caught sight of John Billington sitting on the deck, and walked over to him. He nudged Billington with his foot.

Billington looked up at him with mutinous eyes. 'What?'

Will said calmly, 'I don't know whose spawn you are, or what you think of the delicacy of your wife's upbringing, but most of us are God-fearing folk here, and we do not like to hear language like you just used. In particular, we do not want our wives and children exposed to such language. If the sailors can moderate their speech around God-fearing women, I'm sure you can too.'

'Goddam Bible basher!' Billington retorted, coming to his feet.

Will looked at him a moment longer and then contemptuously walked away.

Billington sat down again in the straw, growling like a dog.

TWENTY-EIGHT
Land!

The Mayflower, November, 1620

The storm blew them off course again, and the winds set in to push the *Mayflower* towards the north. Not that Captain Jones was by any means certain of his position. There was no absolute way to calculate longitude with any degree of accuracy, and dead reckoning—a complicated mathematical equation taking into account the speed of the ship, tidal drag and contrary winds—was, at best, an informed guess. Furthermore, being blown in a more northerly direction, they were not travelling directly west which was what Captain Jones had intended.

'I think it fair to say that we are well past half way to our destination,' Captain Jones told Will when they next met on the main deck during a lull. 'How do your people go on?'

Will shook his head. It had been six weeks since they left Plymouth and the passengers were exhausted. 'Finding it difficult to keep their spirits up,' he said truthfully.

Captain Jones sighed. 'Even sailors find life at sea hard. And your people are not sailors. So far they have borne up very well.'

Will combed his long wet curls out of his eyes with his fingers in a despairing gesture. 'I don't think any of us ever thought the weather could go on like this for days, weeks on end.'

Captain Jones allowed himself a small knowing smile. 'We are in the middle of the Atlantic in November. Pray, what weather did you expect at this time of year, Master Bradford? Calms and sunny days?'

Will shook his head. 'No—but we expected to be there long since. We have been at sea since July. In fact, I experienced something like it when we crossed from England to Holland, a voyage of two weeks in the most terrible tempest. It blew us off course at the time and when the storm cleared we found ourselves in Norway.'

Captain Jones raised his brows, impressed by this little piece of information. 'From England to Holland is not usually more than a day or two.'

Will nodded. 'We survived that. We'll survive this.'

'If your God is with you, we will. I tell you this, Master Bradford, I too have seen worse than this and survived it. True, it has taken longer than it might. I've known this crossing to take just four weeks. But take heart. It is not the worst the *Mayflower* has taken.'

'The trouble is, we have women and little ones with us. Some of them are not strong. We are permanently wet, our clothes wet, our quarters foul.' His own clothes were damp through to the skin and he was always cold, with his feet squelching inside soaked boots. It did little for the spirits. 'We have scurvy too.'

'Well, it was to be expected. When did you board the *Speedwell*?'

'July 20th. Three months ago.'

A diet of fish, biscuit, salt meat, a quarter pound of butter per day and a half a pound of cheese as well as peas was more than enough to keep them from starvation—but not to keep scurvy at bay. There was an expression of sympathy in Jones's brown eyes. '"Tis a long haul for the best of us. It's been one problem after another. I don't understand why your God don't look after you better.'

Will didn't rise to the challenge, but smiled and left him.

On deck the air was icy cold, blowing through his damp clothing, and raising the goosebumps on his skin. He began to shiver. It was enough to give anyone an inflammation of the lungs.

He glanced up at the sky. The weather was changing from autumn into winter. No longer were there patches of blue sky; instead a uniform grey ceiling hung over them, like an omen of doom, if they believed in omens, which they did not. The sea was a heaving, frothing grey mass, tossing the ship about as though she were rocked by a giant hand. And they couldn't expect much better this side of the spring.

The stench struck him afresh as he went below. Brewster waited for him. 'Well?'

Will sighed and sat down. 'Captain Jones has no idea where we are, except that we are heading north-west, sort of. He reckons that, by the sun, when he can see it, we are too far north.'

'You are worried, Will?'

'Aye. You know what happened to Blackwell's group.'

'We are in Jehovah's hands.' He said it with the patience of one who had often repeated those same words. 'If he wills, we shall make it.'

Will nodded, but in his heart he grew despondent. There were many reasons, he reckoned as to why God might not be with them, not least his own sin, for which he still begged forgiveness continually. Day by day, as he watched, the passengers grew weaker. The terrible conditions, the continual motion of the ship, the cold and the continual wet took their toll. Captain Jones also worried about them.

John Carver took to his bed, unable to endure any more.

Then, towards the end of November, the sea patterns and currents and waves changed—imperceptible to the Pilgrims—but observed by Captain Jones. They were approaching the western side of the Atlantic, and he ordered a lookout to be kept for twigs and seaweed blown out to sea from the land.

Below, the Pilgrims were in a desperate plight. They began to fall sick with scurvy and coughs and colds. Will could not but think of the tragedy that had hit Francis Blackwell's doomed expedition. He spent a good deal of time in prayer, and the rest of his time speaking to the others to keep their spirits up.

'I shall die before we make land,' John Carver confided to him weakly.

Will shook his head. 'We are close. The captain says he has seen sights that tell him land is near. You must have faith and not give up.'

John Carver, that great big bluff man, looked up at the deck head in a despairing gesture. 'How much more can we take?' he demanded and his usual booming voice was now only just above a whisper.

Will glanced at Katherine, John's wife, and she raised her brows. 'John is right. We have endured much. I fear we shall all die if we do not soon reach land.'

'No talk like that!' Will told her. 'We are close, very close.'

A scuffle broke out at the other end of the deck, and Will sighed and stood up, with a despairing grimace at John. 'I think you are in the best place,' he said, and went off to see what the commotion was about.

He might have guessed John Billington would be in the midst of it. The man was a bully and boor. He had a fat belly, and a week's worth of stubble on his chin. And an attitude of superiority, of insubordination even, that irritated Will beyond measure. If ever there was a cantankerous, downright annoying man, it had to be John Billington. And there was Christopher Martin, that other pompous trouble-maker, and a regular slanging match had ensued, with John Billington hurling profanities at the other slighter man. 'That will do!' Will snapped, and both men turned to face him, surprised. Thankfully, there was no room to fight here, for the deck head was too low, and they all stooped to look at each other.

'I've told you before, Master Billington, that we do not tolerate such language before Christian wives and children. As for you, Master Martin, you should know better.'

'It was his fault,' Martin growled.

Really, they were like children! Will's patience was at a low ebb. He said curtly, 'Look, don't you think you could set a better example for the children? I know it has been a long hard voyage, and that we are all at the end of our endurance. But we must be patient a little longer. Both of you need to learn to get along together!'

However, it was typical. Arguments and bickering had become the norm, even among those who were Pilgrims. Women burst into tears for no apparent reason, or shouted at the children while the children whined and cried. Some even began to voice doubts that they would ever reach land.

They stepped up their Bible reading, and they prayed. They begged the cook for some hot porridge which did a little to revive flagging spirits.

'We shouldn't have come,' the detestable John Billington said loudly as Will came by.

Will sighed inwardly. Who was the idiot that inflicted this man on them in the first place?

'No-one asked you to come, friend,' he said quietly. 'You chose of your own free will. And you could have gone back when the others did. However, now we are all in this together, and there is no going back.'

Billington met his eyes mutinously for a few moments, and then dropped his before Will's.

The *Mayflower* ploughed on. The weather grew colder still, but blew a fine wind.

Then the twenty-two year old servant of Sam Fuller, William Button, fell sick.

'He has a high fever,' Sam told Will and Brewster. 'And there's a rattling in his chest I don't like the sound of. Dr. Heale thinks it is an inflammation of the lungs.'

Will knelt beside William Button, lying restlessly on a bed of straw, covered by a single blanket. The man moaned and shivered, and then said he was hot. Will felt his forehead, and his skin was hot to the touch.

Button had been well enough when they set out. He had never been a strapping young man, it was true. Now, weakened by scurvy, and the cold, damp, unsanitary conditions, he was unable to fight off whatever ailed him.

They prayed over him, and the weather improved, but William Button died.

On a bitterly cold November day they slid his body over the side into the sea. It was a terrible blow.

Long after the others had gone below, Will stood looking down at the sea, an unspeakable desolation in his soul for one he did not know particularly well, and fear for the rest of them. Captain Jones joined him at the guard-rail standing beside him in companionable silence. Then he said, 'See there, Master Bradford?'

Will followed the direction of Jones's pointing finger. And there, sure enough, was some black seaweed floating on the surface of the water. 'That means we are near the coast.'

Will's heart turned over. 'You mean we have arrived?'

'Just about. A little further north than we intended, I'll warrant. Nevertheless, we are near the coast.'

The next day they saw seagulls circling overhead and twigs and leaves blown out to sea from the shore.

At dawn on Friday the ninth of November the cry from the masthead brought them all up from below. 'Land ho! Land ho!'

It was difficult to see much in the cold grey of a November dawn, and of course the man on lookout had the advantage of being at the top of the mainmast. It took a little longer for the land to become visible to those on the deck, but yes, there it was, a dark grey smudge on the horizon. Will felt his heart skip in his chest and tears come into his eyes. 'Thank God!' He slipped his hand around Dorothy's slender waist. 'We've arrived,' he told her, unable to hide the excitement in his voice. 'We are safe!'

They had been nine long weeks at sea since leaving Plymouth, sixteen weeks or just about four months since leaving Leyden on the *Speedwell*. It had been an endurance test, a trial, but they had made it. This was America. This was their new home.

Dorothy took a deep shuddering breath and gazed steadfastly at the horizon. To her the dark shadow on the horizon was as cold and uninviting as the cold grey sea beneath them. She had come all this way to be with her husband, but her son, and her parents, and her sister, were three thousand miles away. Now she faced the prospect of winter in this inhospitable place. There was no joy in Dorothy's heart for their safe deliverance.

Without a word she turned and left him to go below.

It was as though she had struck Will across the face. His heart sank as he watched her thread her way through the excited passengers, his joy and excitement turning to ashes in his chest. He tried to recapture it. After all, this was what they had striven for, this was what they had sacrificed everything for. Their new life was about to begin.

The others got down on their knees to give thanks to God for safe deliverance, and he knelt with them. His heart was so full that he could not pay attention to the prayer William Brewster offered, but uttered in is heart his own prayer of thanks to his God. They were safe. They had made it.

If only Dorothy could be pleased.

Captain Jones compared the charts spread out in front of him to the land he could see through the telescope. To double-check he took a noonday reading by the cross-staff, and did his calculations, but his first suspicions were confirmed. He called the men to his cabin.

'Well, gentlemen, I have to tell you that the land we can see is Cape Cod.'

It conveyed little to them, so he showed them on the charts. 'We are too far north. Not by much, I grant you, but you asked to be nearer the Hudson River.'

'It would be better to be where we should be,' John Carver said. He had struggled from his berth, hope giving strength to a weakened body. 'Our Virginia patent allows us to settle as much as forty-one degrees

North.' It included Manhattan Island.

'And who is going to stop you settling here if you so choose?' Captain Jones asked, but the question was rhetorical. 'So you want to go south now?'

'About how far is it?' Will asked.

Jones looked at his charts. 'Say, ten or fifteen leagues—approximately thirty to forty-five miles.' It wasn't much, surely. Less than a day's fair sailing. 'We have a fine day ahead, gentlemen and the wind is light, but from the north-east.'

So they agreed to turn south and look for a suitable landing place.

Will stayed on deck watching as the *Mayflower* came about, seeing the land on his right, but far off. For half a day they went on well. Then, as they came down past the bottom of Cape Cod and Monomoy Island the man on the lookout bellowed something Will didn't understand, and he glanced at Captain Jones to see what he made of it. Captain Jones peered ahead of him at the water, his brows drawn together. Turning his attention to the sea ahead, Will could at first make nothing out, but then he saw it, a seething mass of white-crested waves which suggested shallows or rocks beneath. His stomach turned over when he saw it. This could swallow a ship down whole, he thought.

Captain Jones strode swiftly forward to the forecastle, to the head, to see for himself. A moment later he strode aft again, bellowing out his orders.

'Bring her about! Bring her about!'

The mates took up the cry and the crew ran in all directions. To Will it seemed as if they had no idea what they were about, but in hardly any time at all they were a well-rehearsed team, each in his own position, ready to heave on the halyards to swing the sails round so that the ship would turn.

The noise of rushing water increased, and spray came over the gunwale in a spurt, soaking Will. Captain Jones bellowed above the noise. At that moment the ship hit the foaming water and the rhythmic up and down motion changed to chaos, the ship staggering beneath his feet.

The sailors worked doggedly to bring the ship about.

Captain Jones, coming near to Will said curtly, 'Pray, Master Bradford.'

Will obeyed, for the lives of a hundred and fifty people hung in the balance.

Slowly, agonisingly slowly, the ship turned, the crew working as a team, as they had been trained to do, bringing the sails into the wind, two men heaving on the whipstaff, captain and mates overseeing all.

And then it was over, and they were heading northwards again, the noise of water diminishing and the *Mayflower* picking up her usual rocking rhythm.

Looking back, Will knew they had been close to disaster.

Pollock Rip would become infamous in later times, but it was not even on Captain Jones's charts. It was a treacherous sea of shallows and roaring breakers that was known as Point Care, and Tucker's Terrour, and the French and Dutch called Malabar because of the ships they lost there.

Christopher Martin, below all this while, but feeling the turn of the ship, came on deck. 'What are you doing?' he demanded of Captain Jones.

'We turn back,' Jones answered curtly. As captain he had the final say. 'We will shelter in Cape Cod harbour.'

It had to do. The following day the passengers came on deck to see the ship round the hooked claw of Cape Cod, where, protected from the Atlantic by land on three sides, the *Mayflower* dropped anchor.

Once again William Brewster led them in prayer.

The terrible pitching and rolling gave way to a gentle rocking. They could now dry their clothes, and best of all, most longed for during all the weeks at sea, they had the chance to set foot on solid ground where they belonged.

TWENTY-NINE
Cape Cod

Cape Cod, November, 1620

Will realised it wasn't going to be as easy as they thought. Behind them lay three thousand miles of pitching, cold, rolling sea. They were exhausted and they were sick. And there was absolutely nothing here, no houses, no people, just woods, trees and sand down to the sea. A wilderness. And it was cold. Winter was coming on apace. It was going to get a whole lot worse, he was sure.

It should not have been winter, though, he thought. It should have been autumn. Or late summer. If only things had gone according to plan. But almost nothing had gone according to plan. This was not the time of year to be exploring a new unknown land. There was no welcome here.

Looking at it, Will found it difficult to be positive. Never in his life had he seen such an unwelcoming place. The euphoria of arrival gave way to something akin to despair when he thought of the tasks ahead. In this wilderness, they must find a place to settle, and begin to build houses, and plant and harvest. It was daunting. And no-one was going to do it for them. Much as the congregation back in Leyden loved them and prayed for them, their only help now was their God.

Christopher Jones sought him out. 'Master Bradford, I suggest that at the first opportunity, you find a place to settle and begin to build. We cannot leave until you have shelter ashore, but by the same token, we cannot stay indefinitely. Already the provisions are running low. We need to set sail for England as soon as possible.'

Will nodded. He knew that.

But it wasn't just the captain. The crew, too were anxious to be gone. 'If they cannot find a place in time, we will turn them and their goods ashore and leave them there,' they muttered.

The Pilgrims discussed the situation and asked God to strengthen them and give them courage to go on.

'We are few,' William Brewster told them. 'Just as it says in Deuteronomy.' He opened the Bible and began to read. 'So,' he concluded,' we should gird up our loins for work and get on with the work the Lord has given us to do.'

Stephen Hopkins said, 'Before we go ashore, we ought to have an agreement drawn up that every man should sign as to the principles by which the new colony should be governed right from the start.'

John Carver agreed. 'We are not under the Virginia patent here, so we are not subject to their laws. It could well be that some would use their own liberty to do as they wish. If that be the case, then this new land will fall into anarchy and disorder. There ought to be laws and rules which we all abide by and which we all agree to, and which everyone who comes after us shall also abide by.'

'An agreement, then,' Christopher Martin said.

So, in Captain Jones' cabin, they drew up a contract which they called the *Mayflower Compact*, which read:

'*In the name of God, Amen. We whose names are underwriten, the loyall subjects of our dread soveraigne Lord, King James, by the grace of God, of Great Britaine, France, & Ireland king, defender of the faith, &c, haveing undertaken for the glorie of God and the advancemente of the Christian faith, and honour of our king and countrie, a voyage to plant the first colonie in the Northerne parts of Virginia, doe by these presents solemnly and mutualy in the presence of God, and one of another, covenant & combine our selves togeather into a civill body politick, for our better ordering & preservation & furtherance of the ends aforesaid; and by vertue herof to enacte, constitute, and frame such just & equall lawes, ordinances, acts, constitutions & offices, from time to time, as shall be thought most meete & convenient for the generall good of the Colonie, unto which we promise all due submission and obedience. In witnes wherof we have herunder subscribed our names at Cap-Codd the 11 of November in the year of the raigne of our soveraigne lord, King James of England, France & Ireland the eighteenth, and of Scotland the fiftie fourth. An^o: Dom. 1620.'*

Forty-one of the sixty-five adult males signed the document. They were: John Carver, William Bradford, Edward Winslow, William Brewster, Isaac Allerton, Myles Standish, John Alden, Samuel Fuller, Christopher Martin, William Mullins, William White, Richard Warren, John Howland, Stephen Hopkins, Edward Tilley, John Tilley, Francis Cooke, Thomas Rogers, Thomas Tinker, John Rigdale, Edward Fuller, John Turner, Francis Eaton, James Chilton, John Crackston, John Billington, Moses Fletcher, John Goodman, Digory Priest, Thomas Williams, Gilbert Winslow, Edmund Margeson, Peter Brown, Richard Britteridge, George Soule, Richard Clark, Richard Gardiner, John Allerton, Thomas English, Edward Dotey, Edward Lister.

That done, they then appointed their first governor, John Carver. He was to be governor for one year when another man would be chosen.

They dug out the shallop from its stowing place in the hold, but inspection found it to have splits in the seams, where it had been thrown about in the storms. 'You can't go ashore in that,' Captain Jones told the Pilgrims. 'It'll sink as though made of lead. I'll get Master Alden to work on it.' John Alden was the carpenter.

Christopher Martin could not hide his frustration. 'Why wasn't the boat lashed down so that it didn't get damaged?' he demanded.

Captain Jones looked at him and shrugged his shoulders in a couldn't-care-less attitude. After all, he had enough things to think about without worrying about trivialities.

Will, eager to set foot in this new land, said, 'Might we not use the longboat, Captain?'

Captain Jones considered it. 'Aye. Master Parker!'

'Aye, Cap'n?'

'Haul out the longboat.'

With their chant to keep the rhythm of the pull, the crew soon had the longboat out of its resting place on the deck, and in the water.

Will's excitement churned in his stomach as he watched. Quickly he made himself ready, determined to be one of the shore party.

'Must you go?' Dorothy asked in that annoying whining voice that she employed when she wanted her own way.

'You know I must,' Will said, holding on to his patience with an effort. 'We need to find a place to settle, to explore this new land.'

'But what is the point of going today? You only have this afternoon, for tomorrow 'tis the Sabbath.'

'I know.' Absolutely nothing must interfere with the Sabbath, and therefore the trip ashore must of necessity be quick.

'B-but it is so wild—so—so barren.'

Will had regained his usual optimism. 'It isn't barren at all. Look at the forest there! It comes right down to the water in places.'

'Will, you do not know what is in those trees. What if it were wild animals—or savages!'

'We have muskets with us,' Will pointed out. He had done his best to learn from Miles Standish, but he was uncomfortably aware that he was no crack shot. 'Besides, there probably aren't any savages.'

'Please don't go.'

He kissed her lightly on her bare pale forehead, and clambered down the rope ladder to join the others in the long boat. He looked for her among the watching faces, but she was not there, and he felt a pull of dismay inside him. She would sulk again, and he must endure her depression when he returned. Still, the excitement of what lay ahead dispelled Dorothy's depression from his mind.

The *Mayflower* had anchored three quarters of a mile from shore because the bottom was too shoal, so they had a distance to row. It was not difficult work, and Will was grateful for the opportunity to stretch his muscles. He looked around him, trying to imprint on his memory every detail of the landscape around him, for he knew this moment would be fleeting. The excitement in his belly made him feel physically sick. Perhaps it was fear as well, he acknowledged. After all, Dorothy was right about wild animals and savages. They didn't know what might await them. He could see his own emotions reflected in the faces of the men around him. They rowed with their backs to the prow, the English way, and kept craning their necks to get a better look.

A grating sound beneath the keel told them that they had run aground. Robert Coppin, the ship's pilot, announced, 'That's it—we get out and walk!'

Will peered over the side and saw the bottom not that far below. It would be cold and wet, but—well—they had been cold and wet for weeks. Another day would hardly be different. They had a short distance to go—about a bow-shot, and there was nothing for it, but to jump out of the boat and into the water.

It was colder than Will had anticipated and the shock of it took his breath away. The water came up to his knees, and washed over his thighs as he walked, filled his shoes and made his whole body shiver. In England, in this weather, he would have sternly advised against paddling in freezing water.

This is it, then, he thought. Our new home.

It was a bit of an anticlimax, after all the weeks of waiting, to be simply wading ashore in freezing water. There ought to be more than this. A fanfare perhaps. A ray of golden sunlight to brighten the cold grey afternoon.

The shore was heavily wooded with oaks, pines, junipers and other trees, and where the woods thinned, birds in vast quantity. No wonder someone had named this place New England. It was just like England. He took several deep sweet breaths. The air seemed so clean and clear after the foul air of the ship, crisp with the oncoming winter. Birds twittered and shrieked in the trees, alarmed at their approach. Will knelt down and clawed up a handful of good black soil, good earth for cultivation, and let it trickle through his fingers. 'It's good to a spit's depth!' This was good land. Strong land. Land for sowing seed and reaping harvests. His heart swelled within him. This was to be their home. Here, somewhere on this coast, near the sea. And in his heart he thanked God yet again for this most wonderful deliverance, for this good earth.

He looked at John Carver, who had recovered sufficiently to join the shore party. John was no farmer, but a merchant. He would have to become a farmer, as they all would. Will had been bred to farming, knew what it was all about, but not John Carver. Still, he could learn, even though he was getting on these days—at six and fifty it was a little late to be learning new tricks.

'Ho!' John Carver bellowed delightedly, 'the ground rocks beneath my feet! It's like being on the ship!'

Will had noticed it too. When he tried to walk he found he rolled from side to side, the way he had often seen sailors do.

'It comes with being on the ship so long,' Robert Coppin told them. 'It will pass.'

Like children let loose from the schoolroom, they wandered about aimlessly, just looking, touching, experiencing. It was stupid, Will realised, lacking in direction, and thought.

Rubbing the blond tuft of beard on his chin Edward Winslow said, 'This is no place to settle. Too exposed to the Atlantic winds and storms. We must find somewhere more suitable, I think.'

Miles Standish agreed. 'No, this will not do.' He picked up a fallen branch in one hand. 'We should take some of this wood back to the ship, though, and we could do with fresh water.'

Edward Tilley emerged from the woods. 'There's a pond behind the trees yonder.'

Oval in shape, the pond was about a mile long, and hidden from the ship by the trees. Edward Winslow dipped his hand in the water and tasted it. 'Not as salty as the sea, but still brackish. It might do for bathing in, or washing clothes, but not for drinking.'

'We could all do with a good wash,' John Carver observed, and laughed his great belly laugh, slapping Will between the shoulder blades. It was no less than the truth. They must all stink something terrible.

'We must stick together,' Miles Standish told them, taking charge of the shore party as he would a military corps. 'No-one must get lost. We don't know what danger there might be.'

Indians, Will thought, and what he had dismissed in Leyden as mere talk, he worried about here. What if they were not alone? He clutched his musket and peered into the trees, expecting savages to charge them at any moment, his stomach fluttering at the thought. Perhaps there were no savages.

They found sand hills, much like those in Holland, but better, and wooded, and there were swampy places with fresh water, edged by great shady cedars, and red sycamores or maples, and great flocks of birds.

Worried that evening would come on before they had returned to the ship, Captain Standish ordered them back to the longboat. They waded the distance and piled into it, with firewood and fresh water and rowed back to the ship.

Lining the gunwales, the others waited for their return, eager to hear about their new home, yet it was in vain that Will searched for Dorothy. She hung back, not coming forward to hear the news, watching him with sorrowful reproachful eyes, while they told of the things they had found. 'It's like England,' Edward Tilley said, 'with sycamore trees, and cedars, and grass, and woods. So like England.'

Never had it been so difficult to observe the Sabbath, which fell the following day when the urge to go ashore surged through the whole company. However, nothing must interfere with the observance of the Sabbath, particularly as they owed their lives to their God.

'It is good land,' Will told Dorothy when they snatched a private moment together on open deck. 'A place to raise children and praise God.'

She looked at him, her blue eyes huge in her white pinched little face. 'It is a cold place,' she said, her voice strangely monotone. 'Barren and empty. And the wind howls across the land.'

Leaning on the guard-rail, Will watched as whales played in the vivid blue sea, huge flukes slapping the surface of the water and sending spray many feet into the air, blowing great plumes as they breathed. 'It isn't barren. And in any case this is just the Cape. We must explore the rest yet.'

'I wish we had never left Holland,' she said in that same strange voice. 'I hate it here.'

Will was dismayed. 'Dorothy. You will see, it will be a good home, and then we can send for Jonathan, and perhaps your parents and sister if they are willing.'

'I will never see any of them again,' Dorothy said looking straight at him. 'You have robbed me, William Bradford, of my son and my family. You have brought me to a place that is deserted and empty, cold and terrible. And here is where I shall die.'

Her quiet statements, her very calmness, caused a nag of disquiet within him. He didn't like it when she was like this. For she was cold and flat and empty.

He reached out to enfold her in his arms, but she turned away out of his reach.

She took herself below, and depression descended on him like a weight, pricking his eyes, burning in his heart.

Dorothy blamed him. Yet he had offered to leave her at home with Jonathan, to send for them both later. It was she who had insisted on coming. Now what was he to do? Take her home again? He couldn't bear to think of it. He did what he always did in times of trouble, and turned to his God in prayer and after a while felt the peace of God calm him. For that was his strength, his God.

THIRTY
Going Ashore

Cape Cod, November 1620

On Monday, the long boat worked in relay to bring the whole company, men, women, children and the dogs—they had two with them—ashore. Miles Standish as military commander, posted sentries, just in case, and while the children ran up and down on the sand, delighted to play and stretch their legs after such a long while cooped up on the ship, the women took laundry to the pond and began to wash the grime of months out of their clothes. The water may have been brackish, but it was such a relief to be able to get rid of the caked dirt, and with the aid of a little lye, bring the white collars and cuffs and caps back to their original colour. Will hoped the visit ashore would bring some life back to Dorothy, but although she went to the pond, she chose a spot by herself, and did not join in with the chatter of the other women. Even when Mary Bewster and Susanna White came to kneel beside her, she kept sullen and silent.

While the women washed, the men searched for anything edible, and found clams and mussels on the shore. However, they did not know how to prepare them, and by that evening everyone who had eaten them, and that included Will and Dorothy, were vomiting and wishing they had left them alone. They put it down to experience. No-one was seriously ill, and no-one died.

On Wednesday sixteen men volunteered to explore on foot towards the south where Captain Jones thought he had seen a river mouth, and Will put himself forward again. Dorothy protested. 'Let others do it. You do not have to go.' He looked down into her childlike eyes and thought of the misery she brought to herself and to others around her. He had endured enough of her depression, her bad moods, her sullenness, her silences.

Miles Standish armed them all with the five-foot long muskets, and taking hold of his, together with the powder horn, wadding and shot, Will hoped he would not have to disobey Jesus' command to love his enemies.

John Carver, also one of the shore party, stood next to Will as they primed their muskets. 'Don't worry about it, Will,' he said in his good natured way, slapping Will between the shoulder blades. 'The Lord will expect you to protect yourself and your brothers.'

'But should any man have to die for that?' Will demanded, and walked away.

Edward Winslow took his own musket and poured some of the black powder down the muzzle. 'It ain't easy for him,'

'He's a fine man,' Carver agreed, nodding. 'Doesn't shirk his duties.'

'No. 'Tis a pity that wife of his don't support him better.'

Carver looked at Winslow from the height of an older man of experience. 'Watch your tongue, young Winslow,' he warned. 'Mistress Bradford is your sister in the Lord. I know you are worried about Will, but his problems are none of our business.'

Edward paused in the act of ramming the wadding home in his musket, then looked at him with those cool grey eyes. After a moment he nodded. 'No, perhaps not.' The column had set off and now that the muskets were loaded, Edward Winslow and John Carver caught the others up.

Joining Dorothy at the gunwale, Katherine Carver put her arm around her shoulders in a comforting gesture. She felt sorry for Dorothy. That the girl was deeply unhappy she could see with her own eyes, but the reason eluded her. 'They won't be gone long, dear,'

'It doesn't matter, does it,' Dorothy said in a flat voice.

Katherine frowned, dismayed. 'Just what is the matter, Dorothy?'

Dorothy turned and looked at her then, her face tragic, her eyes brim full of tears. 'I hate it here,' she whispered. 'I miss my son, and I miss my family, and it is cold and unwelcoming here. I hate it. The men go off with guns, and who knows if we'll ever see them again.'

'God will look after them,' Katherine said soothingly.

'God! I don't think he even bothers with us. Else why did he bring us here at the start of winter to the most inhospitable place on earth? Don't talk to me about God when I prayed so hard for William Button to live, and he just died. Where was God then?'

Katherine was taken aback. 'Dorothy!'

But Dorothy was in full flow and not to be silenced. 'I hate it here! I want to go home!'

Katherine's patience snapped. 'Well, you can't go home! Be grateful that your son is still alive—mine died remember? I have no sons at all and never will have now. Be grateful that your husband loves you. You will see your son soon. Your place, though, is with your husband. He needs you.'

'What does he need me for? I'm just little Dorothy, not much good to him or anyone. Ask him, he'll tell you! Why, don't you know, I'm not even a proper wife to him!'

'Dorothy, you go too far!'

'That's it. All you want to do is take his side. Everyone thinks he is such a—a saint, so capable. Yet I know what he is like.'

Katherine lapsed into offended silence. Perhaps with no response Dorothy would be quietened.

'You don't know about it, do you? You don't know what he's really like, how he lusts after another woman—'

'Mistress Bradford!' William Brewster's firm male voice cut her off. 'Of all things, I have never heard the like of it! That is enough, before I must publicly punish you.' He was talking of public reproof, not physical punishment.

She glared at him mulishly. But Dorothy was wary of William Brewster. All men made her nervous, but William Brewster had an air of authority about him that made her jumpy in his presence. She could not defy him. Perhaps ashamed of herself for her disloyalty, she burst into tears. 'No-one understands,' she wailed.

Brewster met Katherine's eyes. 'Take her below,' he said.

With Dorothy still weeping into her handkerchief, Katherine ushered her below, as the sailors looked on with interest.

Brewster sought Katherine out later. 'A word, if I may, Mistress.'

Picking up her skirts to climb the companionway ladder, Katherine followed him on to open deck where they could not be overheard.

It was cold on deck, and she shivered, pulling her cloak tighter around her shoulders. She could see the longboat tucked into the shore, and wondered where the men were now. They had lost sight of them ages ago. Part of her was afraid for them, for her husband who she adored, for after all, one never knew what might be lurking in those dark woods. The other part of her regretted that she was a not man and able to go with them.

Brother Brewster faced her. 'What you heard today, I am sure I can depend on you not to repeat.'

'You did not need to say, brother.'

'I know. But this is a small ship in a big land. And we are a tightly knit community. If the wrong people heard such a rumour it would be a terrible thing for Master Bradford and for all of us. One day Will Bradford will govern us.'

She frowned. 'You know this?'

'Do not you? He is strong, capable, well-liked. All he lacks now is years.'

'And Dorothy?'

'Dorothy is young, vain and silly,' he said without preamble. '"As a jewel of gold in a swine's snout so is a fair woman which lacketh discretion"!' as the saying goes.'

Katherine allowed herself a smile. But then she was serious. 'Dorothy, I think, is very sad. Melancholic even.'

'Well, it has been a long voyage, fraught with difficulties.'

'True. But it is more than that. It has been going on a long time. If only there were something we could do to help.'

'It is time Dorothy pulled herself together,' he said bluntly. 'A man does not need a whining wife weighing him down.'

'I will talk to her,' Katherine offered.

'Thank you.'

He turned and left her, but she stayed on deck a little longer, watching the shore for any sign of the men, and pondering over what had happened. Was it true, then? Did Will lust after another? And if so, who? She racked her brains and could think of no-one that might have caught Will's eye. Besides, she could not imagine Will, who she knew to be a spiritual God-fearing man, doing anything sinful. Still, if he had looked in the direction of another woman, it was hardly any wonder. Dorothy was no asset to any man, more of a liability. What Will needed, what all the men needed in this new situation, was a decent supportive wife. Katherine, who prided herself on her loyal loving support of her own beloved husband knew just what a loving wife should be. She would speak to Dorothy at the first opportunity.

''Tis a fine good land,' John Carver said, falling in beside Will.

Marching along with the others, trying to ignore the discomfort of cold wet feet and legs and even his bottom from wading ashore, Will, had been thinking and worrying about Dorothy. Now he looked at John Carver. 'So it is,' he agreed.

John Carver took a deep breath, heaving good clean—and cold—air into his lungs with a sense of well-being unknown since they embarked on this voyage. 'I can see it all. A settlement in this land. We will be successful, Will.'

'Aye.'

John Carver frowned at him, but they marched along in silence for some time. Then he asked, 'What ails you, Will?'

Will shrugged. 'Nothing.'

'No? Well that's a very loud nothing to me!'

Will sighed. 'Dorothy wants to go home.'

'Well,' John wiped his hand across his beard, 'you might have to take her back, then.'

It had crossed Will's mind. Yet it was unthinkable that he should leave the rest here, and go all the way back to England when the *Mayflower* returned. It was the worst possible outcome for him. This emigration, this new land, had been his dream for four years or more. He had worked for it, and prayed about it, and worried about it for all that time. It had been his goal in life, his reason for living, the will of his God. And Dorothy could bring it all to nothing. And he knew that if she did, he would never forgive her.

'Perhaps it won't come to that,' he said. 'Perhaps when we have built a home, and settled down, she will see things differently.'

''Tis not the most auspicious time to be landing here, with winter coming on,' John agreed. 'Perhaps with the spring—hey, what's that?'

Will, who had been studying the sand just in front of his feet, following the footprints of the others, looked up. Half a dozen people and a dog came towards them on the sand. His heart lurched with shock. The shore party came to a halt in their surprise, for they had thought themselves the only ones there.

The other group halted too.

''Tis Master Jones,' Stephen Hopkins said. After all, the captain of the *Mayflower* and some of his men were also ashore.

Will had better eyesight than Stephen Hopkins and he could see they were not Europeans. Clad in what appeared to be leather tabards, some wearing a feather in their hair, they were without a doubt the local inhabitants. Whether they were male or female, they were too far away to tell. 'Indians, I think,' he said very quietly.

Stephen Hopkins recovered from his surprise first, and yelled, 'Hoi!'

Will grabbed his arm. 'Don't frighten them!'

It was too late. Rather than coming towards them, the Indians fled, whistling the dog after them, taking to the woods.

John Carver was disappointed. 'We would have done well to speak to them.'

Miles Standish raised a sceptical eyebrow. 'Oh yes? And get ourselves murdered perhaps?' He looked around him uneasily. 'There could be more of them, lying in wait for us.'

'An ambush?' John Tilley asked also scanning the trees around him nervously. A whole lot of Indians could be hidden in those trees.

John Carver was not in the least nervous. Rather he had it in mind to speak to the natives, for to his mind it was unthinkable that they could be violent people. 'Let's go after them.'

Miles Standish rubbed his red whiskers. 'If we're caught out here on the shore, we're easy meat.'

'Somehow, I wish you hadn't said that,' Edward Winslow remarked dryly, and, clutching his musket tightly, fell in with the others as they marched after the Indians at a quicker pace. Will's fears turned to a strange excitement.

'We might well come across their habitation, seeing that you're so set on conflabbing with them,' Standish said to John Carver as they tramped after the Indians. 'Though how you expect to speak with people who can't speak English is beyond me.'

'There are signs,' John Carver said optimistically. No hurdle was too large for them to conquer. With the Lord's help of course.

'P'raps. But I hope they don't want to kill us before we have had the chance.'

The Indians had vanished. The English, encumbered with armour, swords and muskets, followed the tracks the Indians had left at a much slower pace, all the while looking around them nervously. Here the Indians ran up a hill to see if they were followed. There you could see they were following their own footprints back, trying to fool the strangers. All of this Miles Standish interpreted to them as he studied the tracks with serious intent. Not that any of them could not have come to the same conclusion, Will thought. It was obvious enough.

They had travelled just five miles or so when night came on. There was no going back now.

Miles Standish took control. He appointed three men as sentinels, while others gathered wood and made a fire. They had brought no beer or water with them, and had only a little ships' biscuit and some Dutch cheese and a small bottle of strong liquor called *aqua vitae* made from strongly-hopped beer, well fermented which did nothing to quench the thirst. They rationed it all out. How short-sighted of them not to bring something, Will thought. And even more short-sighted not to shoot one or two of the wild fowl they spotted on the way, instead of chasing Indians. John Carver led them all in prayer, asking for God's protection, before those not on watch settled down to sleep.

Will slept a little, but it was uneasy sleep. Not only did he have one ear open in case of sudden attack, but the cold seeped through into his core. It was a relief when it was his turn to take watch, with Edward Winslow and John Tilley.

Unnerved by the presence of Indians, tales of whom had filled those in Leyden with dread, Will kept very much on the watch, peering into the night, trying to pierce the darkness until his eyes ached. Where were they? Were they skulking around the camp, watching their every move waiting for their chance? Or were they perhaps back in their own village, wherever that might be, discussing the English, drawing up a plan of attack? However, the watch passed without incident, and he slept a little more soundly when, two hours later, he was relieved by John Doty.

The morning found them once more tracking the Indians. They stopped in a valley at mid-morning, ate sour blueberries and whortleberries and drank from a fresh stream. They built a fire to let Captain Jones know they were still alive.

And no doubt to alert the Indians as to their whereabouts, Will thought, and a shiver ran up his spine.

The Indians didn't need to be alerted.

By mid afternoon, Will had to admit he was exhausted. The weight of the armoury, and the unfamiliar exercise took its toll. He was desperately hungry. But when Miles Standish said it was time to continue, he made no demur. If the older men could do it, so could he, even though he now regarded Standish with something akin to dislike!

A little further on they found about fifty acres of flat plain earth with rows of corn stalks left behind when the Indians had harvested.

'What's this?' Miles Standish stood still looking at some sand heaps. One was covered with old mats, and had a wooden top to it, and an earthen pot in a hole at one end.

'What do you think it is?' John Howland asked, and everyone looked at Stephen Hopkins who had been in America before and might therefore be expected to know. He just shrugged however.

Will, though, had a strange feeling about this. The Indians were here. He could feel them watching, feel their eyes boring into his back. Beneath the weight of his clothes, goosebumps rippled on his forearms, the hairs stood up on the back of his neck.

Miles Standish began to dig, and found a bow, and what might have once been some arrows. That confirmed Will's unease. 'They're graves! I think we should go!'

'Do you think so?' John Carver asked with interest. 'Perhaps it would be better not to disturb the graves in case they don't like it.'

Edward Winslow gazed about him fearfully. 'I agree.'

To Will's relief, Miles Standish put the bow back and the sand, and made it up as it was, and left the rest alone.

They went on. There was more corn stubble and some walnut trees still full of nuts after a mild autumn, and strawberries. This was a real find, and they ate some.

Two fields later they came to another field where the stubble indicated that the Indians had worked this land this year, and here they found the remains of a house, five old planks laid together and, surprise, a European ship's kettle.

'So how did this get here?' Edward Winslow demanded.

'There was a tale of a French ship wrecked at Cape Cod,' Stephen Hopkins ventured. 'As far as I heard it, all the crew were saved, and some of their victuals and other things.'

'What happened to them?' Edward Doty asked.

Stephen Hopkins shrugged again. 'Who knows?'

'Perhaps the Indians killed them,' John Howland said.

Miles Standish glared at him, and his voice when he spoke was full of menace. 'Any more of that, John Howland, and we'll leave you here on your own!'

'Perhaps this is indeed all that remains of the French,' Will suggested. Then he spotted another heap of sand, newly done, for the Indians had obviously patted it with their hands, the imprints still on the sand. 'What's this?'

Edward Doty dug this time, and found a small basket of Indian corn, and further down a large new basket full of this year's corn with three dozen ears of corn, some yellow, and some red, and others, curiously, mixed with blue. The basket held about four bushels, or eight gallons, and took two men to lift it from the ground.

'I don't like this,' Will said. 'It's stealing.'

''Tis a gift from God, Will,' John Carver, the optimist, told him.

'And if the Indians are watching?' Edward Winslow demanded.

So Miles Standish posted the rest of the men all around in a ring.

'What shall we do with it?'

John Carver had no doubts. ''Tis a gift from God,' he repeated. 'We take it with us!'

''Tis stealing,' said Will again on a note of reproof.

'We will make reparation to the Indians,' Carver pointed out. 'Give them back the kettle. But we need the food. And it will feed us for a while.'

They filled the kettle with loose corn, and two men carried it on their shoulders with its staff. Others filled their pockets and then they buried the rest, for they could carry no more.

They went on, and found the remains of an old fort, or palisade, perhaps again of European origin, beside which seemed to be a river. But whether the river was of the sea, or whether it was fresh, they did not discover, for a high cliff blocked their descent.

Christopher Jones had impressed on them that they should be no longer than two nights away from the *Mayflower*, and it was time to be going back. But this appeared to be the river that Captain Jones had seen from the ship, with a bank dividing it into two halves. And there also they found two canoes. It was tempting to stay, and explore further, but it was getting late, and they must go back, leaving any further exploration until the shallop had been mended.

At a freshwater pond they set up camp for the night, making a huge fire, and a barricade, partly against the wind, and partly against any sudden attack by the natives, and set three sentinels on watch with a lighted match at the ready—just in case—and settled down to another uneasy night.

Will, struggling to get some sleep cursed the rain which beat down on them, and thought of Dorothy. There was something there that nagged at him, worried him, caused any sleep that he might have to be full of vivid dreams. He knew that with Dorothy the situation was serious, that it would not be easily resolved, that she would make his life—well, hell—in the way only a wife could if she did not get her own way. Oh for a supporting wife such as Mary Brewster, or Katherine Carver or—or Alice!

He banished the thought immediately from his mind. He must try and sleep, no matter how cold the rain, how sodden the earth beneath him.

Not before time, Miles Standish had them all up on their feet in the cold grey dawn, made them trim their muskets, before they set off. No breakfast this morning. There was none to be had. They left the kettle behind at the pond.

They trudged on in tired miserable silence. Everyone was grumpy through lack of sleep, lack of food, and the wet conditions and jumpy from the threat of Indian attack.

'Alright, so where are we then?' Edward Tilley asked curtly a short way on.

Will said, 'Don't tell me we're lost! Faith! How can we go wrong? We have only to follow the shore—'

He hadn't seen the trap set beneath the tree. A cry of shock escaped him as a loop of rope jerked at his foot, swept him off his feet and hurled him into the air. With his heart hammering, and an excruciating pain in his hip, he bounced up and down, swinging dizzyingly, and then dangled like a fish on a line in mid air, upside down from the rope caught around one foot.

The others stopped to look round at him. For a moment he couldn't quite make out what had happened and the new view of the world, as he swung some twenty feet off the ground, confused him.

The others gathered round. 'I was just saying,' Stephen Hopkins said, helpfully, and unable to hide his chuckles, 'that it looks like a snare for a deer.'

'Well, you might have mentioned it a little louder!' Will protested, peering at everyone from his upside-down vantage point. The blood was rushing to his head, and the pain in his hip joint from the sudden jerk was agonising.

John Carver burst out laughing in that great booming voice of his, and the others joined in. It did little for Will's temper. 'Get me down!'

They cut him down, and he fell into their arms, and then in a heap at their feet. 'Are you hurt?' they asked peering at him anxiously.

'Only my pride!' he said getting up and brushing bits of tree off his coat. But his hip ached, and when they set off again, he limped.

Back on board the *Mayflower* they gave their report to the party who had been left behind, telling of fertile land, of game and meat to be had, of fresh water, and of Indians. The talk of Indians made the others anxious.

'I think we should be careful not to take any chances,' Miles

278

Standish said briskly. 'Post a sentinel, that kind of thing. When we find a place to settle, we must build a stockade.'

'Could we not make peace with the savages?' William Brewster asked reasonably.

'Can't always do that,' Stephen Hopkins gave them the benefit of his experience. 'It depends. But we can try. Still, I think we might be at a disadvantage, having taken their corn and touched the grave.'

'For the corn we will make recompense,' Will said. 'Else it would be stealing.'

'Which it is, of course,' Brewster said in mild reproof.

'And I thought you damn Puritans didn't believe in stealing,' put in John Billington. 'After all, you didn't ask. And if you take without asking—well it seems to me them savages ain't going to take kindly to our presence. We'll all be murdered in our sleep.'

'That's enough!' Miles Standish cried, jumping to his feet and glaring threateningly at John Billington. 'I don't recall seeing you on the expedition and able to give us the benefit of your great wisdom!'

'That's it, Captain Shrimp, fire up, why don't you!'

Miles Standish's eyes flashed. William Brewster came between them. 'That will do,' he said in a stern voice. 'We have enough to deal with without squabbling among ourselves.'

Later, when Will sat down next to Dorothy, carefully because of his painful hip, she said, 'I was afraid for you, husband.'

'Were you?' he asked non-committally, wondering what she would say next.

'What would I do if ought happened to you?'

He peered at her in the lantern light. She did not look at him, and her averted face was set, strange. 'Would you miss me?'

'Of course.'

He frowned, perplexed and saddened. She would miss him in the sense that he had the task of providing for her. But he doubted that she would be heartbroken. He wanted to cry out, to protest, to take her in his arms, and tell her he loved her. Yet he doubted the truth of it. Perhaps he did not love her. How could a man feel warmth towards such a cold distant creature, however pretty? And he wondered if he had ever really loved her.

He climbed into their shared bed, weary to the very heart of him, grateful for some kind of warmth, for drier clothes, for food in his belly. And he fell into a deep sleep.

He awoke sometime during the night to the sound of someone near him coughing harshly, a terrible barking cough that seemed to come from his boots. Will went back to sleep, but by the morning it seemed to him that everyone was coughing and sneezing and wheezing.

''Tis the cold weather,' Sam Fuller explained, in answer to Will's query. 'Having to wade ashore to get wood to mend the shallop, we've all got colds, as I knew we would.'

'If only the weather were better,' Will said, but he was loathe to complain. They were alive, and they had lost just one man. It was a blessing from the Lord.

THIRTY-ONE
Exploration

December 1620

As November came to a close, the weather turned wintry. The wind blew mercilessly out of the north-east, off the sea, leaving a coating of glassy frost on the decks. Inside the ship, you could see a man's breath in the cold air, when you could see at all, and the passengers were allowed no fire, either to heat themselves with or to cook with; the potential danger to the ship was too great.

Will was acutely aware of the need to find a place to settle, to get them out of the ship and onto dry land. Every day they delayed brought the agony of winter closer, when it would be difficult to find a suitable place under snow and ice and when the cold which was already penetrating would become lethal. The cramped and difficult conditions made people morose and tetchy and he hated the arguments and niggles that continually broke out between men who should know better. Besides, the coughs and colds had become an epidemic.

So far, the shore party had found nowhere favourable, and it was decided that when the bigger shallop was finally ready thirty-four men—twenty-four Pilgrims and the rest sailors which included the *Mayflower*'s captain—should go ashore again to search out the river they found previously.

The idea was to take a closer look at the divided river they had found on the first expedition, hoping this might prove to be a suitable place to settle. With the weather worsening, and with cross winds which battered the shallop threatening to swamp her they ran into the shore as close as they could but as usual, had to wade in knee-deep water to get to the land.

'We can go no further in the shallop,' Captain Jones said.

'We will go ashore,' John Carver announced. 'Come to us when you can.'

With wet and frozen feet and shoes, they struggled to build a stockade to windward to shelter them from the worst of the gale, while the first tiny flakes of snow bounced onto brown grass blown horizontal in the driving wind. It was sheer misery. Will found it difficult to keep positive and not to curse the biting cold, the stinging snow. Before long a blizzard obscured his vision, stinging his eyes, sticking to his beard and moustache, driving the blood from his fingers and toes.

With the coming of night the cold grew stronger. It froze hard overnight, and the shore party huddled together in the lee of the stockade in an attempt to rest, and Will thought he had never in his life been so cold.

He curled up tight, and tried to ignore the pain in his feet and in his hands, but his teeth chattered, and he could not—dared not sleep. It was a relief to take his turn at sentinel. In the morning the landscape was white with drifting snow that caught in the dips and against mounds, and breath froze in beards and moustaches.

At about eleven o'clock the next day, the shallop came for them, and with the wind direction changing for the better, so that they could use the sails, they made for the river which someone appropriately called Cold Harbour. It was a disappointment. Not fit for ships, only for boats, being just twelve feet deep at high tide.

Leaving just a few men to sail the shallop they got out and marched along the shore, intent on finding the head of the river to see whether it would be fresh water. It was hilly country, hard going in the snow, and at last they gave up, exhausted. It was far too hilly to be of use to them. They camped there beneath some pine trees, and dined on geese and ducks which they had managed to shoot.

'We ought to see whether there is fresh water at the head of the river,' Stephen Hopkins suggested.

'I like it not,' John Carver boomed. 'The land is hilly, too much hard work. And for what? Even if we do find fresh water, the land is too hilly for us to build a settlement.'

Will agreed with this. It would be wasting time and energy to go further up the river.

So they turned instead towards the north part of the divided river.

'A boat,' Will said, surprised, staring at a native canoe, resting on the bank.

Unimpressed, Miles Standish shot some geese, and they used the canoe to retrieve them, and to take them to the opposite bank. Then they tramped to the place they had named Corn Hill.

'There might be more corn here if we look,' Stephen Hopkins suggested.

Will was uneasy. He looked around him, certain that they were being watched, fearful of discovery by the Indians. He ought to have been braver, but the feeling persisted. 'Well, hurry up then.'

They dug around and found another stash of corn, and in another place a bottle of oil, perhaps from the shipwrecked sailors previously spoken of. Yet more corn in another place, and a bag of beans. Altogether they found about ten bushels of corn. It was enough to keep the people in the *Mayflower* alive for some time.

'We should thank God for this,' Will suggested, trying to square it with his conscience. Without it they would starve.

They sent the corn, and some of the company who had become ill, back to the *Mayflower* in the shallop. Eighteen stayed behind however, and waited for the shallop to come back the next day, bringing with it some tools which they badly needed.

Will looked around him, and felt the hairs rise on the back of his neck. 'I think the Indians are here, and that we are being watched,' he said. 'And I think it would be better to make friends with them, than enemies.'

'Then we will follow their paths,' Miles Standish said.

They tramped on, following beaten paths, and at one point got their matches ready for the muskets, thinking they must be near habitation, but they were wrong. They found no signs of the people, and they returned to the coast another way.

'What's that?' Stephen Hopkins asked, pointing ahead.

Captain Miles Standish peered ahead. 'It looks like another grave.'

Will groaned. 'Leave it be, then. We should not interfere with other people's graves.'

'And how do you think we will find anything out?' Standish demanded impatiently.

There was no stopping them. They removed boards from the top of the grave, and dug it up.

Will felt a shiver run up his back. They were watching them, he knew it. He could feel their eyes upon him.

'Leave be,' he recommended. ''Tis only a grave.'

Already they had found a mat, beneath that a bow, and the another mat, and under that a board about two foot three inches long, carved and painted, with three spikes on the top like a crown. Also there were bowls, trays, dishes, and other things. Another mat, and two bundles, one bigger than the other. Opening the larger one, they found a great deal of fine red powder which smelled strongly, but not unpleasantly and was evidently used for embalming, for also inside was the skull and bones of a man.

'It's got yellow hair!' Edward Winslow exclaimed, he who also had yellow hair. 'How on earth—?' Also there was a knife, a pack-needle and some pieces of iron. It was wrapped in a sailor's canvas shirt and a pair of cloth breeches.

'Perhaps it was an Indian king, or lord?' Miles Standish suggested.

'Indians all have black hair,' Stephen Hopkins said impatiently. 'This man was European. A Christian.'

'Well, he must have been of special note,' Winslow suggested. 'Look at all the things they buried with him. And the child.' The child was in the other bundle.

'Perhaps they buried him with all those things to honour him,' Standish suggested.

'Or to triumph over his death?' John Carver put in.

Miles Standish, to Will's intense objection took some of the things, then they covered up the grave again.

'Ho—and who is this?' Carver asked rhetorically as two men came towards them from the sea.

'Sailors,' Will said shortly. He didn't like this interfering with the graves. It made him uneasy.

The sailors came nearer. 'There be two houses yonder!' they told the shore party.

They were two native dwellings, lithe saplings bent over with both ends in the ground to make a framework, and covered with mats inside and out.

Will, curious as he was, did not like being there. This was someone else's house. The people had run off at their approach, which was hardly surprising, for they were a fearsome looking lot with their beards and armour and muskets. It occurred to Will then that the Indians were as afraid of them as they were of the Indians. It did not allay his own misgivings. Frightened people acted irrationally. At any moment the whole tribe could appear and they would be as good as defenceless.

'Come on,' he said, 'let's go.'

But the others were less concerned. They went in the small door, which was another mat, and helped themselves to trinkets that they found—wooden bowls, trays, dishes, earthen pots, and so on. An English bucket stood in the corner. Rushes and sedge, and other stuff were stored for making the mats, and in a hollow tree they found pieces of venison. They did not view it as suitable for human food, however.

And they found more corn, which they attributed to God's good grace.

But the place was unsuitable for a settlement. They came back to the ship with the corn and some of the things they had found.

'Mistress White has given birth to a son while you were away,' William Brewster informed them. 'Peregrine.'

'Is that all that has happened?' Will asked, grateful to be with his old friend again.

'Aye.' Brewster looked at him. 'I would rather the shore party did not keep raiding the Indians, Will.'

Will agreed. 'I suggest you speak to Master Carver about it. He is the governor.' He brushed his hair off his forehead. 'I don't think any of this land here will do for us. The land is not big enough just here on this Cape, for us and the Indians. They were here first and we must of necessity be too close to them.'

'Will, we must find somewhere soon. People are becoming ill.

Edward Thompson has a fever and a terrible cough, and I tell you none of us likes the look of it. His lungs are clogged and his breathing laboured. This ship has served us well, but we must get our people ashore now.'

Will rubbed his hands over his face wearily. 'Then we will have to look farther afield,' he said.

At a meeting on the open deck, others disagreed. 'There is nothing wrong with the freshwater river,' Stephen Hopkins said. 'It is a decent harbour, the soil is good—witness the corn we have brought back—the fishing excellent, and the whaling—if we had the means—and it is a healthy and secure location.'

Captain Jones coughed. 'Excuse me, gentlemen, but I have to say I don't think the river is the best location.'

Edward Winslow agreed. 'It would be foolish to settle in the first place we see without really looking.'

Richard Coppin said, 'Across the bay from here, there is a river which flows into the bay at a place Captain John Smith named as Plymouth.'

'I think that sounds an excellent place,' Captain Jones said.

'Certainly we could look,' Will agreed.

'So you are away again.' Dorothy's face was as white and bleak as the winter landscape around them.

A watery sun had chosen to send forth a few weak rays, but it did little to warm them as they stood together on the open deck. It was the only place to get any privacy, however, something Will knew Dorothy felt the lack of most keenly.

Will said patiently, 'We must find somewhere to go ashore and settle before the *Mayflower* has to leave us.'

She looked at him, her big blue eyes huge in their sunken sockets. 'I want to go home, Will. I want to go back with the *Mayflower*.'

Will felt as though a hand had caught his heart and squeezed. He stared at the icy sea, an impossibly vivid blue colour, as smooth as a pond, like a mirror. And suddenly a spurt shot water into the air and a huge black shape broke the surface sending creaming ripples as far as the ship.

Magnificent beasts, Will thought. With their huge flukes, diving in and out of the water. They often came right up to the ship, and Captain Jones had said many times that it was a pity they did not have the means to catch them, for they would be good for meat and oil, an export the Pilgrims could not afford to miss. Yet it would be a shame to kill anything so magnificent. Dangerous too.

Dorothy was unimpressed by the magnificence. 'This is a terrible place, Will. I hate it here.'

'But when we have our own little house, and our farm, it will be different, you'll see. We will send for Jonathan, and your parents if they have a mind—'

'And when will that be?' she cried, her voice rising shrilly, and she burst into tears. 'When we are all dead of the cold, or the Indians have murdered us all? If you think I want Jonathan or my parents here in this— this wilderness, your wits must have gone a-begging!'

Will's heart plummeted. There was no reasoning with her when she was in this mood, and he did not intend to try. 'We are not going home Dorothy,' he said firmly. 'We are staying and we will build our home here.'

She looked up at him, and her face had that pinched closed expression he had come to dread. 'Well, I am not staying,' she announced. 'I shall go back when Captain Jones returns.'

Will looked at her, and wondered what on earth he was to do. She could be as unyielding as flint. He knew that if she returned without him, it would be the end of their marriage. He thought of living here alone, with no wife and no hope of marrying, and he felt so empty and desolate that he wondered if he could do it. But then, where was his faith? His God had brought him here to start afresh, to give the church a new direction. Surely He would give him the strength to deal with whatever Dorothy did.

But then of course, there was the humiliation. Would Brother Brewster advise him that the place to be was at his wife's side? When he had worked so hard to get here? And nagging in the far recesses of his heart was Alice. He squashed that thought firmly. It wasn't helpful.

'It is your Christian duty to stay by your husband,' he said. 'And neither you nor I have the money to pay your passage back to England. I doubt, too, whether Master Jones will allow you, a woman on your own, aboard his ship with all those sailors.'

'What are you saying?' she demanded.

'That it is not safe. I cannot allow it.'

She studied his face and knew that he meant it. He would stop her going. Forcibly if he had to. He was not a short-tempered or violent man, but he did have an iron determination. She knew it, and for all her bravado, she knew she could not defy him.

He turned away from her, leaving her alone on open deck, and marched smartly to the hatch. *We shall see, Mistress Rebellion,* he said to himself..

He reached the hatch in a black mood, at the end of his patience. He could take no more from her, he decided. She was not going, and that was that.

A huge bang shattered the quiet of the ship reverberating through its structure.

Will halted at the companionway ladder, astonished, and trying to decide what it was. The powder magazine? No. Not loud enough. And besides, they were still afloat. A musket then.

He slid down the ladder the way the sailors did. The air below reeked of gunpowder, and thick smoke, and in the confined space the shouts and bellows and screams of panic hit him like a wall.

Will grabbed young Love Brewster as he came running past. 'What is going on?'

Love paused and looked up at Will with wide eyes. ''Tis Francis Billington, sir. Let off his father's gun he did.'

An unchristian oath sprang to Will's imperfect and sorely tried lips, and he only just managed to stifle it. He pushed his way through the mass of gabbling people, and suddenly Miles Standish appeared holding the fourteen year old Francis Billington by the left ear.

'Fire's out!' Standish announced. 'And here's the culprit. Thought he'd let off his father's fowling-piece. Set light to the deck!'

'We could have been killed,' Mistress Allerton cried. 'We could have lost the ship and our lives.'

'Yes we could!' Standish agreed. He took off his belt and advanced on young Billington with intent.

Young Francis Billington stood his ground bravely. His mother Ellen turned away but John Billington put himself between Standish and the boy.

'You will beat my son?'

'Do you not think your son deserves it? We could all have been killed.'

Billington looked at young Francis. 'Nevertheless, he is my son to discipline.'

Standish glared at Billington. 'Hand the boy over for punishment,' he ordered.

'You have no right to order me.'

'No,' John Carver intervened. 'But I have. Hand the boy over.'

John Billington glared at them all. Then he turned away also. 'The boy deserves all he gets,' he said with a shrug.

Miles Standish gave young Billington a sound thrashing on his bottom and he howled and screamed and kicked furiously.

On the sixth day of December 1620 the shore party of ten men as well as some of the sailors left the *Mayflower* in the shallop to travel south down the coast with a view to discovering Plymouth, the spot across the bay indicated by Captain John Smith on his earlier exploration.

The weather had turned for the worst, the cold extreme. Will sat in the shallop with so many layers of clothes on beneath his cloak that his knees and elbows bent only with difficulty. Yet still he shivered. Steam came from noses and mouths and froze beards and moustaches coating them with frost, making them look old before their time. In England and in Leyden, will had never known weather like it. As the shallop ploughed through the waves, the spray settled on their clothing and froze hard, as if they were glazed.

It called for endurance and faith and determination, but Will was worried about the older ones among them—the Tilley brothers for example were all but insensible from the cold and could not move, and the *Mayflower*'s master gunner became very ill.

'Perhaps we should turn back,' Will suggested, worried by them.

'You'll not turn back on our account,' Edward Tilley said through chattering teeth. So they went on. Will's fingers and toes went dead, his face stiff from the cold. The wind was strong and blew off the sea, and seemed to go right through the layers of clothing. He gritted his teeth and tried to shake off the terrible discomfort, for he knew, they all knew, how desperate they were to find a place to settle.

As night approached they passed what came to be called Wellfleet Bay, and they came nearer to shore, knowing they must stop for the night, but finding the sand flats a barrier to their coming in close to shore.

Will saw something moving on the beach in the half-light. 'What's that?'

Robert Coppin stretched out the telescope to have a better look. 'Indians,' he said. 'About twelve of them. Busy at something. Can't see what.'

'Better not go ashore there, then.'

'No choice, Master Bradford. We be on the flats and have but little choice in the matter. Unless you want to spend the night on the water?'

Will looked at him. He had come to know Robert Coppin well since he had first arrived in Leyden as the *Speedwell*'s pilot. He knew him to be a man of skill where the business of sailoring was concerned. Yet he was uneasy that they must land so near the Indians.

Miles Standish was uneasy too. 'I don't like it.'

The Indians scattered as they came ashore, but Will had no doubt that they hid in the trees behind the shore, watching them haul the boat up onto the sand. He could feel their eyes upon him as he helped build the barricade. It sent the prickles up his neck, and he remembered yet again the stories of cannibals and heathen cruelty. What was it they said? They would skin a man alive? As he sat down with the others to eat a dinner of ship's biscuit and rock hard salt beef, he watched the smoke rising from the Indians' fire only a few miles away.

'We'll all be murdered while we sleep,' John Clarke, another of the *Mayflower*'s pilots grumbled.

A twig snapped outside the barricade, and they reached for their muskets. Will's heart thudded in his throat, as he peered into the growing dusk, but he could see could see nothing. It was unnerving. Will knew they were vulnerable, for the barricade would be of only limited value in the case of an attack.

'They're out there alright,' Edward Winslow whispered to Will, as they kept up their position peering over the barricade.

'They're only curious,' Will whispered back, and he wished he believed it. 'Frightened probably.'

'Frightened people are dangerous people,' Miles Standish said.

They spent an uneasy night. The morning was just as cold, their breath white steam, and ice had formed on the muskets.

'If we split up, one half coasting along the shore by boat, and the other half tramping the coast and we might see if there be a fit place to settle,' Miles Standish announced over a breakfast of ship's biscuit.

Will and Edward Winslow were of the shore party, and went with Miles Standish, Stephen Hopkins and others, following the bare footprints of the Indians. How anyone could walk along in this weather without shoes was beyond Will's comprehension, but he was pleased to be moving—it kept the blood circulating, and stopped him freezing. However, the pain in his hip began to nag him.

They found no Indians. They found another graveyard, and some more house frames without mat coverings, but that was all.

Meeting again with the shallop they built a barricade near what came to be known as Eastham, and set a sentinel and tried again to sleep.

Will dozed uneasily. What with the cold, and the tension, it was impossible to get comfortable. He envied the sailors' ability to drop off at a moment's notice! That, he realised was borne of necessity—when a man has four hours on watch and four hours off, save for the dog watch, which was two and two, then he has to be ready to sleep anywhere and in any condition at a moment's notice.

He thought of Dorothy, and how he had left her weeping this time, begging him not to go. She was so difficult to deal with. So difficult to understand. So hard to please! He drifted off to sleep eventually, and dreamed of Indians.

'Arm! Arm!' The sentinel's voice shook him instantly wide awake and set his heart pounding in his ears. Reaching for his musket he leaned the barrel on the top of the barricade. A whooping or yelling, he wasn't sure what, echoed around them

Miles Standish fired his piece, the noise echoing in the night, as did some others. The noise stopped.

'I've heard that noise before,' one of the sailors said in the sudden hush, 'In Newfoundland.'

'Wolves, very like,' Edward Winslow said prosaically.

Will tried to believe him, but he got no further sleep that night.

It was a relief when morning came and the company roused themselves and made preparations to travel.

The cold was even worse, the wind coming off the Atlantic, cutting at faces and exposed hands like a scythe. Will tried not to let it affect him, but the cold was numbing, and his hip ached like toothache.

Still, they were alive. Joining the others in kneeling on the frozen ground Will thanked God for their deliverance from the terrors of the night.

'Right, we'll load the shallop,' Standish announced.

Will looked out across the sand dunes to the boat. It wasn't far, but when one was labouring with goods, it would be warm work. That would be no bad thing.

'Shall we put our guns straight into the boat?' John Tilley asked. He caused them no little anxiety because he was so obviously ill, and so determined not to let it affect his work.

'No,' Miles Standish said unequivocally. 'The savages could be back at any moment, and if we're unarmed, we're dead.'

'You think they'll be back?' Edward Winslow asked doubtfully.

'Oh yes, they'll be back. Whether we'll be here by then, though, is another matter. So let's get loaded, and get out of here.'

Accordingly, they began carting all their things down to the boat.

However, the muskets which were large and heavy and unwieldy with long barrels, hampered their movements. Once the boat was in the water it was a lot further away than it looked. There is only so much a man can carry, and some of them, despite Miles Standish's constant railing, put their muskets down on the bank. It was certainly a temptation. Leaving them there, they worked until the call for breakfast when they all trooped up the bank again to their little barricade.

Suddenly a sound, a cry, varying in notes, the same voices they had heard in the night, quite near, stilled them. Will shivered, the hairs rising on the back of his neck. This was it. He had his musket, but the other muskets were on the bank outside. At that moment John Howland came running up the bank. 'Men! Indians! Indians!' followed by a shower of arrows pouring out of the sky like murderous rain.

'Arm!' Standish cried, taking control.

Those who had left their guns on the bank scrambled to get them, while Will and others who had theirs by them, gave them covering fire.

With the barrel of his musket resting on the top of the barricade, he looked down the length of the barrel and tried to aim at the trees so that he didn't hit anyone, and pulled the trigger. The report deafened him, the stock kicked back into his shoulder and nearly knocked him over. He expected that. He had practised enough. Only this was different. This was real combat.

The initial shock, gave way to a calm determination. The rush of excitement, like he had taken strong drink, cleared his brain, making his senses acute. He reloaded with painful slowness.

Miles Standish fired into a mass of half-clad bodies rushing towards them, for he had one of the new snaphance or snaplock muskets. These were a step forward from the old matchlock which had to be fired like a cannon. The snaplock used a flint to fire the gun. Will fired again, his brain crystal clear, his whole mind calculating.

Edward Winslow and Edward Doty had by now charged their muskets and stood ready at the entrance of the barricade.

'Aim first. Don't waste your shot!' Miles Standish bellowed like a madman above the sudden chaos.

Will re-loaded again, but it was an agonisingly slow process. A man could cross fifty yards in the time it took to re-load a musket! Again he brought his musket to bear.

Those that had run out to recover their muskets found Indians whooping and yelling and wheeling around them. Will watched in growing horror. The English brandished cutlasses, their armour protecting them from the worst, until they could get to their arms. Then they fired their muskets into the Indians.

To the Indians the crash of muskets and the whiz of balls past their ears came as a terrible shock. They fell back. Only one lusty young man, who they thought to be their leader, hiding behind a tree, continued to fire three arrows at the fort. Three men fired at him, but missed. Then Miles Standish took careful aim and fired.

The bark of the tree flew off into splinters, and the man gave a terrible shriek and took off with all his friends and relatives.

In a show of bravado, some of the sixteen men by the boat gave chase.

'Was anyone hurt?' John Carver asked. Always his first concern was the welfare of his people.

'Not a one,' Miles Standish grinned, well pleased. 'Not a one.'

'No, and only one Indian slightly hurt,' Will said with relief. He looked at his musket with something akin to surprise. 'Not very accurate, are they?'

Miles Standish glared at him. ''Tis the man who shoots who is not accurate, sir!'

'Look at my coat!' John Tilley wailed. It had been hanging up on the barricade, and a dozen arrows looking for all the world like hedgehog spines, pinned it to the wooden wall. In all more than a hundred arrows stuck in the wall, and all the coats hanging there had holes in them.

'Could've been yer head!' Miles Standish pointed out dourly.

'Why do you think they attacked?' Will asked.

'Savages,' Miles Standish said shortly. 'Stands to reason.'

Will frowned, thoughtful. They had stolen corn from the Indians, and disturbed their burial chambers, and taken interesting items that belonged to them. Yet surely savages were not as concerned with such things as 'civilised' white men?

So they gave God special thanks for his help in vanquishing their enemies, gathered up some of the arrows with a view to sending them back as curiosities to England, and de-camped. They called that place First Encounter.

John Carver sighed and leaned forward so that the others could hear him above the wind and the waves. 'There is nowhere here for us,' he said. They had followed the shore line some distance and they were now tired, and dispirited.

'I think we should go on to Plymouth,' Robert Coppin the pilot said. 'There is an excellent harbour there that will serve you I think. We will be able to fetch it before nightfall.'

'You reckon?' Will asked. He did not like the thought of being caught out at sea in this flimsy vessel as darkness fell.

Coppin was sure of it, so they set off in the boat, following the shoreline down the coast and along the bottom of the bay. It was the best way to navigate and they had to put their faith in Coppin and in God.

The weather worsened. Snow came down, turning to rain and sleet. Will groaned within himself, and the sailors cursed. The rain soaked them, finding its way through their clothes and to the skin beneath, making them shiver, and they sank into silent misery. If anyone had dared suggest it, they would have gone ashore there and then, or made their way back to the ship. John Carver huddled beneath his cloak, using his hat like the roof of a tent, and Will did the same. The sailors, however, kept sailing the boat, peering at the coast in an attempt at any kind of recognition with the charts they possessed. However, they passed right by what came to be Barnstable harbour without even seeing it.

The day wore gloomily on. The wind grew steadily, becoming a gale that howled at them, and snapped at the sails, and the sea grew with it, the waves turning into white crested mountains before their very eyes. The shallop pitched about as the sea caught it. It seemed such a small and frail

292

vessel to be at the mercy of such a sea. Surely it would be better to go ashore anywhere than try and ride out the tempest.

As the shallop rose up on the wave and crashed into the dips, Will thought all his bones would break. Icy sea hit his face as if a bucket of water had been aimed at it.

Robert Coppin swore suddenly. 'The damned rudder's broke!' he announced.

They were becoming used to sailors' profanities, but John Carver bellowed, 'I'll thank you to mind your manners, sir!'

Robert Coppin glared at him, outraged that their impending doom was of less importance than bad language.

Will intervened. 'What can we do, Master Coppin?'

Coppin frowned at him without actually seeing him. 'Allerton, English,' he barked. 'Take the oars, use them as rudders, and steer.'

The two men did their best to hold the boat to her course as she bucked and rebelled in the sea, and Will and Edward Winslow came to assist them.

The rest hung on. The snow came down thick and fast, the wind likely to blow them overboard and the waves threatening to capsize the boat. They were in a lot of trouble, and night was coming on quickly.

Even with two men apiece, it was difficult to steer using the oars, much harder than it looked, for the waves hit the oar just as they had the rudder, and jerked it out of their hands.

Grimly the little boat struggled on through the thick grey sea, as John Carver prayed out loud. Will too prayed, but silently, in his heart.

Suddenly, Robert Coppin gave a whoop. 'See that! 'Tis Plymouth harbour.'

All Will could see was a spit of land jutting out across the sea, but Coppin was certain of it. 'No mistaking it.' Then he raised his voice. 'Be of good cheer, you men. I see the harbour.'

However, the wind grew ever stronger, and the shallop, bearing as much sail as it could to get them into the harbour before nightfall, raced along at breakneck speed.

''Tis all she can take!' John Clarke the other pilot yelled above the tempest.

Coppin peered up at the mast and saw it bend. 'We'll have to take in sail.'

Too late! A terrible noise, the splintering of wood, and a crack and suddenly they were covered in canvas. The mast had snapped in three places, and it dangled on its ropes like a strange puppet, narrowly missing John Carver's head.

The sailors were to it immediately, took what oars they could, and began to row, as the other men gathered in the fallen canvas, coiled up the ropes and heaved the fallen mast out of the way

Even so they missed the spit of land, heading instead towards the coast. 'The tide's coming in,' John Clarke cried. 'It's taking us with it!'

Coppin peered about him. 'Lord be merciful to us!'

'What's the matter?' Will demanded, alarmed at the note of panic in his voice. He had to shout above the noise of the tempest.

Coppin tried to wipe the water from his eyes with his hand. 'My eyes never saw this place afore!'

'I thought you said you'd been here before!' John Clarke accused.

'So did I. But I never set eyes on this place.' He looked at Clarke and made a decision. 'We'll run her ashore on the breakers!'

'Damn me you won't!' the man called English swore. He was doing his best to steer, and he knew that without the boat they would be unable to get back to the ship. He added to the rowers, 'You men bring her about, or else we be all cast away!'

The sailors were expert at this. They knew what they were doing, and they brought the shallop about quicker than Will dared hope.

English cried encouragingly, 'Be of good cheer and row lustily, for there be a fair sound afore us, and I doubt not but we shall find one place or another where we might ride in safety.'

The snow had again turned to pouring rain and the light disappeared into darkness, yet they found sand, dry land, with a wood and brush on it, in the lee of the wind.

It was a haven. They were safe.

Will thanked God, and made to scramble out of the boat.

'We should stay here in the boat in case there be Indians,' Miles Standish said.

'Well I'm not spending another minute in that boat,' Will announced. 'I'm cold and I need to go ashore.'

'Ain't much drier ashore.'

'I'm with Bradford,' Winslow said.

'Aye, and me!' John Carver announced.

So a group of them went ashore, and, as usual built a palisade and a fire as best they could. It took many attempts with the tinder box to get the fire lit, and the rain did not help, but at last they sat around a decent blaze.

They were wet and they were cold, but at least they were safe. Will sat and ate his salt beef and ships' biscuit with relish.

Better still, it stopped raining, and they settled down to sleep. But in the middle of the night the wind shifted to the north, and everything froze hard. Those left on the boat abandoned it and joined their friends on the shore around the fire.

When Will woke the sun was already up, and he realised he had slept well, which was surprising, for his clothes were frozen, where they had been damp, and he was stiff from huddling in one position all night. It promised to be a good clear day, and it gave them a chance to recover, to dry their clothes, to make repairs to the shallop, to fix their firearms.

They discovered that they were on an island—Clarke's Island they called it after the pilot, but it was not a place that they could settle, for there was no fresh water, and besides, it was too small for their needs.

The next day was Sunday 10th December, and as a Sabbath it was time to rest, talk about the Bible and thank God for their deliverance yet again. The Sabbath did much to restore Will's good spirits, and it was with good heart that they broke camp early on the Monday morning, and weighed anchor from the island. About two miles and a quarter away, across the bay, they could see land, and what looked like a river. They made towards the river.

Coppin took a depth sounding. ''Tis deep water,' he announced. 'Good for a harbour.'

Will looked over the side as though by looking he could confirm it. Certainly the water looked a dark blue colour. 'You can get a ship in 'ere,' Coppin added.

It sounded good. It felt good. Will had a warm feeling about this, and when he looked across at John Carver, he knew he did too.

The land, on a good sunny day, was inviting. Rising up gently from the beach the wooded shoreline and cornfields, and the fresh-water brook resembled paradise. This, Will knew with absolute certainty, was where the Lord wanted them to be. This was where they would settle. This would be home.

Plymouth. So named by explorer Captain John Smith a few years before.

Will felt a great swell of gladness and happiness rising from the depth of his belly. It had been long and hard, but at last they had arrived.

THIRTY-TWO
Dorothy

As the shallop came alongside the *Mayflower* Will looked eagerly at the faces peering over the gunwale for Dorothy. He had so much to tell her, the images and words bubbling up inside him as he anticipated her pleasure. Already he had decided on a good spot to build a house for her. Her sufferings, her agonies, would be silenced now. She would have her house in the meadow, where they might live out their lives together, bring up more children. Why, they could bring Jonathan over from Holland.

He waited impatiently as others clambered out of the shallop and up the side of the ship ahead of him. He searched for her. But Dorothy's face was not in the line of faces peering down at the explorers, and he felt a sharp pang of disappointment. Was she still angry, still sulking? All at once he was impatient to see her.

As he climbed the ladder he told himself how her sulks would turn to smiles when he told her of the house he would build for her.

On the deck, everyone seemed strangely quiet. William Brewster stood in front of him, waiting for him.

'We have found the perfect place,' Will began excitedly and trailed off at the lack of response. Something was wrong. The sombre expression on Brewster's fatherly bearded face caused a tremor of uncertainty in Will's belly. The others too, all of them, stood silently, some looking at him, some not meeting his gaze, as though they were uncomfortable.

With sudden terrible dread lurching in his insides, Will looked around again for Dorothy.

'I would speak with you, Will,' Brewster said gently, and with his hand on Will's arm, drew him away.

Will went with him meekly, but his hands shook, and his knees felt suddenly weak. 'What's happened?'

The others parted respectfully to let them pass, the silence unnerving.

He allowed Brewster to take him to the stern, to the poop deck where only the captain and a favoured guest might walk. Special dispensation, then. This in itself did not bode well.

When they were alone, Brewster turned to look at him, and his grey eyes watered. Will felt his whole being turn to ice. 'Dorothy?'

Brewster searched for words. 'I don't know how to tell you this, Will.'

Will's heart crashed in his chest, and his legs suddenly buckled. He grabbed the taffrail to stop himself falling.

'What happened?' he asked, and his voice did not sound like his own.

'She fell overboard. There was nothing anyone could do.'

He felt sick. The world seemed to spin before his eyes. 'No.' He shook his head, and Brewster grabbed hold of his arm. Violently he shook him off. '*No!*'

Patiently Brewster went on, 'It happened the day after you left.'

Will's mind raced. His Dorothy was gone. All this time, when he had thought of her, worried about her being depressed, she was already dead, deep in the cold watery depths. 'Could nobody save her?' He couldn't think, couldn't quite understand. 'We saved John Howland, didn't we? Could someone not have thrown a line or jumped in after her?'

'It was during the night, we think. No-one saw it happen.'

He was angry. 'Dammit, there are a hundred and fifty people on this ship.'

'It was icy,' Brewster offered gently, 'slippery. No-one saw it happen. A woman's skirts, you know, hold so much water, are so heavy.'

She would sink, he realised, straight away. Straight to the bottom.

'But she must have cried out.'

'No-one heard. Mary knew she had gone topside, and she was surprised when Dorothy did not return. After a while she asked if others had seen her, but no-one had. So Mary and I went topside ourselves. Then we all searched the ship. She is gone, Will.'

'If I had been here . . .' Will whispered through tight lips.

'You could not have saved her.'

'But I could.' He looked at the cold blue sea—murderous sea. 'She wanted to go home, but I told her that we would not be going. I was hard on her. I should have understood.'

Brewster was horrified. 'You don't think—?' He could not voice the word 'suicide'. Will stared at him with shocked eyes, and the pause stretched as Will fought to dismiss this thought from his mind. Yet he knew it was a possibility—in fact more than a possibility, with Dorothy's state of mind, her endless depression, her anxiety over Jonathan. She would have known just as Will knew that she could not go home. Indeed, he had told her so. He had been hard on her. 'I should not have brought her.' He brought shaking hands up to his face, and the tears came. 'I should not have brought her. It is my fault. Oh, dear God, no! Not Dorothy! Not Dorothy!'

Brewster stood awkwardly by, put a hand on Will's shoulder, and let it drop again. What could he do? What could he say? That she was with God in Heaven? Poor tragic little Dorothy. What if that were not the case? Suicide was a terrible crime, a sin against God, an anathema to all they believed.

But perhaps it wasn't suicide. Perhaps it was just a terrible accident.

As if they had not lost enough people, Brewster thought sadly. Six other people had died of sickness while they had been exploring, among them James Chilton husband of Susanna Chilton and father of Mary, and seven year old Jasper More, one of three siblings brought across at the instigation of the government, ostensibly as a servant of John Carver. A likeable urchin, Jasper More, Brewster reflected. He had been so eager and excited to be going to the New World along with his sister and brother.

He doubted they would be the last, for sickness now had a firm hold on the company.

He left Will, thinking it would be best if he were alone in his grief.

Will had never known pain like it. It was a searing roaring agony that he could not express or get out of his soul. And then a sudden tearing rage. How *could* she leave him like this? His fists clenched; he thumped the taffrail hard several times, bruising the side of his hand, not caring that he did so. Then he wept for a long time until he was exhausted, and his eyes were puffy.

Dorothy, who he had once so loved, the mother of his son, gone now, perhaps in despair at her unhappiness.

As the weeping passed, he became quieter, and stood for sometime leaning on the taffrail, looking down into the deep clear water as if he thought he would see Dorothy's body there somewhere. He prayed for strength to deal with this blow, and he prayed for God's mercy on Dorothy. But mostly he did not know what to say, except to ask for help.

Dorothy who he had fallen in love with when she was just twelve, and married when she was sixteen. Pretty little Dorothy, with her golden hair and huge china-blue eyes. Dorothy, the mother of his son, his wife, his companion. And he had never stopped loving her. Not really. Not even when she sulked and cried and had her tantrums and accused him of terrible things.

Now he was alone. So desperately alone. There was no wife for him, no woman to hold him in her arms, to comfort him. He ached for Dorothy with all her grumpiness and her sadness and her miseries.

Later, as night came on, and he had grown calmer, he went below. They fell silent as he came down the companionway. Perhaps they had been discussing him. Perhaps it was out of sympathy. He ate mechanically because he knew he must, and tried to focus on the discussion of the exploration which continued well into the night. It was good to have something to distract him. However, when he went to the corner which had been his and Dorothy's and he saw her things there—a shawl, a bonnet, a collar—the pain welled up in him again. She was not there. He crawled into his bed and wept, and he had never felt so wretched in his life.

The next morning as the sailors got to the work of putting sail on the ship and raising the anchor to the accompaniment of a strong chant timing the rhythm of the pull, Will stood disconsolately on the deck in the freezing cold. To Will, seeing everything through a black veil of desolation, it was too cheerful. Yet there was reason for gladness. They were moving the *Mayflower* to Plymouth bay where she could safely harbour and they could use her as a base for getting settled on the land.

For Will, though, the joy had gone out of it, the excitement had vanished as though it had never been.

There had been much discussion about Plymouth Bay. Miles Standish thought it a good idea to settle on Clarke's Island so that they would be safe from Indian attack and John Carver had agreed that they should explore that possibility. Wherever they decided to settle, however, their first priority must be to erect a large communal shelter, a storehouse, which would later serve as a meeting place, as a shelter and whatever else they needed it for.

So Will found himself pulled into the plans and preparations, and he knew the best thing for him would be to throw himself into work, which he found helped. However, when he was alone he ached for Dorothy, and his grief was deep in his soul.

The *Mayflower* came within six miles of Plymouth bay but then the wind changed direction, blowing them north-west, and they had to retreat again to Cape Cod.

The following day, 16th December, they were more successful and the *Mayflower* dropped anchor at the entrance to Plymouth Harbour. From here the passengers could see the land that the shore party had selected.

They sent a party ashore, and Will was again one of them.

Will's first impression had been right. It was a good place, with trees of many sorts, fruit trees, plum, cherry, apple, and herbs, including leeks, and onions, flax and hemp. There was gravel and an excellent clay for making pots. Best of all the soil was a soft black loam, rich and fat. There were fish in the sea and also fresh streams, the water of which was as sweet as any Will had ever tasted. He took pleasure in just the act of exploration and it lifted his spirits temporarily. Yet when they camped for the night, his heart was like lead in his chest.

They looked for Indians, saw only where there had once been some inhabitants and where they had planted their corn, but it had been left for some time and there was no sign of recent habitation.

The next day they travelled along the coast and came to a river which they named Jones River after the master of the ship. Will wondered why they were looking further. He liked the first landing place. Others agreed with him when, after travelling three miles up the river, they decided that it was too woody to defend from Indian attack. Clarke Island, also was far too woody and too cold, and there was no fresh water, and they had no mind to be digging wells. As Will pointed out, they had enough to do without that.

Already it was 19th December, they were running low on food, almost half the company were sick, and the need to find a place to settle had become urgent.

'I cast my vote for the land we first saw,' Edward Winslow said. 'On the high ground. The land has been cleared and planted with corn three or four years ago, the brook runs under the hill nearby, and there are many fresh-water springs for drinking.'

Will agreed. 'We can harbour our shallop and boats in the river and there's good fishing too.'

Miles Standish rubbed his face. 'It sounds reasonable to me. We can put a fort on the hill which will command all sides, and we can also see into the bay and into the sea, and also Cape Cod itself.' As ever the military aspects concerned him most.

'But we will have to fetch the wood,' John Carver pointed out.

'Well it ain't that far,' Will said. 'Half of a quarter of a mile. If that.'

'Far enough when one is having to lug it and build with it,' John Carver grumbled, in his bombastic way. Will glanced at him concerned. John Carver was feeling his age, he thought, the rigours of the exploration taking its toll on him.

'So what do we do next?' Christopher Martin asked.

John Carver took charge, which, as governor, he was supposed to do. 'We shall send twenty men ashore to make a start, and then all can come ashore tomorrow to begin building.'

'We must build a guard house!' Miles Standish suggested, and it sounded more like an order.

'A common house,' John Carver agreed, beaming suddenly. 'A good idea. Faith! I wish I'd thought of it myself !' He paused as he imagined it in his mind's eye. 'A house for sheltering in—we can put a fire in there— for meeting in, for storing things in.'

'Once we have one building up, we can start on the others,' Will agreed, his mind set on the fire which would warm them. He hadn't been warm since they left England.

However, the wind got up in the night, blew a ferocious gale, and by morning the rain lashed down and there was hardly enough light to see by. Will, still on land with the shore party, did his best to ignore it, but in a short while he was soaked through to his skin yet again.

'We ought to get back to the ship,' he said through gritted teeth. He'd had enough of being cold and wet, and the ship was the only shelter.

John Carver, crouching down and hunched over in his cloak, the rain beating down on his hat, looked up at Will with eyes as full of misery as his own. 'You can't put to sea in such conditions!'

They spent the day and night on land, wet cold, and hungry.

Will crouched in miserable silence, depressed. He had nothing to do but watch the rain as it lashed down in a steady torrent, and wish that they were somewhere dry and warm. His face and hands were numb with cold, his hair, dripping, and when he tilted his head, water poured off his soggy hat brim in a stream. It was impossible to sleep, impossible to make a fire, and there was no shelter of any sort.

His thoughts were of Dorothy. Poor pathetic, depressed little Dorothy. He should never have brought her here. He should have known she couldn't cope with this, that their marriage was not strong enough to ride the tensions of the journey. But then it would not have withstood the separation either. Whatever the reason for her death, whether accidental, or deliberate—and he could not bear to think of it being deliberate—he berated himself for her plight, for not giving in to her whims. But if he had given in to her, then what? What kind of man would he be to bow to the whims of a silly woman, a woman who did not really love him anyway, made his life difficult, and who would have made it even more difficult had she lived?

Still, no matter how much he reasoned with himself, grief and guilt tortured him day and night while deep in the recesses of his heart, was Alice. A flush of guilt shot through him anew. Dorothy knew.

The nagging pain in Will's hip grew, creeping down his leg and into his ankle. Or was it creeping up his leg from his ankle and into his thigh? He couldn't quite decide, but the cold and wet made it worse. There was little he could do about it. His feet and legs were soaked, his whole body chilled.

THIRTY-THREE
Sickness

Plymouth, New England, January 1621

Mary Brewster had been up all night, and it was morning before she rejoined her husband in their own berth. He had not been there long himself. As she slipped behind their curtain, quietly so as not to disturb the boys who slept still, he reached up for her and pulled her down into the bed against him, wrapping the blanket over her. Softly, in the darkness, in the warmth of his arms, she wept.

'It wasn't your fault,' he said in a low voice.

'No. It was too early. Mistress Allerton said so herself. Such a small little might. Didn't even cry.'

'Richard Britteridge died last night too,' Brewster whispered grimly. 'There'll be many more deaths if we don't get off this ship.' His arms tightened round her. 'What have I brought you to?'

She stopped crying abruptly and looked up at him in the dim light of a distant lantern, suddenly gaining strength. 'To a new world. *"Who hath heard such a thing? Who hath seen such things? Shall the earth be brought forth in one day? Or shall a nation be born at once?"* I didn't think it was going to be easy.'

As the weather abated a little, they managed to get the boat off to the shore party with provisions, but it could not return to the ship.

The weather finally eased on twenty-third December and as many as could went ashore and began the laborious task of felling timber for building. The next day was a Sabbath when no-one did any work, but that did not stop Solomon Prower, the stepson of the odious Christopher Martin, from dying of the sickness.

The following day, was the twenty-fifth of December, but the Pilgrims did not celebrate Christmas for they viewed it as unscriptural, a pagan celebration, the date chosen because of the winter solstice. So they worked, sawing riving, carrying timber, and they began to erect the first building, the common house, a timber-framed affair of wattle and daub, just as they had been used to in England. It was the easiest and the quickest way of doing things.

The common house was twenty feet square, and once they had thatched the roof they intended to move supplies from the *Mayflower* ashore. It was a good sign that heartened them, even though the sickness continued to claim lives.

John Crackston died. Christopher Martin's wife Marie, mother of

Solomon Prower died. Alice and John Rigdale died, and all the Tilleys got ill. Digory Priest died at the beginning of January, as did Christopher Martin who annoyed them all so intensely on the eighth of January.

'We've got to get the people off the ship,' John Carver announced, pausing in the act of chopping at a tree, desperation in his voice.

William Brewster agreed. 'The foul air of the ship breeds sickness. We need clean warm housing.' He swung his axe, and a chip of wood flew out of the groove he made in the trunk.

'It is a waste of time and energy to have most of the shore party rowing back to the ship each night,' Will put in. For although the common house would be good to shelter some of the sick, like a makeshift hospital, there would not be room for everyone.

'Well we can't build any faster!' John Carver snapped, throwing down his axe.

Will looked around him at the trees, good thick wood for building, and sighed. Tempers were fraying yet again, and even good-natured bluff John Carver had fallen victim to the stress.

'Half of the company are now sick,' Will said. 'Daily more become sick, and people are dying.'

'You think I don't know that?' Carver raged. 'Am I God that I should stop a sickness?'

'If we could get some cottages up,' Will pressed his point, standing his ground.

John Carver looked as though he searched for a suitable oath, and his face darkened with anger.

Brewster came between them. 'You are right, of course you are Will, but we are doing all that we can.'

Will nodded. 'I know.' He felt frustrated at the time it was taking. 'I'm sorry, John.'

'We're all anxious about the people who are dying,' William Brewster said.

'Tomorrow we begin erecting cottages,' John Carver announced. 'Weather permitting.'

The weather didn't permit. For half the week it halted their activities completely, while on the ship the sickness became an epidemic.

Everyone grew impatient with the inactivity, and fights became common. Captain Jones decided on some exploration of his own, really to take a breathing space from the ship, and with some men put to sea in the shallop.

He wasn't the only one. Francis Billington, John Billington's reckless son, had climbed a tree and spied what he thought was a sea. He took one of the sailors, one of the mates, and they went to look for it. They found that the 'sea' was actually two freshwater lakes, with a stream coming out of them, full of fish and birds.

'We also found seven or eight Indian houses,' Francis Billington told them excitedly when they returned.

'Aye. And we only had one piece between us,' John Parker agreed, gesturing with his musket.

'But we saw no Indians.'

Will glanced at Edward Winslow, who pursed his lips. So the Indians were not that far away then.

'Ho! You sound disappointed young Billington,' John Carver boomed, laughing. 'I tell you what—we'll call those lakes Billington's Sea, how is that?'

'*Really?*' The lad's eyes grew round with sheer amazement.

His father beamed at him, well pleased.

The work stopped for a storm blew up, and they huddled in the lee of the unfinished common house.

'We need thatching for this,' John Carver declared.

John Goodman massaged the fluffy ears of his spaniel bitch who had endured the voyage with them, as had the other dog, a mastiff. 'I'll go if you like.'

'And I'll go too,' Peter Browne added. Both men were young and strong and healthy.

'Then make sure you take weapons, in case of Indians,' John Carver warned.

'What do you think about the Indians, Will?' Edward Winslow asked later, as they worked in the woods.

Will grimmaced. 'I wish they were not so close.'

'I reckon we ought to try to make friends with them.'

'They're afraid to come that close.'

Edward pulled a face, and jerked his head in the direction of the hill where a plume of smoke rose lazily above the trees. 'Oh yes?'

He picked up his axe again to work alongside his brother, Gilbert and Will picked his up too, both of them watching the smoke as they did so.

Will swung the axe, the muscles tightening in shoulders and back, and trying to ignore the pain in his ankle which had been growing worse by the day, but even so he was pleased to be actually working.

'The Indians ain't suffering from the cold,' Edward Winslow observed.

Gilbert Winslow, peered at the smoke, and said with a little sarcasm, 'They're used to it.'

Will paused in the act of swinging the axe, and let it drop down, his arms suddenly weak. Despite the cold weather, he was sweating in his shirt-sleeves, yet the moment he stopped work, the chill of sickness rose goose bumps on his skin right across his body. He ignored it with an effort, and focused instead on the Indian smoke. He didn't like it. The proximity of lawless savages so close to them made him nervous.

But he felt ill, and serious though the Indian presence was, it could not blot out the weakness and pain that shot through him. Surely, he told himself, all it took was determination. 'Well, let's just hope they stay where they are, and leave us be.' But his voice was faint and Edward glanced sharply at him.

'What's wrong, Will?'

Will shook his head. He picked up the axe but there was no strength in his arms. Taking two or three deep steadying breaths he swung it up, but the stroke that chipped at the tree carried no power.

He dropped it again, brushed the dark hair from his eyes with a shaking hand. The pain in his ankle suddenly grew and shot up his leg from his ankle, a tortuous ache that seemed to be right in the middle of his bones. He had a sudden overwhelming urge to sit down. Right now.

He heard Edward's voice as though far away. 'Will? What ails you?'

Will swayed and clutched the half-cut tree.

'It's my leg,' he said, and he felt sick and faint with the pain of it.

Edward dropped his axe and marched smartly across to him. 'Faith man, you look terrible!'

Pain shot up Will's leg to his hip-joint, like someone had shot him in the joint with a pistol. His leg gave way beneath him, so that he fell heavily to the ground. He could hear himself crying out as the pain flooded his whole being, filling him with white hot agony.

He heard Edward send Gilbert for help. 'It's his hucklebone,' he said.

Will couldn't think for the pain. He knew he was crying out, knew he writhed on the ground like a man possessed, but he couldn't stop.

People came around him and expressed their concern. 'He's going to die,' someone said.

'No-one can survive such great pain,' someone else said, and wrapped him in a blanket.

Then he was lifted up, hands carrying him on a litter across the ground.

'I mislike it,' Dr. Giles Heale said to Sam Fuller.

Across the pain, across the agony, Will knew they spoke of him. Did they think he couldn't hear?

'You think him like to die?' Sam Fuller asked.

Will thought about dying. It held no terrors for him. A short sleep, then resurrected to be with the Lord in the heavens.

'I do not doubt it.'

That was it, then. He was going to die, to be with Dorothy. Dorothy who he had not yet forgiven for leaving him alone in the way she had. Would she be in heaven?

Pain overwhelmed him. It shot through him like a knife whenever he moved, and nagged like toothache when he lay still. He could think of nothing else but the pain. He couldn't sleep, couldn't speak, couldn't think. There was no getting away from it.

He heard himself groan, and he tried to move, to turn on his good side away from it. Dimly he knew he was inside the common house. It was warm here, despite half of the thatch not being in place, and there was a fire in the huge hearth. Even so, he shivered. The light from the fire flickered on the bare earth walls, wattle and daub, still damp not having a chance to dry out properly. Yet it was far more comfortable, than the cramped ship. He did not have the same loathing for the ship as others had, after all it had been their haven since they arrived in this place, but he did look forward to living in a proper building once more, being able to stand up straight when inside, not having the sea beneath one's feet, being able to clean out the dirt, to wash, to cook on a fire.

He moved again and pain shot though him, making him groan and grind his teeth. Did he have the general sickness? He didn't think so. They were coughing and feverish, but he had a pain his huckle-bone. There was a difference.

Mary Brewster raised his head and forced some water between his lips. He opened his eyes and saw her looking down at him, her face a mask of concern. He closed his eyes. How could a man endure it?

'Will, drink this.' She raised his head and forced something bitter between his lips. No doubt a concoction of Sam Fuller, for there were herbs enough around, healing plants as Sam had already told him. Or perhaps it was some of the strange medicine Giles Heale had brought from England.

Whatever it was, it made him sleepy, and a short time later he dozed off, only to dream strange dreams in which Dorothy became Alice and both of them were lost.

John Carver, became anxious. 'I don't know what has happened to the men cutting thatch,' he said to William Brewster.

Brewster frowned and peered in the general direction the men had taken. 'Did you think them to be back before this?'

'I did. 'It don't take that long for four men to cut enough thatch—' He sighed noisily. 'I tell you, William, I feel the responsibility as governor almost too much to bear.'

'You do a good job,' William Brewster told him. 'And you are certainly capable at getting men to do your bidding.'

'Is that because they are afraid of me?' Carver asked in mock amusement.

Brewster grinned. 'Probably.'

'Men coming!' The cry went up, and Brewster and Carver stared at the incoming figures. Were they Indians?

'Two men!' John Carver said, relief in his voice as he identified Englishmen.

They came in panting and anxious. 'Master Goodman and Master Brown are lost! They left us to bind up the thatch while they went for some more, but when we went to follow they were gone. We searched but we couldn't find them.'

John Carver did not hesitate. 'Right! Master Standish! You others, come with me!'

'You go to look for them?' Brewster asked. 'Be sure you do not lose yourselves!'

Carver slapped him on the upper arm. 'I'll be back.'

'They could have been surprised by Indians,' Brewster warned.

John Carver shook his head. 'I hope to God you are wrong,' he said.

Brewster watched them go, and prayed for their success.

They came back later, however, empty-handed.

John Carver sent others out. When they came back without the missing men after dark, Carver was seriously alarmed. 'It could have been Indians,' he admitted reluctantly. 'We saw their smoke yesterday. I do hope you are wrong, William.'

Brewster looked at him seriously. 'So do I.'

Later, as Brewster lay down alongside his wife, Mary said, 'You will go?'

'If they will have me,' he replied. 'But I fear my days of wielding sword and musket are long gone.'

The next day John Carver armed twelve men, and sent them out to search.

They too came back empty-handed.

It was nightfall when the missing men and the two dogs staggered into the Plantation, weak from lack of food and exhaustion, insensible with the cold. They had got lost, they explained simply. John Goodman's feet were so swollen he had to have his shoes cut off. But they were home, safe.

Will tried to make sense of the sounds and of the strange lights that flickered all around him. Thick, choking smoke blocked his lungs, fogged his eyes, made him cough so much he couldn't breathe. People shouting, women screaming—women always screamed in a crisis—and then Brewster's voice, close by, urgent.

'Get up, Will! Get out! Fire!'

Will struggled to move, but the pain in his hip caught him suddenly and made him cry out. He felt so ill, so weak, so warm. He didn't want to leave the comfort, the warmth. Better to just lie here and go back to sleep.

'Will! Come on!' Brewster heaved him into a sitting position. He could hear Brewster coughing, gasping, groaning with the effort to lift him. He must make an effort before Brewster ruptured himself.

He opened his eyes. A thick fog of smoke filled the building. An orange glow through the fog, and drifting in the air, little lights, like fireflies. Dripping down from the roof like liquid fire, the thatch crackled and burned above them. The realisation jerked Will to full consciousness. There, in the corner was the gunpowder store, and men around it with little care for themselves struggling to get it outside.

Will tried to get to his feet, but his legs buckled. He struggled further, and with surprising presence of mind, grabbed his clothes from the end of the makeshift bed.

'Can you walk?' Brewster demanded. 'Will, can you walk?'

Wattle and daub walls swam before his eyes. His head ached. He felt suddenly cold despite the heat. He tried to walk, but when he put some weight on his bad leg it collapsed, and only Brewster's arm around his waist stopped him from falling. Someone grabbed him from the other side, and he was dragged out of the burning building.

Outside the cold made him shake, and his skin reacted in sore goose bumps. His hip and ankle would not hold him, and Brewster and the other man dragged him away from the building to the lee of another half-built wall, and lowered him to the cold icy ground. Brewster found a blanket and wrapped it around him. But he shivered so much his teeth chattered in an agony of fever. For those with the lung inflammation is was likely to be fatal.

Next to Will John Carver coughed and then groaned and moaned. He had taken the sickness just recently.

Brewster disappeared with the other men, for the Common House was so important to them that they must try and save it. Will sank into his own misery. It was a relief later to be taken aboard the *Mayflower* again.

The ship seemed to stink worse than it had ever done. It smelled of sickness, and sweating bodies, of sweaty feet and ordure, all mingled with the ship smells of tar, wet wood and rope. It made him choke as he came aboard with the other sick ones. How he regretted losing the comfort of the common house, to be housed once more on the dark fetid ship, among the coarse ungodly sailors. But others had far more to complain about, for many of them were very sick indeed, including members of the crew.

Here Will languished for two or three weeks in the care of those sisters who were well while the men got on with the task of making habitation ashore.

But at last he began to get well, the fever left him, and the pain in his hip abated. He felt like he had come out of the teeth of a gale into beautiful sunshine and peace. The relief of just not feeling ill was immense.

When he felt able, he went ashore again to help with the building party, and was surprised at what they had achieved in his absence. The common house was finished, and used for meetings as well as for housing those on shore. They had erected a shed to use as a store, so that they could move provisions and gunpowder out of the weather. Several houses had been started too, and one or two were nearly finished.

Will did what he could. He could not do hard physical work, for he was still weak, and he limped on his bad leg, but he could do some fetching and carrying, and some sitting down jobs like riving, or splitting branches. John Carver had recovered from the general sickness and was once again firmly in control as governor.

Just as in old England, New England's weather was changeable. One or two days warm and sunny, like a spring day, even though it was January. The next day wet, and they could do no work. The day after sleet or snow. Then fine and crisp. And like Englishmen wherever they were in the world, the weather was a constant topic of discussion and conversation. What would it do today? Would they be able to work?

At the end of January, Captain Christopher Jones saw two Indians. They came near to the ship, on the island, and then went again before anyone could speak with them.

At the end of January too, Rose Standish died of the general sickness.

They completed other buildings; a little house for the sick, was set alight by a spark catching the thatch in the roof, but they managed to put it out before it caused too much damage and repaired the roof.

The weather in February continued unsettled, stormy, cold, wet. Still, John Carver pronounced himself satisfied with the way things were progressing.

'We have accomplished much,' he told Will and Brewster in his booming voice. 'And we now have shelter.'

Will raised a sardonic eyebrow. 'And that is something that was sorely needed.' He saw a movement just on the edge of his vision and he turned to see a man running out of the woods carrying his musket in a state of great excitement. 'Hey-up—what's this?'

The workers downed their tools and came to see.

Carver and Brewster strode forward. Will hobbled after them, but couldn't see who it was..

The man had been out shooting wildfowl, for he was a good shot, and he did indeed have with him a few geese, which he had dropped in the earth.

'What is this about?' John Carver demanded.

'Indians! I saw Indians. Many of them,' the man cried, struggling to catch his breath.

Carver exchanged uneasy glances with Brewster. They had been expecting this. 'How many?'

'I saw twelve pass right by me, coming towards the plantation, and there were many more in the woods. I could hear them.'

'They saw you?'

'I don't think so. I lay still in the grass until they passed, and then came back.'

Carver reacted. 'Master Standish, call to arms if you please. You boys, quick, find the men who are abroad and bring them home.' The Billington boys raced off with Brewster's eldest son, while Miles Standish bellowed out his orders with amazing gusto for one so small.

Men ran to their muskets and the cannons which they had rather neglected, partly because of the need to build, partly because of the weather, which put the weapons out of temper, and partly because of the absence of any contact with the Indians.

Will hobbled across the plantation to collect a musket, and made it ready, a mixture of excitement and fear growing in his belly. He took up a position behind a partly constructed wall, and waited. He prayed, not so much out of fear but because he didn't want to have to kill anyone. How could he keep a clean conscience with the blood of men on his hands?

All the men who were working outside the plantation rushed in, leaving behind the tools they were using, and they too took up arms, and positions.

Silence settled on the plantation as they waited expectantly.

'Don't shoot unless I give the order,' John Carver told everyone, passing quietly from one group of men to another.

Will's insides writhed like a coiling snake. He was cold in the winter air, but he hardly noticed it.

'Where are they then?' Sam Fuller asked in a low voice beside him.

'Trouble'll come soon enough,' Edward Winslow answered him.

So they waited, tense. Gradually darkness came on.

John Carver gave the order for them to stand down. He shrugged at William Brewster, Isaac Allerton, and Will, the three men he trusted most. 'I doubt they'll come now,' he said.

Miles Standish overheard him. 'Keep several men on watch all night,' he recommended, 'and let everyone else get some rest.'

Sleep, though, was impossible. Tension hung over the plantation. People spoke in whispers, and the women stayed together in one of the new houses with their little ones. Will kept looking out at the surrounding area, expecting to see arrows pouring out of the sky, or figures moving in the darkness. When he put his head down to sleep he listened for the terrible whoops and cries, the unearthly screeches of the Indians. Once he dropped off and jerked awake again immediately, and he could see a glow lighting up the house.

Outside the plantation, the Indians had made a great fire which lit up the whole area, and they could hear them chanting, and making those strange calls and whoops which had so terrified them when they first went ashore. They kept it up all night.

The following day John Carver called a meeting to establish military orders and they naturally chose Miles Standish as Captain and gave him command over the defence of the colony.

Accepting the commission with befitting gravity, Standish said, 'I will do my best to serve the community, and give our women and children protection from the savages.'

The lookout, one of the boys, gave a cry. 'Indians!'

The meeting dissipated in a rush to arms, and everyone took up their positions again, staring grimly at the countryside outside the plantation.

The Indians, however, turned out to be two braves standing on the top of the hill south west of the plantation, perhaps a quarter of a mile away.

The English stood together, watching as the two Indians beckoned to them.

'What do they want?' John Carver asked.

Will frowned. 'They seem to want us to go to them.'

'Why don't they come to us?' Carver asked reasonably. He made signs, inviting them to come into the plantation.

'They won't come,' Brewster observed. 'They are probably afraid.'

Carver said, 'We will have to send someone to them.'

'I'll go,' Miles Standish volunteered, flushed with importance over his new responsibilities.

'And I'll go with him,' Stephen Hopkins added.

Carver looked at them seriously. 'You don't have to do this,' he said.

Standish gave a small smile, and picked up his musket. Together the two men went out and crossed the brook.

All the men in the plantation stood ready behind cover, their muskets loaded, and watched as the two men walked towards the Indians. Will felt his heart beating hard as he watched the two men stop at the bottom of the hill. Then in sight of the Indians, Miles Standish put his weapon on the ground in an exaggerated gesture, a show of peace, and Stephen Hopkins did likewise.

'That's it!' John Carver whispered encouragement as he watched this scene from behind the half-built wall of a cottage. 'Now go and parley with them.'

As if they had heard him the two men began to go towards the Indians. A moment later the two Indians on the top of the hill disappeared and a terrible noise of whooping and calls came from behind the hill. It sounded like a thousand devils and it raised the hairs on the back of Will's neck.

The two men outside grabbed the musket and ran back to the relative safety of the plantation.

They waited a little longer to see if the Indians would return, but they didn't.

Painfully aware that they were unready for any attack, John Carver ordered the cannons to be put in a convenient position; Captain Jones brought ashore a great gun called a minion, and his sailors helped them heave it up to the top of the hill together with another gun, and a saker and two bases, all cannon of various sizes. If the Indians returned they would be ready for them.

But the Indians didn't return. The settlers worked again on their houses, but kept their muskets near them. It was a nerve-wracking time.

Indians or no Indians, the sickness claimed more lives. William White, husband of Susanna, died as did William Mullins and also Mary Allerton, the wife of Isaac. Others too succumbed to the sickness. John Carver decreed that they should bury the dead on what came to be called Burial Hill, and that they should do it in the night so that the Indians could not see what they were doing in case they realised what a weakened state they were in.

THIRTY-FOUR
Samoset

March, 1621

Will sat on the hill by the brook and watched the *Mayflower* riding quietly at anchor in the bay, presenting a picture of serenity in a sea of blue calm. Who could have known of the death within her hull, the misery, the cursing, the agony?

He sighed. So many dead. So many loved ones, wives and husbands, children, friends. Only half the company remained, and only half the number of sailors. Hardly enough to sail her home again.

The worst of the sickness was over now. No new cases for over a week, and many now recovered. Only Elizabeth the wife of Edward Winslow, gave cause for concern. However, it had left them with only a few men and women and a whole lot of children to care for. It would make the task of settling the colony that much more difficult.

John Carver joined Will, sitting down heavily on the grassy mound beside him. 'So now we have work to do, Will,' he boomed.

Will felt a spurt of anger inside him. It was a swipe at Will's protracted convalescence, for those with the general sickness had recovered quicker than he had. His hip still plagued him, and he walked with a stick. Still he had done his share, even if he could not do the heavier work.

He didn't argue with John, but said, 'Aye, there is much to do.'

'So it ain't no time for sitting here and staring at the water.'

'A short rest, sir,' Will snapped, and he came awkwardly to his feet and hobbled away without waiting for John.

John Carver caught him up a few moments later, and fell into step beside him. 'Didn't mean nothing by it, Will.'

Will took a breath. His illness irritated him, and the delays in getting organised irritated him. It had been far more difficult than he had foreseen, and losing so many members of the congregation—particularly losing Dorothy—had been a bitter blow. He glanced at John. 'Sorry. Feeling a bit out of sorts today.'

As they came over the brow of the hill, the plantation came into view. It looked like a regular village, with houses set out in a neat and orderly fashion, two rows of cottages with little gardens. Will lived with the Brewsters, and Mary had been most solicitous, fussing around him as though he were her own son, but nothing could ease the emptiness in his own heart. He shook his head to clear the thought.

It was the loneliness in him that he found so difficult to bear. He had a desperate need for a woman of his own. He could perhaps take a wife from one of those left widowed. Not Desire Minter. Not only was she socially his inferior, but she had a face that frightened children and a voice like an old man with a cough. There was something not quite right about her as well. Priscilla Mullins was too young for him, and besides John Alden had cast his eyes in her direction as had Miles Standish.

There was pretty little Susanna White, Sam Fuller's sister. True, she had two children, one of whom was a baby. However, she was a fine woman, with red hair, and tawny eyes, and quick intelligence, and she needed a man to take care of her and her children. Necessity, survival, could cause him to be that man. It would be a marriage of convenience, for he was not even remotely attracted to her but her brother Sam would be pleased with such a match.

Perhaps, when she had had time to grieve, he should speak to her, he thought without much enthusiasm. And all at once Alice came into his mind, with her chestnut hair and green eyes and freckled nose. He could almost feel the warmth of her kiss, his hand on her waist, and he missed her with a great longing.

'We must have a meeting concerning government,' John Carver boomed at him suddenly, cutting across his thoughts. 'I will call the men together.'

Will nodded, bringing his mind back to the present with an effort. It was necessary to see about these things, and now that it was March and the weather had turned better, the days longer, and settlers more organised, they must make the time to discuss such things.

But Alice lingered guiltily in his thoughts.

At the summons the men gathered together and sat in a circle, perched on whatever came to hand—a lump of tree there, a bench here. Will sat on the ground, which would have caused Mary Brewster to throw a fit if she had seen him, for she was convinced there was nothing so injurious to health as the humours that came up from the ground and seeped into a body when one sat down on bare earth or grass. And if Will wanted to get well he ought not to let the damp get into that leg!

John Carver, having been confirmed governor, opened the meeting by addressing the group, saying a prayer for God's guidance and presenting the reason for their meeting together. 'To discuss military matters and how we are to conduct ourselves,' he announced grandly.

'Well, that's easy enough,' John Billington put in. 'We'll leave that to Captain Shrimp seeing as he knows all about them sorta things.'

Standish fired up at the jocular tone. 'Aye, and it's more'n you do! I don't think I seen you pick up a firearm in weeks, John Billington. As far as you are concerned we could all be killed in our beds!'

'Ain't no Indians here,' Billington said. 'And there ain't no reason to rip up at me!'

'There are Indians here,' John Allerton put in. 'We've all seen them.'

'Well they ain't botherin' us!' Billington insisted. 'I reckon they're all affrighted at our coming.'

'Such fierce men as we are,' Will muttered under his breath.

Sam Fuller raised a brow at him, and Will looked down at the ground between his feet to hide a smile.

'Right then, what do we need to do?' John Carver boomed.

'We need to work out the watches for a start, particularly the night watch,' Miles Standish said. 'At the moment we ain't got no idea what we're doing!'

'That is a point,' John Allerton put in. 'We all need to know when 'tis our turn. As it is some men are on watch all night, and then having to work in the day as well.' He knew because he was one of them.

'And we need a lookout during the day, too.' Standish went on. 'On the hill.'

'I told you there ain't no Indians,' John Billington insisted.

John Carver didn't answer, but his gaze fixed intently on something behind Will. He came unhurriedly to his feet, grabbing his musket which was on the ground beside him.

Will turned his head, and his heart turned over.

A man came towards them, walking straight up the 'street', his head with its long black mane of hair held high. He was almost naked, a leather cloth covering his loins, brown muscles glistening in the sunlight, long straight legs striding purposefully, shoulders set square, and in his hand he carried a spear. He had the bearing of a proud warrior, of a man fearless in the face of possible death.

He stopped in front of them. At close quarters he was an imposing man, tall and strongly-built, his dark skin muscled and honed with hard work, and good-looking.

The English arranged themselves in a line to confront him, and for a long moment no-one spoke. The Indian's black eyes studied the men in front of him. 'Eng'ish—well come.' He said and then he thumped himself on the chest. 'Samoset.'

Will exchanged glances with John Carver. How could this man speak English, however badly?

John Carver laughed loudly with delight, and held out his hand. 'Me—Carver,' he boomed. 'This Winslow, Allerton, Standish, Bradford.'

Samoset grinned, showing a row of even white teeth as the men just named bowed their heads in salutation as they would have done in England. Samoset nodded too, with jerky stiff movements.

'Do sit down,' Carver said politely. 'You will eat with us?'

They made room for him, and he sat down on a log. Carver sent for some food. With typical English concern for the chill wind someone else ran to fetch a coat , for despite his show of hardiness, Samoset's skin had started to show little goose bumps.

'Do you live in these parts, Master Samoset?' John Carver asked politely.

Samoset shook his head and his long black mane of hair which had been cut short at the front, rippled like a waterfall. 'No. Samoset yive Moratiggon,' he told them. In fact they discovered later that he was a native of Pemaquid and chief of what was to become Bristol. He had difficulty pronouncing the letter 'L'.

'Moratiggon?' Miles Standish asked. 'Where might that be?'

Samoset favoured him with a long fierce look, taking in the red hair and beard, and gestured vaguely. 'Many days.' He held out his hand spreading his fingers. 'Five days walking. My people Sagamores. Lords of all country. Samoset here eight moons.'

He had an odd abrupt way of speaking and it was obvious his command of English was scant, but enough.

'How do you speak our tongue, friend?' Edward Winslow asked.

Samoset shrugged. 'Ships come. Samoset meet them. Know many masters. Captain Dermer come six moons past. He save French men.' He meant the shipwrecked sailors. 'Samoset go on ship. Men teach Samoset Eng'ish at Monhegan.' That wasn't all he learned from the English. 'You give Samoset beer?' he asked with a wide grin.

Carver laughed again and slapped the Indian on the shoulders. 'We have no beer, but do have strong water!' They put the horseman's coat on him, and someone else fetched some strong water, and biscuit, and butter and cheese and pudding and a piece of wild duck and watched as he ate all these things. This, he told them, he liked very well.

And while he ate, and they watched, he talked.

'This place here—Patuxet,' he said. 'Pa-tux-et.'

'We call Plymouth.' John Carver said, getting the hang of shortening his sentences of unneeded words. 'Plim-moth!'

'P'im-moth,' Samoset repeated through a mouthful of biscuit, grinning and showing his impossibly white teeth.

'There are other people here?' Will asked.

Samoset shook his long mane again and frowned in a comical expression of deep sadness. 'No. All dead. Four summers.'

'Four years ago, you mean,' Miles Standish corrected him.

Samoset gave him another inscrutable look, and a sharp nod of his head, and bit into the biscuit again. 'Patuxet beyong no man,' he assured them.

'How did they die?'

Samoset frowned. 'Sickness. White man's sickness. Patuxet now beyong Eng'ish.'

'He means we are safe here,' Will translated as much for his own benefit as for that of others.

They talked well into the afternoon, and learned many things from Samoset, even though his broken English and heavy accent were difficult to understand. It required much concentration to piece together the information, and it took a long time too to say anything. However, they learned that he stayed presently with the Wampanoag tribe who, he said were about sixty strong. (He counted only the men.) Their chief, or sagamore, was a man called Massasoit. These were the Indians they had seen near the plantation. Another tribe, the Nausets, were a hundred strong and lived south-east of Plymouth (or Patuxet) across the bay on the Cape, and were the Indians the Pilgrims had first encountered when they went ashore from the *Mayflower*.

'Nauset afraid Eng'ish,' Samoset explained. 'Many days since, man Thomas Hunt trapped Nauset. Took away Nauset to sell.'

'Slaves?'

Samoset nodded. 'S'aves. Nausets hate Eng'ish, kill Eng'ish. Three Eng'ish. Two Eng'ish go to Monhegan.' Monhegan island that is.

Will frowned. 'That would explain it,' he said.

Samoset put his head on one side, his black eyebrows raised, clearly not understanding.

'Nausets attacked us when we first arrived yonder.' Will waved his arm expressively in the general direction of the Cape. Adding to make things perfectly clear to the Indian, 'Set trap for us.'

'Nausets afraid. Eng'ish make many s'aves.'

'We do not take slaves,' Edward Winslow reassured him. 'We come to live here. Come in peace.'

Samoset nodded, pleased. 'Good. Samoset tell Massasoit, sachem of Wampanoag tribe, Eng'ish friends.'

'Is he here?'

'Massasoit camp near.'

'Your people take our tools,' Will said. 'Tell Massasoit we want them back. We need to build with them.'

As Samoset talked on and on the sky began to darken in the east, and very soon the stars came out.

The English did not like to ask him to leave. And he did not seem inclined to go. In fact he seemed reluctant to go.

It was a situation they had not anticipated. They had precious little space to sleep as it was, each house being seriously overcrowded. Besides, they were not sure if they could trust him. He was a native, after all, a so-called savage, which they had been warned about back in Leyden. Everyone knew that savages were murderous cannibals, didn't they? Only Samoset did not look very much like a murderous cannibal, with his friendly open ways, and his wide grin. Still, it wouldn't do to take an unnecessary risk until they were sure of him.

They suggested he sleep on the *Mayflower* which he readily agreed to. However, when they got to the shallop the water was too rough. ''Tis no good,' John Carver said. 'Can't put to sea in this.' Samoset looked at him intently as he spoke.

'So what shall we do with him?' John Allerton asked. Samoset turned his head to study him.

'We'll put him in Stephen Hopkins' house. There is room there.' Again Samoset's head turned towards Carver. 'Master Standish—keep an eye on him, will you? Just in case.'

Standish, who was small enough to tuck under the Indian's arm, bristled with military pride. 'Indeed I will, Governor, indeed I will.' He looked at Samoset. 'Come on then.'

Samoset grinned and trotted along happily with Miles Standish.

Stephen Hopkins' wife and children moved out for the night.

'He won't go,' Brewster announced to Will the next morning when he came in for breakfast. He had been to check on the guest, and had found him wearing the horseman's jacket, and eating ship's biscuit, quite happily at home in his new surroundings. 'I think he likes it here.'

'Well, who would expect a savage to outstay his welcome?' John Carver said and laughed his booming laugh. The Carvers were temporarily berthed with the Brewsters.

'Not so savage, I think,' Will said. 'He likes the soft ways of civilisation. Although I admit he looks fearsome enough.'

'*I* wouldn't argue with him,' Mary Brewster agreed, bustling around in her apron in an effort to feed her extended 'family'.

'Well that's a pity, since someone has to ask him to leave,' John said, carving himself a chunk of salt beef which had seen better days. 'How are we to do that?'

Brewster had an idea. 'I suggest we give him some gifts. A knife. Perhaps trinkets, that kind of thing.'

Carver nodded, and, swallowing his mouthful he jumped up from the rough-hewn seat. Will and Brewster went with him.

Samoset greeted them with a big grin. He looked odd, sitting with his long coal-black hair, draping over the dark blue coat, the rest of him naked save for his loin cloth, chewing on some salt beef.

'Samoset go tell great chief Massasoit that the English are his friends,' John Carver said at his most persuasive, putting his arm around Samoset's shoulders, and gently raising him from his seat. Samoset looked at him, squinting because of the short distance between them. 'Look!' Carver boomed. 'We give Samoset gifts.'

Will had persuaded Edward Winslow to find the necessary gifts, and he came to the cabin now. With great ceremony he presented Samoset with a knife, a bracelet and a ring, not very valuable items, but pretty enough. Well, they pleased the Indian.

Samoset put the bracelet on his wrist, the ring on his thumb, and examined the knife which was a particularly splendid example with a carved bone handle.

'Samoset come again in two nights,' the Indian promised.

'And bring with you some of Massasoit's men,' John Carver suggested, 'and whatever you have to trade.'

'We bring many skins,' Samoset said, nodding and grinning and hardly able to take his eyes off the knife.

He went away happily, not with the swagger of the previous day, but with a jaunty step, evidently well pleased with the English, and very happy with his coat.

Will chuckled, and turned to pick up his tools and go to work in the field. There was digging and seed-sowing to be done.

'That went pretty well,' John Carver remarked as he walked beside Will, 'even if I do say so myself.'

Will said, 'It is a good start. But it is Massasoit we will need to keep happy if we are to have good relations with the Indians.'

Carver clapped Will on the shoulder, as was his habit, and took himself off.

Will walked on, and there in front of him was pretty Susanna White, with her red hair tied in a plait coiling down her back from beneath her white bonnet, her baby firmly tied to her back with a shawl, his little head nodding with the movement, and a basket of laundry in her hands.

He approached her. 'Good day to you mistress.'

She looked up at him in that straight candid way that she had. 'Master Bradford,' she acknowledged.

There was no warmth in her eyes when she looked at him, not like there had been in Alice's. In that moment he knew that he could not marry her, for pretty as she was, he did not love her, nor was he even remotely attracted to her.

She continued walking, and he watched her for a moment, before turning and marching across to the field which had been decreed for digging. No, there was nothing at all between him and Susanna. That spark that he had felt with Alice, just wasn't there. *Alice*! His heart ached for her all the more.

He met Susanna's brother Sam Fuller who was leaving the field, for his work lay in helping the sick. Sam had become something of a physician, spending a great deal of time with Giles Heale, the *Mayflower*'s surgeon, and he had a knowledge of herbal remedies which he had put to good use during the recent epidemic.

'I hear you managed to send the Indian on his way at last,' Sam said by way of greeting.

Will nodded. 'Master Carver did. He was reluctant to go. But a few trinkets persuaded him. You go to the sick?'

'I have been gathering herbs,' Sam said, and held up a bunch of greenstuff. 'The epidemic is almost over, but I fear for Elizabeth Winslow.'

'No better?'

'Her breathing is worse. She rattles in her chest, and although a week ago she seemed much recovered, now her fever climbs. I like it not. I have seen the like in too many of them, and they have all died.'

'Poor Edward.'

'Yes, I fear he will be grieving before a week is out.'

Will shook his head. 'This has been a terrible sickness.'

'Aye. Satan visits plague on us alright. I just hope Mistress Winslow is the last.'

They parted, and Will felt suddenly very low. How many more? He asked himself as he picked up the spade. How many others would die here in this wilderness?

The following day was the Sabbath, but they had hardly managed an hour's meeting before Samoset and five other Indians strode into the plantation.

They were an alarming sight, their dark faces painted with black, each with a different design—one with a large stripe three or four fingers wide from forehead to chin, another with zigzags across his cheeks, a third with a cross. Every man wore a deerskin, and the principal men had a wild-cat skin on one arm. Their legs were covered right to the top with leather leggings, and a leather cloth about their waist so they looked like Irish trousers. They had no facial hair, and their long black hair hung past their shoulders. The one with the black stripe wore his hair tied up with a feather like a fan, while the one with the cross on his face had a fox-tail hanging out of his hair. They came unarmed, having left bows and arrows a quarter of a mile outside town, but they did bring with them the lost tools.

So the English entertained them. And the Indians entertained the English, singing and dancing with strange antics, blissfully unaware that this was what the English considered to be the Sabbath, a sacred day, and not a day for singing, or dancing, or any frivolity. However, John Carver thought it prudent to let the strange singing and dancing continue, reasoning that the Lord would understand. The English provided food and the Indians ate with relish, as though they had not eaten for a week.

The principal man wore about his waist a bow-case which contained a little corn pounded into powder which when mixed with water, hot or cold made a meal. They also had a little tobacco, but no-one smoked it.

'Wampanoag bring skins to trade,' Samoset explained.

John Carver nodded. 'The English thank great chief Massasoit. However, today is sacred day. We worship our God. We do not trade today. You leave the skins here, and bring more in two nights, and we will trade for all.'

Samoset nodded, satisfied with this explanation, and they allowed themselves to be escorted to the place where they had left their bows and arrows. Some of them thought to slink off.

'Where do they go?' Edward Winslow asked. 'They have not taken proper leave.'

Samoset was incensed. He translated and the others called them back.

The English then gave them little gifts and bade them farewell, and so they left with promises that they would come again.

Samoset, however, had other ideas. Samoset had grown used to English comforts, a real house, decent food, sleeping on beds. Civilisation in short. He was not so happy with the Wampanoag's limited facilities.

'Samoset sick,' he told John Carver, pulling a face, and holding his stomach and staggering dramatically. 'Samoset stay.'

So Samoset stayed. And stayed. Until Wednesday morning.

On Wednesday morning, they eventually sent Samoset off to find out why the others had not returned, and they gave him a hat, a pair of stockings, shoes, a shirt, and a piece of cloth to tie about his waist with which he was more than satisfied.

Again they got on with the meeting which had been interrupted to confirm the military orders, and to make laws for the smooth running of the community.

The meeting went on for an hour, arguments as to the details of night watches causing Will to grow impatient. His leg ached sitting for so long in one position and he got up to walk about a little to ease it. Let them argue, he thought irritably.

'What on earth—?' On the hill nearby two Indians had appeared hooting at them and waving their bows and arrows in the air in a show of defiance.

'What do they want this time?' Brewster demanded impatiently.

'We did ask Samoset to find out what had happened to the others,' Will reminded him mildly.

'I'll go and see what they want,' Miles Standish volunteered, grateful to use his military talents, and to show that he was not cowed by Brewster's reprimand.

With Stephen Hopkins, Miles Standish marched out of the compound and up the hill towards the Indians. Both of them had muskets and following behind were two of the mates from the ship.

On the hill, the Indians rubbed their Arrows and the strings of their bows. 'See how they make defiance!' Miles Standish growled.

'What do you think they want?' Hopkins asked.

'I don't know. Just a show of bravado as young men do.' They marched a little longer, up the hill, and suddenly the two Indians turned and fled.

Standish followed them a little further, but they were nowhere to be seen, and there was nothing more to do but return to the compound.

On that day, Wednesday the twenty-first day of March 1621, the last of those who were still on the *Mayflower* came ashore and the colonisation was complete.

THIRTY-FIVE
Squanto and Massasoit

March 1621

The Indians, however, were not done. The following day, the twenty-second day of March was a warm spring day, and once more John Carver called a public meeting for the conducting of business.

'Not again!' John Billington complained. 'Lord, we just get to work, and Master Carver calls a meeting!'

'Not that he ever does any work,' George Sowle grumbled about Billington to Will, as he followed the others to the assembly point.

'What public business now?' John Billington demanded. 'Ain't we had enough of this lately?'

Will said sharply, 'If the governor wants a meeting, we'll have a meeting. You may not see the need, John Billington, but we do.'

Billington glared at Will and turned away. Always a trouble maker, Will thought.

So they sat down around John Carver on anything they could find, like the disciples scattered at Jesus' feet, and John Carver called for quiet, and opened in prayer. The talk this time was of building and laws, but again they had only been at their business an hour when five Indians approached the settlement. While Miles Standish and some others checked that their muskets were handy, John Carver felt no need to worry. Their new friend Samoset had returned, with another four natives, one of whom he made a point of introducing to the English.

'Tisquantum,' Samoset said.

Mishearing, John Carver said, 'Squanto, eh?' And the name Squanto stuck.

He was a tall man, like most of the Indians, naked to the waist and wearing hide leggings. His hair, long and black reached half way down his back. It was difficult to determine his age—perhaps late twenties or maybe early thirties. Probably even he didn't know.

Squanto grinned and nodded, showing a mouthful of white teeth. 'We bring skins and fish. Gifts.' The fish was red herring, dried, but not salted.

'Ho,' John Carver was delighted. 'Another who can speak English.'

Squanto studied him with his black eyes. 'Tisquantum been to Eng'and.' He announced proudly.

'Have you?' Will asked much impressed.

Squanto nodded seriously. 'Me yive with Master John S'aney in Cornhill.

John Carver nodded. 'I have heard of Master Slaney,' he informed the others. 'He is treasurer of the Newfoundland Company. So you lived with him did you?'

'Bought as a slave?' Will asked, but he got no response. 'How did you get back here?'

'Ship.'

Will cast a look at Brewster. 'Serves me right for asking.'

Samoset said, 'Great Sagamore, Massasoit, very near with brother, Quadequina, and many men.'

'Massasoit is here?' John Carver repeated, and looked outside the plantation as though to see these people, but for now they remained hidden. 'I don't see them.'

At that moment a shadow appeared on the top of the hill, and seemed to grow longer. About sixty men lined the brow of the hill silhouetted against the clear blue sky.

Everyone in the plantation froze, neither speaking nor moving. They were dead men, exposed and vulnerable, their women and children dead too. They could not hope to see off so many, not with them in such a weakened state. They had only twenty-one able-bodied men, six adult women, and the rest, twenty-three, were children. In the face of a well-planned attack, they could not win.

'Oh my God!' the godless John Billington swore.

John Carver's face blanched of all colour. Will's heart hammered in his chest, pounded in his head. Suddenly the stories of vicious natives, of cannibalism, of torture, did not seem so far fetched.

William Brewster let his breath go in a whistle. 'May Jehovah have mercy on us.'

All at once Will was icy calm, his head clear, his thoughts decisive. Without realising he did so, he took control. 'We should make defence,' he said. 'Look to your guns.' Turning he saw Squanto still standing beside them with Samoset and the three other Indians, grinning all over his treacherous dark face.

'Have you betrayed us?' he demanded.

Squanto continued to grin. 'You talk with Chief Massasoit,' he said nodding. 'You talk.'

John Carver managed to recover himself. 'They will come to us?'

'No. Eng'ish go Massasoit. Carver go. Carver chief.'

There was a short silence. 'Well I ain't going,' John Carver declared flatly.

Will had a suggestion. 'The best thing is if Samoset or Squanto goes to him to see what we should do.'

'Tisquantum go,' Squanto announced, and marched off abruptly, head held high, black locks shimmering in the sunlight, a proud warrior. Samoset stayed behind.

Squanto came back directly. 'Massasoit say one Eng'ish go. Know Massasoit and tell of Eng'ish governor's mind.'

'I'll go,' Edward Winslow said unexpectedly.

Squanto stared at him in that direct way all the Indians had, fascinated by this fair skinned man with his yellow hair and very blue eyes. Why, he was almost as interesting as the small red-haired man with the red beard!

Will looked at Winslow and asked seriously. 'Are you sure?'

Winslow gave a quick reassuring smile. 'My wife is grievously sick and not like to recover,' he said. 'If it is the Lord's will that I die, then so be it. But you have three Indians you can keep here as hostages. I think the Lord will be with me. Besides, I am curious about these people.'

'You had better not go empty-handed,' John Carver said. They found a pair of knives and a copper chain with a jewel hanging from it. This was for Massasoit. They also sent a knife and a jewel to hang in the ear of Quadequina. They included a pot of strong water and some biscuit and some butter.

'God go with you,' Will said quietly in his ear, as Winslow picked up his offerings.

Winslow looked at him, and his face was paler than usual. 'Thank you, but you are making me nervous!' Indeed, the hand that took Will's in parting, shook. He took a steadying breath, so that the two Indian guides should not see his fear. 'Look after Elizabeth for me.' Then he turned to the two guides. 'Come on then.'

As Edward trundled up the hill accompanied by Samoset and Squanto, he was silent, praying in his heart for God's guidance to say and do the right thing, for His protection too, and he knew that the men back at the plantation also prayed for him. He tried to ignore the churning in his insides, the sudden need for the privy, controlling himself with an effort. Whatever awaited him in Massasoit's camp, he needed God's help.

Massasoit had retreated to his temporary camp, a set of mat-covered dwellings arranged around a central fire. There were children, and women, some of them very beautiful, for all the Indians were a fine-looking race. They stared at this man with the yellow hair and beard as Squanto and Samoset led him through the huts, until fear overcame their curiosity and they fled inside the tents. Their shyness strengthened him, for he realised they feared the white man as much as the white man feared the red man.

Massasoit was a large man, perhaps thirty-five to forty years old. He had painted his face a dull red colour, and his face and the black hair of his head were oiled, so that he seemed very greasy. His lips had a natural downward turn which gave him a forbidding appearance. He wore skins the same as his people did, except that he had a necklace of white bone beads from which hung a little bag of tobacco, and a string from which a great dagger dangled almost to his ample belly.

All his people too were painted, some black, some red, some yellow and some white, some with crosses and other strange symbols, some wearing skins, some nearly naked, all strong tall men. They stood with him while he sat outside his tent, all of them silent, watching as Edward, Samoset and Squanto approached. Edward's stomach turned over.

They stopped and Edward faced Massasoit. The two men studied each other in silence, Edward trying to judge the mood of the king. He decided that if they attacked, he would not die easily. He would take one or two with him. Mentally he worked out how he would do it. He did not have a musket, but he did have the gifts for Massasoit, including the knife, and at his hip his own sword. At the first hint of threat, he would use it, open a way perhaps to his left where he was nearer to the edge of the village, and then away. His senses, sharpened by fear and clear as ice, focused on the men around Massasoit. He listened for movement behind him, watched their eyes, their movements.

The moment had come. He had been silent long enough. He bowed graciously, and said through a dry throat, 'King James of England salutes you with love and peace and does accept Massasoit as his friend and ally.' Squanto translated.

The king bowed his head graciously. 'What do the Eng'ish want of us?' he asked through Squanto.

'Carver, our governor desires to see you and to trade with you and to confirm peace with the great Massasoit as his next neighbour.' Edward managed a smile.

Samoset and Squanto argued over the translation of this and eventually asked for another word for 'governor', for which Edward supplied 'chief', and then Squanto gabbled away in his strange tongue.

To Edward's intense relief, the king seemed well pleased. 'What is that you wear?' he asked, pointing at Edward's chest.

'This is armour,' Edward replied. 'To protect my body from sword and arrow.'

'You give to me. And that?' He indicated the sword in its intricate scabbard hanging at Edward's hip.

This was going too far. 'No.' Edward replied straightly. 'This is mine. But I bring Massasoit gifts.' He handed the cloth-wrapped parcel. 'And also for the brother of the king, Quadequina.'

Squanto gabbled away, and the king gabbled back. 'The King is pleased with his gifts,' Squanto said. 'The King wants you stay with his brother Quadequina.'

Edward's heart sank. The last thing he desired was to be a hostage with the Indians, but he knew he had no choice. He bowed his head in consent and the King stood up.

'I believe it is Massasoit coming over the brook,' John Carver declared, frowning into the distance.

'At last!' Winslow had been gone some hours. Will's anxiety about his safety had kept him hobbling about the compound, unable to sit still. What if Edward did not come back at all? What if the Indians had killed him? Of what value would the hostages have been then?

Will peered at a group of men approaching the brook from out of the trees, a large man in the middle flanked by the others. 'Yes. I can see Samoset and Squanto too, and a large number of others. I can't see Winslow, though.'

'I can't see Winslow, either,' Stephen Hopkins agreed.

'I mislike it,' Miles Standish growled low in his throat. 'We will take some of their men as hostages until we get Winslow back.'

'We already have three hostages,' Brewster snapped. 'Of what value, pray, would more be?'

'Someone had better go and meet the king at the brook,' John Carver said.

'The Indians like to see a chief,' Brewster said bluntly. 'You go.'

Carver glared at him. 'If I am the chief, then I ought to have circumstance, and all due honour! I thought for the King to be brought to the new house that we have not quite finished, and for me to make an entrance, with horns and trumpets. That kind of thing.'

'Beware a haughty spirit, Brother,' Brewster warned him grinning, and marched off.

'I ain't afeared of no Indians,' Miles Standish announced. 'Who will go with me?'

'I'll go,' Isaac Allerton said grimly.

The two men left them and marched out of the plantation towards the Indians.

'How did we get into this?' Allerton asked through tight lips.

Standish did not look at him. 'Because somebody has to do it.'

'We'd have been safer staying in Leyden.'

'No doubt on that.'

They tramped on in silence for a short while. Then Allerton said, 'What do you suppose has happened to Winslow?'

'Dunno,' Standish replied, although deep inside he was sure Winslow was dead. Pretty soon he would be dead too. All of them perhaps. Still, he was a soldier with a job to do.

The two men came near to the brook and waited.

The Indians now were just the other side of the brook, quite a number of them, with brilliantly painted faces, warriors all. Facing them, Isaac Allerton whispered that he felt small and naked. Standish, though, had worked out how, if they were attacked, he would make short work of three or four before they overpowered him. And the big man in the middle, obviously their chief, would be the first, of that he was certain.

The Indians splashed through the brook, and came to a halt in front of the English.

Allerton and Standish bowed civilly.

'I'll do the talking,' Allerton whispered to Standish.

Then, addressing Massasoit, he said, 'The English chief welcomes King Massasoit to their village, and bids Massasoit enter with his men.'

Samoset translated for them.

Pleased with this greeting, the King allowed Miles Standish and Isaac Allerton to escort him into the plantation.

It was Will's turn now to greet the king, which he did with all due solemnity, trying not to stare at the red painted greasy face. He conducted Massasoit to the uncompleted house, where the English had placed a green rug and three or four cushions. No sooner had Massasoit entered than John Carver came in with drums and trumpets blaring, and a few men made up as musketeers. The pomp and ceremony was to impress the Indians, for the English rightly assumed that the more ceremony there was the more highly the King would think of them.

The two 'chiefs' greeted each other, Carver kissing the hand of the Indian king and Massasoit bestowing a kiss on John Carver's unshaven cheek, leaving a greasy smear. Carver imperiously ordered strong water with a wave of his hand, and someone brought it on a tray, with some cups. 'I drink to you, great Sagamore Massasoit,' John Carver boomed, raising his cup.

Massasoit nodded seriously, but he was well pleased, and he swallowed such a great amount of drink, it caused sweat to break out on his skin. Then John Carver called for fresh meat and the king ate, as did his retinue.

Over the food, they concluded a peace treaty which was duly written down.

They agreed, That neither Massasoit nor any of his people should injure or hurt any of the English; that if any of his people did hurt the

English, he should send the offender to them that he might be punished. Also, if any English did any harm to any of his people, the same would apply. They further agreed that if any tools were taken from the English Massasoit should cause them to be returned.

They also agreed that if any should unjustly war against Massasoit or his people, the English would come to his aid. And if any should war against the English he would come to their aid. Further, that Massasoit should send to friendly neighbours to let them know of this agreement that they might not harm the English. And that when their men came to the English they should leave their bows and arrows behind them as the English would do with their arms when visiting them.

Finally, that doing thus, King James would esteem of him as his friend and ally.

All of this King Massasoit and his people seemed pleased with.

Will, watching this solemn occasion, began to feel easier in his mind. This man Massasoit seemed a reasonable sort of fellow, the sort one could talk things over with. Perhaps Winslow was unharmed after all.

Massasoit reached for a cup, and Will noticed that his hand trembled. Not the result of too much strong drink, Will thought with surprise. No, the Indians were as afraid, of the English as the English were of them, if not more so. This agreement was as important to them as it was to the English.

Massasoit left with as much stately honour as he had when he arrived but left behind three more of his men as hostages, making six, and then his brother Quadequina came over the brook to the English.

Quadequina was a tall straight young man, of 'very modest and seemly countenance', as Will put it later in an account of the incident. He enjoyed the entertainment the English offered, and then he too returned to his people.

A short time later Edward Winslow came marching back towards the plantation.

At the sight of him Will thanked God, and John Carver ordered the Indian hostages released.

Samoset and Squanto stayed all night with the English and Massasoit and his men, and their wives and children slept in the woods not half a mile from the plantation. Then they left and went to their home at Sowams (later called Warren in Rhode Island) some forty miles away.

Squanto remained with the English.

THIRTY-SIX
The Southworths

London, 1621

Alice Southworth brushed a tendril of chestnut hair from her face with a floury finger. Although it was still dark outside, the daily task of kneading bread had already begun. She hoped the communal bread oven had been lit and would be hot enough by the time the loaves were risen. Yesterday the dough had collapsed in a heap and the inside of the round loaf had been doughy because it had not been hot enough. That had brought her censure from Edward. It was hot in the kitchen, and she guessed that outside the weather had turned warm.

Not that you could tell what time of year it was, she thought crossly, for here in London there were no fields, no bare earth where a daffodil grew, or a snowdrop, or even a blade of grass. It was a barren dirty landscape of buildings and mud and sewage. Never had she hated a place so much!

Thomas emerged from the boys' bedroom first. Now almost five years old, he had schooling like his brother Constant, a year older. It was a privilege, she knew, that the youngsters had the benefit of an education which was free, provided by the congregation. But she would far rather have been in Leyden.

'Porridge will be ready when your brother gets up,' she said, and continued her kneading.

Thomas came over to her, and she stopped momentarily to hug him and kiss him, taking care to keep her floury hands off his nightshirt.

'Constant is still abed,' he said, and yawned.

'Hand over mouth when we yawn, Thomas,' she reminded him. 'Now there is water in the bucket. Wash yourself, please.'

Reluctantly he moved away from her, and she went back to the rhythmic stretch and pull of kneading. *Stop too soon and you end up with bricks, not loaves,* she told herself. But she watched Thomas and her heart wrenched. That her boys should have to grow up in such surroundings was a source of constant pain to her. As a little girl growing up with her sisters in Somerset, she had had fields to play in, flowers to pick, lambs would be born, and be gambolling in the fields. Now they were hemmed in by bricks, and wattle and daub, all dirty with age, and she hardly ever saw even the sun. *Leyden was better than this.*

Leyden. It had once seemed alien and cold to her. Now it was home, neat and clean with flowers and sunshine. And her parents and sisters were there. She tried not to complain, but her spirit cried out against the injustice of having to be in this place.

Edward came out from their bedchamber next. He looked worse than usual this morning. His light brown hair stuck out at all angles, and he had not shaved in several days. He was as white as new wool, even his lips, apart from a small dab of red at the corner of his mouth. He staggered to his chair and almost fell into it.

She watched him pityingly as she shaped the dough, and put it on a tray to rise. His illness had gone on too long, and while he languished at home, she had to go to work helping in a laundry. And she must go there very soon. She did not have the luxury of nursing him at home herself.

She sighed. She was exhausted with the effort of just staying alive.

She called Constant, and then sent Thomas to get him up.

'How are you Edward?' she asked solicitously.

Edward managed a feeble shrug, but did not answer.

Alice went to the fire, lowering the chain which suspended the porridge pot so that she could give it a stir, then, fetching wooden bowls, for each of them, began to spoon it out. It consisted only of oats and water, and was poor thin stuff. No salt—she couldn't afford that—and certainly no milk.

Constant appeared.

'Hurry and wash, child,' she told him, as she hugged him also.

A short time later they sat at the old table, and Edward managed a short prayer of thanks for their food in a thin reedy voice.

Seated opposite him Alice was deeply worried. He could not keep going like this. He hardly touched the food. In an effort to make conversation she said, 'Is there any news of Brother Carver?'

'You know there is not,' Edward snapped with more strength than he appeared to possess. 'Probably the ship has sunk. 'Tis six months since they left.'

His grey eyes watched her closely to see her reaction, and although her heart sank inside her, she hid it well. She managed brightly, 'There could be any number of reasons why they have not written.'

'We should face the facts. The journey is a mere four weeks. Four weeks there, four weeks back, that's two months.'

'Perhaps the ship stayed for a while. I know they wanted to have the other ship stay with them.'

'All right. Give them another four weeks for that. That's three months.' He paused, and glared at her. 'I know what it is with you. You are worried about Will Bradford.' Immediately he began to cough again, and pulled out the blood-stained rag he used as a handkerchief.

She got up from her food, and found him a fresh one, taking the other from him and throwing it on the fire. Well you couldn't get bloodstains out anyway, and she had enough rags.

She said, 'I am naturally concerned for all of them. We have many good friends on that ship.'

'Well, we should have heard something by now.' He struggled to say the last words for the coughing took him again, a fierce paroxysm that left him exhausted and collapsed.

Alarmed, Alice went to him. 'Boys,' she snapped, 'if you've finished get your clothes on, and be ready to go.' She didn't want them to see this.

As the cough took him again, Alice ushered them into their room. Oh yes, it was a spacious tenement, with two rooms. But she would gladly have exchanged it for one half the size in Leyden.

She helped Edward back into their room, and put him to bed. He alarmed her. He was so frail, so weak.

Back in the kitchen, she kissed Constant and Thomas and sent them off with the girl Phoebe Hicks from upstairs who was also going for schooling.

Then she began to wash the dishes and the cooking pot, scraping out the very last of the clinging porridge and putting it aside for later. She had a little while before she must go to the laundry. As she worked, she realised that she was desperately afraid. Afraid for Edward, afraid of being alone, and afraid for her boys. And she was afraid for those on the *Mayflower*. And most of all, she was afraid for Will.

Oh, Will! Her heart ached for the comfort of his arms, his broad shoulders, his strength. In her mind's eye his face came to her clearly, a strong face, with his kind blue eyes, his soft expressive mouth, his soft small beard, and a guilty physical ache shot through her. And then he was gone again, banished to the edge of her mind and she could not recall him.

Edward coughed again, and then called out to her.

She went to him. The new rag she had given him was soaked with blood, as were his fingers, and blood trickled out of his mouth. His breathing, never good, now rattled alarmingly in his chest.

He gripped her hand, grey eyes wide with fear. 'What's happening to me?'

She swallowed convulsively, tears springing to her eyes. She knew, and she suspected he did.

She sat with him a while. No work for her today, then, so no money either. Shortly he fell asleep and she left him, washing the blood from her hands in the bucket. Later, she took the risen loaves to the communal oven, which, thankfully, was hot enough. She would collect them later.

Back in the tenement, she sat with Edward the whole day, holding his hand as his breathing became more laboured. He did not wake up again, and gradually, as the sun began to set, Edward stopped breathing altogether.

Alexander Carpenter looked around him at the tenement and he was as appalled by the inside as he had been by the outside. Not that Alice had not kept it clean, but there was only so much a person could do with crumbling walls and no money.

Alice stood before him, a shadow of her former self, and he was shocked at her appearance. She was thin, and careworn, looking older than her thirty or so years, her sleeves pushed up to her elbows so she could work, her hands red raw with the lye of the laundry, her clothes old and often mended.

Yet she held her head high. 'You are well come, Father,' she said, and she had a quiet dignity about her. 'Do, please sit down.'

He watched as she rubbed her hands together nervously.

'What are you doing here, Alice?' he demanded as he sat on the old chair Edward used, and she turned her head towards him sharply. Realising he sounded angry, he added a little more gently, 'What has he brought you to?'

'He did his best, Father, but he was not a well man.' He thought she was about to cry, but she struggled to overcome it.

'How do you survive?'

'I pay the rent by working in the laundry.'

'*In the laundry?*' He was appalled. '*My* daughter working in a laundry?'

She quailed at his fury, but continued bravely, 'And—and the brethren give me gifts of food and money when they can afford it.'

Ever since coming to 'the Truth' Alexander Carpenter had never felt so much like swearing. *My daughter living on gifts of mercy. Working in a laundry!* It was totally unacceptable. But he had known how it must be when he got her letter telling him of Edward's death, only he could never have imagined it as bad as this.

'Where are the boys?' he asked curtly.

'At school. The brethren run a school.'

Well that was one good thing then.

Alexander had come with the strictest instruction from his wife that he must not under any circumstances leave their middle daughter to fend for herself and her children in London, and now he had seen for himself how things stood, he had no intention of doing so. Ever since Edward had whisked her off to London with such unseemly haste, Alexander had been uneasy, but Alice's letters home had been cheerful and encouraging—a false cheerfulness he now decided. He was disgusted with Edward for leaving his daughter in this place, this stinking, dark, dirty, smelly London. He was also disgusted with him for dying and leaving Alice and the children in poverty. Well he, Alexander Carpenter, was not going to leave her here a moment longer!

'Right! In that case, get your things together, I am taking you home with me,' he announced.

The gratitude in her face tore at his heart, and all at once her face crumpled. 'Oh, Father!' was all she could say before bursting into tears. He took her in his arms, then and held her, and once again she was his own dear little girl.

They sailed for Holland the following day.

THIRTY-SEVEN
The First Season

Plymouth Colony 1621

Standing beside William Brewster and his wife Mary, Will watched as the *Mayflower* slipped over the horizon, carrying within her hull their letters. It was a strange feeling to watch her go, the last tie with England, their home since July last year. If she had not stayed so long in this place, they would not have survived. To remember the dramas played out within her hull, the life and death struggles, the children born, the people dead, brought a lump into Will's throat. He wasn't the only one; many of those watching wept openly.

Some of the sailors had become their friends, and they would miss them. In fact, two of the sailors, John Alden and a man called Ely stayed with the settlers. John Alden had converted to the Separatist belief, but also he had fallen in love with pretty little Priscilla Mullins, although he had yet to win her.

Even when all that was left was empty sea, they stayed watching. There was no going back now. They had known it would happen, that the ship must go, but it felt as though they had been abandoned, left to their fate, their own devices.

Eventually, Will turned away, along with the others. They had work to do. It was spring, and the task of ploughing, tilling and seed-sowing must take priority over house-building if they were to survive the next winter. At the top of the hill, Will looked back as if to make sure the *Mayflower* really had gone, and had not turned back, and caught sight of Edward Winslow a solitary figure on the shore.

Edward's wife Elizabeth had died two days ago. The death of a wife was a bitter blow to any man, Will thought, and Edward had loved Elizabeth dearly. Now he must, like Will himself, join the ranks of the widowed to face this challenge of building a colony alone.

'Tisquantum show you how plant corn,' Squanto said, appearing suddenly beside Will, as he had formed a habit of doing.

'Oh?'

'Eng'ish not do right. Do as Squanto say or no corn.'

'Very well,' Will said. 'You show us.'

Squanto fell into step beside Will, watching him closely in that way that he had. He had formed an attachment to Will, and followed him around rather like a puppy might. Will didn't mind. Squanto was useful, and he liked his company, his odd ways, and besides, Squanto wanted to know about the English God and asked many questions.

'You need fish,' Squanto explained. 'What the Eng'ish call a-wive, from the brook.'

Will stood still to look at him, figuring out what he meant. 'Alewives.'

'Yes. A-wive.' Squanto looked at him earnestly. 'Dig hole, put in seed, put in fish, cover over. Seed grow.'

'That is the Indian way?'

'Yes.'

They walked on a little further. It was a fine day, with a sapphire sky overhead, and the sun warmed them. Already work had begun on cultivating the field. Will asked, 'Do you not wish to return to your people, Squanto?'

'Wampanoag not people of Tisquantum. Tisquantum woman and children and all tribe dead of white man's sickness.'

Will was surprised. He hadn't known Squanto had a wife. 'You escaped?'

'Tisquantum in Eng'and. When come back, all gone.' He waved his hand expressively. 'Tisquantum not beyong Wampanoag. Tisquantum stay with Eng'ish.' And he grinned showing his beautiful white teeth.

'Very well, then.'

He followed Will into the field. Before long he had the English running back and forth to the brook where they trapped and caught the alewives, so that they could be used as fertiliser for the corn. He worked as hard as the English did, showing them how to dress the corn.

John Carver worked along with Will, bending down, putting the seed in the drill, which had already been made with a plough, as Will followed with the fish, and covered over. The sun made him sweat, for it was surprisingly warm for the season.

John Carver paused. Straightening up, he wiped the sweat from his face with his forearm. Pleased to have a break, Will straightened also, and saw John grimace. 'What's wrong? Are you ill?'

John shook his head slightly. 'The heat I think. My head! I don't think I can carry on!'

In the time it took Will to walk the half dozen paces to him, John's face drained of colour, and he crumpled into a heap, crying out. 'Oh God! The pain!'

Will went to him immediately, caught him before he fell, and held him with difficulty for John was a big heavy man. John Howland came too, helping him, and George Sowle, and others.

'My head! My head!' John complained, and now his speech slurred like he had drunk too much.

'It is very hot,' Mary Brewster said, bringing over the bucket of drinking water and the ladle. She tried to give him a drink but he could not co-operate. 'Take him home,' she ordered the men.

They carried him back to the plantation. Katherine Carver saw them coming and ran from her house to meet them. 'John, John, what is it?'

'My head!'

''Tis the sun,' Will said with more conviction than he felt. After all it was a very warm day.

They got John Carver to his bed in the Brewster house, and laid him down. His face was grey, his eyes closed his hands holding his head. Mary ran to get some cool water, while Katherine sat by him holding his hand and crooning comforting words, but he was incoherent and in a good deal of pain. When Mary came back with the water, Katherine used it to bathe his forehead, but it brought him no relief.

He cried out, and groaned in his agony. Will stood by helplessly, as the women did their best to make him comfortable, and Sam Fuller came in.

'You might as well all go back to work,' Mary Brewster said briskly to them. 'We don't need to starve on account of one man.' They were reluctant to go, but realising that she wanted them out of the way, Will ushered everyone else out.

'What do you suppose is wrong with him?' Will asked Brewster as they walked back to the field.

'A stroke perhaps.'

Will knew how serious a stroke would be to the victim. He had seen the results before. But perhaps it was not that. He tried to think positively, and continued working with Squanto. However, when Brewster went back later Will went with him.

'He is sleeping,' Katherine Carver informed them, and began to cry. Brewster looked at his own wife, who shook her head. Sam Fuller pursed his lips.

Will went to Carver. He was quiet, but his eyes were not really closed, only half-closed, and although he breathed he was very still, his face a terrible ashen colour. He wasn't asleep, he was unconscious.

Sam Fuller followed them outside. 'I think he has had some kind of stroke,' he said, confirming Brewster's own diagnosis.

'Do you think he will die?' Will asked.

Sam shook his head. 'I don't know. But you know a stroke is a serious thing. I can do nothing for him. It is in God's hands.'

Will shook his head in denial. John had been a friend since Scrooby days. He was their governor, a large booming man, bluff and genial, yet strong underneath. His larger-than-life personality would be sorely missed by everyone. He was simply irreplaceable.

John Carver slipped quietly away two days later.

Will sat on the log, his great long legs splayed out in front of him, easing his back and hip from the morning's work. It was another warm day, a day of sunshine and blossoming trees, and birds twittering in them. As the men joined him, one by one, in the circle which had become their meeting place, he watched them. The younger men were strong and fit, the older men weary with work, but grateful to be out in the sun and warmth and fresh air. The confines of the *Mayflower* were forgotten now in the daily work. But it was good work, honest work.

'So—why this meeting, Will?' Sam Fuller asked as he sat down.

Will waited until the last of them, Gilbert Winslow, took his seat beside his brother. 'Thank you for coming,' he began. 'I know you all have work to do. However, we have business to attend to. Since the death of our brother John Carver, we have been without a governor, a man to take control, to lead us, to make decisions. We need now to make a choice.'

'And let me guess who you want to be governor,' John Billington growled in his flat London accent, his eyes narrowing suspiciously.

Will sighed inwardly. Outwardly he met Billington's eyes squarely. 'Did you have someone in mind, sir?'

'Ain't it right you want one of your so called Pilgrims to be in charge?'

There was an uncomfortable murmur among the men. 'So it is written into the agreement.' Will's gaze swept over them all, effectively signalling that Billington's further contribution was not required. 'We need a man who is able to act as magistrate, who is a leader of men, who has good sense and experience.'

'Which seems to me to be Brother Brewster,' Stephen Hopkins said.

Brewster spluttered, and was quick to disclaim. 'I thank you, but no. I am too old to take such responsibility. And I have no wish to set myself up as governor, or leader.'

Will studied him. 'Are you sure? For you do indeed have the experience and the ability.'

'No. I have enough to do. You have the right qualifications, though, Will.'

'I agree,' John Alden said unexpectedly. 'Master Bradford gets my vote. Showed such good sense on the *Mayflower* when that dolt Christopher Martin—God rest his soul—caused trouble.'

'Like I said,' John Billington cut in nastily, 'you Bible men hold the power.'

Brewster said carefully, 'We are the instigators of this enterprise, Master Billington. From the beginning we have had a vision of a colony based on God's word, run by his laws. We have had to tolerate those outside the faith because of financial wants, but you joined us on the basis of our vision, our faith. Therefore, you must expect to be under our law.'

'I recognise no law and no God,' John Billington avowed. 'Else why did he let so many die, eh? If you be so good as you think you be, why did he kill off your people then?'

'Be grateful he did not think to kill you off, sir,' Will said acidly. And could have added that it was a great pity.

Billington stood up, furious. 'Damn you! Damn you all to hell!'

Miles Standish glared at him. 'Ah—you're only jealous, John Billington. Anyone would think *you* wanted to be governor. Still, you needn't worry! There ain't a man here as'd vote for you!'

John Billington growled again and stomped off.

Stephen Hopkins said, 'Well I agree Master Bradford should be our governor. So I think we should vote on it.'

Will, though, had no desire for the responsibility. He did not want to lord it over people. Besides, he doubted his ability to do justice to the position. 'But I am hardly recovered from my illness,' he protested. 'Surely brother Edward Winslow is a much better contender. Or Master Allerton.'

Stephen Hopkins was unimpressed. 'What say all of you men?'

'My vote is for Brother Bradford,' Allerton said.

'He gets my vote too,' Sam Fuller added.

'Let's have a show of hands.'

So Will found himself the new governor. 'But there is so much to do,' he protested. 'And I am still lame, unless you hadn't noticed!'

'Then we'll give you an assistant. What about Master Allerton?'

So Will had to accept. 'Well, gentlemen, you do me an honour. I will do my best to fulfil my obligations, if the Lord continues to spare me.'

'Billington won't be happy,' Brewster observed dryly.

'Oh why did the Lord spare John Billington?' Sam Fuller asked in mock seriousness.

'Better ask why Satan spared him when he took so many good people,' Brewster corrected, 'and then you'll know the answer.'

'So why did not God protect us from the scourge?' John Alden asked. He was always full of questions, for the Truth was still new to him.

Brewster replied, 'And if none of the Lord's people got sick, John Alden, or died, would there not be the whole world wanting to join us? In that case, how will the Lord select his sheep?'

John Alden frowned. 'Aye. Of course I've heard of Job.'

'Tisquantum not know this Job,' Squanto said unexpectedly.

'Come with me,' Will said, 'and I will explain it to you.'

'Sister Carver is greatly unwell,' Mary Brewster whispered to her husband as she put plates on the rough-sawn table.

Will groaned in himself. Katherine Carver had lived for her husband John. Not a strong woman, she had leaned heavily on him. Now that he was gone she could not come to terms with her loss. As Katherine sat down at the table with them, Will looked at her. She looked very old, although only forty. Her eyes had sunk deep into the sockets of her skull, dark purplish bruising around them, the lids puffed and shiny and swollen from weeping. Her cheeks were sucked in, and her cheekbones jutted out. She cared little about her appearance now. Her once jet black hair was now striped with white and escaped her cap, flying untidily about her face. Her pale eyes were unfocussed.

She barely touched the food that Mary had so lovingly prepared, and as soon as she could, excused herself and left the table to sit in the corner by the fire. Immediately Wrestling and Love began to squabble over what she had left, and Mary shared it between them. 'Boys,' she said despairingly. 'Always hungry.' But her eyes were on Katherine, and there was no disguising the anxiety there. She cast a speaking look at her husband, and then went back to her own meal.

Edward Winslow waited by the brook, half concealed in the bushes. He knew Susanna was here somewhere, for he had seen her bring her bucket to get water. She would not be long.

'Why do you linger Edward Winslow?' Constanta Hopkins asked him.

He looked at her, not having seen her come up. She was a fine looking girl, with the glow of budding womanhood. But she was not to his taste. At fifteen she was too young. He said, 'None of your business, young Mistress.'

She chuckled, and laughed. 'I think you have an eye for a certain lady,' she said carrying on by, and giving him a saucy look.

He said nothing, his face inscrutable. But no sooner had Constanta vanished around the bend by the trees than Susanna appeared.

Edward picked up his musket immediately and came towards her. 'Let me carry that for you,' he said, taking one of the buckets from her hand.

'That is so very kind of you, Master Winslow.' Susanna said in her quick way.

He said, 'I have been waiting for you.'

'Have you?'

'I—I wanted particularly to talk to you.'

'Indeed sir? What could you possibly want to talk to me about?

Unless of course you want some shirts washed or perhaps—'

He stopped and put down the bucket and looked at her face, which surprised her so much that she stopped talking. 'Mistress White, I would ask if you would wed me.'

She flushed, but she continued looking at him, her hazel eyes wide. 'Why? Why would you want to wed me, sir? You do not love me.'

He hesitated, for she was quite right. He didn't love her. Not yet. But she was a pretty little thing, and the attraction was there, certainly on his part, and he thought on hers. But more importantly, in this wilderness a man needed a wife, and a woman needed a man to take care of her. And Susanna had children. 'I know you are an excellent woman.'

'Thank you, sir.'

She was certainly a fine-looking woman, he thought. Pretty, young, capable, God-fearing. They would deal very well together, he was sure. He took a breath. The pause steadied him. 'I have always liked you, Susanna. I know you find it difficult with the little ones on your own. And I—I need a wife. I will take care of you and your children, if you will be wife to me. And in time we will love each other, I know.'

She did not misunderstand him. This was a matter of survival. 'So will you wed me?'

She considered for a long moment. 'Very well,' she said.

He grinned. 'Then—then I'll speak to your brother.'

She bristled. 'My brother, sir, is not my keeper. I have been a married woman, and so I make my own decisions. You need not speak to him.'

So Will's first task as governor was to conduct the marriage of Edward Winslow and Susanna (Fuller) White. The Pilgrims did not believe in a religious wedding ceremony. That was for those steeped in Romish teachings. No, this was to be a legal requirement, necessary to establish inheritance laws and laws of legitimacy for the offspring. It established the family as a legal unit, and satisfied the laws of the government they lived under. After all, the scriptures insisted that Christians be in subjection to the superior authorities. To not have a legal marriage would make the couple fornicators.

It was exactly seven weeks to the day that Elizabeth Winslow died that Edward took Susanna as his wife. As he repeated the words so often repeated by the Pilgrims in Leyden before the magistrate, he shut out the picture of his dead wife and of the previous marriage in Leyden, for this was the woman he belonged to now. He wondered if Susanna thought of her previous wedding, and hoped she didn't.

He looked at her. She had on her only good dress, a green gown, slightly old-fashioned in its cut, for it was second-hand, or possibly even third-hand. It had elaborate embroidery on it, and Susanna had filled in the very low neckline with the chemise she wore underneath, and the judicious placing of some lace. Edward, only dimly aware of the alteration, thought she was beautiful, demure, and enchanting, with the modest blush of a new bride, and downcast eyes and shy smile.

Will conducted the ceremony in the open air in the middle of the compound, and afterwards they engaged in feasting, and dancing.

'Do you not think of marrying again, Will?' Brewster asked during a pause in the festivities.

Will shrugged. 'Who is there to marry?'

'Desire Minter?' and he could not hide the merriment in his eyes.

Will cast him a speaking glance. 'A face to give a man nightmares, and a voice to raise all the devils in Christendom. No, I thank you.'

'What about pretty little Priscilla Mullins, then?'

'Too young. Besides, if I am not much mistaken, John Alden has a liking for her.'

Brewster followed the direction of his eyes, and saw John Alden leaning against a tree, trying to engage Miss Mullins' attention without much success. 'Ah, but will she have him?'

'Not to my taste,' Will said.

'And who would be?'

A vision of Alice shot into Will's mind with such force that it made the breath catch in his throat. He moved away uneasily, but Brewster followed him doggedly. 'It is not too soon after Dorothy, you know.'

Will cast him a wry look.

'Edward did not feel that seven weeks was too soon to marry Mistress White!'

Will stood looking out to sea, thinking not of Dorothy, but of Alice, and wanting her with him with an acute ache. It had been a year since he last set eyes on her and the longing did not diminish.

Brewster studied him intently. 'You think of Alice Southworth still?'

How did he know? 'She is not free,' Will said in a voice that was intended to end the discussion. It didn't.

'Edward was very ill last I saw of him.'

'Aye. But Edward is a friend. A good friend. I would not wish ill for him.'

'True. But if you wait long enough—is that what you think?'

Will shook his head, exasperated with the questioning. 'No. I don't know. What do you want me to say?' He looked at Brewster then. 'It is wrong to love another man's wife. What are you saying?'

'I am saying, don't wait for her. You could have a very long wait. And you've no way of knowing whether she would want to come here anyway, even if she were free. You would do better to settle for one of the sisters who are here.'

Will pursed his lips, by no means pleased with this advice. He said, 'I made one bad marriage, I ain't about to repeat the experience. And I'll choose my own bride, if you don't mind.'

Brewster nodded. 'But it's not good for a man to continue by himself, Will. You need a wife.'

'Thank you for your counsel, sir,' Will said and walked away.

Alice. She was three thousand miles away, on the other side of the Atlantic. A great gulf lay between them. And she was married still. Yet his heart ached for her soothing words, her practical abilities, her love. He yearned to see her smiling face, those green eyes, the chestnut hair. Alice whom he still loved with all his being. And he missed her desperately.

They had begun dancing again at the wedding 'feast' such as it was, and Brewster turned away to join them.

Mary Brewster caught up with her husband. 'How is he?' she asked, motherly concern in her face.

Brewster shrugged. 'In need of a good woman,' he said. He slipped his arm around her, and pulled her to him, giving her a huge kiss on the lips. She flushed scarlet and looked around to see who had seen them. 'What was that for?'

'Because I love you, because I am blessed to have you.' He released her, but she stood beside him with his arm around her waist, safe and happy in his arms.

Two days later Katherine Carver slipped away in death, and Mary lost one of her dearest and oldest friends.

Katherine had been dearly loved, as had her husband John, and it was a sad little community that laid her in the ground on Burial Hill where they had put so many dear ones. Will looked down at the body covered just by a sheet, and on which they put black earth. Katherine's death was so tragic because it was a waste. At forty she was not yet old, and she had a great deal of experience to give. She had died of melancholy, Will thought. Of a broken heart.

He walked away down the hill. Death stalked them all. They had lost so many people, so much death. But this was unnecessary, and part of him felt angry because of it.

They were a couple devoted to each other, for they had a rare thing, a good and loving marriage. Now it was over.

Will they be the last for a while? Will asked himself. The sickness now had passed, and everyone seemed to have a measure of health. *Dear God, let it be the last, and let us build a colony here.*

THIRTY-EIGHT
Alice

Leyden, Summer 1621

Alice took her seat between her sons Constant and Thomas and firmly scolded them for arguing. She knew from experience that they were better separated during a meeting. Along the row sat her mother, her sisters, and her nephews and nieces—Julianna's children—and across the aisle the men, her father, her brother and her brother-in-law. She smiled to herself. It was like a family outing! But then there were others with large families, she thought. The Robinsons had five children of varying ages.

Expectation hung in the air. Everyone was seated early in readiness, willing the meeting to begin, for they knew that there had been letters from those who had gone to America. The *Mayflower* had come home with news, and rumours had been rife. Snippets of information flew around the congregation, but no-one was quite sure of the details. They all waited on John Robinson. Even those families with one or more members in America had to wait.

Constant, aged six, fidgeted beside her, and turned around to five year old Fear Robinson and pulled a face. Catching him, Alice tapped him on the knee. Just ahead of her in the men's section she could see Sabine Staresmore. He had come back to Leyden with his wife and child when he had been released from prison, but the experience had cost him. He looked older than his years, and his health had deteriorated. Digorie Priest's wife Sarah, sister of Isaac Allerton, sat in front of Alice, with their young daughters Mary and Sarah. Digorie was in America. So was Allerton and all his family. Beside the Priests were Fear and Patience Brewster, the two daughters left behind. Patience was now a comely girl of twenty-one and Fear was a promising fifteen-year-old, presently staying with the Robinsons. They were desperate for news of their parents and brothers. Then there were the Cookes, Esther whose husband Francis had gone to New England with their son John, leaving her with the children Jane and Esther and Jacob who they considered too small to undertake such a journey. Bridget Fuller, Sam's wife, too wanted news, as did Bridget Robinson whose sister Katherine Carver was one of the emigrants. But then, perhaps Bridget already knew. If she did, she was giving nothing away.

And Alice wanted news of Will. She knew he belonged to another. She knew she should not care. But she did. It would be enough to know that he, and all of them had survived such a perilous journey.

After what seemed like a lifetime, the meeting began with a sung psalm and a prayer and John Robinson took his place in front of them. Settling herself down again, her Bible on her lap, Alice tried to read his face. He certainly did not look happy, she thought, and she felt her insides coil and uncoil. *Oh, dear Lord, let it be good news!*

John Robinson began with a scripture which they all dutifully followed along with in their own Bibles opened on their laps. *'To all things there is an appointed time, and a time to every purpose under the heaven: A time to be born and a time to die; a time to plant, and a time to pluck up that which is planted; a time to slay, and a time to heal; a time to break down, and a time to build, a time to weep, and a time to laugh; a time to mourn, and a time to dance.'*

Alice had a very uneasy feeling about the choice of scripture, and the coiling of her insides did not dissipate, but grew. When John Robinson read another scripture, also from Ecclesiastes, but this time chapter nine, she knew, as they all did, that the news was bad. *'I returned, and I saw under the sun, that the race is not to the swift, nor the battle to the strong, nor yet bread to the wise, nor also riches to men of understanding, neither yet favour to men of knowledge; but time and chance cometh to them all.'*

She felt sick, and tears started to her eyes. *Oh God, what has happened to them?*

John Robinson cleared his throat. He was not that well these days, unsurprisingly, for the Robinsons had buried a child three years ago and another in February. They had their share of problems and the continuing efforts of John to find a ship to take more colonists to America had met with yet more difficulties. However, as he paused and looked at them all with sorrowful eyes his sorrow was not for himself.

'Brethren,' he began, 'as most of you know, we have news from America. Captain Jones of the *Mayflower* has kindly taken it upon himself to bring back news himself and also letters. A colony has been established at Plymouth, New England, and he says the brethren there were planting for the new year when he left. They have been able to trade with the local peoples for corn and other necessities.'

Alice began to breathe again. The ship had not gone down.

'However, the brethren and their companions have struggled,' he went on. 'It is my sad duty to tell you that half the entire company—ship's crew and passengers, some of our dear brethren—have—have died.' He choked as he said it, and a gasp came from the congregation. Half! Alice felt her insides turn to ice, and her hands began to shake. 'I have here a letter written by Brother John Carver who is now their governor, and he lists those who died. I will read out the list. Not all of them are known to us here, but many, sadly are.'

There was another pause as he took a steadying breath. Alice sat frozen, rooted to the spot. Then he began to read the list of the dead.

The congregation sat in stony silence, as he named one after the other of those who had died. Mary Allerton, William Button, Richard Clarke, Digorie Priest, Edward and Ann Fuller, Sam's brother and sister-in-law, the list went on and on. And then she heard the name Dorothy Bradford. Dorothy was dead! She couldn't believe it. But she had no time to stop and think about it, for John Robinson was still reading and she had to listen to the rest. Several times John Robinson's voice broke, and he wept openly. They all did. But the one name she had dreaded hearing he did not mention, that of William Bradford.

Relief flooded through her. But John Robinson was still talking. He spoke of the hardships, of fevers, of sickness, of a harsh winter. He told how they had to cut the timber to build houses, clawing civilisation from the wilderness. He told about the Indians.

But the congregation could only take in so much information at once. They were so shocked at the death toll, of the loss of dear brethren, of husbands, brothers, wives, sisters and brothers, and some children, that they struggled to assimilate more.

John Robinson knew it, and took pity on them. They prayed together, for the lost loved ones, for those who suffered loss, for the survivors that they could continue to build a colony. Alice could hear sobbing throughout the hall, and her heart wrenched for the ones who had suffered loss. Then John Robinson dismissed them.

They did not want to return home. They wanted to stay and comfort each other. Alice sought out Sarah Priest, Digorie's wife, and put her arms around her as Sarah sobbed on her shoulder.

'What shall I do without him?' she asked through lips that hardly moved. 'And poor Isaac losing his poor dear Mary. Those poor motherless children! How could God be so cruel?'

'Jehovah has not done this,' Alice said. 'As Brother Robinson pointed out, it is time and chance.'

Sarah nodded in Alice's arms, and then pulled herself together. 'You are right, of course you are. It is just one of those things. I must get the children home.' Alice took this to mean that she wanted to be on her own. She could understand it. She had felt the same when Edward died.

It was some time before she could seek the sanctuary of the room she shared with her boys in her father's house. Everyone in the family wanted to discuss this turn of events. George Morton, Julianna's husband, expressed what Alice herself thought. ''Twas the time of year,' he said. 'They arrived in November. It snowed. They had no shelter, only the ship. They had no food. Scurvy. Coughs and colds. They were weak.'

'They were delayed in leaving,' Alexander Carpenter added. 'It was not a good time to set out. It took too long to cross the Atlantic Ocean.' He and the other leading men had spoken with John Robinson after the meeting and they had more details.

'But so many died,' Julianna said. 'So many! God could not have been with them!'

Alice had been thinking the same thing.

Her brother John had a thought, 'No, but the devil was!'

Alice shuddered, but she thought of the mismatched company, of the people Thomas Weston had inflicted on them. Could Satan have stricken the company through them? She didn't understand it.

''Tis no more than time and chance,' Alexander said firmly, and Alice felt relieved. ''Twon't happen again, for there will be people already there with shelter and food to welcome the next ship. We all knew it was a dangerous situation, we knew that they were going to where there were no inns, no shelter, no people—excepting savages, of course. Why did many leave the children and wives at home? They knew what they were going to. But it will be different for the next ones.'

'You think so, Father?' Julianna asked.

'Oh yes.'

As soon as she could Alice fled to her room. Her mind was in turmoil, and her stomach seemed to want to match it. *Dorothy is dead. Will is free!* But she was shocked, not rejoicing. Her brain seemed incapable of processing the information. *Poor Will! How he must have suffered.*

Hard on that thought came another one. Now they were both free—and he was the other side of the Atlantic Ocean!

Will. She had no doubt of her feelings for him. She loved him still, and she always would. Her mind drifted back to London, how he had held her, and (she blushed to remember) kissed her. Stolen guilty moments that should never have been. In her imagination she could feel his hand on her waist, taste his lips on hers.

She gave herself a mental shake, and asked forgiveness of her God for even thinking such thoughts.

Her father knocked on the door and came in. 'I know you were fond of Dorothy,' he began cautiously, sitting beside her on the edge of the bed.

'I was *not* fond of Dorothy. I tried to help Dorothy become a good wife to Will—to Brother Bradford.'

'You have always loved him?'

She nodded dumbly.

'Dorothy Bradford fell overboard. She did not die of the sickness.'

Alice looked at him, shocked. 'Fell overboard? How? Did she slip?' *Or did she jump?* Alice knew from experience that Dorothy had been prone to depression, that she was unhappy. And it did not take much imagining to realise that being cramped on a ship in winter would not improve her state of mind.

'We do not know. John Carver does not tell us. It seems that Brother Bradford was away with the shore party, and it happened the day he left.'

'Poor Will!' She imagined him learning the news, and she saw his grief in her mind's eye, grief like her own for Edward. 'It must have been terrible!'

'They have suffered much, but they wrote of building and planting so I expect they have a village by now. Julianna and her husband intend to go on the next ship.'

'I would like to go with them, Father.'

'I cannot allow that. You have no husband. And you have no money to pay your passage.'

'I could apply to Brother Robinson.'

'Not without my agreement, daughter. You have to have a husband to look after you. I will not allow you to go to a new country—to a wilderness even—without you have a husband.'

'If Julianna is going—'

'Julianna has a husband to care for her,' he snapped. 'You do not. I will not agree to it.'

Alice clamped her mouth shut. She wanted to argue, but she knew better than to cross swords with her father. Not only was Will in New England, but also since the day she first heard of the project, she had thought it so exciting to help build a new world. She liked the very idea of being free, away from the stinking cesspool of London, and the disease-ridden canals of Leyden, but most of all free to worship God in the way she wanted without anyone telling her she could not. And she knew that if she married again it would be to a man who loved God the way she did.

Her father stood up to leave her, and then, remembering something, felt inside his doublet, pulling out a letter. 'This was addressed to Edward, but John Robinson thinks you should have it.'

'For Edward? Who would write to Edward?' she asked, puzzled, but taking the letter and looking at the writing. She did not recognise the hand.

As he left her, she broke the seal and after reading the salutation to Edward, she looked at the bottom of the page and her heart turned over. It was from Will. She hadn't recognised his hand, because she had never seen anything written by him. Of course he did not know Edward had died when he wrote the letter. He told Edward of some of the hardships, but it was clear he left much out. He told of Dorothy's death, and Alice's heart went out to him. He told of his own sickness and how the common house burnt down. But he ended on a note of optimism, how they had now got houses and were working in the fields.

In her mind's eye, Alice could see it all. And she knew that she wanted to be part of it. But she could not see how that could happen while she remained a widow.

She sat down at her father's desk a little later, and wrote a letter to Will.

THIRTY-NINE
The *Fortune*

Plymouth Colony, Autumn 1621

The harvest had been good Will thought as he looked at the food piled up in the storehouse, good enough to get them through the winter. They would have to be careful, but he was satisfied with their first year. Not only did they have a good store of grain but they also had apples and plums and other wild fruit, and the women had dried as much as they could over the cooking fires. The men caught fish, and fowl which were plentiful, and hunted deer. What they could not eat immediately they salted.

'I think it is time for a feast,' Will suggested to Brewster.

Brewster agreed. 'An excellent notion. It will make them feel as if they have achieved something, make them feel good, and also we can invite Massasoit and his braves. It will help our good relations with them.'

Will sent Squanto to Massasoit with a message, and the women began the task of making ready for the feast. Four men went out fowling, and they came back with wild turkeys and other birds.

Massasoit came with rather more people than Will had expected. He had with him some ninety men.

'How are we going to feed all this lot?' Will asked John Allerton, aghast.

That was the trouble with the Indians. If they thought there was the chance of a free meal, they would take advantage. Look at what had happened during the summer. With monotonous regularity groups of up to six or seven Indians would drop in on the colony, and because the English wanted to keep on friendly terms with the Indians they felt obliged to feed them yet at that time before the harvest, the colony had little enough to feed themselves, let alone others. So Will had sent Stephen Hopkins and Edward Winslow to Massasoit with gifts and a plea to stop the intrusion. Massasoit, much softened by the gifts, understood their predicament, and the visits stopped.

Now the Indians were here in force.

'Well we can't turn them away,' Isaac Allerton pointed out. 'You did invite them.'

Will gave a wry smile. 'So we had better entertain them.'

Massasoit and his people stayed for three days feasting, and dancing their strange dances, and singing in their odd chanting way. The English also demonstrated how they danced the roundels and reels common in England, and had Indian braves and women dancing around with them in a ring. They sang, too. Not psalms, for that was religious worship, but common folk songs with rousing choruses, which the Indians enjoyed a good deal. Conversation flowed easily in such happy conditions, Squanto and Samoset interpreting, and Edward Winslow began to get the hang of the Indian language, trying it out on Massasoit himself with great hilarity. However, when Will dared to suggest that they had nothing more to feed them with, thinking that perhaps Massasoit and his people might take the hint and go home, Massasoit went out with some of his men and killed five deer which they brought back to the plantation. The Indians knew how to feast!

At last Massasoit went his way in peace, satisfied, and the English too felt happier in their new home, safe with the Indians who they had come to view as friends.

Will and Brewster came in together, the boys Wrestling and Love close behind, all of them muddy from where they had worked in the field, ploughing with a hand-held plough to the best of their ability. It was hard work, for they had no horses and no oxen to pull the plough, and the men were exhausted as they battled with the land.

They washed in the bucket, and then sat down at the table, leaning on it and resting weary heads on hands, almost too tired to eat. Mary bustled about, bringing them the food she had prepared, venison stew and corn bread. 'Elbows off the table,' she admonished, and began ladling the stew out into wooden bowls.

Then she sat down and waited while her husband asked for God's blessing on the food. Now she had the opportunity to say what had been on her mind.

'I went down to the brook to wash today,' she began generally.

'Oh?' her husband's interest was cursory. After all what did women's washing have to do with him?

'Everyone was there. All the women. You know the women grow resentful, do you not?'

Will rubbed his hand over his face and focused on her with an effort. 'Why is that, Mary?' he asked. He spoke out of politeness, yet inside he felt irritated that he must hear this now.

She frowned, thinking how to put it. 'The sisters are upset that they must do washing for men not their own husbands and not their children.'

Will frowned. 'But *we* work all day in the fields. Is it not women's work to look after the home?'

'Some of you work hard,' she acknowledged. 'Others of you take their ease. But that is beside the point. The women also have the house to keep clean, the meals to cook, the children to take care of, and—oh yes— they also are expected to work in the fields!' She paused to let this point sink in. 'They view it as slavery to have to work also for men who do not belong to them, but yet live in their house.'

'And the men don't like it either,' William Brewster put in, unexpectedly rallying to her cause. 'My wife was a lady, and had servants to look after her in England and in Leyden. Now she has to do the washing for us and for others. And frankly, Will I don't like my wife washing other men's smalls! 'Tain't right!'

'Is it too much to ask men to wash their own clothes? It's not as if one man's things are too much, but put it all together and I tell you, Will, it becomes nothing short of hard labour!'

'All right, I shall do my own washing from now on.' Will said wearily.

Mary's eyes widened. 'I didn't mean you! You know I didn't! You are like a son to me, and always will be. Better than some sons!' She meant her eldest, Edward, whom she had not seen in many years. He had left the faith, and it had caused her much pain. 'Besides, do you not have enough to do with the governorship as well? I was talking of the others. Susanna White—I mean Winslow—is ready to cause a revolt.'

Will frowned. He could see her point. 'Let me think about it,' he said. 'I can't think now. I'm too tired.'

'And that man John Billington beats his wife,' Mary added.

Will stared at her hard. 'You know this?'

'I saw the marks on her neck. Like he had tried to strangle her. And she too frightened to say anything. The man is a bully.'

'The law does not allow me to intervene between a man and his wife,' Will said wearily. He took a deep breath. 'We must keep an eye on him though.'

'Which we've always done.'

'Aye.'

He raised some corn bread to his mouth and bit off a chunk. It wasn't like English bread, but you could live on it.

A noise outside made him look out of the open door. 'What on earth—?'

'Ship! Ship!'

Will sprang to his feet, weariness forgotten, and ran out of the house ahead of Brewster. A half-dressed Indian brave came running up the street with the news and pointing towards the sea. 'Ship! Ship!'

Will frowned and went with the Indian to climb the hill. They ought to have a lookout on the hill, he thought, and indeed there had been a lookout once, only their friendly relations with the Indians had made it seem unimportant. It was more important for everyone to work in the field.

Before he got to the top of the hill, he could see the ship in the distance in full sail coming into Plymouth.

'It could be the French making raids from the northern settlements.' Will said to the men who had followed him. The English had never liked nor trusted the French, their natural enemies, along with the Spanish, both nations staunchly Catholic. 'Fire the cannon to warn those in the fields to come into the settlement. Master Standish—make ready defence, if you please.'

It was a precautionary measure, and by the time the ship came into the harbour, they were ready, every man and boy bearing arms, waiting to greet the visitors. As the ship came closer the flag ran up her mainmast and fluttered out in the wind—the red cross of St. George.

'English!' Will said, much relieved.

They abandoned their arms, and went down to the shore, where the ship had anchored in the bay, as the men on board began the laborious task of hauling out the longboat.

'If I ain't much mistaken, that is Master Cushman standing on the deck,' Brewster said, screwing up his eyes in an attempt to bring him into focus. He slipped his arm around his wife who had come to stand beside him. Perhaps some had come from Leyden. Perhaps their other children among them. He knew Mary missed her daughters and son Jonathan desperately.

They could hardly bear the suspense, standing on the shore, looking eagerly for loved ones.

The sailors made long work of the laborious task of lowering the long boat, but finally some of the passengers clambered into it.

'Can you see?' Mary asked. 'Are they there?'

'No women in that group,' Brewster said.

Mary swallowed her disappointment. Her husband squeezed her waist. There was nothing he could say.

Slowly—so very slowly—the men in the boat lowered the oars and pulled for the shore.

Mary almost held her breath. Then, 'Is that not Jonathan?' she cried, and the tears started to her eyes, and emotion welled up in her throat. 'It is! It's Jonathan!'

Brewster peered at the faces of the men in the boat as they neared the shore. 'Yes—yes it is. It's Jonathan!' He started to cry himself.

Mary clasped her hands to her bosom, hardly daring to breathe in case something should snatch this beloved son from her sight. 'He has come, oh, he has come! Perhaps the girls as well?'

'Wait and see,' Brewster cautioned, for he had scanned the passengers on the deck and could see only one woman.

The boat pulled up to the rock which they had used as a landing stage, and the passengers piled out.

Jonathan stood on the shore, tall and straight and dark, just as Mary remembered him. She ran forward and into his arms, and had a good cry. Brewster was behind her, but he too put his arms around his son and his wife and hugged them both, while Wrestling and Love stood back shyly.

'Are the girls with you?' Mary asked.

'We could not afford to bring them,' Jonathan told her. There was trouble with money and Master Weston. Master Cushman will tell you. But they are well, and they are hoping that soon they can come to you.'

There were just two women on board, one Ellen Adams, wife of John Adams who came with her, and the other Martha Ford, whose husband William had died on the journey, and who had given birth not a month since. Richard Warren's wife and five daughters had not come, nor Sam Fuller's wife Bridget. And Will, who had nursed a vague guilty hope that Alice might have become a widow by now and taken it into her head to join the colony, was disappointed. Neither was there any sign of John Robinson nor any of his family.

Will came forward to greet Robert Cushman and his son Thomas aged fourteen. 'You are well come,' he said, shaking Cushman's hand, and also Thomas's. Then he turned them away and walked with them up the hill to the Plantation, explaining what they had done, what they had built, all of which Cushman surveyed with interest, and then on into Brewster's house. 'What did you bring with you?' Will asked.

'Letters. And ourselves, of course,' Cushman replied, surprised at the question.

'No provisions?'

Plainly he had not thought about the settlers needing provisions. 'We have been three months at sea, Will, and we had enough difficulty in raising victuals to see us through the journey.'

Will stared at him. 'You bring us all these people to feed and house, but you bring no victuals with you? How do you think we are to feed them? We only just have enough to see ourselves through the winter. What about clothes?'

'Do you need clothes?' Cushman asked artlessly.

Will uttered a despairing sound in his throat which was nearly an oath. 'Ours are in holes, sir, and we do need clothes, yes. Or cloth to make clothes with.'

'We sold our last things to make the journey,' Cushman said. 'There is nothing left.'

With iron self-control, Will turned away from him, for an extremely unchristian expletive had come to mind which he was within an ace of uttering. His jaw knotted with the effort it took to hold it back. 'Did it not

354

occur to you Master Cushman, to bring supplies to us here?' he demanded.

'Well—no,' Cushman admitted. 'But if it had, we could not have afforded them.'

Will had formed an opinion of Cushman when they were in Leyden of a man who had little in the way of sense. It had not always been obvious, but in little things, he had thought him wanting. He had been certain of it when he had agreed to Weston's changed terms of agreement, harbouring the suspicion that Cushman had not realised the content of the new agreement and again when Cushman had insisted on making provisions in Kent, not in Southampton. That had not been the act of a rational man. He had not done it out of wickedness, Will knew, but because he simply lacked the wit to understand and foresee these things. Now he had not brought with him so much as a ship's biscuit, they had come at the end of the harvest, when there was no increasing the yield, when the settlers had worked so hard to provide for themselves, and when there was just enough to see to those already here. It really was too much!

It transpired also, that the newcomers had not brought bedding, or any household goods of any sort.

Cushman looked around him. 'Where is John Carver? I have a letter for him from Master Weston.'

'Master Carver died,' Will said shortly. 'I am governor.'

Cushman looked extremely shocked. 'Dead? John Carver dead?'

'That is what I said.'

'I am sorry for it.' And he looked like he would break into weeping. Will remembered then that Carver and Cushman had spent long months together in London working for the cause.

Will added, 'And his wife.'

Cushman grimaced and shook his head. 'Well, you had better have the letter,' he said after a moment, fishing it from inside his doublet.

As they had by now reached the Brewsters' house, Will took the package and broke the seal and spread the sheets on the table.

Thomas Weston began his letter with a salutation to Master Carver, and then began a long complaint. About the situation that had arisen at Hampton, and the *Mayflower* being so long in America, and the fact that she had gone home empty, saying,

'That you sent no lading in the ship is wonderful, and worthily distasted. I know your weakness was the cause of it, and I believe more weakness of judgement than weakness of hands. A quarter of the time you spent in discoursing, arguing and consulting would have done much more.'

Shocked by the ferocity of it, Will uttered an explosive sound in his throat. He looked at Cushman. 'Have you read this? Do you know what it says?'

Cushman shook his head. 'It was sealed.'

'But you must know that Weston is rebuking us for not returning anything in the *Mayflower*.'

'Well, yes.'

'Did not Weston read Master Carver's letters regarding the terrible hardship we had to overcome? We have lost half our people to sickness and we had winter coming on. What was he thinking about?'

Cushman shrugged, and Will thought that Cushman had shared Weston's opinion. Will read on.

'*And consider that the life of the business depends on the lading of this ship, which if you do to any good purpose, that I may be freed from the great sums I have disbursed for the former and must do for the latter, I promise you I will never quit the business, though all the other Adventurers should. We have procured you a charter, the best we could, which is better than your former, and with less limitation.*'

Weston added his good wishes and finished up '*Your very loving friend, Thomas Weston.*'

Will struggled to control his temper. He was furious with the man. Of course Weston had invested money, but did he not know how people had died, how hard life was here?

He said to Cushman, 'We had no skins to trade then, for we had no dealings with Indians. We do have trade with the Indians now.'

'You do?'

'Oh yes,' Will assured him. 'We have a very good friend in Massasoit, the Indian chief here. And Samoset, and Squanto are English interpreters, and a new man called Hobomok. Squanto and Hobomok live with us often.' Hobomok, a member of the Wampanoag tribe, a strong man in the prime of life, and renowned among his own people for his courage, had wandered into the English plantation one day with his wife, and simply stayed, rather like Squanto had done.

Will frowned again. 'How are we going to feed you all?' he asked. 'We have just enough for ourselves for the winter. And how will we provide for you?' He shook his head.

Cushman said stiffly, 'Well I am sure that we are sorry to be a drain on you! We have suffered much at the weather and in the ship and this is all the welcome we get!'

Will shook his head again in dismay. 'You are well come, Robert. It is just that we are desperately short of life's necessities. We needed supplies.'

'It is Master Weston,' Cushman said, excusing himself. 'He said that because we did not get any skins, we cannot invest further except for the ship itself. We have had to scrape together enough to make provisions for the *Fortune.*'

Brewster came in then with his family, and shook Cushman's hand. Quickly, Will outlined what had happened and showed the letter to him.

Brewster read it and then let his breath go in a whistle. Will said, 'There is only one thing for it, we will have to ration the food strictly, or we will starve before the end of the winter.'

'I think that is all you can do,' Brewster agreed.

As Mary dished up some more venison stew from the pot for Jonathan and Cushman, Will looked over the other letters Cushman had brought with him. He ignored their talking, for he wanted the news. He could question Master Cushman himself later.

Each of the settlers had letters from home. John Robinson had written, and was sorry that he had not come to them this time. He was needed at home, especially as he had buried a child in February last. Even so, Bridget his wife had another child on the way. He could not leave her, nor expect her to take the journey to New England at this time.

The voices of the family filtered through. 'The girls are well,' Jonathan said. 'They send you letters.' And he produced some.

Will returned to John Robinson's letter. The colony would no doubt be sorry to hear that Edward Southworth had died in London, and that his widow and her two sons had returned to Leyden to live with her father Alexander Carpenter.

Will stopped when he read this part, his stomach suddenly twisting in knots. Edward was dead. He re-read the terse statement. Edward was indeed dead.

He was sorry for it. He had to be sorry for it, for Edward had been a friend for many years. Now he was gone. No doubt he had suffered in his illness. A mental picture of Alice, careworn but doing her duty towards the sick Edward, came into his mind. He would have expected nothing else of her. Poor Alice. How she must have suffered nursing Edward, and then having to go back to Leyden to her parents. But she was free! His heart soared.

Had she written?

He sifted through the heap of papers and letters on the settle beside him. He didn't know her handwriting, couldn't tell if any of them were from her. The Mays had written, telling him that they would look after young Jonathan as long as he wished. It was the least they could do for him, and for their dear dead daughter. Among the other letters was one written in childish hand by his own son Jonathan. He would be six years old now. A letter also from George Morton, his friend, who said he would definitely be bringing his own family to New England at the next opportunity. There were other letters addressed to John Carver, but then one that caught his eye, addressed to himself. He broke the seal, and spread the sheet.

Alice began with the words, 'Dear Friend,' and expressed her sorrow at learning about Dorothy. She went on to inform him of Edward's death. He had suffered, she said, and died of the slow consumption. She had transferred to Leyden where she and the boys were in the care of her father. She gave him other news—of the death of the Robinson child, and that Sabine Staresmore and his wife and child had tuned up in the Leyden congregation.

He read the letter and then re-read it. His mouth had gone dry, and his hands shook. Alice was free! Yet he looked in vain for some encouragement that she might accept an offer of marriage from him. Did she want him? Did she love him like he thought she did? Or had he been mistaken? She used the phrase *Dear friend.* Did she mean more than friend?

'What do you have, Will?' Brewster asked.

Will re-folded Alice's letter. 'There is a letter from John Robinson,' he told him, and gave it to him. Then he said, 'Sister Southworth has written. Edward Southworth has died of consumption.'

Brewster met his eyes for a long moment. 'I see,' he said.

The news of rationing did not go down very well with the settlers, although they swallowed their complaints and tried not to resent the newcomers who would cause them to starve after all their hard work. Furthermore, the single men, who would presumably expect the women to care for them, much to everyone's annoyance, had to be distributed among the houses and families, setting them back into overcrowded conditions. It was a difficult situation, but they would have to manage.

'What do you think, Will?' Brewster asked after Will had dismissed the meeting. In the moonlight, they walked together down the hill from the fort to the clutch of houses which had become something of a village.

'I think it grossly unfair of Weston to do this to us. You would think he wants us to fail.'

'Perhaps he does.'

Will peered at him in the darkness. 'You think so?'

'Notice how he sends so many of his own people in the ships, and hardly any of our own. He does not want us to succeed. Rather he wants to put his own man in as governor.'

Will nodded. 'You could be right.'

They walked on in silence. Somewhere out in the blackness a wolf howled, that long mournful sound, and another answered some distance away. It was a common occurrence, but eerie in the dark.

'What of Alice Southworth, then?' Brewster asked suddenly.

Will felt himself flush and was grateful Brewster could not see that.

'As you read yourself, Edward has died, and she is living in Leyden now with her father.'

'She wrote to you?'

'She did. A very polite letter, informing me of the death of my friend Edward. My friend,' he repeated not looking at Brewster. 'Yet I coveted his wife.'

Brewster paused as they came to the house, and put his hand on Will's shoulder. ''Tis a hard thing to love a woman.'

'It is when you can't have her,' Will agreed. 'I am sorry for Edward. Of course I am. But she is free.'

'She has two sons.'

'And so?'

'And you will take the responsibility for them?'

'Of course.'

'Then you had better write to her and ask if she is prepared to come to New England and marry you,' Brewster recommended with a chuckle.

'You think so?'

'Don't you?'

Will nodded. 'I suppose so. What if she won't have me?'

'Leave it in God's hands. If it is His will she will come.' He turned to leave, but he paused in the doorway and looked back. 'Oh—and pray about it first, won't you!'

'Naturally!' He had prayed about it every day. Still, once more would not hurt.

The outcome might have been in God's hands, but the letter writing was in Will's and for once, he did not know what to write. He put it off as long as possible, mulling it over when he had a quiet moment. And while he tarried, he tackled Thomas Weston first.

He wrote Master Weston a long, furious, letter, first apprising him of John Carver's death and then explaining again what difficulties they had encountered. True, he acknowledged that Weston and the other Merchant Adventurers had been put to a great charge, and had made nothing out of it so far, but then the settlers had suffered a great deal more. It had taken them a long time to get shelter in the middle of winter, he told him, and on top of that so many had died and so many had been sick that there were hardly enough left to bury the dead. His censures towards them discouraged them greatly.

He went on to tell him of the accounts, how they had agreed to the conditions how the ship was now laden, and in what condition the situation stood. Moreover, if they did not send provisions promptly, as Master

Cushman could tell him, they would all starve. Perhaps now that he had what he wanted, all offences should be forgotten and he should remember his promises.

He wrote also to his son, to the Mays, to John Robinson, to George Morton. Lastly he attempted the letter to Alice.

He agonised over it, prayed over it, wrote and re-wrote it. Either he poured out his love for her to the extent that he was sickened by his own rhetoric, and then he curtly asked her to join him in New England with no hint of love. Neither was what he wanted to achieve. But in the end, he managed to get it written.

'*My Very Dear Sister Southworth, I thank you for your letter and am sincerely saddened to learn of the passing of my dear friend, your husband Edward. May he find his reward in the resurrection according to the will of Jehovah. He was a man of faith and love for God.*' He paused here, chewing his lip, and wondering what to say next. As inspiration came again, he dipped the pen in the ink and continued, '*As you know, I have a high regard for you, and you are well spoken-of by all. It is commonly known that you are an excellent woman, one fearing God, and one who would deal well with the rigours of New England. No greater helpmeet could a man have than a capable woman, such as I judge you to be. I would be honoured, therefore, if you would consent to come to Plymouth Colony to become my wife.*' He paused again, and re-read it, but not entirely satisfied with it. He wanted to tell her how much he loved her, how his life would be desolate without her. But he was not a man of flowery poetic turn of phrase. He dipped the pen in the ink again and went on, '*I am building a house which will be ready soon, for you and Master Constant and Master Thomas. Please come to me, my dear one, and may Jehovah continue to be with you. I remain, sincerely and truly your friend, William Bradford.*'

He read it over again, and wished he could put into words what he truly felt. He hoped she would know. He thought of that day when he had left London for the last time, when he had slipped his hand around her waist, and a great longing washed over him. He could taste her kiss, feel the warmth of her body through her dress. He gave himself a mental shake. Another man's wife! He had prayed long and often about it, agonised by guilt, suppressing all thoughts of her. But now she was free and he could think about her without his conscience goading him. So now Alice invaded his thoughts all the time, and the longing he felt for her came close to desperation.

What if his letter came too late? What if she married another? What if she would not have him after all? The doubts could drive a man mad.

Fourteen days after she arrived, the *Fortune* weighed anchor and sailed for England, taking Robert Cushman, who had not intended to stay, back to Leyden, together with timber, furs, and the letters the colony had written to those in England and Holland. As the sails disappeared into the distance, Will thought of the precious letter she carried, and he wondered what Alice's answer would be. He knew he had an agonising wait to find out.

He put his hand on the shoulder of fourteen year old Thomas, son of Robert Cushman, who had decided to stay in New England, for the boy fought back unmanly tears at his father's departure.

'Come, Tom,' Will said kindly, 'let's go home.'

FORTY
Threat and Challenge

Plymouth Colony, Winter 1621-2

'So, you think Weston will send us what we need next time?' William Brewster asked, leaning on the large rough-sawn beam which served as a mantle shelf.

Will's lips tightened. 'He'd better. He owes it to us, and we have done nothing that he can use as justification for not helping us.' He picked up the new *Authorised Bible* lying on the rough-sawn table, a gift sent by John Robinson, and went towards the door where he paused and looked back. 'More to the point, we have all these extra mouths to feed and I doubt very much whether even half shares will be sufficient to get us through the next six months. I can't understand why these people came without provisions.'

Brewster took a deep breath. 'Well, you know we've never been able to rely on Weston, save to get us into the most difficult situations. I would that Brother Robinson had had nothing to do with his offer. We'd have been better off with the Dutch. Everything Weston does has cost us. Look at that agreement he made with Cushman.'

'Aye, and Cushman hasn't the wit to see it or to put things in our favour,' Will said with typical forthrightness. 'He dances around Weston as though he is afraid of him.'

Brewster followed Will out of the door and into the early winter sunshine. 'Perhaps he is. Certainly he is afraid of losing Weston's support for us. If Weston pulls out, we are sunk.' They fell into step and began walking towards the Common House. There was an air of order to the plantation now, houses standing in two rows either side of the street, little gardens, surrounded by open fields on every side.

'I know it. But if Cushman were to stand up for us occasionally instead of giving in to Weston's every demand . . . sometimes I think Cushman lacks understanding of the situation. He could not have read that amended agreement, or he would never have put his signature to it.'

Brewster was inclined to be less forgiving. 'Cushman fails to understand anything, and that's it! I'll be da—' he pulled himself up short. 'Sorry, old habits and all that. What I mean is, I don't know why Brother Robinson put so much trust in him when the man is clearly deficient in the brain area!'

Will laughed despite his anger. 'Jehovah save me from imperfect men!' They crossed the street together. It had been a damp autumn, and the ground which wear and weather had turned into a sea of mud, squelched and slurped under foot. 'Weston's gone back to London now with all our letters and all our requests.'

Brewster glanced at him. 'Did you write to Mistress Southworth?'

Will felt his colour rise. He tried to sound off-hand, but failed. 'I did.' He glanced at Brewster and found him grinning.

'And now you wonder if she will have you. Ah it is ever the same with young love.'

'I am scarcely young, sir. I am two and thirty, and so is she.'

'Young Will,' Brewster said softly, teasing.

Will found himself chuckling in response, and allowed himself a little daydream as to what Mistress Southworth would say, or do, or think when she received his letter, always assuming she did receive his letter, of course. And that was by no means a certain thing.

He ducked to avoid hitting his head on the door lintel as he went into the Common House. Everyone else was present, except for the lookouts, awaiting the elders who would conduct the meeting. Will sat down on the men's side as Brewster took his place at the front. As the teaching elder it was Brewster's responsibility to conduct religious meetings.

Suddenly the sound of voices outside, the cry of 'Indian!' at the other end of the settlement made Will look around, and Brewster frowned at the door as though to see what was going on. Will got up and went out. Everyone else followed him.

An Indian not a Wampanoag, but of another tribe, walked proudly up the street towards the English, his head held high, his black locks blowing in the cold off-shore wind. The Indian stopped in front of Will and threw down a bundle of arrows tied up in a snakeskin at his feet

Deliberately Will bent down and picked up the bundle, and then looked at Squanto who had appeared at his elbow. 'Ask him who he is and what he wants.'

'Hobomok know who he is,' Hobomok said before Squanto could speak. Everyone had come to see what the visitor wanted, and Hobomok, ever distrustful of Squanto's influence with the English, was there too.

Squanto glared at him, and, determined to prove his usefulness to Will, spoke to the visitor.

Hobomok said, 'This man Narrangasett.'

Will looked at Squanto for confirmation. 'This man from Canonicus, sachem of the Narrangasett people. He send threat and challenge.' Squanto cast a smug expression at Hobomok. The English gathered behind Will murmuring to each other.

Will met the Indian's challenging dark gaze squarely. 'We have done no wrong to Narrangasett. Why does he send threat and challenge?'

Squanto shook his head knowingly. 'Narrangasett want to rule Wampanoag, but Eng'ish help Massasoit, so they cannot. Eng'ish in way.'

Will looked at the messenger standing with his arms folded across his chest, his head held proudly erect. This was certainly no friendly visit. 'Tell him I shall give him my answer directly.'

He left the visitor standing there and went with Miles Standish and Squanto and Hobomok into a house together. He remembered that Squanto was not a Wampanoag, but had come originally from Patuxet or Plymouth. Hobomok on the other hand was Wampanoag, of Massasoit's tribe, hence the antipathy between them. 'What do you think I should do?' Will asked.

'Answer challenge,' Squanto said, sticking up his chin and Hobomok nodded agreement.

Will thought about it, and then said to Miles Standish, 'Some musket balls, if you please, sir.'

Miles Standish raised a questioning ginger eyebrow, but he felt in the leather pouch which hung from his belt, and poured the lead pellets into Will's open hand. Will, put the balls in the snakeskin, and tied it up. Then he returned to the messenger with Standish, and with the two Indians at his heels. 'Tell Canonicus that if he would rather have war than peace, he may begin when he chooses. But we have done them no wrong, and neither do we fear them. And they will not find us unprovided for!'

Squanto translated, and Will deliberately turned away from the visitor signifying his contempt of this challenge. He drew Miles Standish aside. 'I think a paling fence and gates and some arrangement for defence should be looked to.'

Standish stroked his chin. 'Very well.' He thought for a moment. 'We have enough men now to arrange into four squadrons, each with their own appointed quarter, where they will go if we are attacked.'

Will agreed to it. 'And a guard night and day. We must keep on the watch.'

Will turned to see the retreating form of the visitor as he walked proudly from the plantation. 'We begin tomorrow.' He strode into the Common House, and the others followed him, for nothing should interfere with the meeting.

It had been a cold night, and the morning air was crisp with the threat of snow, but Will called everyone out as usual for work, expecting to see men and women taking up whatever tools they needed to build the palisade. So far the Indians had not attacked, but Will had lookouts on the watch day and night, for the threat remained. Their first priority must be protection. The construction of the palisade was dog-wearying work, but urgent and necessary.

As he bent to pick up his axe, a deposition of perhaps twenty of the newly arrived men approached Will, and pushed a reluctant spokesman forward. Will stood up straight and looked at them all wondering what this was about, and then focused on the spokesman. 'You have something to say, Master Pitt?'

'We do not work today, Governor,' William Pitt said.

Will raised his brows. 'Why not?'

''Tis Christmas day. We do not work on Christmas day. 'Tis a matter of conscience.'

Will glared at them. 'A matter of conscience, is it?' He found himself torn between a desperate need to get the palisade finished for security reasons, and the necessity of allowing other men to worship God as their consciences dictated. Fairness to their consciences won. After all, he could not force a man to act in a way contrary to his religion, for he had suffered that himself. Still he didn't like it, for he had a loathing for Christmas which he viewed as pagan idolatry, part of the false religion he had come to New England to avoid. It underscored the fact that he had men here who were not of the Separatist persuasion. They were Weston's men. He said curtly, 'In that case, Master Pitt, I will spare you until you are better informed.'

'Thank you, Governor.' The men departed into their homes and Will marched the rest out to work.

'Christmas!' he said with loathing.

'You should make allowances for ignorance, brother,' Sam Fuller said in his gentle manner. 'You know how misled people are.'

'Well I'll not have pagan idolatry here,' Will fumed.

'Then the sooner they are better educated, the better,' Brewster said on his other side, his manner deliberately calm to take the heat out of Will's anger. 'But you cannot force men to conform.'

'I know that,' Will snapped.

They came back later to the plantation after the morning's work. Hard work, and fresh air had cooled Will's anger, but as he walked in the gate, he stopped.

'What is this?' he demanded awfully.

The men who had begged off because of their religious holiday, were in the street, playing ninepins, pitching the bar, or stool-ball. They looked up at the sound of Will's voice.

Furious, Will strode forward and grabbed the skittles, the balls, the bats, and tucked them all under his arm. The men looked at him, amazed. 'It is a matter against *my* conscience that you should play while others work!' he told them roundly. 'If you make the keeping of Christmas a matter of devotion, then do it in your houses. But there shall be no gaming or revelry in the streets. It is not fitting devotion!'

William Pitt looked at the others, and then without a word they turned around and went back into their houses.

'Christmas!' Will said again as his fury subsided. 'A licence to shirk one's duties!'

FORTY-ONE
The Letter

Leyden, 1622

Alexander Carpenter looked up from his *Geneva Bible* as his middle daughter came in, an empty basket over her arm. Alice looked much better these days, he thought, studying her. The dark shadows had disappeared from her eyes, and she had put on a little weight, which filled out the deep hollows in her cheeks. Good food, and an easier life had given her back that glow of health which had been wanting in London, thanks to Edward Southworth. Alexander forcibly stopped his thoughts there, corrected himself hastily. Whatever he thought of Edward, he had not intended to put Alice through so much poverty and drudgery. It had not been his fault that he was ill. And he was a Christian brother to boot.

'How is Julianna?' he asked her.

Alice smiled, and her green eyes lit up. 'Waiting for the chance to go to New England. Otherwise she is well, and the children, and her husband.'

She came over to him and planted a kiss on his forehead. She smelled of lavender and fresh air. 'Are the boys home yet?'

'No. Priscilla said she would be taking them to the Robinsons' home after school.' She moved towards the stairs, but he stopped her with, 'Alice—John Robinson has been here. He has brought a letter for you from America.'

She paused, one hand on the banister, her green eyes growing round. 'Oh?'

'Were you expecting a letter?'

'No, not particularly.'

'Then who would be writing to you?'

She came towards him then, and took a steadying breath. 'Perhaps if I open it, I shall find out.'

He put his hand inside his doublet and pulled out the packet with the red wax seal and held it out to her. He was curious as to who could have written to his daughter from New England. Susanna now-Winslow was a possibility, but the handwriting did not look female. It sloped forward, not backward, indicating a man's decisive hand.

As she took it and looked at her name written there, he saw the expression on her face change. She recognised the hand, and she said to him, 'I will read it in my room, Father.'

Alexander was disappointed, but she was of age, so he smiled. 'As you wish, my dear.'

In privacy Alice sat down on her bed, and looked at her name written in Will's decisive hand. *Mistress Alice Southworth.* Her heart had lurched within her when she saw the writing, but now she feared to open it. What was he going to tell her? That he was sorry to hear of Edward's death? That things went on much the same in Plymouth? That he was pleased to tell her he had married—who?

A lead ball of dread formed in her stomach and reached as far as her throat. Taking a shuddering breath, she broke the seal and opened it.

What a short letter! Yes, as she suspected, he was sorry to learn of Edward's death. What was all this about her being an excellent woman? And then her heart stopped altogether and then raced on. Did she read that correctly? Had he indeed asked her to marry him? She blinked to clear away any fog, and re read it.

A shadow fell across her and she looked up to see her father standing in front of the small window. 'You cried out,' he explained. 'Is ought amiss?'

For a moment she could not speak, and tears filled her eyes.

'Oh, my dear child, is it bad news?'

She shook her head. 'No,' she managed and her voice was a croak. 'It is from Will Bradford. He—he has asked me to come to New England and become his—his wife.' She held out the letter to her father, and he came forward to take it, his face inscrutable.

It didn't take him long to read before giving it back to her. 'I do think he might have asked for your hand from me!' he complained.

'Father, I am two-and-thirty and a widow with children of my own. I do not belong to you!'

He nodded, acknowledging the truthfulness of what she said. 'As you say.' Then, 'What happened between you in London?'

She turned away so that he could not see her face. 'I know not what you mean.'

'Alice, you are my daughter. Do you think I can be so easily duped? Was not Will the reason Edward moved you all to London?'

'My feelings for Will have been no secret, Father,' she said truthfully. 'From the day they came to Amsterdam.'

'Then I pity Edward.'

'You have no need to pity Edward,' she retorted with more vehemence than propriety dictated when one addressed one's parent. 'I never played false to Edward. He knew I did not have the same intensity of feeling for him as he did for me. He told me so. And I have never done anything that would have given Edward cause to—to—regret marrying me.'

'But something happened in London,' Alexander insisted. 'Bradford calls you his dear one.'

Alice stood up then, dignified, her head erect, and looked him straight in the eye. 'Father, whatever happened in London I keep in my heart. It is nothing for you to fear, for I have not played false to Edward, or to God. That is all I have to say on that subject.'

Alexander was angry. 'But you expect me to allow you to go three thousand miles to marry this man?'

'This man, I may remind you, Father, is one you thought highly of. He is a fine man, a man of God, a dear brother in the Lord. And he has done me a great honour in asking me to marry him.'

'And will you?'

She folded the precious letter and put it in the pocked in her petticoat, but she did not answer him. After a moment he uttered an angry sound in his throat. 'Do you not answer me, madam?'

'No, Father, I do not. You must wait for my answer, as must brother Bradford. When I have decided, I will let you know.'

And with that, Alexander had to be content.

Later, after supper, Alice left the house and went to the Robinsons' at the *Groeneport*. Bridget, astonished to see her, let her in.

'Why Alice, 'tis late for you to be visiting.'

Alice smiled, for Bridget held her newborn in her arms, and said what was proper about the new baby. 'Bridget, may I speak with your husband?'

John Robinson, overhearing, called from another room. 'Come in, Sister Southworth.'

Alice went into a small room that she knew to be John's study. It was small, wood-panelled, and dark, but two candles burned in the sconce. She did not close the door, for that would not have been seemly, and she stood just inside the threshold, aware that Bridget hovered somewhere outside. John sat behind a desk littered with papers that he could hardly see, and stood briefly and with difficulty as she came in. He was sick, she knew, with an illness that seemed to go on and on. It showed in his face, hollow cheeks, sunken eyes, but those grey eyes continued bright and sharp as they focused on her.

John Robinson raised his brows invitingly. 'What can I do for you, sister?'

Alice took a breath. 'I would ask you, brother, to find passage for me and my boys on the next ship to New England.'

John Robinson frowned. 'You have no husband, sister. I cannot allow you to go without a husband.'

'I will have a husband,' Alice said. 'William Bradford has asked me to marry him.'

The shock on John Robinson's face was extremely satisfying.

Bridget came into the room then, any pretence of not overhearing forgotten. 'You are going to marry William Bradford? Why that is wonderful news!'

John Robinson scowled at her, but she paid him not the slightest heed. This was women's gossip. 'Did he write to you?' she asked.

Alice nodded. 'Brother,' she continued addressing John again, 'You know that I this day received a letter from America. Brother Bradford wrote and kindly asked if I would become his wife. So if you could arrange for me to go on the next ship?'

'Your brother-in-law Morton is going with the next departure. But it will not be until the spring. You may travel under his care, if he is willing. Will you be able to contribute to your fare?'

The spring? That was nearly a year away. 'In truth I am unsure, brother,' she said. 'Perhaps my father may help.' But she doubted it.

'Well, leave it with me,' he said, and wrote something down on a piece of paper.

Alice thanked him and left.

Bridget was excited, as she showed Alice to the door. 'Brother Bradford is a fine brother, and good-looking too. You are indeed blessed, Alice,' she said.

'Oh, please, Bridget, don't say anything.'

'Fie on you!' Bridget cried, not allowing herself to be talked out of the best piece of gossip she had come across in ages. 'Of course I will tell *everyone!*'

Alice groaned, but she left the Robinsons' and crossed the garden to the tenement where Julianna lived.

Julianna was overcome with pleasure at the news. 'Oh Alice! At last! I must say, it has taken him a long time to make his mind up!'

'It is the first letter since he knew of Edward's death.'

'May I see?'

Alice handed the letter over. Julianna frowned as she read it. 'Well it is not the most romantic letter I've ever seen.'

'Will Bradford is not Master Shakespeare,' Alice agreed.

George Morton coughed, and Alice felt herself redden. 'Of course, I have not been to the theatre,' she told him, 'But I have heard some of his work read.' She took the letter back, and looked at it with Julianna. 'He calls me his *very dear* sister, though. And he also says here that I am his *dear one*. Oh Ju, he loves me!'

'Well, you would have thought a man in love might have said a bit more than that,' Julianna said, disgusted.

George looked at his wife. 'Woman, you do not know Brother Bradford. He is not a man of flowery eloquence. If he asks your sister to marry him, and calls her his dear one, then that must be enough.' He turned to Alice. 'And will you agree to marry him?'

'I do not know until I see him again,' she said truthfully. 'I will not give him a direct answer until then. For he may not be as I remember, and I may not feel—' she hesitated for she was going to say 'the same as I did' but realised she would be giving herself away to George who may not know her feelings for Will. So she finished lamely, 'I may not feel that he is right for me.'

Julianna looked at her sceptically, her brows raised. 'Really?' was all she said.

Back home, she sat down at her father's desk and wrote to Will.

Watching her, Alexander asked, 'So what is your answer to him, Alice?'

Alice looked at the letter. 'I will go to New England. But I have not yet said I will marry him. He must ask me in person, and then if I think it would be right for me, I will agree, and if not, I will bring my boys home again.'

Her father nodded. 'Good, for I do not want you to be in the sore straits you were in with Edward ever again.'

'Will is a good man, Father. He will take care of me, of that I am sure.'

'Then I will find the money for your fare.'

FORTY-TWO
Indians

Plymouth, 1622

They finished the palisade in March. It was eleven feet high and a mile long, and enclosed houses and little garden plots and a portion of the Mount or Fort Hill. Now they found time to call a meeting in the common house for governmental matters. At the meeting they re-elected Will as Governor, an honour which he would have been pleased to pass over to another. It was strange to think that it was already a whole year since John Carver had died, a year and three months since they landed here at Plymouth.

They got on with other business. 'We have an appointment for the Massachusetts Indians to come and trade with us,' Will said. 'We should begin to prepare for that.'

Hobomok stood up. 'Massachusett and Narrangasett fight Eng'ish. Together.'

Will felt his stomach slide. 'Do you mean that the Massachusetts and the Narrangasetts have joined forces?' Will asked.

Hobomok nodded. 'Squanto know.'

Will took a deep breath. This was serious. With two tribes against them he knew they couldn't stand. It looked as though they would be wiped out. 'If Squanto knows about it, why has he not told us?' he asked abruptly.

Hobomok shrugged his shoulders. 'Squanto not Eng'ish friend.'

Will simply did not believe it. Squanto who had attached himself to Will and followed him around like an enthusiastic puppy would surely not betray them. Furthermore the antipathy between Squanto and Hobomok had more than once boiled over into open battle. They were always scoring points off each other. It would suit Hobomok to set the English against Squanto.

He said to Hobomok, 'Leave us.' It would be better not to discuss their plans in front of the Indians.

Hobomok looked at him, nodded briefly, and left.

Will looked at the men around him. 'Well, we cannot fight two tribes. What do you suggest, gentlemen?'

Isaac Allerton had the first say, 'We cannot stay holed up in the town. Our store is almost empty, and we must go out and hunt and seek food.'

Brewster agreed. 'That's true. Besides we do not know when, or even if, they will attack. Furthermore, if they see we do not come out, they may well view that as a sign of fear or weakness and attack.'

'You think they will attack?' Stephen Hopkins asked.

Miles Standish answered him. 'We have to assume that.'

Sam Fuller scratched his head. 'What about Squanto?'

Will frowned. He didn't know quite what to make of Squanto. He had developed a fondness for the Indian, but he was not blind to his faults. 'Hobomok and Squanto have each been trying to outdo the other in currying favour with us. While Hobomok may be right about the Narrangasetts and the Massachusetts, I don't know what Squanto has to do with it.'

'You are too friendly with Squanto,' John Billington growled. 'You see no fault in him.'

Will let it go. He was used to Billington's snipes at him. Besides, he did not think either Squanto or Hobomok would betray the English.

'We will send the boat to the Massachusetts to trade, just as we planned,' Will said. They were desperately short of provisions. 'Hobomok and Squanto can go too.' They were required as interpreters.

Edward Winslow raised a surprised brow at him. *Both of them?* But all he said was, 'I think it a good idea.'

Standish approved also. 'It'll show them savages we ain't afeared.'

Squanto was delighted to have been chosen. He went off to make his few preparations.

Hobomok, however, resented that Squanto was to go with him, but it had ever been so that the English needed both interpreters, for neither man was expert at English.

The following morning Will watched as the boat with ten trusted men, Standish among them, and the two Indians sailed out of the bay and behind Gurnet's Nose, the point at which it would disappear from view.

Then he turned away to pick up his tools. There was seed-sowing to be done.

'Indian!'

He looked up. Out in the meadow, a man came running from the south, looking back behind him as though he had pursuers hot on his heels.

Will recognised one of Squanto's relatives. *Now what?* 'Let him in!'

The Indian had been running far. His oily skin was damp, his long black hair sticking to his face with sweat. He stopped in front of Will, and stood there bent over, and panting.

'Narrangasett,' he said and pointed to where he had come from. 'Narrangasett!'

'They come here?' Will asked.

The Indian nodded. 'Corbitant come.' Corbitant was the Narrangasetts' sachem, or chief.

Will was perturbed. The Narrangasetts were not friends. The Indian gasped a few more breaths then said, 'Massasoit come also.'

'He comes too?'

'War. Much blood.'

'How came you here' Will demanded, suspicious.

The man looked behind him fearfully. 'They come! They come! I escape!'

'What do you mean they come?'

The man looked behind him again. 'They come!'

Will couldn't take a chance. 'Cause the men to take arms, and stand to their stations,' he commanded the men who had come near to hear, 'and fire two shots to warn the boat to come in.'

The boat was near enough for the men to hear the shots and turn back.

While the boat made its leisurely way back to Plymouth, Will paced impatiently, his eyes scanning the surrounding countryside for movement of any sort. The problem with Indians was their stealth. You might never see them until it was too late. The English were ready, though. The men lined the palisade, muskets lodged in the joins between the palings, watching, waiting. The normally bustling settlement had settled into unnerving silence, the women waiting to reload the muskets, the children safely inside one of the houses in the care of Susanna Winslow.

'Send Hobomok and Squanto to me the moment they set foot on dry land!' Will ordered the boy Love Brewster who raced off on this important mission.

The sun had begun its downward path by the time Hobomok and Squanto marched up to Will.

'Your relative is here,' Will told Squanto abruptly, his anger evident in his voice. 'Speaking of War by Wampanoag and Narrangasett against us. What do you know about it?'

Squanto's eyes grew round. 'Tisquantum know nothing!'

'Massasoit not make war,' Hobomok said with certainty.

Will frowned from one to the other of them, his lips compressed, his anger growing with his impatience. Something here wasn't quite right. These Indians knew more than they said. Squanto was up to something.

'Wampanoag not fight Eng'ish,' Hobomok added.

Will's eyes scanned the surrounding countryside again. There was nothing to see but the usual trees and fields. All seemed reassuringly quiet. He made a decision. 'Hobomok, send your wife to Massasoit's village to visit her relatives, and see what she can find out.'

Hobomok grinned with delight at having so useful a wife. Squanto had no useful woman. 'Hobomok woman go,' he said.

The woman went, and all the English could do was wait.

The sun went down, and Will did not sleep, anxiety for the people in his care keeping him wandering about the compound, his eyes peering into the darkness in case the men on watch missed something. An attack now would wipe them out. The Indians must know it. Certainly he knew it. However, the morning came without incident.

Hobomok's wife came back, but she had nothing to report. Massasoit certainly did not make war with the English.

Will was beginning to suspect Squanto of working for his own ends. He discussed it with Miles Standish. 'What think you of this whole thing?'

Standish frowned, his red brows drawing together above his nose. 'I think Squanto seeks good things for himself.'

Will nodded. 'I think you are right. This is the way I see it. The Indians are a superstitious lot. They think we are white devils, ready to sell them into slavery. I reckon Squanto has told them that he had influence with us, that he could stir up war between whom he wishes, or bring peace if he wishes.'

'But why?' Standish demanded.

'My guess is that our Squanto wants to be more important with his people than Massosoit himself.'

'Cheeky beggar!'

'It seems to me, Master Standish, that if I give ear to Squanto and you give ear to Hobomok, we will learn more to our advantage.'

Standish grinned. 'Aye. That seems good to me.'

Once more Will sent Standish and his men out in the boat out to trade with the Massachusetts.

'Well I hope Standish trades well,' Brewster said. 'We are out of everything. We must scrape around for shellfish, and lobsters to put in the pot.'

'Standish knows what he is doing, and he is quite unafraid. Hello, now what?'

Brewster turned to follow the direction of Will's gaze. Massasoit came marching towards Plymouth with a number of his men.

'Looks like Massasoit has discovered Squanto's perfidy,' Brewster said wryly.

'I don't like the look of this,' Will murmured.

He came forward to meet the visitors with a smile, but Massasoit did not return the smile, or the greeting. There was no mistaking the anger of the chief, and no mistaking the message, either.

'You give Tisquantum to Massasoit,' Massasoit demanded through the interpretation of Hobomok.

'Why?'

'Because he cause war between Eng'ish and Wampanoag. He want be bigger than Massasoit. For this Tisquantum die.'

Will was dismayed, but not surprised. Squanto had sought his own interests, playing one against the other. And there were the terms of the agreement, which Squanto had definitely broken. Under that agreement Will ought to hand him over.

However, Will had become fond of this Indian who followed him around and chatted away in his appalling English. Without Squanto to teach them how to dress corn they would have died. Without his help they could not have become friends with Massasoit in the first place. They needed his translation skills.

'We will deal with Squanto,' he said.

'Tisquantum must die,' Massasoit insisted.

'We will deal with him,' Will said again, a determined note in his voice that Massasoit understood without translation.

By no means mollified, Massasoit departed, muttering darkly to his braves under his breath.

Isaac Allerton was uneasy. 'I don't like it,' he said to Will as they watched the retreating Indians. 'You may have to hand him over.'

'I will not if I can help it,' Will said. 'I will not hand a man over to his death for anything less than murder.'

'It would have been murder if he had succeeded in his ploy,' Allerton pointed out.

'He did not succeed.'

'No. Thank God for that.'

'Massasoit will be back.'

'Then you may have no other option than to hand Squanto over. After all, we cannot risk the lives of the women and children.'

Will knew it.

A few days later Massasoit sent a messenger and then a whole company of painted braves.

They had gifts with them—a knife, and a large present of beaver skins.

'You give to Massasoit Tisquantum's head and hands,' they said.

Will looked at them, and then pointedly looked down at the skins and the knife lying at his feet in the dust. 'You bring me gifts,' he said, his voice low and vibrating with outrage. 'You insult me! It is not in the manner of the English to sell men's lives at a price. When they deserve to die, they will die. Tell Massasoit I do not accept his gifts.'

And he sent the Indians away again with the skins and the knife.

When the boat party returned, having traded well, much to the relief of the colonists, Will sent for Squanto. 'What is this that you have done?'

he demanded.

Squanto hung his head. 'It was Hobomok. 'Hobomok has caused this to happen to me,' he complained.

Will said, 'Squanto, you have caused your own difficulties.'

'Then you must send Tisquantum to die.'

Will looked at him. 'I have no choice. Massasoit will kill us all, and I have women and children to think of.'

'Tisquantum understand.'

Will was exasperated. 'Squanto, why did you do it?'

Squanto did not reply.

The Indians came back, this time painted braves, angry and insistent, demanding Squanto's life.

Will knew he had procrastinated long enough. He must make a decision. If he failed to hand Squanto over, then under the terms of the agreement Massasoit could attack and wipe out the colony. He had to hand him over.

As he stood facing the Indians, he uttered a prayer to his God. The moment had come. He took a breath and opened his mouth, but the words died on his lips.

'A ship! In the bay a ship!'

Indians and English all looked at the triangle of white sail on the impossibly blue water, and Will thanked his God. He turned to Miles Standish standing beside him. 'What are they?' he snapped.

'I don't know. French maybe.'

Will turned his attention to the Indians as though they were of small importance now. 'I cannot deal with this now,' he said impatiently. 'I must first of all know whether this boat is friend or enemy. If it is enemy, I must deal with it first.'

The braves responded in a rage, but in the manner of a great chief, Will had dismissed them, turning away from them, and ignoring any posturing on their part. Will said to Miles Standish, 'Call the men to stand to arms.'

The Indians had no choice but to go. They left Plymouth in furious mood.

Will had managed to save Squanto. For now.

FORTY-THREE
Newcomers

New England 1622

Armed, with the heavy musket in his hands, Will stood on the beach with the other men and waited as the boat sent out from the ship turned back—for it had missed the settlement. It halted just offshore in the shallows, and seven men got out and waded towards them.

Will marched forward, still clutching his musket. 'Who are you?' he greeted them.

'Englishmen,' came the answer from an ordinary looking man with a beard showing tinges of grey.

Will looked back over his shoulder. 'Stand down, they are English.'

Immediately they lowered the muskets which had been held at the ready and came forward to greet them. After all it had been a long time since the last ship. 'We bring with us letters from England, from Master Weston.'

'You have brought supplies as well?' Will asked.

'No, no supplies.'

Will's heart sank. 'No supplies,' he repeated, and his dismay must have sounded in his voice, for the man's voice and stance became apologetic.

'Our commission is to form a colony to the east. We have come with a fleet of fishing ships presently anchored at an Island. We are merely messengers, and Master Weston has asked that you feed us.'

Will glared at them. 'Oh, he has, has he? And what, pray, does Master Weston think we will feed you with?'

'It is all in the letters,' the man said imperiously and searched in his doublet.

Will took the letters and turned and strode up the hill towards the home he still shared with the Brewsters. He hadn't even asked the man his name.

The letters, dated 12th and 15th January 1622 were from Thomas Weston and addressed to John Carver, which told Will that the *Fortune* had not yet arrived home by that time. That was a worry. Still it was a long journey and unfavourable weather might slow up the ship.

As Will read quickly, he felt the blood seething through his veins. Weston complained about the Merchant Adventurers who were funding the plantation in Plymouth, particularly about one Master Pickering, the same Master Pickering whose wife had been a member of the Leyden congregation. But of particular concern to Will was that Weston expected

Plymouth to entertain the seven men with whatever they needed, even though these men were sent out on Weston's private account. Of course it would have been of no concern had they had the means to feed them, but when they were in desperate straits themselves, even one extra mouth became an imposition.

As Will read on, he found that Weston's presumption did not end there. Another ship was to come with passengers also on Weston's private concerns who were also to be entertained while their ship went on to Virginia. And the next ship after that would contain still more persons to join with the first in setting up a new colony under a different patent. All of these people the Plymouth colony, which struggled to feed themselves and the thirty-five newcomers in the *Fortune*, had to somehow provide for. The *Fortune* passengers had just about brought the colony to starvation. And Weston blamed it all on the Merchant Adventurers, the financial backers, when Will knew that Weston himself was to blame.

Further, Weston hinted that the Merchant Adventurers had decided to dissolve the joint-stock company and desired a confirmation from Plymouth.

Will bit back an unchristian oath. This was not good. A pattern had emerged. The wild young men from the *Fortune*, and these arrivals by shallop and those who would come later were all Weston's people. They were not Separatists, and they now formed the majority. Perhaps Weston had it in mind to overthrow the Pilgrim governor and put in one of their own. Clearly Weston did not want the Pilgrims to rule the colony.

Will saw the danger. Everything they had fought for, and risked their lives for, namely the freedom to practise their own religion and live by its precepts was at risk.

He called his council together: Brewster, Allerton, Standish and Winslow and showed them the letters.

Edward Winslow let his breath go in a whistle. 'What kind of man is Weston, then?'

'He is a merchant,' Will said his voice heavy with irony. 'And a merchant exists to benefit only one person—himself.'

'We have no choice but to feed these people,' Brewster said. 'It would be unchristian to do anything else. After all we can't let them starve.'

'What with?' Will countered. 'We have nothing. And he isn't going to send us anything either. We cannot look to England for supplies.'

'We had better not reveal these letters to the colony,' Isaac Allerton put in.

Will shook his head in agreement. ' *"Put not your trust in princes,"* much less in merchants, *"nor in the son of man for there is none help in him.'"*

There was a short silence. Then Edward Winslow said, 'What is this letter here from a Captain Huddleston?'

'I haven't read them all yet,' Will said.

Allerton read in silence for a moment. 'He has one of the fleet of fishing ships of which the *Sparrow*—that must be the ship these men came to us in—is in convoy. He tells us that four hundred settlers have been massacred by Indians recently in Virginia, and that we ought to look to our defences.'

Will groaned. He had to take the warning seriously, especially in light of what had occurred with Massasoit. Perhaps the Narrangasetts or the Massachusetts Indians were of the same mind. Maybe all the Indians were going to rise up and massacre every last one of them.

Miles Standish, however, did not appear perplexed. 'And so?' he asked.

Allerton answered him. 'Captain Huddleston is fishing. We are starving. And the tone of the letter is friendly. Perhaps if we sent a man to him with furs to trade for fish and supplies . . .?'

Edward Winslow looked heavenwards. 'That's me, I suppose.'

Well, he had become trusted in the manner of diplomacy, and he was particularly astute at getting the best exchanges.

Will approved it. 'Why not you?' he countered.

They sent him off in the shallop with furs, and hoped for the best.

Meantime the settlers waited, and the food ran out. They hunted what they could, and they ate shell-fish which made them sick, and yet there was no corn, no fruit, nothing of the ground.

They became increasingly sick. Will saw them fading before his very eyes, men who had been robust now becoming little more than skeletons with skin on, and trying to work to sow the seed for next year's crop. There were just too many mouths to feed and not enough to feed them on. Others, particularly the women and some of the small children, became swollen in their bellies with gas. They were in a desperate plight. If Winslow failed to return, or if he failed to secure any food, they would all die.

Will was furious with Weston for doing this to them, and furious that Weston had intended to take over the colony through his own people. Well, there was nothing new in that. The devil ever did seek to destroy the Lord's elect. However, their weakness made it difficult to counter. Worse, starvation had a depressing effect on the spirits.

Daily he prayed for help and guidance, and for help for Edward Winslow to have a safe journey and make a good exchange. However, as the days passed, he felt himself growing weaker. He found it difficult to work in the fields, difficult to build the fort so necessary for their defence.

He had no energy. The little food they could find did not go far enough. And he was constantly hungry. In England this period in the spring, when everything began to grow was deceiving. Everything appeared lush, and good, but there was no fruitage yet. They called it in England the hungry gap. And hungry it certainly was. They would have to work better at providing for this time of year in future.

At last the shallop returned and Edward Winslow brought with him fish and other provisions, which would tide them over for the time being.

At the end of June another ship arrived from Weston called the *Charity* with more letters, and a further sixty colonists.

Weston wrote that the *Fortune* had arrived, with all their letters, but that it had been robbed of all the furs and other goods the settlers had filled her with. However, the promise of so great a wealth was good in the he eyes of the Merchant Adventurers. But Thomas Weston himself, who had promised he would never desert them, had pulled out, selling his share of the venture to others. Further he admitted that he had intercepted a letter from the Merchant Adventurers to the governor sewn into a shoe, from Master Pickering and a Master Pierce, and tried to defend himself from the accusations therein.

Master Pickering's letter was quite blunt. The company of Merchant Adventurers had bought out Master Weston and were glad to be rid of him. Further among the sixty men who had come ashore was one Andrew Weston, Weston's brother, described in the letter as '*a heady young man and violent and set against you there and the company here; plotting with Master Weston their own ends, which tend to your and our undoing in respect of our estates there and prevention of our good ends. For by credible testimony we are informed his purpose is to come to your colony, pretending he comes for and from the Adventurers, and will seek to get what you have in readiness into his ships, as if they came from the Company; and possessing all, will be so much profit to himself. And further to inform themselves what special places or things you have discovered to the end that they may suppress and deprive you etc.*'

Weston wrote yet another letter, a disclaimer to this, but Will recognised that everything they had hoped for from him was gone. And they had another sixty mouths to feed. And none of the people were from their congregation in Leyden or in London.

Robert Cushman also sent a letter, hidden in the letter of Bridget Fuller to her husband Sam who brought it to Will.

He told them of the French pirates who had robbed them, and taken them to France and held them fifteen days, so that they got home the on the seventeenth day of February. He hoped to come again to Plymouth the following year.

He warned Will not to trust the men that were coming—ramshackle fellows he called them—and to keep separate from them. He advised Will to warn Squanto to tell the Indians that the newcomers were nothing to do with them.

Those in Leyden sent their love, and many intended to come on the next ship.

Will pondered all these things. There were many other letters besides. From Alexander May with news of Jonathan, Will's son. From John Robinson encouraging and with news. However, there was a letter there also from Alice addressed to him personally. His heart skipped a beat when he saw it, but he hid it in his jerkin to wait until he had told his council about the things of Weston.

Later he went for a walk up the hill to the square fort they had built for protection and which had also become their meeting house, and sat down on the ground, before pulling the letter from his pocket.

'*Dear Brother Bradford,*' she had written. It sounded very formal, and his heart plummeted. '*I thank you for your letter, and I am glad to hear you are in good spirits and well, despite the travails you have been put to. I thank you also for your kind offices towards me.*' Will stopped reading, folding the letter in half to hide it from his eyes, hesitating to read the rest. If she turned him down, and he would not blame her if she did, he could not imagine how he would go on. He realised just how much he hoped for her 'yes' to his proposal, how much he wanted her here. Yet it was an awful lot to ask of any woman, and perhaps she had found someone else. He took a large breath, gritted his teeth, and unfolded the letter again. '*I am making plans to come to you at the first opportunity. My sister Morton and her husband and family intend to come also, so I shall travel under their protection. I pray God keep you safe, until we meet again, I remain Alice Southworth.*'

His heart turned over. She was coming! Oh, when would she come? He could not wait to see her. He re-read the letter. She had not said she would marry him, but that she would come. It would do. Perhaps she would reserve her plans until she arrived. Perhaps if she did not like it, she would return. Perhaps she was unsure if she still loved him. What if she didn't?

He rested his head on his forearm on his knee and tried to calm his thoughts. She was coming. It was enough.

The newcomers were trouble from the outset. 'Lusty young men' Will called them, young unprincipled, undisciplined ruffians. Some of them were sick, and so they took the best places in the colony, which meant others who had built their own houses now had to sleep in the Common

House. Will put those of them who were well enough to work with the corn, and they stole it. They treated the women in the colony disrespectfully, which caused Mary Brewster to speak out forthrightly against them.

'Will, you must do something! Susanna Winslow was grabbed by one of them in her own garden! She slapped him soundly and he ran off, but Master Winslow was furious! If you don't deal with them, some of us will do it ourselves!' She waved a ladle at him, in vivid description of just how the women would carry out the threat.

Brewster raised a speaking eyebrow at Will. His wife was more than capable of sorting out recalcitrant young men. However, he said, 'You know that if they continue to run riot, we'll have trouble.'

Will stood up. 'This is Weston's doing,' he said through his teeth. 'He must have known they'd be trouble. Well, I'll not have them making sport with Christian women!' and grabbing his hat he strode out of the cottage.

Will called the trouble-makers together in the street and they came reluctantly, shuffling in the dirt, swaggering scoundrels every one of them. They stood with hands in pockets, or arms folded, heads on one side, regarding Will as though whatever he said was of no significance to them. Their attitude brought the indignation in Will to boiling point.

'Just who do you think you are!' he demanded awfully. 'You come here to join us, benefiting from our labours. We are a colony, and we have fought to make a living in this wilderness. Who are you to come in here and assault decent women with your wickedness, and to steal from those who have given you succour?'

They continued to regard him with an uncomprehending stare. There wasn't an ounce of shame in any one of them. One of them said, 'So what are you going to do about it?'

Will snapped, 'Well, Seeing that you do not wish to obey the laws of the colony, we must ask you to leave.'

They didn't seem to care. 'Don't worry, we ain't desirous of staying with men who are forever quoting the Bible at us! We intend to find ourselves a place to live.'

'Then I am glad to hear it,' Will said tersely, and marched away from them.

'This rabble comes from Weston!' he fumed later to Brewster.

'Perhaps they will be gone soon,' Brewster said.

A few days later, the ship which had left them at Plymouth and then voyaged down into Virginia came back and Weston's company of young men removed themselves from the sphere of the Separatists.

'Where do you go?' Will asked as they climbed into the boat that would take them to the anchored ship.

The man Sanders, who was slightly older than the others, and appeared to have a little more sense than they did, paused to look at Will. 'North to Massachusetts Bay to a place called Wessagusset.' Wessagusset later became Weymouth.

'Among the Indians?'

'Do you think, Master Bradford, that you are the only ones who can build a colony and deal successfully with the Indians?' Sanders retorted. 'Are we not healthy men who can do our own building and planting?'

'I suggest Master Sanders that you find a leader for yourselves, and that you make laws for yourselves. If you do not, you will have an undisciplined rabble who will achieve nothing. This is a hard country, and everything we have we have to work for, and then there is no guarantee of success. Your young men are interested in having an easy life. They will not get it here, but there will be hardship and work, and heartache and danger.'

'You wish us ill, Master Bradford?'

'Not at all. I wish you well, Master Sanders. But we are pleased that you are going.'

384

FORTY-FOUR
Trading

Plymouth 1622

With the departure of Weston's men, life returned to some kind of normality. At last the harvest came round. However, it was disastrously small, and although they had enough to eat for now, Will knew with certainty it would not see them through the winter.

'Why?' Will demanded of his council.

'Because we are not yet well acquainted with the manner of Indian corn?' Isaac Allerton suggested.

Sam Fuller pursed his lips. 'The brothers and sisters were too weak to tend it properly when it needed tending, to fish and then dress it properly, to weed it, and see off the vermin. Remember we had famine then, and we could not work, most of us.'

'And don't forget Weston's men stole quite a bit even before it was ripe.' Stephen Hopkins put in.

Will said pointedly, 'That is only part of the problem. If we suffer another bad harvest next year, that will be the end of the colony. We must turn this thing around or we are finished.'

'So what is the answer?' Edward Winslow asked.

Will frowned thoughtfully. 'Part of the problem is that we are asking men and women to work for the common good.'

Edward Winslow raised his brows. 'Is that not what the agreement is all about?'

'Yes it is—but it sells us as bond slaves. We are allowed to own nothing for ourselves. We all knew it was not a good agreement from the first. Every man has a different ability, a different talent. When that talent is recognised and he gets the blessing for his work, then he is happy. Is there not a scripture which says, *"They shall not plant and another eat."*? And *"There shall sit every man under his vine and under his fig tree."* Jehovah knows that what people need to do is plant for themselves, not for someone else. Look how they complained when the women were expected to work for other men in washing their clothes and cooking and so on. And the young men resent having to feed another man's children. It is understandable. No-one wants to be someone else's slave! Everyone needs to see good for his or her hard work.' He paused and looked at them. 'The vanity and conceit of Plato—who thought up this idea and never actually put it into practice, and that was applauded by some men of our own generation—was that the taking away of property and making everything a commonwealth would make people happy and successful. As if he were wiser than God! Patently, it does not work. It is against man's nature.'

'Plato weren't a Christian,' Hopkins grumbled.

'And so?' Brewster prompted Will.

'And so my suggestion is that we give land to each man in proportion to the number in his family, and let him work his own land, and let his wife and his sons help him. Hitherto, the women and children have often begged off because of weakness, and no man can be such a tyrant as to force them to work. It is my guess, however, that they will go into the fields, willing to work for their own families on their own land.'

'What if someone does not work his land?' Stephen Hopkins asked.

'Then he will starve,' Will said bluntly. 'The scripture says, *"if there were any which would not work, that he should not eat.."'* He added, 'However, I reckon that if men work for themselves, they will indeed work, and perhaps there may even be some produce left over to trade with or for others who come here.'

'I think it an excellent idea,' Isaac Allerton put in.

Winslow too liked it. 'I think my wife and her son will be pleased to help in our own field rather than to feed others.'

Will nodded. 'Then that is settled. Before ploughing and seed-sowing come around, we will apportion out the land. Meantime, we must trade to buy food for ourselves.'

'What with?' Stephen Hopkins demanded. 'We have no goods.'

'Jehovah will provide,' Will predicted.

Francis Billington stood up angrily. 'Jehovah. Huh! Can't you come up with something better than that?'

Will compressed his lips and glared at the man. 'Can you?' he countered.

Evidently not, for Billington made a noise in his throat and stalked out of the Common House.

Stephen Hopkins growled, 'He's got a point. It seems to me that we ought not to have to rely on God for everything.'

Will took a deep steadying breath, deliberately ignoring him, and then said, 'So if that is agreed, gentlemen?'

'Agreed,' they all said at once.

Will sat down immediately and drafted up a plan of the land allotment, with William Brewster's help. 'You think it will work?' Brewster asked, surveying their handiwork.

Will looked up from the paper, and met his eyes straightly. 'Don't you? We have scriptural backing.'

Brewster nodded thoughtfully. 'Aye. And talking of scripture, what think you of the new Bible, Authorised by his majesty?'

Will pulled a thoughtful face. 'Have you seen it?'

'Aye. That's why I'm asking.'

'It is similar to Whittington's Geneva Bible in some ways. It's got the verse numbering, and running headings across the top of the page. But there are no notes.'

'Well you know why, don't you?'

'I expect someone didn't like the notes!' The Geneva Bible contained extensive notes on 'hard bits' of the Bible, many of them challenging widely held beliefs.

'Well they did challenge the idea of the divine right of kings! You can't expect King James to take that lying down!'

Will chuckled. 'No indeed!'

A commotion outside ended the conversation, caused Will to put the pen in the standish and for them both to go outside. From the lookout, one of the boys, the cry of 'Sail ho!' in imitation of the sailors on the Mayflower, brought everyone to the shore.

As Will, standing with the others, watched the ship coming in, his lips set in a grim line, and he wondered if it had pleased Master Weston to provide some victuals for them. Yet that was not the only hope in his heart. Maybe, just maybe, Alice had been able to get aboard this ship. Had she come to him? His heart leapt at the thought. Were there other friends on the ship? It would have been good to see friendly faces, people they loved and missed, like wives and children and other congregation members, rather than Weston's worldly people. Yet they had hoped for that before, and been disappointed. It did not do to get one's hopes up too high.

The ship proved to be the *Discovery*, Thomas Jones master. She came from the Virginia Company, on a mission to discover the harbours along the coastline. To the settlers she was just a visitor, but she did carry a store of English beads which were good for trading, and some knives and other metal goods. It might not have been exactly what Will had hoped for, but it would certainly help. These things they could buy, and then trade them with the Indians for food and more skins. Trade, it seemed, made the world go round.

'The captain wants an inordinately high price for his goods,' Isaac Allerton told Will later, standing on the *Discovery*'s deck.

'We have no choice, and he knows it,' Will said, making the best of a difficult situation. 'We need the goods to trade for food, or we will not survive. It is called business, Master Allerton, the law of supply and demand!'

'I don't like it,' Allerton said.

Overhearing him, the master interrupted him. 'We are not a charity, Master Allerton,' he said acidly. 'And there are many along this coast as will happily buy our goods from us. Even the Indians.'

'We have eked out a living here, sir,' Allerton said heatedly, 'and we do not need men to rob us blind!'

The captain was unperturbed. He knew they must buy. 'Take it or leave it, sir.'

Will sighed resignedly. The captain took their beaver furs and gave less for them than the going rate. It made the goods very expensive. However, the Plymouth colony was now solvent. They would not starve this year.

Later, when the ship had gone, Will and Allerton discussed with Edward Winslow and Miles Standish how and where to trade.

'We cannot go far,' Standish pointed out. 'Without a decent ship we are confined to the bay. The shallop cannot take the seas beyond the Cape. I fear we will not be able to buy much from the local Indians.'

Will clicked his tongue, for he knew Standish was right. The *Speedwell* which they had chartered in Leyden, but which they had left behind in England, had been commissioned for just such a task. 'Well, we will have to do what we can,' he said.

'Master Bradford, Master Bradford!' Love Brewster came running up the street. 'A man from Wessagusset, Master Bradford, asking to see you.'

'An Englishman?' Will asked.

'Yessir!'

Leaving the others to follow at their own pace, Will strode down the street to meet the man, Love Brewster trotting along beside him as if to show him the way. Will felt a spark of impatience. Weston's men. Huh! Trouble-makers. He had little time for them. No doubt their imprudence had brought them to want, and they expected help from Plymouth! Well they would not get it!

The man was thin, and he needed a wash and a shave. Despite his youth, he looked like some old vagrant that occupied the backstreets of London.

'What do you want?' Will demanded abruptly.

'I come from Weymouth.'

'Wessagusset, you mean? How goes it up there?'

The visitor evaded the question. 'We have heard that you have goods to trade with.'

Will regarded him stoically. How on earth did they know about that all that distance away in Massachusetts Bay? News certainly travelled fast. 'What of it?'

'We thought that we might join with Plymouth in trading. We have a ship that you could use.'

A ship! Now Will was interested. However, he did not let his interest show, but said, 'What ship is that, pray?'

'The *Swan*.'

Will was thoughtful. 'But we supply the trade goods, eh?'

'Well, when Master Weston comes, or we get supplies from England, we shall repay you.'

Will pursed his lips, appearing reluctant, but thinking quickly. He could not expect payment from Weston. Still, the ship was worthy of hire. He said, 'Improvidence brings you to want, I see.'

He had seen it coming. Without proper leadership, young men without experience, without the disciplines that belonged to the Pilgrims, indeed, without the knowledge of the Truth, could not stand. They were starving, so they stole from the Indians or they fought each other, or some even became the servants of the Indians, bringing wood or working in the fields for them. The indignity of it made Will wince.

However, the *Swan*, a thirty-ton pinnace, would make it possible for the Plymouth men to make a longer voyage than they had been able to do in the pinnace. They could in fact go right around the Cape and then southward towards the fishing fleets or other settlements. It was a good idea now that they had goods to trade with. It was just a pity that they must pay for the use of the ship. 'Very well,' he said at last.

It took a week to make the *Swan* ready, and finally men from both colonies set sail.

Will watched them head towards the Cape and prayed for God's blessing on it. He knew how treacherous the waters here could be, knew that there were treacherous shoals. He didn't expect them to get as far as Pollock Rip, which had nearly been the end of the *Mayflower*. However, even as he watched the wind got up, and the seas grew, and blew head on into the *Swan*'s sails, so that they collapsed. She came back to Plymouth.

'Call themselves sailors?' William Brewster declared disgustedly as he watched the little ship drop anchor. 'Even I could do better than that, and I am no sailor!'

Will's lips twitched. 'No doubt on it,' he said.

The following day the ship went out again, when everyone could see the wind was just as contrary. Yet again the ship had to come back.

This time they hauled out the ship's boat and brought Miles Standish ashore. The man was hardly able to stand, and his skin was flushed.

'What ails you?' Will asked, surprised, for Standish had the constitution of a bull.

Standish looked at him with over-bright eyes. 'A fever of some kind,' he said, leaning on Isaac Allerton who had come to help.

'He's been dreadfully seasick,' one of the boat crew told Will.

Will took a resigned breath. 'Then I'll have to go in his place.

Tomorrow. Squanto—you know these parts well?'

'Tisquantum know shoals and tribes here,' Squanto told him proudly.

'Good. Then you can come along too.'

Two days later they set off again. This time the wind was with them, and the *Swan* rounded the Cape. Will felt good about this. Standing on the deck, watching the colony from a distance, he thought how much they had achieved. Yet he knew that if they did not trade well, this would be the end of them.

They left the bay behind. Hugging the coast they made their way southward. Here the water was certainly rougher than in the protected bay, the waves large and crested white, the sky overcast and leaden. Will stood on the deck the whole time. He was not affected by seasickness, but others retched painfully over the side. They intended to make landfall before dark, and Squanto assured Will that this would be possible. He knew where they were he insisted.

From his place on the deck, Will saw the water change, imperceptibly at first, little waves white with foam appearing all around them. The captain ordered the lead lowered.

'We're in the shoals,' he told Will. 'I don't like it.'

Will turned to Squanto. 'You told us you knew the way through,' he accused.

Squanto shook his head, and spread his hands apologetically. 'Tisquantum not know what happen!'

'I do! You don't know the way at all!'

Squanto peered at the coastline, hiding his guilt in offended silence.

Will said, 'So where do we go, Squanto?'

At first Squanto didn't answer, and Will thought he had decided to be unco-operative. Then suddenly he said, 'Go ashore here,' and pointed to a river mouth opening invitingly in the golden sand. 'Good trade here.'

'Are you sure?' Will asked, as the captain ordered the anchor lowered, and the longboat hauled out.

Will and the shore party with Squanto piled into the boat. They rowed into a narrow and crooked channel at a place later called Chatham, flanked on both sides by trees.

The boat party fell silent, everyone watching the trees, as the boat slid quietly up the river. 'Where are they?' Will asked, thinking aloud.

'They're here somewhere,' someone muttered. 'I can smell 'em!'

'Indians watch from trees,' Squanto told them unnecessarily.

Will couldn't smell them, but he could feel a hundred pairs of eyes boring straight into him. 'Why don't they come out to meet us?' he asked. He felt the hairs rise on the back of his neck, and goosebumps crawled over his skin. Here, in the boat on the river, they were sitting targets. At any moment, a murderous rain of arrows could come flying at them, and he knew that if that happened, no-one would survive. Gripping his musket, he peered into the trees and caught a glimpse of movement. 'There!' he cried.

Everyone turned to look, but the Indian slid out of sight.

The boat came gently to the shore where Squanto indicated, and gripping his primed musket, Will got out into dense undergrowth with the others. No-one spoke, for all their senses were focused on the slightest movement. Above them the grey sky parted and allowed a glimmer of sunlight to trickle through the dense trees.

'Where the devil are they?' someone whispered.

Again Will thought he saw movement in the trees, the shadowy hint of a man. Perhaps even as they walked slowly forward, the Indians surrounded them.

'Squanto,' he ordered. 'Come to the front.'

Obediently, Squanto came forward, holding up his knife, and speaking in the strange Indian language.

Seeing an Indian with the English and, more to the point, seeing an Indian with a weapon, reassured them and they began to creep out of their hiding places, but keeping well to the trees.

'We come in peace,' Will told them through Squanto. 'We come to trade.'

Cautiously the Indians came towards them, some holding bows and arrows ready, others with knives.

'We have goods to trade,' Will told them. He beckoned and two men brought a box of beads and metal goods—dishes and plates and cups, and bowls, things the natives could melt down and turn into nails, or knives, or perhaps arrow heads.

They came closer to have a look at these treasures, and grew bold enough to pick some up.

Now they were pleased to welcome them. The English suddenly found themselves as honoured guests, and the Indians brought out venison and other food in great abundance to entertain them. Sitting on the ground around a camp fire, eating the first decent meal he had had in a while, Will reflected that there were perks to trading with the Indians.

'Why don't they take us into their village?' Will asked Squanto.

Squanto shrugged his shoulders. 'Tisquantum ask.'

He came back a short time later. 'They make excuses,' he said with disgust.

'They do not want us in their village?'

'That is not welcome for Eng'ish,' Squanto said.

'But they feed us!' Will remarked, puzzled.

'Ah—'tis manners!' Squanto explained. 'Not send Eng'ish away empty. 'They bring food here, trade here.'

'Why then don't they want us in the village?'

It was understandable, though, Will reflected, as he ate succulent venison. After all English and French and Spanish raiding parties had gone up and down the coast taking Indians for slaves, and slaughtering others. They had no reason to trust the white man.

'Tell them English sleep in their village tonight,' Will told Squanto when they had eaten, and stood up to march right into the village.

Squanto's dark eyes grew round with surprise.

'Tell them!' Will commanded.

So he did, and the Indians disappeared.

The English followed at their leisure, conducted by one or two guides.

In a village of tent-like dwellings, the whole tribe appeared to see these strangers who strode in. 'They hide everything,' Squanto explained. 'Not want Eng'ish to take them.'

Will nodded, understanding.

The chief greeted them, made them most welcome, and put two tents over to their use for the night. It was cramped, but it kept them out of the wind and the cold.

The following day they purchased eight hogsheads of corn and beans.

One of the Wessagusset men approached Will. 'I found their things,' he said.

'What things?'

'The things the Indians hid from us. Furs and horns, and shells. Come and see.'

Will followed him out of the camp and into the trees. 'Right here!' he said, pointing to a hollow tree.

Will looked in. 'There is nothing here.'

The man also looked in, astonished. 'They've moved them again.'

Will raised a brow at him. 'Probably with good reason,' he said.

Later that day, the party boarded the *Swan* and set sail to continue their southward journey.

They spent a rough night at sea, and Will was pleased to be able to get up and go on deck the following morning. But when he went down for breakfast, he realised he had not seen Squanto.

'Where is Squanto?' he asked the cook.

'Dunno!'

It wasn't like Squanto to miss a meal, or to be a lie-abed. Surprised,

Will carried on eating his corn porridge, but when he had finished and Squanto still had not appeared he went in search of him.

He found the Indian still in his hammock. Peering in the between-decks gloom, Will could just make out his shape, and was ready to prod it and to tip its inhabitant out onto the deck, when Squanto groaned.

Concerned, Will tried to look at him, and, taking a lantern off its hook, held it up so that the beam fell on Squanto's face. 'What ails you, friend?'

Squinting at the light, Squanto groaned again and shivered violently. 'Tisquantum sick,' Squanto murmured. Will put his hand on the Indian's and felt the skin hot to the touch. He touched his face. 'You are burning up,' he said. 'How long have you been like this?'

Squanto merely groaned. Perhaps it was the same sickness that Miles Standish had gone ashore with.

Will fetched some fresh water in a cup, and helped the Indian to sit up enough to sip. He bathed Squanto's forehead with a cloth dipped in water.

One thing was certain, he could not carry on with the journey with Squanto so sick. Remembering the horrors of the *Mayflower* when the sickness raged, he was not going to submit Squanto to that, nor risk everyone else. He had served them well, and without his efforts they would have starved in the early days. Besides, without Squanto to interpret, they could not trade.

Will sought out the captain. 'We must turn back.'

Back in Plymouth, Will himself nursed Squanto, who did not improve, and indeed became very frightened when he began to bleed from his nose. 'Tisquantum die,' he told Will, clutching his hand.

Will could not deny that his friend was desperately ill. It seemed probable that he would die. ''Tis a little sleep,' he told him gently.

Squanto looked intently into his eyes. 'Pray for Tisquantum to go to Eng'ish God Jehovah.'

Will felt the tears prick his eyes, and he did indeed pray with him. They had concentrated so much on merely staying alive that there had been no time to preach to the Indians, but Squanto, Will's shadow for the last two years, had talked with him and listened to him, and asked many questions. Now, Will regretted that this man had never been baptised, but he said to him, 'You will be in paradise, Squanto,' trusting his God to do the rest.

Squanto nodded. 'In paradise.' He wasn't quite sure what paradise was, but it was enough to know that he would sleep, that the English God would look after him.

Will sat and held his hot hand, as Squanto bequeathed his few belongings to his English friends, and gradually Squanto the Indian slipped away into death.

Will wept for him.

FORTY-FIVE
Preparations

Leyden, End 1622

Winter had come early in Leyden. The sky was leaden, the air crisp from threatened snow, and the wind cut like a scythe as it whistled up the canals and through the gaps in the windows. Even the Carpenters' house, which was larger than most, was not exempt, and the only warm room in the house was the kitchen with the large fire.

So, when George Morton came in without knocking, bringing with him an icy blast which caused all the candles to gutter, everyone huddled around the fire glared at him with ill-concealed disgust. He may be a beloved son-in-law to Alexander and Mary, and brother-in-law to their children, but no-one took kindly to being frozen half to death. He hastily closed the door behind him.

Alexander set aside the Bible he had been reading to his family and stood up to welcome him. 'You are well come, George. Come and sit by the fire. Alice, make a place for George if you please. Some mulled ale?' Unlike Edward Southworth who had taken Alexander's daughter to London and to his mind then failed to care for her, George did his very best for his family, which endeared him to Alexander.

'You must be frozen, brother,' Alice said, relinquishing her place by the fire to find a stool for him, and everyone shuffled along to accommodate him.

'Thank you. I come with news,' he said, taking off his cloak to hang it on the peg by the door, and taking Alexander's hand. 'No, sister, no ale for me, thank you. I cannot stay long.'

Alice's heart skipped a beat. *News!* She placed the stool between herself and her Father and sat down herself, being careful to leave a suitable gap between herself and Julianna's husband.

'What news?' Alexander Carpenter demanded, resuming his seat in the armed chair.

George sat down, with a nod of thanks to Alice. 'Brother Robinson has secured two ships to take us to New England.'

Alice's heart began to hammer in her chest.

'What ships?' Alexander asked.

'The *Anne* and the *Little James*. They are to sail in the spring. Brother Robinson has paid for the passages, and has ordered the making of provisions.'

'And are we to be going?' Alice asked.

'Yes, we are all to go on the *Little James*. You and Constant and

Thomas, and Julianna and me, John, Nathanaiel, Patience and Sarah. And we are taking my brother's son, Thomas. Brother Robinson had at first thought to put you on the *Anne*, but I pointed out that you would be better off with your sister, and where I can take care of you.'

Alice's mind raced. She was going to America! At last, she was going to go to Will. Oh, how she longed for the moment they arrived! And how she feared it also! How could it be otherwise. She had not set eyes on him for nearly three years. What would he think of her now? She had put on a little weight, but not much. Her face had filled out and she had become more matronly. Her hands shook when she thought about it. What would she say to him? Would he be altered?

Her father was speaking and she made an effort to listen. 'Has Brother Robinson thought to make provisions also for the colony?' he asked.

'Indeed he has, and has in mind to send much more besides. As much as we can carry on the ships, I understand. The brethren have been most generous in the last months with their contributions.'

'Well, as the rest of us intend to go over, it is in our interests to help the colony. It has been hard on them.'

'True, but we no longer have Thomas Weston to consider.'

'Bah! Thomas Weston. That scoundrel!'

'He is no longer a problem, and we have different people to consider. But Jehovah provides.'

Alice thought of her boys currently asleep in the room above. They were to undertake a perilous journey, she knew. But she had no intention of leaving them behind. Nothing would separate her from her children, she decided. Not like Dorothy Bradford who left her son behind. But she had to go to Will. He had asked her, and she would go.

Priscilla, the younger sister next to Alice in age, burst into tears. 'Oh Alice! We will never see you again! Or Julianna! Or your dear children!'

Alice looked at her father, and then at her mother, sitting dutifully beside him, sewing. Mary Carpenter looked up, straight at Priscilla. 'I daresay you will all go in time, and leave your dear father and myself quite alone.'

'You will not come, Mother?' Alice asked.

'No, I think not. It is too much for us at our age to up sticks yet again and move. Your father's business does well enough, and we are not strong enough to cope with the rigours of building a home out of nothing. We are not farmers.' She smiled bravely, but Alice could see the quiver to her lip, the tears in her eyes. Just as Alice herself hated to be parted from her sons, so she knew how her mother must feel at being parted from her daughters and grandchildren. And Alice did not want to cause either of her parents pain.

'I should like to go,' Priscilla added. 'I would like to farm, and to have space around me.' She looked into space dreamily, and hugged herself.

'That's because William Wright is there,' the youngest daughter Mary put in. She was now twenty-six years old, but had not learned much tact.

'Will you go, sister?' George asked to spare Priscilla's embarrassment.

Young Mary shrugged. 'I really do not know.'

George stood up to go. ''Tis late, and Julianna will be worried for me,' he said.

Alice's mother detained him. 'Before you go,' she said, putting her sewing aside and standing up herself, to come out of the circle of her family and to face him, 'is it so that Julianna is with child again?'

George's face betrayed his discomfiture. 'How did you know?'

'I am her mother,' Mary said, pulling herself up to her fullest height of five feet, and looking him straight in the eye. 'A mother knows these things. So you intend to take my daughter on a ship across the Atlantic when she is with child?'

George looked down at his feet. 'She has only just become aware of it herself.'

'But such a perilous journey! How can you consider it?'

George looked from his mother-in-law to his father-in-law and back again. Mary Carpenter, mostly a mild mannered woman, was a tigress where her children were concerned. And George knew it. He said, 'If we do not take this opportunity now, who knows when we will be able to go? You know how difficult it is for us to make a living here in Leyden, and Julianna and I feel it would be a good move for us and the children.'

'You are depriving me of my grandchildren,' she pointed out.

Alexander stood too, and put a hand on her arm. 'My love—'

'And I will never know this new grandchild.'

George frowned. 'I am sorry for that,' he said stiffly.

'And I am to be bereft of children, am I?' Mary demanded hotly.

'My love,' Alexander tried again, 'you know we have to let them go.'

Mary glared at him. 'But I do not have to like it, husband,' she snapped.

She turned away then in an attempt to busy herself with putting her sewing into the basket, but catching sight of Alice said, 'And you too will take my grandchildren from me.'

Alice stood up and folded her hands in front of her. In the last few minutes she had realized just how much her grandchildren meant to her mother. It seemed too cruel to remove them from her all at once. She took a deep breath, aware that everyone watched her. It would be a perilous journey for little ones. But she had to go to Will, she had no choice. Not to go was unthinkable. Yet, to leave her children behind . . . And all at once she came to a decision. 'I am not taking Constant and Thomas with me, Mother. I do not know what awaits us there. I ask that you will take care of them until I can send for them.'

Her mother nodded, tears of gratitude in her eyes. She looked back at her husband, an odd look on her face. Alexander jerked his head at George, indicating that he should go. Seeing a storm brewing George grabbed his cloak and took himself off with alacrity.

Priscilla and young Mary decided to retire, and Alice went with them just as their mother burst into tears, and their father took her in his arms.

In her own room which she shared with her boys, Alice unpinned her hair, ran a brush through it and plaited it, then undressed in the dark, slipped on her night shift and, shivering, slid into bed beside her sons, the sons she would now be leaving behind.

She tried to say her evening prayers, but her mind would not settle, wandering off at a tangent. She was going to Will, in not that many weeks. She imagined how he would greet her, what he would say. She longed for the comfort of his embrace, the feel of his lips on hers. Even in the dark, she blushed, remembering how he had kissed her in London, and she had responded. Whatever must he think of her to betray her husband so blatantly? But he must have thought something good, for he had asked her to marry him! The thoughts went round and round in her head. Her stomach churned continually with excitement, and she knew she would get no sleep.

Yet her happiness also brought sadness. She must be parted from her sons, and that would cost her, but she could not risk them on such a perilous journey until she was sure the new colony would survive. She thought with a shudder of those who had died, and knew she could not risk it. But she ached to leave them.

And she must leave her mother and father and would probably never set eyes on them again. It would hurt her to leave them, and it would hurt them too, and she felt a guilty pang until a scripture came to mind, *Therefore shall a man leave his father and his mother, and shall cleave unto his wife: and they shall be one flesh.*

It was the way that God had spoken it. She need not feel guilty at all.

FORTY-SIX
Wessagusset and Massasoit's Sickness

New England, 1622-1623

Standing beside Hobomok on the edge of the clearing, it struck Will that the village was unnaturally quiet. A scruffy dog came towards the newcomers, barking, and Will eyed him warily, but the alarm did not bring anyone out of the little houses the Indians occupied. 'Where are they all?' Will asked Hobomok, frowning. It wasn't what he expected, nor what he desired. This journey northward on the *Swan* had been specifically planned to trade with the Massachusetts Indians, but it seemed that there were no Indians to trade with.

Hobomok frowned, his black brows drawing together above his glorious nose, just as mystified as Will. 'Hobomok find out,' he suggested and without waiting for a reply he loped off.

Will and the other English kicked their heels. Edward Winslow looked about him. 'Pity Standish isn't here,' he said uneasily.

Will too was uneasy. 'There are fires in their houses. I can smell the smoke.'

The trouble was these northern tribes had been antagonised by Weston's men (the young men he had asked to leave Plymouth and who had set up a colony at nearby Wessagusset) and those tribes were unpredictable. Not like their friend Massasoit, who they trusted. Right now they could be creeping up on them from behind, hidden by the scrub.

Hobomok came back presently. 'They sick,' he said. 'Fever. Many sick.'

Will relaxed a little, and at that moment the chief, Wituwamat, came out of his house to meet them. He evidently was not sick, for he stood tall and proud and muscled in front of Will, only half-clad. A few of his men came with him.

Will and Edward and Hobomok went forward to meet them. 'We wish to trade,' Will told him.

Wituwamat glared at him. 'No,' he said flatly.

Will did not need Hobomok to translate that. 'Ask him why not.' So Hobomok spoke.

Wituwamat answered. 'Eng'ish bad men,' he announced in English. 'Take from us.'

Will sighed heavily. Weston's men at Wessagusset had damaged their relations with the local Indians. 'That's all we need,' he said half to himself.

He did his best to pacify the Indian. 'We asked them to leave us,' he told them. 'They are young, inexperienced, suffer hardship.'

'They bad men,' Wituwamat insisted.

In his heart, Will had to agree. But bit by bit he calmed the chief down. He offered him gifts. Then he tried to trade.

Somewhat mollified Wituwamat agreed to trade, but asked exorbitant rates. Immediately Will realised what had happened. The men at Wessagusset, starving, desperate, had paid too high a price for corn, and ruined the trading. Simply put, Plymouth could not afford it.

Furious, Will tramped to the English settlement at Wessagusset.

John Sanders met him as he approached, and Will could not hide his dismay as he looked around him. The colony, if it could be termed a colony, consisted of half-built timber houses in a haphazard plan, with no protective fence, and even the forest had not been cleared around the camp. It was a sitting target for Indian attack. No fields appeared to have been cultivated. And the state of the men that met him told of starvation.

'Your improvidence has brought you to this,' he told Sanders forthrightly. 'I warned you that if you did not have discipline you would fail.'

'We have skins,' Sanders said sullenly. 'We can trade.'

'And how much do you pay for your corn?'

Sanders did not answer him directly, but dissembled.

'Well I can tell you that you have paid far too much! You have ruined the trade with the Indians here!'

'We needed the food.' Sanders said simply. 'We are starving here. You don't know what it's like—'

'I know exactly what it's like!' Will snapped. 'And that is why we do trade so we don't starve.' He ground his teeth in his exasperation. 'Where are your fields under cultivation?'

Sanders shrugged in a don't-know-don't-care attitude.

Will turned to walk away from him in his agitation, but turned back again. 'Do you know what you have done? You have ruined the trade here for us as well, and the good name that we have patiently built up with the Indians. We will have to go south to trade now.'

Sanders' eyes widened. 'Take us with you, so we can trade, too.'

A second time Will walked away from him and then came back again to face him. 'Tell me this, just why should I even consider you?'

'You have our ship, the *Swan*. You said we could share the trade.'

'I remember no such thing,' Will told him awfully. But he considered it. The Wessagusset men were in a pitiful state, and no matter what he thought of them, Will could not find it in him to leave them to starve. And he knew they would starve for he knew they could not for long pay the exorbitant prices for the corn that Wituwamat wanted. True, they had brought their problems on themselves, but how could he leave these dangerous children to die? He looked at them all, a pitiful sight if ever he had seen one, worse than he'd seen his people in at Plymouth.

He took a breath. 'Very well. We will set out for Nauset in the morning. Now I assume you can find us somewhere to sleep for the night?'

'What on earth possessed you to take Sanders' men with you?' Brewster demanded two weeks later as Will sat down wearily on the bench in the Brewsters' cottage and heaved off his shoes and hose.

'What else could I do? I couldn't leave them there to starve, which they would have done. They were almost starved as it was. Wituwamat would not trade except at inflated prices, and neither we nor they could afford it.'

'It was their own fault,' Brewster said and paraphrased a scripture, 'If a man doesn't work, then he shouldn't eat.'

'Well Jehovah does not say that to us, thankfully. He knows we're stupid and that we make daft decisions. But he keeps giving his love to us. Why should we not do the same to our fellow Englishmen?'

Mary Brewster brought a bowl of hot water for Will to put his feet in. 'I am pleased to hear you say that, Will,' she told him nodding approvingly, but with a withering look at her husband. 'We should show love to all of God's creatures, however silly they are.'

Will put a blistered foot into the bowl, and winced with the pain of it, then the other foot. 'I take it they haven't arrived yet with the ship?'

'No. Did you expect them to?'

'Well yes,' Will admitted.

Brewster shook his head at Will's naiveté. 'You won't see the ship or them again.'

'I don't think they dare cross us a second time,' Will said.

Mary put her hands on her hips. 'What happened?' she demanded of this almost-adopted son of hers.

Will took a breath. 'When we found we couldn't trade in Wessagusset, we took Sanders' men on the *Swan* to Nauset.'

'Where is that, exactly?' She had heard the name, but couldn't place it.

'South of here, at the bottom of Cape Cod Bay. We did some trading there, and with some other Indians nearby, but the sea was so rough, and it all but swamped the shallop, so that we could not take the corn aboard the pinnace. So, we stacked the corn, bought mats from the Indians, and covered the corn with them, and some sedge, and left it there.'

Mary put some cornbread in front of him. 'So where is it now?'

'Still there. I am paying an Indian who lives nearby to keep vermin and others away from it. Other Indians found the shallop buried in the sand at the high water mark with the things in it still in good condition, so I arranged for the Indians to keep an eye on it until I could send for it. We could not get back to the ship, for we had no boat, so we walked home. No doubt the ship will arrive here by and by.'

'No wonder you've got blisters,' Brewster remarked. 'But you don't really think the Wessagusset men will come here with our corn, do you?'

Will nodded, always ready to think the best of people. 'Yes I do.'

Brewster turned away and shook his head.

Thankfully, Will's faith in humanity was not misplaced, for the ship came in three days later.

But Will wasn't done. He knew they would not have enough even once they had retrieved the corn, so he set out again with Winslow and Hobomok and others and went inland to Nemasket where he traded with Corbitant, who he had once threatened to behead, and also arranged for the Indian women to take the corn back to Plymouth. Then he went to Manomet where he again had to leave the corn behind to be sent for later.

Once Standish recovered from his fever, Will sent him out to retrieve the shallop and the corn.

A short time later John Sanders sent a letter to Will from Wessagusset. They suffered so much from starvation, he said, might they take food from the Indians by force?

Will growled in his throat. 'Read that!' he invited Brewster, putting the letter in front of him.

Brewster read it, and then looked at Will, alarmed. 'They will bring the whole Indian nation down on our heads.'

'How can they even consider anything so blatantly suicidal?' Will demanded.

He wrote back that they should not under any circumstances take anything by force from the Indians. 'You have already endangered Plymouth as well as yourselves by stealing from the Indians and you must learn like Plymouth to live on ground nuts, clams and whatever else can be found until we are able to get provisions,' he told them roundly.

Standish returned from Nauset two weeks later, and sought out Will who was working in his new house to make it ready for Alice. The weather had turned bitterly cold, and there was no working in the fields until the ground softened in the spring.

'The Indians kept the corn and the shallop safe for us,' Standish reported, taking Will's hand, 'but they had taken some of our beads and some scissors and some other trifles. I made a show and marched some armed men up to Sachem Aspinet and demanded the return of everything. I refused too, their offer of hospitality, showing I was very offended. And sure enough the next day Aspinet came to me, bowing and licking my hand if you please, all the way up to the wrist, returning the beads and assured me that the thief had been punished. I tell you, these Indians are queer folk at times!

'And then when we got to Cummaquid the same thing happened! I told Iyanough I was not happy, and he suggested we send a man to look in the shallop—and there were the beads!'

Will chuckled. 'They had put them back there when you were not looking.'

'Aye! That's the right of it.'

Will was thoughtful. 'They are afraid of us, I think.'

'More than we are of them,' Standish agreed. 'But I think now we are on friendly terms. Perhaps they fear us less now that we trade with them, and they can see we mean them no harm.'

'Well let's hope the Wessagusset men hold to that,' and he told him about Sanders' letter.

Standish let his breath go in a whistle through his teeth. 'Them children at Wessagusset don't know what they do!' he said. 'They won't be here long at this rate. Either they will leave, or they will be killed.' He glanced out of the door he had left open. 'Hey! What's this?'

Will turned at the words, in time to see an Indian brave come running into the camp. Will dropped the plane he had been using and went outside, and the brave came right up to him. Someone grabbed his musket and took aim, but Will stopped him with a raised hand. 'No!'

The Indian, blissfully unaware that his life had almost ended at that moment, looked at Will with earnest black eyes. 'Massasoit, he sick, much sick.'

'Will he die?' Will asked.

'Massasoit die,' the Indian confirmed with an expressive gesture of his hand.

Will felt his heart sink, not only because they needed Massasoit's friendship, but also on account of the man himself, for whom Will had a liking. He said to the brave, 'It would be an act of kindness to send such things to Massasoit as would make his passing comfortable.'

Brewster who had joined Will and now stood beside him asked, 'Who will you send?'

Will's eyes fell on Edward Winslow, for he had found favour with Massasoit, and could speak a little of the Indian tongue.

Edward Winslow nodded, answering the unspoken question. 'Alright, I'll go.'

'You are the best man for the job,' Will told him bluntly, ignoring a protest from Susanna, Edward's wife.

Winslow raised a fair eyebrow. 'And if Massasoit dies?'

'Better hope he doesn't. Indeed, we are offering only to give him succour for his passing. Better take Hobomok with you.'

So, armed with blankets and some medicine made up by Sam Fuller, Edward Winslow and Hobomok set out for the Indian village.

Edward had been to the Indian village many times before, and had even been Massasoit's special guest on one occasion. Then he and Stephen Hopkins had slept with Massasoit and his wife and a couple of other braves in the one small house. That is, he had tried to sleep. The fleas, the lice, and the Indians' strange habit of singing themselves to sleep had prevented much more than one or two short naps. Still, as he walked into the Indian village, it became clear that he remained an object of curiosity to the women and the children and not a few of the men, not just because of his European origin, but also because of his yellow hair, pink-and-white skin and intensely blue eyes. They came out of their houses to watch and stare, and he felt his insides churn with that hint of fear that always assailed him on coming into Indian villages for he knew that if he should do something they disapproved of, he stood no chance.

Edward though showed no outward fear. He strode confidently up to Massasoit's house, from inside of which he could hear many people raising their voices in grief. He glanced at Hobomok who nodded, and pulling back the door covering, and, stooping to get through, he went inside.

The only light inside came from a fire in the middle of the house so large that the air was thick with heat and damp, and the smoke mingled with the acrid stench of unwashed bodies. Massasoit lay to one side from the tent opening, and the rest of the space was taken up by a multitude of people, chanting and wailing, and acting out acute grief.

'Who is it?' Massasoit asked in a weak voice, and the chanting and wailing stopped abruptly.

'Winsnow,' someone said.

They parted to allow Edward to edge through them to the bed. Massasoit lay there with his eyes closed, his face a picture of extreme suffering but he held out his hand. 'Are you Winsnow?' he asked his voice pathetic with sickness.

Winslow took his hand. 'Yes.'

'Oh, Winsnow, I shall never see you again!'

Having come to the end of his abilities with the Indian language, Edward spoke through Hobomok. 'Tell him that while the Governor himself could not come, he has sent some useful medicine which he hopes will make Sachem Massasoit well.'

'Ah—Eng'ish friends of Massasoit,' the chief whispered. He then invited him to sit on the edge of the bed which was better for Edward because he no longer needed to bend over to speak to the chief.

Seeming quite the officious doctor, Winslow inquired through Hobomok who stood beside him, 'When did you last sleep?'

'I sleep little,' Massasoit told him. 'I have a pain in my belly.'

'Hmm. When did you last eat?'

'Two days.'

'Hmm. When did you go to stool?'

'Six days.'

'Aha.' It did not take a genius to guess that Massasoit suffered from nothing worse than constipation. Anticipating something of the sort, the medicines Sam Fuller had armed him with contained just the very thing. He took a piece of the medicine on the point of his knife, and forced it between Massasoit's teeth. He gave him a good draft of medicine, and then Massasoit lay back as though half dead.

Everyone waited, peering at the chief, including Edward who was suddenly half afraid that he might have killed him. Then Massasoit let out a big sigh and opened his eyes.

'If you will send a messenger back to Plymouth, I will ask them to supply chickens and other medicine,' Edward said. All Englishmen knew from their mothers and grandmothers, that chicken broth was the sovereign remedy for just about any ill.

Massasoit weakly waved a hand in agreement, and Edward left him so that he could scribble a note on a piece of paper and send it with an Indian messenger back to Will.

However, Edward knew that the messenger would be at least two or three days in the dispatch. He wanted Massasoit to have the benefit of the broth now. Perhaps duck, which was also fowl after all and not so different to chicken, might do the trick. He went out hunting with some Indians and shot a duck at some six score paces which impressed the Indians no end.

Of course duck contained a good deal more fat than chicken. Cooking the broth over the fire, the scent of such a delicious food brought the much improved, and now starving chief from his bed.

'For Massasoit?' he asked.

'Yes indeed,' Edward told him. 'But I must draw off the fat first.'

'Never mind fat!' Massasoit announced, and grabbed the broth in the bowl from Edward, and ate the broth, fat and all. As Edward could have predicted had he been asked, it made the chief very sick and he brought up the broth again which started a nosebleed. To the Indians, a nosebleed was the sign of doom. Massasoit was obviously destined for the happy hunting grounds. They again started up the lament, the strange chanting, the wailing.

Edward looked up to heaven and prayed for patience. The nosebleed did not bode ill. 'Massasoit will not die,' he announced with such certainty that Massasoit looked at him intently. Surprised, the others stopped chanting again.

'Winsnow very good man, friend of Massasoit,' Massasoit proclaimed, much impressed. He was even more impressed when the nosebleed stopped a minute later just as Edward had predicted, and so did the wailing.

Then Massasoit slept. Edward stayed with him, just in case.

When he woke Edward bathed his face. 'Massasoit much better!' the chief announced delightedly, and suddenly plunged his whole face into the water, choked on it, snorted and started off the nosebleed once more. The other Indians once more gave up all hope, and began the wailing and chanting all over again. Edward could have cried with vexation.

'It will soon stop,' he told the chief. The Indians didn't believe him. They knew that when the nose bled, the patient would die, and they didn't let up on the wailing and dirges.

But the nosebleed did stop, and by the time the chickens came from Plymouth, Massasoit was so well that he decided to keep them for breeding. Wisely, Edward stopped nursing him or giving him any more medicine, for plainly the chief was as healthy as he was himself.

While Edward had been busy with Massasoit, the chief had other visitors. The news of the sickness of the great sachem Massasoit travelled far,' they said. 'We come to wail with the Wampanoag tribe.'

'There is no need,' Massasoit told them, coming from his tent to greet them. 'My friend Winsnow has made me well. Now I see the Eng'ish are my friends and do love me,' Massasoit announced. 'I will never forget this kindness they have shown me.' He beamed on Edward.

Edward was pleased with the accolade, for in being able to help Massasoit he had given Plymouth a strong ally, one that may prove invaluable. 'I shall leave now that the great Massasoit is well,' he announced.

Massasoit would have none of it. 'Winsnow stay, Winsnow feast with Massasoit,' he announced.

It would mean another night sharing the chief's tent with Massasoit, his wife and their friends, being serenaded to sleep, and being bitten alive. But Edward smiled. 'Thank you, that would be a pleasure.' He knew his where his duty lay when it came to cementing relations between the English and the Indians. *Ah, the things I do for Plymouth!* he thought.

FORTY-SEVEN
Wituwamat

New England, 1623

Edward stayed another day, but then insisted on making preparations to leave, packing up his things into a portable bundle, watched by a fascinated brood of Indian children. He no longer wore armour to come to the Indian camp, but the children were fascinated by his sword, which had been given to him by his father, an ornate affair with cut ironwork on the hilt.

'You like?' he asked, showing them the hilt, and the ornate scabbard.

They giggled at his atrocious accent, and then suddenly ran away to play.

'Children think Winsnow strange with yennow hair,' Hobomok explained as they trudged through the forest back to Plymouth.

Edward stepped over a fallen log, and glanced at Hobomok loping along beside him. 'I saw you talking with Massasoit,' he ventured. 'I think Massasoit spoke about me. What did he say?'

Hobomok took a breath. 'Massasoit speak well of Winsnow. Winsnow Massasoit's friend. In friendship Massasoit say to tell Winsnow Massachusetts Indians kill Eng'ish.'

Edward's heart turned over and he stopped walking in surprise. 'Why?'

Hobomok carried on walking, and Edward then had to run to catch up. 'Eng'ish steal corn from Indians.'

There was no denying it. Will had told him that he feared the Wessagusset men were raiding the Indians. He felt anger well up in him. Well, they had brought it on their own heads.

'Kill Eng'ish at Patuxet also,' Hobomok went on after a long pause.

The blood turned to ice in Edward's veins. Plymouth was in danger too. 'But why? We haven't hurt any Indians.'

'Because Patuxet brothers of Wessagusset. Patuxet Eng'ish kill Indians for kinning Wessagusset Eng'ish. Massasoit say Eng'ish Governor must seize chief ones at Wessagusset.'

'This is serious,' Edward said.

'Eng'ish all die,' Hobomok agreed matter-of-factly.

They tramped on in silence for a while as Edward chewed this information over in his mind. The men at Wessagusset deserved all they got, in his opinion, but to bring calamity on Plymouth at the same time was a different matter. He thought of the plantation, the women and children, of his own wife and step children, and Edward's anger seethed through his body at the injustice of it. However, the Indians were right. The English at

Plymouth would avenge the massacre of their people at Wessagusset. That was justice.

'Did you tell Massasoit that we have nothing to do with the men in Wessagusset?' Edward asked Hobomok.

'Massasoit know, so warn Winsnow.' He paused. 'Tell Eng'ish chief to take chief Indians at Wessagusset first.'

It had grown dusk, and they came to a clearing in the forest where another tribe had set up a village. 'We stay here tonight with Corbitant sachem of Narrangasett,' Hobomok announced, and Winslow understood that Hobomok had said all he intended to say on the matter of the impending attack.

On his return to Plymouth, Edward sought Will out and found him reading his Bible in his now-finished house. This was the house Will had built for Alice, a large room with the bed at one end screened from the rest of the room by a curtain, and above it two more beds behind a gallery. A huge stone fireplace stood against one wall, and a welcoming fire burned brightly in the hearth.

Will looked up as Edward came in the open door, then came to his feet, extending his hand in greeting. 'You have been successful?' he asked.

Edward took Will's hand in his, and shook it. 'Aye. Massasoit lives. Nothing worse than a bound up bowel.'

Will chuckled. 'Still, I have known men die of such a thing.'

Edward raised his brow. 'Massasoit was convinced he would die. And so were his people. You should have heard the noise! Wailing and warbling.'

'But he is well now.'

The smile vanished from Edward's face. 'Massasoit has sent a warning that the Massachusetts Indians intend to wipe out Weston's men at Wessagusset. Then, when we avenge their massacre, to wipe us out also. He advises you to deal with the trouble-makers, the head ones.'

'Who is behind it?'

'Hobomok didn't say. But the chief of the Massachusetts Indians is Wituwamat.'

'I mislike it,' Will said, rubbing his hand over his small beard thoughtfully.

Edward said, 'Massasoit is not with them in this. He makes it clear that he is our friend.'

'Then we must take his warning seriously.'

'This could be the end of us,' Edward said quietly.

'God is with us,' Will replied. 'Who will be against us? Have faith my friend, and we shall deal with this also.'

Will knew that he must take decisive action. He considered the situation from every angle. As a Christian he had no wish to kill anyone, whether Indian or of any other nation. All life came from God and was therefore sacred. But equally, the lives of those within the two settlements, here at Plymouth and there at Wessagusset, were just as precious. To allow the slaughter of so many settlers when it was within his power to do something about it would be an act of criminality in the extreme. How could he justify such negligence before his God? He had to act, and quickly, to avoid a massacre the like of which had happened in Virginia. There the Indians had wiped out the colony by all accounts.

The one person he most needed to discuss it with was Miles Standish, but he had been away for several days on an expedition to bring back the corn Will had left at Manomet, and Will had no idea when he would be back. If Standish did not make haste, Will would have to send someone else, someone not so fitted for the task. Only Miles Standish had the experience as a soldier, and the training and ability to carry out what Will had in mind.

Will prayed and fretted about it for another day so it was with profound relief that he heard the lookout announced the return of the trading party, and then saw Standish striding confidently up the street towards his house.

Will met him at the door. 'You had a successful trip?'

Standish nodded. 'Aye. We traded well. Is all well here?'

'Massasoit had a bound up bowel and was convinced he would die. Master Winslow took some medicine with him which has made him well again.' He looked closely at Standish. 'What is it? Something has happened?'

'Aye.' Standish propped his musket against the cottage wall. 'We went to Manomet, to trade, and this Indian chief came into the camp, Wituwamat by name. He's a big fellow, an evil-looking beggar if ever I saw one, a warrior.'

'I know him,' Will told him grimly.

'He went up to Canacum, the sachem, and gave him a dagger which he took from around his neck.' He imitated the movements of the Indian, strong definite movements. 'I guessed this boded ill, especially as he kept looking at us in a meaningful way. I tried to listen, but I couldn't make head or tail of it, though I know a little Indian now. He spoke too quickly for me, and in a different dialect. But I didn't like the sound of it, or the look of it. No.' He paused thinking about it. 'He was very audacious towards us—hostile even.'

Will's thoughts flitted to the warning Massasoit had given him. He said to Standish, 'Wituwamat, is the chief of the Massachusetts Indians, near Wessagusset. What did you think all this posturing meant?'

Standish met his eyes squarely. 'I think he means war against us, and he was trying to drum up Canacum's support.'

It agreed with what Massasoit had told Hobomok. Will looked up at a clear blue sky and let his breath go through his teeth. He felt that coiling in his insides, that serpent of dread, which warned him of big trouble. Then he focused again on Standish. 'Massasoit warned us of this. The men at Wessagusset have caused real problems with the Indians because of their thievery. Wituwamat has reason to seek vengeance. However, by attacking Wessagusset, Wituwamat hopes to provoke us into coming to their aid, or avenging them, for that is what the Indians would do. Then they have the perfect excuse to wipe us out.'

Standish let his breath go in a whistle. 'The dirty . . .'

'Just so.'

'What'll you do?'

Will compressed his lips. 'What do you think I will do?'

'Man coming in!'

Will's heart turned over at the lookout's warning. Perhaps it had already happened, and they not ready. He grabbed his musket from the place by the fire and ran outside ready to give orders for defence. However, it was an Englishman with a pack on his back running from the direction of the north. He ran for all he was worth, looking behind him all the while. He stumbled in the gates and all but fell at Will's feet.

'Close the gates,' he cried. 'I am being followed!'

'Close the gates,' Will ordered. 'Men to arms!'

Immediately the settlers burst into activity. Women grabbed the children and took them inside the common house. The men ran for their muskets, and hurriedly primed and loaded them, and then took up positions on the palisade. Will searched the trees for any sign of life, his heart pumping in his ears. Perhaps he had waited too long. *Dear God, how can we defend ourselves?* He remembered all too vividly the tales of the massacre in Virginia. Surely they had not come all this way to die in the same way.

'I think I lost them,' the man said coming up beside Will as he leaned against the palisade with his musket trained on the distant trees.

Will looked at the man. He was no more than twenty, unshaven, and dirty, and his clothes were rags. Will knew him for one of those who had gone to settle in Wessagusset. Will's eyes narrowed suspiciously. 'You said you were being followed.'

'I was—but I lost them.'

Will glared at him. He could do without panicking his people unnecessarily. He lowered his own musket. 'Keep a lookout,' he ordered

Miles Standish.

He marched off to Mary Brewster and the man trotted along behind him. 'You have some cold venison?' he asked her curtly.

She raised her brows at him, and then glanced at the visitor. She knew Will well enough not to be offended when someone else had upset him. Without a word she brought out food, and gave it to the traveller, and he wolfed it down like some starved animal.

Will sat opposite him at the table and watched him eat, assessing him. Ah yes, he was one of the trouble-makers of Weston's group. 'So what has brought you here?' he demanded abruptly.

'We are in terrible danger in Massachusetts Bay,' he said chewing noisily on the meat. 'We are starving, many of our people are sick and some have died.' He swallowed and then drank some of the water they had provided. 'Daily we are threatened by the Indians. We will all be knocked in the head shortly, I reckon.'

'And why do they threaten you?' Will asked.

The man looked at him, then looked away shiftily. 'I dunno.'

Will's jaw knotted. He didn't have much time for these lazy undisciplined idiots who put themselves and others in danger. 'I think you do. I think that despite our warnings, your people steal from the Indians.'

'Some do.'

'Then what do you expect?' Will's voice vibrated with suppressed anger, and the man quailed before him. 'Tell me,' he went on through gritted teeth, 'what man, whether Indian or English, wants to work the land and plant and weed and dress corn only to have some ne'er-do-well steal it from under his nose?'

The man's eyes widened. 'But we were starving.'

'And so? Can you not do as we do, and eat lobster and ground nuts? Are you so useless that you cannot even do that? Improvidence brings you to want. You are all of you ramshackle fellows, thinking you can live off other men instead of working for yourselves. Have you ploughed and tilled the land? No? I thought not. No, your people stole from us, and you still steal. Thieves all of you, and your thievery will kill us all!'

The man stopped eating at this tirade and fixed fearful eyes on Will. 'So you will not help us?'

Will folded his arms across his broad chest. 'You have brought your misfortunes on yourselves.'

There was a dreadful silence where the man could only stare at Will. Mary Brewster, hovering in the background, working at her women's work, also stopped and looked at him, waiting.

Will ground his teeth. 'But no, we will not stand by and see you murdered, even though 'tis no more than you deserve.'

The man shuddered visibly. 'I wish I had not come to this God-forsaken land.'

'Do not blaspheme! Better wish you had come with men of wisdom and intelligence,' Will said acidly.

He left him, and called the council together in the Common House where they sat down around the rough-sawn table.

They began with a prayer. Then Will, his elbows resting on the table, his chin on his fists, addressed them. 'As you already know, the man from Wessagusset has confirmed what Massasoit has told us, namely that the Massachusetts Indians intend to seek recompense from those men who have stolen from them and who have caused them anguish. Their sachem Wituwamat has decided to get rid of the settlers there.'

'Well 'tis no more than they deserve,' Billington observed flatly.

'Even so we cannot stand by and allow that to happen, Master Billington.'

Brewster stepped in. 'The fact is, Master Billington, the plot by the Indians is to annihilate us as well, simply because we are white too.'

'In that case, we strike first,' Miles Standish announced.

Will pursed his lips. 'I am unwilling to go to war, gentlemen, for we came here to teach these natives, not to kill them. However, we cannot stand by and let the men in Wessagusset be massacred without some kind of effort to stop it. So I ask you for your guidance, as to what I should do.'

In fact Will already knew what he ought to do. However, he needed their agreement, so he waited for their input.

'Can we not bribe the Indians?' Isaac Allerton asked.

'What with?' Will demanded. 'We have little enough for ourselves.'

'Or perhaps we could go to them and sue for peace,' Edward Winslow suggested. 'You know—talk with them.'

'Are you willing to try?' Will asked, impressed by this bravado in the face of almost certain death.

Winslow puffed out his cheeks, turning it over in his mind, and Will could see that he was willing, but not eager, to try.

'No,' Will said, 'I will not send a man to his death.'

John Billington put in, 'I reckon we should go north to Wessagusset and kill the lot of them Indians before they kill us.'

'I've already said I don't like that idea,' Will countered. 'It's murder, especially when there are women and children involved.'

'Not them—just the men.'

'And what do you think those who are children now will do when they grow old enough, eh? Besides, it is not in accord with justice. The rest of the people had nothing to do with Wituwamat's decision.'

'I could go,' Standish said, his eyes glowing at the thought, 'and challenge Witwaumat, the sachem to a duel. He is the ring-leader, I'll wager.'

'If they all attack we will not stand a chance,' Isaac Allerton said. 'The way I see it, you have no choice, Will, but to send someone to deal with this Wituwamat.'

Will rubbed his hand over his face. 'I don't want any man's death on my conscience,' he said.

Brewster said, 'Better for one man to die than for all to die.'

Will thumped the table with a clenched fist. He didn't want to do it, but he had been manipulated into an impossible position and he had to act.

Everyone looked at him nervously. Then Brewster said calmly. 'You are our Governor. You take whatever steps you think necessary.'

Isaac Allerton agreed. 'Whatever you do we will support you.'

Will put his head in his hands for a long moment. He prayed silently, for he knew what he must do. The lives of every Englishman in New England depended upon him. He looked up. 'Master Standish, are you willing to go to Wessagusset and deal with Wituwamat as you said?'

Standish bristled with pride. 'Yessir.'

'Do you think you will have success?'

'I have dealt with worse than that Indian can offer.'

'In that case, I will send you Captain Standish with eight men to Wessagusset, under the pretence of trading with the Massachusetts. Bring me back the head of Wituwamat.'

Standish stood up and nodded. 'I will, Governor, I will.'

'For all our sakes, May God go with you.'

As Captain Standish approached the clearing at Wessagusset where Weston's men had built their settlement, he uttered an oath in his throat. For where Plymouth boasted a house for every family and a plot of garden, all in nice neat little rows with a street down the middle, the Weymouth men had just a few half-finished buildings, all in a huddle. It smacked of disorder, and slapdash work.

John Sanders met Standish as he entered the compound at Wessagusset. Sanders, looking dishevelled and careworn, was the leader of this rabble. Quickly Sanders told him of their plight.

'We have been threatened by the Indians. They come here posturing and making noises like war.'

'We have heard the same.' Standish said. 'Is there anything to eat here?'

'We have nothing.'

Standish had expected as much. 'Powder and shot?'

'We are sick, starving.' They were not interested in powder and shot.

They were all unshaven and unwashed too, men who had lost all self-respect. Standish was disgusted. 'Come we will show you and your men to your quarters.'

The others surrounded them, and cheered as they marched through their village to the half-finished house allotted to them.'

'We are here to stop Wituwamat,' Standish told Sanders.

John Sanders' eyes seemed to pop out of his head. 'You are going to kill him?'

'If the good Lord gives me strength.'

'How?'

'You shall see. We must stop him before he slaughters the lot of you! Not that it's not what you deserve! I am only surprised he has taken so long for him to come to that decision. Your thieving, and plundering have brought us to this.'

'Don't pretend you've come for our sakes,' Sanders said bluntly. 'You've come to save your own skins!'

'Aye. Once the Indians have finished with you, they'll come to Plymouth.' He leaned on his musket and fixed Sanders with his eyes. 'At any rate, the Governor says we cannot stand by and see you slaughtered, though for myself I don't see why we should interfere. If the Indians want revenge then so be it, I reckon.'

Sanders glowered at Standish's forthrightness, but fear overcame ire. 'What makes you so sure we're in for attack?' he demanded.

'You have an undisciplined rabble here, Master Sanders. And you would do well to look to them better in future.' He ran his eyes contemptuously over the man. 'We have received reports at Plymouth—notably from Massasoit.'

'So you think that will be the end of us.' He sounded as though he did not believe it.

Standish sighed impatiently. 'Master Sanders, The Indians are quite within their rights to deal with you as they see fit. Now, if you wish to die at their hands, that is your problem. But the people at Plymouth are our responsibility. We have women and children to protect. Now I suggest you co-operate.' He took a deep breath and his eyes wandered to the forest surrounding the colony. 'I suggest you bring in any of your men who are out in the woods for their own safety.'

Convinced at last, Sanders compressed his lips thoughtfully. 'The Indians come here often,' he said. 'Ostensibly to trade. More likely to see what we're up to, I reckon.'

'When are they likely to come again?'

'Any time. Two or three days perhaps.'

'Well, when they come next, we will deal with them,' Standish replied, and wandered off.

While he waited for the next Indian visit, Standish bullied the Wessagusset men into some sort of order, splitting them into two watches, naval style, and making sure their muskets were in order. However, they did not have enough muskets to go round. A disorganised rabble, he thought contemptuously. All around him the want of women showed in the lack of hygiene, in the general disarray. Good women kept their men in order.

To their credit, and Standish's surprise, the Wessagusset men did not dissolve into weak-kneed fear. Instead they listened to Standish's instructions, and responded promptly by working on their defences. Even so, it was too little, too late.

Surveying their efforts Standish knew that if the Indians attacked in force, not a man would be left alive. They could not fight them off, for their defences were not of the calibre of those at Plymouth. In the time it took to load and fire a musket the Indians could run hundreds of yards, and breach any defence. They were vulnerable. No, Standish knew that his only hope lay in a one-to-one combat with Wituwamat. If he could defeat the chief, the Indians would be shocked into disunity, while his own standing as the victor, the white man, would grow enormously. But if he failed, then the life of every white person in New England would be forfeit.

Yet he was unafraid. Excited by the prospect, yes, and anxious that so much hung on him. Yet not actually afraid.

Although impressed by the efforts of the Wessagusset men, Standish would never be satisfied that they were ready. So it was with foreboding that a few days after his arrival, Standish was called from his scant breakfast by the cry of 'Indian!' from the lookout.

He was joined outside by Sanders. 'That is Pecksuot, one of the Massachusetts braves,' Sanders said.

Standish had seen him before with Wituwamat in Nauset. Pecksuot, a man in the prime of his life, swaggered into the camp, posturing and pouting and uttering dark threats in his Indian tongue. He certainly had not come to trade.

While the Wessagusset men looked on fearfully, Standish stood with his arms folded, wholly unimpressed by this arrogant display.

Recognising Standish, Pecksuot gabbled more threats this time walking right up to Standish, and with gestures and proud tosses of his head no doubt told him what he thought of him. Then he turned and walked away.

Standish did not move, but continued watching the Indian as he left.

A short time later Wituwamat, strode haughtily into the village, with Pecksuot and stood in the middle of the clearing, his black eyes sweeping over the men there. Then his eyes rested on Standish, once more standing with his arms folded across his chest.

'We know why Eng'ish come here,' Wituwamat said to Standish.

Standish had enough of the Indian language to understand him if he spoke slowly, which he did.

'And why might that be?' Standish asked.

'You come to defend Eng'ish brothers.'

'And so?'

Pecksuot spoke up, with emotional bravado at variance to Wituwamat's cool arrogance. 'Though you are a great captain, yet you are but a little man.'

It was true enough! Standish, always embarrassed by his lack of inches, and especially so when faced with tall enemies, bristled. Pecksuot continued, 'I am no sachem, yet I am a man of strength and courage. You are weak like a woman!'

'You have courage enough to fight and kill me? Man to man?' Standish challenged.

'I kill a little man like you, no trouble!'

'We shall see!'

'Tomorrow!'

'Tomorrow!' Standish agreed.

This was what Standish had been waiting for. He turned his back on the Indians dismissively, and Wituwamat and Pecksuot walked away.

'You can't fight Pecksuot,' Sanders said appalled. 'You don't know what these savages are capable of.'

Miles Standish smiled slightly. 'I think you don't know what *I'm* capable of, Master Sanders!'

Sanders glared at him. 'You bring them all on us! They will slaughter us because of your audacity. I wish you will leave us.'

'You are a cowardly nave!' Standish told him roundly, and marched off.

Despite the coming duel, Standish slept well. Only in the morning did he think seriously on what he attempted to do. Then his blood was up, the fighting spirit strong in his veins. Fear did not come into it. He was confident of his own abilities, and confident that God would help him in this, that right was on his side.

He knew the lives of everyone in New England rested on him. It was a huge responsibility, and he took a leaf out of the Pilgrims' book and prayed to a God he only dimly knew about.

When Wituwamat and his younger brother, and Pecksuot and another brave strode purposefully into the English camp, Standish did feel fear snaking in his belly sending the blood pumping in his veins, heightening his senses, focusing his brain.

Wituwamat, dressed for combat, wearing only a loin cloth despite the cool weather, was also calm, hatred for this arrogant little Englishman burning in his eyes. Wituwamat was much bigger than Standish, an accomplished fighter, probably the victor of many such duels.

It had been a long time since Standish had fought in hand to hand combat. For though the Pilgrims might be God-fearing and peaceable men, wherein lay their strength, Standish was not one of them, and never would be. His military training told him that force was the only thing bullies like Pecksuot and Wituwamat knew.

'You are brave fellows,' Standish challenged. 'You come together to fight one man.'

'We are brave men,' Wituwamat insisted angrily. 'Indian fight man to man.'

'In the house?' Standish dared them indicating a cottage that was not yet complete.

There was room in the cottage for only the combatants, and perhaps some onlookers. He did not want any of his men in there interfering. He did not want their calls and cheers and encouragement. He wanted to concentrate on the foe.

Seeing that this might be to their advantage, the Indians took up the challenge. 'In the house,' Wituwamat agreed.

To show that he was not afraid he tossed his head, and marched ahead of the others to the house.

'You are mad!' Sanders hissed in Standish's ear as he strode towards the cottage. 'They will murder you.'

'If they do, my men will kill them all,' Standish told him.

'I beg you to cry off from this.'

Standish stopped walking and turned to fix the man with clear grey eyes. 'Cry off? Don't you know the lives of nearly two hundred people rest on me? You, man, have your brains addled!'

'But if you are beaten, we will all be dead!'

'Then,' Standish replied resuming his walking, 'you had better hope that I am not beaten!'

Wituwamat and the other Indians as well as all the men in the Wessagusset settlement, waited for Standish outside the cottage.

'Little Eng'ish afraid,' Pecksuot said with a look of smug satisfaction on his face.

Hearing him as he approached, Standish met his eyes with a fierce unblinking gaze. Then, quite deliberately, Standish took off his coat, and his shirt, and stood bare-chested in the cool breeze.

Standish spoke to Wituwamat. 'You and me and your men in this house,' he said slowly and distinctly so that Wituwamat could understand his use of the Indian language. Then he addressed the Englishmen. 'I am going into this house with these Indians. No-one is to come in unless any of us calls from inside. Understood?'

They murmured and looked at each other, and shifted uncomfortably. 'Understood?' Standish repeated.

The moment had come. Wituwamat, Pecksuot, Wituwamat's eighteen year old brother, and the other brave filed into the cottage. Standish took a deep steadying breath, stilling his suddenly coiling insides, and followed them.

'Lock the door!' Standish commanded over his shoulder, and he heard the sound of the wooden bar being fitted home.

The half-clad Indians looked about them, quickly assessing the confined space, then turned to face him. It was quite dim in the cottage, only one window, unglazed, and covered with oil-soaked paper, giving enough light to see by.

Standish stood in the middle of the floor, quietly, waiting, his eyes on all the Indians at once. He didn't dare take his eyes off any one of them. His fear had vanished. He was icy calm, determined. He uttered a quick prayer and drew his large hooked Damascus blade from his belt.

Pecksuot came forward first, knife in hand, menacing, circling, looking for advantage in light or surroundings. Pecksuot had challenged Standish first, had called him small and insignificant. A mere Englishman. Probably Wituwamat, the chief, had thought Pecksuot would make short work of the Englishman.

Standish gripped his own knife in his fist, and circled too, keeping the Indian in front of him. Then he attacked. Pecksuot danced back out of the way, his eyes wide with surprise at the speed with which the blade came within an inch of his bare brown skin. Hatred flashed into his eyes. Standish smiled grimly. He knew that hatred and anger were the enemies of victory.

They circled again. Pecksuot attacked, and Standish side-stepped neatly, ready to lunge with his own knife.

The battle was deadly and silent. Only the heavy breathing of the sweating combatants, of men evenly matched in strength as they wrestled together, filled the room. Again Pecksuot came at Standish, and Standish grabbed his wrist. They pushed apart and stood facing each other, bodies tensed, feet spread to balance. Then Pecksuot came at him again. Standish had knowledge of his opponent now, saw it coming, side-stepped and his knife blade slid in between the Indian's ribs. Pecksuot went down without a sound, his eyes wide with surprise.

Standish pulled the blade out with an effort and stood still watching the man's blood pumping over the dirt floor. The killing madness pulsed through him, predatory, deadly. He was not done yet. He faced the others, waiting for the next challenger.

The Indian brave pulled Pecksuot's body away, and Wituwamat the chief came forward, knife ready. He was wary, his eyes watching Standish's every move, eager to avenge Pecksuot's death.

Standish was ready for him. He did not underestimate the Indian. Wituwamat was a skilled fighter, and he moved with the grace of a cat, with deadly precision.

He waited for his advantage, saw it, and with lightning speed, the knife flashed. It caught Standish's bare sweating arm a glancing blow. But his senses were tuned to the Indian and he hardly noticed it, even when the blood began to flow.

The Indian danced out of the way of Standish's great hooked blade, and Standish began deliberately to gasp, as though short of breath. The Indian smiled. He could taste victory, and it made him careless. He came at Standish, the blade raised high, leaving his belly undefended.

Standish found his mark and Wituwamat died.

It was the turn of the other Indian brave. He did not give Standish time to recover from Wituwamat's death, neither did he remove the body, but came straight at Standish. In a flash Standish pushed the man's arm out of the way with his own arm, bringing the Indian in close. His blade severed the man's jugular and sliced through his windpipe, almost decapitating him. He fell to the earth, not killed outright, but writhing, eyes wide with terror. In a few seconds his lifeblood puddled on the floor and he too slid into death.

That left the eighteen-year-old brother of Wituwamat.

He stared at the fallen men, and then at Standish with shocked eyes. He was a young man. Almost a child, Standish thought. Not yet full grown. He made no move to engage Standish in a fight.

With the dead men at his feet, their blood soaking the dirt floor, Standish looked at him. 'I ain't into killing babes,' he said disparagingly in the Indian tongue, and in truth the killing madness already cooled in his veins, and a sudden excruciating weariness washed over him. He knew a moment of regret that men's lives had ended, but he was a soldier. He had done what he had to do for the good of the colony, to save the lives of others.

He called to those outside to unbar the door which they did, and then Sanders and others came in. They stopped on the threshold, seeing the three dead bodies, the boy standing in the corner, the blood soaking into the dirt on the floor, and Standish victorious, his sweating oily torso and his hands drenched in the blood of the dead men. As they watched, he calmly picked up his Damascus blade and hacked the head off Wituwamat's body, severing it between the vertebrae. This same man had insulted him at Manomet not too long ago. It satisfied a grudge as well as the governor's orders.

Sanders vomited on the dirt floor.

Taking the head by the hair, Standish walked out of the cottage. 'What about this one?' someone called after him.

Standish turned around. 'Let him go, he's just a boy.'

He was too weary to do more. With the head swinging grotesquely at his side by its long black hair he marched to the cottage where he had spent the night. Behind him he heard the men turn into a mob. There would be no mercy for the Indian boy. He had killed three Indians by himself. It would take a mob to kill one Indian boy.

They took away the young Indian and hanged him from a tree.

'What'll you do now?' Standish asked Sanders as he picked up the blood-stained canvas bag.

Sanders took a breath and looked at the hills and the forest around the colony. 'We will go home.'

'Home?' Standish was disgusted. 'Home? It'll be safe now with Wituwamat dead. They ain't going to bother you now.'

'These men, they can't take any more. We are sick of struggling to eke out a living in a wilderness, of being in daily fear of either starvation or massacre. We're going back to England.'

'I see.'

'We will leave immediately for the Maine coast to seek passage home.'

'Then God go with you,' Standish said.

'And with you, sir.'

Standish headed back to Plymouth with his men and Wituwamat's head.

Will waited for him, and was pleased to see the little band come out of the trees and stride confidently into Plymouth.

The people lined the single street, and clapped and shouted their approval as Standish marched up to Will. He dropped the bloodstained bag in the dust.

'That is Wituwamat's head,' he said.

Will took a deep thankful breath in which he could smell the stench of rotting meat, then he picked up the bag, opened it, and tipped the contents on to the dirt.

The skin had shrivelled and developed a greenish glow about it, and the eyes stared sightlessly back at Will, the black hair matted and caked with blood and earth, and the final wound where it had been taken from the body, like a piece of maggoty rotting meat. Yet Will recognised the chief of the Massachusetts Indians.

It had no effect on him except relief that the threat had passed. 'Fix it to the fort,' he said.

And there it stayed until it was unrecognisable, just as London bridge was decorated with the heads of state criminals.

The English victory brought a reaction throughout the area. The other tribes who had also been in the conspiracy were so amazed and terrified that one white man could kill three strong and experienced Indians that they left their homes and hid themselves in the swamps and other uninhabitable places. Many became sick, and died, including three friendly sachems: Canacum of Manomet, Aspinet of Nauset and Iyanough the gentle hospitable sachem of Mattachiest (Cummaquid). It had the effect of ensuring that the Indians were fearful of crossing the English. Evidently the English had a powerful God. Plymouth entered into a new period of peace.

However, the victory sat ill on Will. While Standish may have been the executioner, Will knew he was responsible, and he could not see it as a great victory. He had acted because he had to protect his people, and he had done it in a way that cost the fewest lives. All-out war would have cost many more. Even so, he regretted it, and found it difficult to justify before his God. Had not Jesus said *'Love your enemies'*? Love did not allow for killing them!

Yet, he was the governor. His was the responsibility to protect these people. He had acted as he must. He groaned within himself. He did not want the responsibility. He had never wanted to be governor, did not want to have to make these decisions. But someone had to do it. He leaned his elbows on the table in his small cottage and put his head in his hands in something akin to despair, and he prayed.

FORTY-EIGHT
Thomas Weston

Plymouth, 1623

The storage house was just about empty. In dismay Will looked at the dwindling heap of corn and shook his head. 'It isn't enough!' he said to Isaac Allerton. 'It will not get us through to the harvest.'

'Then we'll have to trade again,' Allerton said.

Will made a noise in his throat. 'Let us hope that this year, with the different system, we will have a better harvest.'

'It would be good if we had enough to feed any newcomers, since we always seem to be feeding an army!' Allerton observed. He stroked the whiskers on his chin. 'Another bad harvest will see the failure of this colony, Will, and very likely all of us either dead or gone back to Leyden.'

'I know it. We cannot go on as we are.' And really who had a wish to when it was so difficult just to survive? Weak as they were, death in the shape of sickness, or vulnerability in the face of attack, was a real prospect.

They left the store room, and Will closed the door. He did not lock it. He had to trust the settlers. After all, it belonged to all of them. Were it not for hunting and fishing they would have starved long ago, but a man needed more than meat to live on.

He stood with his hands on his hips looking at the compound. It had become a small village now, a single street with houses and little gardens off each side, all enclosed by a palisade and huge gates. On the hill overlooking the village, was the wooden fort with the big guns. It would break his heart to leave it now, after all they had gone through, to give up and go back to Leyden and the city. They had achieved so much. Reliance on God, discipline, and good organisation had brought them civilisation in a wilderness. When he thought how the men at Wessagusset had failed because of not having discipline, he was justly proud of his little group. He thought of the trials and the hard work, and the sickness which had claimed so many lives. It was nothing short of a miracle that they were still here. It would be a disaster to lose it all because of famine, after all that sacrifice.

He went into his cottage. The cottages, were small, like the peasant cottages in England, single-roomed affairs. At one end was the entrance, and the storeroom for dried vegetables and fish, and whatever else the housewife needed. The fireplace, built of what stone they could find, cemented with the same clay that they made pots from, stood in the middle and was the hub of family life. Here the housewife would cook, and the family would sit and talk in the evening. At the other end of the cottage, was the sleeping area. Two full-sized pallet beds fitted end to end across the width of the house, divided in the middle by a wooden screen, and above them on a wooden platform or gallery, were two more. You could just about fit eight adults in if they didn't mind sharing, or even more children. And there was room for guests on the dirt floor. There were two windows, on either side of the room, but no glass. They used oiled paper, for that was all they had, and shutters kept out bad weather.

Will sat down at the large refectory table, where he had an assortment of books and papers. He lived here alone, and did his own cooking, when he didn't eat with the Brewsters. He had built the house with his own hands ready for Alice and her boys if she chose to come. And for Jonathan his own son too. There was space enough for everyone, plus some, and no doubt that too would be needed, for indeed with newcomers arriving unexpectedly as they had a habit of doing, housing was always at a premium. For the moment, though, he enjoyed his new-found solitude.

He opened the journal, his record of life at Plymouth, and dipped his pen in the ink. He was writing at this moment about the difficulties they had in getting away from Leyden, finding a ship. He paused as he read the last part he had written, and suddenly remembered how he had gone to London to help sort out the stalemate between Weston's group and the Leyden Pilgrims. Of course that was when he had stayed with Alice and Edward Southworth.

Alice. The thought of her made his stomach slide. Just thinking about her made him want her here with him so badly that it became a physical pain. He had asked her, and she had said she would come. Oh how he wanted her to come! He needed her by his side as his helpmeet, his wife.

But what had he asked her to come to? A half-civilised country, with savages, and starvation, and petty quarrels. How would she cope? What if she hated it here?

Yet he knew how she would cope. She would be practical, and efficient. She would not cry like Dorothy would, because she had no new dress, no hat, or because she couldn't get the linen whiter than snow! She wouldn't panic because they were on half rations, or complain when her husband already had enough to deal with. He had seen her cope with poverty and sickness in London, and he knew she had the qualities required of a wilderness wife. But that wasn't why he had asked her to come. His asking her had nothing to do with logic and ability. He wanted her with a deep instinctive need, which even three years and an ocean's distance had not dimmed.

How long must he wait? How much longer till he could ease this gnawing hunger inside him?

With a struggle he brought his mind back to the task in hand and re-

read the last few lines of what he had written in his journal. He decided to include a letter that he had in his possession which Robert Cushman had written at the time, when he had angrily remonstrated with them over the affair of making provisions. Now where had he put it? He knew exactly and he frowned at the chest standing in the corner. The letter was in there, but it would be down the bottom, beneath hundreds of other documents.

He had just willed himself to get up and get it when a commotion outside took his attention.

'Stranger! Stranger coming in!'

Will frowned. If this had been an Indian visitor, the lookout—the boy Billington in this case—would have said so. As for an Englishman, well, the men at Wessagusset had all gone home. Wherever had this one come from?

He put down his pen, closed the book and went out of his cottage into the cold of late winter to gaze down the single street to the gates. Everyone else too came out to look at this rare occurrence.

The visitor staggered towards the gates, and then leaned against the paling fence, hardly able to stand. As people rushed to help him, Will strode down the street wondering who could possibly have come here. With all the Wessagusset men gone, there were no other Englishmen for over a hundred miles. Or so he thought.

The visitor had evidently travelled some distance, and undergone extreme hardship. Will could well believe it. Without a guide, this was no place to be wandering about. His clothes were ragged, and he was dirty and unshaven, and his hair hung 'like eagles' feathers'. But as Will peered into the thin shrewish face, he realised that he knew the man.

'Master Weston?'

Thomas Weston looked back at Will through pitiful little black eyes. 'Master Bradford! Thank God!'

Taken aback, Will looked him up and down. Could this possibly be the swaggering overbearing man who had dealt so haughtily with them when they tried to leave Southampton? And what on earth was he doing here when they had thought him safely in London? 'What has happened?'

'I have fallen on hard times, Master Bradford, hard times. Can you spare a little food?'

Two men helped him into the Brewster house and sat him down at the rough-sawn table. Mary Brewster brought some cold roast fowl, and some corn meal bread, which Weston ate greedily without even saying thanks either to Mary or to God. Will and Brewster sat down with him, and a speaking look at the door sent the others back to their work.

'This has not been an easy journey,' Weston told Will and Brewster, wolfing down the meat as though he had not eaten for at least a week. 'I came on one of the fishing ships, under an assumed name, and pretending to be a blacksmith.'

'Why under an assumed name?' Brewster asked, surprised, but he got no answer. Weston only shrugged. The man liked his secrets.

'I left the ship in a boat, but we were wrecked in a storm. I tell you those fellows in the boat didn't know what they were about! Indeed, the boat is now at the bottom of the bay, and had I not been able to swim, Master Bradford, I would not be here now! No not at all.' He tore a leg from the fowl and bit into the flesh with relish. 'I was thrown up at a place called, I believe, Piscataqua—' later called Strawberry Bank and then renamed Portsmouth '—and fell into the hands of the Indians, who took everything I had managed to rescue from the sea, and even my very clothes, and my shirt! I was mother naked! And an amusing sight they thought it too!' His little black eyes kindled as he recalled this insult to his dignity. 'Eventually, I got to the settlement at Piscataqua and borrowed a suit of clothes and managed to come here to you.'

'And what do you want with us, Master Weston?' Will asked, his anger igniting in his belly as he remembered all his grievances against this man. 'Because as you can see we have little enough for ourselves. And as for the men you sent to us, they have eaten up what little we did have!'

Weston bit back whatever retort came to his lips. He was not stupid and knew that now was not the time to air his own grievances if he wanted help. 'I would borrow beaver from you.'

'Borrow, Master Weston?' Brewster looked him up and down meaningfully. 'And just how do you think you would repay us?'

'I have hope of a ship with supplies coming to me here, and then you may have whatever you need.' He smiled in what he hoped was a winning way.

Will did not believe him. He had long ago learnt to distrust anything Weston said.

Weston had finished his meal, so Will stood up. 'You had better billet with me,' he said and, without waiting for his guest, left Brewster's house and marched up the street.

Belatedly remembering his manners, Weston thanked Mary Brewster for his food, and then ran after Will, struggling in his pitiful state to catch up with him.

'We have nothing, Master Weston,' Will snapped as Weston did his best to fall into step beside him. He was a short man with short legs, and they could not keep pace with Will's long angry strides. 'Not supplies, not even much beaver. For it may have escaped your memory that you have sent us nothing but people, to eat what little we do have!'

'Now I told you in my letter, Master Bradford, that was not my fault.

The Adventurers—'

'A plague on the Adventurers!' Will exploded, stopping to look at him. Weston, out of breath, also stopped. 'All of them, you included Master Weston, are out for nothing more than monetary profit at the cost of other men's lives.' He resumed striding towards his cottage and Weston ran after him again.

'Come now, Master Bradford, be fair. We were in this for the money from the beginning. We made no pretence to do otherwise. *You* and Master Robinson and the others had higher ideals. Well, that was fair. But you can't expect people to invest in a venture if they get no return from it.'

Again Will stopped to face him, just outside the cottage. 'We invested our lives, sir. And men have paid with their lives. Yet when we are on the brink of starvation you do not help us. Oh no! What do you do? You send us more mouths to feed! You demand from us returns of furs and skins and wood, and complain when we are too busy struggling to survive through sickness and death, and cold and want, because we didn't have the chance to get any!'

'Well yes, but we didn't understand that in England.'

'Well you should have done! Did you think we would come here and it would be easy? We arrived in cold and snow and rain and ice. We were attacked by Indians, and in daily threat of our lives. The ship was like a plague ship. Everyone was sick, including the sailors. It was cold and damp and unhealthy. The humours from the ship were enough to kill any man off. Our first priority was to get shelter on land, dry, warm shelter, houses, before the seed-sowing came, so that the *Mayflower* could go home.'

'But you sent her back empty-handed.'

'We had no choice!' Will stormed, and Weston quailed before the onslaught. 'We had nothing to send in her. *Nothing!* Every piece of wood we cut was needed for our own houses. *And* you expected us to work as bond slaves for seven years—*seven!*—with nothing for ourselves. That policy has brought us to starvation. Don't you understand? No man wants to think he is working for another's profit. So, contrary to what you would like us to do, we have changed our policy. We are allotting land to each man, in accord with his family's needs, and we are working it accordingly.'

Weston rallied and stuck to his guns. 'That is contrary to the agreement.'

'To hell with the agreement!' Will bellowed. 'It ain't worthy to kindle a fire! And I don't see how your men in London can enforce it.'

'Well there is no need to be like that, Master Bradford,' Weston replied, affronted. 'In any case, I have pulled out of the agreement myself. Others have bought me out. So it is nothing to do with me what you do. You must deal with Master Pierce yourself.'

'I am not interested,' Will said flatly. 'I am interested in the welfare of these people. I am interested in seeing that they do not starve to death. For if they do, Master Weston, your Adventurers will have no return whatsoever for their investment.'

There was a short silence. Then Weston said, 'So you will not give me anything?'

There was an explosive sound in Will's throat. 'If we let you have what we have, there will be a mutiny among the people, for we need the beaver we have hunted to procure food for ourselves, and clothes too.'

Weston asked simply, 'Then what am I to do, Master Bradford?'

'I honestly do not care, Master Weston,' and Will turned away from him and went into the cottage.

Will discussed it with William Brewster when they were alone later.

'What can we give him?' Brewster asked.

Will pulled a face. 'I fear we will never be rid of him if we don't do something. And if there is one person I do not want here, it has to be Weston.' He leaned on the rough-hewn mantle shelf, and tapped his front teeth with his thumbnail. At the moment Weston was out, looking around the plantation, but he would be back to share Will's house, for that was the only one with room to spare. It was not a prospect Will relished. He said thoughtfully, 'We do have a few beaver skins. If we were to let him have some, then he can trade and get himself back home.'

Brewster didn't like the idea. 'We haven't got much, and if you give him any, our people will be in revolt! As it is they are not happy that he has come here, and some—that is to say John Billington—have suggested that he stands trial for defrauding us so blatantly.'

'No,' Will said flatly.

'So, what then?'

'If we don't let him have the skins, then he will continue to be a burden on us. And believe me, the likes of Billington will not like that! Neither will I! I tell you, if we don't get the man away from here I shall be the first to commit murder!'

'I sincerely hope you are jesting!' Brewster replied, giving him an old-fashioned look.

Will said, 'If we give the skins to him, then he will go away.'

'We can't afford to let him have any. And you won't see return for your generosity.'

'I know it.'

'And if you think to put him in the way of helping us when he gets back to England, then you are far out.'

'I know that too.'

'In that case, do what you think fit.'

'If we help him, we must do it secretly.'

'Then so be it.'

Will felt he had no other choice than to let Weston have a hundred beaver skins which weighed about 170 pounds. He was rewarded for his generosity for when a ship came by, Weston left Plymouth.

Having put up with him for two weeks, Will was heartily glad to see the back of him.

FORTY-NINE
Ships

Plymouth, 1623

As soon as Weston departed, they apportioned the land, and began the job of digging and seed sowing.

The people worked well now that they worked for themselves and they had a good deal more land under cultivation. They hauled up the buckets of alewives from the Town Brook, and dressed the corn as Squanto had taught them, and set a guard each night to keep off the wolves who saw the alewives as a cheap meal. However, between seed sowing and harvest there was the hungry-gap to consider.

Edward Winslow had purchased a fishing net off the friendly Captain Huddleston when he went to visit the fishing fleet some months earlier and they put the net to use. Working in groups of five or six men, they took out the boat, and let down the net into the sea, not returning until they had caught something. To return empty-handed when they had nothing on shore would be worse than not returning at all. As soon as they came ashore, the next group went out, and so on. Furthermore, each group tried to outdo the other in the amount they brought back. A little healthy competition did no harm.

The whole colony searched the sand flats on the shore for shell-fish until they were heartily sick of them. Their best hunters searched for deer, or fowl, and shared it between them all.

However, after a promising start, and a good seed-sowing and planting season, the weather turned hot and sunny, and from May onward they had a drought. Not a drop of rain. The first sowing of the corn sent out ears too early, before it was half grown, and the rest stood limp in the field, and just about dead. The beans also dried up, some giving up altogether.

It looked like another failed harvest, and Will despaired.

'Just look at it,' he said to Brewster, as they surveyed the limp yellow shoots struggling for life. 'We are doomed in this place.'

Brewster put a consoling hand on Will's shoulder, but he could think of nothing to say.

At the end of June 1623 a ship arrived, called the *Plantation,* captained by Francis West who had been made Admiral of New England, and had a commission to restrain interlopers, that is ships trading without a licence, from the Council of New England for which they should pay a large sum of money. However, he was ineffectual in this, for the interlopers were too strong for him, and he found the fishermen to be stubborn fellows.

The Plymouth people traded furs with him for two hogsheads of peas.

'We came across another ship bound for this plantation,' Captain West told Will, as he ate with him in his house. 'With passengers.'

Will's insides contracted as hope shot through him. 'Men and women?' Will asked, thinking immediately of Alice.

'Aye. We did go aboard her. Puritans, like you are.'

'We are not Puritans,' Will snapped, offended, 'We are Separatists.'

The admiral raised his brows, but continued, 'We lost her in a storm.'

Will's heart turned over. 'Lost?'

Not recognising the look of panic in Will's eyes, the admiral said, 'She might have gone down, or she might have gone off course. Pray God it is the second.'

Will felt the colour drain from his face. *Oh God, Alice! I must have been mad to ask her to come here!*

Other men too had wives and children that they hoped might come. God would not allow them to lose everyone, surely? He felt sick. *Oh dear Father, no! Jehovah, please do not let it be so!*

The next day the *Plantation* left to go on to Virginia.

In an agony of worry, Will thought of Alice night and day, and prayed about her and the others constantly. He tried not to count the days. In the time it had taken the *Plantation* to come and go, the other ship could have done the same. With each passing day, the dread grew, and he searched the horizon at every opportunity.

He wasn't the only one. Sam Fuller, already bereaved of two wives, waited for his Bridget. The Brewsters looked for their daughters.

Will did his best to keep everyone busy, organising people to get the plantation moving forward. Yet he looked at his people and he saw them lean and starving, and the drought continued unabated.

'Has God decided to bring us to ruin?' he asked Brewster.

Brewster shook his head. 'It would seem we do not have His protection. The Devil is determined finish us off.'

'So why do we not have Jehovah's protection? Have we done something to offend him?'

'I cannot see how. We have done our best to live according to his good orders. We have kept his laws to the best of our ability. We have done our best to come closer to the way of life suggested in the Bible than any have. Unless . . .'

'Unless?'

Brewster met his eyes squarely. 'Wituwamat.'

Will was appalled. 'But we had no choice.'

'It was still a man's life. Three men's lives.'

'I have begged Jehovah to forgive me for that.'

'Perhaps we all ought to ask for forgiveness. There is such a thing as community guilt you know.' Brewster looked at him, waiting.

Will hesitated. 'Perhaps we should humble ourselves before our God by fasting and prayer.'

Brewster gave a wry smile. 'Well the fasting bit won't be that difficult!'

Accordingly Will appointed a day in July—just as hot and dry and cloudless as all the others. Everyone, John Billington included, walked to their meeting house, dressed in their best clothes. All day they prayed and meditated, and no-one except the children ate anything.

On coming out of the meeting, late in the afternoon, Will looked up at the sky.

'Look!' he said to Brewster.

Brewster looked up and saw the first little clouds gathering over the sea. 'I hope you didn't doubt Jehovah!' he said with a delighted chuckle.

As they watched, the clouds grew bigger and soon blotted out the scorching sun. In England Will had disliked grey overcast days, and in Leyden too. He thought of them as depressing, but now the clouds lifted his spirits, and he felt hope rising in his heart. The next morning it rained. Sweet, moderate showers continuing on and off for fourteen days.

An Indian, stopped by. 'You have good rain,' he said. 'Make corn strong.'

'English God make rain,' Edward Winslow told him.'

The Indian was impressed. 'When medicine men ask for rain it comes heavy, with nightning and thunder and f'attens corn!'

For Will it was an assurance that his God had heard his prayers, that He had forgiven them, and had not deserted them. It gave him hope also that the constant prayers he uttered on behalf of those still at sea would be answered.

The ship sat on the horizon, a tiny triangle of sail visible against a cloudless blue summer sky, a fragile speck in the vast frothing waters of the Atlantic.

Will had his eyes on it as he strode down to the water's edge to join the rest of the colony. The sighting had stopped the work and he did not expect anything else out of them for the rest of the day, even though he knew it would be some time before the ship dropped anchor off Plymouth. They all hoped loved ones would be on board. Will, too, had plenty of things he could be doing, yet he stood beside the Brewsters, as mesmerised as any of them by the sight.

An air of excitement surged through the group, and the children jumped up and down excitedly. This might well be the ship Admiral Francis West had spoken of. And if it were, who would they find aboard? Would Alice be there? Had she at last come?

Will's stomach twisted itself into knots as he watched the sails gradually growing larger. *Oh, dear Lord, please may she be aboard!* And if she were, what would she think of him? Did he look like a ragamuffin, like some of the others did? He tried to keep his beard trimmed, and his clothes mended, but they were threadbare and patched. Besides, he had no looking-glass

He waited with growing impatience his heart thudding in his throat as the ship sailed gradually closer. He had no idea how he should greet her, what he should say. He was so nervous his hands actually trembled.

By the time the ship dropped anchor he was in an agony of suspense. His stomach churned continually, and his heart continued to thud in his chest. He stood mutely beside the others, watching as the sailors hauled out the longboat.

'Can you see them, William?' Mary Brewster asked as the first load of passengers clambered over the side and down the rope ladder into the boat. Of course, the Brewsters hoped to find their girls aboard.

Brewster, already shielding his eyes from the sun with his hand, stared at the distant ship until his eyes watered. 'I don't know,' he said uncertainly.

Will too strained to see. At that distance it was impossible, for the passengers were a jumble of forms. He watched with unendurable impatience as the now-full boat set off for the shore.

Thomas Blossom who they had last seen in Portsmouth, and his daughter, and his wife Anne came ashore first. The Conant family, the Bangs family, John Faunce, the Dixes, Timothy Hatherly and his family, Manasseh Kempton. And an assortment of young men. Alice was not on the boat.

They sent back the boat and another group came ashore. Francis Cook found his wife Hester and three children. Sam Fuller's wife was in the crowd, as was Thomas Morton's son, and Richard Warren's wife and five daughters.

Still Will hung back, feeling suddenly desolate among the happy hugging families, unable to see Alice.

They sent the boat back a second time. His heart was in his mouth. He knew suddenly that she wasn't here. More people descended the ladder into the boat, women and men, and the boat pulled again for the shore.

He felt sick in his insides, his eyes filled with tears, with a mixture of desperation and hope. *Please, dear God, let her be here.*

But there was no sign of Alice among the passengers. Nor of the Brewster daughters.

Mary Brewster burst into tears. Jonathan Brewster went to enquire of one who would know, Bridget, Sam Fuller's wife. Will watched him hang back until Sam released her from the embrace he had enfolded her in, then he asked her.

A few minutes later he was back with his father and mother. He spoke quietly. 'There were two ships. The girls, and George Morton and his family, and Mistress Southworth, were on the other ship. They lost sight of her in a storm some weeks ago.'

Will felt the ground rock beneath his feet. *Dear God, no!* He felt suddenly bereft. They had lost the ship. Had it sunk? Still, if the *Anne* had only just come in, there might still be hope. He tried to think so, but he knew that hope was only a tiny flickering candle in a gale. The sea had claimed one wife, had it claimed his bride too? He bit his lip to fight back sudden tears.

Mary began to sob, and William Brewster wrapped her in his arms, and led her away from the happy throng on the shore.

Will took a deep breath, and went to seek out the ship's captain.

'We sailed in company with the *Little James*,' the captain told him. 'We lost sight of her in a storm, though.'

'Sunk?' Will asked, trying not to let his agony sound in his voice.

'Pray God that is not so.'

I pray every day! Will thought.

Desolate, he returned to his house, to solitude. He closed the door firmly, and stood looking around him. This house he had built for Alice. Perhaps now she might never see it. He touched the table that he had lovingly made for her, and thought of the hours he had spent planing and sanding until the top was smooth. The benches also, and a chair, as John Alden had taught him. All for her. The fireplace with its huge shelf, and the crank for hauling cooking pots up from the fire. All this he had built for Alice, the love of his life. He tried not to think of her drowning in a turbulent sea, terrified, battered, cold, yet he knew that there was little chance of the ship's survival.

And there was George Morton, his dear friend, and his wife, Alice's sister Julianna and their children. And the Brewster lasses. He felt cold and shattered inside, tortured by fear for them all. Alice. He could not lose Alice. *Not now. Please God, not now.*

A week dragged by. Every hour of every day, his eyes went to the skyline, searching a depressingly empty sea for that hint of sail that would tell him the other ship had made it. Brewster did the same, and Mary became sullen and morose, puffy-eyed with grief. No-one spoke of possible disaster, but when they held their meetings, they prayed for the lives of those still at sea.

The passing time was agony, and Will's insides churned sickeningly all the time. He had to have faith, but with each passing day it looked more unlikely that the *Little James* had made it. He felt himself sliding into a black hole of depression. His life stretched ahead of him in this inhospitable place, bleak and empty. He wondered how he could possibly go on without Alice.

''Tis more than a month since the *Plantation* told us of the ship they had seen,' Brewster said to Will one day as they went out into the field to inspect the corn. Since the rain, it had grown good and strong and it was now just about ready to harvest. It would be a good crop this year after all, one that would keep the colony from starvation. 'Ten days since the *Anne* arrived.'

Will knew it. 'What do you think?'

Brewster hesitated. 'I think she must have gone down, Will.' His voice cracked. Hearing it, unmanly tears sprang into Will's eyes.

He looked at this man, the one who stood in place of his father, this man who had taught him so many things, and saw that he was old, and haggard, and hurt with life. 'I am so sorry, sir,' Will said, putting his hand on the older man's arm.

Brewster nodded, and tried to smile, but his lower lip wobbled, and his grey eyes filled with tears. 'They were beautiful girls, my girls,' he said, his voice breaking. 'Patience and Fear. They would have been twenty-three and seventeen.'

Will felt his own lip tremble. 'Perhaps there is still hope,' he said, but he didn't have much of it himself.

Brewster looked into his eyes. 'I am sorry Will. I was forgetting about Mistress Southworth.'

Will's self-control nearly deserted him. 'Aye,' was all he said.

Will looked at the ground, at the good black earth which had given substance to their crop. It had been hard backbreaking work, and they had nearly failed. Brewster bent and picked out a weed, a habitual motion these days, and threw it to one side.

Will picked up a hoe and began the job of cutting out the weeds. He had to keep busy, but this kind of work, laborious and requiring little concentration, allowed him time to think, and thinking right now, was not what he needed.

A musket fired from the plantation brought his head up. Up on the fort hill, the lookout pointed in the direction of the sea, and Will and Brewster tried to see through the trees that lay between them and the sea.

'A ship!' Will cried, and he left Brewster, racing back towards the plantation, stopping as soon as he had a view of the sea and, shielding his eyes, he peered out at the shining vivid blue water. Brewster caught him up, panting.

At first Will could see nothing. Then his eyes picked out the tell-tale triangle of sail on the horizon. His heart skipped a beat, and hope renewed. 'There!' *This time, this time Father, please let it be The Little James!*

'Thank God!' Brewster left him to seek his wife down by the brook. Will raced to his house and poured some water into a clay basin to wash in. He knew he had time, for the ship would take hours to come to the anchorage, but he rushed anyway. He brushed his long dark hair, combed his beard, and put on his only other shirt, which, although it was clean, was unfortunately threadbare and torn. Rooting through the books and papers and assorted junk in the huge travelling chest, he found his precious red coat with the gold buttons, and put it on, carefully teasing the ragged frills of his shirt through the cuffs. Together with a clean white lace collar, the finest thing he had, he thought he might look well enough to greet Alice, although the others might stare.

Trying to keep from hurrying, he strode purposefully down to the sea where everyone else awaited the ship.

The anxiety he had felt when the *Anne* came in assailed him again. Only this time it was worse, coloured by thankfulness that the ship had at last arrived. This had to be the *Little James,* surely.

As the first boat-load of passengers rowed towards the shore, his insides coiled and uncoiled.

The passengers spilled out of the boat and onto the rock which acted as a landing stage. William Brewster and his wife hugged their two daughters Fear and Patience and sobbed. Francis Cooke's family were there too, laughing and crying together. Others who had no connection to anyone stood uncertainly on the shore. Of Alice there was no sign.

Will felt sick with fear. Had she died on the journey? Had it been too much for her? He shouldn't have asked her to come.

The boat returned to the ship, and he waited still, watching anxiously, wishing he had vision that would allow him to see the details of the passengers as they climbed down the ladder to the boat.

The boat pulled away for the shore.

Desperately he searched the faces of those in the boat as it came nearer.

Then he saw her, sitting in the middle of the boat. A white cap obscured her face, but he would know her anywhere. She had come!

His heart jumped into his throat, and he felt suddenly nervous, more so than he had done confronting hostile Indians. It had been madness to ask her to come! After all this time, would it be the same? What if she found him altered in some way? No doubt he was different. Would he still feel the same about her? With an effort he tried to calm his panicking thoughts, taking deep breaths. But his hands trembled, and tears had come into his eyes.

The boat came into the rock, and a burly sailor helped everyone clamber out. George Morton, and his children, and his wife Julianna, Alice's sister, and others that Will didn't recognise, and then Alice.

She stood uncertainly beside Julianna, her eyes eagerly searching the sea of welcoming faces.

Will strode forward, pushing rudely through tightly packed bodies in his impatience. She looked up to see him bearing down on her, and her green eyes widened and her lips trembled. 'Will!'

For a long moment he stood looking at her. Her face was more rounded, and her skin had turned brown in the sun. But she was the same dear woman he had fallen in love with. In a single movement, he gathered her into his arms, unmindful of her gasp of surprise, or the astonishment of everyone around them. 'I have waited too long for you, Mistress,' he said in her ear. 'Will!' she managed again.

This was the woman he loved, the woman he had once thought never to see again. Over Alice he had suffered agonising guilt. He had tried to forget her, tried not to love her, yet his need for her nagged at him day and night. Now she had come to him. She would be his. As he held her, feeling the warmth of her slender body through the bodice of her dress, her breath in his ear, breathing in the heady scent of her, he felt as though an agonising weight had been taken from him.

'And not even married yet!' Julianna Morton's voice brought him back to the present. He looked up over Alice's head and grinned.

'You are shocked Mistress?'

She gave him an arch look. 'Setting such a bad example to the young ones! And you the governor, I hear! How are you, Will?'

Keeping his arm around Alice's waist, he released her enough to plant a kiss on Julianna's cheek. 'Well enough,' he told her, unable to stop grinning. 'George!'

George Morton shook his hand. It had been three years since they last spoke, but George looked as though he had aged ten. His hair had started to recede, and it was streaked with grey.

'Good to see you Will.'

'You had a difficult voyage, I fear?'

Alice spoke then. 'I hope I never have to repeat the experience.'

'Me too!' Julianna added with feeling. 'Storms and seasickness and we thought we were lost for good. There was a time when we though we might never get here.'

Alice said, 'We went so far north that I thought we would be put ashore somewhere hostile and we would never find you! Then the captain managed to discover our position.'

Will's hand tightened around her waist.

Julianna looked for the children who, enjoying a sudden bout of freedom after the tortuous weeks on the ship, had wandered away. It took her some minutes to round them up, and to present them to Will. 'You remember Nathanaiel, John, Patience and Sarah.'

'And we're soon to have another,' George said proudly, glancing meaningfully at his wife's over-large abdomen.

She cast shocked eyes on him. 'Not in public, George, if you don't mind!'

Will laughed. 'Come. You shall stay in my house, all of you.'

Their belongings would come ashore later.

With his hand still around Alice's waist he led them all up towards the plantation.

The plantation that they had built out of the wilderness. With their bare hands and the most rudimentary tools, they had sawn and hacked and built their houses, all nicely set out in two rows, with gardens, and thatched roofs, and on the hill the fort, all surrounded by the palisade. Over there the corn grew strong and straight, almost ready to harvest. Here they had beans and peas growing, and other vegetables. It was a going concern now. His fears over the survival of the plantation had faded.

They had much to talk about. Will wanted to know all the news, all the details. He wanted to know about John Robinson, the congregation in Leyden, those in London. The questions were endless.

Much later, as Will walked with Alice he told her what he had been thinking. 'I should not have asked you to come.'

She looked up at him in the balmy evening light. 'Why did you, Will?'

He stopped walking and looked down at the ground, then into her eyes, unexpectedly shy. 'Don't you know?'

'No, Will, I don't,' she replied unexpectedly. 'Tell me.'

He bit his lip. 'You must know that I've loved you a long while, Alice,' he admitted. 'Though I know I should not have done. It has been a sin for me these last three years.' He paused, unable to express a heart that was so full he thought it would burst.

She took his arm and urged him to walk, for it was easier to talk that way. 'And it has been my sin these last thirteen years. I've always loved you Will, since you first came to Amsterdam. You just didn't notice me.'

'I must have been mad.'

'You were in love with Dorothy,' she reminded him.

'I was infatuated with Dorothy,' he admitted. 'It was foolish. *I* was foolish to think a girl that age would make a suitable wife.'

She said after a moment, 'I knew you were unhappy. I knew from the outset how it would be. I tried to help you, you know.'

'You did?'

'I taught her to cook. To clean. To keep house, among other things.'

'What other things?'

She flushed in the darkness. 'Women's talk. Never you mind! I did it to help you, so that you may have a happy life.'

He thought about what she said, about how their lives had been. He said, 'You must have loved Edward.'

'I tried. I married Edward because he was persistent in his asking. Because you made it plain that you wanted Dorothy. But Edward was ill. I was impatient with him, for he brought us to poverty. I thought—may God forgive me—I thought he was malingering. You know, a cry for sympathy, and I ran out of sympathy. Poor Edward. He could never match up to you in my eyes. And he knew it. I don't know how, but he knew. He was jealous of you.'

'But he let me stay with you in London.'

'He didn't have much choice, did he? You turned up suddenly on our doorstep! What was he to do, send you away to sleep on the streets? Besides, he trusted both of us.' She smiled. 'He loved you too, in his way. You were his friend.'

'Fine friend I was, falling in love with his wife!'

She was quiet as they walked in the half-light. The sun set late, so it was just light enough to see by, and he looked at her, wondering if he had said the wrong thing. Trying again, he said, 'It was in London that I realised. I didn't want to leave you, knowing I might never set eyes on you again. I wanted to take you with me.'

'I know. I—I—would—might have gone if you had asked me.'

'I should be shocked!'

'I'm human, Will.'

'You would have broken Jehovah's law?' He was surprised.

'No. No. But it would have been a strong temptation. I am glad *you* didn't break His law.'

He stopped walking then. 'But I did break His law. In more ways than you know. This place, this plantation, has brought me to breaking point. It has nearly killed us all.'

She took his hand. 'He knows, Will.'

He slipped his free hand around her waist, feeling the warmth of her body through the bodice. She was intoxicating. And he wanted her with a deep aching longing. He pulled her against him in an embrace which would have shocked the rest of the colony had they witnessed it. She did not resist, but came into his embrace, leaning in to him. He kissed her forehead beneath her cap, and she raised her face to him, waiting. 'I told you I would not have stopped you,' she told him softly, her eyes shining, but he felt her trembling in his arms.

His lips brushed hers, and she did not complain, or pull away, but he felt the soft response in her.

Her hands rested on his shoulders then wound their way around his neck, gently pulling him down to her.

'Oh, Alice—'

And he kissed her with all the pent up longing and passion that he had held in check all the years. He kissed her with all the love in him, and with his whole being. He kissed her from the depth of his soul.

'I love you, Alice Carpenter,' he said.

'And I love you William Bradford.'

He cradled her head against his broad shoulder. 'Marry me, Alice, please.'

'Yes, Will. It's what I came here for.'

The *Little James* stayed with them to work as the *Speedwell* should have done. They loaded the *Anne* with skins and clapboard and sent her back.

Unlike the men who went to Wessagusset, the newcomers were strong determined people, useful to the colony. For the most part they came from the Leyden congregation. John Robinson, however, could not come. His efforts seemed to be blocked at every turn, he wrote to Will, and to Brewster. Perhaps next time he and his family would come. They were in his prayers.

House building went on apace. George Morton built a house for himself and his family which was ready in time for Will's wedding, which was just as well for up to that time they all stayed in Will's house, Alice included.

They had other weddings that year. John Alden married Priscilla Mullins, Miles Standish married Barbara, his dead wife Rose's sister who had come on the *Anne*. Will conducted all the weddings except, of course, his own. That privilege was given to his deputy, Isaac Allerton.

As Will waited for Alice outside George Morton's new house, he thought he had never known such simple happiness. He tugged at his red coat, rubbed at the brass buttons and knocked on the door. Alice, clothed in a green dress, with a large white collar and cuffs decorated with a little Flanders lace, emerged from the Morton's house with Julianna behind her.

He thought she had never looked so beautiful. She had a radiance about her, a glow of happiness which brought a pink blush to her freckled cheeks, and caused her green eyes to shine. The sight of her took his breath away.

She slipped her hand in his arm.

'Ready?' Will asked.

She smiled up at him. 'At one time, I didn't think this moment would ever come.'

He bent his head and kissed her lips. 'Neither did I.'

'Do you two think I am here as chaperone for nothing?' Julianna interrupted.

Will glanced at her. 'You, Mistress, talk too much,' he told her severely, but he turned to lead his bride up the hill.

His step was sure, her hand in his arm did not tremble, as they climbed the hill together to the fort where the whole town now waited for them, where Isaac Allerton married them. A simple exchange of promises, a signing of the register of births, marriages and deaths, and it was done.

They had a great party, a feast, made possible with a bounteous harvest, which went on late into the night.

Will had never felt as proud as he did with his new bride at his side. She would give him the strength to continue, to battle against the elements, to deal with the Indians, to keep the colony in order. With Alice by his side he could bear the burden of governorship, and build a colony.

In time the colony would grow, and others would come. In time it would give birth to a new nation, a great nation.

As Will wrote himself: *'As one small candle may light a thousand, so the light here kindled hath shone to many, yea in some sort to our whole nation; let the glorious name of Jehovah have all the praise.'*

AUTHOR'S NOTES

Although much research has gone into the writing of this book, the reader will appreciate that this is a work of fiction, so a few notes might be worthy of consideration.

History does not tell us every detail of a person's life. Indeed, how can it? Many of William Bradford's letters have been destroyed, and that was nearly the case with his memoirs *Of Plimoth Plantation.* Those memoirs, however, do not give us any personal information, therefore, we have no way of knowing exactly what happened to Dorothy Bradford. She may have jumped overboard, or it maybe that she fell. Certainly the stress of the journey could have taken its toll. While history does tell us that Will set his heart on Dorothy from the moment he first saw her, we have no way of knowing the state of their marriage, whether it was happy or not.

Likewise, we have no way of knowing what went on in the Southworths' marriage. Heneage House is known to have been a slum dwelling, its grandeur sadly faded, by the time the Separatists moved in. So, we can assume that financially things were not good. When Bradford learned of Edward Southworth's demise, he had no hesitation in asking Alice to marry him, suggesting that he had admired her back in Leyden, or London, or both (adding weight to the idea that perhaps life with Dorothy was not that happy), and she had no hesitation in travelling to Plymouth when he asked, even leaving behind her children, to do so, which could mean that she admired him also. Of course, it could have been a marriage of convenience, but I like to think they were a love match. Needless to say, Will's letter asking her to join him, and her reply, are from my imagination. However, all other letters quoted are from the originals.

William and Alice Bradford went on to have two sons, William and Joseph, and a daughter Mercy. William senior died in 1657 aged 67, while his wife Alice died in 1670, aged 80. William Bradford junior had fifteen children. Jonathan Bradford, son of William and Dorothy, came to New England in 1626, and Constant and Thomas Southworth, Alice's boys arrived in 1627.

Sadly, John Robinson, whose dream it had been to move to America, did not make it to New England, but died in Leyden in 1624. However, his son Isaac emigrated to New England in 1632.

Fear Brewster married Isaac Allerton, in 1626, and Patience Brewster married Thomas Prence who later three times became governor of the colony. Priscilla Carpenter, Alice's sister, moved to New England and married William Wright.

John Billington was hanged for murder in 1638, William Bradford acting as judge, and his wife Eleanor married Gregory Armstrong.

The peace that William Bradford made with the Wampanoag people lasted for twenty-four years.

Unfortunately, the dream of the Pilgrims, namely to create a colony based on their faith was unsustainable because people who did not subscribe to their faith joined them and watered down their ideals. By guaranteeing freedom of worship, Bradford had to allow others their own consciences, and some of their consciences were very liberal indeed, both in doctrine and in morals. By the end of the century, the Separatist ideals had been swamped by the Puritans and others who came to Plymouth.

We can see how the English population grew by looking at a few statistics. First, Plymouth Colony: 50 people survived to start the colony in Plymouth in 1620/21. By 1691 there were 7,000 people when the colony was absorbed into the Province of Massachusetts Bay. In New England as a whole, the English population rose from the first fifty people to 91,000 by the end of the century. Between 1630 and 1643 approximately 20,000 Puritans went to New England, settling in the Massachusetts Bay Colony around the Boston area. After that, fewer than 50 immigrants arrived per year, the population growth coming from births.

From this, we can see how the two or three hundred people who were Separatists arriving from Holland were swallowed up by the mostly Puritan immigrants. Their beliefs were not the same. As the older ones of the colony died off, the coming generation did not have the same intense love for their Separatist religion. Gradually, they were absorbed into the Puritan fold, and the Separatists ceased to exist as a distinct religion.

All scripture quotes are from the *Geneva Bible* of 1560, which is the Bible the Pilgrims used, as the *King James Authorised Version* was not published until 1611 and was not widely distributed by the time the Pilgrims emigrated to New England.

Please note that while the word 'Indian' is no longer correct, no offence is intended by its use. I have used the word to denote native Americans because that is the word the Pilgrims used.

BY THE SAME AUTHOR

GENTLEMAN OF FORTUNE,
The Adventures of Bartholomew Roberts, Pirate

"Evelyn Tidman has done a superb job of bringing the adventures of the infamous pirate Bartholomew Roberts to life."

"Readers are more demanding about historical novels and expect to be taken back in time so that they can visualize the sights, hear the noises and smell the smells. Evelyn achieves this."

"Brilliantly written and the characters and details are so realistic you feel like you are there on the high seas."

"Because the story was based on such meticulous research the author writes with great confidence and that inspires the reader."

Historic characters come to life in this swashbuckling epic about the pirate Bartholomew Roberts.

Learn about pirate laws and customs.

When pirates capture a slave ship on the West African coast, third mate and ex-British naval seaman Bartholomew Roberts is forced to join the company. The death of the pirate captain catapults him into office as leader of a drunken, rebellious crew. His first act of piracy sees him on the Coast of Brazil, taking a Portuguese treasure ship, and capturing the beautiful Lúcia. As Roberts takes the pirate company into adventure and fabulous treasure in the Caribbean and on the Slave and Ivory Coasts, he becomes so successful that he brings British trade to a standstill. Can the Admiralty stop him? Will his love for Lúcia threaten the pirate company?

GENTLEMAN OF FORTUNE is a swashbuckling adventure and is based on the true story of Bartholomew Roberts.

Available from Amazon

BY THE SAME AUTHOR

FOR THE KING
The Adventures of Roger L'Estrange, Cavalier

"One of the few books I have purchased rather than borrowed, and it was worth it. Some romance, some war, some family issues, all in a historical context."

The English Civil War puts Englishman against Englishman, Cavalier against Puritan, Royalist against Parliamentarian. East Anglia lies firmly in the control of Parliament—or so they think.

When King's Lynn in Norfolk, under governor Sir Hamon L'Estrange, declares for the King, Parliament reacts by sending Lord Manchester, Oliver Cromwell and 18,000 troops to retake it. Can Sir Hamon and his sons hold Lynn until help arrives? Can they keep King's Lynn for the King?

Roger L'Estrange, son of Sir Hamon, fights for the town and for the King. Yet his heart is captured by beautiful Puritan Ruth Pell. Can they overcome their differences in allegiance? Can their love survive the siege?

FOR THE KING is a swashbuckling adventure and based on the true story of the siege of King's Lynn in 1643.

Available from Amazon

BY THE SAME AUTHOR

REBELLION
Roger L'Estrange and the Kent Petition

"This is a thoroughly enjoyable read, and for readers who are unfamiliar
with aspects of the Kent Petition, this sheds light on the dark times of
Parliamentary oppression of those who dared to challenge its right to rule
without a monarch."

English Civil War.
Kent, 1648

With Parliament victorious and King Charles in prison, England suffers
under oppression. In Kent, the Royalists, led by Edward Hales, draw up a
petition to Parliament demanding the release of the King.

Enter Roger L'Estrange, newly escaped from Newgate prison, eager to
promote the petition with Hales while Parliament works to suppress it.

As Fairfax's army bears down on Kent, can the Royalists take the petition
to London? Can they save the King?

And in the resulting bloodbath, can Roger save feisty Beth Wotton, Hales'
beautiful sister-in-law? Can he save himself?

The second Roger L'Estrange adventure, **REBELLION** is a
swashbuckling adventure based on the true story of the Kent rebellion.

Available from Amazon

ABOUT THE AUTHOR

'History is another land.' I learned that at an early age as Errol Flynn swashed many bucklers and flew across our TV screens on a rope, dagger clenched between his teeth. Yet, somehow, teachers in school managed to drain the life from history. It became a list of dates, kings, laws, and events that had no relevance to my life and was as boring as watching paint dry. Still, I had a certain fascination for our ancestors. How different their lives were to ours! If only it were not all so tedious.

Then I discovered Jean Plaidy's books, like '*Light on Lucrezia*' and '*Madonna of the Seven Hills*' about the Borgias, and her books about Henry VIII's six wives. She brought history out of the past and made it *live*! I had discovered a whole new world—another country. I wanted to write those kind of stories.

While much historical fiction is about fictional people, and I am certainly not one to miss out on those tales, I wanted to know about actual people. Just who were these pirates? Murdering cutthroats or conquering heroes? Why did the people on the *Mayflower* decide to go to America? We'd all heard about them, but what made them do what they did? I wanted to know, so I did the research, and that led me to write about them, to share their stories.

Writing was my other passion. I've been writing since I learned to read, but, you know how it is, life gets in the way. When the kids finally flew the nest, I settled down to write *Gentleman of Fortune* quickly followed by *One Small Candle*. *For the King—The Adventures of Roger L'Estrange*, and the sequel *Rebellion—Roger L'Estrange and the Kent Petition* about the English Civil Wars, came next. All my stories so far are based on real events and real people.

Oh, in case you wanted to know about me, I'm English, born in London and now living with my husband in Norfolk, England.

I hope you enjoy reading my books as much as I enjoy writing them.

Made in the USA
Monee, IL
23 November 2024

70974745R00249